ILLEGITIMATE-ADVANTAGE

ILLEGITIMATE-ADVANTAGE

A Novel

KIRK GOLLWITZER

ISBN: 1519115229
ISBN 13: 9781519115225
Library of Congress Control Number:2015921011
CreateSpace Independent Publishing Platform
North Charleston, South Carolina

To the innocent in danger

PROLOGUE

To my loving sister Golareh

It is all a blur--because my memories have been so very altered by the amount of sleeping pills I have consumed during my lifetime. There are things I would love to remember but simply cannot, and conversely there are things I wish I could forget but will remain in my mind's eye forever. One memory, however, travels with me everywhere I go, every single day of my life.

I was only nine-years old when I, along with my parents and twin sister Golareh, were vacationing at our lovely villa in Noshahr, the "summer capital" of Iran, on the southern shore of the Caspian Sea. I can still remember my father sitting on the shoreline that day appearing as if he were watching us but clearly sleeping under the hot afternoon sun.

I saw my mother carrying what appeared to be a large tray of food down the stone pathway from the villa towards the shoreline. She was wearing a cream colored silk scarf which she had just purchased in a restaurant lobby the day before. She looked so beautiful with her long dark hair blowing in the breeze while containing a level of freedom I rarely saw anymore.

Everything seemed so peaceful to my parents from my vantage point offshore. Yes, it was the sort of calm that had been hard for my parents to find those days because of the dangers at home. The dangers had crept up on us slowly, like a cancer invading a body and finally becoming so obvious that the condition of our country had become terminal.

My sister and I were just a few meters off shore, when the ocean floor dropped off from beneath our feet dropping us into the deep, bone chilling, angry waters below. The world of the sea moved us around as if we were suspended in time. I remember vividly seeing a huge school of starfish being battered against the rocks by the same force of water and I thought the site to be quite odd.

Even though we were so close to the shoreline we might as well have been on a different planet. We were now one with the ocean, wrapped around us like a huge blanket of death. I can recall feeling as if we were tiny pieces of fruit suspended in a thick chilled gelatin dessert.

Golareh's face was grimacing with pain as a plume of rust colored fog escaped from her nose and darkened the water around her. We were both being slammed against the unforgiving surface of large jagged rocks as if we were being punished for some past sin. All I could feel was the tight grip of my sister's hand on mine as I struggled to keep her from being torn away from me.

Golareh's grip was like nothing I'd ever experienced before; it was like a connection to my only lifeline. Even though we were both struggling for our lives our fingers were tightly interlocked. The pressure from my loving sister's hold seemed to bind our souls at the palms of our hands.

The dark blue sky above and the distant shoreline flashed in front my eyes for a split second as I spotted my father turning his head in the direction of my mother. She was walking towards him with a smile on her face as she carried the tray of food. Our worlds were now completely separate from the safety of the beach and we were caught in a world of death.

We were now on our own at the complete mercy of the sea and totally helpless. There was no way our salt water voices could reach our parents over the roar of the surf. We smashed against the jagged rocks relentlessly, time and time again in the same company as our neighboring starfish.

I felt the warmth of my own blood streaming from my shoulder followed by white-hot jolts of pain. My sister's face had gone blank as our world swirled away and diminished into an abstract. All reality of our lives changed into a dream-like vision while our hands remained tightly interconnected.

We had lost our strength to protect ourselves against the outside world. The only thing we had left was our genetic link to each other through our fingertips. We were now one person, just as we always had been and will always be. Our minds were suddenly interlocked just like our long dark identical braids of hair.

Suddenly our worlds transitioned into a whitish-yellow day light and the movement of the blanket of water drastically changed. My face was now being pressed against the body of a large, living being of some kind and I began to lose consciousness. The movement of the creature shifted into the cadence of a marching soldier as I felt the warmth and strength of something akin to a huge fish-like creature carrying us both out of the water towards some unknown destination.

The cloud of death began to subside but I could still feel the tight grip of my sister's fingers on both of my hands. We were both riding high above the sandy shore-line, wrapped in the arms of a giant human being as our panicked-stricken parents ran towards us with their arm and eyes wide open in shock.

My mother threw her arms around my sister and me and screamed in our native tongue of Farsi at our giant savior. *"Khodaye bozorg, mamnoun k bachehaye bi bahaye mano nejat dadi!"* *"My God, my God, thank you for saving my precious daughters! Thank you so very much."*

The huge creature that was carrying us began to comprise itself into a gentle-mountain of a man with broad shoulders, massive arms, and an unbelievably trusting and charismatic grin. Our bloody and bruised bodies collapsed in exhaustion as the giant delivered our shivering souls to the safety of my parent's beach blanket.

My sister and I had escaped death and we began to realize we were safe once again. God, if there was such a being, decided to spare us for another day.

Through it all, even though we were both barely conscious, my sister and I never once let go of each other's hands. It was only until my mother gently spoke to us while parting our fingers beneath the warmth and comfort of a soft blanket under the Persian sun that we felt safe enough to release our hold. *"Bekhabine dotarhaye golam. Ba tamame esgham mohafez shoma hastam."- "Rest my beautiful children. Rest my lovely girls, you are both safe within our loving care. Sleep my darlings, sleep,"* my mother crooned.

The vision of that massive man filled my heart with both admiration and trust from that day forward. Might that giant of a man be God himself, I asked myself. I would never forget that powerful but haunting trust of that man's human spirit, powerful energy and beautiful wonderment. I somehow knew from that day forward that I would one day see that giant savior once again, but I never dreamed it would have such a different face.

I re-live that vision in my dreams every single night with no aspects of the event exaggerated through embellishment. Only the caring grip of my sister Golareh's hands would change as they became stronger and more protective during the difficult years to follow.

Golareh was so much more to me than my identical twin sister; she was and will always be the deepest part of my soul.

Chapter 1

HOMAYRA: A CHANGE
IN THE PROGRAM

The Palais Garnier Opera House - Paris, France — UNESCO Foundation dinner - 8:00 p.m. present day.

Although I am thoroughly exhausted, I am quite impressed by the amount of renewed mental clarity I have and if I were to put my hand on my chest, I would be actually able to feel the exact location of my renewed power source. It's as if a massive weight, which I have always considered to be *a way of life* for me, had been completely lifted away.

Over the years my entire upper torso has become cranked down so tightly that I now see myself as an old woman. Now that I am 52 years old, I feel so much older than my actual age. My lower back curves forward and my shoulders have started to resemble the protective shield of a hermit crab. All of this has been due to exhaustion, stress, loss and rejection. I have even found myself relying upon a cane, however, as of *six months ago*; I no longer need the assistance of a crutch or anything for that matter, as the aches and pains of my mind and body have been relieved.

I have been a hermit crab ever since that day my sister and I came to Paris, back in 1979. Even worse, ever since my dear sister left me it became almost impossible for me to even look at my own image in the mirror.

Although I have been told all too often by men and woman alike that I am beautiful, the compliment repulsed me. I hated everything about the word *beautiful*. I viewed myself as despicable, undesirable, sick, and far from beautiful. The fact is, I have been a beautiful mess for my entire adult life.

I realized not too long ago, when I finally got enough courage to look at myself in the mirror, why it was I hated to look into my own eyes. It was because all I saw was anger, contempt, disgust, and anxious humiliation for who I was. One word could best describe my life, for as long as I can remember, and that would be the word "*furious.*" I have been furious for my entire life, ever since the day I was born.

My father saw it in my eyes and heard it my voice when he caught his first glimpse of me in the neonatal intensive care unit, this fat, identical twin baby girl, with a cry like no other kid in the nursery. My cry was different, my father would say, it wasn't a cry for help or attention, it was a deep cry of anger, resembling the sound that a prize fighter might make during the final rounds of a boxing match.

My crying was intense, reminiscent of a boxer who was finally coming to terms with an opponent who had earned a reputation for brutally beating others opponents to death. I had the fury alright, but even more, I had the determination of a fighter whose goal it was to not only win, but to wipe the *loathsome monster* entirely off the mat.

In my culture all of our first names carry a meaning. My father's name was Amin which in Persian carried the meaning of "king", and a king my father was in my eyes. My mother's name was Souri which also carried a meaning that most eloquently described her, that being "sunshine."

The source of my fury at such a young age served as mystery even to my parents who would often say, "We never raised that child to be this way." For that reason my parents followed suit with the naming convention and gave me the name "Homayra" which in Persian meant the "*hottest part of a flame.*"

Golareh, or *Goli*, as I called her was so very different than I was, even though we looked exactly alike in every shape, form, and nuance. I would call her a *human mirror,* having these eyes that could reflect back towards the onlooker their own personal makeup.

She had the gift of vision that would allow her to look forward into the soul of humans, whether they allowed her to or not. My sister, as a general rule, was distrusting of others and was always looking over her shoulder at those who might be trying to take advantage of us. Golareh was my protector who always made sure that we both made it home safely and always had an exit plan away from danger.

She had the eyes that resembled a mysterious one-way mirror. Golareh's eyes were more reflective of the person looking into them than the other way around. It was as if when people looked into my sister's eyes they saw nothing of her, but everything of themselves and for many, that was extremely disconcerting.

For most people, the human eye is a window into a person's soul but in my sister's case, one would get the distinct impression, when gazing into her eyes, that she could see more of them than they could see of her. My sister's eyes did not disturb me in the least but provided a sense of comfort to my otherwise burning heart. For when I looked into her eyes I saw exactly who she was but moreover I could see who I was, in a perfect reflection of our balanced souls. It is for this reason my parents named my twin sister "Golareh", which in Persian meant the "pupil of the eye".

Just six months ago I could completely understand after all of these years, 32 to be exact, why it was I hated to look at myself in the mirror. It was because I would see the image of my dear sister, whom I had ironically grown to despise and all but disown for leaving me behind to fend for myself.

Why on God's earth, if there is such a place, did she leave me, I wondered time and time again. For when she was gone, I became a helpless empty slate, a pitiful remnant of who I once was. Loneliness could not even begin to describe the feeling of the loss I experienced. In losing my identical twin sister, it was as if my heart was pumping on the single and weakest valve. It felt as if my soul had been ripped out of my chest.

I didn't even know how to view life as I once knew it. I drew inward and completely hid from the world around me, that is until the dreams began visiting me only a few months ago. Those powerful nightmares, that somehow originated from my lost sister, of those lost and forgotten children, who had been removed from their loving parents, just as we were, and hidden away from everyone who could help, including *God* in heaven. I have since become a fixer, a corrector, an adjuster, and more than that, an independent soldier on a mission of furious mercy.

Tonight is different though, for now the power is in my hands and I have the power to correct with a renewed understanding of my own destiny. For the first time in my adult life, I'm beginning to feel attractive and perhaps maybe even beautiful.

I all but stopped believing in the old adage, what goes around comes around. From my standpoint, I have seen the other side of the human race, the side where what goes around does *not* come around perhaps ever. I have seen way too many people accumulate massively imbalanced winnings at the expense of far too many losers like myself, who have spent a lifetimes of being beaten down by those selfish individuals.

⸺⧉⸺

SO AS I STAND ON THE STAGE, LOOKING OUT AT THIS VAST CROWD OF SOCIETY'S UPPER CRUST, I SEE A VISION OF HENRI IN A SURPRISINGLY NEW LIGHT THAN IN THE PAST. Do I feel anger towards Henri, like I thought I would? I think not, if anything, I feel an odd sense of pity, even though Henri deserves none. If there ever was a person who deserved to be hated, it would be Henri, and even that emotion wouldn't do him justice.

I'm almost shocked as the strange vision appears, as I look down at this horrible person. My imagination brings to light a clear vision of Henri taking on the form of a filthy pigeon with a surprised and stupid face. I imagine him suffocating under the weight of a huge hawk that is quietly perched on his weak back.

The hawk sits on Henri with such a prominence while everyone around him seems oblivious to the fact that this spectacle in my imagination is even taking place, but then again only I am viewing this drama.

To the other people, in this high fashion collection of the country's rich, spoiled and famous, one of the world's most famous Irish rock band from Dublin is titillating their limited attention span. It is now midway through their closing number as I continue to watch Henri, who is sitting only nine meters away from me, just part of the crowd of many dignitaries surrounding him.

I continue to watch the mighty hawk bearing down on Henri like a helpless pigeon, with his powerful claws sinking deeper into his muscle mass and finally around his skeleton.

The powerful hawk sits there amidst the oblivious crowd waiting for something special to happen. Whether it's because he is playing with Henri or simply trying to conceal his prey from the other predators circling high above becomes an odd question in my mind. Henri has now become a helpless and defenseless prey, totally submissive to the grip of the large hawk shifting its weight on his back.

Suddenly the hawk's massive wings begin to spread out into an explosion of incredible lift, snatching the flabbergasted Henri out of his seat and towards the ceiling above. I see Henri's face full of fear, akin to the same level of fear I've seen all too often in those poor, battered women and children in my daily nightmares. A fear of impending doom as the massive bird steels Henri by his razor sharp claws out of his seat, higher and higher into the heavens until he is gone.

The crowds, still mesmerized on musical entertainment in front of them, never see the drama playing out in my imagination as I continue to examine his face. Henri once owned every aspect of me as well as so many others in his sick kingdom. Now here he sits sipping his expensive red wine with few cares in the world as to what is about to unfold.

Even the well-known dignitary from the United States, along with his attractive wife sitting right next to Henri, didn't notice that the hawk had come and gone in my imagination. They continue to see Henri as one of the world's most prominent statesman just sitting at the table with those broad shoulders, cheshire smile and massive appeal.

Now I alone see Henri for who he really is, as I begin to make my way toward the darkened microphone and podium on the right side of the stage. Directly to my left, on the other side of the stage, sits a second podium and microphone, cloaked in the darkness facing the huge curious audience.

As I stand at my dark vantage point waiting for the dramatic music to reach a conclusion, I am taken back by the beauty of this classic opera house, known as The Palais Garnier. From the day the famous opera house opened on the 5th of January 1875, talent from all over the world has entertained the most appreciative of patrons along with the most haughty and arrogant world leaders of almost every continent in the world.

The opera house is massive in stature where above me hangs a 7-ton bronze and crystal chandelier designed and hung by Garnie himself. It was the very same chandelier that was written about in the classic Phantom of the Opera.

The theatre has completely sold out this evening with more than 1,979 seats on five levels with at least 20 private box suites. The control of the program is almost entirely run by a production crew of only 12, with the heavy lifting of the massive stage backgrounds and lighting systems being controlled by computers.

Even with all of the majestic beauty and visual acrobatics the public seem so perfectly bored with it all. I have grown to recently know a large percentage of these people and I am continually reminded of the fact that they expect so much from these benefits but give so little in return. For this reason alone, I feel that my message to the audience this evening will be one that will stay in their minds at least until they read the headlines in the paper tomorrow morning as they nurse their champagne hangovers. I'm reminded that during times past, my messages have been totally lost to the passing cleavage of a cocaine soaked movie star or a ridiculous tattoo on a far-from-sexy pop phenom's lower back.

Time and time again all I'm left with is that unmistakable expression *of passive interest*. Perhaps tonight will be different? Perhaps they will take note and remember what they learn tonight and become active to the spirit of my message? Most likely they will not, I admit to myself, realizing full well that most people will never be able to relate to the horror of an abused child trapped in the mechanics the human trade industry.

Just before the song comes to a conclusion my eyes are drawn straight down to the narrow center line of the ground floor aisle towards the back of the opera house. I see Zooli accompanied by a young gentleman whom I've never met but feel as though I know so completely well.

They enter the large room and both confidently walk hand in hand down the red carpeting towards their own reserved seats to my right of the stage. Zooli looks so incredibly radiant, containing a social confidence that has been vacant from her mannerisms for as long as I have known her. Her eyes are now alive with excitement, as she walks so purposefully through a sea of society's super-crust, towards her destination.

Now only 15 meters away from me, I see her eyes piercing my emotions with deep love, extreme pride and profound gratitude, as her instructive voice reaches my soul and says, "Excellent Homi, good job girl! We did it!"

The song has now reached a completion point as the light and sound architecture of the theatre begin to rotate in my direction.

I poise myself to begin an intense education of my life experience and why I am standing before them tonight in the first place. I'm about to tell the audience that there has been a slight change in the evening's program.

The light falls upon me and illuminates my body like a bright star, as I begin to fill my lungs with fresh oxygen and push the first words of our incredible story out of my now powerful diaphragm and into the live microphone.

The completely unknowing, sold-out theatre in front of me becomes a sea of ears and eyes. I am eager, alert, and wide awake and also in the company of someone who feels the exact same way as I.

The podium to my left suddenly becomes illuminated as well, as a flawless carbon copy of myself stands motionless, silently studying the audience with her beautiful knowing eyes. I feel the entire opera house gasping in disbelief and holding their collective breaths as they gaze at the duplicate spectacle of my sister and me.

My dear sister Golareh stands proudly upright, silently studying the audience and most especially Henri with obvious hateful intensity. She is wearing the exact same dress as I have on, a long, red draped satin dress by John Galliano, very sculptural and vividly dramatic. The audience and most especially Henri stare in disbelief at the duplicate sisters studying them from the stage as our story begins.

THEN AND THERE

.

Chapter 2

HOMAYRA: MY NEAR-
DEATH EXPERIENCE

Tehran, Iran — 3:10 p.m. - June 19, 1979

I left my body that morning and retreated to the safety of the heavens above. The *first* explosion blew my sister's and my unsuspecting six-teen year-old bodies violently to the ground and so very close to kingdom-come. My vantage point suddenly switched to about 10 meters above our backyard, looking down on my sister and myself lying on the ground in a semiconscious mess. The rest of our childhood friends were scattered, shocked and motionless next to the fence line while the other two boys stood screaming at each other in disoriented confusion.

Just seconds before, Golareh had pulled me from the top of this boy I was choking. I was so angry at him for telling me that I could no longer hang out with them because I wore a bra! I could not believe the nerve of that boy, who I considered to be one of my best friends, abandoning me just because I was a girl. I threw myself on him and began to strangle him with anger. Why was I so much different from him and why did he suddenly consider me now the enemy, just because I had breasts?

My sister grabbed me from behind and with all of her might pulled me off the boy. I felt my anger slowly diminish when I heard my sister laughing uncontrollably. She covered my mouth with her hands for fear that our mother would hear the most inappropriate words spewing from my lips.

"Be quiet Homi! Forget about him! You don't need to worry about that boy, he's a jerk anyway", she said. "Besides, I know who really likes you---he does," she said, pointing at this gorgeous boy on the other side of the yard.

I had always admired that wonderful boy, who never seemed to pay attention to me in the least. "He has a crush on you Homi! I'm sure if it. I can read him like a book! I can see it in his eyes!"

It was almost as if the explosion of knowing this exciting new fact was more than my mind could handle as an intense pressure wave began to mix with the environment all around us. The cool sunny day suddenly turned into a grainy horror picture as my sister and I were thrown to the ground with such force that all I could see from my *new* safe position in the sky, high above the turmoil, was that the world around us had just been turned inside out.

I panned my view point across the street to the neighbor's house, where I saw a screaming woman in a bloody nightgown running towards a burning automobile in the center of the street. Her husband lay broken and lifeless by the curb next to their mail box. I suddenly vacated my position from my elevated perch, back to the ground below, where I felt my sister grabbing my wrists, as my confused mind and body was being jerked into a standing position. We staggered in some dream-like dash towards, somewhere, anywhere, than the direction of the blast. Falling debris of fence posts, glass, nails, dirt and roof shingles, showered down upon us from the sky, splintering our bodies as we both ran towards an indistinguishable point of safety.

My mother appeared out of nowhere, still gripping her paint brushes and wearing her stained artist smock. She grabbed us both by the scruff of our necks so hard that I thought I would scream, but nothing would come out of my mouth.

My sister and I violently tumbled down the narrow wooden stairs of my father's makeshift bomb shelter, which doubled as my mother's art studio. As she pulled the door down over us, the *second* explosion amended the sound of the first one, as my face hit the concrete floor and I witnessed a drop of blood dripping from my sister's left ear.

Paint from my mother's art table filled the room in a horribly tasting cloud of red, white and green misery, covering our faces like comic book characters. I remember calmly thinking how cool the floor felt and how lucky we were to have no windows in this underground dugout, as we would have been cut to shreds.

The three of us lay there on the floor in a deafening silence, a silence created not only by the world around us, but also from our own buzzing and disabled eardrums. My sister and I had no idea what had just happened, as we lay there motionless, staring up at the ceiling. There were no police sirens or emergency personnel, nothing but the loudest silence I had ever heard in my entire life.

I don't remember sleeping that night, but I do recall sitting on the couch the next morning, holding my disabled sister's hand and nursing my splitting headache. My mother and father stayed up all night long making sure that Golareh stayed awake during that crucial period following a concussion.

The phone rang in the kitchen and I heard my father answer it. He was talking to my uncle, who was the current region governor of our small-town near the capital of Iran. He didn't say much more than: *bashe, vali na, mifahmam, bashe, yes, no, I understand, okay.* My uncle was telling my father that his son Jalal, who had taken on the name *Frédéric*, was interning as an attorney at the State Trade Department in Paris and that he and Jalal had arranged for my sister and me to leave Iran and travel to Paris.

My father gently hung up the phone and returned to the living room and sat at the base of the couch. He gazed at the two of us with the most sorrowful eyes and said, "I must tell you both, that you will to be going on a wonderful adventure to a land far away from here called Paris. There you will live in a *castle*. You will be at peace there and most of all, you will be safe." At that very instant, I became confused, scared and dreadfully nervous from then until this very second.

Chapter 3

GOLAREH: TO THE FRENCH CASTLE

*"Je n'ai plus que mes yeux pour pleurer" - So
now I have only my eyes to cry*

I noticed at a young age that people had trouble looking me in the eye. At first I thought it had to have something to do with me, as they looked off into space when they talked me. I asked my sister Homayra or *Homi*, as I called her, why it was that no one ever looked me in the eyes when they talked to me, and she said, it's because they're afraid that you will *see* who *they* really are.

I know now why my mother became so very sick during the week prior to our leaving for Paris. Homayra was convinced that she was dying of some unknown malady, for when she wasn't sobbing uncontrollably, she was throwing up violently. Looking back, I believe that she couldn't bear to even look at my sister, and most especially into my own eyes, during the days before we left Iran.

I could hear her moaning in terror, day and night, as she flailed around in her bed, tearing thick tufts of hair out of her scalp, in a futile attempt to purge some horrific poison out of her system. Her suffering resembled a self-induced exorcism, in a feeble struggle to rid her own soul of some terrible spirit.

My father told us not to disturb mother as we left for school that morning, *"khahesh mikonam - bezarine madaretoon esterahat koné - ehtiaj be khab dareh"*, meaning *"she needs to sleep,"* he said, *"she must rest,"* he pleaded. I firmly believe that my mother was having a full and complete, physical and mental breakdown. Her most cherished and beloved twin daughters were being torn away from her, and there was absolutely nothing in the world she could do about it.

Although Homayra wanted to believe that we would see our parents soon or that we were only going to be gone for a fortnight, I knew better. She believed my father when he would solemnly tell us, *"Na tarsid. Be zoudi ba ham degar khahim bood,"* which meant: *"Don't be afraid. We will come and join you as soon as we can!"* I could see in both my father's and mother's eyes the horrible truth that I would never see our dear parents again.

Homayra and I were sitting in the backseat of the car after my father picked us up from school on that dreary, gray morning. The excuse that he gave the school was that we were going to the dentist. But as we drove away from the school, with the radio quietly reporting the breaking-news from the dashboard speaker, I saw for the first time in my entire life, my father crying as he navigated the car out onto the busy expressway.

When we arrived at the airport we moved through the jungle of chaos with apparent ease. We sat together on a wooden bench holding hands as we watched our father present our identification papers to the military police.

I remember listening to the news about the Shah on the radio, as I stared at a square wooden speaker box mounted on the wall above the security guards. I can recall looking at the fabric on the speaker and actually seeing the words of anger being projected to the soldiers standing guard at our final checkpoint. My sister was numb with fear, as I held her wrist tightly and walked towards the plane.

I realized that day, that the pain my parents felt during that entire week before we departed must have been absolutely incredible. As we taxied away from the gate, we saw our distraught father running along the entire length of a fence line desperately trying to keep us in view as we disappeared out of sight. It just broke my heart.

It was our first time ever on an airplane and it should have been exciting but it was far from it. As the heavy plane flew high above the mountains, plateaus and broad basins of Iran, the two of us gazed out of the window and wept. Our homeland and those beautiful mountains which had shaped our country's rich political and economic histories for centuries were now becoming a part of our past. We held each other's hands tightly together for the entire flight and said nothing. We were simply too shocked to talk.

We arrived in Paris and spent the night. Early the next morning we boarded another small private airplane bound for Dijon. Once we landed, we were instantly taken by a policeman to an awaiting limousine. We never stopped to pick up any luggage and I never thought about that until after we arrived at the castle. Our parent had sent us with no luggage whatsoever, in order to minimize scrutiny.

My sister and I learned English in school; however French was another story. We could speak very little French at first and found the language extremely difficult to learn. However, from the moment the wheels of our plane touched down in Paris, we forced ourselves to learn it because we had no other choice.

⸻

Yes, it was called the *Castle*. We were going to live in a castle in France, sure we were, I thought as my sister and I sat in the backseat and l looked out the window at the beautiful countryside. After about 45-minutes we arrived at the small town of Montbéliard which served as the primary supply source for the castle.

The driver stopped the car and pointed with pride at a massive stone fortress just below the snow line. It was breathtaking. The structure appeared as if it had grown naturally out from the rocks it sat upon. The massive stone and glass castle was simply magnificent, with sparkling gas lights that could be seen for kilometers. Surrounding the fortress I could just vaguely make out tennis courts, swimming pools, and rich green fields.

The wheels of the limousine bumped to the rhythm of a long medieval wooden drawbridge as we slowly approached the entrance way and came to a stop beneath a massive portcullis that loomed above us like an evil inverted iron fork. An officer of the French security force, wearing an earphone, carefully checked our identification and glanced suspiciously at my sister and me, as we sat with our duo pony tails and timid identical dark faces in the back seat.

"Bonjour Monsieur, ces jeunes femmes sont des invitées très spéciales de Dr. Henri Lepan, il devrait être en train de les attendre" - *"Good afternoon sir. These young ladies are the very special guests of Dr. Henri Lepan. He should be expecting them,"* announced our driver, as we were quickly allowed through. What was this place, I wondered, and why was the security so tight?

We were soon directed on to a service road dedicated to some sort of equestrian riding area, according to a yellow sign on the side of the road with a figure of a horse on it. A long line of wooden fencing seemed to stretch for thousands of meters, as beautiful horses peacefully grazed on the rich grass of meticulously manicured fields.

Groups of riders, dressed in colorful clothing, stood together laughing and conversing as they sipped from small crystal glasses. I remember having the distinct impression that these people were preparing for some unusual hunt, but had little regard for the animal they were hunting or the horses they were sitting on. It was the way they held their heads, with the noses positions so high.

Our limousine came to a stop along the fence line as a large, square truck following behind us made its way through an entrance gate and came to a stop. Homayra and I stepped out of the car and stood on the rich grass by the fence line watching as the strange truck came to a stop in the center of the paddock. A crowd of colorfully dressed riders on horseback were gathered, and I distinctly heard the sound of what reminded me of human voices screaming from the interior of the truck, it was a strange haunting sound of trapped creatures begging to be freed.

A stumpy black man dressed in a red and white uniform accompanied by a young boy, lifted the heavy iron latch on the back of the truck and as he began to raise the door a sea of dogs came charging out of the cramped and crowded inner quarters of the truck. The numbers of dogs were incredible, as they literally poured out of the overstuffed interior, desperately gasping for air while urinating and defecating all over the rich grass.

The crowd of fashionable dressed riders on horseback seemed oblivious to this dumping of animal life on the carpet of this incredible portrait, which served as a main stage in front of the majestic French Alps in the background. Walking through the assemblage of horses, dogs and humans was an interestingly attractive woman, carrying a riding crop and moving with a sense of purpose. As she walked she moved her head from side to side carefully inspecting all of the activity surrounding her.

She appeared to be in her late twenties with long beautiful brown hair pulled into a tight braid that ran through the back of a dusty ball cap and down to the small of her back. She was truly beautiful and had a perfect posture with a dancer's body. Her face contained a bright smile with a toothy grin, as she recognized us and walked in our direction.

She had on black riding pants and tall brown riding boots with straps which showed a marked contrast to the smartly polished boots on the riders around her. Covering her eyes were dark aviator sunglasses which complimented a leather flight jacket.

When she first noticed our car she began to walk towards us, but quickly made a beeline towards a worker with a horse. She snatched the water nozzle from the confused farm hand and signaled him away as if she were protecting the horse from a stray, aggressive dog.

Homayra and I stood next to the fence line like two peas in a pod, transfixed by the vision of this commanding woman and the activity surrounding us, as she made her way towards us. Before she even formally acknowledged our presents, I heard her mention under her breath in perfect Farsi, *"Az roubah chekarkonan bizaram!"* meaning *"I hate fox hunters!"*

"You must be Homayra," she said to my sister with an impressive confidence. "And you", she said, looking deeply into my eyes, "you must be Golareh."

"Yes ma'am, but you can call me Goli and my sister's nickname is Homi. We just love your dogs," Homayra and I said in unison.

How could she identify us so well I thought to myself? I realized at that very moment that she was probably the first stranger in my life to look directly into my eyes with a sense of purpose.

"My name is Zooli and I have two things to tell you. First of all, don't ever call me 'ma'am' again, and secondly, never refer to those animals out there as dogs; they are foxhounds to these hunters. Do you like horses" she asked?

To which we both replied in unison, "Why yes, yes we do, very much," even though neither of us had ever seen a real horse in our entire life.

"Good" she said with authority and a broad smile, "for the two of you now work for me!"

"Ma'am---I'm sorry, I mean-- Zooli," I said, remembering her rules. "May I ask what they are doing with all of those foxhounds," I timidly asked, as I curiously watched about 50 of them follow the old black man on horseback off to side in a noticeably orderly fashion.

Lowering her voice to a whisper while producing a noticeably contrived smile, Zooli put her arms over both of our shoulders and gently nudged us over to the fence line.

"Well right now these lovely people over there are sitting on their horses drinking liquor. Soon my good friend Stash, the hunt master, is going to release the foxhounds and off the drunken riders will go after a tiny fox," said Zooli, as she leaned back against the wood fence board and watched the riders in the distance.

Homayra stared at Zooli with a curious expression of wonderment. "Well what do they do when they catch the little fox, do they get to keep him for a pet?" asked Homayra.

"Well if the fox is cornered by the hounds the little thing is usually killed."

"What!" my sister and I screamed in unison. "That's horrible," my sister yelled with alarm, loud enough to be heard by others.

Zooli smiled and, moving her face close to my sister and me, began to whisper. I could see both of our surprised faces reflecting in her dark sunglasses.

"But don't worry girls, Stash and his precious son Becker will never let that happen. Half of those foolish riders will fall off their horse anyway, while the other half are too stupid to even recognize a fox when they see it. Now aren't you so happy to be here at the castle," Zooli asked, while laughing and patting us both on our faces.

My sister and I felt an instant closeness to this woman from the moment we set our eyes upon her. She was a total breath of fresh air with a wonderfully natural way about her. There was a safety feature about Zooli that was palatable, as if she were our own personal lifeguard sent to us from God to keep watch over us.

From that day forward, she never mistook one of us for the other. It didn't matter whether we were far away from her in some distant pasture or standing right next to each other in pitch black darkness; she always knew who each of us was.

I remember asking her, how she was always able to distinguish us from one another so well, when the rest of the world, including our own parents, sometimes had trouble. She threw her head back and laughed and said, "Girls, let's just say I have damn good horse sense!"

Zooli led us through the huge entrance and into the magnificent *castle* that was alive with activity, laughter and beautiful people everywhere. As we entered what was to be our suite, I felt as if we had been adopted by a king. The room was huge with three large beds and a large crystal chandelier hanging above us in the center of the room. The windows were panoramic and presented a spectacular view of the equestrian grounds with the snowcapped mountains in the background.

We noticed that our clothing had been picked out for us and neatly arranged on our beds. "Well, it appears that tonight you are expected to wear these dresses to dinner; however, right now, I want you to put on those clothes and follow me back to the stables," Zooli said as she pointed to a matching pair of riding boots, stretch britches, short sleeve shirts, gloves and riding helmets.

Suddenly the door sprang open and a strangely dressed black girl blasted into the room, swearing obscenities in a thick cockney accent, "Fuck them all! I hate those fucking assholes," she blurted as she threw her purse across the room. Realizing she wasn't alone she switched up and tried to act dignified.

She had long brown hair and was wearing a short knitted top, showing off her flat belly and extra short black shorts. Her face was simply beautiful, complete with high cheekbones, large greenish-blue eyes and a clearly disgusted expression.

She stood at least two centimeters taller than my sister and I and had a figure to die for. She glanced at us and wiped what appeared to be tears from her eyes. She looked deeply into my eyes with a level of depth that shocked me and seemed to touch my very soul.

"What's happened to you? Why are you so upset," Homayra asked, while breaking a very odd moment that the black girl and I seemed to be experiencing.

"Well, you must be Homayra Parastou," she said, while turning her head at my sister, "and you must be Golareh," she asked, as she directed her full attention to me.

"Girls," Zooli said, "I want you to meet your suitemate, Danielle Elba."

As I looked into Danielle's beautiful eyes, I saw a profound level of beauty that was covered in noticeable pain. I remember feeling my body shiver with a strange chill as I studied her beautiful figure. At that very instant I felt that I had been struck by an intense and uniquely distinct attraction to not only who Danielle was but everything about her.

"Sorry for my words girls, but this place sometimes really fucking sucks! So please call me Danni."

Zooli tapped the floor with the tip of her riding crop and waved her head in a sort of humorous frustration. It seemed evident that Zooli disapproved of Danielle's language but could do nothing to prevent it. Up until the moment I met Danielle I had never even heard what were known as swear words.

Zooli then lifted her sunglasses, revealing her beautiful brown eyes. "Girls," she quietly whispered, "I want to tell you something and this is meant for all three of you. I want you to stick close to me, very, very close to me! Now go put your work clothes on and meet me in the barn in thirty minutes, we've got some mucking to do."

Before long, I was taught the definition of the word *mucking*. My sister and I, along with Zooli and Danielle were down in the stalls raking horse manure into a dark blue muck-bucket with rope handles. For the most part, there were few others tending to the horses, except for few farm hands slowly cutting the tall grass fields in the distance and an elderly woman who kept to herself, grooming a large black horse in a stall across from us.

The smell of the barn was like a fragrance I had never experienced before; it was the smell of both protection and life. We worked all day at the general orders of Zooli, who labored alongside of us, scrubbing out water buckets, swatting flies, sweeping off the aisles and lifting heavy muck buckets of manure onto trailers. But it was those magnificent horses that provided a way for me, for at least the moment; to put away my pain, loss and deep concern for our parents.

There were 20 full time horse stalls in total, along with two riding arenas at the complex. Zooli told us that she took care of all twenty horses herself each day, mucking out each stall, twice a day, managing the health and hoof care of each animal. She watched over every single rider with a strict eye, even though she had little control over the guests.

Every single day, rain or shine, in sleet or snow, Zooli was out working those huge animals, riding as many as 10 horses. She was in better shape than anyone I had ever seen in my life. I was constantly amazed by her perfect athletic posture and bright smile that appeared as fresh as farm land around us.

I'm quite sure that she was constantly admired and perhaps pursued by the many guests at the castle; but she projected a countenance of being off limits to the many men and women who took personal riding lessons from her.

Danielle was a natural rider and even though her eyes contain so much sadness, the joy that she expressed on horseback was unbelievable. Zooli would instruct her from the center of the dusty arena, wearing her heavily weathered ball cap and sunglasses, while holding a riding crop in one hand and flag in another.

She taught the way a ballet instructor might dictate movement to her students in short phrases.

"Sit up straight," Zooli said, while making a clicking sound from the side of her mouth. "More left rein! Sit up girl and look forward Danni. I said look forward girl! Good, Danni, very good, excellent, good job---girl!"

The power of Zooli's instruction permeated my mind, as I'm sure it did both with Danielle and my sister. In the years to follow, Zooli's voice would often take the place of my own conscience whenever I was considering my direction and movement in life. This completely unselfish desire to improve the welfare of her students is what I most remember about this fine woman with the strange name of Zooli.

It was almost dark when we finally got back to room and stripped off our filthy clothes that smelled of sweat, hay, manure, and those wonderful horses. We showered, fixed our hair and put on some of the most beautiful dresses I had ever worn.

It was as if we were preparing to go to the king's ball. However, although it seemed as if we should all be excited, Danielle appeared far from enthusiastic about the evening ahead of us.

"Tonight the two of you are going to meet Henri," said Danielle, "he has been looking forward to meeting you for weeks. Be very mindful of him and watch my lead," she said in a thick cockney accent. "Follow my fucking lead," Danielle said, with a level of warning which traveled through my mind like a warning flag but completely over the head of my sister.

Chapter 4

HOMAYRA: A FIRST LOOK: ATTENTION TO DETAIL

*B*ayade bakereh bashi, was a phrase in Farsi which became common place in my household when my sister and I started coming of age. It meant "remain a virgin", and this was the only education or advice my parents would ever give the two of us with regard to the divine changes that were taking place in our quickly developing young bodies.

My sister and I never once questioned this sacred rule of passage, nor did we even ponder the significance of what men and women did within the privacy of their own bedroom. Sex education was not left to the responsibility of our schools, or even our own parents for that matter. While our schools were advanced in so many ways, our curriculum was meticulously designed by the leaders of our country to keep us at a certain level of ignorance.

My sister and I had a limited understanding of the historical and sociological world outside the borders of our massive country of Iran; there was never any mention of the World Wars, the plight of the Jews, or even Adolf Hitler. Even our parents were restricted from enlightening us to the social mores of the outside world, not to mention, how we should act around adults.

All of those teaching were reserved for the sole responsibility of our future husbands, who had full discretion as to how much we needed to know about human sexuality and when they thought we should be enlightened. Knowledge, it seems, was considered evil in those turbulent times in my country.

So it was for this reason that nothing Golareh and I were about to witness at the castle, in days and months to follow would come as any sort of shock to us because our minds were literally blank slates. We were naive and uninformed twins neatly arranged on a platter for the selfish motivations of the people surrounding us, whose appetite consisted of money, power, sex and greed.

It was about 7:30 p.m., when my sister and I had finished our baths, fixed our hair and put on our long white evening gowns. When I looked at Golareh, it was always as if I was looking at myself, and vise-versa, as neither of us required the use of a mirror. I was always adjusting her clothing and hair, as she would do the same with me. We both shared a high degree of obsessive compulsive disorder, but not to any level of detriment. Our disorder was confined to our daily rituals, patterns, and tasks, which were invisible to us.

That first night at the Castle, both my sister and I looked stunning. We each wore long, white and extremely elegant evening gowns, which were made of sheer layers of rich silk. Our arms and shoulders were bare down to the midpoint of our chest, exposing our smoky brown skin.

Our skin tone was not olive in color, as Italians or Greeks were, but a unique color of earthy brown. The contrast of the white material against my sister's mysterious skin color became vivid to me that night, as I saw both of us as young women for the first time.

We each had broad cheekbones with large, light-brown feline shaped eyes. Our physiques were delicate in nature, with clearly defined feminine features, including our full breasts, which came to us as an odd wakeup call at a young age, and because of these new features I noticed people communicating with us differently. I can recall people gazing at my sister and me with odd expressions. Men would noticeably become awkward in their speech patterns, while their attention scattered to multiple focal points on our bodies. The women, on the other hand, reflected an expression of jealous appraisal, which soon soured to a frown as they leered at their husbands' gazes.

The doorbell suddenly rang, waking me from my momentary trance, as Golareh rushed to the door and opened it. Standing directly under the door frame, was this stunning looking woman in a beautiful, dark gray evening gown. She was leaning against the door frame, with her legs crossed over one another.

Whoever she was had an expression of someone who had been waiting too long for an elevator to arrive. Her shoulders were bare and tan, revealing her slender but muscular arms, a beautifully sculpted neck, delicately carved collar bones, and attractive shoulders.

The mystery woman appeared to be a minimalist and wore very natural jewelry comprised of a simple silver bracelet and a delicate necklace, with a single quartz stone gently lying against her toned chest. We both had no idea who this woman was or why she was even there, until she began to speak, then it all came rushing back to us like a wake-up call.

"Listen to me girls," she quipped, "never open the door without asking who is on the other side. Do you understand me," she demanded. "My God", I thought, "this couldn't be?" The blood in my head felt like it was emptying and my vision began to blur as I was desperately trying to connect this very familiar voice to the completely unrecognizable woman. In my total disbelief, I finally realized that this woman was in fact Zooli.

But the Zooli I remembered from earlier in the day looked nothing like this beautifully angry woman standing in our doorway scowling at us. That woman was cloaked in dark sunglasses, tight riding pants, rugged work boots and a dirty ball cap. What gave her away now were her rugged and strong hands. Zooli had the hands of a worker that were not primped and manicure, but hands that were meant to grab reigns, lift buckets and work.

This Zooli, however, looked absolutely radiant as she walked past my sister, who stood in the doorway with her mouth half open. The back of her dress was very low cut, exposing her flawlessly tanned back. She had long, golden brown hair, with hints of sun bleached highlights, that burst away from her head with the rage of a lion, and tumbled over her shoulders and down her back. She had a fragrance of a mixture of mineral water and natural soaps, while sporting a quizzical expression on her face.

"Well they certainly have you both dolled up beautifully don't they", she said, with an appraising eye, "but damn if you two don't look as if you're going to a christening!"

She walked over to the shadow of a large window box and looked off in the distance, while turning her face away from us. After an awkward moment of silence, she called out loud, "Danni, we will see you down in the Grand Ballroom later, alright? From inside the bathroom we heard a subdued voice replying in return, "okay."

Zooli turned towards us as if she was recapturing her original expression, and it became clear to me that she was holding back some deep emotion. She cleared her throat and said with a newly constructed smile, "Now come with me girls."

I remembered thinking to myself, that Zooli had a chameleonic quality, able to totally change her outward appearance from one extreme to another, but still hadn't quite mastered the ability to fully control her emotions.

As we left our room, we followed a long private hallway that emptied into a large mezzanine area exposing a huge terminal-like quadrant below. The smell of fresh cut flowers, expensive international perfumes and rich tobacco smoke wafted upward.

Large crystal chandeliers camouflaged the ceiling above a massive semicircular staircase that led downward to where people milled around on shiny white marble floors and huge oriental rugs that stretched out of sight. I can recall thinking that this must be what heaven looks like.

It seemed as if everyone in the castle were moving in three-quarter time, from the way they walked and spoke to one another, to their slow, relaxed way they controlled the movement their eyelids. A tall blonde woman with thick makeup glanced at us as we entered her space. Her empty eyes reminded me of the blank eyes of a doll.

The smoke from her slender dark cigar gently emptied through the relaxed openings of her bright red lips and floated towards the overly artistic heavens above. Her hand was gently touching the small of the back of an elderly woman with unnaturally colored red hair and a detached interest. The women with the overly produced hair sipped slowly from her drink, while paying more attention to another equally disinterested woman on her other side.

I turned my head to the other side of the hallway and noticed an elderly man with short cropped gray hair and a long face sitting alone in a dark bar. He had a rather apathetic look on his face, with his legs carefully crossed over one another, revealing his richly polished half boot on his calf. His whole demeanor was that of a contrived pose, almost as if he perceived himself as the center of attention.

On the table in front of him was an unopened, leather bound notebook with a gold pen perfectly positioned in the exact direction as his book. Directly next to his notebook sat a large martini glass, completely full of clear liquor with a lone olive sitting motionless on the bottom. The side of the glass had a noticeable amount of perspiration, signifying to me that he was in no hurry to go anywhere and that perhaps the drink itself was a mere prop in his own private play.

He had the look of an extremely educated man with no need for idle conversation or even company for that matter. He seemed to be there to observe others and not to interact with them. It was as if he considered the people passing by him as open season for some sort of hunt.

He seemed to be tracking me with an unimpressed interest, almost as if he wanted to acquire me as some sort of play toy. But as the three of us walked past him, I felt his interest level begin to intensify. When we were almost completely out of sight, I glanced back and noticed him slowly lifting his glass to his lips while never compromising his gaze on me whatsoever.

Zooli quickly navigated my sister and me to the top of staircase by her fingertips as we descended to the floor below. I noticed an overly-protective look on her face as she leered back at the man at the table behind us, while not breaking full contact with him. She appeared to be telling this strange gentleman to stay away from her pack with a level of protectiveness that I will never forget.

As we moved to a more rapid pace Zooli mentioned to me, "Be at the barn tomorrow morning a 6:30 sharp, and be ready to work. I'm going to give you girls your first lesson in dealing with large and unpredictable creatures."

I wasn't sure why Zooli seemed to walk so much faster than everyone else in the castle, but she certainly did. It was as if she was on a mission to get us to where we were requested to be, get it over with, and then get us out as quickly as possible.

Chapter 5

HOMAYRA: THE AMULET

"For clothing I should say Versace and Cavali, for jewels, I just adore Graff and Harry Winston", I heard someone mention as we walked swiftly down a large and very active hallway. Everything about this castle was huge, from the giant ceramic vases that lined the corridor, to the massive amounts of flowers that exploded out of them. Mounted on the wall, at about every five meters, were large original paintings, portraying stern men and aristocratic matriarchs with cold expressions, standing next to their strong horses awaiting their beckoning call.

Custom clothiers and fine dress shops, within the castle, had their doors wide open with women trying on expensive dresses, while modeling in front of their mildly impressed friends. Smart looking women dressed in scant metallic evening gowns weaved around the customers carrying what appear to be silver trays of neatly arranged appetizers. But as we moved closer to the scene, I noticed that these appetizers were not morsels of food at all, but larger arrangements of diamond necklaces, golden bracelets and precious stones.

Zooli was herding us even faster now, pushing past the high-class feeding frenzy. Her watchful eyes and protective wingspan widened around us as we turned the corner and moved deeper into this thick sea of money and power. My body shivered and I noticed a palpable taste in my mouth, when a vision from my childhood experience on the streets of Tehran reunited with my memory:

A pack of angry dogs were fighting over a huge piece of fat that a butcher had just heaved out a second story window on to the dirty street below. The animals ran after the filthy fat with such an aggressive passion that they seemed totally blind to the world around them.

A well-designed looking man wearing a white turban sat on a wooden throne-like platform with the index finger on his left hand gently curling the blonde hair of a young woman at his side. I presumed that the girl at his side was his daughter, but could not tell because of the expression on her face.

She had an odd look, not reminiscent of a daughter at all, but a kittenish look that seemed hungry for his attention. An elderly black man dressed in a white shirt and black tuxedo worked at his feet, aggressively buffing his already shiny shoes, while two other women, about the same age as his daughter were fawning over his every move.

Immerging from an open door on the opposite side of the hallway from Mr. Turban were colorful lights and pulsating music, which I now remember as being disco music. Two shirtless and perfectly tanned young men wearing tight sequined pants maneuvered what appeared to be a cylindrical birdcage into the center of the hallway in the direction of Mr. Turban.

Mr. Turban appeared to be suddenly repulsed by the harem of women surrounding him and pushed them away. One young woman, who was desperately trying to remain with him, refused to leave and was quickly dragged away by one of the shirtless-blond young men. Just as she started to make a scene she vanished through a door on the opposite side of the hall.

A thick cloud of low hanging fog crept across the floor at the base of the cage and exposed a stationary female human figure. A crystal-white spot light positioned high above beamed down upon the creature in the cage with pinpoint accuracy. My eyes slowly regulated to the quickly changing lighting as I decoded what appeared to be a tall, beautiful black woman with long black hair. She was slowly moving her head in the direction of Mr.

Turban, who watched her with passive interest, as he casually lit a cigarette and slowly pulled the white smoke deeply into his lungs.

The top of the cage lifted towards the ceiling, revealing a lone black figure sitting on a chair with her back positioned towards Mr. Turban. The woman appeared very young and had beautiful ebony skin that appeared to be entangled in only a single white cotton rope, and draped over her left shoulder was a large golden amulet. The woman looked at Mr. Turban as if she were a large black cat, alluring but mysteriously protective of her body and soul.

Mr. Turban's interest built as the onlookers in the area, including the three of us, were gently urged to move on down the line. As the round platform turned clockwise the woman appeared to be inviting Mr. Turban to come into her domain.   Orbiting around her were two photographers quickly snapping shots of this half-human temptress, bound in a web of white cotton rope.

I felt a sharp pain in my left arm which reminded me of the claws of an animal pulling me away. It was Zooli yelling, "move along girls! Do not stop and look any longer!"

Zooli channeled us down the hallway that was rather empty of people while the sounds and smells of the menagerie melted away to a quieter and more subdued atmosphere. I could tell that Zooli was relaxing as her breathing slowed to a normal pace.

"In a moment you will meet Dr. Henri Lepan", Zooli said.   "This is the man that arranged for you to leave Iran at your parents' request. Your cousin Frédéric works for him at the Department of Trade. Henri is an extremely powerful man in both government and social circles. My sweet little ones, I wish to tell you that you will see many people here at the castle in the days ahead," said Zooli, "heads of state, presidents of large corporations and even ladies of apparent royalty. I want you to promise me one thing," she continued, appearing dreadfully serious. "Please treat every single person here at the castle with the same level of respect that you would pay a wild animal. Always keep everyone of them at an arm's length away from you and never let your guard down, not even once," said Zooli, motioning with her hands. "I'm telling you this, girls, for your own good. You are no longer at home in Iran with your parents, you are now in the real world," Zooli whispered, with her eyes narrowing.

We came to a stop in front of an entrance which appeared to be a formal office of some sort. Zooli pressed a button above the brass latch while producing no noticeable report from the room inside. Within a few seconds we heard the sound of the mechanics of the door lock as the huge wooden door opened.

A dignified and well-dressed elderly woman who appeared to be in her mid-sixties greeted us with a welcoming smile. She was of tall stature with a kind face and a long white hair tied in a braid behind her back.

"Oh my god, Zooli," she exclaimed, with genuine pleasure. "It is so wonderful to see you away from the horses, you look absolutely stunning." The woman embraced her. "My heavens, these must be our brand-new visitors from that dreadful country of Iran, I've heard so much about the two of you," she said, looking at us with a level of confusion.

"I am Golareh," my sister exclaimed, "and this is my sister Homayra."

Goli was always the bold one who introduced us both to every one we met. The woman appeared slightly embarrassed for not knowing exactly who was who, but quickly composed herself.

"Girls, my name is Catherine Lepan, but please call me Miss Cathy. I am Henri's mother and he has been so eagerly awaiting your arrival and simply can't wait to see you *again*," Miss Cathy said.

"Well you can call me *Goli*, and this is my twin sister *Homi*," instructed Golareh, while proudly pointing at me.

I had no choice but to ponder what she meant about her son being happy to see us---*again*? What did she mean by again? Zooli also realized that this must have been some sort of mistake on her part, as we followed Miss Cathy down the rich hallway towards an open office.

As Miss Cathy walked, she draped her arms around Zooli lovingly, as if she was extremely fond of her.

"How is my dear *Atticus* today," Miss Cathy asked, with a level of deep concern.

"Oh, he's doing okay Miss Cathy, but he's still a little lame on his back hooves."

"I am so upset with that blacksmith," Miss Cathy quipped. "Every time that man comes here our poor Atticus goes lame. I'm sure he clipped way too much off those hooves mind you. I do hope he doesn't abscess," said Miss Cathy, with a distinct level of intolerance.

"Why can't he see that the poor horse is simply not balanced properly?" Miss Cathy added, "Oh, how I miss my dear Rosedale so much", Miss Cathy said, rather sadly. "He is the best blacksmith we've ever had. Why on earth did he leave us? I just cannot understand!"

"Now dear Miss Cathy, please my love, you mustn't forget that Rosedale died years ago," Zooli said, while gently patting Miss Cathy's face.

"Tell me Zooli," Miss Cathy asked, not referencing Zooli's mention of Rosedale's fate in the least. "Is Atticus still biting that son of mine?"

Zooli, chuckled, while rolling her eyes, "always my dear---the man is clueless."

"I keep telling, Henri," Miss Cathy said, "that he must be gentler to that poor horse. Why just this morning I caught Henri washing him with ice cold water with a hose! I felt like knocking him over the head with my muck rake. Atticus is such a gem, he rides through so much pain and does whatever that boy will tell him to do."

It's suddenly occurred to me that this dignified woman standing before us was the same woman I had seen mucking out stalls earlier today.

"Some men never learn, ladies," Miss Cathy said, as she gently smiled at us. "That is why we horse girls must to stick together," she said, moving us further down the hallway.

As we entered a richly decorated office, I noticed an extremely dashing man with a dignified well-groomed beard, deeply involved in a telephone conversation. He was speaking in a language that sort of reminded me of Spanish, but a little different. But this I could make out: "Oh stop my brother, please, you must come to France. I will treat you with the cream of your crop. You will not believe the uplift I given these babies," Henri boldly said, directly into the blue phone.

The phone he was using was the color of the sky with a long baby-blue cord tethered to a receiver on the other side of the room. I remember thinking to myself that the cord looked like some sort of leash, holding him against his will.

He was wearing a dark suit, crisp-white shirt and a handsome dark tie. His dark brown hair was combed meticulously but with an elegant flair. As we entered the room, he gazed up at us over his reading glasses and smiled. Henri continued his conversation but quickly terminated his phone conversation.

"Please my brother, you will enjoy the improvements I've made in your *objects*. Goodbye my brother and live well," Henri said, as he hung up the phone.

He walked toward us with a stylish grace and a welcoming smile, almost as if he owned the floor on which he stood.

"I am so happy to see you both", Henri said, as he extended his hands to my sister and me. "Just this morning I assured your uncle that you had arrived safely, and he is very much relieved.

I so hope that you're enjoying your time with Zooli? My mother was so adamant about you both spending time with her. You will learn so much from that horse woman as she is the best in the world," Henri said, as he smiled at Zooli.

"Well, I wish you would learn something from Zooli, my son," quipped Miss Cathy, with a chuckle, to which Henri began to laugh out loud, almost uncontrollably.

"Ladies," Henri announced, "these two wonderful women are always trying to set me straight. Now you two young ladies appear to be very hungry," Henri said, motioning towards the door. "We have a wonderful dinner planned for you both in the Grand Ballroom. I can't wait to introduce you to the rest of our guests."

Henri gently held my hand while struggling to reach my sister's fleeting hand as we walked to the dining room.

I felt an unknown familiarity emanating from the touch this huge man's hands. I was also flushed with attraction to his stature and handsome features. He owned such a giant demeanor and I remember feeling safe in his presence as we walked hand in hand towards the ballroom.

To my surprise, however, when I glanced over at my sister's face, I noticed a totally different expression than mine, one of almost complete distrust. It was as if Golareh instantly disliked Henri for reasons I simply failed to understand. Zooli picked up on Golareh's temperament as well and playfully stole Golareh away from Henri as if she were dancing, almost like she might save a freighted horse from a sudden panic attack. The dance was contrived and I remember seeing Henri taking note of my sister's protective and untrusting nature.

The lights from a spotlight from the ceiling of the Grand Ballroom shined down on us as the five of us entered and to my astonishment everyone in the room stood in applause.

"Ladies and gentleman," an announcer's voice boomed from hidden speakers. "Please stand and welcome, Dr. Henri Lepan, with his beautiful mother along with their very special guests of honor."

I was shocked and highly embarrassed, but yet extremely humbled, as we walked into this large room with all of these magnificent looking people standing at attention. How lucky we were to be entering this fabulous dining room of a massive castle, in the very same company of this handsome prince and queen. I became totally overwhelmed and quite happy to be a part of it all and I realized that I wanted more.

As we slowly moved from the back of the room towards our table up front, the band began to come alive. Henri and his mother were shaking hands with everyone along the way. When we reached our beautifully appointed table, which was adorned in a white linen table cloth, priceless china, crystal goblets and golden flatware, an usher pushed his way through the crowd holding a microphone on top of a burgundy velvet pillow, while carefully trailing a long black cord on the floor behind him. He politely handed the microphone to Henri, who began to speak.

"Ladies and gentle, welcome," Henri spoke with a level of grand eloquence, "this is a very special evening for both my mother and me. We both want to first extend our sincere appreciation to Chef Michael Schrez for preparing such a wonderful dinner for us this evening."

The room exploded into applause and quickly went quiet.

"And now it is with great pleasure to introduce our newest guests here at the Castle, who have journeyed from a land so far away; Iran, ladies and gentleman that dreadfully war torn country of Iran.

Please welcome Homayra and Golareh Parastou, to our dinner this evening," said Henri, as the room exploded in applause. I blushed with humility as I stared at the beautiful people standing around me with their massive wealth. The sight so aroused me that for a second I completely lost sight of my wonderful homeland and I have regretted that moment ever since.

"I want to also introduce one of the world's most esteemed equestrian trainers who recently completed her assignment with our beloved Cavalry of the French Republican Guard, the most lovely, Miss Zooli Trahm."

The crowd applauded with an ever building intensity, but still the excitement grew stronger.

"Now my friends," Henri spoke with pride, "I would like to introduce our next guest, who has just come directly from a concert at the base of the Egyptian Pyramids! Ladies and gentleman," Henri's voice boomed with excitement. "I am so very humbled to welcome my very close and dear friend, Frank, who has just turned the young age of 64. Happy birthday my young friend," Henri said with pride.

The crowd went wild, with a roar so loud that I thought the ceiling might collapse. "Ladies and gentlemen," Henri announced again, "please welcome and help me celebrate this wonderful man's birthday this evening, the crooner himself, Mr. Frank Soriano!"

To everyone's delight, slowly strolling across the stage, under a white hot spot light appeared Frank Soriano, a famous singer and movie star from the United States of America, holding a microphone in one hand and a fedora in the other. The band began to come alive as he waved to Henri with a school boy smile, and began to sing.

As the voice of the beloved crooner put the entire crowd into a deep trance, I noticed in the corner of my eye, Danielle entering the room, through a side entrance. She was dressed in a long backless red evening gown with her hair neatly tucked under a delicate black shawl. Her persona seemed almost unknown to me, as she slowly walked completely unnoticed to our table. She appeared defeated and terribly sad.

As she came into view, Golareh stared at Danielle with a look of shock. I felt a cold chill shoot up my spine as I clearly recognized a large piece of jewelry hanging like a piece of artwork from over her left shoulder. It was then I realized that piece of artwork was the same golden amulet that hung from the shoulder of that half-naked temptress which was tied in ropes in the hallway with that strange man in the turban.

Chapter 6

HOMAYRA: LESSON 1: PASSIVE PERSISTENCE

"Calm, forward, straight"

- *ALEXIS L'HOTTE*

The next morning at 8 o'clock, after we all, including Miss Cathy, fed all 20 horses and lightly picked out each of their stalls, Danielle told me to report to the large pasture for my first lesson. As I maneuvered my body through the center slat on the wooden fence and stood up straight, I saw Zooli standing far off in the distance appearing to be waiting for me.

She looked so different that morning from the way she had appeared at dinner the night before, suspicious and uncomfortable. She had a renewed level of confidence that was accompanied with her refreshing sternness. Zooli was clearly back in her element and I could hear it immediately in the tone of her voice.

"Get rid of your gum, Homayra", she demanded. "And --- please don't throw that gum on the ground", she said, as she handed me a small piece of paper from her pocket.

"Homayra, I want you to have your riding helmet on before you come for a lesson and not after you arrive! When you come out here in the morning, I want you to be ready to work, do you understand me?"

"Yes ma'am," I said, biting my tongue.

"These horses will not wait on you to put your helmet on as they knock you on your butt and cause you to choke on that gum in your mouth. --- And will you please stop calling me ma'am, I am Zooli!"

I noticed that when Zooli was teaching any of her students, it didn't matter whether they were rich guests at the castle, Danielle, Miss Cathy or my sister and I, she would completely switch over into the role of a serious instructor. Anyone who dared to interrupt her during her lessons was either totally ignored or firmly instructed not to interrupt. She was always fair and never angry with the horses or those students who tried their best. Zooli was always complementary when we were performing properly.

The lengths of our lessons were variable and always linked to the condition of the horse. "The horse comes first," she always would say. She was also there for everybody, paying complete attention to her students. It didn't matter whether she was teaching one student in the early morning or a group of people at the end of the day, her energy level was always peaking and spot on.

"Now Homayra, today I'm going to give you a life lesson of sorts on managing creatures that are much larger than you. I want you to pay particular attention to what I'm about to teach you because you will use these principles as a way of life and not just with these horses. Do you understand me, young lady?

Now, the horses that you will be working with here at the castle will all be an average of 16 hands and at least 500 kilos. Each one of these horses is able to put you down by a simple turn of their head. So if you are not watching where your body is with respect to the many parts of the horse, you could be knocked completely off your feet, simply because a leaf falls off a nearby tree. Are you following to me, Homi," she demanded as I quietly nodded.

"Now when you are in the same space as these animals, you need to let them know that you are firmly and fairly in control of the task at hand. The moment they think you are not sure of yourself, that will be the moment they will step in and attempt to gain an advantage over you. It's not what you say around these creatures that matters, it's the confidence that you employ when you interact with them. These horses will test you in ways that you can never imagine and the moment they see you drop your guard; that's the moment they pop down and clean your clock!"

I was beginning to think that Zooli was desperately trying to teach me something important and that the lesson she was giving me pertained to the dangerous forces around us that didn't necessarily stand on four legs.

"Now I want you to step out there on the top of that hill over there and call for Atticus!"

How do you call a horse, I wondered? "What do I call him; do I call them by their name?" I asked, as I timidly walked up onto ridge of the hill.

"Of course you do," she said laughing. "How else do you think you will call them, by their breed?" Zooli lifted her dark sunglasses and eyeballed me.

So I cleared my throat and started to yell, "Atticus! Come!"

"Louder Homi, they have to hear you, girl. Now---call them like you mean it, and as if you really want them to come to you!"

I remembered feeling touched, by Zooli actually calling me by my nickname "Homi," which was mainly reserved for my sister. So this time, with more confidence, I really raised my voice and yelled, "Atticus, come!"

From out of nowhere I watched not one but two huge horses in the distance charging down the hill directly at me. I felt the sudden urge to start running for my life.

"Oh, I forgot to tell you," said Zooli, laughing into the sky, "horses are herd animals and they hate to be left alone, so if you call one, you can usually expect others to follow!"

"How do I stop them?" I yelled, as I felt my knees beginning to weaken.

"Well, first of all Homi, stand tall, look big and believe that you are larger they are. Remember they have to actually see you, so stand up straight young lady," instructed Zooli, still laughing. "You don't want them to trample over you and never know you were even there do you? Now raise your arms above your head and tell them to stop with your hands.

Now this is very important part, Homi---and I want you to listen to me very closely! As these horses approach you at full gallop, you must completely believe in your mind, that you are bigger than they are, and when you tell them to stop, you had better damn well mean it," exclaimed Zooli, from a safe position on the hill.

"You are not just hoping that they will stop, or that you are praying for them to stop. Homi, you're not even *asking* them to stop! You are willing them to stop! Do you understand what I'm telling you, Homayra? They must see in your eyes that you are calm and that you mean business!"

With the sound of the powerful hooves pounding on the grassy terrain in front of me, I felt far from calm, collected and in control. I felt like peeing my pants. But something changed in me; I suddenly adopted a new mindset, it was either meet the challenge head on or face certain death. Zooli continued to instruct me from the sidelines as her voice permeated my entire being. "*Stand your ground, make yourself bigger than the charging force, and mean what you say,*" I confidently told myself.

As I raised my arms above my head and began to wave them, I began to actually feel in control, because there was no way out of this situation, it was either stand my ground and control these raging creatures, or let them trample me down into a bloody mess in the grass. I felt my entire personality change that morning, as I waved them down to a slowing pace. I simply could not believe my eyes. These two huge thoroughbreds began to melt down to a safe pace before my, *now very giant*, body.

Simply adjusting my demeanor and confidence caused the fire in their eyes to soften to a peaceful calm. This became my first lesson in managing larger-than-life dangers, and I could see a sense of relief in Zooli's eyes as I realized this lesson.

Zooli slid one of the halters off her right shoulder and smoothly but slowly approached Atticus, the darker of the two horses. Atticus was a very large thoroughbred male, with dark black eyes and a dusty black face. He had the look of a huge war horse.

As she softly began to guide his nose through the center of the halter, I noticed how gentle but purposeful Zooli's movements were. She wasn't spastic or timid, but respectfully cautious, confident and ever so patient.

"Homi, I want to teach you a life lesson, and I want you to remember from this day forward. It's with regard to living around dangerous creatures that may try to control and destroy you. Some of these creatures appear extremely threatening, and turn out to be angels, while others seem very safe and trustworthy, but will try to trample over you just because you're in their space.

Some of these creatures are very smart, while others are actually not that bright at all; but, each can pounce on you in a split second, teeth first, and make you wish you were going to the morgue, rather than to a hospital.

You must treat the size of these creatures with respect. But you always have to let them know that *you are in control*, even though your small body cannot physically fend off the power of any of them.

When Zooli moved to the left side of the horse and gazed directly at the horse's hindquarters, Atticus stepped aside as if he were looking into her eyes and doing exactly what she wanted him to do, without her saying a single word. I found this lesson amazing.

"If I want him to move his body sideways, I gently provide a small bit of pressure with both of my hands to the side of his body and hold it there until he moves."

With only the tips of her index fingers, she was able to move this giant creature in a dance like pattern around the field.

She then called me over and told me to do the same. I could hardly believe what was happening; by applying a constant amount of gentle pressure, I could send a firm message to the brain of this powerful creature, to move in the direction that I wanted.

"Young lady, this is what I call *passive persistence* and this is what I want you and your sister to learn from me as soon as possible. If you master these lessons you will be able coexist in the same space as these beautiful horses and the many people you will meet in the days to come. You did great, girl."

Zooli put her arms around me and gave me a hug.

"Tomorrow I'm going to show you what to do when these creatures try to pounce on you," Zooli said, as she turned and fed Atticus a tasty hay cube.

"Great, I can't wait for that lesson!"

"Now go find your sister and send her out here to me, then you and Danni go rake the big riding arena!"

As I ran towards the barn I felt so wonderfully alive, as I inhaled the fragrances of the pastures and that early morning air. I thought about what I had just learned as I listened to Zooli yelling at me from the grassy hill behind me.

"Tell your sister to spit her gum out too---but in the garbage can in the barn---and to put her helmet on before she comes out here to work!"

I left Zooli standing with the two thoroughbreds, and as I turned and glanced back, I noticed her gently holding the massive head of Atticus in her arms, while patting the other mare's ears. I fell in love with the soul of Zooli that day. That powerful woman of such profound beauty along with that very strange name made a powerful impact on me that day.

Her lessons served me well during my stay at the Castle. I know now that Zooli was desperately trying to arm me for the dark and dangerous days to follow.

Chapter 7

HOMAYRA: OBSESSED HORSE SISTERS

When I arrived back at the main stable, there was no one to be found, only the horses which were quietly standing in their stalls focusing solely on their morning grain rations and evenly distributed flakes of hay. Each horse would quietly and periodically raise its large head with a curious glance towards me and then quickly return to eating.

I sat down on a large bale of hay, loosened my chin strap and removed my riding helmet while fluffing my hair away from my sweaty forehead and resting my riding boots on an overturned water bucket. As I was setting down my riding helmet, I noticed a white piece of bailing twine sitting on the hay next to me. I picked it up and began to gently wrap the twine around my arm.

The barn was very peaceful with horses quietly munching away. Periodically the silence would be broken by the sound of a large horse relieving himself in the woodchips at his feet. "Thanks", I mumbled under my breath, imagining five liters of urine flooding the relatively clean stall that I had picked out earlier, "that will be one more task for me to do today."

As I looked at the white bailing twine around my arms, I remembered Danielle the night before, posing in that strange position, on that round platform in front of that mysterious man in the turban. I couldn't reconcile the image I had witnessed of Danielle in this odd setting with the Danielle that I had cleaned stalls with just hours earlier because her appearance and demeanor had been so shockingly different.

Everything about her appearance was skewed, from her overly styled hair, to the thick eyeliner that enhanced her equally strange look. I believe it was the expression on her face that shocked me the most. For that did not belong to that obedient student I had seen following the coordinated instruction of Zooli, as she so confidently sat on the back of her favorite horse that she affectionately referred to as "Cookie." The new visual I had of Danielle was a deviant double, or some sort of intense prisoner sitting on a desert plate in front of a selfish glutton. This new Danielle appeared to be hollow and extremely vacant, while being held captive by a mysterious power much larger than she was.

I remember seeing exotic dancers in the street back in Tehran, moving in time to the mysterious rhythm and sounds of ancient drums and strings. The images of these beautiful but mysterious women broadened my limited understanding of both the arts and a new phenomenon which can only be described by single word known as *erotic*.

My mother and father would look upon these dancers with great pride and admiration, but also with an evident level of personal interest and intrigue. I was told they were acting out ancient stories that were written by our forefathers centuries ago. My mother was fascinated by this expression of dance, and actually owned some of the exotic costumes that were mostly reserved for the more male audience.

Even though my family was a true melting pot of religious cultures, music and dance broke all barriers. My father was Chiite, my mother was Sunite, and one grandfather was Catholic, while the others were Kurdes. Love and respect was the binding thread that sowed us all together and music and dance was never restricted in our household.

I remember hearing the sound of tambourines, finger cymbals, and four stringed lutes, sneaking from beneath the closed door of the living room in our home, as my father laughed quietly with his hands gently clapping. My mother would dance in front of him exposing her beautiful belly to my father as he gently touched the beads that swayed from her curvaceous mid-section.

My mother would *never* dream of dancing in front of us, but Goli and I were extremely motivated, and quite familiar with the crawl spaces and hidden architecture of our home. We would watch complete shows and sometime double features of my joyful parents entertaining themselves by this ancient art by peering through a crack in the door or the aperture of a keyhole.

Once Golareh totally lost her composure and exploded into a loud belly-laugh causing the music to came to an abrupt halt, as my father's feet could be heard banging across the wooden floor towards the door. Goli and I flew away like birds to the far off recesses of the house before my father even turned the door knob. I remember thinking how lucky we were to have witnessed my lovely parent's private moments, and *also* how lucky we were to have *not* seen much more. But the vision I saw of Danielle the night before seemed quite contrary to the memories of my happy mother, playfully dancing in front of my proud father.

Danielle's scene was far from happy and totally devoid of any romantic expression whatsoever. Even the music itself was empty of any sort of artistic meaning. There seemed to be no storyline associated with this dark act that Danielle was playing on that rotating stage with her angry and frightened look. She contained the look of a cornered cat, trying to lure an enemy into striking distance.

The man in the turban resembled nothing like my father watching my mother with playful delight. This man had the look of passive annoyance and disinterest. Each character seemed to be playing a game of sexual brinksmanship, which now provided me with a skewed and dirty definition of the word erotic.

The golden amulet that hung from Danielle's shoulder was clearly the most disturbing thing I had witnessed. In my homeland these sorts of relics were used to arouse demons and evil spirits. In no order of imagination would that amulet be used to conjure up romance or love. Just the thought of my mother wearing this spiritual remnant during one of her performances would be something impossible to imagine. So the word *evil* would be the most accurate word to describe Danielle's strange performance the night before.

Reality began to reenter my day dreaming as I heard the sound of a distant tractor slowly making its way towards the stables. Coming out of the woods, from across the stone bridge, on the far side of the main grazing area, were my sister and Danielle. I could hear them laughing uncontrollably as they motored their way into view. Their faces were beaming with delight as the old farm tractor slowly moved through the tall, mid-summer grass towards the barn.

Goli was sitting at the wheel of the dark red tractor, as Danielle stood behind her with her arms draped over my sister's shoulders, smiling broadly while yelling driving instructions into Goli's ear. Trailing behind the tractor was a small flatbed trailer with six empty multicolored muck buckets, stacked on top of one another. Goli was laughing so hard that she could barely steer the tractor in the right direction. And as the two girls came closer, I noticed that they were both completely covered in horse manure and soiled woodchips.

The two girls looked very happy as they ran up and wrapped their smelly bodies around me. The three of us laughed and danced in the dusty alley way, for the entertainment of all of the horses which were staring at us with remnants of hay hanging from their motionless lips. The laughter and smiles on the faces of my sister and Danielle were so infectious that I totally forgot about my confused thoughts.

"Oh shit", I suddenly thought, I almost forgot to tell Goli that Zooli was waiting for her up on the hill in the upper pasture. With a broad smile on her face and a fresh stick of gum in her mouth, Goli snatched up her riding helmet and ran for the upper pasture. As she ran towards the distant figure of Zooli carefully ground-working the two horses in the distance, I suddenly remembered the instructions I failed to tell my sister regarding spitting out her gum and having her helmet on when she arrived.

Danielle also taught me to drive the red tractor that day as well, as we made revolutions around the large, dusty sand arena, making imaginative fresh designs with the landscaping rake that scratched the surface behind us. We worked and played all day like obsessed horse sisters, straight through lunchtime and up to sundown. As the three of us slowly walked towards the castle that evening, exhausted, sweaty and sun-drenched, all concerns regarding the strange world around us vanished from my mind.

For the next several months we had our own horse-world to apply ourselves to, complete with Zooli, Miss Cathy and those wonderful horses. The evil and dark forces within the castle and all around us didn't stand a chance in piercing the armor of our equestrian paradise.

INTERTWINED

The dreams started happening to the both of us when we were only nine years old, and at first I thought the visions belonged solely to me. But as I grew older, I realized that many of the odd dreams were comprised of Homayra's actual impressions of the world around her, and not necessarily my own.

There were times when I was totally convinced, that I absolutely did not like a particular person, but then I would go to sleep at night and have the most vivid dreams of attraction and appreciation for that person. I would suddenly wake up in a cold and confused sweat, trying to decipher fact from fiction. How could I dislike something so clearly during the day, but love it in my dreams at night? This strange anomaly happened to both of us, and would also extend itself to everything else in our tightly linked world, like food, clothing, art and music. I remember absolutely hating the taste of cantaloupe while knowing full well that Homayra loved it, and sure enough, my dreams would be based on the lovely taste of that horrid fruit I despised.

These odd dream sequences became less frequent as we grew older, but would reappear during times of increased excitement and stress. As we became more familiar with this strange phenomenon, we started to look forward to them occurring. I valued this communication linkage, and thought, how lucky I was to have a secret passage into my beautiful sister's soul. I'm sure that Homayra shared that same access as I did.

Chapter 8

GOLAREH: ANIMAL INSTINCT

C*hemistry* is the word that came to mind when I saw Atticus in the company of Henri, and unfortunately, especially for Atticus, the chemistry was not good. Henri would frequently come to the stables, always dressed impeccably, with his boots perfectly polished, riding pants neatly pressed, shirt and riding jacket appearing as if they had never been worn.

He appeared at the most inappropriate times of the day to spy on us both, often early in the morning before the horses were fed, or in the evening, when it was completely dark. I can recall the first time Zooli ever confided in me, even though it was most likely by mistake and under her breath. She said, "Damn, it's Henri again, and he's going to ride that poor horse tonight!"

Henri entered the stable area as if he owned every single flake of hay. On one occasion one of Zooli's favorite dogs named "Kizzie", a Rhodesian Ridgeback, Pit-Bull Mix, came running up to Henri to greet him and without any reason what so ever, Henri kicked the poor dog in the stomach as if it were a soccer ball. Squealing in pain Kizzie tumbled across the dusty pathway and beneath an occupied horse stall door.

Zooli was not around at the time to witness that sinful act and had she been, I could only imagine what she might have done. Henri didn't know that I was watching him until I made myself visible by stepping into the alleyway. He glanced at me with his light blue eyes, and quickly looked away, as if he'd been caught in the act of torturing an animal. I continued to stare at him with an uncontrollable measure of contempt. I believe that Henri knew from that day forward that I understood what he was all about. Henri was a pushy inconsiderate bully who liked to inflict pain on others for his own sick pleasure.

Once, when Henri arrived unannounced, I thought that Atticus was lame or in some sort of pain. He stood off in the distance, along the fence line, at the far end of the pasture, with his rear end facing us and his head hung low. He looked as if he were trying to make himself appear invisible, gazing downward, clearly rejecting his time with Henri.

Henri respected horses the way a spoiled teenager would treat the family car after he stolen it away for a joy ride. He performed little preparation for his ride, unlike a responsible rider, who would check for soundness and the overall mood of the horse. Henri would simply mount up and ride those poor horses as hard as he possibly could while leaving them sore and completely exhausted afterwards.

Henri's treatment of all animals, especially Atticus, was a huge source of consternation to Zooli, who at times could be heard pleading with Henri not to ride an injured horse with such intensity. "He's sore today, Henri. I think he might've stepped on something that bruised his sole," she would try to explain. "Well he looks just fine to me, "Henri would say, smiling as he snatched the poor horse away.

It became clear to me, and obviously Zooli, that Henri had little compassion for horses, considering them insignificant creatures, which were available to humans for their frivolous pleasure. Ride them until they are useless and dispose of them at the point of any noticeable decline in performance, was Henri's motto.

Homayra was well aware of the fact that I did not like Henri from the very first moment we met, and it was also very clear to me that Atticus and Kizzie shared the same contempt for Henri's forceful nature. Homayra, on the other hand, was so taken with Henri, that she appeared to melt in his presence, and while her attraction for Henri was not necessarily romantic, she was definitely in awe of his powerful, handsome and debonair stature.

Henri watched my sister ride with an admiration more for her rear-end than the talent she exhibited on horseback. He was constantly touching Homayra when Zooli was not around and my sister seemed to welcome it. She was naive with delight and completely oblivious to Henri's true contents. My sister had never felt the touch of a man and had nothing to compare him to. She and I were expected to be taught by our selected mate, and somehow I think Henri knew that about us and worked it to his advantage.

Homayra and I never felt the need to explain our independent impressions of Henri, or any person we met, for that matter, because we each were so keenly aware of each other's thoughts. I also believed that if I voiced my negative opinion of Henri it would burst this happy bubble that surrounded her. I therefore made it my mission to let her live her dream, while I stood guard with a protective eye. I never told Homayra or Zooli about that incident with Kizzie and I have regretted that decision ever since.

Over the weeks and months to follow, it became evident to me that Danielle's and my interest in horses were not as intense as Homayra's had become. My sister spent much more time in her lessons with Zooli, advancing her equitation skills and spending time with the horses which she had come to love. This shift in Homayra's attention gave me more time to spend with Danielle, to whom I was becoming so very close, by a measure that was unexplainable to me at the time. I just knew that when I was in the presence of Danielle I just felt wonderful, beautiful and like a complete woman.

Chapter 9

GOLAREH: RECONNAISSANCE

Danielle and I began to notice that we each had a common talent, the ability to move in a stealthily way through throngs of people at the castle, without being noticed. My talent of maneuvering through danger-ous situations had been developed when we were just children satisfying our curiosity of the world around us, but knowing full well that we were sometimes in places we should never have been. Our poor mother and father would have punished us severely had they have known that earlier in the day we had been crawling under the tables of the fruit markets in the lower end of Tehran's market district.

Danielle's expertise had been gained when she was just a child left alone on the streets of London by an alcohol-drenched, disabled father, who slept all day long at home. The one habit Danielle simply could not control was her unyielding and never ending use of swear words, which seasoned her speech with no regard to the people around her. Zooli and Miss Cathy tried relent-lessly to curb her speech patterns, but found it impossible and finally gave up. Swear words were just a part of Danielle's personal makeup, and they loved her regardless. So it was with these sets of skills, coupled with our intense curiosity, which motivated us to investigate the large and mysteri-ous castle in which we lived.

I had another more plausible reason to investigate my surroundings and that was for my sister's and my safety and wellbeing. I was taught at a very young age, by my parents, no less, to always be aware of the entrances and exits in the buildings and homes in which we ventured. I felt it my responsibility to clearly know the boundaries surrounding my sister and me. So with careful attention to timing and detail, Danielle and I secretly slipped into the inner world of the castle, while leaving Homayra and Zooli deeply involved in their activities.

Both Danielle and I had our behaviors down to a science, and I especially appreciated Danielle's instruction in the way we appeared to the people around us. "Simply put," Danielle said in her thick cockney accent, "you must fucking take on the mannerisms of the people around you. Make yourself look more like them, by appearing like you belong there. Never stand still wondering what to do next, but always appear that you have a purpose for every single move you make.

When you speak to me," Danielle said, "you must speak at a volume and a purpose, exactly like those around us. Do not appear overly happy, but match your mannerisms to the cadence and the mood of those around you. If someone approaches you with any hint of suspicion," Danielle instructed, "approach them with the exact same fucking manner of tone, with a direct question about an item that might be missing, or a thing that should be replaced, or that something was not at all to your goddamn satisfaction. Now remember this Goli," Danielle said, "If they approach you in a fucking threatening manner, always walk through them, causing them to back up, and yield to you. When you back people up, you disarm them temporarily. Treat these approaching forces just as Zooli taught us to respond to the charging horses in the pasture." This lesson in purposeful movement, allowed us to gain access to the most secretive side of the castle.

We would meticulously plan out our dress and travel-itinerary to the various parts of the castle we planned to visit on the following day. Since Danielle was so frequently dressed for so many occasions, which was beyond my understanding at the time, she had accumulated a vast inventory of clothing, which could be worn for any occasion. Even though she was taller than I was, with minimal adjustments, we could accommodate each of us for any venue we chose to visit; however, we had to watch our schedule and make sure that we were back at the stable exactly when we needed to be.

We fashioned ourselves as reconnaissance soldiers, on a mission to slip into enemy territory to gain vital intelligence and then to exit safely.

All of our actions during the preparations, whether it was in the changing our clothes or our movements to the obscure entrances in the castle, were fine-tuned, and well planned, but once inside we had to match our movements to the pace of the people within the danger zone and this is what caused us problems.

On our very first excursion into the castle, we made it our objective to reach what we thought was the midpoint point of the massive building; however, we soon found that the castle was much larger than we expected, and we barely made it back to the stable in time to meet Zooli and Homayra who were coming in from the upper pasture.

The castle itself was huge, with more than seven restaurants and bar areas noticeable up to only our halfway point. We soon learned that the castle was made up of more than 105 beautifully decorated suites, some of which were enclosed in towers on the many corners of the huge building. We also understood that there were at least three massive penthouse suites, complete with their own service staff, which provided spectacular views of the surrounding grounds and French Alps in the distance. This first trip taught us a lot with regard to the scale of the property and how we would plan our more efficient trips in the days to come.

Chapter 10

HOMAYRA: WE MERE ORPHANS

Danielle was sitting on her horse "Cookie," while Goli and I were perched on our mares. The horses stood still, with their eyes lowered to half-mast, while allowing the sun to gently warm their bodies. I loved these opportunities to blend with the horses, listening to the sound of hooves working the footing in the large riding arena, as Zooli, warmed up Atticus during his early afternoon workout.

Watching Zooli ride was truly amazing; her body was built to be on top of a horse. Her seat blended in perfectly with the saddle on Atticus, and her motions were so incredibly fluid, as she walked, trotted and cantered her way around the huge dusty arena.

She rode as is if nothing else in the world mattered to her. She wore a serious and sophisticated expression on her face. Her dark brown eyes watched carefully as she examined every movement of the horse, while navigating a pattern that was dynamically designed in her mind. Atticus bumped along with his lazy but labored look which was caused by some unknown soreness somewhere in his body, and Zooli was determined to find out exactly where that source of pain was coming from.

Every part of Zooli was tuned in to the motion of Atticus. She listened to the air enter and exit his large lungs as the massive bones and musculature moved beneath her saddle. Zooli could read the physical and emotional expressions of a horse by the position of its ears and the intensity in its eyes, which were becoming "soft," a term which described as being relaxed. Zooli knew when the conditions of the horse were right to canter, gallop, and even jump, but most importantly, she knew when it was vitally necessary to dismount the horse and move to safety.

As we sat watching Zooli travel around the arena with her ponytail bobbing up and down to the rhythm of the gait, we noticed a large black limousine slowly turning the corner, moving down the gravel road, and stopping just outside the gate. After a few minutes a driver emerged and slowly walked around the back of the car to the side facing us.

When the driver opened the center door of the limo a young man with curly, dark-black hair rotated his hips and planted his feet on the dusty road beneath him. At about the same time, Henri stepped out of the front passenger seat and the two men positioned themselves side by side. The young man looked shy, while Henri sported the look of a proud father, as they watched Zooli bring her routine to an abbreviated conclusion in the center of the arena.

Both of the distinguished gentlemen approached the fence with enthusiasm. "Hello girls," Henri announced with a smile, "I have someone here that I would like you to meet. Come say hello to my handsome young friend." Zooli walked Atticus past our horses while each of our horses followed along with their own level of curiosity.

I didn't recognize the young man's face at first but there was something about him that seemed oddly familiar. He had absolutely gorgeous brown eyes and a physique that was beautiful. He appeared to be in his early to mid-20s.

Henri stood there grinning at us with that cheshire grin, which was becoming his featured trademark. "Do you girls know who this young man is?" Henri asked, as he placed his large hand on the young man's back. Goli and I stood there examining the young man, feeling that we knew him, but couldn't quite place him. Henri's grin began to broaden with excitement as he announced, "Girls, I would like to introduce you to your cousin Frédéric."

Suddenly it all came rushing back to me, this skinny boy whom we knew as *Jalal* once chased us around our backyard back in Iran, while our entire extended family celebrated *Nowrouz*, a Persian celebration for the New Year, marking the first day of spring. It was a time when all of the women would remove the rugs from their homes, and beat them clean in the noon-day sun.

I remembered Jalal leaping over a fire that was built in the center of our yard, and my being so angry with my father for not allowing me jump over it with him.

"Oh my god," Golareh screamed, "Its Jalal!" I stood thinking, how cute he was then, and how absolutely gorgeous he is now!

Goli and I slid off our horses and ran towards the gate. Frédéric fumbled with the latch and swung it open, greeting us with open arms, as we gathered into an intense group embrace.

The three of us clung to each other for what felt like a lost life-time, as tears of emotion streamed from my eyes and soaked into his expensive charcoal suit. Golareh was burying her face into his chest, her own tears staining his royal blue oxford shirt.

Out of nowhere I had a mental vision of my parents, as if they had been positioned offstage and neglected for weeks. As I held Frédéric I felt waves of deep guilt build and boldly impress themselves upon me. I suddenly felt the full impact of my parents back in Iran, dealing with their daily trauma alone, while we were in this fantasy land of sorts, with all of these haughty, upper-class snobs. "How dare you, Homayra," I thought to myself, "that you feel as if you have the luxury or even the right to rest at night, while your poor parents are left in their country, which was now buckling at its knees."

I felt my knees become numb and lifeless as I dropped to the ground. I knew I wasn't acting out some teenage drama as I lost complete control of my emotions. I felt so neglectful for giving such little thought to my suffering parents back in Iran.

I thought of my mother, vomiting on the polished wooden floor next to her bed, as her suffering body rolled around in misery, while she witnessed her little girls departing to a castle somewhere so far away. So here we were, my spoiled sister and I, living this life of riches, and riding these expensive horses that probably cost as much as my parents' home. "Shame on me," I cried in desperation, "Damn--my soul!" I screamed, as I began to *fade to black*.

I soon felt the gentle touch of Zooli's hand on each side of my perspiring face, as she massaged me back to consciousness. To my total disbelief, I suddenly came to the realization that I had fainted. My sweet cousin Frédéric came into focus and a thick level of nausea set in. "Bring her some water and get some ice!" Zooli yelled to a few bystanders, as the quiet horses grazed carefree nearby.

As my wits slowly began to return, embarrassment moved in to take the place of my confusing thoughts. I could not believe how juvenile I must have appeared in front of my dear cousin Frédéric, who I suddenly remembered having a huge crush on as a child. I sat there in a daze staring at everyone standing over me as my composure began to re-inflate my lifeless extremities. For the first time in weeks, I felt the incredible feeling of family again, for as I looked into Frédéric's surprised but comforting eyes, I saw my wonderful parents, looking down on the three of us with pride.

After my most embarrassing and highly charged emotional implosion, things began to normalize, as my sister and I, along with Zooli, went back to our rooms to wash up and change into some casualwear. We later joined Henri and Frédéric for lunch at an absolutely beautiful café overlooking the tennis courts and pool on the eastern side of the castle.

For the first time since we arrived at the castle, I caught my initial glimpse of our surroundings during its normal summer operations and what I saw seemed strange, but by today's moral standards, completely inappropriate. Zooli made sure that we stayed within her view and away from the castle grounds.

Up until that day I never really looked at the guests of the hotel as they moved through their activities of the day. I simply considered the guests as just wealthy couples enjoying a luxury vacation where they, at their worst, might get a bit dizzy from their drinks.

Below us I noticed many pretty women in tiny bikinis sunning themselves by the pool. Many seemed much younger than my sister and I of perhaps 13-years of age. Some of the young teenage girls were mingling with men old enough to be their own fathers. The swim suits they wore seemed almost invisible as they applied suntan lotion all over the gross hairy backs of the fat older men.

The fact that the girls were so young made an impression on me for reasons I was unsure of. I was never taught about what was considered inappropriate between children and adults. However when I noticed an elderly man walking away from the pool with his arms around the waist of a young woman with the face of a child, something inside of me told me that there was something just not right about the castle.

Two bare-chested teenage boys in tight fitting tennis shorts were playing mixed-doubles with two curvaceous elderly women about the same age as the fat, hairy man by the pool and were dressed in clothing that seemed entirely inappropriate for women of their ages. Short tennis skirts revealed their older white legs marked with varicose veins and cellulite. However they each seemed so very proud of their overly exposed large breasts which they flaunted to the young boys as if they were trophies.

The boys were both very handsome but noticeably young, having not a hair on their chests and legs. They seemed almost handpicked for their elderly tennis partners as they danced around the tennis court for the tantalizing pleasure of the rich silver haired women. They flirted with their adult partners in an unconvincing and almost contrived manner.

As one side would score both women would laugh out loud and reach over and touch the private parts of the young boys as if they had purchased them for the day. The young boys would retaliate with their own almost rehearsed flirtations as they bent over in front of them to stroke the older women's ego.

"What a wonderful day it is today ladies," Henri mentioned, with an appreciation that almost seemed as if he might have ordered the weather personally. Henri gazed at the dark blue sky above and said, "these days are just perfect for the pool and soon we will all have the great pleasure, of seeing you young ladies at poolside in your tempting little bikinis as well. Those two handsome men on the tennis court," Henri said, while turning his chair in the direction of the activity in back of him, "will most certainly have their eyes glued to you little beauties—ho! ho! You had better bring along your little riding crops so you can swat them away," Henri said, with an odd grin.

When I glanced over at Zooli, I noticed that she was not at all amused by Henri's comments and the activity around us, as she sat in a tight and restricted manner. Henri realized Zooli's apparent displeasure and quickly changed his demeanor, as he repositioned his body into a more formal posture.

We ate a wonderful lunch and had a lively discussion with Frédéric, who had become quite animated about his new position as a young staff attorney at the State Department. He was so cute, as he referenced Henri with such pride and admiration. He spoke of Henri's immense responsibility as the sole directorship over the entire global trade systems of France and the surrounding European nations.

Frédéric was also becoming increasingly knowledgeable about the laws surrounding logistical taxation, tariffs and trade regulations. He glowed with enthusiasm as he looked at Henri.

"The last few months, working as an intern for Henri has been so valuable to me and I truly feel that I will always owe this man who has given me an opportunity of a lifetime."

Henri placed his hand on Frédéric shoulder and looked at him with a fatherly smile.

"Well, my son, it has been my honor to watch you come along so very well, for when I look at you, I see aspects of myself in my younger days. But Frédéric, you simply must improve your French--young man!" said Henri, with a deep laugh. Frédéric's eyes began to pool with tears as he awkwardly composed himself while started to laugh as well. "New languages have always been so difficult for me. I don't know why," Frédéric admitted, with a cute smile.

For the next three decades Frédéric's and Henri's devotion to one another would only intensify to the level of father and son. Henri would never have a child of his own, nor did he ever want to be a full time father. His rough relationship with his own father bothered Henri terribly, making him believe that his child raising abilities might be similar to the brutal hands of his own father. I also know that Frédéric's love for Henri would serve as a major challenge to him in the years to follow.

"Well you two girls look absolutely wonderful," Frédéric said, while clearing his throat, "and I certainly am very happy to see that you are both so happy to be here, and safe as well. I will be talking to my father tomorrow afternoon, and I will be surely sending him a wonderful report. Your parents will be so relieved to hear how well things are going for you here," Frédéric said, as he winked with gratitude at Henri.

"Good---my boy, I hope your father tells his brother that his beautiful young twins are safe and sound with me!" Henri said, as his eyes slowly surveyed my breasts.

We all had a pleasant conversation through the remainder of lunch, and afterwards, Golareh and I walked privately with Frédéric around the equestrian grounds, telling him about all of the wonderful lessons we had learned from the most talented Zooli. At each stall, we stopped and provided Frédéric with the complete profile of the personality, traits and behaviors of each horse, all of which we had come to know and love. It was also clear to us that this was one of the first times Frédéric had ever seen a horse close up. He appeared to pay a lot of attention to each horse, as he gently touched each horse on its nose and face.

Upon leaving, we held each other in another group hug, only this time I didn't collapse into an emotional mess. It felt so wonderful to finally reconnect with our long lost cousin, who had left Iran just two years earlier, to possibly never return.

Frédéric, Goli and I, shared a unique familial bond which glued us together from that day forward. For when we looked into each other's excited but desperately sad eyes, we realized that we were mere orphans, desperately clinging to a country which we each had to say goodbye to, and would most likely never return to again.

Chapter 11

GOLAREH: IMPORT-EXPORT: REFUGEES

"Suddenly you realize that you're being treated like an object, and the danger to your psyche was that, if you didn't pay attention and you didn't stay clear, you'd begin to behave like one. And if you did that too long, you might end up becoming one."

- ROBERT REDFORD

*S*hadowing-- is what I believe they call it, in the resort industry, when you have two people essentially doing the same job at the same time. I didn't notice it at first but the more Danielle and I made our way in and around the castle, the more we both became aware of it, especially in the area of service personnel. There always seemed to be two maids walking together, or two bellman, two waitresses, and even two masseuses, working side by side. Little did I know, back then, that what I was witnessing was an extremely well planned form of on-the-job training for the human trade industry.

With the castle as being the ultimate resort model, it also served as a perfect training ground for the captive prisoners caught up in the machine. Basic language training was provided to those low level grounds personnel who were being positioned for export to select countries for factory work and other menial labor.

Sadly, however, the castle was the prime sexual boot camp for the young boys and girls just entering puberty, to be trained in the art of sexual gratification. The castle was a highly popular feature and exciting luxury for those special guests who were there to test-drive their future human sex objects.

The manpower required at the castle, was enormous with at least one hundred grounds personnel, constantly grooming the vast landscape and riding areas. The service staff, which included level upon level of guest support, was immense, with only the top tier workers being customer-facing and only a select few being allowed to speak directly to the guests.

As a cardinal rule, no staff member was ever allowed to say a word in the presents of the guests, even to their own fellow workers. They were expected to know exactly what to do at all times and to require no verbal instruction. If there ever was anything akin to a resort boot camp, the castle certainly would be it.

Since the castle was a sophisticated training hub in the industry of human trade the true underlying operations had to be completely invisible to the guests. Only a chosen few knew that almost half of all the people working at the castle were in training, while the fully competent other half were being prepared for out-boarding to locations around the world.

One nagging question always remained in the back of my mind as Danielle and I studied the youngest of the adolescents and pre-teens mixing and mingling with the adults. Where were they all coming from and how on earth did their parents allow them to be there in the first place?

Never once did any of them approach the two of us as they smiled, flirted and seduced the guests, like well-trained sexual robots, always dressed in scant and shockingly provocative clothing.

Perhaps each one of these pitiful young men and women believed early on that they were all part of some legitimate educational exchange program, providing them the opportunity to learn the life and customs of a foreign country. However the way they allowed the guests to fondle them and examine their young bodies very much confused me, and I'm sure it confused them as well.

Danielle and I had made at least a dozen trips into most of the public areas of the castle; and the more we became familiar with our surroundings, the more we noticed the continuously changing staff around us.

We would slip into our matching bikinis, large sunglasses, and designer straw hats, and sip pink lemonade at poolside, while thinking that Henri was indeed correct, when he suggested that we should bring along with us our riding crops to fend off the guests. Every time we stood still for even for a moment, some handsome man, older woman or distinguished grey-hair gentleman, would dominate our time.

On this particular mission into the castle we realize that it was becoming much more difficult for us break free and get back to the stables on time. One reason was because time got away from us in the luxurious surroundings, and the other reason was, Danielle and I were having so much fun being together. We were the center of everyone's attention, while meeting so many people who seemed to like us so much.

Never in my life had I ever been found so pretty by so many people, and I must admit that the attention made me feel special and good. In a funny sort of way both Danielle and I felt like movies stars until the frequent touch of their fingers and hands slowly became more personal and private in nature.

"I've never seen you before," a dignified gray headed gentleman said, with a British accent as he approached me and invaded my space. "You must be one of Henri's special offerings, may I check your tag-number you sexy little thing," the man asked, as he placed his hand on my rear end and pinched my cheek. I backed away from him by my automatic protective response.

"Tag number, what does he mean by that," I asked Danielle, who was pulling my arm and whisking me away. "I hope to see you sexy thing again," the man yelled as he stood on his tip-toes and lost track of us in the crowd.

"Goli---never let anyone touch you like that again," Danielle scolded.

"But Danni, what did he mean by my tag number? What tag number, I have no tag number?"

"Keep quiet Goli, you don't need to know anything about any goddamn tag number. Just don't get so close to those people! Do you understand me, Goli? Damn girl, sometimes you scare the shit out of me," she scolded.

At about 4:30 p.m. Danielle and I left the pool area were on our way back down to our secret changing room in the lower parking garage beneath the tennis courts. The tiny and seemingly unknown restroom served as our inbound and outbound wardrobe changing center, where we would switch in and out of our fashion attire and back into our smelly riding boots and dusty britches.

Suddenly I felt a firm grip on my shoulder, and as I quickly glanced down, I noticed an older woman's hands spinning me around to face her.

"Oh my god---you girls look so cute today, in your adorable pink swimsuits and straw hats. Tell me darlings, where are Homi and Zooli, are they here with you as well?" asked the unknown person, as I swung around in total terror. To my relief, I was shocked to see that is was Miss Cathy standing there with a broad smile.

I had no idea what her reaction might be, while catching us in the act of sneaking around the castle as if we were invited guests. To my relief, I realized that Miss Cathy was not concerned about it in the least.

"Girls, please come with me! I simply must introduce you both to my friends," Miss Cathy said, as she swiftly maneuvered us in the opposite direction from where we were going.

"I simply cannot tell you, just how smashing you both look! Oh---my son's eyes will pop out of his head when he sees just how truly adorable the two of you are," Miss Cathy said, as a feeling of dread set in on me.

"Oh my god, what do we do" I said with my eyes, as I glanced at Danielle in horror.

We both stood there in a daze, realizing that our days were now numbered. I had no idea what Henri would do if he saw us helping ourselves to the luxury of the castle, but my instincts told me that it would not be good. On the other hand, I knew exactly what would happen if Zooli found out that Danielle and I had snuck away from our duties and ventured deeply into the castle.

I knew that I had better think fast and come clean with Miss Cathy. Had it not been for the fact that we and Miss Cathy had worked together so much in the stables, I would have probably just broken free of her grip and bolted for an exit.

"Oh, Miss Cathy," I said to her, with a pleading expression on my face, as I moved the three of us off to the side. "Please understand Miss Cathy! We are not at all allowed to be here, we were just so curious and just wanted to see the castle for ourselves," I said.

"Oh nonsense, girls," Miss Cathy said, with a comforting smile, "you girls are always welcome to be here in the castle, especially with me!" Miss Cathy said, holding her head up high in an aristocratic manner.

"No, no, Miss Cathy, please, you don't understand," I shuttered, watching Henri suddenly appear in the main thoroughfare, with his view partially blocked by a large plant vase.

"Oh my god," I whimpered, shielding myself and Danielle in the shadow of Miss Cathy. "We simply must leave, Miss Cathy! Zooli will be so upset, if she knew that we were here, please understand," I exclaimed with a level of pure terror.

"Oh very well, now you girls hurry and run along if you must," Miss Cathy said, with an understanding look. "However, the two of you should always remember, that I will show you around the castle any time you wish."

Danielle grabbed my arm and pulled me through the closest doorway. We snatched off our sandals and began running like barefoot wild girls through the service hallways in a direction of the parking garage. We had a total of thirteen minutes to be completely changed and be back on the equestrian grounds. Zooli and Homayra would be waiting for us and the thought of making it back in time was beginning to seem impossible.

As we moved through the inner hallways of the castle, there seemed no way that we could avoid bumping into people, who were moving around us like drones through of a massive ant hill.

We saw busboys carrying pans of dirty glasses, maids pushing linen carts, janitors holding mops, chefs with stern faces, and workmen pushing tool carts. There the two of us stood in our scant little bikinis, straw hats and dirty bare feet. It soon, however, became obvious to us that everyone around us was speaking in different languages, and each from a different country, as everyone struggled to complete their intense mission of getting to their next task.

There were Latin Americans cooks, Japanese sushi chefs, and shapely American waitresses with curvaceous bodies and white-blonde hair. Every one streamed through the inner hallways as if they were the life-blood, surging through the main arteries, oxygenating the entire castle. Everyone was traveling so quickly and focusing so intently on what they were doing that they never once took the time to notice the two us running alongside of them.

A huge metal door opened up, causing the blinding daylight from outside to fully illuminate the service alley. I caught a quick glimpse of the edge of the lower level parking garage and felt a sense of relief.

"Thank God --we're almost there, this way Danni!"

I grabbed Danielle by her arm and suddenly, just as we were about to dash across the alley, a black, mid-size, Mercedes-Benz bus pulled up and totally blocked our pathway to the parking garage.

Danielle and I stood in the doorway completely vulnerable in the bright sunlight, like sitting ducks, in our pool attire. On impulse I turned and ran in the opposite direction as Danielle snagged me by the straps on my bikini top and yanked me through a doorway of a small vacant office. The office appeared to be uninhibited for the time being with just a wooden table and two chairs facing a large square observation window. The people on the other side of the window milled around as the two of us stared at them in terror.

"Shit, Danni, we can't hide in here! Those people will surely see us; we look like stupid fish in an aquarium?"

Danielle was locking the door behind us.

"Goli, will you shut the fuck up and stop worrying! That's a one-way mirror and they can't see shit. I noticed this room the other day!"

"Well how long can we stay in here before someone comes in?"

"As long as we need to---or until I'm fucking ready to open the goddamn door."

Danielle had a cocky smile and was sliding the deadbolt closed.

As my heartbeat and respiration began to normalize, Danielle and I watched the activity on the other side of the glass. We noticed a tall, slender woman with tightly cropped, platinum blonde hair slowly emerging from the door of the bus and descending down the steps to the ground. She looked as if she had been poured into her tight fitting black dress with close to nothing on underneath.

Her low-cut dress was split up the side almost entirely, revealing her, noticeably, ample breasts, well-toned body and chiseled biceps. Although she was pretty, her persona projected a dichotomy of both power and evil, encompassing the look of erotic muscular enforcement.

At first I thought that she might be a model preparing for a photo shoot somewhere, but when she bent over to examine her six inch heels, I realized that she was meant for something more than just a walk on a runway. Her extremely short dress appeared to be designed for frequent revealing previews of what I later learned was called a thong. The least amount of movement at all, whether forward, backwards or sideways, would produce a vivid view of her shiny metallic colored undergarment.

But it was the ivory handled pistol protruding from a shoulder holster positioned under her left arm which both startled me and made a distinct impression on me. This mysterious temptress appeared to be armed and extremely dangerous.

The gun on her side was oriented strategically for quick retrieval by either hand, with the barrel pointing to the ground in back of her. The gun was no tiny pistol either, but one of significance, reminding me of the same high caliber firearm my uncle would brandish back in Iran when he served as an officer with the government police.

As she straightened back up, she appeared to notice a puddle of dirty water a bit too close to her expensive shoes, at which she delicately moved into safer territory. Appearing to be waiting for someone, she impatiently glanced at her watch and then turned around and made her way back up the steps and into the bus.

Just before she dropped out of sight, Henri suddenly appeared from a doorway only about six meters down from us. His immaculately groomed gray beard and perfectly tailored suit seemed to conflict with the dirty surroundings of the loading area.

"That's Henri," I whispered to Danielle, "he must be looking for us! Miss Cathy must have ratted on us!"

Danielle appeared to be asking herself the exact same question, while she moved towards the door preparing for plan-B, which was for the both of us to run for the hills.

"Wait! Quiet!" Danielle said, as she gently put her hand on my neck and squinted at Henri through the glass. "I don't think he's here after us."

Henri slowly walked up to the bottom stair of the bus and with ease he climbed the steps and entered the bus, closing the door behind him. My shoulders began to relax, as I realized that Henri had something else he was interested in rather than chasing down two trespassers in swimsuits.

We sat in the office staring out the window for about five minutes, waiting for something to happen so that we could finally make our way around the bus and back to the stables. Slowly the door of the bus re-opened, and we saw Henri and the mysterious woman emerge. As they stepped down onto the street and slowly walked in the direction of the door where Henri had come from, we saw, to our surprise, trailing out of the bus behind Henri and the woman, a line of frightened children.

"What the hell are those children here for," I quietly whispered to Danielle. Each child appeared to be between five and seven years-old; all were dressed in school clothes, and walking in a single file line, holding hands with one another. Their faces seemed drained and washed out as they walked in a quiet and organized procession towards a room just to the right of us.

That day in the alley, Danielle and I counted sixteen children in all, each paired off with one another, girl-boy, boy-girl, in the sort of a buddy system. The chilling sight of those children holding their little back packs and stuffed animals stuck with me until today. It reminded me of the field trips I would go on during my early school days, except my teacher never looked like that strange women, with her gun and flashy attire.

Our childhood faces had been filled with delight, excitement and sense of adventure while theirs were filled with a doom and dread. When the last child disappeared through the doorway into the castle, Danielle and I made our move, across the alley, and into the darkness of the underground garage.

It was 5:25 p.m. when we finally got back to the stables. Zooli and Homayra were both sitting on a bale of hay when we rounded the corner and came into view.

"Where have you girls been?" Zooli demanded, with both a combined look of alarm and anger.

Homayra sat by her side in her shadow, with a look of forlorn confusion on her face. Danielle and I slowly slithered across the dirty alleyway, staring down at the remnants of hay and small pieces of manure which we were supposed to have cleaned up hours ago.

"Zooli," came a cheerful voice in the distance, as Miss Cathy walked around the corner with a noticeably contrived limp. "I am so sorry for steeling these precious girls from you this afternoon," Miss Cathy announced, as she stood in front of us wearing her dirty riding pants and soiled muck boots.

"I simply had to borrow them while you were teaching Homi." Miss Cathy said, as she put both of her over-worn gloved hands on our shoulders. "I know it was entirely rude of me to take them from their chores, but I guess I'm just getting a little too old for this sort of work." Miss Cathy said, while dropping her eyes to the ground in a rather pitiful manner.

"Yesterday that old mare of mine spooked while I was cantering around an obstacle on the cross country course and before I knew it, I planted my foot the wrong way in my stirrup and twisted my ankle. I thought I might have broken it, but it feels much better today. I don't know what I would've done without these two strong and helpful young angels." Miss Cathy said, so convincingly, that even I almost believed her.

Zooli's expression began to slowly change into a counterfeit smile. It appeared that she might have actually bought Miss Cathy's story, but by how much, we didn't know.

"Well, okay then," Zooli said, with one eye burning a hole in my forehead. "I'm glad that our little angels could be of such help to you today, Miss Cathy. I am sure that they were so very glad to lend you a helping hand."

Zooli motioned us over to the empty water buckets. "Now would you, ever so helpful ladies go finish your chores and get back to your room and change, for there's another stupid dinner planned for us this evening."

Stupid, was the right choice of words, I thought, as the three of us walked back to our room that late afternoon. I realized just how stupid we must have looked standing in front of Zooli with that cheap alibi. I knew full well that Zooli knew precisely where we had been that afternoon. Zooli was completely aware of the daily heartbeat of everything that happened on the equestrian grounds every single second of the day, including the distant whinny of an anxious horse frightened by the sight of a new pile of brush on the far end of a pasture. Top the entire story off with a potential injury of Miss Cathy, Henri's mother, while on Zooli's watch, and you end up with a *stupid* story that was completely unbelievable and absolutely insulting at the very same time.

As the sun slowly set in the distance, my mind ventured to the request for my tag number by that dirty old man in the castle. What were tag numbers used for and why did Danielle seems to know about them, I wondered. Most especially, it was the vision of those 16 children walking together, gripping the hands of their fellow travel-mates that haunted me the most. The scene triggered vivid memories of my sister and me leaving our home not too long before.

We were deathly scared when we were outbound just three months prior, as our devastated father guided us through the crowded Mehrabad International Airport on the outskirts of Tehran. We had a similar look of freighted bewilderment.

We were snatched by the claws of that powerful hawk, which pulled us high into the cold heavens above and away to a distant land. My sister and I were not that much different from those small children. But we were all vulnerable refugees being exported from one country and imported to another with the ironic blessing of our own loving parents.

Chapter 12

HOMAYRA: MY EARLIEST TOUCH OF PASSION

More frequently than ever Danielle's presence in the evenings was becoming increasingly required at the request of some unknown power in the castle and with each directive came an increased level of emptiness in Danielle's once spunky personality. While we knew that Danielle had a large inventory of exotic clothing, I rarely saw her model them.

For that matter, we rarely saw Danielle leave or even return to our suite. However, the toll on Danielle was really taxing her personality and physical strength. As the weeks and months passed, the dynamic and sparkly little tom-boy we knew shrank away before our very eyes. The only outlet she seemed to covet was her time with my sister.

My relationship with Goli had always been sound, so I never experienced any level of jealousy or envy over the amount of time they spent together. Our sibling bond was baked into our souls genetically during our gestational development within our mother's womb as we clung to each other for dear life. So the amount of time that Golareh and Danielle spent together, along with the rich closeness they each shared, provided me with a level of comfort because I loved to see them both happy.

I loved witnessing their shared joy. If anything, I felt a little guilty for not spending enough time with them, as I was becoming totally involved with Zooli and the *horses. I also must admit that I was extremely excited by Henri's apparent interest in me and enjoyed showing off my equitation skills whenever he visited the equestrian grounds*

—⚬⚬⚬—

On that afternoon, when I saw Danielle and Goli arrive late to the stables, with the fear of god in their eyes for skirting their chores, I also saw a renewed level of spirit in my sister.   Danielle, however, was showing clear signs of falling into a serious depression for reasons I had not a clue.

As usual, Danielle stayed in her room alone dressing for her mysterious evening duties, while Goli and I were outfitted in alluring outfits provided to us for the evening's event, which was to be held in Henri's penthouse on the top western corner of the castle. We never knew who selected our outfits, but whoever it was, thought things out with an apparent sense of purpose.

On this particular evening, Goli and I were expected to wear matching outfits which included a pair of pants made of a strange material that I'd never seen before and a type of sleeveless shirt that was referred to as a tank-top. As Goli and I began to dress, a new and exciting sort of look emerged in our physical beings.

Goli's thin but shapely figure filled the odd pair of pants which were called *Levi Strauss* jeans and they fit like nothing she'd ever worn before, much like a glove.   The jeans were expressly delivered that morning by special courier from England. The labels said that they were low-rise, prewashed denim, slightly faded, fashionably flared and tight to the fit.

Goli was instructed to wear a tight white tank top which was a little too short and showed off her belly button; after she put it on, she looked rather cute. We were also given frilly bras and brightly colored thongs which the French referred to as *strings*. My string was teal and Golareh's was red and we each could hardly determine how to put them on.

The purpose of the tiny garments, which consisted of a thin waistband and a tiny piece of material, was unknown to me because it lacked any sort of functional purposes. Never the less, once I had them on, I felt as if the strange contraption moved around my body as if it had a mind of its own. My sister and I giggled out loud as we examined the strange underwear, saying the inventor of such an item must have been clearly mad.

Regardless of the odd fitting clothing and our revealing look, my sister and I were both smiling and laughing as we finished dressing for what we thought was to be some sort of strange costume party. I had little concern about what to expect because I didn't know any better; it was all some sort of fantasy for us. We both looked very grown up as we danced in front of the mirror, picturing ourselves as famous pop stars.

I was to wear a pair of beautifully embroidered low-rise jeans that were very similar to my sister's. However, instead of a tank top, I was provided a teal silk top which was backless and very revealing, leaving me with a feeling of vulnerability. I had similar earrings but was given no necklace, as my sister had, and I wasn't sure why.

We were each provided fabric tan sandals, in a very comfortable peasant style. Even though the heels were a bit too high, they were actually fun to wear, as we happily left our suite and skipped down the corridor towards a private glass elevator. We were on our way to a king's penthouse for an exclusive party and I, for one, was excited.

A security officer in the elevator, wearing a thin wire running from an earphone to a two-way radio attached to his belt, pressed the button and we were on our way to the top floor. As the elevator swiftly whispered to the top of the massive castle, I gazed down at the guests casually walking across the rich white marble floor below in wonderment. For the first time in my life I felt an odd sense of unearned wealth. I couldn't help but think of my parents so far away from us at home in their small house. I questioned our new found life and asked myself why must anyone feel the right to live in such lavishness?

Zooli had earlier instructed us to go directly to the penthouse and wait for her but she never arrived. After waiting around for several minutes the operator finally pushed the doorbell and we heard chimes softly ringing from behind the hand carved Brazilian mahogany door.

The door opened and there greeting us was Miss Cathy.

"Oh my god, you both look so delightful in your cute little American blue-jeans," exclaimed Miss Cathy, wrapping both of her arms around us. "Won't you please come in," Miss Cathy said, while moving to the side and welcoming us into a broad entrance way.

Miss Cathy was wearing a white turtleneck top under a button-down blue blazer. She had her hair parted on the side, tied in a fashionable bun behind her head. She wore slim fitting, off-white pants, with smartly polished riding boots, and in her hand she was holding three very decretive riding crops with golden tips.

"Oh Miss Cathy," I exclaimed, "You look so wonderful this evening. I must say it was so nice to see you today," looking into her eyes, and dramatically pausing for my next statement. "I'm so happy that Danni and Goli were able to help you so much today," I said with a wink, knowing full well she was covering for my sister.

Goli's face flushed with embarrassment yet Miss Cathy's expression appeared oblivious to my comment, as she put her hands on both of our cheeks and said, "Oh you sweet thing, what on earth are you talking about? You girls are simply so very humorous," said Miss Cathy, supposedly having no understanding of what I was talking about.

I noticed a look of surprise on Goli's face as well, not knowing whether Miss Cathy was joking with us or not. Might it be possible that she didn't remember covering for Goli and Danni earlier in the day?

"Girls, before we go in, I wanted to give you each something that I think you both should have," Miss Cathy said, as she approached us with the most gracious smile.

"Yes Miss Cathy, what is it," we both replied in unison.

"Girls I want you to have these riding crops as a token of my appreciation for putting up with an old, forgetful, lady like me. Since the two of you came here to the castle, I actually feel younger and so much more fulfilled," Miss Cathy said, as she handed me the one of the riding crops and the other to my sister. "I just love you girls so very much---and where is my sweet Danni, I have one for her as well," Miss Cathy asked with a look of concern.

I was so touched with my Miss Cathy's kind gesture that I forgot to answer her question about Danielle's whereabouts as we both approached her and kissed her on the cheek.

"Now, I want you girls to use these crops wisely whenever you need to make a vivid point with a powerful force. Be gentle with them when needed but firm when required," Miss Cathy said, as she moved us along.

As we entered the penthouse, I became captivated by the extraordinary room, which looked as if it were custom designed for the evening's event. The walls were at least 10-meters tall and made of Italian white marble. A huge stain glass dome overhead filled the room with an aquarium-blue color.

One magnificent pane of crystalline glass formed an outwardly protruding panoramic window, which captured a breathtaking view of the sun setting over the vast equestrian grounds in the distance. I stood in disbelief, taking in the richness of the surroundings. My sister, on the other hand, seemed not impressed in the least, as she surveyed the grounds below as if she were looking for an escape route.

The room was filled with the wonderful aroma of appetizers, which were meticulously presented on several tables throughout room. I remember thinking that each tiny morsel of food looked like an individual work of art. Standing at attention behind every serving table were attractive young women and men, silently serving rich delicacies including duck foie gras, milk poached sweetbreads, wild turkey, and veal.

As I soaked in the new world, I noticed an eclectic group of people, with distinctly different nationalities and interesting expressions. I also had the distinct but mild feeling that many of the people in the room looked strange, with a tint of ugliness. I could not put my finger on why I felt that way. My intuition just told me that the people around me were there to sample something more than just food and drink.

People moved around the room gazing at each other with artificial expressions as if they were appraising not only the value of one another but the cost as well. Cocktails of every size and color, ranging from fine wines, champagnes, martinis and rich creamy drinks were being served on silver and gold drink trays by the young beautiful men and women.

An overly made-up and extremely well endowed woman in her mid-20s sat on a stool next to a full-size grand piano playing a beautiful classical guitar. She had bleached blonde hair and thick rose colored lipstick. She resembled a mannequin while her classical guitar scarcely concealed her unnaturally large breasts from the gawking eyes around her. Her fingers traveled the neck of the guitar with ease and the music permeated the room with a sensual and soothing sound.

Making his way through the crowd as if he were the king of his own castle was Henri with his classic, carefully groomed gray beard and graceful style. He was dressed in a perfectly tailored charcoal blazer and stone blue shirt, which matched his eyes. His collar was unbuttoned to the midpoint of his chest where he proudly displayed a golden chain and an Italian-Cornicello. He wore a beautifully tailored pair of light colored raw silk pants and loafers with no socks.

Clinging to his left arm was a remarkably attractive woman with platinum blonde hair and a rather severe expression. She had on an extremely short, sleeveless, one-piece black dress which was slit up the side, barely coming to a stop at the base of her stocking's *safety* lines, prominently displaying her long shapely legs. A dark seam traveled from the back of her heels up the center of her legs and terminated under the back of her dress. I also could not help but notice her black and pink patent-leather pumps which had six-inch heels that matched the color of her fingernails.

Many of the people around her starred at her in amazement and moved in for a closer examination of her extraordinarily well toned body and prominent breasts. One man in particular came in a bit too close to the blonde spectacle and was suddenly discharged away by an extra-poisonous glare.

Goli had a speechless and almost shaken expression on her face, as she studied the unusual woman with a visible gap in her front teeth. It appeared as though Goli recognized the woman but from somewhere before.

"Hello young ladies," Henri said with his deep voice, "It is so nice to see both of you beautiful girls here this evening." Henri said, while slowly examining every millimeter of my body. After a prolonged moment of inspection, Henri said, "Girls, I would like to introduce both of you to my dear friend Ari who has just arrived from her shopping trip this afternoon.

Ari is our expert in the area of guest services and is meeting with the Castle's board of advisors. She provides us with our most beautiful luxury objects, which keep our most demanding guests, shall we say, fulfilled." Henri said, with an over amplified laugh.

Ari stood for the longest time not saying a word, examining the both of us with noticeable level of disapproval.

"Well if it isn't Henri's little Persian play toys, don't you two look so, how shall I say---fun?" Ari asked, as she stared directly into my sister's eyes and suddenly looked down to the floor as if she didn't like what she saw in the least.

Golareh never broke her stare at the woman's face as if she were reading her like an open book. Ari avoided my sister's eyes but held her nose high and talked down to us as if we were mere children.

Henri broke the moment of thick awkwardness by saying, "isn't Ari simply beautiful, girls? Would you know that the name *Ari* actually carries an ancient Spanish meaning of---*a beautiful looking creature?*"

My sister and I glanced at each other as if we both agreed that the woman was a beautifully unpleasant creature.

"Ari my dear, Homayra and Golareh are becoming invaluable at our equestrian center with my mother and our precious Zooli, who unfortunately could not be with us this evening. She is currently tending to our latest equine arrival from Carmel, California, an impressive and ultra-expensive, warm-blood stallion. I'm sure you know how dedicated Zooli is with those horses, there was just no way that she could leave that new horse unattended this evening."

Goli and I glanced at Miss Cathy, who had a shocked expression on her face. "Oh my heavens---son, I had no idea of the arrival? Why on earth was I not informed of this?" Miss Cathy gasped, "I must go to her at once and help that poor child." Miss Cathy announced.

Goli and I looked at each other with uneasiness; wondering why we were not told of a new arrival as well. Certainly, had we known of the new horse on it's way we would have been preparing a new stall that very morning, if not days prior.

"I must go with you as well," I announced, as I followed Miss Cathy towards the door.

"Oh nonsense, girls, don't be ridiculous, let my mother go and tend to that spoiled beast," Henri demanded, as Miss Cathy left the room.

Henri was now alone and free from his mother as he stood there with an enriched level of excitement, turning and smiling broadly into my eyes.

"Girls, I think it's way past time for you young ladies to enjoy a nice glass of champagne with Ari and me," Henri said, with a sneaky laugh.

Henri guided us over to the bar and placed his hand on the small of my back and gently tugged on the exposed strap of my thong, pulling it taunt beneath my jeans.

The touch of Henri's hand unnerved me and caused me to stiffen in both surprise and excitement. I found his touch to be both remarkable and shocking at the same time; for this was the first time in my life I ever felt the touch of a man's hands against the bare skin of my lower extremities. His hands were both handsome and impressive, but also soft and warm, with a hint of familiarity.

Having never been instructed on how to act around older men, no warning alarms went off. I felt no need to pull away from him, nor did I have the impression that he was being inappropriate in the least. For the first time in my life I experienced the existence of a huge dose of butterflies as my sensual emotions surged.

As we walked over to the wine table my mind was reeling with a mixture of anxiety and confused familiarity. His hand transmitted a vivid feeling of déjà vu, relating to a time I could not identify. All of my shyness vanished when Henri placed a rather large glass of bubbly champagne in my hand and lightly kissed me on my lips.

I giggled as I looked at my sister sneezing as the sparking champagne tickled her nose. She and I had never experience the taste of champagne before and for that matter any alcoholic beverage. But as I noticed the surprised smile on my sister's face I started to let down my guard and relax.

The sun was setting over the mountain range to the west and so did my anxiety and concerns of our magical new surroundings while the cocktails kept coming my way. While I finished at least three flutes of champagne, an adorable young man carrying a silver tray of creamy drinks replaced my empty glasses just as each was consumed. I had no idea that the creamy drinks contained any alcohol in them until the young server informed me that they were called Brandy Alexander's.

The minutes passed quickly as the music switched from soft classical guitar to disco without my even noticing it. The room became alive with laughter as people danced with one another and the momentum of the party began to intensify.

The blonde guitarist was now out from behind the cover of her guitar, as her large breasts proudly bounced to the rhythm of the pulsating music. The young men and women who had been serving drinks and appetizers were now dancing and mixing with the elderly crowd and becoming noticeably tipsy.

As everyone danced, their hands fondled one another's private parts as if the wall of privacy had collapsed. The whole scene reminded me of a room full of juvenile delinquents raiding the sacred liquor cabinets while their parents were away.

I fell into a relaxed stupor after my ice cream drink made me dizzy and a bit nauseous. Goli was snatched up to dance by a stumpy bald man in a seersucker suit and an overly perspiring red face. She appeared to be as relaxed as I was while we both blended into the folly of the evening. Goli had a full glass of champagne in her hand as her tank top strap slipped off her left shoulder while she was being pulled out onto the crowded dance floor.

The female guitarist, who I privately named *Miss Boobs*, began to humor me as I watched her through the blurry slits in my eyes. Although she was quite the guitarist she lacked the ability to dance, as she hopped up and down to the music like an idiot. Her top was disheveled and hardly covered her independently moving breasts, which resembled two wild animals wrestling under a blanket. Drunken men were now crowding around her with hopes of taming them.

On the other side of the room I noticed Henri watching me with and an interested eye. I was being swallowed up by an overstuffed couch with a look of drunken bewilderment, I'm sure. He broke away from Ari, who still seemed to be leering at me with distain, as he moved through the room of drunken debauchery.

He extended a hand as if he was inviting me to dance, an invitation I declined. It wasn't that I didn't want to dance with him. I thought he was the most handsome man on earth. I was simply losing the sensation in my legs and was about to pass out. "No worries, young lady, but would you please join me on the patio for some fresh air, I believe you could use some."

As I rose to my feet I felt the blood leave my head and mix with the rest alcohol flowing through my body. I followed Henri into another room, listing to one side. He opened two French doors and led me out on to a beautifully decorated slate patio. The sun was about to disappear over the mountain range in the west and the evening air felt refreshing to my very cloudy and twirling mind.

"Sorry for all that madness in there, Homayra," Henri said, while removing his dark blazer and draping it over my shoulders. "I guess everyone's just letting off a little steam from the day, and I love their playful antics and wonderful faces, don't you?" he asked with a broad smile, exposing his perfectly straight white teeth.

Henri wrapped his arms around my shoulders and rested his intertwined fingers on the midpoint of my chest just above my breasts. I could smell the aroma of his rich perfume and felt his beard brush against the back of my neck. I became a bit uncomfortable, but at the same time quite special as my thoughts softened to the mood of the moment.

"I am so happy that you and your sister have come to live here with me," Henri whispered, as he gently pressed his face against my hair which was tucked beneath the blazer. "In a strange sort of way, I feel like you and your sister are a part of my own family." Henri moved both of his hands to the back of my neck and gently lifted my hair from beneath the blazer.

We stood in silence watching the sun go down until Henri gently removed his blazer from my shoulders and draped it over a chair next to us. He placed his hands against my bear arms and gently massaged my biceps.

"My darling Homayra, I noticed that your sister had such a beautiful necklace on when you both arrived," said Henri and his lips pressed against the side of my neck. "I thought I should probably balance things out a bit and give you something you can show off to her."

He removed a velvet pouch from his pants pocket and carefully placed the most beautiful diamond and pearl necklace around my neck. I glanced down and could not believe my eyes.

"My dear, sweet Homayra, please accept this treasure as a welcoming gift from me to you. This wonderful necklace is a one of a kind. It *was* my mother's and one of her most favorites. Its call the *Emperies*, a 4-carat European diamond necklace with more than 48 cut diamonds. I want you to have this."

"Oh no, I mustn't take something that rightfully belongs to your mother," I said, as I gently touched the valuable stones with my fingers.

"My dear, I'm sure that my mother would want you to have this treasure, I promise you this. Besides, she has most likely forgotten she ever owns it," Henri said, as he started to laugh. I took the precious necklace with both apprehension and a very cloudy mind. As I took the jewelry I made a mental note to return the item to Miss Cathy one day when and where the opportunity was right.

"Your sister seems a bit untrusting of me for some reason. I'm not at all sure why that is, do you believe that is just her nature? Might she have a bit of a selfish streak in her?"

"My sister is quite like my mother," I said, slurring my words, "She always takes time to warm up to people. I would just give her some time, Henri."

"Well then, my dear Homayra, I am so very happy that you feel comfortable with me." Henri said; clearly knowing that I was becoming blotto.

Henri's right hand slid down the side of my arms and moved inward towards the lower part of my body. His entire hand was completely resting on my exposed belly just above my belt buckle. The chill of the evening air did not prevent my entire body from breaking into a sudden sweat. I felt embarrassed as his fingers glided over my moist belly as my shyness was replaced with a new level of excitement.

I lost myself for a moment as I looked off into the distance and watched the last thin remnant of the sun disappear behind the mountain range. The alcohol in my head combined with the intensity of Henri's mysterious touch, launched an intense feeling of excitement, which I'd never experienced before.

Never in my life had I felt the powerful sensations I was experiencing at that very moment. My entire body began to shutter with butterflies and I became covered in tiny goose bumps. I came alive with a mysterious desire for something that I could not explain while at the same time thinking that my mother would have killed me for what I was about to do.

Henri's large right hand moved across the lower regions of my belly and stopped on my left side as he gently rotated me around to face him. His fingertips were smooth but firm as they pressed into my lower back, just above my beltline. Henri's breathing intensified as his embrace tightened.

The cloud of alcohol in my brain thickened as Henri looked deeply into my eyes. Even now I must admit that he had the most beautiful light-blue eyes with an extraordinarily handsome face. I was speechless with desire, as this intensely debonair man stood there for what seemed to be an eternity gazing into my young but very vulnerable eyes. Might it be possible that he was falling in love with me, I naively asked myself? I hope so, I most surely do.

Slowly Henri began to remove his hand from my back and place it against the side of my face. The palms of his hand felt strong and wet from my own perspiration as he stared into my eyes and captured my complete attention.

"My god, Homayra, I am humbled by your beauty." Henri said, in an almost apologetic way, "You have grown up to be the amazingly beautiful women."

The sound of his words were both comforting and confusing as he hinted to the fact that he might have once known me from years past. Where had I met this man before? I faded in and out, and my body felt weak and submissive. I was now saturated with a mixture of both hazy confusion and intense desire as my new sexuality came alive. I became tearful for a longing of something I couldn't comprehend. A strange pressure was building deep in areas of my body I never knew existed. The more he caressed me the more I came close to exploding with joy.

But exploding from where and how, I questioned. Could this be what my childhood girlfriends referred to as the beginning of an orgasm? My mind was racing, trying to determine the source of my new found muscles which were pulsating and flexing within the fluid regions of my pelvis.

Up until this point in my life, I had absolutely no frame of reference as to the female anatomy, for I had never been counseled by my parents or anyone, to the mysteries of sex. Panic slowly began to set in because I could feel my interiors starting to burst with excitement. Somewhere in my body, somehow, something huge was going to happen and very soon. I found myself completely out-of-control of my actions as Henri's mouth moved closer to my now open lips.

Henri gently placed his left hands on the cheeks of my rear end and pulled my body against his lower extremities, as he maneuvered his right hand under my top and up my side. His fingers slipped underneath my shirt with the palm of his right hand coming to rest underneath my dampened bra and entirely covering my sensitive breast.

"My god, Homayra, you have no idea how much I want you at this moment."

"I felt my nipples harden as his fingers lightly pinched them and gently massaged my breast in the palm of his warm hand. I moved into him and felt his other hand grab a generous portion of my rear end as both of his hands began to work them in unison. I felt my inner regions become moist with a foreign desire.

I detected what felt like a mountain suddenly inflate underneath his belt line as he began to slowly grind my pelvis against the bulging front parts of his pants. His mouth touched my open lips and activated my excitement as my eyes completely closed. I saw visions of flames, sparks and stars bursting in front of me as I completely let go.

I was now yearning for something bigger than anything I could ever imagine, as Henri's lips touched my wanting but totally inexperienced mouth. Henri pressed his mouth against mine with a passion that began to uncouple all of my defenses. I accidently moaned out loud as caution signs began to appear once I felt Henri's beard brush across my face causing a sudden wakeup call of warning.

I was reminded of the fact that Henri was considerably much older than I was, but oddly I didn't seem to care that much. I actually visualized myself watching Henri and me from a different vantage point on the patio. I clearly saw this activity as being entirely inappropriate but still advancing towards something not at all right. However, still I wanted it and I almost demanded and prayed he would move to a next step, whatever in God's name that was.

I wondered what nerve I had to be almost as equally aggressive for the passion as Henri was. I asked myself, was I really that starved for this sort of attention and what was happening in my life to cause me to desire this so much?

I placed both my hands on the front of Henri's chest and began to gently push him away, but as I increased my pressure against Henri, his embraces tighten around me.

Even though I was resisting I realized that there were aspects of this highly charged moment I actually extended for. How ironic, I thought, it was that even though I was fully aware of the fact that what was happening was utterly wrong, I still wanted it and was actively asking for more. Just how far would I let these selfish temptations take me, I wondered, and would I even have the ability to stop it if I needed to?

Suddenly, from inside the castle, I heard a voice that jolted me out of my drunken, dreamlike state, like a bolt of lightning and crack of thunder.

"Who did that," a woman's voice charged from the room inside. "Did you do that?" a demanding and extremely sober sounding voice from inside the room exclaimed. The unknown woman was deflating the party atmosphere like helium from a balloon.

Henri's mood suddenly changed and in an instant he took on the behavior of a totally different person. He smiled confidently and spun me around as if we were twirling to the sound of classical music. In a split second,

Henri changed from a sexually charged male on a mission to the most congenial host, able to face his next situation with ease.

Henri had suddenly disappeared from my side and was nowhere to be found, as I was left completely alone on terrace by my lonesome. My mind was now lost as the adrenalin quickly left my body and I began to come to the conclusion that I was entirely drunk and hardly able to stand.

To my surprise, when I staggered back into the room, I found Zooli standing directly in the center of it all, advancing towards the man in the seersucker suit, with a look of surprise on his face.

"Did you just do what I thought you did?" Zooli demanded, as the drunken fat man began to lose his composure in front of his friends, "Did you just grab my ass!" Zooli questioned, while standing in the center of the room, as if she were standing in the center-ring of a circus tent, with a menagerie of wild animals circling around her.

The voices in the room dropped to a silence, with nothing but awkward dance music playing in the background, while everyone stared at this spectacle of a woman, in a dirty leather jacket, tight black riding britches and dusty leather riding chaps. Her braided ponytail, which flowed through the back of her ball cap, conflicted intensely with the other high fashion drunken ladies in the room, who were now awkwardly covering themselves with their disheveled clothing

Zooli lifted her dark sunglasses from her eyes and positioned them on top of her ball cap while moving directly into the fat man's personal space. The embarrassed man came close to falling in the lap of the now totally drunk guitarist who sitting right behind him.

"Why yes I did, little lady," said the jolly, fat man with a selfish grin, while desperately trying to regain his composure. "Hey, it's my birthday", he said, with a joking look. "I'm sorry, what can I say?"

Zooli looked at the fat man as if she was about to smack him down, causing everyone in the room to tune in. "You do that again, and I'll knock your fucking lights out!"

I noticed Henri reappearing on the other side of the room with his hand around the Ari's waist and his arm on her shoulder. Ari looked at Zooli with a cool interest while Henri watched Zooli with a humorous expression, showing not the least bit of concern.

Zooli directed her eyes at both Goli and me and said, "What in God's name are you two girls wearing, you look like common trollops out for a good time!"

She panned the room for Henri but failed to locate him---and lucky for him, I thought. Returning her eyes on us, she issued a seething command to exit the room at once. My sister and I staggered in the direction of the door, as if she was removing two mares in season from a pasture full of wild stallions.

Goli and I stumbled out of the room like the drunken teenagers we were, as I noticed Ari slip away from Henri and move into a position within Zooli's view. She appeared to be squaring off with her. The two locked eyes, with a matched intensity, while sizing each other up until Ari finally broke her gaze and politely backed down.

"Do you have a problem with something here, lady?" Zooli asked, while moving directly into Ari's domain. Ari didn't flinch in the least, but casually stepped back and glanced at Henri as if she was placing Zooli on her personal watch list.

Zooli herded us out the room and on to the open elevator with a look of complete control. The dedicated security guard stood next to the elevator buttons with a totally complicit expression on his face, as he turned a key and pressed the button for the ground floor. On the floor of the elevator I noticed remnants of his broken two-way radio, which, as I think back, might have been stomped to death by the heels of Zooli's riding boots.

As the elevator door opened, exposing the white marble floor on the busy main floor, my sister and I staggered a few steps and that's when my night suddenly came to a nauseous and spinning end.

The next morning I was jolted into semi-consciousness by the nudge of a riding crop digging into my side. It was 5:30 a.m. and my stomach whirled with nausea while my head pounded with a pain that was reminiscent of the day after a bomb went off in my yard back home in Tehran.

"Girls, I want your collective asses down at the stables in 15-minutes, do you understand me? If you think your hangovers are bad now, just wait until you are on the backs of your horses. Unfortunately ladies, it appears that you both didn't learn much from my lessons about passive persistence!" Zooli's dark brown eyes were drilling holes into my sister's and my souls.

Standing behind Zooli, was Danielle who appeared fresh, fully dressed and ready for the day. She was bent over, with one hand over her mouth and the other around her waist, desperately trying to hold back an explosion of laughter.

Zooli, swung around, and shot a look at Danielle but backed off once she saw Danielle's smile begin to fade. Zooli was so happy to see Danielle's enthusiastic attitude that she refused to spoil it. As Zooli walked out of the room, I noticed a satisfied smile on her face, as she confidently turned and saluted us.

"*Thank you---girls,*" she said as left the room.

Chapter 13

GOLAREH: THE MENAGERIE

R aptio - Abduction; a carrying off; a large scale abduction of women by groups of men.

Henri obviously knew that Danielle and I had been making frequent trips to the castle. His staff was certainly following every move we made and while at the party the other night he would gaze upon Homayra with such fatherly love, he would glare at me disapprovingly, as if he knew full well where we had been, and just how much I loathed and despised him. Henri had a difficult time making eye contact with me, starting from the very first time we met, and while I had an almost palatable familiarity with him, like my sister, I absolutely could not understand where I had met him before.

I saw a man who felt the most comfortable with people much younger than he, or those individuals completely under his control. I had an instantaneous dislike for Henri, at a level that I would consider terminal, completely based on intuition. He had a contrived and out-of-control laugh, and while others found him so charming and distinguished, he actually made my skin crawl, and cause even my own perspiration to smell differently than it normally did. To me, Henri was oddly, and markedly, a real threat to my sister and me.

The other night at the cocktail party, Henri reminded me of an over-dressed juvenile delinquent, especially when I noticed him watch his mother exit the party to aid Zooli. I am sure that he planned the whole goddamn thing, just to have my sister and me alone with him, in our racy little outfits. 'Oh good, my mother's gone, let the party begin,' I'm sure Henri thought.

Poor Miss Cathy, what a wonderful soul and caring older woman she is, but so very forgetful at times, for reasons I did not understand. She simply idolized Zooli, with a clear level of appreciation that was based on honesty and respect. I was convinced from the day we met that Miss Cathy looked upon her son Henri as a gentle young boy, a little spoiled, but shy for the most part. Perhaps he was a bit too forceful with animals, but far from a danger to human beings.

I saw Henri watching me from a distance, as if he were hiding a window to his own madness and so very far from the way he looked at my sister. He gazed at Homayra with needful, puppy love, while lusting at my anatomy with a perverted dirty thirst. Henri purposely ignored me, because he would not stand for any form of distrustful insubordination. He had good reason to distrust me too, because I hated his guts.

<hr />

Over the last several weeks Danielle was gone most every single day, leaving me both confused and deeply concerned about her whereabouts and welfare. Danielle had also sunk to a new level of depression, sometimes not speaking to anyone but me for days at a time. So as I finish my chores on that fateful day, I devised a plan to enter the castle on my own and try to locate my dear Danielle and see first-hand what was going on.

Homayra and Zooli, together with Miss Cathy, we're planning to work well into the evening, bathing the horses, braiding their manes and tails, and preparing them for a foxhunt early the next morning. I worked as hard as I could that day, pulling their thick long hair until my fingers became so sore they bled. I was also experiencing menstrual cramps and my exhaustion clearly evidenced no disguise on my part.

Miss Cathy noticed my discomfort and said, "Oh child, you need to go back to your room and rest, you look simply pitiful."

Zooli glanced up at me from behind the long line of horses as she and Homi were braiding and said, "Go back to your room, Goli, and get some rest. But we need you here by 4:30 a.m. to present the horses to the foxhunters.

"I know Zooli and I'm so sorry," I said, with a true level sincerity to all three of them.

As I left the stables and walked up the path towards the castle, I had the hardest time visualizing myself working by my sister's side the next morning. I was on a one-way mission of my own to explore the unknown mysteries of the castle and life beyond that did not matter.

I noticed a crowd forming near the base of the tennis courts on the eastern side of the castle. There appeared to be a rather large and well organized group of hotel workers armed with cameras moving swiftly towards the alleyway between the tennis courts and the loading docks behind the castle. I quickened my pace up the path and came within view of the source of the photographers' interest.

A group of around 20 women dressed in scant swimsuits, appeared to be involved in some sort of fashion show near a loading dock in the back of the castle. The early fall air was changing and the girls appeared to be cold as they stood in line. I soon realized that their shivering was not entirely due to the autumn breeze but anxiety as they each faced the office with the one-way observation window.

I entered the alleyway in my normal fashion of *purposeful intent*, and walked up just behind the group of onlookers who were all snapping photographs. Why were these food service personnel tasked with taking pictures of these girls? I watched the line of young women standing at attention with their backs to me and their faces towards the photographers. They all appeared to be Latin American with a mounting anxiety which soon clearly changed to fear.

As the women stood shivering in their scant swim suits and painfully inappropriate high heels, I suddenly noticed Ari emerge from the door of the office with the one-way mirror. My heart skipped a beat as I quickly put two and two together, and realized that this was the same woman I saw unloading the bus full of children with lost expressions. She was also the same women who seemed visibly annoyed by our connection to Henri during our drunken party in Henri's penthouse.

I quickly moved back under the shadows of the parking garage hoping that she wouldn't see me. Luckily for me she didn't, as she proceeded to inspect the young women, who appeared to be in their early teens, in the way a horse trader might examine thoroughbred horses. She examined their symmetry, posture, feet, hair, skin, and teeth. She wrote down their measurements and inspected the front of their panties as if she was verifying their gender.

After Ari was done appraising the poor girls, she began a process of elimination. The chosen ones were stamped on their wrist with a number. The rejects were pulled out of line and ordered to stand at attention. After everyone had been evaluated, she instructed the chosen ones to follow her through a doorway into the castle.

One of the girls in the front of the line looked back with confused terror at the remaining three rejected girls shivering in the cold. With a look of trepidation she broke out line and rushed to the girls standing off to the side. In an instant, Ari was on her with the most poisonous look in her eyes. She grabbed the frightened child by her hair and ratcheted her arm around her back into a painful contortion. Now at the end of the line, and with everyone in order, Ari and the struggling dissident herded the young girls through the heavy metal door way as if she was driving livestock into a slaughter house.

The three remaining women on the outside suddenly broke protocol and raced towards the now closed door and began beating and clawing at the flush edges of the door. They cried and howled as the blood from their broken fingernails combined with their flowing tears of terror painted the side of the door with a symbolic coat of loss.

In an instant, Ari rushed out of the observation office with a look of controlled rage. She gathered the women up with a peculiar ease and moved them towards the parking garage in my exact location. I instantly retreated to the only place of safety I knew of, the hidden changing room which Danielle and I had used so many time to dress for our castle adventures. I slung open the door and twirled into the darkened restroom while quietly closing the door behind me and turning the bolt lock.

I threw my back against the door and sat in the dark with my hands on the filthy floor as the group of female prisoners walked passed by my door. My heart was pounding as I listened to the sounds of their sobbing and pitiful heels echoing off the concrete walls as they moved deeper into the dark parking garage. My concern for the welfare of these poor young girls became overwhelming as I opened the door and reentered the dark garage, following the sounds of the group in the distance.

When I came into viewing range again, two women were sobbing out of control, while one seemed to be pleading with Ari in a language that might have been a form of Spanish.

Ari provided no sympathy to the trembling women as they approached the same Mercedes-Benz bus that was used to unload the children a few weeks before. Two heavily armed security guards escorted the now screaming women onto the bus as Ari stood guard, with a gun in her left hand.

I cursed at myself for not preparing for the bus to come back out of the garage in my direction. I retreated backwards to the safety of my changing room as the sound of the approaching bus began to intensify behind me. I struggled back up the hill and turned a corner while slipping on the concrete and falling painfully on my left side. I clawed the course cement with my fingernails as the approaching bus closed in on me. The lights of the bus began to illuminate the wall next to me, as I limped in pain on all-fours, clawing my way to the handle of my changing room door.

I swung myself into the dark room like a frightened mouse and pushed the door closed. The bus rushed past my door as I opened it a crack. My eyes refocused on the back of the bus, and to my disbelief, I saw a woman's back being pressed violently against the back window of the bus by the forceful Ari. She struck the out-of-control woman over the head with a wooden baton, rendering her instantly into a lifeless doll. The horror intensified as Ari continued to bludgeon the poor woman's skull. The woman's blood spattered against the inside of the window of the bus like a scene from a movie.

The bus stopped in the alleyway just next to the observation office as Ari casually disembarked, straightening her shirt and fixing her hair. She calmly lit a cigarette with her metal lighter and walked through the door of the observation office as if nothing had ever happened.

I turned the light on in the changing room and stared at my filthy face in the mirror. Sweat was pouring down my face as my hip and fingertips burned with pain. My god in heaven, what had I just witness here? I didn't want to accept what I had just seen. I choked with fear and suddenly become nauseous, as I became quite certain that I had just witnessed a murder.

I suddenly thought of Danielle being held captive in that horrible castle. Might this sort of cruelty be meant for her as well, and what in the hell were these women supposed to be used for? I had no clue, as my mind raced for some answers. I slowly opened the door and exited the changing room and tried my best to walk unnoticed toward my suite in the castle. I had to go find my sweet Danielle and warn her, and I had to do it that instant.

Once I returned to my suite, I had to determine what I was going to wear, on my emergency search for Danielle. I knew full well that if I simply walked around the public areas of the castle, dressed as I had before, I would immediately be spotted by some of Henri's security people. So as I looked through Danielle's supply of clothing, it became clear to me that every young woman in the castle was dressed with the same exact theme: skimpy, tight, and overtly revealing.

I was still confused as to exactly why that was the case, but I knew that I had better dress in something that blended in with the rest of the female population. I soon came upon what appeared to be an erotic cocktail waitress uniform, complete with a tight black skirt, which was functionally too short with a white-lace low cut top over a hot-pink frilly bra. I looked both ridiculous and stupid; resembling what my father would call a *faheshe*, that is, a prostitute.

I thought about choosing something else, but the rest of outfits had the same ridiculously provocative look. Luckily for me, this particular waitress uniform had more reasonably heeled dress shoes. I braided my hair extra tightly, which was clearly different from my usual look.

Even though the outfit was clearly suggestive, I made the mistake of assuming that usually the bartenders and cocktail waitresses were considered service personnel and possibly off limits to the lecherous grabs of the guests. While I was now convinced that most men were pigs, I also thought that few would get in the way of a customer's drink order. I applied an overly dramatic swath of eyeliner and thick blush with strong overtones along with extremely feathery eyelashes. I added extra color tones to my face while changing my natural color. In the end I resembled a cross between a street walker and a show girl in a dance lineup.

As I left the suite and headed down the main corridor toward the mezzanine floor, I knew full well that I needed to stay out of public sight so I decided to circulate around the castle by the means of the service corridors and elevators, which led to every nook and cranny. My main concern was that while I knew my way around the castle by way of public access, I didn't know anything about the layout of the internal service arteries. I also only knew one safe way in and out of the behind-the-scenes pathways which Danielle and I done several times in the past.

It was an easy jaunt to the changing room, where I stepped in and composed myself, and then I quickly walked across the alley way and through the door next to the observation office. The hallways seemed safe and as usual streaming with the activity of waiters, waitresses, and staff members briskly moving from here to there. I quickly snatched up a round serving tray as a prop and for the next 30-minutes; I decided to simply let the flow of the people take me on my own observation tour.

Hallways and corridors split off from the main hallway like tributaries to the many venues in the castle. Elevators and service-stairways were purposely built for exclusive access to the many entertainment areas of the castle which branched off here and there. Soon my mental landmarks became familiar to me again as I completed my first entire revolution of the main-floor service corridor.

Since the main hallway had people coming and going in both directions, I decided to map out my second revolution in the opposite direction, only this time paying particular attention to where the secondary hallways branch off. I broke off from time to time and examined where the short hallways lead to and quickly rejoined the main flow.

Since the castle was built during the time of the Roman Empire, its guts were used for all sorts of purposes. Also, many of the rooms in the old castle were each designed differently for the many different purposes I hated to even imagine.

At about three quarters of the way around my second revolution, I miraculously spotted the familiar sight of one of the bikini-clad new arrivals. She had regained her composure and was standing with her back to me while facing a dark hallway. Poised directly in back of her was a woman that appeared to be dressed in what can only be describe as an erotic version of a lion tamer's outfit, complete with a bull whip draped over her shoulder. She was in her own world busily adjusting a tiny piece of material barely covering the breasts of the dreadfully young girl with a now overly made-up face. As I moved closer to the two women they began to simultaneously move in the direction of the dark hallway as I followed without missing a step.

Luckily the hallway leading to the unknown entertainment venue was very dark, and I could hear the sound of circus orchestra music becoming louder as I moved closer to the source. I was now only three meters behind the made-up bikini-girl and the lion tamer when the doorway opened and the three of us entered a large room with ice-blue lights and a white center spotlight. I stepped in and stood by a door while trying to decipher what it was I was looking at. There was a large ring of rotating ladies either naked or wearing sheer veils.

Just outside the circumference of the ring the audience was cloaked in darkness, as a directional pinpoint spotlight illuminated each figure with complete precision. As my eyes began to adjust, I surveyed the room, noting that it was a perfectly round circle resembling the look of a "big-top" tent at a traveling circus.

On the far side of the room there was an orchestra pit containing six musicians all dressed in white shirts and black vests. A mixture of semi-familiar vaudeville tunes and circus music continuously played tune after tune without pause. The young ladies in the circle slowly rotated the room in a clockwise direction.

The erotic lion-tamer stood in the center of the ring cracking her whip dreadfully close to the exposed skin of the now fully trained women-creatures. At the end of each song the trainer lifted a silver whistle to her lips and emitted a shrill tone signaling the pitiful young girls to come to a stop and slowly rotate in a standing position to the apparent study of the poorly lit audience members.

Men and women of different nationalities stepped out of the audience and onto the floor of the stage, closely examining the twirling women. Some of the spectators appeared drunk and on a different mission, as if they were seeing something for the first time in their lives. Others acted as if they were there on business to appraise the ladies as if they were judging contestants in a dog show.

During the twirling display period four suspended pedestal stages arraigned in a square surrounding the entire circle, began to come to life with their own dedicated spotlights. Independent lights focused on strange animalistic-human figures, now pacing within their own cages, naked and kneeling to the apparent exotic entertainment of the audience. The lion tamer in the center of the ring periodically cracked the whip directly at the naked figures in the overhead platforms, causing the women to growl like tigers and swipe their hands in the air, as if they were lashing out with their claws.

With the added lights from above slightly illuminating the audience, I started to see a way to navigate around the room. I walked over to the first of the many steps, leading up the coliseum style seating system and briskly climbed the steps while studying the people seated to my right and left. I soon arrived at a mid-way walking level that circled around the entire arena. I surveyed the entire room and noticed men and women casually sitting in spacious seats, watching the strange, naked menagerie on the floor below, while sipping cocktails which were served by noticeably young girls and boys.

From my new vantage point, I noticed that each of the girls on the floor had a round white numeric label, clearly displaying a three digit number. Frequently, an audience member raised their own distinctly colored card to the attention of a circulating waitress. The waitress would quickly retrieve the card from the audience members and run it down to one of two judging tables, which sat across from each other, on each side of the circle.

For the life of me, I could not understand what I was witnessing, so I continued to follow the main walkway around to the other side. I soon realized that this process of retrieving and delivering customer tickets was becoming systematic and routine. The process of simply taking the ticket from the customer and dropping it off at the apparent judging table seemed rather simple, so I decided to take it upon myself, to retrieve one of these tickets and run it to its destination point.

I noticed a hand raise, about two rows down and three seats over from where I was standing. I moved in on the customer and started to pick up a few of his empty glasses and set them on my serving tray, while accepting the customer's blue ticket from his extended hand. The customer glanced over at me with a level of interest that surprised me, so I backed away from the table.

The man had a sick grin that appeared gross as he quickly grabbed me by my inner thigh with his fat hand and pulled me in to him. He moved his hand up the inside of my leg and under my skirt as if he had a complete liberty to do so. "Why don't you pick up a couple of vodka martinis, honey, and come back to join me?" he asked as he boldly moved his hand further up my inner thigh and directly under my crotch.

His body and breath smelled of saturated liquor and cigarettes, and his eyes had a dangerous look to them as he pushed the base of his hand forcibly upward against my vagina. My defenses jumped to full alert and I came remarkably close to jamming the rigid side of my serving tray into his fleshy neck, with glasses and all, but I luckily didn't, as I quickly backed away from his reach.

As I walked away, I found myself astounded by that man's nerve, and total lack of human decency. It was as if he believed that he had the right to touch any part of my body as if he owned me. As I walked, I positioned the card under the lights above, and noticed a three-digit number, corresponding to one of the women on the floor, a customer number, apparently associated with the pig above, along with a monetary amount. It was then I realized that what I was witnessing was a competitive bidding process for the ladies on the floor.

I briefly considered discarding my tray of dirty glasses, along with the ticket and getting the hell out of there---but I didn't. What if the pig in the bleachers was watching me from his seat? I could disregard his drink order, because of the hideous way he ordered it, but thought I had better not throw out his ticket, or he might leave his seat and come down looking for me. With relative grace, I turned the corner and moved down the main stairways leading to the judging table.

Each table consisted of four rather attractive ladies who accepted my card without even looking at me. On the table in front of them were piles of customer tickets neatly arraigned in organized rows, resembling a complex game of solitaire? One of the women was quietly dictating numbers to the lady next to her, as she notated the numbers on a sophisticated accounting worksheet.

At this point I realize it was time for me to leave this fantasy bidding circus and make my way back to my suite before it was too late. As I was walking toward the exit hallway, I suddenly noticed Ari walking in front of me, wearing a belted, oversized beige sweater which exposed her shoulders and an extremely short cream colored skirt with a single brown strip. She had on exotic leather sandals with very tall heels, and I remember thinking that while she was a very attractive woman, she was also a brutally dangerous one as well. Luckily, she appeared to be moving in the same direction as I was, with her back to me.

Since I still had a tray full of glasses, I decided to make another quick revolution around the arena, allowing time for Ari to move out of the room all together. As I turned the final corner towards my exit, I looked over at the *pig*, who was now becoming noticeably upset that I had not returned with his drink and my company. He rose to his feet, and began to step across the people to his right, while pointing in my general direction. Almost expectantly he lost his balance and fell backwards on to the table directly in front of him. The surprised customers underneath him, grimaced and screamed as they found themselves buried under the smelly mass of the drunken *pig*, as their own colorful drinks covered them in a strawberry and cream, sticky mess. I picked up my pace while heading to the exit and to my surprise I ran directly into Danielle, who was also serving drinks.

"Danni", I gasped, with my own look of surprised relief, "I was looking for you" I said, reaching for her arm.

"Goli, What in the fuck are you doing here? Goddammit Goli, you need to get the fuck out here, now!"

"But Danni, you need to come with me, we need to get out of here. What the hell is going on here?"

"Well I certainly can't tell you here, Goli," Danielle whispered, as she moved me along.

"Get out here, before you get us both killed! Do you fucking understand me? This is some serious business in here, and something you should not know anything about! I'll tell you more tomorrow but you need to get out of here this instant!"

"Tomorrow might be too late," I said with anxious dread, "I have to tell you about what I saw outside in the alleyway just now! I saw a woman murdered. I saw that--that blonde woman kill someone! Danni please come with me now, I'm so dreadfully scared for you."

Behind Danielle's left shoulder, I spotted Henri walking through the crowd, shaking hands with the customers at nearby tables. I shuttered as I saw him make direct eye contact with me, as I swiveled on my feet in the other direction. I had the feeling that I had been most certainly caught as I walk towards the exit, fully expecting to hear Henri call my name. My body was shaking with fear, waiting expectantly for his voice, but to my relief, he never called.

I was soon running down the dark hallway leading up to the main service corridor, I swung the door open and immediately blended into the sea of rapidly moving service personnel. At least at this point, I thought that Danielle and I were safe, but what about tomorrow and the next day? I just had to make it to the door next to the observation office which was not too far away.

What were those people buying and selling in there, and what the hell is going to happen to Homi and me? What sort of hell are we all trapped in, I wondered. What about my poor Danni, I thought, as if panic was about to completely set in on me. Suddenly I felt the steely grip of sharp fingernails sinking into my bicep and to my complete surprise I looked up and saw Ari bearing down on me with the look of a massive and threatening hawk who had just caught its pray.

Chapter 14

GOLAREH: INNOCENCE LOST DURING A NIGHT WITHOUT END

"So you couldn't keep away from here, could you, you stupid little Iranian bitch?" Ari said with a shocking level of assertive meanness. It was as if she had an instantaneous hatred for me which I thought was completely unwarranted on her part and far from my understanding.

I considered breaking free from her grip and running but I realized that her grip was way too powerful. I felt like screaming for help at the many faces that were standing right next to mine as we both traveled through the crowded hallways of the inner castle but each face appeared totally void of any level of humanness.

"Did you think you could just come and go anywhere you wanted to around here, little girl?" Ari asked, with an evil chuckle. "Did you think we wouldn't see you and your stupid nigger girlfriend as you both strutted around here making yourselves at home? Oh--I'm going to enjoy this; I am really going to enjoy this, you little hot bitch!" Ari said as she turned a sharp corner and pushed me into the dark entranceway.

Ari slid her left hand up the base of my neck and grabbed my ponytail and tightly wrapped it around her wrist as if she was going to tear it completely from my scalp. We approached the end of the short hallway and she slammed the right side of my face directly against the cold metal surface of the door, while turning the doorknob with her other hand. As the door burst opened inward I felt a sharp pain on the base of my tail bone as her harsh heel cut through the flesh covering my spine. I twirled to the ground in writhing agony as the pain shot completely through to my abdomen.

Tears poured out of my numb right eye as one of my fake eyelashes partially dislodged and curved into my eye blocking my vision. I felt the impact of Ari's left foot smash into my ribcage as my body spun to the right a second time. Her tight fingers intertwined with my hair braid, twisting and almost separating my hair from my scalp. The unbelievable amount of force that originated from this hideous, female monster shocked me, as she yanked me to my feet and hurled me forward.

The motivation of this woman to inflict such forceful pain on me was both confusing and terrifying to me as I flailed around like a helpless rag doll under her complete control. She shoved me from room to room calling me horribly vulgar names until I realized that I was in Henri's ground-floor office.

"You are one haughty little *hot* Iranian cunt, do you know that you selfish bitch, I can't wait for this, you little wayward spoiled tease," she yelled, as she heaved me backwards and forwards by my braids.

She violently dragged me through the large dining area and into a kitchen while passing a large collection of pots and pans, gas stoves, and wooden chopping blocks. Her fingernails dug deeper into the back of my neck as she shoved me through a final doorway into another room. One final kick to my lower back tripped me up and propelled me forward into the center of a large living room and onto an oriental rug directly at the feet of Henri.

All I could focus on was Henri sitting on a spacious U-shaped couch with two women, one on each side of him resembling bookends. He was drinking something from a snifter and grinning at me with a whimsical expression as if he had been presented with an injured rat that had just been captured in his kitchen.

He was dressed in a dark silk paisley robe with matching pants and leather slippers. A fire was burning in the fire place to the right of him and the fact that he had moved so rapidly from the circus room to this room defied my sense of time and space.

"Hello Goli," Henri said, as he slowly lowered the crystal goblet from his lips. The two girls, wearing revealing lace negligees and no underwear, with crossed legs and leaning into Henri, were unfamiliar to me. The contrived expressions on their faces, coupled with an almost choreographed group pose made me wonder if the entire scene was staged for my benefit.

"Come Goli; please join us in a nightcap?" Henri said, as he looked down at me on the floor by his feet. "How about a glass of cognac, my darling," Henri asked, as he signaled Ari to bring me one. "Oh my dear child, you do appear to be a little rough for the wear! Darling Ari, would you please try to be more careful with these precious youngsters, in the future? We simply cannot have them blemished---don't you know?" Henri scolded, as he looked at Ari with a hint of joking discipline.

I was so terrified I couldn't speak as I lay on the floor in front of Henri. My face burned with pain and I wondered if my scalp was bleeding from the brutal grip of Ari's nails. I felt like I was about to be initiated into some strange cult, as Ari slowly prepared a drink for me.

Ari orbited around the room and delivered a crystal goblet of cognac directly into my trembling hand, while scanning the position of the ladies with an odd level of interest. She then came to rest on the couch directly across from me. Ari's expression completely dissipated from that of a brutal henchman to a desiring participant in a sexually charged theatrical production in which I was to be the star character.

"Goli, may I ask you a question? Why is it that you seem to dislike me so much, and why do you distrust me so?" Henri asked, slowly raising the cognac to his lips. "Have I ever harmed you in any way, my dear, have I? I just want to know, is all?"

Ari began to appear extremely anxious by her position outside of the central activity of Henri and the posing ladies. She stood up, and in an overly-seductive manner, untied the belt around her sweater, and allowed it to slowly drop down over her shoulders. She walked over to Henri, and sank to her knees, while rotating her body around at the base of Henri's feet to face me. She then spread her legs and purposely showed me her shaved vagina.

Henri's gaze didn't break from me, showing no interest in Ari and the three women flanking him on all three sides. "Why is that, Goli?" Henri asked in an elevated voice. "What have I ever done to cause you to dislike me as much you apparently do? Henri's demand reminded me of a schoolyard bully, upset with his neighborhood friends for refusing to play with him.

I found myself dumbfounded as I starred at the glowing embers under the burning logs in the fireplace. The hot coals beneath the logs seemed to come alive as if they were tuned to the activity in in the room.

"You were such a beautiful child," Henri reminisced, with an odd level of appreciation. "You and your sister stole my heart that day so long ago," Henri said, as his eyes wandered to the ceiling. "How can anyone so young and so beautiful contain so much distrust and apparent hatred for someone who---," Henri halted as his sentence and quietly trailed off to a barely audible mumble.

"I saw that look in your eyes then, and unfortunately I see it now", Henri said, as he emptied the entire contents of his glass into his mouth, the liquor dripping down the center of his chin.

My throat was dry as I faced this odd inquisition panel, while Henri moved between spiteful anger to the tones of an apologetic fatherly figure. I began to feel like I was a victim of mistaken identity, feeling as if I owed this mad-man some explanation for the crime of simply seeing him for what he truly was.

I knew that my feelings for him were purely instinctual on my part, and not based on anything he had ever done to me, but more for the selfish evil I clearly saw in his eyes. Henri oozed a self-centeredness that seemed to thrive upon breaking the weak souls of others, and I began reading him like a book right then and there.

As I looked into Henri's eyes, I could clearly see the depth of his evil, and through my instincts I was able to determine the root cause of his design, stemming from a mystifyingly, overbearing guardian. I knew that it certainly could not have been Miss Cathy, so I determined that it must have been his father.

He noticed me examining his demons, as my staring eyes pierced into his pupils, and he became visibly uncomfortable.

"Why do you stare at me like that, Goli? Tell me what you see!" Henri demanded, shoving Ari away from his feet. "What do you see in my eyes Goli; tell me! I want to know!" Henri anxiously demanded as he stood up and began walking in my direction.

I was spellbound as I sat looking at the now confused animalistic female creatures, cowering together on the couch behind Henri as he advanced on me. My body was limp with fear and although I felt the urge to flee from this impending predator, my limbs felt paralyzed by the dominant force of Henri's power above me. He stood towering over me like a mountain.

"Tell me goddamn it! I want to know what you see in my eyes?"

Henri snatched me up off the floor by my underarms. My body was completely off the ground with my feet dangling above the oriental rug below. The heavy crystal glass flew out of my hand, showering the carpet with alcohol and quietly bounced across the thick rug. He moved my face directly in front of his eyes and pressed for me an answer.

"I saved your life by bringing you here to my home, you ungrateful little tramp!" he yelled, as his angry eyes struggled to focus on mine.

Suddenly I felt a level of confidence fuel my mind, as I detected a crack in Henri's powerful armor, as he struggled to understand how I was able to look so closely into his private world.

I drilled a hole through both of his eyes as my confidence in what I saw increased. It was almost as if I could reach in and touch the actual demons in Henri's mind, and *he* knew it.

"Why do you hate me so, Goli? I have treated you and your sister as if you were my own family!"

Sweat was dripping down his forehead and hanging on the base of each of his earlobes.

"You must tell me why you dislike me so!"

Without fear, a well-constructed speech visually presented itself in my mind's eye, one that I could actually read from like a script.   I began to perfectly and completely unload Henri's profile, which was the basis of my distain for him. I paused like an actress on a stage and leered intently into his confused eyes as if I were going to plant a reflective mirror directly in the center of his soul:

"Because you are a hateful monster hiding behind a gray beard. Underneath your thin and revoltingly facade lives a manipulative, pitiful man, with a hatred for everyone else in the world, and most especially the loving parents of the humans you take advantage of! You despise those caring parents that you have convinced of your virtues, because of your own jealousy of them!

You believe everyone around you is an imbecile, especially the women and children who you secretly hate! You are a goddamn misogynistic pervert!" I exclaimed, as I pulled words from a vocabulary that I never dreamed existed. *"Why do you draw such enjoyment out of secretly hurting those young girls and the parents of the vulnerable people you supposedly help? Shame on you, you selfish man!"* I shouted.

"I see you as a bearded pudgy boy who feels entirely inadequate, a childlike bully in a human suit, wanting to torture everything around you, in an effort to keep the voice of your father away from your soul," I screamed. *"The truth hurts doesn't it, you monster? The truth hurts--you sick animal,"* I said, admonishing him at the top of my lungs.

The room fell silent as we both considered every word I just said. I was also astonished by how quickly I had crafted such a complete monologue about what I had seen in Henri's personality. I was fully aware that I always had a higher than normal facility with composition, and an intense sensitivity for easily recognizing behavior in people. However, it was the forceful way that Henri demanded that I tell him completely why I didn't trust him that provided me the fuel to artfully craft such a demeaning character profile.

Henri stood there staring at me in shock with his eyes still locked under the relentless control of mine. Perhaps I was the only other person outside of his father who had ever talked to him in such a way that would cause him to become disabled. At that very second I felt in complete control over Henri as I poked and prodded the inner most recesses of his mind with the fingers of my sight.

Ari sat on the floor in back of him with a look of shock and awe as she measured the condition of Henri's helpless state of mind. She sprang to her feet in Henri's defense, pulled him around and tried to bring him back to a reasonable point of consciousness. "Leave him alone you selfish fool! You don't know what you're talking about! Stop it! How dare you insult this poor man," Ari screamed, as she attempted to control Henri's building temper. But it was too late; the eruption had begun as I felt a massive explosion take place.

In an instant, I felt my entire body being launched towards the ceiling as I traveled through the air with my back above the floor and my feet trailing behind me. My lifeless body landed violently in a mass on the floor about four meters away from him as my head curled forward blocking my airway. Henri stood there with a horrid look on his face as he glared down at me. His expression appeared broken while an odd muscle spasm began to activate and contort the right side of his jaw. He flexed his face over the base of his collar bone, in an effort to prevent the onset of a strange nervous tick.

"Henri, please sit down over here and relax, my darling, let me get you a drink. You poor, poor boy," Ari pleaded, as she sat Henri down in an almost catatonic stupor.

"Don't call me a boy---*mother!* Henri mumbled as he sank deeper into a dreamlike state. He was now drifting away into a semiconscious state of oblivion. Henri appeared done for the evening, resembling a child who had been beaten up by the neighborhood boys.

"Ladies," Ari said sternly, "help me show our little tramp just how horrible you have been treated here at the castle by this sinful man".

Both girls stood up and began to move in my direction while dropping to their knees around my collapsed and contorted body.

"Do you like these girls, Goli," Ari asked, with an evil tone.

"Aren't they beautiful," she asked, as she moved her hand underneath Henri's silk robe? "I can tell that you like those women, you horny little bitch," Ari taunted, as Henri sat on the couch moaning to himself as if he were experiencing a childhood nightmare.

"In fact, dear Goli, I think that you actually like women in general a little bit more than you wish to admit, don't you, you little tease."

The room went silent for a long time, as Henri's fog began to lift, while he soaked in the view of the three of us sitting on the floor in front of him. A single pop from the from the embers in the fireplace distracted me from her last comment as the girls began to shed their clothing like snakes and congregate around my body. Using their hands, the girls began to work my tense muscles as if they were clay.

"Nicola, please standup and face the man who saved your life!" Ari ordered. A tall naked Greek woman with olive skin and ample breasts stood up at attention.

"Nicola, can I ask you a question, my dear, please? I'm sure that you know how much Henri loves you? How much does Henri care about your welfare?"

"Oh---so very, very much, please never ask me this again Miss Ari!" Nicola answered, with a thick Greek accent, as if she was on trial as well.

"And doesn't he provide you with everything that you need each and every single day of your life at the Castle? Does he not dress you so beautifully in expensive clothing? Doesn't---he actually work for---you?"

Henri was beginning to come out of his daze.

"Oh my dear Henri, of course you do, I couldn't ask for anything more! You certainly do work entirely so much for the benefit of us all. I owe you my life Henri," Nicola answered, as if the inquisition were shifting entirely in her direction.

Ari slowly moved her hands under the belt line of Henri's silk pants and wrapped her fingers around his flaccid penis. Henri's face was beginning to inflate from the whimpering little boy back to a viral man, growing more confident by the second.

"Nicola, aren't your parents so grateful for you being here, and so very happy for your safety?" Ari asked, as if no other answer would be accepted. "How would each of your parents feel if they knew how some of you treat this fine man," Ari scolded.

"Don't you see Goli," Ari said, as she massaged Henri's now erect penis.

"If it were not for Henri---all of you ungrateful women would be on the street, addicted to drugs, starving to death in poverty or dead all together! Your own miserable parents pleaded with Henri for help. And for this, he receives your selfish insubordination? Shame on you all!" Ari scolded, with an ever increasing level of command, as she moved her face over Henri's bulging penis and inflated testicles.

Henri pulled Ari on to his lap and aggressively raised the bottom of her skirt up to the midpoint of her back, completely revealing her naked rear end and a pistol that was parked in a white leather holster around the upper part of her thigh.

"I hope you understand that your level of distrust makes us question the lot of you! We will never tolerate all of your disrespect," Ari said, warning all of us, as she arched her body over Henri fully engorged penis while glancing back at the group of us with a nasty expression as if she was priming him for something yet to come.

"Well unfortunately for you in particular, Goli," Henri said, coming back to life with a newly enriched cavalier voice. "I have ZERO tolerance for your misconduct."

Zero tolerance, I wondered what he meant by that.

"You should have never been where you were this evening. You had no business being in that room. Do you understand me Goli?" Henri asked. "Why were you there?" he demanded, as Ari grabbed his fully erect penis and pointed it directly at me.

"Why did you feel that you had to go to that room, tonight of all nights?"

I tried to speak but my throat was dry as the girls around me began to claw at me with mixture of fear and excitement. I tried to stand up and escape but I was convinced that my legs simply wouldn't work. All I could feel was the huge gravitational pull of my own fear and the surrounding girls grinding my body into the fabric of the rug, pulling at my clothing in every direction, seemingly waiting for some attack-signal from Ari, who was now moving her mouth closer to the head of Henri's erect penis.

"She had to go check on her little colored *girlfriend*, Danielle, Henri." Ari said in a sort of baby voice, as she lowered her mouth around the head of Henri's engorged penis while gazed up at him from below.   The sight revolted me as I closed my eyes and clenched my jaw.

"Oh my lord," Henri growled in a baritone power of a grizzly bear. "Is that why you were in there? You were looking for that little foul mouthed black bitch?" Henri bellowed, as he stood up dropping Ari to the floor in front of him. The girls on top of me began to become aroused as they slid me around the room like a helpless fish out of water. Ari began crawling in my direction while poking and prodding her vagina in a sick cadence.

Henri dropped his robe and stepped out of his pants while he advanced across the room towards me, with the large shaft of his penis extending in front of him like the bowsprit on a sailing vessel. I suddenly felt a horrible feeling of vulnerability in my lower regions. Ari moved closer to the horrid pile of writhing bodies, sitting upright on her knees masturbating and laughing like a wicked witch as she watched the mass of slithering women and Henri's naked body closing in on me.

I felt a sudden boost of power return to my body as every level of protective measures moved to full alert. I flipped over onto my stomach and gathered myself up into a tight ball. The girls scratched at my back, ripping and stretching my clothing in all directions. I reached for a girl's hair with my left hand and pulled it so violently that I felt a joint in her neck crack, but instead of hearing a scream of pain; I heard an ironic moan of pleasure.

I fumbled and fought violently as I felt my bra being torn from the side of my breasts by Ari and to my horror my body was tossed completely over onto my back. I lay there on the ground totally vulnerable and helpless, but never stopping once to resist their advancements. My tight black skirt and panties were violently stripped from my waist and thrown across the room as if Henri was desperately clawing for a sinful treasure, as my insides were now totally exposed to the outside animals surrounding me.

"I think we have ourselves a menstruating little virgin here Henri," Ari said, with a sarcastically, hideous smile.

"Well then---that makes me want to preserve that delicious part for a more celebratory time." Henri exclaimed, as he positioned himself over the center of the grinding mass of sweaty humanity, as I violently hurled my body back on to my stomach for the last time.

My eyes snapped tightly shut as my mind attempted to block the terror of my horrible reality. I kicked at whatever I could make contact with, and grabbed anything I could grip. I wrapped my arms around the necks of the bodies surrounding me and tried to rip their heads completely off while adrenalin flooded my defense mechanism.

I fought with every ounce of strength in order to avoid my body from being in any one position for too long. My eyes were full of stars and bright with flashing lights as I felt the mouths and fingertips of the girls clawing, licking and biting my entire body like rabid dogs.

Suddenly I felt a massive object enter my rectum as it seemed as if my entire lower body had been broken into and burglarized. A foreign object of no defined shape or size suddenly began widening the inner recesses of my colon. I felt as if I were being ripped wide open and stuffed with the most hideous object imaginable.

Raw pain shot though my body like bolts of lightning, as if I were being dismembered internally. My body moved to the massive rhythm of the monster inside of me, advancing to a sudden feeling of either ice cold or scalding hot fluid, which filled my body with a forceful saturating injection.

My mind slide into another time and dimension and I found myself, once again, being smashing against the jagged rocks of the Caspian Sea. I saw my sister's hand reaching for me through the ice cold water, but it was impossible for us to stay together, as the force of the sea continued to demolish my lifeless body against the jagged edges of the rocks.

Homayra was below me, drifting deeper into the abyss, as her helpless eyes dimmed and the last remnants of life vacated out her lungs and bubbled past my face. I witnessed all life leave my poor sister's body that moment, as the energy source within her soul timed out and her lifeless form twirled down into the cold darkness below.

"Your sister is dead---Golareh! You sister was killed by an animal! You will never see your sister again! Your sister has passed away and you will never--never, ever-ever, see Homayra again!" the voice of God told me as I drifted into unconsciousness.

The storm of trauma reached a conclusion almost as fast as it started and I felt my body being lifted out of the stormy waters by an oddly familiar savior of my past. Salt water washed across my face and I began to open my burning eyes to the human that must have saved me from the sea, leaving my poor sister to perish. My eyes slowly focused as I watched the monster who savagely raped me, transform into my new savior and the only person I had left in my entire world. It was Henri, now holding me like a baby, as he walked across the floor with a look of confident love on his face.

"There, there, my darling Goli, you are safe now." Henri said, as he sat down on the couch with my naked and battered body in his arms. His words sounded reminiscent of my own mother comforting me after a terrible nightmare. He parted my sweat soaked hair from my eyes with his fingers, and placed his massive hand on my cheek.

"Oh, my sweet Golareh, you do have such passion and power. I love that fight in you, so very much," Henri said. "You are now one of us, young lady, for you have nothing to fear for the rest of your life."

Ari, now dressed in an evening robe, stood by his side, gazing down at me, warming her hands around a cup of tea, with a look of motherly love.

"I think she was our winner tonight, don't you Henri?" Ari asked, while looking over at the other girls who sat on their knees, thoughtfully smiling at me. "She is our little *superstar*; she really put up a great fight." Ari said, as she kissed me on the cheek.

"You were so scared my little fighter, I almost felt sorry for you," she said as I laid there in disbelief, realizing that I must have been unconscious for an extended amount of time.

Henri gently pulled my face against his chest and began to stroke my bare back. "Yep, she certainly is tonight's winner, our little *superstar*. Now rest my little superstar, rest, there, there".

As my dismembered reality began to return to my broken mind, I realized that I had been entirely, physically and emotionally compromised. Every fear I could think of, including my now dead sister Homayra and my lost parents began to thrust upward and out of my chest. I burst into an explosion of tears, as my voice for the first time that evening came alive with deep and bellowing cries of need.

I buried my face in Henri's chest and cried my heart out, as my broken body ached and leaked beneath me. I was confused as to *why* I was now embracing the very same monster who had just taken me completely apart; but at the same time, I felt that I was totally alone, desperately reaching out for the only caregiver I could find and that person was Henri.

I screamed and clawed for him, as my heart completely emptied out into the now comforting and powerful chest of the very same man who completely annihilated my innocence.

HERE AND NOW

THE NEW NOW

Job 18.5-6: "The light of the wicked shall be quenched...and his candle shall be out with him."

I wake up and find myself sitting on the floor of the inside of my mind. It's dark and lonely and dreadfully scary. I feel the warmth of my own blood surging through the inside of my skull. I gaze around the dark, oval architecture of my confined area and wait for the many aggressive thoughts to invade my drowsy space.

I first came to the room thirty-two years ago. Then I was gripped with anxiety, fear, anger and confusion. The walls of my mind are alive with bright, cinema graphic images of the most painful moments of my life. There are things that I must to do, accounts I need to reconcile and gods I need to square off with. There is just too much to tend to in the darkness of my horrible chamber.

Some of the memories appear to be in motion affecting my stomach, making me feel sick, nauseous and bloated. Others attack the interior portions of my heart in the form of deep stabbing pain, causing me to grip my chest and press the tips of my fingers deep under the shallow edges of my rib-cage as I desperately try to relieve the heavy pressures within.

Every night I wake up under the same miserable blanket of darkness and despair which surrounds my bed. The entire world seems unbearably dark and unfriendly. Logic whispers to me that I am safe--but only for the time being. But I am still terrified of the dark and furious at my nightly obligation to sleep.

I am pursued by a force I can't identify, a dark force that is full of never-ending, fuming energy. A spiteful force charged with a mission of hurting me, of rendering me completely useless and of little worth.

One by one, I spend my time with each of my many painful memories, scrubbing them down to a stain that will never quite go away, but at least I can tolerate. The attention I devote to each stain pays off, as one-by-one they are removed enough from the walls of my soul that I may rest and see another day.

Chapter 15

GOLAREH: 32 YEARS LATER
AND SIX MONTHS AGO

Details surrounding the first ten years following my relocation from the castle, can be summed up by the visual of an entirely blank calendar. As for the next twenty-two, all I can say is that life passes by in a blink of an eye. My sister was dead and my parents were far away in a remote land. I was convinced that Homayra was dead just as much as I knew I was alive. No question. Case closed.

I was relocated by Henri to the city of Oxford in central southern England and was immediately entitled to magical scholarships that paid for my entire education. To my surrounding collection of classmates, teachers and academic advisors, I appeared to be an Iranian war survivor. I was also an intelligent but maladjusted foster child of the state of France.

I took up smoking entirely too early and was attracted to the relaxing effects of marijuana. I didn't smoke to get high, well I take that back, I did smoke to get high, most especially to get stoned as hell. I always needed to calm that ever present tightness in my chest caused by the loss of my sister. I simply could not put my finger the other sources of my pain, I just knew the size of the scorched fields of my life were massive. I missed my sister terribly and wished on so many terrified nights that I could join her in heaven, hell, or wherever she had ended up.

All need for money was taken care of by the country of France, and any concerns about making ends meet simply didn't exist. I was provided with the funds that I needed under the rules of France's social protection system. If I had a need for additional funds for clothing, entertainment or whatever, I would simply submit a voucher. I would send it directly to UNEDIC, France's National Union for Employment in Industry and Commerce, and *voila*; an electronic transfer would almost immediately show up in my bank account with no questions asked, ever.

As far as I was concerned I was some sort of unchecked ward of the state that fell outside of normal audit procedures. I was not a spendthrift and disliked people who were. As a matter of fact, I despised wealthy people for reasons I couldn't understand at the time. I just knew that whenever I was around them I would feel my skin crawl.

I loved the university and the city of Oxford, a very old town with large dark buildings that looked as if they had been sheltering students for centuries. Oxford University was not your typical campus setting at all. It had a large footprint which spread throughout the entire city. Oxford was and still is the second oldest university in the world next University of Paris and just being a part of it was wonderful.

I lived in a simple flat completely alone and for that reason; I found that I didn't have the time to even contemplate my new environment. I made my bed every single morning, went to class every single day, studied hard and worked my ass off. All I did was smoke, work, eat and sleep.

I got a job writing for the *Cherwell*, the Oxford student newspaper. I felt very comfortable around the writers at the paper, mainly because everyone seemed as maladjusted as I was. I started out writing about local news events in and around the town, but soon wrote a weekly column about politics, which interested me greatly.

I formally enrolled in the Oxford School of Journalism and earned a master's degree. I found that I simply loved to write about political figures and soon was recognized by at the Enterprise and recruited as a staff writer.

The Enterprise was widely distributed but had a reputation for speaking out about political figures, academicians and celebrities. I didn't realize it at the time, but I now believe that when my editor moved me off political topics to general and more local news, it was because of Henri's influence.

I rarely ever saw Henri anymore and for that matter I never even thought about him. However, the only person who would occasionally check up on me was Ari. She would appear out of nowhere at the most impromptu times and ask how my studies, workload, and social life were going. Ari always referred to me as Henri's superstar and I hated it. "How's Henri's little *superstar* doing," was the first thing that came out of her mouth every single time I saw her. I was not sure why it was, but every time she used that word, I cringed and experienced cold chills.

Actually anytime I heard the phrase "super-star," no matter if it was in reference to a well-known musician or even Jesus Christ himself, the word made me curl up inside and want to hide. Thank God for the balancing effect of marijuana and my wayward friends at the Enterprise for keeping me going during my twenties.

Ari was indeed correct about one observation that she had of me years ago and that was the fact that I was gay. I can't remember her actually ever saying anything specifically about it; I just felt that she always knew it.

I never had an interest in men what so ever. I also never struggled with my sexuality in the way others might when they realize that they are homosexual. I just simply always felt more comfortable with females.

I guess I always knew growing up that I loved the touch of a female, but since in my culture, the whole notion of sexual intimacy was left to the controlled teachings of a future husband; I simply rejected the possibility of having a heterosexual relationship. Especially in light of the fact that a man, any man for that matter, was supposed to dictate to me how I was supposed to love. "Fuck them all," I always said, which was a phrase I seemed to remember learning from my dear old friend Danielle whom I'd lost track of many years earlier.

In the fall of 2008, while covering a press conference regarding the legiti-macy of a famous dignitary's child, I was sitting in the back of a taxi cab in the thick London rush hour. My driver suddenly slammed on the brakes to avoid hitting a pink taxicab. My very vocal driver, who was from India, spared no words as he rolled down his window and screamed at a black fe-male driver at the wheel of a cab adjacent to us.

The driver of the hot-pink taxi squealed alongside of us and rolled down her window. She was an extraordinarily beautiful black woman with large thick sunglasses and a tremendously self-confident behavior. She was perched up against her steering wheel as if she were driving a bumper car at a carnival.

"Fuck you---George! This one's for egging my taxi last week you shit-head! Magda will be directing a washing notice your way soon," she yelled, in a thick cockney accent as she spit a large wad of chewing gum direct-ly into the thick beard of my driver. She then revved up her engine and screeched around us as if she were going to drive over the top of us. In the midst of the excitement the wild black woman's eyes met mine and to my utter amazement, I realized that she was my long lost and most treasured friend Danni.

My driver sat in his seat spellbound as Danielle peeled off in the distance.

"That woman is a Cockney bitch," said my driver, in his thick Indian accent, "She is the terror of London I tell you---a terror!"

I sat in the back seat giggling uncontrollably, as I watched my driver pounding on his steering wheel and tossing her sticky gum out his window.

"So you think that this is funny, do you?" my driver retorted, as he turned his head and glanced back at me.

"This is not funny in the least, why must you laugh me?" he yelled. "Leave my taxi at once! Get out of my car you heartless and ungrateful bitch!"

I was laughing so hard that I was afraid I might wet his already smelly back seat. I exited the taxi and stood on the center median as the rush hour traffic sped by me. I stood bent over on the concrete median completely overcome by one of the most intense cases of the laughter I'd experienced in years. As the driver sped away I realized for the first time in my adult life that I had a chance for happiness.

One thing that was evident to me, as I considered the whereabouts of Danielle, was that tracking down a female taxi driver in a pink Mini Cooper taxicab in the heart of London might be an easy thing to research on the World Wide Web. How on earth, did Danielle end up driving a taxi, I wondered as I hailed my next cabby home.

Once I arrived back at my apartment I immediately began scanning the internet for the existence of a taxi company that employed female drivers and utilized pink Mini-Cooper automobiles. I found no listing for the name Danielle; but I did find a website called *Impeccable Transit* which showed a group photo of 14 very attractive female drivers posing for a group shot. Standing in the shadows on the bottom row, directly next to a very stern looking elderly woman, was Danielle, who was using the name *Jessie James*.

Later, on that momentous day, I placed a call to *Impeccable Transit* and requested this Jesse James character to come pick me up. To my surprise the driver who came to my door was not at all Danielle or Jesse James, but someone else entirely, a young red head with the most beautifully adorned freckles and gorgeous figure, who went by the name "Lucy."

"Where is Danielle, I mean---Jesse James?"

"I'm dreadfully sorry mum, but I know of no Danielle."

"She's a feisty black girl, with absolutely horrible language," I said, thinking that Danielle most likely has retained her signature use of the word *fuck*.

"Jessie sent me here to pick you up and is very excited to see you again. Well---I guess I can tell you now. We had never witnessed our Danni cry like that before, but when she returned to the office for her shift change she was in tears. Tears of relief, I might add---mum. We had no idea what had happened, until she told us all about you," said Lucy.

We left my flat and took a 45-minute revolution around the mid-section of London, in an apparent effort to confuse someone who might be following us. Why that was necessary was beyond me, but I attributed it to the fact that Danni had most certainly changed her name for some reason.

We soon approached another pink cab about to be washed in a long drive-thru carwash.

I hopped out of Lucy's car and entered Danielle's cab, slamming the door behind me. We stared at each other in amazement as our hands gripped each other's with the most touching emotion I'd ever experienced. Our faces touched as tears flowed out of our eyes in a joyous flood of love.

For the next several minutes, I wrapped myself around Danielle's body, not saying a word, feeling her wonderful heartbeat and taking in the warmth of her sweet breath. I devoured Danielle as I gathered up handfuls of this scrappy but beautiful woman's lovely features.

In total we made three revolutions through the car wash that day, hugging and caressing each other as our feelings for one another blossomed to full flower. I could not believe the intensity of the feeling of my body against hers. It was as if we were electrified with a current of the most wonderful voltage.

The beautiful qualities of Danielle made me see just how lucky I was to be chosen to be the recipient of such a wonderful woman's touch. I examined Danielle's face and body with such intensity, remembering her as a tough fourteen-year-old kid.

What had happened to her, I wondered as I laid my face against her trembling chest, feeling the soft touch of her nipples pressing against my eye lids. A combination of intense love, protective nervousness, and erotic pleasure emanated from the both of us, as the powerful streams from the water nozzles blasted against the outside our tiny pink space capsule.

I wanted to consume Danielle as she situated my tearful face against hers. She moved her body over mine and straddled me in the passenger seat, as the heat and sweat of our bodies fogged over the wet interior windows while we slowly advanced through the car wash cycles.

I gently caressed her beautifully toned body and placed my hands on the small of her back. I felt the tight musculature surrounding her carved spine and slowly placed my hands on her beautiful rear end. The vision of Danielle awakened senses in my body that I thought never existed and made me desperate for more of her. I moved into a journey of profound joy, gently taking time to feel the tiny hairs that covered her body like a fresh layer of peach fuzz, and the feeling of her pulse pushing her blood through her veins.

Danielle slid her hands over the top of my chest and around the edges of my shoulders, catching the straps of both my tank top and bra in her clenched fists. Down went the top of my shirt and the cups of my bra causing my breasts to unload. Danielle sat starring at my bare breasts in amazement. I felt so very beautiful and alive as I gazed at her.

Streams of passion flowed from her eyes, along with uncontrollable moans of buried emotion as she gathered my breasts in her hands and moved her mouth against my nipples. She pressed her face deep into the center of my chest and began to weep inward against my pounding heart. Her body heaved as her exhausted mind opened and aggressively unloaded years of repressed pain and untapped desires deep into the welcoming depths of my soul.

During the short time Danielle and I were together as young girls, I never once kissed her, even though I clearly wanted to. That time was not our time. We were both very young and under the supreme pressure of society's most selfish population segment, which neither of us could understand nor recognize.

As Danielle raised her soulful face towards mine, she released her hands from my breasts and placed them around my sides of my face. She gazed at me as tears dripped from her cheeks and said, "Oh Goli, I am so sorry! I don't know what to say."

I looked up at her crumpled face contorting into a frown as she cried in an out-of-control, choppy cadence. "I don't even know where to start," she bellowed. "I tried to find you through the years, but simply gave up. I was told that the both of you were dead! I don't know what to say, my dear Goli! I'm so sorry!"

"Oh, Danni," I said as I studied her beautiful soulful lips. Her eyes were staring downward as if she were completely embarrassed.

The daylight from the end of the carwash snapped us back into reality. As Danielle struggled to reposition herself back into the driver's seat, we became tangled and knotted up together, losing our race against our ultimate appointment with the general public.

All at once the driver side door swung open as daylight blasted in along with excess water. In dropped our savior Lucy. "Danni, I can't take my eyes off of you for a second---can I?" she asked, as she took the wheel and turned the key to the ignition.

"You should have seen these blokes on the other side of the glass in there. They were moving up and down the observation hallway, cheering the two of you on as if you were actors in a slow moving triple-X car wash," Lucy said. "I just hope no one captured you guys on video! Let me ask you something----Danni! Do you think you missed this girl or what?"

Lucy laughed, pressed down on the clutch and slipped the car in to first gear. We slowly immerged from the exit of the watery car wash like children being born.

The vision of the two of us coming out that day to a world of applauding on-lookers wrapped in our pink cocoon of love, reminded me of an immaculate birth that was both perfectly clean and free from flaws.

"If the public had caught us on video, they would have missed the best part to follow," said Danielle, laughing and looking down on me with her caring eyes.

She pressed her beautiful lips against mine and completely overwhelmed me with our most passionate first kiss. I melted beneath her, as the applause from the entire wash crew faded in the distance. I will never, ever, forget the intimate and tender touch of Danielle's small tongue making contact with mine on that first day of rest of my life.

The conversations to follow from that day forward would serve as a catalyst for unlocking my past. We met constantly and shared wonderfully intimate times together feasting on our beautiful chemistry. Danielle was also a stickler for our privacy. She seemed overly cautious as to how we would rendezvous for reasons I still did not understand, but as time marched forward I would learn about our always and ever present predator.

Chapter 16

GOLAREH: DANNI'S BREAK TO HIDDEN LONDON

*O*ur pathways split off on that fateful evening at the castle as my crushed mind and demolished spirit were transported into an academic setting while Danielle's life was thrust onto the fast moving runways of the fashion world. Danielle was very slow to tell me why she changed her name, but after a few weeks of reuniting she shared only the following:

She said that her painful past of being used and abused by the controlling characters within the high fashion modeling industry, coupled with drugs, alcohol and crash diets almost killed her. She was constantly propositioned by businessman, powerful women, and the dregs of society, all under the bright lights of the beautifully-ugly modeling industry. She found herself in positions of forced rape too many times to count as her drug and alcohol consumption pushed the upper limits of physical toleration.

Danielle was not protected by the pimps of the fashion industry who were referred to by the French as *Mecs*. "We work for you," they would tell her, pretending that they cared about her best interest and personal safety. "No man or woman who uses a person for sex has their fucking best interest at heart," said Danielle. "They were all pimps to the industry and there is no such thing as a caring pimp!"

At the height of her despair and the darkest depths of her addiction, Danielle escaped from the clutches of her pimps back to the world she once knew as a child. Off she ran, deep into the dangerous Angell Town community of London's Brixton district, in the Borough of Lambeth. She slept on a cot in the back room of a bar that her father once frequented, called the Hoot & Nanny. Squirt Terhune, the proprietor, knew her as child and took her in from her darkest side of darkness. Her street smarts and knowledge of London's roughest neighborhood provided a blanket of coverage she most desperately needed.

She had finally dropped off the radar of Henri's fashion pimps and the occasional brutal oversight of Ari. However her addicted mind could not break free from the drug she depended on so much; the very same drug that provided her the ability to adorn a fake smile during a photo shoot or a walk down a runway.

When Danielle's use of heroin increased to a critical level, her dear friend Squirt thought it was necessary to call the only person in Brixton that could help. Her name was Magda Hulls, the one legitimate female force residing in the drug soaked dark land with a reputation of a savior.

Originally from Austria, Magda had a thick German accent and a very demanding way about her. People either loved Magda or hated her, and she shared the exact same intolerance for others. Magda was a loner in the business world, highly demanding of everyone from the tax offices to the local licensing commission. When local politicians received a telephone call from Magda, they often wished they had never picked up the phone. Everything about her was demanding, but also extremely fair and accurate.

Magda ran her own female taxi cab company with shrewd business savvy. Armed with a master's degree in accounting, coupled with a sharp business mind, she grew her pink taxi cab company to an impressive fleet of 18 cabs. The all-female drivers' personalities covered the gambit, but they each had one thing in common, they were all extremely beautiful, lovely, picture-perfect women who looked as if they had just stepped off a magazine cover. Each woman had been rescued from the streets of Brixton, and each had stories of profound tragedy, having once stared into the eyes of the devil. They were all devoutly loyal to Magda, owing their lives to the brash personality of the woman who had caught them all as they fell from grace.

Magda didn't know who Danielle was, when she first saw her, as Squirt and his busboy carried her shivering body out to the back seat of her awaiting cab in the pre-dawn hours of the morning. It didn't matter who the sick black girl was anyway as Magda looked at Danielle's troubled and drugged sapped face. For behind Danielle's faded body was a beautiful angel that Magda could see from a distance. Magda once later told me that with Danielle, she could almost reach out and touch her sensitive and loving soul.

Danielle lived quietly undercover with a brand new name, as Magda nursed her back to health and gave her a job in dispatch. Magda was despised by the competition in the Greater London taxi industry, but she could care less. She was completely devoted to her "girls" as she called them, and came to love Danielle as if she were her own daughter. She provided Danielle with tender nurturing love at a time she most desperately needed it.

Soon Danielle decided that she wanted to try her hand at driving her own cab, so Magda took it upon herself to train her personally. Magda, who was once married to one of the world's leading French mechanics and stunt car drivers, had been taught everything about high performance driving techniques and the principles of a high speed driving.

Magda had the most wonderful relationship with her husband Hartley up until the day he died of a sudden stroke. Hartley placed it upon himself to fit each car with the most powerful engine packages and braking systems available. He once was the lead mechanic for John Cooper himself and had the inside connection to some of the most sought after high performance engine parts available, many of which he designed.

Hartley fit each Mini Cooper taxi with the most powerful engines applicable to the automobile. He then spent years teaching his wife, Magda, every aspect of his driving technique which he had developed on performance tracks and movie sets all over Europe.

Hartley knew that his treasured wife along with their family of beautiful drivers would be tested every single day on the highly competitive streets of London. He firmly believed that if Magda's team were skilled in the art of high performance driving, they would be able to survive their dangerous competition that was always out to sabotage them.

Hartley's technique of driving, blended the force of engine power with suspension and early stage torque. The main principles of his method were incorporated into short burst maneuvers or *movements* as Hartley called them. Each movement was a show of dance on the roadway and each accomplished a specific objective of confusing a determined enemy. Each routine required the right amount of speed along with the help of wind, water and gravity.

In a celebratory graduation ceremony, when Magda deemed Danielle confident enough to have her own car, Danielle burned every stitch of clothing that she had from her past life, in a steel barrel in the back lot of the taxi cab company as the girls and a few close friends cheered her on.

Henri's troops tried in vain to keep close tabs on Danielle for years until she dropped out of sight and into the protective hands of Brixton's most renowned savior.

Chapter 17

GOLAREH: TOTAL RECALL

*Haghighateto begouh, tchonkeh azadet
mikoneh ...The truth will set you free*

Scientists believe that the adult human brain has between 10 and 100 Billion neurons, with each having a specific purpose with regard to voluntary and involuntary behavior. Through electrochemical impulses in the brain, which weighs only between 1.0 to 1.5 kg's, the mind has the shrewd capability of exercising some neurons while purposely isolating others, perhaps for the sheer protection of the soul that inhabits it.

In my case, the neurons that controlled the replay button housing the horrible memories of my adolescence were almost perfectly set off limits. It is also absolutely amazing for me now to imagine how effectively those poisonous thoughts were kept at bay. For more than three decades, I never once examined even a shred of memory that may have recorded that violent night in which Henri completely intruded on my shivering mind and body.

The long forgotten memories that lived within the dark recesses of my mind were awakened suddenly one rainy afternoon by a single song and a flashing image. One song was all it took to activate that microscopic neuron, which my mind had assigned so much power to, commanding it to hold the truth and my horrible past completely at bay for most of my lifetime.

I had just finished interviewing a physician who just completed 14 hours of reconstructive surgery on Stephanie Krueger, a beautiful young circus performer in her mid-twenties. She had been viciously mauled by a creature that she completely trusted and believed to be her gentle giant.

Perry was her precious lion's name and for most of her life she dedicated her faithful moments awake to her huge cat. She spent endless hours seeking to understand its extraordinary mind and many nights sleeping with her exposed body pressed against the warm, massive frame of her beautiful beast.

Krueger had come from a family of lion tamers, some of whom were still in the trade, while others had tragically met their demise outside of the ring. Ironically, both her father and her eldest brother were not killed by animals at all, but by being careless at high speeds in automobiles and motorcycles.

Her father, Stephane Kruger Sr., was test driving a lightning fast motorcycle and lost control, striking the bottom car of a carnival ride appropriately named the *Domain of Death*. The family was stunned and the press had a field day with the irony of it all.

Two months later, Stephanie's brother Philippe was killed after drinking at an all-night bar and striking a utility pole with his Dodge in a quiet urban neighborhood. Officers on scene said that the car had flipped upside-down severing young Philippe's drunken body in half.

Miss Kruger had seen the ironic twists of fate with both her father and brother, and had since paid extra attention to her own safety measures. Stephanie believed that she had her act down to a science as she would place her entire head within the sharp confines of the massive jaws of Perry.

Stephanie knew that being in a cage with a group of lions required a large degree of attention so she strictly adhered to that age old adage that *lions are never tamed*, although she clearly loved her lions and most especially Perry. Stephanie also knew that it was her job to always be more attentive to her surroundings then the lions were. It is vitally necessary, that at all times, she had to capture the animal's full and complete attention and never let it go. Never should there be a second when a trainer is in a cage when either lion or human becomes distracted by something else.

The sexy circus ringmaster was about midway through her second act, which was called *Gentle Jaws*, when a peculiar distraction that she never considered made its way through the iron bars of Stephanie's menagerie and came to a stop within centimeters of Perry's fluffy tail. A 14-year-old spectator, whose name must remain anonymous, thought it would be funny to see if he could distract the huge lion with his laser pointer.

Miss Kruger's head was completely engulfed in the orifice of Perry's huge jaws, when the beast noticed a bright red dot slowly advancing across the floor towards his tail. The young brat, month's later, admitted to the police, that he had tried the very same trick with his own cat at home and had solicited the most exciting response. His little domestic short-hair was so frightened by the sight of the strange red light that she jumped towards the ceiling lights in a show of contorted panic. To the surprise of the brat, the stupid stunt triggered the exact same response with Perry, but this time with horrible consequences.

The 11-year-old, 700 pound, East African Lion which Krueger had trained for his life time had never advanced on her once, but the strange red predator caused him to launch himself towards the top of the cage like a missile. The powerful upward thrust of his legs elevated the cat into the air about four meters carrying his precious cargo along for the ride. Kruger screamed once and only once as her limp body swung from the jaws of the frightened beast.

There was a frightful panic among the spectators as the other lions in the cage became confused and advanced on Perry. One of Kruger's assistants was severely injured as he successfully moved Perry and the other lions away from Miss Kruger's torn body using hooks and iron bars.

My assigned job as a reporter on the beat that day was to determine whether Perry had viciously mauled the young lady on purpose or was absent of malice and simply trying to protect himself from danger. The fate of the poor cat's life now hung in the balance, depended upon whether there was a component of intent-to-harm. After replaying the video of the awful event time after time, with the sound off, I decided to revisit the incident again, but this time with full audio and within the privacy of my earphones.

It had been raining all morning and I was sitting on a cement bench just outside of the entrance of Whittington Hospital in Greater London smoking a cigarette and squinting at the tiny screen of my cell phone. Did Perry really want to kill this young lady, who had deep lacerations to her jugular vein? Or was the injury caused by a sudden upward compression of the lion's teeth against the young girl's neck?

The audio track of the video segment proved to add much more information to the many factors leading up to the injury then I ever imagined. I could clearly identify Stephanie's blood curdling scream and the lion's roar. It seemed easy for me to determine whether the sounds emitting from the lion contained the tone of aggression. Freakishly, I suddenly realized that I had heard that sound sometime in my past, but from where I had no idea.

With regard to Perry, the sounds coming from his diaphragm were not that of viciousness, but only a huge defensive effort to move his body out of harm's way. I could also distinguish a sound of compassion with regard to the possible injury of his helpless trainer. "Not guilty! Absence of malice," I yelled out loud, not realizing the volume of my voice within the privacy of my headphones. "He didn't mean to hurt her!" I yelled.

I took another long, nervous drag off my cigarette and pressed the right arrow icon to play the segment one more time, but this time with a different set of ears. As the video started, my attention was drawn to the sound of the circus orchestra in the background playing continuous music. I suddenly began to shiver with a sick familiarity with the song itself, but I simply could not understand why I hated that song so much.

The song that was playing during the struggle was a tune by Frank Sinatra called *World on a String*. The song gaily played as the bloody events within the menagerie cage unfolded. Along came the questionable groans of the lion violently twisting the body of the helpless trainer high above the ground. I felt a sudden kinship with the trainer and a sensation that I'd experienced a similar event when I was just a teenager.

A chill invaded by mind as I mentally combined the single scream of the woman with the groan of the animal on her back, all against the backdrop of that dreadful melody. I was convinced that I had heard those horrid sounds before as I fumbled through my handbag for another cigarette. It occurred to me that the growls from the creature in my memory were not that of a defense creature, but of a vicious, nasty monster on the attack.

I became light-headed with a barrage of images that flashed before my eyes, as I held an unlit cigarette against the burning embers of my other one. It was blatantly obvious to me, that the strange combinations of images and sounds were reawaking hidden memories of my past, which had been buried in a cryogenic state for more than 32 years.

My mind ventured back to that dreadful evening in the circus room, which had long since vanished from my conscience, and was completely shrouded in mental scar tissue. I dredged up the erotic lion tamer, at the time, cracking her long whip against the violated backsides of those poor women who were being sold to the highest bidder. I also revisited Ari, that horrible brute, on the back of a bus armed with a billy club, relentlessly bludgeoning the brains out of that helpless young woman who was only trying to save her sister from some sick evil madness.

Everything at that moment began to push out of my buried memory like the delivery of an overdue after-birth, which had been sitting and rotting in my dark past for decades promising to make its way out to the light of day. My mind's antirejection capabilities had finally worn off, simply by the combination of that song and those images acting like a key in the ignition to my dormant past.

The vivid nightmares I had been recently having about my dear sister Homayra suddenly began to make perfect sense to me. She was somehow alive and living somewhere on the same planet as I had been. All of the memories of my encounter with Henri and Ari, on his living room floor with the two other sexual soldiers visited me with increasing vigor, along with the details of the weight of them all on my back.

"She's gone Goli, you selfish bitch! I couldn't save your sister," the voice of Henri chanted over and over as he pushed his disgusting appendage deep into the recesses of my rectum. This was no minor crime at all, but a brutal unadulterated rape of the highest degree, upon my young body and untrusting soul.

"She's dead Goli; you need to remember that and never forget it!" Henri repeated. "She dead you foolish, selfish little bitch," he yelled with intensity, as he worked himself up to a sick, filthy and disgusting orgasm.

Everything about Henri started to resurface as I sucked the smoke out of two cigarettes at once. I abruptly understood why Henri and that mean bitch, Ari, would constantly reinforce their hypnotic suggestion every time they saw me using that powerful keyword that I hated so much: *superstar*. *Superstar* was the term they always used to reactivate my mind's response to tighten up around my buried memories.

Ironically though, the more I remembered the details of my days at the castle, the more the threats that Henri and Ari had placed on me became less potent. I suddenly felt a healing power of the truth strengthen my mind and resolve.

I awoke to a beautiful sunny day in the smoking section just out-side the hospital doors, holding two spent cigarettes in my fingers and a renewed view of my life. I felt refreshing energy filling my soul, as I smiled broadly like a crazy person as my fellow smokers nearby stared at me. I was suddenly convinced that Homayra was not dead at all, but very much alive.

I wondered where Frédéric had been all of these years; might he be aware of Homayra's whereabouts as well? I hadn't talked to him in decades. Could I now simply call him up on the telephone? Might he still remember me? Is he also part of Henri's lies? Why had he never tried to contact me?

All of the questions flooded into my anxious mind as I realized that it was vital that I find Frédéric and get his help in locating my sister. Besides, Frédéric is family and I should always be able to trust him? Shouldn't I? Maybe yes, but then again---maybe no?

I stood up and gazed at the crowd of curious onlookers and laughed out loud like a psychotic woman in a public forum, mumbling her own private monologues to everyone within range. "She's alive my dear friends," I yelled with glee. "My sister Homayra is very much alive! I just know it!" I flung my cigarette butts into the air in separate directions and began dancing around in circles like a gleeful gypsy girl.

Out of nowhere an elderly Persian woman approached me with the kindest smile. She placed the wrinkled palms of her hands against the sides of my face and said something to me in Farsi that I will never forget for as long as I live. How ironic I thought, that an old woman who was a total stranger, would speak to me so tenderly in my native language at a time of such an epiphany: *"Haghighateto begouh, tchonkeh azadet mikoneh." - "The truth will set you free."*

"My dear, the truth will set you free!" she whispered to me. "Somethings in life, my dear child, are worth fighting for! Now you must go find your sister, my dear child, go to her at once!" the old woman ordered, as I threw my arms around the old woman and hugged her as if she were my own mother!

The ironic goodness that came to me on that rainy and fateful afternoon was the result of that poor injured female trainer and her kind but terrified lion. Those two foreign souls unlocked the gates to my new life that was about to unfold.

Incidentally, Stephanie Kruger and Perry, her lion companion, survived the ordeal and returned to under the big top as I moved on to my next position of locating my sister.

Chapter 18

GOLAREH: TIMOTHY

Zelebritiez - *Oxford City*

" *W**ell you see, Golareh, I have special powers and something tells me that you might be interested in them," Timothy said, with an arrogance of pompous, technical superiority, while miserably mispronouncing my name and overtly examining my breasts with his eyes.*

Timothy was one of the newer reporters at the *Enterprise*, who was transferred in from one of our sister companies, a retail and news distribution arm in the town of Dartford. He first appeared at *Zelebritiez* only a few weeks ago, and had been trying to get me in his bed every day since.

Timothy Edwards had wondering eyes, a stupid, choppy laugh, and was a compulsive liar. He was the epitome of a player, who was trying to screw any woman he could get his hands on in London proper. Even though Timothy had heard that I was gay, he refused to believe it and pursued me constantly, since the moment I was introduced to him on his first day at the *Enterprise*. Perhaps he thought that he was the one thing I had been missing for my entire life and had I met him earlier, perhaps my life would have been quite different.

Zelebritiez or *Zelz*, as we reporters called it, was a popular night spot in the town of Oxford where many of the editors and staff writers at the *Enterprise* gathered after work. I had many friends at the paper even though the material I wrote was considered dry and mainstream by my peers. But still, I had a good reputation as a talented reporter and was well liked. There was plenty of dancing, decent food, and live bands, some good and some not so good. Everybody knew everybody at Zelz, the good, bad and the assholes.

Timothy was a high ranking member of the asshole party and a complete bullshit artist who exaggerated every single detail of his life by a factor of ten. He claimed he was bowlegged because of the many soccer injuries he had sustained when he *was* a young Olympic hopeful. He wore entirely too much cologne and had a belly that made him look as if he were entering his second trimester.

Somehow or another, he was always able to demonstrate to the many women he hounded that some of his attributes were attractive and because of that he always had some clueless women at his side.

Somehow Timothy forgot to tell most everyone he met that little detail about his wife, who had come to London only once when Timothy was being recruited in for his new assignment. She was a full figured Greek woman with a strong outgoing attitude, jet black hair and a loud mouth. She talked constantly and clearly drove Timothy mad.

Timothy undoubtedly had a fair amount of money but after I met his wife I was convinced that she had him by his golden balls.

"She and I are done," Timothy always said, after she returned to their home near Dartford. "The divorce is a done deal, just a few details to clean up and I'm a free man." That his wife shared the same opinion seemed implausible, but I just wrote it all up to Timothy's long line of bullshit.

Timothy sat with his various dates for most of the evenings, appearing completely bored with them all, while constantly gazing at my ass with his lustful eyes. He claimed that he had homes all over the world and had very close friends with people in parliament. He was also a litigious bastard, claiming that he was suing everyone from his realtor to an 89-year-old neighbor over land rights.

Whenever he had the opportunity, he would announce to me that, "one day soon---girly girl, you and I will be together in bed." To which I always replied with a friendly smile, "Yeah right, in your fucking dreams---asshole!"

One floor of the *Enterprise* was referred to as the *Killing-Floor*, where those reporters who were responsible for generating the bulk of the revenue for the 128 year-old news publication worked. With a huge budget, the *Killing-Floor* was dedicated entirely to ruining the lives of crooked celebrities, politicians, priests and corporate kingpins with the news of their dreadful deeds and paying huge sums of money for the stories. Forget the good news that I covered, that never sold papers, for it was the shocking smut that the Killing-Floor went after which met revenue forecasts.

Timothy was at the top of the food chain of the Killing Floor and the person most of the staff members loved to hate, because he was the best at his job and everyone knew it. He was transferred to *Enterprise* mainly because of his stories which were always so shocking that every one of us questioned how in the hell he able to obtain such smut on so many people.

His cornered victims always followed the same formula, crying foul at first, in the form of a public rant, full of fury and blame. However, always, not sometimes, but always, the victims would come clean with a full admission of guilt and go down in glorious flames. They even coined a name of cell block at the Wandsworth Prison after the Killing-Floor, with many inmates vowing revenge on Timothy if and when they ever got out.

Timothy came up with everything from exactly how much a judge won while betting on a dog fight down in Brixton to what the Vice-Chancellor of Oxford was suggesting on buying his underage male prostitute, while he was screwing him in room 1457 of London's most prestigious hotel. Not only were his facts straight, but they often came accompanied with video, audio, exact times, and locations of each crime committed.

At times, the executives of the *Enterprise* were so shocked by Timothy's stories that they were almost afraid to run them, but each was so hot and his details so concise and factual, that the story simply had to reach the light of day. His success rate was well over 100 percent and the sheer number of stories he produced were so amazing, that he had become the most feared investigative reporter in the United Kingdom. Further, the managing editors of the *Enterprise* would simply point him at a particular target, and very shortly he would return with breaking news about the poor slob on every newsstand and media platform in the country.

On this particular night, Danielle was working late and I had more than enough white wine. Two of my friends met me at Zelz for dinner, along with one of their cute sisters named Kara, who was considering leaving her husband and was even more inebriated than I was. She was on the hunt for a new man and Timothy was a prime target. Timothy had finally taken his eyes off my ass and was all over Kara, and Kara didn't seem to mind it in the least, which totally blew my mind.

Timothy invited Kara to his flat and like a fool she accepted, but there was no way in hell that Kara's sister, Liz and her partner Eileen would ever allow that happen. They were going to follow along no matter what Kara or Timothy had to say about it. So being a caring friend, and a spiffed one at that, I went along for the ride knowing full well that Danielle would be around to pick me up whenever I needed her to.

When we arrived at Timothy's flat, he was almost foaming at the mouth with delight, the sheer thought of bringing home four smoking-hot women from Zelz was more than he could ever hope for. Never mind that three of us were gay and so close to kicking his fat ass if he made one slight move on Kara.

We looked at all of Timothy's artwork, which he exaggerated about completely, and toured his boring flat that was huge but contained little imagination. The wine was starting to get to my head and it was late when I suddenly found myself alone with Timothy. Elizabeth and Eileen had just left, but notified Danielle as to my exact condition and location, so they felt reasonably safe when they pulled their overly stimulated sister away from the grip of Timothy's wandering hands and drove away.

Albert Einstein — 'I fear the day technology will surpass our human inter-action. The world will have a generation of idiots.'

Chapter 19

GOLAREH: THE POWER
OF EXPRESSION

Timothy was now clearly drunk and slurring his words, he topped off my wine glass and said, "Well good looking, are you now ready to hear about my superpowers?"

He appeared to be leading up to just how he was able to get the many juicy facts on so many of his shocking stories. I must admit that I was intrigued so I made the decision to stay a bit longer and take the chance that he just might reveal the secrets behind his fact-finding techniques.

"Back in the early 70s," Timothy began, "there was a theory presented by a well-known author by the name of Alvin Toffler who wrote a wonderful book named *Future Shock*. In the book he examined a unique phenomenon which he firmly believed might happen to the human race when overwhelmed by the pressures of extremely rapid technical advancements.

Back then, Toffler, who was a fucking futurist by the way, theorized that the human mind would be outstripped by the overwhelming capabilities of the sudden onset of super technology. It was thought that computers and machines were advancing at such a fast clip that the human brain would go haywire trying to keep up with it all, resulting in some sort of mental breakdown. In other words, Toffler believed that too much technological change, in too short a time, was bad."

Timothy leaned back on his leather sofa with a look of cheap self-admiration, as if what he was about to tell me had the power of maneuvering me directly into his bed for an evening of unbridled sex. However, I needed him to get to the damn point, so I fueled his ego with a seductive smile and a quick glance at his crotch, which caused Timothy to beam with delight.

"Well simply put," Timothy continued, while adjusting the inseam of his black denim jeans. "The *Future Shock* theory, which Mr. Toffler presented, has already occurred, but exactly opposite of the way Toffler predicted. Rather than humans being outstripped by technology, it was technology that became out stripped by consumer demand. Society was not overcome with all of this new technological shit---they were enchanted by it. Consumers didn't give a fuck about how it was created, they just wanted it! As far as the consumer was concerned it was all magically created by some goddamn wizard!

Then came the cellular telephone," Timothy said, as he waved his shiny new cell phone directly in front of my face. This little piece of shit has become the sugar water for today's consumer. Right now there are more than 4.7 billion of these fucking things out there and people's lives are completely controlled by them."

"Oh my God---I simply must have one! Why, you may ask? Because they're new! That's why!" Timothy dramatized his words by getting down on one knee and staring at his phone as if it were a communion wafer. "Just because these fucking things are new, every goddamn person in the world has to have one!"

"And guess what? I want the newest of the new. I want the latest version out---and I want it right now! Oh hell---guess what? I more than want it right now; I demand it even before now. I want the goddamn newest shit---yesterday!" Timothy shouted like an actor on the stage.

"Toffler's theory of helpless impudence didn't happen to humans, it has happened to the entire fucking communications industry! Simply put, the world's unquenchable appetite for the very latest of *everything* has outstripped the industry's ability to keep up with the fucking demand."

Timothy put his hands over the back of his neck, exposing his fat pectoral muscles under his tight black T-shirt. "Golareh, you pretty thing, in trying to satisfy the selfish demands of the consumer these big ass companies have brewed up a horrible problem right under our noses.

"And what problem is that," I asked, hoping he would get to the point before he passed out.

"The problem is, you sexy thing, that there is now a fucking, goddamn security hole large enough to drive your car through!" Timothy said, as he fell back against the back of the couch and rolled his eyes.

"Golareh, sweetie," Timothy continued, while flexing his bicep, "let me make this simple enough for even you to understand. No one is inventing anything new anymore with regards to cell phone technology. They've hit the proverbial brick wall, and they're making a fucking mess out of what they already have." Timothy said.

"Think of it this way," Timothy said with a grin, "It took Bell Labs 45 years to go from rotary dialing to touchtone. But today the spoiled consumers, along with the financial markets, demand ground breaking enhancements on a weekly basis!"

The once most innovative country in the world, the United States, has fired most of their developers and shifted the responsibility of all innovation to third-world countries like India and China, just because they can mass produce shit better than we can. Golareh, those countries can mass produce things perfectly---but they can't invent a goddamn thing! So what we have here is this big-ass lag between software and hardware. Research and development has come to a fucking halt in the areas that really matter---like security, while the relentless consumers scratch and claw for more."

"These fancy *smart* phones, as we now so affectionately call them, are running on software that has been reused over and over again," Timothy went on. "Where there was once quality and secure software dedicated to a single manufacturer like Motorola, we now have the same code running on every single phone out there."

What was he talking about? I thought, as I struggled to understand him. "What do you mean Timothy, I'm not following you?" I asked.

"Well in order for the big companies in the industry to give the consumers something new to suck on, they decided to pass everything over to what is known as the application market, or *app market*, as the youngsters now call it. This was all done so that the big companies could focus on the real important things that mattered like life-saver colored phones, games, protective cases, video cameras and big-ass screens.

The app market is a fucking disaster! It's like some reality television game show putting anything in front of the consumer to play with. The app market is made up with a bunch of underfunded, fly-by-night companies that all have these get-rich schemes of being the next biggest thing on the planet.

Apple and Nokia hoped that this unchecked industry would fill the void of consumer demand---and man, were they were right. Almost overnight, app companies flooded the supply chain with millions of worthless apps, most of which are garbage and thrown together as an afterthought with this *shared code* I was telling you about.

The big thing that drove the final nail in the coffin of the security layer was when a handful of underground developers started taking drastic measures into their own hands, by creating huge shortcuts for the app market.

A universal command set was developed that overly simplified the integration of newly created applications, allowing an avalanche of untested bull shit to enter the secure domain of the smart phone's restricted layer. The rogue software developers called their shortcuts *Expressions,*" Timothy said moving closer to me on the couch.

"Expressions, what are they? And why are they called expressions?" I asked almost completely lost in all of this technobabble.

"Expressions are auditory tones that allow all new apps the ability to communicate or integrate seamlessly with the rest of the primary applications on the cell phone. Most importantly the ability to dial someone up and talk to them! Expressions can be either manually sent through the keypad or programmatically executed by the applications themselves like fucking magic.

Couple this whole technological mess with the fact that the big companies began designing in marketing obsolescence---to sell more of them!

You know, cycle them through the system! Consumers all over the world are forced to retire their unsupported cell phones as frequently as possible in order to stay current. Today no teenager in the world is going to be seen walking around with an outdated cell phone. Talk about being so uncool," said Timothy, while acting the part of a selfish teen.

"We even see pictures of half-naked natives in third world countries using the latest version of the smart phones, for Christ sake," Timothy exclaimed, as he placed his hand on my knee. "Everybody thinks that the communications industry is getting so much better, when in fact, it's taking a fucking nose dive towards disaster.

Every cell phone user in the world now has the latest and greatest version of the most dangerous communication software possible, complete with a largest security flaw in the history of telecommunications." Timothy preached.

"So---guess what happened next--- Goli? These little child hackers have gotten their hands on these *expressions*. Do you understand what I just said---you beautiful thing? These goddamn kids have mastered the power of *expressions* and are controlling other people's cell phones," said Timothy, with a crazed look on his face.

"Golareh, my darling— my dear! Today's cellphone manufacturers never dreamed that anyone, most especially a kid, would have any interest in exploring the inner sanctums of a cellular phone's operating system--- but, oh my god, were they ever wrong.

When these fucking kids, including my own son---mind you, started to figure out how to control other people's cell phones, I simply just had to step in and investigate." Timothy was getting drunker by the minute and starting to slur his words.

"I can---I mean, these kids are able to control everything on your phone, including activating your phone camera, reading your email, and tracking you with your own GPS."

Timothy realized that he now had my full attention as he moved around the back of me and placed his hands in the lower regions of my belly. I could smell his wine saturated breath as he whispered in my ear.

"Alright Golareh," Timothy slid the palms of his hands along the sides of my waist. "I bet you like people taking advantage of you a little, don't you? How would you like a little demonstration of my superpowers?" he asked, with an evil look.

I thought, no way would I let this creep try out these so called *expressions* on me, but I realized that he already had my cell number so there was not much I could do.

"It sounds like you need a little bit more scientific background, girly girl," he murmured as he brushed his lips against the side of my face. I was beginning to get nauseous by the things that I had to do to extract more information from Timothy, but I forced myself to endure it for a little bit longer, as Timothy continued his story and took more and more liberties with my body.

Timothy continued, as he maneuvered his body around mine. "So the story goes, that most people, up until recently, thought of hackers as those sleazy people who sneak through the rear entrance of a computer system and lay a golden egg," Timothy said, as he pressed the lower part of his body against my rear end. "The golden egg would later hatch and perform some hideous acts of destruction as the totally vulnerable computer system lays flat on its back with its legs spread wide open for the sheer pleasure of the hacker.

There now is a more sophisticated hacker out there, one who can simply slide straight in through the front door like an invited guest," he said, while placing one hand completely over my breast and the other down my arm to grip the outside of my hand which tightly held my cell phone.

Timothy slowly rotated my body around so that I was now facing him, "all I have to do now is press a couple of tones on my cell phone and begin working my way up to your sweet spot. I can explore the inner reassess of your privacy and learn everything about what turns you on and makes you itch for more.

I can view all of your erotic pictures of your naked body. You know, the ones that you sent to that cute little black girl you hang out with. Man, is she ever a hottie! I can follow you around like a hawk and even record you singing out loud as you're driving down the road," Timothy sneered.

I was about to explode with anger after realizing that the fat son-of-a-bitch has already hacked me!

Timothy continued. "Imagine me calling you, but instead of leaving you a message, I punch in a few *expressions* and I am inside of your moist little world. If I need a story about you, I simply listen to every single fucking voice mail that you have, and read every single text and email you ever wrote. Or let's say I don't want you to receive that most important message from your sexy girlfriend, I can slow it down or maybe even delete it all together! How do you like me now---Goli?

Check this out Goli, I can even control your GPS, activate your voice recorder, and use your fucking camera without you even knowing it. I can even shoot a movie of you in bed with your hot girlfriend doing whatever it is that the two of you two do together," Timothy said, now resembling a serial killer.

"And guess what, you hot little thing," Timothy said, with an air of complete control, "There is absolutely nothing, at all, that you can do about it. Think of this as the perfect crime that can never be detected or even proven. Imagine a real horny peeping-tom being welcomed into the bedroom by a hot lady in another country.

All I have to do is dial you up," Timothy said, as he pressed a single digit on his phone, to which my own phone made no respond. "I bet you were expecting your phone to ring weren't you?" Timothy asked, while looking at me like a psychopath.

"I'm slowly unbuckling your pants and pulling down your zipper this very second and you don't even have a clue---do you", Timothy asked, as he typed in a series of tones on his phone.

I could feel perspiration build on Timothy's forearms as his breathing intensified. My cell phone sat completely dormant as Timothy pulled my body closer to his and turned the face of his phone in my direction, "Now, let me see if I can find my favorite one of you. Oh here it is! I just love this one!" In an instant he demonstrated ownership of more than 500 of my own private pictures.

There I was in all of my glory, in one of the most seductive pictures Danielle and I had ever taken together. We were joking around one night in the privacy of our own home just a few weeks prior! We were just having a little fun is all. I should have known better then to have taken that picture of us with my phone!

Timothy mistook my look of shock and anger for a level of intense desire. He was now convinced that he had completely captured my full attention and that I was melting under his control. His hands were now aggressively moving over my entire body as he gripped a large portion of my rear end with his despicable claws. Timothy was now king of the world in his mind, as he positioned his head for the most romantic and erotic kiss of his lifetime.

"You could have this power too if you really want it---girly girl. We could work together as a team," Timothy offered, with a sly grin.

It was then I had *enough* of this unwelcomed pervert. I was so pissed off at him for invading Danielle's and my privacy that I could barely see straight, but at the same time, I was totally enamored by this powerful capability he had acquired. It was now time to call it a night so I employed an old maneuver that I learned as a child when I was being groped by the neighborhood boys.

I slowly moved my head backwards into a fully cocked position, and then drove my forehead deep into the bones of his chest, causing Timothy's remaining libido and tobacco laced wind to vacate parts of his body that he never knew existed.

He stood in total shock, wondering what had just occurred, and how I was able to formulate such a powerful blow.

"That one was from Danni---you perverted bastard and the next one will come from me if you don't back the fuck off," I said calmly.

A new type of *expression* appeared on Timothy's face along with the desperate realization that through his own stupidity and selfish male urges he had completely provided me with every detail of his hacking capability.

Timothy knew that I now had the potential to make him part of one of my own stories, and could, if I chose, send him to the very same cell block that housed the many targets of his own investigative reporting. Timothy stood there with a look of bewilderment on his face, resembling a schoolboy who just experienced his first premature ejaculation.

During the weeks and months to follow, as I struggled to put my life in order; I considered the power of Timothy's hacking techniques, which Timothy referred to as *expressions*. Perhaps the unethical power of Timothy's tools might help modify my sorrowful life and do some actual good for humanity and those I love.

Timothy, on the other hand, would become a central and much more important part of my life in ways that neither of us would have ever imagined. The arrogant, flirtatious bar room, bull shit artist, with hopes of taking advantage of me that night, would soon become one of most valuable staples of my soul.

Timothy was about to provide me with an illegitimate advantage. It was the advantage that I needed at the single most important turning point of my life, as I began to understand the memories of my terribly scorched existence.

Living the soul of my dearly departed

-GOLAREH-

I had my most vivid and lucid of nightmares to date:

I dreamt that I was actually occupying the soul of my dead sister and living in some far off land. I'm quite certain that it was Henri who was chasing me around a large cold and mysterious home. He had a revolting smile on his face as he shadowed me around the hallways from room to room.

"Where in the hell do you think you are you going---you spoiled bitch," he bellowed at the top of his lungs.

"I'm leaving you Henri," I screamed, as I ran from room to room, desperately trying to get away from him. I could not gain any distance from Henri as he scrutinized me from every corner.

I was tightly gripping, of all things, the very same riding crop that Zooli had given me when I was just a kid. I was standing at the top of the staircase gazing down at Henri in terror.

"Get out of my way Henri and let me pass---this very instant," I screamed.

Henri stood at the foot of the stairs holding a crystal shot glass and snarling at me like a maniac. He suddenly exploded into a wild rage and hurled his drink directly at my face.

I dipped to the left as the glass flew pass my right ear, missing me within centimeters and smashing against a painting on the wall in back of me. Shards of glass showered down on the wooden steps, as I summoned my courage to descend the stairs and walk directly into Henri's domain.

My hallucination's visual acuity tightened enough for me to actually see and hear Henri referring to me by my sister's name.

"You will never leave this house alive Homayra! Do you hear me, you selfish bitch," thundered Henri.

My latest nightmare was one of the very many reoccurring visions I had been having on a nightly and each time I was living the life of my dead sister Homayra. Afterwards I would find myself sitting naked on the cold bedroom floor, staring off into the darkness and feeling my heart racing out of control. I then would tuck my knees against my abdomen and attempted to squeeze the fear out of my body. Over to my side I would roll, and then on to my stomach, then to my back again. I continued to feel the phantom pains of that hurtful Henri as vividly active as they have always been and promised to always try to be. "Not this time," I whispered into the darkness.

I returned to safety of my dark bed and lay stunned, staring at the ceiling in a cold sweat. As my heart regulated back a normal range I slowly rolled over on my side and press my forehead and eyes deep into Danielle's sleeping body, and quietly sobbed aloud, "Oh my lord! What do these dreams mean and where are they taking me?" I press my face deeper against my sweet Danni's dark warm sleeping body and quietly receive the answer.

...to my dear sister---I'm now completely sure of it.

Chapter 20

GOLAREH: IN LIKE FLYNN

Timothy was stunned when after almost three months I called him on his cell phone and asked him to meet me for coffee. He sounded pretty confused and embarrassed, especially since the last time I saw him I almost cracked his sternum with my head. Thinking back on that night, I admittedly felt bad. I really should not have gone to that extent of a punishment, because I probably could have injured him. He just really pissed me off by owning up to the fact that he had hacked into my own smart phone and still had the nerve to use his super-powers as some sort of leverage to get in my pants.

It wasn't difficult for me to gain his attention, when I asked him to meet me to talk about his so-called *expressions*.

"What expressions," Timothy asked, while acting as if he had no idea what I was referring to.

"Calm down, Timothy, your secret is safe with me; meet me at The Attendee downtown on Betterton St.," I politely ordered, as I hung up the phone.

I arrived at my favorite coffee house just after the lunch hour and sat at a table in the back of the almost vacant coffee house. I always felt comfortable at *The Attendee*, Freddie the owner was from Lebanon and had a cute Iranian wife named Shard. He would occasionally speak to me in Farsi, when no one was around, and offer me some wonderful Iranian deserts that his wife would prepare only for themselves and a few select friends.

The clientele at the Attendee were friendly and for the most part minded their own business. I was the only one in the room at the time; the rest of the patrons were sitting outside on the sidewalk sunning themselves, drinking coffee, smoking cigarettes and watching the people pass by. I ordered a decaf latte and checked my phone for messages.

In walked Timothy, appearing as if he might had lost a few pounds since the last time I saw him. He was still wearing that nauseating cologne and projecting his trademark grin, only this time he appeared to be much more humble. He politely moved a chair nearby and sat down across the table from me, reminding me of a person entering a confessional, with a tall order for the priest.

"Hi Goli, I mean Golareh" Timothy greeted, while looking down at his folded hands in the center of the table, "I just wanted to apologize for my behavior the other night. I simply wanted to tell you how dreadfully sorry I am for what I did. I must have been just completely smashed out of my gourd, and I assure you that I will never behave like that again."

His eyes still remained fixed on the hands as he continued with his shallow apology.

"Also, it occurred to me that I probably should not have served you with that whole line of debris about this stupid superpower, which I truly don't have, mind you. It was all really a simple sleight-of-hand trick, you know? I'm sure that you are well aware of the fact that there is completely no ability out there these days, that can invade someone's smart phone, no matter what I said---and if there was, I wouldn't have the foggiest idea how to harness such nonsense. I am a simple featherbrain when it comes to that sort of technical bling. Oh and by the way---if I had such a power, I simply would never---ever, use *it* to spy on anyone, and oh my lord, especially not you," said Timothy, clearly not even wanting look up at my eyes.

Timothy continued. "What I vaguely remembered showing you at my house that dreadful night was a simple bar trick that I was taught from a couple of blokes at Zelz's. Goli---I was so drunk that night, my darling girl. I must admit that the trick served me well in the past with other women, but totally flopped with you.

Please believe me, darling girl, that all of my stories come to me from only the most legitimate methods and sometimes an overabundance of luck," said Timothy, now running out of things to say.

I leaned back in my chair and slowly lifted the cup of latte to my lips and stared intensely into Timothy's most telling eyes. His mind was scrambling for more to say, while having a dreadful time making eye contact with me.

I quietly set my coffee cup back down on the glass table top and slowly leaned into him while forcing eye contact.

"Timothy," I said, looking directly through his pupils, "cut the crap and never insult my intelligence ever again! Do you understand me? What you showed me that night was no magic trick whatsoever. I have enough on you right now to send you to prison. But I'm not going to do that Timothy--- and do you know why that is, Timothy? Because despite of the fact that you are the biggest player I have ever met--- there is something that I sort of like about you. As a matter of fact, Timothy, I could really use your help on a project I'm working on."

Timothy sat back with a look of relief, as I slowly watched his face normalize. As I studied his eyes, I noticed deep inside there was a spirit of a man who had somehow lost his heart. Perhaps there was a deeply troubled soul deep within Timothy, who was desperately holding himself at bay with an excessive life style of alcohol, pride, and sex.

I also recalled a training maneuver that Zooli taught me to use when horses get out of hand. Zooli instructed us to back up the unruly horse a few steps to let it know who was in control. Backing-up an unruly horse was a physical order that caused the animal to submit to the trainer. "Back him up girl, and *disengage his hind quarters*", Zooli always said.

This very same training tactic that Zooli taught me, seemed to work well with Timothy, but it had to be consistent with Timothy every time he got out of hand. Timothy was beginning to realize, by the look in my eyes, that I could always disengage his hind quarters every single time he got *snooty*.

"Relax Timothy, I really do need your help and I want to talk with you about a person that I want to learn a little more about."

Timothy dropped his shoulders and his eyes began to soften, just as Zooli would often describe a horse that was safe to mount. Timothy's expression showed a level of humility that I had never seen before.

"I do need your help Timothy---and for a very important mission. This man that I would like you to investigate is very powerful and extremely dangerous and I'll certainly understand if you decline to help me."

"Do you want to write a story about this man," Timothy asked, as he lowered his voice and checked to see if anyone else was around.

"I'm not sure yet, Timothy---I just want to see what I can find out about this man," I said. "But I have to tell you that this is one target that could snuff both of our lights out in an instant. If anyone writes about this man, it must only come from an anonymous source to an unknown reporter on the Killing Floor, and certainly not you or me. This man should never know who broke the story, much less who even reported it," I said with a look of profound warning.

"Well, who is this guy anyway, girl? I'm curious, Timothy asked, with a look of complete interest.

"Timothy, have you ever heard of a man named Henri Lepan?"

"Oh sure, Dr. Lepan, the Minister of Trade in France. Who doesn't know him? What's your beef with him?"

For Timothy's wellbeing, I decided not to step into the details of my past, which were only beginning to burst to the surface of my mind.

I needed to take this process one step at a time with Timothy, while always reminding him that Henri's power was almost imperial and unlike any other person he's ever investigated.

"Timothy," I said with a smile, "how about an ice cold beer?"

There seemed to be very little Timothy had problems with when it came to determining telephone numbers of high ranking officials anywhere on the globe. When I told him that very possibly Henri's number would be difficult to obtain within the government walls, Timothy leaned back and laughed out loud while bragging, "My dear---those are the easiest targets of all!"

—⚬⚬⚬—

I had barely gotten home and it was early evening when I received a telephone call from Timothy telling me to meet him for a drink at Zelz. He sounded like he was in the midst of a party and already plastered. At first I said, "Timothy, I don't have time to meet you for a drink, I have an early morning interview and must prepare."

"Oh no girly-girl, you don't understand, we are *in like Flynn!*" Timothy bragged.

I suddenly felt a cold shiver climb up my spine and cause my head to spin.

Danielle called me and demanded that she drop me off at Zelz and wait for me in the car, but I ever so politely declined. I felt extremely uncomfortable about involving her at that point, especially in light of the fact that she was living underground and off the proverbial radar of Henri. This was going to have to be at my risk alone and an activity that would never, ever endanger my sweet Dannielle.

I walked into Zelz at about a 7:15, right in the middle of happy-hour, and said hello to the drummer of the house band, who was quietly unloading his drums for a long evening ahead. I gave him a quick hug and then walked to the table where a party was in full gallop. Timothy was sitting at a table with four buxom blondes on the far end of the room and back to his own ass-hole behavior. Behind Timothy stood two male acquaintances of mine waiting for their first chance to take Timothy's spot at the table.

The table was littered with wine bottles and martini shots as the girls leered at me while I slowly approached. Timothy had his right arm drooped over the shoulder of one of the *bimbos* with his fingers lightly grazing her cleavage. As I approached him, I was astounded to see, first hand, just how of much of a dog Timothy really was as he spoke nonsense into the woman's ears and drooled over overly inflated breasts.

"What a complete idiot you are," I thought, as I approached him from the side. The sun hadn't even set and Timothy was already shit faced, as he gazed up at me with a surprised look and a wine stained mustache.

"Wow good-looking---you are looking hot! That was fast! You must be really horny for me," announced Timothy, loud enough for every person in the bar to glance over and take note.

I hovered over him, holding back my desire to slap the shit out of him.

"Jesus Christ, Timothy, you are something else, don't you ever stop this shit?"

"What, Goli? I've been a very busy boy," Timothy said, as he rolled his head over and starred directly at the large set of boobs under his chin.

I realized then and there, that Timothy clearly was a functional alcoholic and most likely a sex addict as well. Had it not been for his self-described super-powers, I was quite sure that Timothy would be out of a job and living on the street.

"Have a seat, pretty-girl, and join us, we need to calibrate---I mean celebrate our new partnership. Let me pour you a nice glass of this red wine, baby---Uhm...yeah...you are looking so hot!!" he said, emptying the last remnants of the bottle into the glass of the bimbo to his right.

"I've *already* popped into your man's secret life and you won't believe what I've found; besides you owe me, girly-girl! You owe me---big time," he bragged.

"What do you mean you popped into my man's secret life," I asked, with a sudden feeling of panic.

"I infiltrated the target---baby girl, and we are *in like Flynn,* we have achieved our goal," Timothy gurgled, with a drunken smile.

"Oh---I just don't get any respect," Timothy yelled out loud, as the girls next to him started to giggle.

"Goddamn it, Timothy," I whispered. "You were supposed to wait for me before you did anything. You are going to get us all fucking killed!" I said, as I pressed my face within centimeters of his.

"Ease up, girly-girl; I've got that shit down to a fucking science. It's all good---you sexy thing. Now come on baby---sit down here and let me introduce you to my friends. Goli, this is the most beautiful Sheila and her best friend Julia. I can't remember the names of these other hot babes at the table, but it doesn't matter, because by the end of the night I'm sure I will know them all---very well. If you know what I mean," Timothy bragged, as each one of the bimbos cut me a mean look.

I felt my skin get clammy, imagining Henri already being aware of his snooping; Timothy could be dead before he even paid his bar tab.

"Don't worry, Goli---you have nothing to worry about! I'm captain of this goddamn ship! Do you think I just figured this shit out yesterday?" Timothy asked, while signaling the waitress for two more bottles of the same wine.

The woman sitting next to him was becoming disturbed by my presence. "Hey, who's the downer-bitch anyway---Timmy," Sheila asked, while her friend scanned my clothing and mentioned, "Hey, sweetie, I just love your shoes."

"Hey, are you his wife or something?" Sheila asked. "Hey Timmy, you didn't tell me that you were married! You said that you were divorced, you fucking asshole," the bimbo said, as she moved away from him as if she had just learned that he had a sexually transmitted disease.

Timothy's eyes widened as he realized that I was the only person in room who knew that he was, in fact, quite married, and that his wife lived up north, not wanting to move down here because she thought London was full of unsophisticated people.

"Listen to me sweetheart," I said, looking down at the smashed women face, "I'm your fucking guardian angel---bitch, and I'm here to save you from this asshole." Sheila moved her head towards Timothy with a drunken and shocked look on her face and said, "you are married aren't you---you fucking asshole?"

I spun around on my heels and began walking towards the front door. Timothy finally realized that he had invested way too much time and money on the table full of bimbos while completely wearing out his welcome in just the last two minutes.

"Hey, girl, wait for me, I was just playing with you," yelled Timothy, as he stood to his unsteady feet and staggered after me.

Sheila, who was clearly trashed, suddenly became belligerent and began bantering at Timothy for the entertainment of the entire bar crowd.

"Hey, you married asshole, you forgot to pay your fucking bill!" mocked Sheila, while accepting two more bottles of expensive red wine delivered at table side.

A skinny French man with a puppy face along with an elderly Austrian gentleman quickly moved in for the kill, taking Timothy's seat, just as Timothy was called over by the bartender to cash out.

"Hold on Golareh! Wait for me! I was just messing around with you, everything's cool baby," I heard Timothy yelling, from the noisy bar, as he was trying to settle up his tab and make it out of the bar with any dignity he still had left. The entire drunken crowd inside the bar began chanting at Timothy as if it were a standing ovation curtain call: asshole, asshole, asshole, asshole!"

I stood on sidewalk in front of Zelz completely frozen with fear, asking myself, what had I just done. I lit up a cigarette and was trying desperately to steady my shaking hands as panic set in. My god, I thought, what if Henri noticed something, anything I thought. I took another huge drag from my cigarette and inhaled the smoke deeply into my lungs, burning almost a third of it at once. I was really beginning to detest smoking, but I really needed the nicotine to calm my frazzled nerves.

What sort of danger, might I have just put myself in, not to mention everyone else in my pitiful world? I thought of poor Danni and my dear sister whom I had just determined was alive. What about my blank and completely unknowing parents, now very much older and living undisturbed in Iran? I suddenly began hearing Henri's voice pushing a warning directly into the darkest reassess of my panicked brain.

"Your dear parents think of you as their little superstar, don't they, Goli," Henri voice resonated as if he was standing right there next to me.

"Well they are so very wrong, for you are my little superstar---you little bitch," he said. "It would be such a shame to see anything happen to your helpless father and mother. I would hate to see them both spend their final days in prison, wouldn't you? I'm not at all sure they could survive such a life. Tell me you love me---my hot little superstar, tell me you need me. Tell me you will never disrespect your elders, my sweet little superstar," Henri chanted as he raped me from behind.

Chapter 21

GOLAREH: THE DEMONSTRATION

I went into my own world when I left Zelz, smoked several cigarettes and just started walking into to the night. I reached the corner, turned left, and walked over a railroad crossing and just kept on walking. Without knowing how long I had been walking down a dark street in a complete daze, I was finally brought back to my senses by the sound of a distant car horn.

I could still hear the sound of the band's drums and its muffled bass guitar in the night, reminding that I was still within range of the bar. My mind had been racing ever since I left the bar with visions of horrible circumstances in my future, all by the hands of Henri and his potential army of henchmen. I thought of Homayra taking the initial brunt of Henri's anger by deeply punishing her poor mind and body with every force necessary to pay me back. Then I thought of my parents being sent to prison or perhaps to the execution chambers for what I had just done. My god, I thought, I have no courage for this sort of thing whatsoever. I simply can't go on with this insane plan.

Again I heard the sound of that same familiar car horn, but this time much louder as its bright narrow lights lit up the dark neighborhood in back of me. It was Danielle, driving up the road with her lights flashing at me. Her pink taxi pulled up alongside of me as the passenger window slowly powered down. In the back seat, holding a bloody tissue over his nose was Timothy.

"Hold your damn head back, asshole," Danielle ordered. "I told dickhead here, that if I didn't find you I was going rearrange his testicles. His nuts were on the line---big time, I'll tell you," Danielle quipped. "Now get in the goddamn car, girl, you have a lot of explaining to do here."

I opened the passenger door and gave Timothy a nasty look as if I wanted to give him a black eye on top of his possible broken nose.

"Alright Goli, I want to know what the fuck the two of you are up to here? Girl, if the two of you think that you can play Sherlock Holmes, and Dr. *Fucking* Watson, without me knowing it, then you have another goddamn thing coming to you! Cause you are in my life, lady friend, and I don't want to get a call one night and find out that you are dead!" Danielle yelled and halted her rant as she stared down at her lap and burst into tears.

Timothy and I simultaneously dashed our anger over the last hour and moved forward to comfort her.

"Oh Danni, I wanted to tell you but I just couldn't, I was so afraid about your own safety, I didn't want to involve you in my problems."

"It's Henri, isn't it Goli, the two of you are going after Henri aren't you," she asked as she pounded her fists on her steering wheel in anger. "We need to be so fucking done with Henri. That's all I think of every fucking day and night, Henri, Henri, Henri," she bellowed.

"I'm sorry Goli, she forced me to tell her about Henri," Timothy offered from the back seat, in an attempt to calm her down. "I thought she was going to smash my head through the glass window of Zelz, Goli," he said, pointing out fresh scratches on his neck and face. "She threatened to push me through the front window, just as the freaking band had started their first song," said Timothy, beginning to whimper with a slight giggle.

"You are fucking; goddamn right I was, Timothy, and tell me this---asshole, what sort of a man has a name like Timothy anyway. Timothy *this* and Timothy *that*. Get that stupid smile off your face! Do you think this is funny? You know what Timothy? Fuck you---for not taking my girlfriend here seriously!" Danielle vented, fully expelling her anger into Timothy's wine and blood stained face.

We sat in silence for several minutes with the engine running as I tried to conceal my fear, Timothy nursed his bloody nose, and Danielle finally calmed down. She then reached for her radio and pressed a green button on the microphone emitting three short tones. "Jessie James is inbound from Oxford downtown, with the idiot and the ball," she announced in some sort of secret code, while releasing the button. "10-4," returned the metallic voice of a female dispatcher. "Atlas, Dominic, and Brooke, break your formation and return to the home field. Thank you, girls," the voice ordered.

The three of us managed to relax as Danielle picked up speed onto the M40 highway towards Brixton. Timothy dropped back in the seat and checked to see if his nose was still bleeding as we drove for the next hour and a half to the southern reaches of London.

I was half asleep when we came to a stop in the back yard of *Impeccable Transit.* Timothy peered through the window with his eyes opening at the wide variety of beautiful women who were changing shifts for the night. "Wow," Timothy whispered, "where in the hell are we? Have I died and gone to some sort of taxi heaven," he asked, sitting up in his seat.

Danielle glanced around and faced Timothy while grabbing him by his blood stained shirt and said, "Now you listen to me, *Girly-girl;* if you so much as talk to any of those girls out there, the woman in that office up there will be on your ass like a fucking tornado, because those girls are my family and they are off limits to you! Also, if you ever tell anyone where I live, I will come after you with a vengeance and kick your fucking ass." Danielle tightened her grip on Timothy's shirt.

Timothy started getting Danielle's message as he lowered his eyes and slumped forward. "Alright you two, let's go in and talk this over and put some ice on that nose of yours," Danielle ordered.

Timothy's brow furrowed, finally understanding her concern for me, but clearly confused about the apparent hold Henri had on the both of us.

"Danni," Timothy said, "I just wanted to tell you and Goli that I'm sorry for tonight. I shouldn't have taken Henri so lightly, and it won't happen again. I have no idea what this man has done to the two of you. But I know what I'm doing with these *expressions* and Henri doesn't have a clue about what I did today, I promise."

We closed the doors of the car and began climbing up the old iron fire escape to the make shift patio attached to Danielle's apartment on the second floor of the taxi company. Magda stepped out on the stoop outside of the dispatch office and asked, "Is she safe, Danni?"

Danielle smiled and yelled, "Yes, mum, thank you, Magda."

"Is he safe and does he know the house rules," Magda asked, referring to Timothy, with her thick and authoritative Austrian accent.

"Yes mum," Danielle replied back, "and there's no need for you to come up here and educate him."

Magda turned off the outside light and closed the door while saying, "Okay, my sweet girls, good night and be safe."

"Wow, thanks for clearing me with her, Danni, she sounds strict," Timothy whispered as Danielle unlocked the door of her dark apartment.

"Strict is an understatement for Magda," Danielle mumbled.

"Do all of those women out there live here with you?"

"Yep, every single one of them," Danielle said proudly.

"Man, this has got to be one of the most awesome taxi companies I've ever seen. It's like a freaking girl's dorm."

Danielle walked away rolling her eyes, as she let that last comment pass. She then switched on a light above the stove and tapped a power strip on the floor next to the couch with her toe, turning on two lamps in the living room in back of the couch. She carefully took her shoes off and placed them neatly by the door. "Goli, will you take your damn shoes off, and you too Timothy! Where were you two raised anyway---in a barn?" she quipped.

Timothy watched Danielle with a renewed, but modified, sense of awe, as she removed her New York Yankee's ball cap and hung it on a chair. Without pause she shook out her long black hair and pulled her white tank top off over her head, revealing her smooth dark back and beautiful figure, as she walked into the bedroom and closed the bathroom door behind her.

"God almighty, Goli, I now see what you like about her. She is absolutely, freaking, gorgeous. But damn, I think she almost broke my nose," Timothy said, as he smiled and gently touched his face.

Danielle emerged from the bedroom wearing a white V-neck cotton tee shirt and baby-blue pajama shorts.

"Goli, let's use your cell phone so you might understand what I do first hand. You need to be in the driver's seat anyway. Now don't worry, this is very safe. I'm just going to show you how to gain access to Henri's cell phone domain and then we will exit."

Timothy and Danielle sat on opposite sides of me as I carefully squinting into my smartphone.

"Okay girls, I'm going to show you how I actually perform the magic of *expressions*. I don't expect either of you to remember how to do this. I just want you to understand the general concepts, just in case either of you ever have to do it yourselves. Also, just so you know---I have never showed this to anybody else in the freaking world, so we will each share a common set of secrets, so to speak."

"Wait---I have to take some notes, Danni, could you grab a pad of paper and a pen? I have to write this stuff down if I'm going to remember it," I said.

Danielle got up and walked over to her desk and began searching for a pen and paper.

"Girls, please listen to me, and with all due respect, I must ask you, for our own safety, don't write any of the shit down. I just want the two of you to get the feel of what I'm doing here, okay?" Timothy said. "What I'm about to show you is very proprietary to only a few of my very trusted friends, all of whom are teenagers. One, most importantly, happens to be my own son---Adam."

"My god, Timothy, did your son teach you this stuff?" I asked.

"I know, Goli, you might think I'm an ass-hole husband, but I'm very close to my *only* son, a freaking genius when it comes to this stuff. He and his friends are part of this multiplayer game club. I'm sure that you've heard about these kids today playing these goddamn games all night long with one another? Well, these kids are spread out all over the world and they play these computer games just like they're sitting right next to each other in the same room. Everyone knows everybody, but only through their usernames. Let me tell you about these kids! These damn kids are smarter than shit with computers and also, you got it, telecommunications!" Timothy said, as his excitement grew.

"So you're saying that these damn kids invented this shit?" Danielle said.

"Not exactly, Danni, they just found what was already out there and now they know more about the *expressions* then the actually inventors do. These damn internet battle-games are now beginning to use aspects of the *expressions*. I'm telling you guys, it's getting really scary out there!" Timothy said, as Danielle and I looked at each other in disbelief. "So, this is why the *expressions* must remain a secret only between us. Hey, I'm just trying to keep my kid safe, okay girls? Okay, here we go," Timothy began. "Have you ever wondered how telecommunication companies can check the status of your phone without you even knowing it? I mean without your phone even ringing. Well this is the sort of principle behind the *expressions*. My kid tells me that they use these things called 'super-pings' which can be sort of thought of as a handshake or a tap on the shoulder between communication devices. You know, to see if someone is awake or not.

If I was to ping you, for example, you would respond back to me with a visual or a verbal response, telling me both if you are awake and who you are, so to speak.

Well these *expressions* do the same thing; they send these super-pings to other people's cell phones. However the expressions aren't just pinging them for the hell of it, they are pinging them with a purpose," said Timothy, checking to see if we were following along. "Girls, these kids are now controlling all of the functions on other peoples' fucking phones!

I like to think of the term *expressions*, as a way of traveling somewhere to retrieve something. Sort of like what you do, Danni, you move people down the road and drop them off. Or you might pick them up and deliver them someplace else. However what I do with my expressions is a hell of a lot more than that. I look through that person's pockets to learn about where he's been or even plans to go. Shit! I can give that same damn customer a physical examination and even check his prostate if I want to!" Timothy exclaimed.

"Now before we start, I need to bore you with a little Computer Science 101. Consider a line of 132 characters, where each character has a specific meaning. Now in order for us to express into Henri's phone, we must enter his domain with a very important greeting known as a *start*-command. Within this long line of letters and numbers you will recognize Henri's phone number, and everything else won't make a damn bit of sense to you.

Now as I was saying, there are two very distinctly important commands that must be issued every time you express somewhere. The first line of characters serves as your open-and-enter command and the last command line is your close-and-exit. The first line, which includes the phone number, opens our communication tunnel into Henri's domain; and the very last command, which also contains his phone number, closes our session down safely and exits back out of the tunnel. The importance of these two unique greetings is that they allow us to enter Henri's domain without his domain controller ever being aware of it. Does that make any sense at all?" Timothy asked.

Danielle seemed to be following Timothy's discussion much better than I was. She was wired that way with all of this high tech stuff. I, on the other hand, was better with faces, names and people's behavior.

"Everything that we do once we're in Henri's communication domain must be done by issuing a variety of short commands which are now menu driven, thanks to the kids! Okay, now, with regard to how we can get into Henri's cell phone domain without him even knowing it---here's the idea.

Think of the data in his cell phone domain as individual data records in a database. Normally when you check your voice mail, text messages or emails, the system retrieves the data and then marks each data record as being *read*.

The beauty of the *expressions* is that we can retrieve the data from Henri's cell phone without marking any of his records as being *read*? Does that make any sense to you guys at all? God, I do hope you are following all of this," Timothy said, as he stared directly at me.

"All right then, let's take a little trip into Henri's world, shall we?"

A thick level of anxiety suddenly came over me as Timothy positioned his body towards me. I hadn't seen Henri in years, and here I was about to hack directly into his private cell phone.

Timothy slowly began dictating the opening command to me, which was made up long line of alphanumeric characters. I typed in each character one by one until we had completed all of them.

"Okay, love," Timothy said, "now press: SEND. Almost instantly I received a cryptic response message back from Henri's phone that read:

--EXPRESSION. V.4.3.134—SESSION 23.43.1.A.L.%

ENTER-START-BIT-COMMAND>

"Very good Goli, now type in this command at the end of the next prompt: *OPENLOCALDOMAINMANAGER#TXTZONE*

ENTER-START-BIT-COMMAND> OPENLOCALDOMAINMANAGER#TXTZONE <ENTER>

"Congratulations girls---welcome to Henri's world! We are about to check our man's text messages," Timothy proudly announced.

The following message automatically appeared on my phone:

DOMAIN.CONTROLLER.ID$>LEPAN,HENRI,A*** Ce message a été envoyé depuis un terminal BlackBerry de Bouygues Telecom

TEXT MESSAGE MAIN MENU: >>>>

INBOX>1 SENT>2 DRAFTS>3 VOICEMAIL>4 MOBILE IM>5 EXIT>6

Okay, love, now let's just take a peek in Henri's inbox---shall we? Type "1" and then press your send button.

>>1 <SEND>

Immediately 10 of Henri's 468 private text messages filled my screen as if they were all meant for me to review. Timothy sat between us grinning like a big fat smiling cat that had just caught a canary.

"Okay, Goli, that's quite enough for now, press the 6 key then press *send*. Let's leave this place, shall we?

Now, love, type this closing command when you are ready," Timothy said, carefully dictating to me another list of alphanumeric characters, with his last instruction for me to press *send*.

DOMAIN.CONTROLLER.ID$>LEPANN,HENRI,A***   Ce message a été envoyé depuis un terminal BlackBerry de Bouygues Telecom

*****SESSION*ENDED*****DOMAIN*INSTANCE*GHOSTING-PROCESS**COMPLETE WITH$0ERRORS

--EXPRESSION. V.4.3.134—SESSION 23.43.1.A.L.%

>>>>>SHAREWARE AND OPEN SOURCE GO TOGETHER LIKE MILK AND COOKIES**PLEASE DONATE TO OUR CAUSE**<<<<<

I was suddenly so excited that I reached over and kissed Timothy on his cheek, completely surprising him. I powered off my phone and then fell back against the couch staring at Danielle in disbelief. Danielle's eyes were wide open, as she quietly whispered "holy fuck!"

It was now very late as we each laid our tired heads back against the overstuffed pillows and closed our eyes. Timothy dozed off first, completely exhausted from a day of excitement, wine, woman, and the hard knuckles of Danielle's fist.

I moved him over and placed a pillow under his head while Danielle covered him with a blanket. Timothy was completely asleep as the two of us crawled into bed and slipped away into a restful slumber in each other's arms.

Chapter 22

GOLAREH: THE SHOT HEARD FAR AND NEAR

*F*RENCH TRADE MINISTER CLAIMS RECORDINGS ARE FALSE AND MALICIOUS

June 13 — (REUTERS) In the space of a week, Dr. Henri Lepan has jumped from near obscurity to outwardly becoming France's most talked about man. French Trade Minister Henri Lepan cut his vacation schedule abruptly short yesterday and returned from Mexico City to his Paris office. The visibly embattled Socialist politician reportedly thought a podium microphone was off when he issued a sarcastic remark about Louise Hebberling, the openly gay Deputy Prime Minister of the United Kingdom.

Lepan had just delivered a passionate speech during a summit meeting at UNESCO on the topic of immigration reform when a stage microphone captured Lepan's offhanded remarks meant for a fellow staffer.

"It's too bad Hebberling is a goddamn dyke. I'd love to bend her over my knee and teach her a lesson about the male anatomy," were his remarks that were swiftly captured on tape and broadcasted to the news wire services.

Following his comments the recording went viral on the internet, spawning gay and lesbian groups in the U.K and France to cry foul and demand for Lepan's immediate resignation.

The trade minister's press blunder surfaced just four days after Lepan was caught bragging on yet another 'hot' microphone, in which Lepan described lavish dinner parties at a little known French government retreat, referred to only as the Castle.

During a press conference in London, Lepan can be heard bragging to Lord Branston of Parkhead, the Minister of State for Trade & Investment, about a lavish dinner party at the Castle which by all measures was over the top. The estimated cost of a seat at the table was said by sources to be "staggering," according to a spokesperson for the Minister of Economy, Finances and Industry (France). The 16-course dinner reportedly included Duck Foie Gras Terrine and Handmade Buratta with black truffles.

The wine at the dinner party ranged in cost from €2,200 for a Petrus 1990, to several bottles of 1945 Chateau Mouton-Rothschild, each carrying a price tag of €29,340. Lepan also bragged about the sheer number of available women at the party as well.

Initially, Lepan laughed off the comments about the women and scoffed at costs by saying that he was the target of calumny. However, last evening, Lepan admitted that the numbers were true and an apology was forthcoming.

News about Lepan's lavish lifestyle couldn't have come at a worse time for the French economy, with rising taxes, a bulging budget deficit and deepening spending cuts.

It had been only two weeks since the night Timothy demonstrated his super-powers and already he was hard at work, mining for gold and splashing the most unflattering pictures of Henri all over the media. Timothy was continuing to be a good sport about following our rules about not reporting anything under his own name, but I could tell that he was itching to get his own name out there as the famous reporter.

To say I wasn't scared to death after our first shots across the Henri's bow would be an understatement, but it felt so justifiable. To think of Henri and all of the pain and suffering he has inflicted on my family and so many others only fueled my commitment to do more.

What were my motivations, I wondered, as I closed my eyes and thought of the Henri that I knew so many years ago but hadn't seen in several years? The only connection I had with Henri these days had been through Ari, and even her visits were becoming almost a thing of the past.

I quietly folded the paper and laid it on the coffee table next to the bed and began to relax.

"Well that should get his attention, I'm sure," I softly whispered, as I turned over on my side and spooned my body against Danielle. I cupped her breasts in my hands and gently caressed her toned belly. I loved the touch of Danni's beautiful ebony skin against my body as I lightly warm my chilled breasts against her bronze back while gently kissing her on her neck.

"Who's attention," she mumbled while half asleep.

"Henri's," I quietly answered, giving her time to wake up slowly.

"Who ran it?"

"Some staffer at Reuters---thank god!"

"Did they cite a source?"

"Nope, just staff. I tell you Danni, Timothy might be a pig, but he is really good with the news wires. His stories are going everywhere," I said, looking up at the ceiling fan slowly turning as I rolled over on to my back.

Danielle slowly turned her body around facing me and opened her sleepy green eyes.

"Good morning you sweet girl," I said, as I kissed her on the tip of her nose.

Dannielle always had the ability to wake up much faster than I was ever able to; it always seemed that I needed at least 30 minutes to come to life in the morning. She gracefully moved her body over mine and covered me like a wonderful naked blanket. I placed my hands on each side of her lower back and gently stroked the delicate bones of her ribs. I absolutely loved the feeling of her body on top of mine.

I moved of my hands over each side of her rear-end and kissed her smooth throat. Danielle looked down at me from her perch and said, "Good morning my love."

It never mattered what time it was, day or night, Danielle's breath always was fresh and inviting, as she planted her traditional morning kiss on my lips, which had become our daily ritual.

"What are *you* doing today," she asked, as she did every morning.

"Well, whatever I do, I'm sure it will be one interesting day," I said, just as the phone began to ring.

"Oh damn, who the fuck is calling us this damn early in the morning," moaned Danielle, as she moved over to the edge of the bed and reached for the screeching phone. I always loved when she contorted her body while reaching for the phone on the floor by the bed; I pinched her ass playfully as she answered the phone.

"Now who in the hell is calling my house this early in the damn morning," Danielle blurted in a half serious tone.

"Well hello to you too---sexy, Danni girl," came Timothy's voice from the receiver. "You know you really must watch your language at this hour of the morning; it sort of blurs that erotic image I have of the two of you lying in bed together doing whatever it is that the two of you do. You know, I was just thinking of the two of you in bed---and I would love to be in there with---," Timothy continued as Danielle rolled her eyes and placed the phone next to my ear.

"---no really girl, just imagine the three of us in bed together," Timothy continued.

"The three of us in bed together? Stop it, Timothy!" I blurted into the phone.

"Whoops, caught again, sorry about that Goli, what can I say?"

"Well, all I can say is that your wife must really have you by the balls to put up with all of your shit," I commented, with a grin.

"I know it, I know it---I'm sorry girl. Hey, how'd you did like the lead story this morning, Goli-girl, the phones on the killing floor have been going freaking mad all morning," said Timothy. "I heard that Lepan never slept last night and had to fly to London to prepare for a personal apology, scheduled for a noon press conference."

"My god, Goli there is so much I can get on this guy, I just know it. I can't wait to write my next story."

"Slow down Timothy, you need to slow down," I said, as Danielle rolled over and slid out of bed.

"I'll go make coffee," she whispered, as Timothy kept talking. I watched her flirtatiously shake her butt at me as she walked out of the room and into the kitchen. She stretched her arms and shook her long hair out, as I tracked her naked form walking across the wooden floor.

"How in the hell did you get those recordings Timothy? How were you so lucky to capture them?"

"Well I'll tell you, but then I'll have to kill you! I was sitting at my desk on the floor watching a live television feed of the *UNESCO* budget meetings. At about two minutes prior to Lepan's speech I *expressed* into his smart phone and activated his digital voice recorder."

"Without him knowing it? Are you kidding me?"

"Baby, I had his recording downloaded to my computer before the next speaker even took the stage! I didn't even know that Henri had his phone with him." Timothy laughed. "But the guy is such a sleazebag; he's so predictable that he's going to show his ass."

When I giggled Timothy picked up on it, "What? Oh---I know what you're saying--- you think he's just like me---right?"

"Right!"

"Oh come on, Goli, you and I are on the same team now, cut me a break!"

"How did Reuters pick it up," I asked.

"I published it anonymously to World News Network and within minutes, Reuters picked it up and ran with it. I uploaded the recordings with a cut-line saying, 'Trade Minister caught slamming openly gay UK official on live microphone', and the news aggregators went wild! Goli, I know there is so much more. I haven't even started with this guy. God damn, I can't wait to write a - -"

"Timothy, Timothy, Timothy, slow down, we need to talk. You can't publish your damn name; you don't know who you are dealing with here. Look---meet me for coffee at *The Attendee* in an hour. We have got to have a strategy here or you're going to get us all killed!"

"Yeah, yeah, yeah---you're right. I'll see you there," Timothy said, ending the call.

I slid the covers over and popped out of bed with a feeling of excitement that I hadn't felt in years. It felt so good to think of my morning with Danielle, about to enjoy a nice cup of coffee, while at the exact moment in time in France, Henri was concerned about his political future. I made the bed and walked across the floor towards the kitchen, following the scent of fresh brewed coffee.

I turned the corner and to my surprise I found myself standing completely naked in front of Magda.

"Well it appears that I caught the both of you in your birthday suits this morning," Magda said with a smile.

"Danni, why didn't you tell me that Magda was here?" I scolded as I quickly turned and skipped out of the room.

"Oh Goli, dear, don't even give it a second thought, kiddo, if I had a body like either one of you girls, I would give up clothing all together," Magda laughed as she sipped her coffee.

I reentered the kitchen in a light robe and kissed Magda on her forehead.

"My god, Magda, what will I ever do with Danni? Sometimes I think she does that sort of thing on purpose, just to get my blood boiling."

"Oh sweetie, you get my blood boiling every single day," Danielle said, as she handed me a cup of coffee and kissed me on my nose.

"Baby, just look at what Magda brought for us this morning," Danielle said, while pointing at the table, "wonderful organic muffins."

Magda sat there at the table and, removing her glasses, reached for a tissue and pressed it against her eyes.

"Oh my, Magda, what in the world is wrong, why are you crying?" I asked.

"Just looking at the two of you, makes me so very happy for you both. Just seeing you and Danni together makes me think of my dear Hartley. He would gaze at me with the same passion that you both have, every single morning. I just love you girls so very much," said Magda, looking down at her coffee cup.

Danielle and I quickly placed our coffee cups down on the counter and rushed over and hugged Magda. This tough woman with such a stern business disposition had a soft side to her. She saved Dannielle's life with her kind and giving heart which few, with the exception of the other girls in the taxi service, even knew existed.

"Okay girls," Magda said, slapping us both on our butts. "Let me go, I have to make sure the rest of my sleeping beauties are up and moving. We've got to get this team out on the playing field!"

I glanced at the clock, and said, "Oh my god, I'm late, I have to go meet Timothy downtown and I haven't even washed my face!"

I gulped the rest of my coffee and ran into the other room as Danielle chased after me, pounding the floor with her bare feet, as if she were a monster of love in pursuit. Into the bedroom we went as she shoved me down on the bed and pinned my wrists against the cotton sheets.

"I have to go Danni, Timothy's waiting for me," I protested, trying to move her strong arms off my body.

"Well he's just gonna to have to wait---now isn't he, *girly-girl--until we're done—doing whatever it is that the two of us do to one another!*"

Danielle was clearly mocking Timothy as she slowly released her grip and began unbuttoning her silk rope, revealing her plump and ever inviting breasts.

"Well -- I – I - guess he just may have to wait after all."

I watched Danielle's robe fly across the room as my excitement grew.

I looked up at Danielle as she sat on top of me, shaking out her long beautiful hair, letting it drop down against her lower back.

"Oh god Danni---you know what happens to me when you let your hair down like that?

Danielle seductively teased me with her breasts as she arched her back and urged me to touch them.

"Well, why do you think I do it?"

Soon time stood still and meeting Timothy on time didn't matter, as we both drifted off into our rich dance of intense love making.

"If Timothy could only see us now," Danielle whispered, as she moaned with delight.

Forty-five minutes later I opened my eyes and glanced at the clock; Danielle was already in the bathroom getting dressed for the day.

"Danni, I've got to get my ass out of here---now!"

I slid out of bed for the second time that morning. "Okay babe, wait, let me kiss you goodbye," Danielle said, as she opened the bathroom door, poked her face out and puckered her lips.

I gave her a quick kiss and turned around and began to leave. "Hey Goli, you forgot something---girl," Danielle announced.

"What," I asked, turning around to look.

Danielle spun around and shook her beautiful butt at me and said, "I hope you know what you've got waiting here for you tonight---baby?"

"I can't wait, I just can't wait," I said, as ran towards the door with a huge smile on my face.

"Love you---Danni,"

"I love you more!"

"Damn girl, you are glowing," Timothy said, as I walked through the front door of *The Attendee*. "I'm not even going to ask why you were late. If it were me, I would never even leave Danni's apartment."

"Sorry I'm late, Timothy."

I sat down and began searching through my hand bag for my cigarettes. "Dammit, I just got this pack last night and I'm already out! These damn things are going to kill me," I moaned, as Timothy stood up and led me outside for a smoke.

"Decaf mocha latte, Goli?" Freddie asked from behind the coffee bar.

"Thanks Freddie," I answered with a smile and a wink.

We stepped out on to the side walk in front of the coffee house and joined the crowd of early morning tobacco and caffeine addicts, as Timothy lit two cigarettes at once and passed one my way.

"Thanks, I needed that," I said, taking a long drag from my cigarette. I leaned against the painted brick wall of the coffee shop and let the nicotine soak into my morning mind. The sun felt nice as it warmed my face, and I began to relax as the two of us blended in with rest of the customers.

I glanced over the back of the elderly man sitting in front of me and saw the front page of the *Enterprise*. There it was in bold print, the same article I had just read about Henri about two hours earlier.

"It's amazing how much more news seems real when it's printed on paper," I whispered to Timothy, scanning the bold print brightly illuminated by the morning sun. "I guess that old sayings true about front page news withstanding the light of day."

"Sure is," Timothy said, as he leaned back against the wall and took a sip of his black coffee. "But I suspect Henri won't have much of a problem fending off this story," he whispered, as we moved away from the people.

"Why do you say that?"

"Because politicians like Henri deal with this sort of shit on a daily basis," Timothy said, as he took another long drag off his cigarette.

"But not Henri, he's never been in the press for stuff like this."

"It doesn't matter, girl, it's just an accidental gaff. He'll make a few apologies to the gay community and kiss the ass of the deputy prime minister over the phone, and it will all be forgotten by tonight," said Timothy. "Nope, Lepan should be able to handle this one just fine.

"Well then, why take the risk if you think it won't make a damn bit of difference?"

"Because it's a process, Goli; we want to start with a slight itch and slowly build up to a full blown weeping rash. I'm just fucking with him right now. Nope, we have just scratched the surface on this old chap, I just know it. I'm going to ease into this dude slowly and start to make him sweat. Just wait until I start rearranging his appointment schedule, and delaying his emails," Timothy said, while blowing a smoke-ring into the breezeless morning sky.

"You can do that?"

"Girl, the things I can do with this dumb fuck will astound you."

"So when can we read some of his emails?" I asked, lowering my voice and glancing over my shoulder.

"All in good time, my little pretty, all in good time," Timothy chanted with a high voice. "You see, pricks like Lepan are well practiced in the art of deflecting embarrassing news, but the more often news like this appears in the press, the sloppier they become. The egos of these high ranking government officials will astound you. People like Henri fly so damn high that they begin to think that their own shit doesn't stink."

Timothy shot a glance at the rear end of blonde bending over and tying her shoes. "We need to make Henri think that he is under some sort of attack by his adversaries. You know the people who have been his enemies for years. We want to be subtle with how and why he becomes newsworthy. Recorded slip-ups are fun, but they don't buy us anything. It's the volume of embarrassing fuck-ups that will begin to pay us a return. I want him to start thinking he's being jinxed with some kind of bad luck, then we will modify our plan and amp it up for the attack," Timothy said, as I followed him back into the coffee house for a refill.

Timothy sat in the booth just as Freddie delivered my latte. "You certainly look very pretty this fine morning, Goli," Freddy said, with an appraising smile.

"*Techmhatoun ghashang mibineh!*" – "*The beauty is in your eyes!*" I responded to Freddie in Farsi with a smile.

"She's glowing isn't she, Freddie," Timothy asked, as he gave me a light pinch on my cheek. It's amazing what a little early morning sex can do for you! Isn't that right girly-girl?"

Freddie shook his head in dismay.

"That will be quiet enough---Timothy," I snapped, acting like I was going to pour the contents of my cup into his lap.

"Thanks, Freddie, and guess what, that's one thing that Timothy here will never experience," I said, smiling.

"Oh, that's a low blow, girl---low blow," Timothy laughed, while acting as if he'd just been kicked between the legs.

Freddie smiled and walked away as we both sat stirring our coffee in silence.

"You know, Goli, the other night when we were at Danni's, I realized that there's a lot about this guy Henri, that you're both not telling me. Now

I know that you think I'm a real pig sometimes---okay most of the time, but I really like you two girls.

Even though there's never going to be a chance in hell that I might be able to have my way with either one of you. But the two of you just make me feel as if--- for the first time---since my life turned to shit, I'm starting to do something, you know---meaningful."

"What do you mean Timothy," I asked, leaning in towards him, "I thought you loved smearing people."

"Well, I did, up until I got to know you and looked into those all-knowing eyes of yours. It was as if I could see myself for the creep that I truly am," Timothy said, as he looked deeply into my eyes.

"Oh come on Timothy, don't be so hard on yourself. What is it that caused your life to get so out of control?"

He evaded my question. "Goli, I'm not that much better than these creeps that are screwing the tax payers," Timothy said while looking down at his coffee. "And the things that these people did, yeah, they were bad and all, but nothing like what I think Henri must have done to you girls."

"What makes you say that, have you seen something that you're not telling me about?"

"Not yet. I can just tell that there is something big going on with this guy. Just as you've got me figured out with those big brown eyes of yours, I know that this Lepan dude has a lot going on that the public is unaware of. Now you don't need to tell me now about what happened to the two of you until you are ready. But know this--- at some point you may need to tell me everything."

"Timothy, Henri Lepan is a very bad man, is all I can tell you now," I said, as I took a sip of my coffee. Timothy leaned in and placed his hand on the top of my palms. "My whole family has been completely destroyed by Henri. What that man did to me and so many others is only now coming back to me. I can't even begin talk about it."

I looked down at my hands and started to choke up. Timothy acknowledged my pain with the gentle touch of his hands. "Once we have something on him, I will tell you more. But for now, I want you to come up with the facts naturally. But you need you to promise me one thing, Timothy," I said, as I placed my right hand over his. "Please do not publish anything under your name, because I promise you Henri has the power to destroy us all."

Timothy looked at me with his eyes wide open.

"Goli, trust me when I tell you, I know what I'm doing, and when I, no---I mean, if I ever publish something on him, it will be at the right time and I will ask you first—okay?"

"I mean it, Timothy, Henri is someone you don't want to mess with. Please proceed with the utmost caution, and keep me in the loop."

As I stood up to leave Timothy looked at me with his puppy eyes and half smile.

"Call me when you get more and be very careful, Timothy." I bent over and kissed him on his cheek. I then turned and walked up to the counter to pay my bill when I heard Timothy yell, "Hey Freddie—put her coffee on my tab."

I glanced around and winked at Timothy.

"Hey, Goli," Timothy yelled, in an even a louder voice. "Tell Danni that I said that the two of you are the hottest bitches in Oxford, and one day when this is all over, you guys will be begging me into your bed! You just wait and see--you sexy thing!"

I rolled eyes as I walked past Freddie and said in our native tongue, "*Yek bar heyvan, hameye omr heyvan*"-- *"Once an animal, always an animal."*

Chapter 23

GOLAREH: POCHA: THE DEAD, LIVES

For the next three months the Killing Floor had the ride of a life time with anonymous news tips about Henri's character being loaded into the news aggregators as fast as Timothy could stuff them in. Everything from Henri's derogatory comments about the Catholic Church to how much he hated French automobiles appeared in every news outlet in France.

Call-in telephone banks were swamped at talk shows throughout France and England. *The Times, Daily Mail, The Guardian, The Observer*, and the BBC were all trying to cash in on the feeding frenzy by deploying their own reporters to Paris in search of Henri, and especially the unknown source of the meaty news.

The BBC began referring to Henri as being bullet-proof because nothing could be traced back to him.

"So what," Henri would say in response to the news outlets. "I plead guilty to having a loose tongue, but do you think I would ever take advantage of the taxpayers? Never in a million years." He bragged.

"So what if I drank a little too much expensive wine, what the hell, at least it was French wine. And so what, if I think some lesbian in Britain is a hottie, who would argue? I was paying her a complement," he quipped. "But let me say this to all of you ultra-liberal media groups out there. I know that you are watching me, just waiting for a chance to get your lead story on the front page of your worthless rag. Be careful what you print, for one day it may backfire on you. I have nothing to hide and I dare any reporter to come up with just one shred of evidence pointing to me taking advantage of anyone, most especially the taxpayers of France."

Henri, for the most part, was dodging each report with relative ease, claiming that it was all media fabrication. "It's all politically motivated by France's far left-leaning National Front! They are the people responsible for the true waste of *my* beloved country! They are the ones trying to destroy the reputation of *my* party's true values," Henri said in his defense. "I defy anyone," speaking within centimeters from the nose of a nervous reporter for CNN-France, "to produce a shred of evidence suggesting that I've ever misused any of the taxpayers' money! My god, I bring money to this god-forsaken country, I don't take it out!"

Henri seemed to revel in the sudden spot light on his character, welcoming interviews with any news source that dared to question him. His debonair qualities coupled with lightning fast rebuttals were so effective in disarming his critics, that he soon became a French entertainment reality show. It was as if the detached public couldn't wait for the next unarmed reporter to publically attempt to corner Henri.

He even became the talk of the men's fashion industry with his charming good looks, expensive conservative suits and meticulously groomed gray beard. Custom tailored clothing sales shot through the roof.

During what were supposed to be Henri's most embarrassing and lowest moments, he made the cover of GQ France. He had just made a fashion statement without even knowing it. There in all of his glory was a grinning Henri Lepan, sporting a wine stained white shirt, with a glass of expensive wine between his fingers as he appraised the sexy backside of an unknown government official.

Just when Danielle and I were about to fall asleep while lying in bed watching Fashion-Week on late-night television, she appeared. The mysterious women, who had been living in the shadow of the trade minister for years but had never been seen in public before, just showed her face.

The reporter described the woman as Pocha, a recluse, an invisible marketing genius, and a *never-before-seen* trademark in the fashion industry. It wasn't what was being sold that made Pocha sought after; it was how women's treads were spawned, that made this beautiful but reclusive women intriguing.

The video clip showed a black Roll Royce limousine slowly approaching a private Gulfstream jet on an exclusive tarmac at the Aéroport Charles De Gaulle in Paris. The door of the jet slowly opened and a woman in a black leather coat, brown tight fitting top, and black denim jeans immerged and slowly stepped down the stairs of the jet way. She had long brown hair hand styled over her forehead and oversized dark sunglasses blocking most of her face. Her expression was one of profound privacy and deep thought as she gripped her leather briefcase, lowered her head, and walked quickly to the waiting limousine.

The fashion reporter said: *"In both a stunning and never before seen public appearance, we see Pocha, who has now been identified as Ms. Homayra Parastou, the rumored long-time, live-in girlfriend of Henri Lepan, arriving from London today after delivering a passionate speech at the U.N. Parastou and Lepan have been reportedly working closely together to substantiate the need for a new government human rights organization whose mission would be to crack down on human sex trafficking."*

Danielle and I jumped out of bed and stood naked in front of the television as if we had both seen a ghost. "Holy shit---that's Pocha?" Danielle, screamed, "That's Homi? My god baby, that's Homi! She is alive!"

"Did they just say that she has been living *with* Henri?" Danielle asked.

"I knew it---Danni! I just knew!" I screamed at Danielle as I stood frozen---staring at my sister. It was no surprise to see Henri still in the equation, as shocking as it was, but then that was probably the main reason I had been having these terrible nightmares.

The reporter continued, *"Although Pocha has been a major figure in the development of woman's fashions, she has always been hidden away from the public eye, never appearing on public television. It certainly appears that Ms. Parastou has been hiding her beauty at the expense of the world; looking so beautiful in those stylish Onassis framed sunglasses. I'm sure we will see a spike in sales of those glasses in the not too distant future, not to mention that beautiful leather coat and shirt."*

"Damn, Goli, that's our Homi? You were right girl, she is alive, I can't believe what I'm seeing here," Danielle gasped. "She is so fucking beautiful Goli." She kissed my cheek and hugged my neck with delight.

"Oh my lord, she most certainly is," I whispered while not even wanting to blink my eyes. "My sweet Homi is alive!"

"Goli, I can't believe how she still looks so much like you, she's like your exact fucking double," Danielle exclaimed.

The two of us danced around the apartment totally naked, screaming at the top of our lungs as the lights came on in the rooms below.

Soon the girls from the apartments below began peering through our windows from the fire escape, all smiling, laughing and demanding to come in. Magda soon appeared next to them, pushing them aside and telling them to go back to their rooms, but there was no stopping them. Danielle tossed a blanket over both of us and opened the door. The girls piled into the room in a wave of giddiness. "What's going on," they all asked. Magda entered the room and said, "Girls, stop it---this moment, and let them talk. Now tell me girls, who's alive and who's so beautiful?"

"My sister," I said, "my dear sweet sister, Homi, who I thought was dead! But she's alive, very, very much alive! We just saw her on television and oh my lord she is just so beautiful. I must go to her now!" I began to exit the blanket.

"Calm down child, be calm, my dear Goli, take a breath, you will see your sister in time," said Magda.

The girls rushed in and threw their arms around us and chanted, "She's alive! Homi's alive and beautiful!"

Danielle escaped from beneath the blanket and ran into the bedroom and moved the television around the corner in full sight of the girls in the living room.

"Danni, put on a nightshirt," I laughed, as she stood naked in front of the television screen changing the channels hoping to catch another glimpse of the famous Pocha.

"There she is again! Guys! It's Pocha! Pocha is Goli's fucking sister! Can you just believe this shit?" Danielle yelled, blocking the screen with her naked body.

Brooke ran up to Danielle from behind and covered her in another blanket as we all stood in front of the screen in the dark room watching another news clip of Homi.

"In an unprecedented show of solidarity," the report began, *"the U.N. today heard closing arguments as to the final justification of budget allocations. Trade Minister Dr. Henri Lepan and Pocha, his apparent longtime girlfriend and fashion icon, now known to be Homayra Parastou, spoke for more than five hours today trying to convince a 12-member panel of the French budget office to allocate funds for the creation of a child protection program.*

The International Society for Prevention of Human Trafficking and Child Neglect and the World Health Organization are wanting to ban together to devise a strategic plan for cracking down on the human trade. Pocha, Ms. Parastou, has been positioned by Dr. Lepan to be the face of the newly created organization. Henri Lepan has also been asked by committee members to serve as the board chairman."

"Are you hearing this shit---girl!" Danielle belted out, as she beat her fists on the wooden floor. "Goddamn Henri-Fucking-Lepan, is going be the chairman for a group that is supposed to stamp out the sex trade? Are you fucking kidding me, that's like the goddamn fox overseeing the proverbial hen house," she yelled.

"Oh my god, look at her, Danni," I said, staring at the television screen displaying my sister's face.

There was Homayra in file footage shot earlier in the day, sitting at a microphone in front a bunch of bored looking French stuffed shirts, speaking so passionately.

"Damn girl, her French is much better than ours," said Danni, as we all crowded around screen. Homayra appeared serious as she sat at a table speaking into a small microphone positioned in front with of her pursed lips. She wore a dark business suit with large framed reading glasses and had her hair styled over her ears. She was speaking with a pronounced level of passion as she stabbed the air in front of her with a golden pen as if she were piercing at each point individually.

As I looked at my sister on the television screen, I saw a deep level of loneliness as she labored through the facts about the immense amount of pain and suffering child sex slavery inflicts on the human spirit. Around her neck I noticed the same diamond necklace that was given to her by Henri shortly after we both arrived at the castle.

As I looked closer I noticed another necklace with two separate charms that had been fused together, the very same charms that our mother had given us when we were infants. Each charm was a golden carved sculpture of identical twin girls facing each other, with their hand pressed together in unity.

"Oh my god", I said, as I touched the screen with my tear soaked fingers. "She's wearing both of our charms," I cried, as I broke down and dropped to my knees. "She must still think of me! My god---Danni, what am I doing here, I have to go to her this instant," I screamed, as the girls surrounding me held me down and cried.

"She can no longer remain with that horrible man. I think she is trying to get away from him too---Danni! Why is she with that man? Why? Why? Why? He is a demon and must be stopped," I cried as Danielle sat on one knee and held my tearful face in her hands. "We have to stop that man, Danni! We have to stop Henri and get my sister back home where she belongs," I cried

Chapter 24

HOMAYRA: FLAWLESS DEPRESSION

My life was circular, rotating through the bumps and grinds of the next thirty years. Imagine that? It's been thirty-two years of following a meaningless pathway in to a future which looked so unwelcoming. Goli's disappearance from my life left me in a confused state of mind that congealed into a formation of deep hurt and spiteful anger. I simply could not reconcile the fact that she had actually left me, and as the years passed and my loneliness grew, so did my anger towards almost everyone, most especially Golareh.

The first five years preceding the sudden disappearance of Golareh and Danielle, were blank and void from my memory. I was so traumatized by the loss of my sister that I have no recollection of ever leaving the castle for college.

"She left you, Homayra! She wants nothing to do with you!" Henri told me the morning after she ran away.

Every single day was as exactly as vacant the as the day before, and each night I woke in the darkness and pined for my parents and distant sister. Nothing would break the vicious cycle which seemed to go around and around and around.

I dreamt about Golareh and Danielle ever single night. I could never claim my own independence. I believed that they had survived, while I crashed on the jagged rocks below and bled to death.

I considered myself as a rejected stranger always wondering where they had gone to and what I had done to deserve such despair. I imagined them both smiling and laughing within their comfortable worlds.

I imagined Golareh living in a big home somewhere with the love of her life. Each day would be productive for her, doing exactly what she was meant to do. Then there was me in my daily rituals, always standing in some other dimension, sight unseen, an observing third wheel, tagging along with my sister completely ignoring me.

I would wake up at the same time every single god-forsaken night and stare up at the ceiling, thinking that there must be a solution to my miserable existence and that the key to rejoining my sister was somehow within reach. One day I would find Golareh I thought. It's not possible to feel this horrible for the rest of my life. The rain can't go on forever---can it?

I yelled at God directly, as if I wanted to slap him in the face.

"Alright God, you win! I've lost! Okay? Are you happy now? Now stop it and change the goddamn channel!"

Losing was the story of life and depression was the one thing in my existence that was perfect. Flawless depression, it was, that covered the days of my life in a suffocating blanket.

Growing up, I never once imagined ending my own life. That was simply not me. I wasn't put together that way; I always believed that life could be a lot worse. I did, however, spend a lot of time thinking about more comfortable ways of snuffing out my pitiful life.

If it were to come to it, I sure as hell wouldn't want to inflict any more pain on my already suffering body and soul. The thought of jumping out of window was out because I was terrified of heights. Shooting myself in the temple seemed too painful and extremely messy.

I did, however, consider one way of ending my life. I noticed that the more depressed I became, the more I enjoyed the smell exhaust from a passing bus, or the strange but oddly attractive scent of my automobile's fumes. What was it about these harmful fumes that appealed to me? I think it was the organic nature of these burning fuels that made me feel a certain chemical kinship with them. It was as if we were both sharing a joint cremation.

Perhaps it stemmed from my childhood days in the church, where the mean nuns and the fat priests defined the rising smoke of incense as our joint prayers reaching for the heavens. Yeah, right! Whatever the reason was, the more depressed I became the more I wanted to envelope myself in those very dangerous and carcinogenic fumes of death.

How easy it would be for me to simply feast in a sauna of those poisonous fumes and escape through my headphones to another world. There I would be found, sitting in my car within the privacy of my own garage, wearing my best fitting jeans and the sexiest tank top ever. I would watch the garage door lower down in back of me as my engine ran and filled my world with that wonderful scent. When the time was right, I would slowly inhale myself into another world, all within the confines of my cute little Audi R8.

I was living a reclusive life with Henri in his spacious home in the town of Neuilly-sur-Seine, just a short distance west of Paris. This particular night was no different than any other, as I had returned home from an art show that a friend invited me to. I had pleasant conversations with everyone and actually enjoyed myself.

I had planned go there for a little while and simply pay my respects and then return home early. But before the food was even served, I had already consumed three large glasses of white wine. I should have known better, for there was something about the effects of white wine that always rendered me useless.

After my fifth glass of wine I made the unwise decision to drive home. The mixture of wine and loneliness changed the backdrop of the entire world around me. I slowly pulled into my garage and lowered the heavy door above me. I sat there in complete silence visiting every nook and cranny of my inebriated dark mind.

The faces of my family moved in on me with varying expressions. There was my father running alongside the fence line at the airport in Iran, then my sister holding my hand on the plane and finally the sight of my mother weeping on the day we left home. My sadness elevated into a fit of scornful and exhausted anger.

"Why in the hell did you leave me Goli? I thought you loved me! Why did you abandon me?" I banged my fists on the steering wheel, slumped over to my side and cried myself into a stupor.

The gentle purring of the engine dissipated into the ambient sounds of my surroundings. My eyes closed and quite suddenly my reality switched off like a light. I woke up staring at a paramedic through the goggles of an oxygen mask.

After my sister and Danielle disappeared from my life I clung to the only person that was there for me. Henri increased his care for me and constantly pledged his deep love for me. Since I was an emotional wreck, I must admit that I became a kept woman and perhaps an added accoutrement for Henri's social appearance.

He showered me in gold, diamonds, beautiful clothing and luxurious automobiles. He bought me a beautiful flat in Paris where he gladly paid for my entire education at the world renowned Institut d'études politiques de Paris (Sciences Po). While at Sciences Po, I earned a master's degree in fashion merchandising.

While also studying foreign languages and completing my studies, I had little time for anything else in my life. I now speak five languages: Farsi, French, English, German and Spanish. Aren't I the lucky one, for I'm now fully able to understand all of the many voices in my horrible nightmares?

I never felt any measure of romantic love for Henri even though his exterior qualities were what most women would dream of. He was extremely good looking, charming, dignified and enormously wealthy.

Any interests in the matters of the bed were neatly folded up and locked in a safe deep in my soul. While there was a time when I was young that the touch of Henri caused fireworks to explode, the loss of my family erased my need for any human touch. Sexual gratification was a gift meant for those who were content with themselves. I looked at myself as a pitifully disgusting woman.

Henri never stopped trying to reignite some possibility of normalcy in the intimacy department, but simply couldn't, and it frustrated him greatly. He bought me silk evening gowns, sexy bras and panties, but the pilot light on my libido had long since gone out.

I sometimes slept with Henri and allowed him to go through his routine, but the mere feeling of his body inside of me actually made me want to vomit. Afterwards, I would move completely away from him, not wanting to feel even the touch of his skin against mine. I now realize that regardless of the amount of pain and emptiness in my life, I simply would never love Henri.

The mere mention of sexual intercourse seemed utterly ridiculous to me and my desire for it was non-existent. What was it about the act of a man's erect penis moving in and out of my body in some meaningless attempt to solicit an orgasm? For that matter, what was an orgasm anyway? I always considered it some meaningless biological feature that belonged only to the selfish needs of a man?

I always felt that the most sensual part of romance fell into the act of the kiss, which we called *boos* in Farsi. I loved every aspect of kissing, stemming back to the key-hole days, when Golareh and I spied on our lovely parents. They would simply lie on the rug of their bed room, after my mother had completed her exotic belly dance for my father. They would gaze into each other eyes under the slow moving blades of the ceiling fan for what seemed like hours.

My father would place his hand on my mother face as they both rested their heads on oversized pillows. I could hear my father softly telling my beautiful mother in Farsi: *To kheili ziba hasti, Bi had doostat daram, Ba tamam khalbam.* This wonderful phrase, as beautiful as it sounds means: *You are beautiful. I love you so, with all my heart!*

My parents would move their bodies together as if they were woven together by a yarn created by God himself and then they would begin to kiss. They would kiss for the longest time, and many times fall asleep in the mid-afternoon while in mid-kiss.

Thank God mother and father never advanced to any other acts of sexual intimacy, and it never would have happened either. Both were keenly aware of the fact that maybe, just maybe, two nosy little girls were spying on them. On a few occasions, either my sister or I would make a slight sound and we would watch our parents lift their heads off the pillow and smile at each other, as if they thought it was cute. I didn't think my mother and father were cute at all, I thought they were absolutely beautiful.

Henri would give me anything to open my heart and let him in. If he became aware of any hidden passions or interests he would provide me with whatever I needed to fulfill my desires. As a teenager I had always had an interest in fashion design, and even received a scholarship at a college in Iran; however my father was against that idea. Iranian women who were interested in the fashion trends outside of the boundaries of our country were considered outcasts, and although change was happening, my father did not want me to risk our safety.

Henri knew of my interest in clothing design and with his massive wealth, I set off to build one of the largest fashion marketing firms in Europe. I adopted my public brand *Pocah* which was short for Pocahontas. I always loved this mysterious woman that people have been talking about for more than 400 years. I believe what I liked about her the most was how she guarded her privacy and never spoke of her values and beliefs to anyone.

I represented some of the top fashion designers in the world always sight unseen. It was here I was able to bury myself within the beauty of women's clothing and remain completely invisible to the public eye. I found that I simply had a knack for being able to recognize design trends that would appeal to women around the globe.

One reason for having such an interest in woman's fashion had to do with my upbringing. In Iran, the only place a women could display her own beauty was within the confines of her own home. My cultural restrictions were normal for me and I never questioned it but after my sister left, I found myself angry at the amount of oppression leveled upon women. I dreamed of the opportunity to provide women with the colors, textures and designs that would paint their souls, bring them alive, and make them a true part of the human race.

With Henri's capital I was able to position myself in the epicenter of the French fashion industry, and after a few years my abilities to spot and sell clothing to major retailers became apparent. Designers from all over Europe contacted me for the opportunity to draft their creations in our studios. I was never a rude critic, and I loved the designers who tried to bring out the true beauty of women.

Conversely, I had zero tolerance for anyone who was abusive to the women in my industry. If ever I saw any person, man or women, denigrate any of our models, I would immediately disassociate myself from them.

On one occasion, a German designer by the name of Marc Slootz, creator of the Opus-Slootz denim lines became so irritated by one of my model's weight that he actually spit in her face. Although Slootz was becoming a household name in Britain, and poised to open at New York Fashion Week, I terminated our relationship within the same moment of his assault. His lines never made it to America and he ended up disappearing into the mass of other fashion failures.

I opened up major lines of business between the world's largest retailers like Bloomingdale's, Abercrombie and Fitch, and the Gap, all within the confines of my own office. I never attended high society parties, never mixed with industry leaders around the world and still the name Pocha, not my own, became a world renowned name in fashion. Henri made sure that I was never hounded by the press and paparazzi as I moved invisibly around the fashion circles.

I was constantly in demand to appear on the talk show circuits but never agreed to an interview. I became a major topic of conversation on entertainment talk shows. Who was this hidden woman behind the brand name Pocha? I was a mystery to the media and press considered me an eccentric paranoid. The public scrutiny had no effect on my efforts, because the clothing had a life of their own.

Chapter 25

HOMAYRA CAPITALIZING ON HORROR

About six months ago I began having vivid nightmares portraying teenaged girls being sold for sex. At first the dreams were so foreign to me that I considered them irrelevant and thought of them to be associated with some movie I had seen or an article I had recently read. But night after night, the dreams attacked my all but hollow existence.

My dreams consisted of long lines of young females in their early teens being led, in single file, through an entrance of a long dark tunnel. The girls were dressed up to appear much older than their actual age and projected deeply sad and blank expressions.

During my imaginings I was able to move close to the human figures and study their features closely, watching their forms dynamically change the closer I looked. Their faces would morph from frightened young teenage girls to what appeared to be circus lions.

The backs of the children were scarred and beaten with bloody open sores which were apparently caused by whips, fingernails and teeth. The dreams were also accompanied with a dreadful chorus of both children screams and adult groans of carnal pleasure. A crack of a whip followed by the sound of a suffering child stabbed me so deeply that I expect to live with those memories until the day I die.

As my dreadful dreams lingered, I noticed two men with rifles dressed in safari clothing. One faceless man was leading the injured prey of young boys and girls down a dark hallway into what appeared to be a one ring circus tent as the other man turned towards me and reached out for my hand. It was then I realized that the man reaching for me was none other than Henri.

The dreams confounded me as I desperately fought to avoid them by any means possible. I began combining a vast collection of prescription drugs into my own customized cocktails with which I thought might help me avoid the REM stage of sleep which I was told contained dreams. But my drug theory failed miserably and positioned me directly in the center of my nocturnal horror shows.

One terrifying dream, I'm quite sure, lasted a full 24 hours, rendering me useless and unable to get out of bed. It was then I began mixing in time-released amphetamines which I thought might counteract the powerful effects of the sedatives, enabling me to wake up. The effects of all of these drugs were horrible, draining me of all energy and amplifying the nightmares.

My days were spent in miserable state of exhaustion. I became useless at work, so I backed away from my responsibilities and retired my duties to my staff. I couldn't talk to anyone about the dreams because they were so deplorable and sickening to recall. Further, conversations relating to dreams of sexual abuse were the last thing anyone wanted to think about.

One night, out of desperation I finally broke down in Henri's presence at the dinner table and told him about my private hell. Henri appeared shocked after I described my dreams to him. His response was filled with anger and devoid of any human comfort. It confused me terribly.

"You haven't heard from that selfish sister of yours have you," Henri asked, with a look of rage. I was stunned by his remark, and began to back away and retract what I had just admitted. Why would he ask such a question about my sister whom I had all but written off? The thought of my dreams having any connection with my long lost sister seemed utterly ridiculous.

However, it soon occurred to me that Henri might be on to something, because everything about my dreams seemed seasoned with the loss of my sister, Golareh.

"Oh, Henri," I said as I closed my eyes and looked into the darkness of my own mind. "You may never understand what I'm about to say to you, but sometimes I wonder if my sister tries to contact me through my dreams." I admitted this for the first time.

Henri now looked mortified. He stood up from the table, stormed over to the window and stared off in the distance. "Oh don't be ridiculous you naïve thing! Your sister has never cared about your welfare in the least. Why do you think she abandoned you? Although you and your sister look alike, you are both drastically different."

"What do you mean," I asked as I watched Henri sip his cocktail and avoid eye contact with me.

"You are the loving and kind one, the one I have fallen so desperately in love with. But your sister, she is the confused one who never loved you. She is the angry little soul who lives like a rabid animal striking out at the very people who try to help her. She cares nothing about your wellbeing! Why is it that you will never accept that?" Henri continued, as he lowered his head and looked at the floor. "She was always so inconsiderate of you, when she left with that-that foul-mouthed colored girl. The two of them were more interested in sneaking around the castle and flirting with the guests then being with you. Homayra, why have you never been able to let that selfish bitch go? And why will you never allow me into your heart?" As Henri pouted as I felt my blood begin to boil.

I stood up and glared at him with anger, "How can you say such a terrible thing about my only sister? I know that she left me, but I---I also know that she still loves me. I know it Henri---now stop it!"

Henri sat his glass down and rushed over and held me in his arms.

"Oh my dear, I am so very sorry, I should have never been so harsh. I just think that you are mistaking the real source of your dreams," Henri said, as he kissed me on my neck. "My darling, I have never told you this before, but I, myself, have a horror that I must divulge. You see, my dear, I believe that it has been my horrible nightmares that have been reaching out to you, not your dreadful sister's.

Darling, I am the one tortured by those very same demons, not her. I'm not even sure your sister is even capable of feeling the pain that I feel almost every single night after I lay my head to the pillow. My darling, the things that I have seen in my travels---Homayra, you just have no idea," Henri said, as his face turned distorted with an expression of profound sadness as tears came to his eyes. "The things that I witnessed people doing to those poor vulnerable girls and boys, my god, Homayra, if I could only tell you, it would break your heart."

When Henri told me that perhaps his dreams might be the source of mine, I naively accepted it and began to see him in a different light. I also accepted the fact that the faceless hunter in the dream perhaps was Henri reaching out to me for help. Over the weeks and months to follow, I began to relax a bit just knowing that I could at least share these horrid night-terrors with someone, anyone. Henri began treating me with much more respect almost as if he were finding solace from his own apparent nightmares.

Certain aspects of our romantic life began to awaken and Henri was realizing it. For the first time ever we began to hold hands and talk more freely about our private fears. Henri told me about some of the most horrific things he had witnessed in Taiwan and China, describing in detail how families sold their innocent children in order to put food on their own table. Brutal rapes of young women at the hands of both their pimps and customers. He told me that many of the images were so gruesome that he would wake up in the middle of the night, in a cold sweat.

Over the next few months following our discussions, Henri's mood began to brighten considerably. I don't think I ever saw him as excited about his work and our future potential of being a real couple. His smile was broad, and his eyes twinkled when he looked at me.

Even though we were having closer conversations and feeling mildly romantic towards one another, I could not ignore the impressive hatred he had towards my sister. Further I could never let go of the possibility that my sister was out there somewhere reaching for me in the most profound, metaphysical way, because she was now appearing in my daily thoughts.

A driver picked me up at my office one day and took me to a local airport. The limousine passed through the security check point without slowing down and moved west along a secondary taxiway. We slowly drove around the other side of the tower and headed towards a beautiful jet. Henri was standing by the steps of the aircraft next to his chauffer who was holding a bucket of ice and a large bottle of champagne. I'll never forget how he looked as he stood there leaning against the railing in his dark suit, immaculately groomed gray beard and dark sunglasses.

A smartly dressed pilot appeared at the entrance of the bulkhead door with a welcoming smile. I stepped out of the car and walked towards Henri as he also smiled and handed me a glass of sparkling champagne.

"Hello you beautiful thing, I am so happy to see you. You look so absolutely stunning."

I started to blush and look down at my feet. "Oh Henri, what's going on here, you know that I can't handle this stuff."

Henri put his arm around me, raised my eyes to his and said, "Oh sweet Homayra, I would never let anything happen to you. I love you so very much. Besides," he chuckled, "I like when you get a little buzzed. Perhaps then I can finally take advantage of you. Sweet Homayra, I hope you know how much you mean to me," Henri said as he lightly touched my back with his large hands. "Since the night we both admitted to each other our private fears, I have never felt so very close to you. I have never, ever been this much in love with anyone in my life and I pray that perhaps one day you may feel the same way about me. My dear, after much thought and deliberation I have decided to provide you with the most proper way to fight these selfish demons that claw at your soul each night. I want to ask you a very important question, and you don't have to answer until you are ready. So let me simply present it to you."

The chauffer stepped forward and topped off my glass with the fresh champagne as Henri continued. "Darling Homayra, I would like to ask for your hand--."

Oh my god, I thought, Henri's going to ask me to marry him. I began to experience a mixture of terror and anxiety.

"Homayra, I want you to be the acting president of Europe's next largest multinational agency that will wage war against the horrible industry of human slavery," Henri said, as he dropped down on one knee and began lightly kissing the top of my hand.

I looked at him and felt the hair stand up on my head. I thought the responsibility of battling an industry I had little to any knowledge of would be impossible and almost irresponsible.

"Why me?"

"Because I need you, my darling Homayra, to help me shed a light on this horrible activity that is happening right under our very noses. I want the people of France to look up at you with as much admiration as I do, and realize that we need to stop these despicable people before they start. I need your help fighting this corruption so that we both can sleep again in peace."

The pilot, who had such a kind face, made his way down the steps of the aircraft and stood at attention next to Henri.

"Darling, I would like to introduce you to Captain Richard Edward, consider this man your personal pilot. I recruited Richard all of the way from the United States where he was a fighter pilot in the U.S. Navy and then later served as the Chief Flight Instructor at Embry-Riddle in Daytona Beach, Florida.

"It's a pleasure to make your acquaintance Ms. Parastou," said Capt. Edward, as he extended his hand. "However, I must tell you that I can't speak a word of French other than *bonjour*, *bonsoir* and *au revoir*."

Henri laughed and patted the captain on his shoulders and said, "Well my boy, that's quite alright, because Ms. Parastou speaks many languages fluently, and probably speaks English better than most American's do. I would suggest letting her do the talking for you!"

"Oh, Henri, please don't tell this kind man that I speak his native language better than most, I don't want to offend him," I said, as I shook the captain's hand, feeling the pressure of his grip match mine exactly. As I looked into his eyes, I was surprised to see a level of sadness in the way he seemed to gaze at me, almost as if he had experienced a major loss of some kind in his life.

"Darling Homayra," Henri proudly said, as he looked up at the huge aircraft next to us. "This is a Gulfstream G650; it is among the newest in the Gulfstream family. Consider this your new twin-engine business office. This will be at your complete disposal to travel between France, Switzerland, Germany, London and the United States, whenever you desire," said Henri, pulling my head closer to his chest. "I need your help my darling, now more than ever. We have much to do to establish in this organization, but I need you to stand with me now to tell the world that we want to stop these selfish demons wherever they may be hiding."

Chapter 26

HOMAYRA: HIGH SPEED EXPLANATIONS

After weeks of fruitless meetings with ministries of every branch of government I felt that we were making little progress in moving our organization ahead. I had just stormed out of a meeting with the committee members who controlled the purse strings of France, at the Fontenoy Building within the place de Fontenoy and was about to scream out loud.

The purpose of the meeting was to summarize our funding requirements for UNESCO, but somehow our message was lost in distraction and disinterest. Although Henri was making major strides towards establishing our organization, I could hardly get the attention of the high and mighty decision makers. Not one of them appeared to take me the least bit seriously.

Our new organization was designed to provide aid to the victims who were rescued from human trafficking and forgotten by any support services. The one official who pushed me over the edge and caused me to call my meeting to an immediate end was the now deceased Jules Perrault, who was the Minister of Finance at the time.

Perrault made little eye contact with me during my entire justification plea but stared often at my breasts. He then made the most shockingly sexist remark that I had ever experienced in a public forum: *Ma chere dame, je dois dire que parler avec cette passion vous rends encore plus sexy - - - My dear, I must say that I think that you are quite sexy when you speak with such passion.*

I slammed my notebook down on the table and stormed out of the room to the sound of my heels on the marble floor. I actually heard laughter from the chambers as the mostly male attendees joked and snickered. I wondered if the topic of human slavery was just some stupid joke to those pompous ass-holes.

When I think back on what I actually knew about the human trade industry, I have to cringe with embarrassment. I was so passionate about a subject about which I knew so little about. I expect I did appear like an uninformed and quite naïve person to those fat bastards. But what I was about to learn over the next twenty-four hours would eclipse everything I ever believed might be possible about the evil side of the human race and most especially the man I lived with.

———

I was walking to my car on the second level of the parking garage, deep in thought, when a bright-pink taxicab screeched around the corner and came to a halt right next to where I was standing.

A black female driver rolled down her window, and with a thick English accent began yelling at me in a tone littered with profanity. "Homi, get in the fucking car--- right now!"

I had no idea who this person was and why she was so demanding. For a split second, I had the feeling that I was being abducted in the same way children were plucked from the streets.

"Homi, I said get in the goddamn car!"

Suddenly my childhood nickname resurfaced from my suppressed past: *Homi.* Only a handful of people had ever called me by that name and that was many years ago. However in an instant it struck me. The rude cabbie with her pretty face was none other than my long lost Danielle.

I felt portions of my body shiver with excitement. The same sort of excitement I would experience riding a rollercoaster. Without even considering my own safety, I opened the car door and launched myself into the backseat right next to an attractive man with curly black hair and a boyish face. "Frédéric!" I screamed, as Danielle stomped on the gas and squealed around the dark corners and out onto the sunny streets of Paris.

"Danni! What in the hell are you doing here?" I shrieked, holding on for dear life and grasping for swear words that I had originally learned from her.

"We have a whole lot to talk about, girl, so just sit back and enjoy the fucking ride.

Danielle maneuvered her Mini Cooper through the traffic as if she believed we were being followed by someone. We weaved in front of a truck and squeezed behind cars at speeds that exceeded 125 kmh.

"Are you a taxi driver?" I asked, as the street signs buzzed past by and the G-forces tossed me against Frédéric.

"Girl, there's many things you don't know about me now, but you're about to find out. Oh, by the way, buckle your fucking seatbelt girl, because I have to shake this son-of-a-bitch on my tail!" Danielle yelled, as she surveyed the traffic through the rearview mirror.

The little sports car entered the fast moving four-lane Boulevard Périphérique expressway and screamed down the middle of the highway at a speed that felt as if we were lifting off the ground. I pulled myself forward with all of my strength and glanced at the speedometer and to my amazement saw that we were rapidly approaching the speed of 239 kmh.

"How fast will this little car go?" I asked, as I fell back against the back seat dumbfounded.

"Don't rightly know, but I'm sure faster than those pricks behind us."

"Where have you been all of these years, Danni, and why now? Why did you guys leave me?" I asked, without pause, as we continued our trip to an unknown destination along the motorway that circled Paris.

"Goli sent us---Homi," Frédéric said excitedly, as he tightly gripped his briefcase in the center of his lap and hunkered down with fear.

"What do you mean Goli sent you? Why would she care about me?" I asked with both confusion and anger. "She doesn't give a shit about me!

Never has and never will! I gave up on her a long time ago!" I screamed, lying through my teeth.

"She's trying to protect you, Homi," Danielle said, from the front seat, as the car darted between a slow moving tanker truck and a semi.

"Watch it! Danni!" I screamed, as an angry driver in the tanker truck blasted his air-horn, flashed his lights and shot us the bird.

I pulled my body up against Danielle's seat back and yelled, "Where are you taking me? Are you trying to get us all killed?"

Danielle stomped down on the clutch and shifted through the gear ratios as if she was a seasoned sports car driver.

"Because Henri is scared---shit! For the first time in his goddamn life, girl, and he is watching you like a fucking hawk, Homi. I bet that you don't even realize that do you?"

"Danni---that is utter nonsense!"

Danielle kicked the accelerator as if she were having a spasm on the right side of her body. The tuned carburetors under the hood began to sound like two oddly paired wild animals growling at the top of their lungs. The front tires screeched in unison as they gripped the asphalt in front of us and pulled us into the emergency lane, passing congested traffic on our right.

I unfastened my seat belt and twisted my body around to search the traffic behind us and to my amazement; I saw a familiar gray Ford Town Car drop into the emergency lane and pick up speed in pursuit of us.

"Homi, will you please sit back down and fasten your damn seat belt! Have you ever seen that car before?" Danielle asked, as she jumped back over into the middle lane, punching the clutch, yanking the emergency brake and downshifting, causing us to feel like we were hopping backwards.

"I think so, but I'm not sure," I said, gripping the door handle with all of my strength to keep myself from being thrown into the front seat.

"Well you might want to start looking behind you from now on, girl, because Henri keeps tabs on you every time you leave your fucking house!"

"What? That's ridiculous! Why would he do that?" I asked, as Frédéric and I spun around to try to identify our tail. "My god, I think I do recognize that car, I think that's someone from Henri's detail."

The small taxi dropped between a panel truck and a cement mixer like a pinball from a spring launcher. To the left of us I saw the gray Ford shoot past us, the driver and confused passenger appearing frustrated as they overshot their mark.

"Yes," Danielle yelled with delight, "I just love that trick! Magda calls it *bury the hatchet!*"

"Who's Magda, Danni, and where the hell are you guys taking me?" I yelled to deaf ears.

Like a rocket, we shot out of the hole and back over into the left emergency lane and began rapidly gaining on the car that was previously tailing us. Danielle was clearly enjoying this as she chomped on her chewing gum and sat up close to her steering wheel with a wild expression on her face.

"How does this feel now---you stupid bastard," she muttered as she moved up to within a centimeter of the rear bumper. Suddenly we shot sideways-right, through a tiny notch in the congested traffic like a stick shift moving through the neutral position.

To the right we darted, brushing against the mud flaps of an 18 wheeler and then squeezing along the right side of the highway with emergency lanes within centimeters of the concrete barriers.

Frédéric buried his eyes against my neck and hair as if he were desperately trying to avoid watching his own death. But Danielle was beaming with excitement as she popped the clutch and down-shifted one notch. The small powerful engine groaned loudly as if it were begging for the maximum amount of fuel, sparks and oxygen.

The car shot forward like a rocket and blasted along the side of the truck like we were threading a needle. "Kiss my ass, you mother fucker!" Danielle yelled with delight, as Frédéric and I jointly screamed, "Ohhh—myyy—godddd!"

We shot like a pink rocket out of the side hole of the truck and the concrete barrier, directly onto an exit ramp to another highway system. The driver of the car that had been tailing us glanced over at us in shock and mouthed the words "what the fuck?" The three of us began laughing uncontrollably as if we were kids on a carnival ride.

"Later, asshole," Danielle yelled, as she shot him a bird and pushed us forward like a rocket into a new solar system.

The three of us sat in silence, gathering our senses as Danielle winked at me in the rearview mirror.

"Henri, why would Henri want me followed, and why the hell would Goli give a damn about me after all of these fucking years," I cried, as my emotions began to burst to the surface. "She---no---both of you, ran away from me! You left me! She abandoned me!"

"Sweetie, there is so much that you don't know," Danielle yelled, as she studied the rear view mirror for any signs of a tail.

Danielle continued to put distance between any possible tails as the traffic became less congested. Frédéric moved closer to me and put his arms around me in an effort to calm my nerves.

Danielle eased off on the screaming engine and executed a series of braking and down-shift maneuvers. The car skipped and skidded to a masterful racing stop as the dust from our wake blew over the top of our roof and followed the sea of traffic rapidly passing by.

"Homi, look at me." Danielle fastened her intense eyes as she unfastened her seatbelt and spun around to face me. "Goli did not leave you and she never abandoned you! She has always loved you with all of her heart," Danielle said, as her eyes began to fill with rage.

"Well then why the fuck did you both run away from me? How could you both leave me when we were so young and vulnerable? How could you both do such a horrible thing to me?" I screamed, completely confused. "How could you?" I began to lose it.

"Because of Henri," Danielle yelled.

"Henri, why Henri, he loved us! He told me that you and Goli just wanted to be together and away from me!"

Danielle threw open her door and stepped out into the emergency lane. The never ending line of cars, truck and motorcycles moved past us, spraying the car with debris, hot wind and exhaust. Danielle strained as she slung open my door, pushed the release button on my seatbelt, and yanked me out of the car by the lapels of my coat. She then pulled me around to the back of the car and slammed me against the rear window. The pungent scent of the exhaust and highway debris blasted against my face as Danielle gripped my coat and shook me in anger.

"Now you listen to me, Homi, and you listen good! Henri is what this all about! It's all about Henri! He's a fucking, goddamn demon---Homi! He is so fucking horrible! You have no idea! He moved Goli and me out of that horrible castle on the very same night he realized that Goli had seen way too much more than she should have. He knew that we both had explored the castle way too often and had seen what in the hell was going on there!"

"What do you mean---way too much? What was going on where? What in the hell are you talking about here, Danni? Oh my god you are not making any fucking sense here!"

"Henri sells people for money---Homi!"

"What in God's name do you mean----Henri sells people? How could Henri of all people, be involved that sort of shit?"

"He's a modern day slave owner, Homi, and every person at that castle was for fucking sale! He buys and sells people to the highest bidder! Every single person at that castle, from the busboys to the cocktail waitresses---are for sale! Henri owns every goddamn one of them and sells them like sides of beef to people all over the fucking world!"

"Of for Christ sake, Danni, that's ridiculous. I know the man, he saved my fucking life! He's working with me trying to stamp out human slavery! Henri wants to stop that sort of thing! How in the hell can you say such a terrible thing about Henri?"

"Well for one thing, he tried to sell me back when I was only 14-years old! Every single night he pawned me off on his filthy friends! Don't you remember seeing me dressed up in all of that---shit? Come on---girl! You have to remember that? He would have sold me into sex slavery, if it weren't for Zooli and Miss Cathy."

Suddenly I remembered Danielle as a naked child sitting on a round platter wearing nothing but a rope in front of that strange Indian man in a turban.

"Henri hurt Goli so horribly, Homi! He did some real bad things to her! He fucked up her mind up for years! He brainwashed her into believing all of these lies! Henri totally convinced her that you were gone," pleaded Danielle.

"What do you mean---gone? So what if I was gone! She could have at least tried to find me or call me something! For Christ sake, Danni---you both could have at least tried to find me," I screamed, as I beat her in her chest with my fists.

"Henri threatened her! He said he would kill your parents if she ever tried to look for you! She was told that you were dead, Homi! Dead! Do you fucking understand what I'm telling you? Henri said that you were killed by a horse! He said that you had gotten in an accident by a confused horse. He said that a horse trapped you on the inside of a horse trailer and crushed your body. Homi, I'll tell you everything tonight, but you have to believe me when I tell you that Henri completely molded your sister's mind into thinking that you were dead!"

I felt my legs give way as I fell towards Danielle in shock. She caught me in her arms and held me tightly, rocking me like a baby as a sea of traffic passed by us.

"Hell, I thought you were dead too, Homi," Danielle sobbed. We didn't think that you even existed up until just a few months ago until Goli started to remember it all!"

"Danni, I want to see her now! When can I talk to her? Please take me to her this instant!"

"Homi, the two of you cannot be seen together; it's way too risky right now. I had to keep Goli from running out of the house and chasing you down the other night, but we have to plan this right.

It is vitally important that Henri and that Ari bitch continue to believe that you two are completely out of each other's lives. Right now Goli is off the radar and we have to keep it that way. Look at me, girl, do you understand me? We need your help now, girl, do you understand? Because we are going get that son-of-a-bitch and fuck him up bad! Are you with us, Homi?"

I couldn't talk anymore; I just stood there stunned and numbed, nodding my head like a puppet in agreement.

Frédéric appeared from the right side of the car and put his arms around the two of us and moved us further away from the traffic. Frédéric was also crying as the three of us stood together in a tight group on the side of the highway.

The sea of traffic sped past us not showing the least bit of concern for our safety. No driver made any attempt to stop, or even slow down to ask if we needed any assistance. We were simply human clowns dancing alongside of the highway of life.

We left the urban boundaries of Paris and traveled into countryside as a light rain began to fall. A thin layer of fog covered us with a cozy blanket. We turned next to a barn and drove further down long gravel road to a driveway with a secluded red barn in the misty distance.

"This is my secret getaway," Frédéric said, as we came to a stop. "This is the one place that no one knows about, and the very place where I plan to bring my parents and possibly yours one day, if I can ever get them out of Iran."

We drove up a pea gravel driveway past a beautiful pond on our right and came to a stop in front of a horse a barn with large living quarters above. Danielle turned the keys to the ignition off and stepped out of the car. The quiet sound of the evening was wonderful as the crickets and spring peeps chirped all around us while the daylight began to disappear.

I felt a level of comfortable warmth as I looked into Frédéric's eyes as he held my hands in the quiet backseat of the car. "We have a lot of tell you about, Homi, and much of what you will hear will be very hard for you to come to terms with, but we must get through this."

After an extended pause, Frédéric opened the door and stepped out and held the door open for me as I scooted off the back seat and stood on the gravel driveway.

"Well it's about damn time the two of you get out of my damn cab," Danielle joked, as the three of us slowly walked through the center isle of the barn.

I looked over at Danielle, admiring her beautifully carved feminine features and thought about how they collided so perfectly with her signature profanity.

"Danni, has anyone ever told you that you have one very dirty mouth," I commented as I slapped her on her butt.

Chapter 27

HOMAYRA: A PRELUDE
TO THE AWAKENING

The home was simple with a four-stall horse barn below, and a comfortable loft above. It was situated in the center of a 20-hectare horse farm surrounded by beautiful fields and wooded trails. Off the back deck was a wonderful view overlooking luscious green fields with snowcapped mountains in the distance.

"This is beautiful Frédéric. How long have you had it?" I asked.

"Oh, I think for about 28 years now," Frédéric said, as he looked off in the distance. "I don't come here often because I don't want people to know that I have it. I usually rent it out to the local equestrian community."

"Why horses, Frédéric?" I asked.

"I don't know, I guess it all started when I visited the two of you at the castle and watched you girls ride under the instruction of that beautiful horse trainer. I still remember that day. You showed me around the grounds and introduced me to all of those wonderful horses. You both seemed to love them so much, almost as if they were part of you. Some memories just stick, I guess. But I've been coming here more often lately."

"Yeah, especially after he got a call from Goli and received a load of shocking shit!" interrupted Danielle.

Frédéric looked up at the sky with a pensive expression. "It's all about Henri now Homi, it's all about him."

The three of us leaned against the railing as Frédéric continued. "I didn't want to believe it at first when Goli first contacted me. As a matter of fact I almost hung up on her and told her to never contact me again. I thought she was crazy! I would shake my head in disbelief and say, 'this couldn't be! anyone but Henri.' He was like a father to me. This man saved my life. He put me through law school, and gave me my first job. I worked for the man and respected him more than anyone in the world. He groomed me for success. I was closer to him than I was to my own father. He was my mentor, my friend, my savior and I was so very proud to be in the company of this powerful man."

"Frédéric, I'm sorry to ask you this, but I feel that I simply must. But why did you never try to contact me, or check on both of our whereabouts?" I asked.

"Because Henri, told me that Goli had run away and wanted nothing to do with any of us."

"But Frédéric---what about me? Didn't you ever try to get in touch with me either?"

"Henri told me not to, and I did what he told me to do. I always did what Henri told me to do. He said that you were a mental, basket-case and wanted to be left completely alone."

"Left alone? Frédéric, you could have at least tried to contact me. My god, you are my cousin! Why Frédéric? Why didn't you at least try to find me? It's been more than thirty-years?"

"Look, Homi, I don't know! You tell me?" Frédéric's face exhibited a mixture of guilt and frustration. "Why didn't you ever try to reach out to find me either---Homi?"

There was an extended and very awkward pause.

"You know, I think a glass of wine would be good for us all right about now, don't you think so, girls?" Frédéric said, as he wiped his eyes, opened the screen door of the porch and stepped into the kitchen.

I stared off into the distance and thought about what Frédéric had just said. Why had I never reached out to him either? I could have done the same but chose not to.

"Because Henri told me not to, and I always did what Henri told me to do. My god, Danni, Henri was right. I really must have been a true basket-case!"

"Listen baby, Henri kept all three of us, including Frédéric, under his thumb, and the bad thing was, we all did what Henri told us to do," Danielle said, as she put her arms over my shoulder. "But those days are gone---girl. We've all been woken up, thanks to God, Mother Earth or some other damn entity out there."

Frédéric returned with a bottle of red wine and three glasses and continued to fill in the blanks of our lives.

"When Goli began telling me all about what Henri was into, I was mortified. I thought, no way could this be possible. I didn't want to believe it, and chose not to at first. I thought that Goli was just lashing out in some insane effort to hurt us all. Also, I couldn't even picture the crime---I mean human slavery, child abuse? What is that? My mind couldn't even go there. I couldn't even picture those sorts of crimes. Hell, I still have problems imagining it.   It was only after Goli showed me what she and her friend Timothy had uncovered that it hit home with me. She said that they just stumbled upon all of this shit. Homi, she was only trying to find you, but in doing so she caused a geyser in Henri's criminal oil field.   That's when she dumped all of this shit in my lap. The initial information was so shocking that I was required to contact Interpol for their help. Interpol then brought in ICE and then we all jointly opened up a huge investigation effort into Henri's past."

"Ice, what is Ice?" I naively asked.

"Well since Henri has been sourcing people from the United States, Interpol and Europol were required co-operate with the U.S. Department of Immigration and Customs Enforcement. Thus ICE."

"Oh my God! Are you telling me all of these people are investigating Henri? You have got to be kidding me?"

"You have no idea, Homi; we have a dedicated investigation team studying Henri's life, 24/7 at Europol's headquarters in the Netherlands.   The leaders of France, to this day, have no idea what is about to be brought forward, but they soon will, and when that happens, there will be one hell of an explosion. Bottom line, girl, Henri has been running a human trade organization of a massive scale. It's so huge that it has become completely invisible to the human eye. Oh and, Homi, here's the best part! Every bit of it has been funded by the state of France!"

The four of us stood and listened to the sounds of the evening as my thoughts shifted to the significance of my sister and me. How were we so lucky to get snagged into this nightmare? "Frédéric, one thing that doesn't make any sense to me, is, why us?"

"Well, what do you mean by—why us?"

"What I'm asking is, why us, out of all of the people on earth. Why did Henri bring the two of us to that castle? What was so special about us? I mean why would this powerful man with so many resources at his fingertips want to have anything to do with two lost Iranian souls? How did it happen, Frédéric, what was his attraction to Goli and me?"

"I have asked myself that exact same question, Homi," Frédéric said, with a perplexed look. "But I can still vividly recall the day that I received a letter from my father that contained those picture of you two girls. My father was pleading with me to help your father move the two of you out of Iran. He thought that I would be able to do something, because I was the only person he knew outside of our country. Iran was on the verge of collapse and those series of bombs that went off on the sidewalk in front of your house that day, convinced your father to get the two of you out of there. Homi, the neighbor who lived right across the street from you set off those bombs. I mean everything was crazy during that time."

Frédéric placed his hands on the wooden rail of the deck and slowly continued to recall a day deeply entrenched in his memory.

"I was only 16 months into my apprenticeship detail with the in-house legal counsel at the Department of Trade and scared to death about my ability to do my job. My French sucked, having come from Iran and I thought I would never learn this stinking language. Henri took an instant liking in me and today I'm not even sure why. Perhaps he just got a kick out of watching me struggle with French." Frédéric gave a slight laugh.

"The day I took my father's letter into the meeting room and showed it to Henri, his eyes almost popped out of his head. He moved over to the window and held the picture under the sunlight, and said, 'Oh my lord, it simply can't be them? They are so beautiful.' He spoke as if he already knew you, but from where, seemed entirely impossible to me. He stood for the longest time staring at that picture as the silence became awkward. He then carefully placed the picture back in the envelope and handed it back to me, and said, 'Bring them to me, Frédéric, I want those poor girls home with me.'"

Frédéric prepared a wonderful dinner along with assistance of Danielle as we sat on the back deck of Frédéric's hidden country home. The hills were beautiful in the distance as the darkness enveloped us.

For the first time in what seemed like a lifetime I felt as if I could breathe again, and although my sister was not there with us, the understanding that she still cared about me was overwhelming. Even though my mind was derailing with confusion, the truth caused me to pull the information in with a forceful tug.

With the relentless nightmares I had been experiencing, everything started to fit together like some sort of mental puzzle. What I was about to learn from Frédéric in the next sixty minutes regarding the man to whom I had surrendered my body and entrusted my most private nightmares to, was in fact a monster of the highest magnitude.

After dinner we cleared the table and prepared some espresso as the three of us sat close to each another while Fredric lit an oil lamp and opened up a thick government folder.

Chapter 28

HOMAYRA: DOS·SI·ER-
HENRI AUSTIN LEPAN

*C*hildhood struggles
Frédéric begins: "Okay guys, what I'm about to read to you is a compilation of research from a wide variety of sources. This is a rough draft and much of what you are about to hear, I haven't even read myself. So please bear with me as I work my way through this report:

"Bulletin No. 3 - Henri Austin Lepan – Biographical Sketch – V1.4.6"

Most of the information contained in this report pertaining to Dr. H.A. Lepan's childhood years was pieced together from records obtained from notes of Dr. Lepan's child psychiatrist, Danièle Canorenni, who was later found murdered by one of her patients in December of 1979. Also, please note that many of Henri's past tutors, coaches and advisors have either been incarcerated or are missing altogether.

It has also been discovered that Henri's longtime administrative assistant, Davner Leinfried, was found shot to death against a garage wall in Paris on September 5, 2009. The rest of the details surrounding Henri's criminal activity were pieced together by the Organisation Internationale de Police Criminelle (Interpol), and the NYC Office of Immigration and Customs Enforcement (ICE).

Please note: this is a highly confidential, work-in-process report:

Henri Austin Lepan was born in Étain, France on April 4, 1941. His father Austin Chalmers Lepan was a highly decorated French General. Dr. Lepan was the only child of Catherine Elizabeth Godignon, a notable equestrian athlete.

Serving as a young cavalry officer during World War II, Gen. Lepan earned the Oder of Merit, and ultimately took over the helm as the chief-of-staff of the French Army.

Gen. Lepan served at several posts around the world while leaving young Henri and his mother at their primary residence in Versailles. In many ways living in one home for most of his childhood was good for Henri because, as he said, he was able to maintain a close relationship with his mother. However, Henri's father was a brutal man who left his mark on Henri during the times he returned home from his many outposts.

Henri idolized his father and tried to mold himself into a son his father might be proud of but painfully Henri fell quite short. His mother Catherine or *Miss Cathy,* as she was called, was the true prize in his father's eyes and he treated her like a princess from the day they met.

Catherine was an Olympic equestrian hopeful, nicknamed the Jumping Diva, who was well on her way to stardom, until a head injury sustained during competition brought her eventing career to an abrupt end. Today Catherine suffers from the neurological effects of anterograde amnesia.

Gen. Lepan fell in love with Catherine after witnessing her equitation skills under the big top of a French traveling circus company. Although Catherine struggled with memory retention, she was a tremendous athlete and showed little difficulty caring for her horses. She was a master in the art of *voltage,* in which she and other riders would chase after horses at full canter and vault upon their backs.

Although Austin Lepan was a highly recognized military figure, he was reportedly vain and extremely homophobic. He had zero-tolerance for homosexuals and publically referred to them as *freaks of nature.* He was once quoted by the *French Free Press,* following the discovery of a high ranking officer's homosexual lifestyle, as saying: "These perverted queers are the most hideous creatures under the light of God."

As a young teen, Henri Lepan had few friends and spent more time in the company of adults. His schoolmates spread vicious rumors about him being the teacher's pet, a *tattle-tale* and a fairy. Henri was constantly in the company of teachers, coaches and church leaders. As a result of his personal connections, Henri was treated to an exclusive education which would be unaffordable for any other students of his locale. He traveled to distant lands with many of his teachers, staying in lavish hotels and dining at the most exclusive restaurants in the world.

When Gen. Austin Lepan returned home, Henri's life of luxury would come to a sudden halt while his world was ripped inside out. Gen. Lepan made up for his time away while ruling the home with an iron fist of zero-tolerance. Gen. Lepan had little regard for formal education and considered Henri's friendship with the adult teachers as being strange and a bit *queer.* When the General was home, Henri's life rotated completely around the rule of respect.

The strange preoccupation that Gen. Austin Lepan had with regard to zero-tolerance confused Henri, causing him to feel profoundly inadequate. "You are a honey-boy!" Henri's father always barked before a beating was about to arise.

Henri knew what it was like to be beaten down with a velocity that was far from a slap in his face. Whether Henri's punishment came in the form of a kick in the stomach or a punch in the nose, the intensity would be massive, many times resulting in hospital visits for what his father said were careless injuries.

His father had little regard for blemishes, bruises and lacerations. It was the way he was brought up, his father would often tell his mother, and very much appropriate for that little honey-boy. It wasn't the number of beatings Henri received that confused Henri, but it was not knowing when they might happen and what would provoke such violent outbursts.

One memory that Henri's spoke of during therapy sessions was a time he witnessed his mother setting the table and humming a light hearted patriotic song while Henry was being beaten within a hair's thickness of his life. Henri described the feeling of being raised high above the lamp shades and then slammed down onto the living room floor as his mother sniffed the flowers on the dinner table for freshness.

Henri's mother's short term memory deleted every occurrence of Henri's horrific beatings. Within minutes following a beating, Catherine would forget all aspects of the attack. All details of the travesties were expunged from Miss Cathy's mind as Gen. Lepan capitalized on his wife's convenient disability.

Some of the most severe beatings came from the most innocent of crimes, like a disappearance of a piece of salami from the top shelf of the icebox or a rug found ruffled beneath Henri's chair. Henri's father would burst into his room in the middle of the night and yank Henri out of the bed by his hair and kick Henri in the mouth with his leather moccasin. Henri spoke of watching one of his teeth skip across the bedroom floor as his father called him a: *Espece de sale pedale! - Disgusting little faggot!*

When Henri was nine-years old his father was doing some repair work in Henri's bedroom, while young Henri sat on the edge of his bed. Henri began pulling the chain on a lamp which sat on his nightstand.

"Stop that Henri," his father snapped.

Being bold, Henri decided to explore the boundaries of his father's tolerance. Henri disregarded his father's orders and continued to turn the lamp off and on.

His father set his tools down and walked over to young Henri. He picked up Henri and repositioned him on the edge of the bed with his feet dangling over the side.

"Henri, when I was about your age, I was taught the meaning of respect. Now, although many of my lessons were painful, I've grown to appreciate the importance of being respectful to one's elders."

Henri listened as he watched a light bulb heat up under the lamp shade. The longer his father lectured the hotter the room became.

"Son, it is now your turn to learn those same valuable life lessons that I was taught by my own father."

Henri was now sweating profusely as his father reached over and re-trieved a tissue from the night stand.

Henri watched as his father carefully unscrewed the burning bulb from the lamp as the expanded bulb squeaked as it was being twisted from the fixture.

"Son, sometimes you have to learn the meaning of respect and your time is now."

Gen. Lepan seized Henri's wrist and pressed the burning element against Henri's wrist.

Henri later told his therapist that he could hear the sound of his own flesh sizzling beneath the hot bulb, as his father rolled the burning bulb around his blistering skin. Henri also described the expression on his fa-ther's face as being peaceful as he purposely cooked Henri's flesh.

"You---my son, are now excused," his father chucked as he finally re-leased him from punishment. "Now run off, you little honey-boy. Run to your momma. Run, I say---you little faggot!

Henri could hear his father laughing as he ran down the stairs. "Have your momma spread some butter on your hand, you little faggot!"

Henri ran pass his startled mother and dove headfirst into the couch in the living room. His mother gently applied butter to his disfigured skin while humming a childhood nursery rhyme as Henri wailed into the dark-ness of the couch.

When Henri was 17-years old his father was struck in the head by a flying piece of metal that was launched from a lawnmower. Gen. Lepan was sitting on a bench on the grounds of Central Command Headquarters having lunch when the foreign object flew into the side of his face.

Gen. Lepan was soon relieved from command and sent home as a mere remnant of who he once was. The flying piece of metal had seriously lac-erated his left eye and two thirds of his brain. While cognitively normal, he was left with limited mobility, broken speech, and poor vision. Henri's care of his father during the last months of his life appeared gentle to the community at large, but behind closed doors of Henri's new domain, his care was apparently quite brutal.

Young Henri now in his late teens was suspected of taking complete advantage and total revenge upon his father's wilted body. While Henri cradled his semi-functional but loving mother, vowing to take care of her for the rest of her life, he was suspected of exacting severe punishment on his then helpless father.

At the age of 56, Gen. Austin Lepan died. The coroner's report was obtained from classified military files, at the request of Interpol, and it was found that his death was due to natural causes. The report included a stamped order: *Cremation Without-Ceremony.*

Henri's new found freedom soon launched him into a forceful, upward trajectory towards future success in both his professional and private interests.

While Henri was an extremely handsome man, he was never known to have a girlfriend. He threw himself into his studies and advanced quickly in the areas of linguistics and international trade.

Henri attended Panthéon-Assas University and earned a Master's degree History and a PhD in political science, presenting a dissertation on international trade barriers. Henri's first job after graduating from college was serving as the director of the French Diplomatic Corps, where it was his job to promote French trade markets to the rest of the world.

By the time Henri was 29 years-old, he had become highly recognizable in international circles as being a dapper young man with a quick wit, and a very popular topic of conversation among the wives of the ultra-rich. Henri was prematurely grey and sported an immaculately groomed beard which some adversaries joked that he hid behind.

At the age of 32, Henri was named head of the Ministry of Foreign and European Affairs. He was the youngest person ever to take the helm of one of the most powerful governmental agencies in Europe. Henri's authority began to spread through many branches of government ranging from immigration reform to vital worldwide embargo decisions considered during times of war. Henri's formal installment into this position was one of a few appointed by the prime minister himself.

Some criticized the massive agency in which Henri oversaw, as having a lack of appropriate internal controls. Regardless of the criticism, Henri became recognized internationally for his effectiveness and administrative command.

Henri controlled huge revenue funds stemming from timeworn tax laws. Massive funds that ran through the account categories were rumored to have gone unchecked for decades. Internal auditors who attempted to examine the obscure interest bearing accounts were quietly terminated from their positions as others were jailed for interfering with public policy.

Henri modified the systems of work visas and the process of contracts of asylum. His office also developed a fast-track emergency work-visa system, which Henri designed himself.

In his off time, Henri traveled extensively in Japan and Taiwan. According to travel records, it was his fascination with Mexico that made ICE suspicious. Lepan formally reported that his trips were largely spent learning an obscure central Mexican language known as Huasteca Nahuatl. The language, which is remarkably complex, originating from the Aztecs, and was made up of a blend of extra-long words with complex meanings. Henri became fascinated with the language and most especially the town of Tenancingo, Tlaxcala Mexico. It was in this tiny town, just 128 Kilometers northwest from Mexico City that Henri became affiliated with the infamous Santo Gordo.

Chapter 29

HOMAYRA DOS·SI·ER CONTINUED–
THE MEXICAN CONNECTION

The townspeople referred to Santo Gordo as a *Chiclet*, who was not just from Mexico; he was Mexico. When Henri first met Gordo his esti-mated wealth was $399 Million Pesos - $26 Million (US).

Gordo was born and raised in the small town of Tenancingo, which today has a population of only sixty-thousand where at least one-thousand of the residents are pimps. Santo's extended family is the largest and most well organized crime families in Mexico, but in the town of Tenancingo the Gordos were considered to be the Über family and the residents' only hope for financial wellbeing.

The community at large revered the Gordo family and considered them their only savior. If there was any possibility that a son or daughter was given the opportunity to work as a pimp or a *delivery-girl* for the family, the parents would be consider it a gift from God.

Parents from all over town proudly flaunted their young daughters to the community at large and tourists during festivals which glorified pimps and prostitution. They were well aware of what their children were in for by the hands of their pimps and customers. The young *delivery girls* spent their days in the Tenancingo "security houses", where they were forced to have sex up to an average of fifty times during a 24-hour period.

Santo's father, Emilio Gordo, however, knew the value of an education along with a rich cultural upbringing, so he sent young Santo to school in Venice at The Venetian School of Music, where he studied language and vocal performance.

Santo mastered the Italian language and devoured their customs. When he returned home, his father completely mistook him for a disrespectful young Italian punk, after the Italian-speaking Santo entered his father's restaurant and jokingly criticized him about the pasta.

Santo Gordo was an extremely handsome man with a profoundly beautiful outward appeal. At age 24, Santo, along with his brothers, sisters and cousins, left for major cities throughout the United States. Santo positioned himself in train stations, singles bars, and concert venues, dressed in the finest clothing, while proudly displaying his wealth.

He was a master pick-up-artist and always caught the eye of many vulnerable young women yearning for the opportunity to be swept off their feet by a young prince charming. He lured young women with jewelry, clothes, money and sex. The young women fell hard for Santo, while desperately hoping for a proposal.

Many of the women came from middle and upper-class families and were carefully singled out and handpicked by Santo for their exceptional beauty. Santo was hunting for *delivery girls*, who were built for a life of sexual performance and able to withstand intensive work loads. The incentives were high for the family with most girls selling for lump sum payments of between $35,000 and $65,000 (US) apiece. Others were leased out and treated as long-term annuities until the day they were used up and disposed of.

Santo mastered the ability to capture his prey. He worked the bars and restaurants to apprehend the most attractive women and successfully lure them away, no matter who they were with, including their husbands or boyfriends. Santo believed that everyone had a price and so he would approached each woman well-armed with tools of the trade.

Santo had an intense appetite for sex and excellent attention to time management, while simultaneously engaging with as many as a dozen women at a time. He covered three boroughs of New York City, including Manhattan, Brooklyn and Queens. He spoke English with a flawless Brooklyn accent, Spanish, and French, but it was his Italian, which provided Santo his most prized packages of high class of women on the west side of Lower Manhattan.

Santo always hunted for the rich, high maintenance women, who were often the black sheep of their families. The targets were flawless on the outside, but emotional wrecks on the inside, starving for male attention, especially from a highly educated and extremely wealthy man. He was the master of seduction within the confines of a bar or out on a loud dance floor, and once they saw his Midtown Manhattan penthouse, they were begging him to be captured.

All of the targets within his acquisition process were in various stages of closure. The women anxiously awaited any shred of attention from Santo who appeared to have the world on a string. Each desperately hoped that one day soon young Santo would present them with a huge engagement ring and invite the young women on a long journey to gain the blessing of his parents in Tenancingo, Mexico. Each had a vision of standing next to the kneeling young Santo in the presence of his wealthy parents, as he humbly asked for their hand in holy matrimony.

All of the women Santo set his sights on received their wish, paid in full, and none were ever heard from again. All were devoured by the intensely brutal power of the Gordo criminal empire and circulated to customers throughout the world. Most of the women were infused with drugs and alcohol to the point where they became pleasure zombies under the complete and total control of the most heartless pimps.

Among the most noteworthy of *madams*, who was personally introduced to Henri during his last visit to the region, was a woman named Consuelo Ari Balencia, whom the industry dubbed the *blond-maiden*. Ari is Santo's first cousin and like a mirror image of him had also mastered the art of the trade.

Ari was deployed by the family to Los Angles, where she set up shop and recruited both men and women into the sex trade. Ari was virtually identical to Santo, especially with the power of attraction, but significantly more violent than all the other family members put together.

She used sex as a tool to lure young women and men into the trade and was assigned the leader of the family's disposal unit. Police in Los Angeles considered Ari a serial rapist/murderer who left a trail of mutilated bodies up and down the California coastline until the day she left the U.S. never to return.

Ari was known to beat both men and women into complete submission often in public. She once killed a woman by smashing her skull in full view of a café during the lunchtime rush. Guests watched in horror as she violently smashed the women's bloody head against the marble floor.

The Gordo family became suspicious of Henri's frequent visits to Tenancingo, because of Henri's huge spending activities. Santo, who watched all of the big spenders, was so curious that he ran his own security profile on Henri and was surprised to find out that Henri was a well-known French government official.

Santo's opinion of Henri completely changed one night at Zócalettos Wine Bar near the center of town. According to the bartender and restaurant staff members, Henri was dining alone at the bar, when one of Santo's men tapped him on his shoulder and suggested that he join Santo in the back room for some conversation.

At first Santo disliked Henri as he took his seat directly across from him. Henri sat with a pompous expression on his face which projected a look of blatant superiority. Santo's men didn't frisk Henri because it was clear he was unarmed, wearing only a cotton shirt, shorts and sandals.

Santo slid a shot glass across the table directly into the hands of Henri, while nodding to the waiter to fill both glasses with tequila. Since, at this point, Santo knew more about Henri then Henri knew about him, Santo thought he would shake Henri up by questioning him in French. Henri didn't even raise an eyebrow as Santo's questioning became more interrogative. For that matter, Henri didn't say a word for the entire time, making each of Santo's thugs, including Santo himself, extremely uncomfortable.

Henri's mastery of body language was well tuned, especially with the art of silence, which he controlled with precision. Thick and nervous energy filled the room with a palpable charge as everyone was hoping for Henri to say something, anything. Slowly Henri lifted his glass to his lips and held it there for an entire minute, savoring the aroma of the tequila. Finally he smiled faintly, threw his head back, swallowed the entire shot, and then began to laugh loudly.

Santo and his men flinched with surprise and backed away from Henri, thinking he was a lunatic. Two of Santo's men reached for their knives and moved in from the rear, just waiting for the order to bag him.

Henri casually reached in his shirt pocket and presented two Cuban cigars, sliding one across the table to Santo. Henri bit off the tip off his cigar as Santo did the same. Santo signaled for the waiter to light their cigars. Henri continued his deafening silence as he savored his cigar, and then spoke.

Henri began asking Santo the same questions Santo had asked him, but in Santo's native language of Nahuatl. Santo was so surprised by Henri's command of his obscure language that he instantly became disarmed and began to smile. The two smoked cigars, drank tequila, and discussed almost every aspect of their lives entirely in Nahuatl.

Santo was aware of Henri's immense wealth and legitimate control over European trade systems, but how they might ever work together seemed complicated. It was during dinner the next evening at the Paulsa Presidential Hotel, as the two discussed a business arrangement beneath a 24-carat gold ceiling overlooking the pool with a stunning view of a volcano in the distance, that Santo swallowed Henri's hook.

The two struck a deal that was far beyond than any other opportunity that Gordo had ever dreamed of. The two devised a plan that would broaden the definition of human trade to include everything from industry labor and family adoption to human experimentation. The huge segment of sex slaves was actually the smallest percentage of the entire captive population, but most exciting for both men who each craved the taste of their own inventory.

All transportation costs and living expenses would be covered by the French Government. All concerns relating to customs, border crossings, work-visas, medical/dental costs, passports, housing, transportation and security concerns were all covered by Henri's control of the French trade infrastructure.

Henri required only three demands for his side of the deal; he wanted the healthiest crème of the human crop available, with no venereal diseases, a 50/50 split of all revenue generated from the "objects," as Santo referred to the human cargo, and an efficient disposal services of any unwanted object anytime and anywhere in the European market zone.

From Santo's side, in order for the deal to be sealed, Santo's cousin Ari was to be installed as the third player in the operation. Ari would be responsible for the disposal of obsolete units and the coordination of traffic between Tenancingo, Mexico, and Henri's future castle in the mountains south of Paris. Henri was fond of the idea, admiring and desiring Ari's striking beauty and also because of her take-charge intensity in bed.

Santo also required Ari in the mechanics of the business primarily for his own insurance policy. Santo was known to trust no one, except for Ari. She had proven her knowledge of the family business, which included a remarkable talent for the human disposal, and intense loyalty to Santo. At any instant, Santo could simply give Ari the order to eliminate Henri and it would be done.

Ari would have no problem blowing Henri's brains out with her pearl handled revolver, while he was in the shower; or by driving a silver desert knife into the center of his chest while serving him a cognac.

Henri and Santo had a hand-shake operating-agreement. Henri knew full well, that he had better play by the rules of engagement with Santo or the consequences would be swift and punitive. While Henri held the mantra of zero-tolerance, dating back to his childhood beatings, he was well aware of Santo's ultra-thin line of toleration.

Financial accounting was to be handled separately. Henri would direct service revenue to Santo electronically in and out of an international bank account within the bowels of the French Treasury. Henri knew that while government accounts were heavily scrutinized by examiners, international accounts destined for the International Monetary Fund (IMF) were only topically examined, mainly because of their auto-balancing characteristics and the fact that the accounts had a reoccurring revenue feature. Further the massive task of making any sense of the huge accounts was considered almost impossible to undertake. Money flowing to Santo pockets represented just a single thread of transactions within the huge web of overall trade.

Chapter 30

HOMAYRA: SHOCKINGLY REVELATORY

The strangely recognizable remnants of reality began to slowly return as Frédéric gently closed the file on Henri's life. The three of us sat in silence for several minutes pondering what Frédéric had just read. Not realizing that I was shaking, I felt the loving arms of Danielle settle around my body as my shattered world lay in shambles in front of me.

Nausea overtook me, causing me to lunge forward and vomit over the banister into the darkness below. I was trying to purge my body of everything possible, including all of the active memories of Henri's filthy hands upon my body. I sat staring into the darkness not knowing at all what to say.

How could I have ever let Henri into my life, make love to him and even adore him, when he had done such terrible things to my sister and so many others. The same man who was pushing to establish a human rights organization based on my own feeble attempts to try to save the prisoners within my own dreams. How could Henri be so audacious as to stand in front of the United Nations and deliver such emotional speeches, pleading to the world for the creation of a mobilized force dedicated entirely to cracking down on human slavery?

Henri recognized the characters in my horrible dreams and sought to take advantage of even them. His eyes showed such honest compassion as he passionately spoke to dignitaries from every nation in the world about the need for stricter controls on such a shameful industry. Henri described with tears flowing from his eyes as he told horror stories of a young women who had been found beaten to death; and a 12-year-old child who was forced to perform hideous sexual acts the day after she had lost an eye from being severely beaten by a psychotic customer.

I finally understood why Henri would attempt to do such glorious things for humanity. It was not because he wanted to eradicate the world of such sins. He didn't give a shit about those poor souls. It was only because of how he would stage himself to the world at large. He would have more control of certain aspects of law enforcement, by leading enforcement forces on a goddamn wild goose chase. What a picture-perfect position Henri would be in as he led his own government agency in the eradication of his own competition. Further, it was also what Henri thought might be the key to my cold and broken heart.

How could I have been so blind not to have seen Henri's evil side, and what would have been the true effectiveness of our new mission had Henri prevailed? The organization would have been a fruitless farce, a toothless giant with our master-of-disguise at the controls.

Danielle showed me to my room, and led my exhausted body into the bathroom. "Oh my sweet Homi, your days of living with the enemy will soon be over, I promise you. Tomorrow will be a new day. You just wait and see--- we're gonna get that fucking son-of-a-bitch!"

Danielle's patented cockney-seasoned profanity lifted my spirits and reminded me of when we were kids at the castle. Slowly, I felt the power to form a genuine smile for the first time in my whole pitiful life. We held each other for a long time as she moved my crumpled face towards hers.

"Homi, there is something that I need to tell you. We are....I mean—I am..," Danielle said, with the most sincere expression but clearly clogged with emotion. "There's only one way for me to tell you this, baby, so here it comes."

"I know Danni; you are in love with my sister, aren't you?"

Danielle eyes filled with tears as she stared at the lights above the mirror.

"Yes Homi, yes I am. I love your sister with all of my heart."

I put my hand on Danielle's beautifully chiseled face and kissed her lightly on her forehead.

"I fell in love with that girl the very moment I first set eyes on her," said Danielle. "It was her eyes, Homi; she had these goddamn eyes---right? You know the eyes that could just see right straight through you. And those lips of hers, I fell in love with those rich beautiful lips."

Danielle and I sat there in my bathroom leaning against the sink, looking at each other in the mirror for the longest time.

"Homi, I have to tell you something else, that will be very hard for you to take, but you must know."

Danielle looked down at the floor and studied the ceramic tiles. Her beautiful brown toes lightly traced the grout lines as she struggled to continue. Her voice cracked and her chest heaved as she summoned the strength to speak.

"Oh Homi," she bellowed, throwing her face forward over the sink.

I put my hand on the back of her perspiring neck and pressed my face against her back. I didn't know what to expect, but I knew something horrible was forthcoming. Danielle's body was retching with pain as she desperately tried to regurgitate her horrible news.

"Oh Homi... Henri, he raped your poor sister," Danielle cried, as she dropped to the floor. I fell back against the wall and slide down until the small of my back came to rest on the cold tiles. I covered my eyes with the palms of my hands in an effort to hide from what was yet to come.

"He and that horrible woman---Ari, raped her so brutally. Homi they---they---" Danielle turned around and fell against my chest and poured her heart out to me. "They sodomized her, Homi; they fucking sodomized my lovely angel!"

For the second time in the evening I found myself speechless. I was completely stunned by what Danielle was telling me. I smoldered on the floor and pressed my fingertips against my eyelids as though I was trying to stop my imagination from processing more images.

I moaned as my gut burned with an intense fire. I rolled over onto my side and began to cry uncontrollably. My face was now lying in a pool of my own mucous, saliva and tears. Finally my safety barriers gave way, opening my mind to the climax of the worst horror film imaginable. Powerful waves of buried dreams resurfaced in my mind and come ashore, one after another. I felt throbbing agony building in all quadrants of my brain. I could also feel the horrid rhythm of a man's engorged penis invading my insides from behind, with no regards for human mercy. I saw unknown female hands tearing off my clothes and felt them biting at my back with their jagged teeth.

Suddenly the identity of the monster riding me from behind was Henri! Henri's face burst forward in my mind with supreme clarity. Henri glared down upon me with a mocking expression and a wild smile as he glued small pieces of chewed up garbage all over my naked body, as if I were a paper-Mache piñata. He chortled at me while vandalizing my entire body with his sticky fingers.

I broke away and ran for my life through the hall ways of my mind covered in all of this putrid graffiti, hoping I could escape, while all the while hearing Henri's hysterical laughter in the distance. He was closing in on me like a panting beast.

These were the hidden dreams that emptied out the fuel of my daily life. These were the intense nightmares received from my sister, which would collide with my own dreams. These were the vivid images that jolted me awake in the middle of the night in a cold sweat, as my heart pounding in terror.

These were horrible thoughts that would cause me to grind my teeth and bite my lips until they bled. The very same messages that my mind had deemed too horrible for me to remember during my waking hours, up until now!

"It was Henri! It was Henri!" I screamed out loud as I grabbed Danielle in desperation.

The room began to go out of focus, but rather than fall completely apart, I felt an inner strength building in my soul. I was waking up to a new reality with an enriched strength to do something about that horrible creature.

Henri was not going to be the predator any longer, I vowed. Henri was now going to become, for the first time in his filthy life, the prey. I pulled myself to my knees and lifted Danielle's sobbing body to a standing position.

Danni turned the water on in the sink as we both stared at our faces in the mirror. I looked at Danielle, whose makeup had mixed with mine along with our smeared lipstick.

"We look like sick clowns! Don't we Danni?" I mumbled under my breath.

I glanced up at Danielle and noticed a hint of comedic irony, "Well sister, don't we just look like shit?"

We studied each other's pitiful profiles and slowly began to smile.

Danielle looked at me with a face of confidence and said, "Let's go get that mother-fucker and kick his goddamn ass!"

"I love you so much Danni, and I'm so happy for you and my sister. I want us all to be a family again."

"I do too, Homi! I want us to be a family again as well."

After Danielle left my room I stared at my exhausted face in the mirror for the longest time thinking how long it'd been since I had the nerve to even think about my dear sister. Through my eyes I began to see and feel the comfort of Golareh's soul absorbing back to where it belonged. I crawled into bed and turned my body towards the moon. I felt my body come alive again with a sense of true purpose.

I drifted off into a deep sleep and for the first time in what seemed a lifetime I slept soundly. My dreams were pure and pleasant. I no longer felt vulnerable or haunted.

The next morning I awoke to the smell of rich coffee and enticing bacon. I eased myself out of bed with a renewed vigor, threw fresh water on my face and rinsed the taste of the night away.

Frédéric was busy making breakfast in the kitchen and Danielle had just returned from a morning run. The site of the two of them lifted my heart as they both looked so fresh.

Frédéric's curly brown hair along with his cute smile made me feel like a child again. I was ready to take on the world with a rehabilitated sense of confidence. I knew, however, that there was more to talk about this morning. There would be many hurdles to overcome before we could bring our nightmare to an end.

"How did you sleep sweetie," Danielle said, as she kissed me on the cheek and placed a coffee cup on the table under my nose.

"Like a baby, Danni. Guess what, Danni, last night was the first night in almost ten years I didn't take a single sleeping pill," I said, tasting the rich warm coffee blend.

"How often do you take a sleeping pill, Homi?" Danielle asked, as she sat down in front of me and sipped on a glass of fresh squeezed orange juice.

"A sleeping pill? My god, Danni, I have my own customized pharmaceutical cocktail. I didn't even think about the fact that I was being kidnapped by the two of you. I have no luggage!" I laughed.

"Well cousin," Frédéric said, as he kissed my forehead, "all I have to say to you on this fine morning is that you look a lot better in my old robe than I ever did."

"Why thank you my dear cousin---and guess what? I have never felt more comfy."

"My god," I said, setting my cup down on the table and realizing where I normally would be at this time of morning. "Henri must be wondering where I am and what has happened to me!"

"Not to worry yourself sister, Goli has got your ass covered. Timothy sent him a text from *your* phone yesterday afternoon as we were leaving Paris," Danielle said, as she set a plate of poached eggs, grilled bacon and two slices of lightly buttered rye toast in front of me."

"How in the world did he do that?" I asked, in bewilderment.

"Timothy can do anything with those damn *expressions*. As far as Henri's concerned, right now you're in Paris, sitting in the dining room of the Saint-Michel's Hotel sipping coffee and about spend a relaxing day shopping for boots," Danielle said, winking at me over the top of her coffee cup.

"Did Henri buy all that?"

"Homi, that man is so busy this morning with press problems, he can't even remember whether he even wiped his own ass," Danielle blurted out, causing Frédéric and me to stop chewing.

"Goli look, he's on TV! Henri's on CNN-Paris trying to explain his way out of calling the winner of Prix Goncourt, one of France's most prestigious prize winners -- a *goddamn nigger!*" Danielle exclaimed while clapping her hands above her head.

"When did that happen?" I asked.

"Yesterday, at about the same damn time we were high-tailing it out of Paris!"

"Homi, Danni, listen to this," interrupted Frédéric, as he turned up the volume on the television:

LIVE CNN-PARIS-BREAKING NEWS. "—— [senior reporter] Sir, I would prefer that you respond to my question openly when I ask you, if you are in fact a racist? My dear boy! [Henri interrupted laughing] I consider this negro-woman to be almost a member of my own family, and she and I are both terribly offended by such a ridiculous line of inquiry. I ask you, sir, to watch your mouth in deference to that woman's family. [Senior reporter] But sir, that is what you called the woman a…" Sir, why don't you ask her if my comments offended her, you disrespectful little brat? She has more spunk than any of you in this room. I believe it's the press that is spreading this continuous denigration of [those] people who require the love and assistance from people like [me]. Sir, what is your name? No—wait just a damn minute here. I demand to know what this little prick's name is? Who allowed a clown like you access to this press conference anyway? I want some answers here or I'll sue every one of you bastards for a public lynching!" [CUT TO COMMERCIAL]

"Henri can deflect anything," Frédéric said, shaking his head and turning off the television. "He's a master at forging public opinion. I've watched him do this for years. He loves it."

"Well he can only do it for so long, he's been caught on tape one too many times during the last few weeks, and pretty soon the public will begin to look at him like some sort of idiot," Danielle said, taking her dishes to the sink.

"Is Goli doing all of this?" I asked.

"No sweetie. Henri is doing *all-of-this*, the fool is so used to denigrating people it comes second nature to him. He's just speaking his mind just a little too close to his own cell phone. Henri's the one who's running his big old ugly mouth," Danielle said, as she turned her back and looked out at the morning sun.

"Wow, I just can't believe this, Henri's world seems to be coming apart as we eat, I mean speak," I said, shaking my head and looking down at my food. "I swear this is the first time in years food has ever tasted so good to me."

"Hey Homi, Timothy hasn't even begun to fuck with Henri yet. You guys---aint' seen shit yet!" Danielle said, still starring off at the farm land.

"Now who is Timothy again," I asked, as I thoroughly enjoyed my farm fresh eggs. "Frédéric, where on earth did you get these wonderful eggs, they are incredible," I interrupted.

"Can you guy believe this, with all of the events of the last 24-hours and Henri's latest gaffs; here I am sitting here in a country kitchen with the people I love enjoying my bacon and eggs? I feel so much more alive today? I can actually smell food again!"

Frédéric picked up his plate and patted me on my head while watching me clean the remaining eggs off my plate with my toast.

"Girls, mimosas are now being served on the deck. I would be honored if the two of you joined me," he announced.

I gathered up my dishes and took them over to the sink, as Frédéric struggled to remove the cork from a bottle of champagne.

"Here, let me help you with that", I said, kissing his cheek. I felt incredibly relaxed as I slipped the cork out of the bottle, producing a delicious "pop."

When I stepped out onto the back deck and saw the remnant bottles of wine from the night before, I suddenly remembered the intelligence report on Henri. The seriousness of Henri's inhuman activities rushed back like a dark cloud.

Frédéric and Danielle, holding our mimosas, stepped out on the deck after me.

"Cheers, girls," Frédéric said, as he handed me a drink and touched our glasses together under the morning sun:

Mesdames buvons a la belle lumiere de ce jour et a la liberte pour tous! - *"To the light of day ladies, and to freedom for all!"*

"Okay, so where are we with Henri?" Frédéric asked, as he sat down at the table and studied a rabbit running across the dew soaked pasture grass.

"The answer to that question is, we are somewhere and we are also nowhere at all," he continued, as he scanned the woods behind the racing rabbit for a possible early morning predator.

"What do you mean Frédéric?" I asked, studying his expression. "I thought you said that Timothy and Goli haven't even scratched the surface yet on Henri?"

"Well, we know that there is a lot there, but nothing we can use to nail his ass to anything Interpol or ICE has uncovered. If we can only come up with something substantial, showing an actual business deal going down between Santo Gordo and Henri, then we might have some evidence. Santo Gordo will be even a larger catch than Henri, but I seriously doubt that we will ever snag him. He's built a wall by the name of Mexico around his empire. If you think our politicians are corrupt in France, you couldn't even imagine what they're like in Mexico. But, if we can at least get Henri out of the equation, then at least that pipeline of human blood will be cut.

"Henri has been a master at having other people run his machine for him. It's been fun to publicly catch him in embarrassing acts but Henri is still so revered by both the public and all branches of government, his missteps are actually making him more appealing. I often wondered why Henri never considered being Prime Minister, but now I know why. He's much too happy with everything he already has.

"The only person who interacts with Henri on a regular basis is Ari, but even their conversations have been too short and cryptic. Homi, do you remember the last time you saw Ari?"

"My god, I hadn't thought of that woman in years. My recollection of Ari goes back to my days as a teenager at the castle. I remembered her as a very rigid woman with killer looks and a cold disposition. Henri introduced her as being some sort of hotel consultant."

"Here, take a look at this recent picture of her and see if it jogs your memory," Frédéric said, as he handed me a picture from his file.

"Wow, she looks like this---now? She hasn't aged a bit!" I exclaimed, examining her attractive face and gorgeous figure. "She is Henri's social secretary and fully dedicated to the events at that castle. I see her from time to time, but never realized it was the same person. Perhaps I purposely tried to forget her, she was always so kind to me that I totally mistook her for who she really was," I said.

The more I looked at her picture the more I was shocked to think of her as a brutal pimp, practiced in the art of murder.

"So she cleans up pretty well doesn't she?" Frédéric asked, as he looked at her picture from over my shoulder.

"Damn, she looks like the girl next door, someone who I could even be friends with," I said, as I squinted at her picture without my reading glasses. "Why have the police never apprehended her?"

"Because, she is a fixer, and a master of movement," Frédéric said. "She lives her life moving both her clients—or sorry---her *objects*, either to high-class parties or to their death. She kills with pinpoint precision, extremely quickly and disposes of their bodies while they're still warm."

I looked over at Danielle as she stood against the rail staring down at the grass. I got up and stepped over to her side and wrapped my arms around her. She was quietly crying. She turned around and faced me as she directed her eyes at her hands with a look of despair. She didn't have to say anything; I knew full well that she was thinking about Ari maliciously raping Goli alongside of Henri.

Danielle remembered Ari from her own days at the castle and luckily never experienced the vicious and animalistic hands of that woman.

"Danni," I said, as I pulled her head over to my fluffy robe and pressed her eyes against my chest. "Quiet, Danni, don't even try to speak. You've said enough already. I know what you are feeling, I do." I held her tightly.

Frédéric knew that we needed a private moment together and stepped away. I placed my hand on the back of her head and allowed Danielle to cry into my robe.

As she wept, I gazed out on to the pasture in the distance to where we had previously seen a rabbit running from its prey. I then noticed two wild coyote traversing across the pasture in direct pursuit of that frightened rabbit.

Each coyote seemed so wild and aware of its own mission to hunt the rabbit down to a kill, but at the same time both also seem so very fearful of their own volatility. They awkwardly meandered across the open pasture and dropped under the dark cover of woods.

They would find that rabbit, I thought, as I held Danielle's weeping body in my arms. They will most likely rip it to bloody pieces, consuming only what they want, while discarding the rest for the scavengers. But they will meet their own demise one day when they least expect it. I'm sure even they know that fact all too well. I could see their end-days approaching by the expression on their nervous faces. "In time they will meet their demise," I softly whispered into Danielle's ear. In time, I prayed.

Chapter 31

GOLAREH: AN EXPRESSIVE CHALLENGE

OXFORD, UK

"Holy shit, Goli, meet me at the coffee house at 7:00 p.m. Things are really starting to heat up on Henri's end," was the theme of the last four voicemail messages Timothy left on my answering machine. It was 7:20 p.m. when I checked my messages and texted him back saying that I would be there in twenty-minutes.

When I arrived, Timothy was in front of the Attendee, lighting two cigarettes at once and crossing the street towards me.

"Walk with me, Goli," Timothy said, as he handed me a cigarette.

"Talk to me," I said, skipping alongside of him in the general direction of Zelebritiez.

"Fuck coffee, I need a goddamn drink," Timothy said, as he reached for my hand and picked up our pace.

We dodged traffic on the busy street in front of Zelz and opened the glass door to make our grand entrance. The bells hanging from the door frame jingled, announcing to everyone in the bar that the man who had earned the name "ass-hole" a few days prior had just entered the building, escorting me. Michelle, my puppy-face, skinny French friend, who was always trying to watch over me, and of course Hans, the elderly Austrian

Casanova, who wanted to watch over every women in the establishment, glanced at me suspiciously as if I'd lost my mind, coming in like a couple with Mr. Ass-hole.

Timothy made a quick bee-line across the bar to the same women that he had been sitting with the night he barely escaped with whatever dignity he had left. It was as if the girls had never left the bar. Sheila, the apparent leader of the blonde bimbo-squad, smiled at Timothy and flirted with him as if he were her long lost lover returning from the sea.

As far as the bimbos were concerned, they didn't care whether he was married or not. Timothy was just another guy who paid attention to them and had cash in his pocket to spend.

"What are you doing with him, Goli?" Michelle asked, with his thick French accent, as he gave me his traditional cologne saturated hug. "I hate that man. He is a pig! He cannot be trusted," Michelle protested, as if he had somehow been a past victim of Timothy as well. "I try to tell my friends to stay away from him, but will they listen to me? No! No!! No! Do you know why they don't listen to me—Goli?" Michelle searched my face as if he were sniffing me for an answer.

"Because he told Sheila and Julia, that I am the one to watch out for! He tells them---that I am the *pig!*" He scowled at Timothy at the far end of the room. "Damn that pig! Look at him. He has no respect for women. I love all of my friends here at Zelz, but now they are calling me a pickup artist, a pig---a player! Tell me---why are you with that man? He is just a shit--- Goli, be careful with him!"

"Thanks Michelle---darling", I said, cutting our conversation short.

"As if you're not a pig as well," I thought, as I walked to the back of the room and corralled Timothy from the herd of mares in heat.

"Alright Timothy, what's going on?"

"Ok, here it is. I think I'm on to something with this prick---Henri. I've been tracking him on GPS for the last 24-hours. He has been meeting with this Ari chic, several times a week," Timothy said, as his eyes tracked Michelle and Hans moving in on his table of women. "At first I thought they were just meeting for some good sex and oh-my-lord was I right about that?"

Timothy said, rolling his eyes. "Let me tell you about the fun they are having! This Ari chick, whoever in the hell she is, sounds like she screws Henri within centimeters of his own life. The sexual intensity that bitch brings on his ass, oh my god! I have got to meet this hot bitch---someday," Timothy said, now watching the Austrian sit down right next to Sheila.

"Timothy, damn it," I snapped. "Can you talk to me and shut up about how hot you think Ari is? You have no idea who you are dealing with here."

"Why? Do you know her or something," Timothy asked, as if he wanted me to set him up on a date with her. I felt as if I was about to be sick as I thought about just how much I knew about that horrid monster.

"Do I know Ari? Get me a glass of chardonnay before I give this whole thing up with you! And please stop staring at that table over there! Can you do that for even a damn minute?"

Timothy shot a signal at the cocktail waitress for two glasses of wine as if he were a catcher telling a pitcher what ball to throw next.

"Wow baby, I mean this Ari chick sound so damn hot, I have got to find out more about her. I'll tell you baby, I could use some of that rough sex. I'm so bored with everyone else---except for maybe you." Timothy said, with a wink and a smile.

"She's so not your type, Timothy, believe me! If there is one woman on this planet that you do not want to mess with---it's Ari. Do you understand what I'm telling you, Timothy, or do I have to write it on your stupid forehead?"

"Okay Goli, don't worry about me, I'm just playing with you. Listen, here's the deal with Henri. Everything was going hot and heavy for Henri and Ari up until about three hours ago. That's when she received a message from this Santo Gordo dude. He's telling her that he's about to come to Paris and kick Henri's ass," Timothy accepted two glasses of wine from the buxom waitress.

"Thank you sweetheart---and hot-damn girl you are looking so good tonight," he said, speaking directly to her breasts.

"Timothy! Pay attention to me--here! Now tell me how did you get all of this information?"

"Through Henri's handy-dandy voice recorder app, that's how. Plus I hijacked a few of Ari's voicemails," Timothy said, as he lowered his voice and covered his mouth. "Hey, dig this baby; she probably hasn't even heard them yet. Am I good or what?" Timothy continued with a sly smile, "Apparently Henri has been ignoring Gordo and missing some- -- shall we say--- important communiqué. Hmmm---I wonder how that might have happened. This Ari bitch drilled him a new asshole for missing some real important conference-calls on their private communication link. I'm not positive, but I think Henri and Gordo have scheduled conversations using a dedicated cell service, which I think is a two-way satellite connection."

Timothy suddenly stood up with an alarmed expression. Wait just a damn second Goli; I've got to go piss on my turf!"

There he goes again, I thought as Timothy stormed over to the table of women. Just as Timothy starts to get serious, he reverts back to being a shit head.

Timothy zeroed in on the table of women, bent over and kissed Sheila on the back of her neck.

"Yuck," I thought.

"Just give me a minute, baby, and I'll be all yours," Timothy promised, as he reluctantly turned around and headed back to my table. Michelle shot him a mocking expression from the far end of the bar.

"So anyway, girl---where was I? Okay---I know. If Gordo was just threatening to come here or was just blowing smoke up Ari's little sexy ass, remains to be seen. But he certainly sounded pissed at Henri." Timothy said, with his eyes pinned to table of bimbos.

"Timothy, will you please forget about those girls over there and give me at least some of your limited attention?"

"Okay Goli, hey, seriously---do you know what? Here, the general public couldn't give two shits about Henri's behavior. Hey, any news is good news for him---so what! But this Santo guy on the other side of the world, wants to kick his lights out." Timothy said, as he stood up and tried to slide away.

"Will you sit the hell down with me, Timothy," I demanded, reeling him back in like a dog in heat.

"Tell me what you know about these two-way satellite things you just mentioned?"

"Oh yeah that. Well, I think that Henri and Gordo are doing all of their business deals over dedicated satellite-phones. Not just any communication service either. Those guys are using some real secure and extremely narrow frequency links between Gordo's office in Mexico to some place in the mountains of southern France."

"Well so? Can't you just hack into that phone like you do with the others?"

"It's not that easy, these sat-phones are a different animal altogether. They are commonly used by news organizations and the military and are highly restrictive. The phones themselves still fall victim to the same security breach as the rest of them, but--" Timothy furrowed his eyebrows and paused. "And this is a big---but. Getting those phone numbers and passing over their encrypted security barriers will require us to pull the SIM card from his actual phone."

"Well how are we going to do that, Timothy? And what in the hell is a SIM card?"

"Goli---I'll explain more to you later when I have more time. But a SIM card is this electronic chip in his phone that contains all of his information. If I can copy the information on that chip to my phone, then we are home free!"

I was now totally confused, wondering how we were ever going to be able to get our hands on Henri's SIM card. I mean taking some chip out of his satellite phone and copying the information off of it onto Timothy's phone? Was he kidding me?

"But, first things first, girl, we have got to locate his sat-phone and then figure out a way pull his SIM card. Oh here's another thing, baby. Ari keeps telling Henri to use the phone at some strange castle, somewhere in southern France. Do you have any ideas about where this castle is?"

Timothy stood up, barely waiting for my answer, and began backing away, like what we had to do was nothing more than child's play.

"Hey, we'll figure all of this stuff out later. See if you can find out about this castle place? Sorry baby but I have an entree about to be eaten by another customer, chow baby."

Timothy stopped midway to the table then suddenly returned and kissed me on the top of my head.

"At some point soon, Goli, you need to tell me more about what you know about these people. I'm sure that you know something about this castle too. You need to tell me everything soon."

"Soon---Timothy! I don't want you to jump the gun and run off half-cocked. I have to manage you! Right now, the less you know the better off you are. But Timothy, I want to warn you again, don't you ever write a story about Henri using your own name," I said, looking at him directly in the eyes.

"No worries, girly-girl. You can trust me on that one," he said, as he moved in on the table of bimbos. Then, from across the room, he yelled, "Hey Goli, You are still the hottest bitch in this place. You know that don't you? You and me---baby, one of these days, girly-girl, one of these days."

"As soon as Timothy left, Michelle dropped down and quietly claimed his seat. We sat in silence and watched the crowd intensify as the band assembled their equipment on stage. My mind began to drift to visions of my sister. I thought about how much I wanted to call her and talk to her again. Knowing that she was alive was a true blessing, but not being able to contact her was sheer hell.

What was she like these days I wondered, and how could she have become so successful in the fashion world without my even knowing it. I admit that I crawled into myself and hid in my own work, but not knowing that my own sister was a trade name in the fashion industry was a surprise to me.

"Look at that pig would you! Goli! Goli," Michelle said, as he snapped me out of my momentary dream. "This man should get off the dance floor and get a room," Michelle complained, lifting his beer bottle to his lips while watching Timothy slow dancing with a curvaceous blonde on the dance floor. "Oh, my god, look at his hands," he said, as we watched Timothy move his hand over the right side of her rear-end.

"Forget about it, Michelle, there's no hope for that man. Go find someone nice to dance with," I said, as my cell phone began to ring. I squinted at the name on my cell phone and was excited to see that it was Danielle calling in from France. I stood up and pressed the answer button, and began walking towards the door.

"Hi baby," I blurted, while Michelle looked at me inquisitively.

"Hi sweetie," Danielle said, as I worked my way past the band playing entirely too loud.

I stepped outside the bar and fumbled through my purse for a cigarette. I popped one between lips and walked over and bummed a light from another smoker. "Thanks," I nodded as he lit my cigarette.

"Where are you, baby," Danielle asked.

"I'm at Zelz with Timothy the pig," I said, as I took a long drag of much needed smoke. "Did you find Homi? How is she?"

"Oh my god, Goli, she's so--," Danielle said.

"What's she like, Danni, please tell me? Is she there, my god I want to talk to her so badly? Tell me Danni, tell me all about her!"

"Oh Goli, she is so completely wonderful. She looks exactly like you. I'm mean entirely like you, except for that tiny little difference."

"What---tell me Danni, tell me how she looks different from me?"

"Do you remember that tiny mole, Goli, you know--- that little love mark on the left side of her face?"

"Oh my god, yes, she has one on the exact opposite side of her face as I do. That's the only physical difference between the two of us!"

"Oh Goli, yes, she is so absolutely beautiful, just like you baby! And she is exactly like I remembered her too. And, girl does she ever want to talk to you! Oh baby, she wants to see you so badly."

"My god," I said as I moved into a corner of the building away from the other smokers.

"Goli, we dumped a whole lot on her yesterday and today. But she's so unbelievable strong and supportive."

"Did you tell her about us," I asked, as I saw Michelle exiting the bar and searching for me.

"Oh, baby, yes I did, and she was so completely wonderful about it."

I began tearing up as I thought of Homayra accepting Danielle's and my deep love for each other.

"She said that she is so happy for us, almost as if she knew from day-one that we fell for each other."

"Well, I'm sure that she knew about us back then too, baby. She knows me like no other person in the world," I said as I wiped the tears from my eyes. "Danni, I love you with all my heart, but Homi and I are almost identical in thoughts."

Michelle rushed back into the bar and then returned with a hand full of bar napkins to dry my eyes.

"Get away from us!" he shouted, spinning on his heals to face Timothy who was heading towards us.

"Leave her alone, you – you pig," Michelle ordered, standing guard between us both. "She does not wish to talk to you, Timothy, beat it!"

"Who's that in the background, baby? Are you okay," Danielle asked.

"Oh, it's just Michelle trying to fend off Timothy," I said, as I pressed the napkin into my eyes. "Damn it, where did my cigarette run off too," I complained, as I watched it roll towards the edge of the sidewalk and drop into a puddle. A fellow smoker offered me another one, which I openly welcomed.

"Goli, you need to stop smoking."

"I know, Danni, just not yet though. When you're away I smoke almost twice as much," I said, as I nervously, took another long drag and inhaled it deeply into my lungs. "I'm just so damn scared Danni! I know that we are on the right track with all of this, but it seems like such a long shot to stop Henri. All I ever wanted to do was get enough on Henri to scare him away from us, but now! I never dreamed that we would be learning so much more about this bastard. I feel like we are making this up as we are going along, and I don't even know what to do next," I moaned.

"I know baby, but we are making progress, Goli. Every single day Timothy finds more details on Henri, and we haven't even started looking."

I kissed Michelle's cheek and said, "Thanks for helping darling, please tell Timothy to give me a few minutes, okay."

Michelle looked at me with his eyes flaring and lips pursed while nodding his head in approval. "You must give her a few minutes, okay, Timothy—you pig!" He held out his hand in front of Timothy as if he were directing traffic.

I started to walk and talk, "Listen, Danni, tell Frédéric that Santo Gordo is beginning to get concerned about Henri's missteps in the press, and might be heading to the castle to have a word with him. But also tell him that Timothy thinks that Henri and Gordo do all of their business over a 2-way satellite phone which is at the castle. We have to come up with a plan to go back to that castle!"

"Oh my god! We have to go back to that castle? Are you kidding me?" Danielle whispered.

"Baby, listen, tell Frédéric, that we also need to start keeping tabs on Ari, she appears in the middle of Gordo and Henri. Plus, Timothy is beginning to really get out of hand! He wants to screw every person in this entire mess, including Ari herself," I yelled, as Timothy tapped me on the shoulder.

"Do me a favor baby, put that jack-ass on the phone with me right now," Danielle demanded.

"Okay, baby, here you go," I said, knowing that she was going to give him a verbal lashing.

"Timothy, Danni wants to talk to you for a second," I said, handing the phone to him as if it were a live grenade.

"Well hello there, Danni, do you miss me?"

"Timothy, I want you to listen to me----you little fuck head. You had better straighten your gnarly ass up and start taking this shit a little more fucking seriously, do you understand me? Stop thinking this is all some sort of goddamn joke! These people we are dealing with here will crack your ass in half, and that means Ari too! Help us, you little prick. Will you please work with us? Do you understand me, you oversexed dickhead? Get your head out from between your legs Timothy, playtime is over!"

"Okay, Danni! Okay, okay, Danni! I'm sorry, I will. Here's Goli," he said, handing the phone back to me while rolling his eyes. "Jesus Christ, that girl is really something else, you know that? That woman can stop an erection faster than a patrolman at a license check," Timothy said, as he walked away in search of his next party girl.

Chapter 32

GOLAREH: HITHER GREEN

Give me thy soul — said the Angel of Death to Moses
I had just returned to my flat in Oxford where I had been spending entirely too little time these days. My original plan was to spend every other weekend in Brixton at Danielle's apartment, but as the weeks clicked by I soon began breaking my own rule by staying almost exclusively with Danielle. Visits from Ari had become rare and I was beginning to think that perhaps I might have dropped off Henri's list of priorities entirely. That clearly was the wrong assumption on my part.

I entered my dark condo not even thinking about turning on the lights. The actual thought of illuminating my boring apartment made me anxious and frustrated about my ridiculous partnership with Timothy and being away from Danielle. I stood in the darkness staring off at the city lights in the distance, still wearing my coat and holding my handbag.

Suddenly my silent thoughts were interrupted by a rapid metallic tapping on my front door. I stepped into the dark living room and studied the door. Three more quick taps convinced me that the caller was not just some ordinary visitor; this one was on a mission to learn if the apartment was empty. I cautiously approached the door from the side and squinted through the peephole.

I'd been spending so many days in a row at Danielle's that my newspapers and junk mail had been piling up in the hallway by my door. From the outside, my apartment was dark so most people would assume that the resident was away.

Whoever was standing in front of my door was so close to the peephole that it was difficult for me to distinguish who it was. Suddenly the unmistakable sound of a key being inserted into the lock transformed my feeling of security to that of terror.

My hands sprung away from the side of the door as if they had been electrified. I flinched backwards into the shadows of my dark living room as I stared at the doorway. As I listened to the intruder trying key after key for the correct fit, I wondered who in the world it might be.

Finally the winning key worked as the lock gave way and the door began to slowly open. I had no place to go but backwards, to the far end of the room, against the sliding glass doors. The door opened wide and a dark human figure entered. I searched for some semblance of cover, finding only a large drafting easel with a large blue tablet of paper draped over it. I slipped behind it and prayed that I would be invisible.

The moonless night in Oxford rendered my small studio apartment unusually dark as I stood motionless behind my barrier measuring every breath I took. For some odd reason and perhaps it was because of my childhood upbringing in Tehran, my protective instincts kicked in, shielding me from complete panic.

I knew that I had no suitable form of protection against the monster in the room, so I began taking an inventory of what I could develop as a weapon. I had nothing in my handbag for protection, of course. A stapler was within reach along with a package of staples that I might be able to throw at him. So I quickly realized I was completely defenseless.

I expected the monster to turn on the overhead lights but instead he, she or it, switched on a flashlight and began examining the walls and ceiling of my living room. The intruder worked diligently in a world of his own, convinced that he was completely alone.

His neutral white LED light climbed the wall illuminating the seams of the ceiling and corners and came to a stop on a smoke detector. He then reached into his appliance bag and produced what appeared to be another smoke detector which he then swapped out with the existing one. The monster then preceded on to the kitchen and then dining area, replacing one smoke detector at a time until he had covered every room.

Could this mysterious dark figure be a maintenance man attempting to catch up on his work schedule? Not hardly, this guy was clearly in the process of bugging my apartment.

Astonishingly, I heard the monster actually lift the lid of my toilet bowl and begin to urinate. When the flush occurred, that was my queue to escape through the front door and out of the building entirely.

Once outside, I tried to call Timothy but noticed that he had also made several attempts to contact my phone which was hopelessly buried in my handbag. His last text to me read: *Come to Zelz now! We have some work to do!*

It was 1:15 a.m. when I arrived at Zelz. I needed a smoke badly so I took the opportunity to light up as I peered through the window in search of Timothy. The house band was playing some overplayed dance tune to the drunken patrons on the dance floor, and there was Michelle, my French bodyguard, kissing Sheila's neck. The *pig,* as he was now called, was hanging all over the same bimbo that Timothy was trying so hard to lure home to his bed earlier in the evening.

A burgundy Jaguar parked about nine meters away from me on my side of the street tapped its horn twice. I bent down to examine the driver and recognized Timothy's typing something into his cell phone. I tossed my cigarette into a receptacle and approached the car.

"Where in the hell have you been?" Timothy barked, as I opened the door of his Jaguar and slid in. "You couldn't even answer your damn phone, Goli? I must have called you about ten damn times!"

"I saw that you did but I couldn't get to my phone---sorry," I admitted, as I rested my exhausted mind on the head rest.

"Well, where in the hell was your handbag anyway? You know that we need to keep in touch with each other!"

"Look, Timothy, forget about it! I was having some damn company! Okay? I was visited by a professional tonight. Some surveillance monster, probably sent by Henri to check up on me---would be my guess. The guy planted some pretty sophisticated bugs all over my flat. The ass-hole made himself at home in my own damn apartment. He even had the nerve to use my own toilet. These guys are too much!"

"Didn't he know that you were in there too?"

"No, thank god, he never turned on the damn lights. He just assumed that he was alone."

"Well you know what happens when you assume," Timothy said, as he typed something into his cell phone. "And I'll tell you one damn thing; you're sure as hell not staying there tonight. You're staying with me, girly-girl."

"Yeah right, I was waiting for you to say that."

"All right, girly-girl, are you in for a little surveillance this fine morning?" Timothy asked, as he banked his way onto an exit ramp to the Lambeth Palace Freeway.

"I finally got a GPS fix on Ari and I think she's up to something big tonight. I'm also dying to check this hot bitch out first hand," Timothy said, as we increased our speed and joined the early morning traffic.

"I'm done telling you, Timothy. Be careful what you wish for."

"Sorry, Goli, no time for advanced notice on this one. A reporter's day is never done. Ari is apparently expecting a pick-up and delivery over at the Hither Green Hump Yard."

"Will Henri be there?"

"Well he sure as hell better be there, if he knows what's good for him. If he's not, that Gordo dude will kick his ass," said Timothy as he squinted at his GPS navigation map. "By the way, Goli, Hither Green Rail Yard is one of the oldest and most actively traveled transfer points in southeastern London. It's different than all of the other rail yards because it's what they call a marshalling yard, where trains can be easily separated, reconfigured and redirected to other licensed transfer points. In essence, a train can arrive in one configuration and depart a totally different animal with a brand new bill-of-lading. Oh---and listen to this, Goli, Frédéric contacted me and told me that Interpol has just discovered a train belonging to our

Dr. Lepan, which he has ingeniously reclassified for his own personal use. Perhaps this will be our chance to see it in action."

I felt myself coming alive with energy as Timothy handed me another lit cigarette. "Are you trying going to kill me with these damn things," I mumbled, the cigarette bouncing between my lips.

"No, I just know what you need, baby."

Both of our minds were reeling in over-time as we drove south into the dirty industrial floor of lower London's freight district. It was lightly raining and the fog was settling in, providing a dank shade to the already dreary and dilapidated remnants of London's industrial past. The lifeless visuals combined with my mood set the stage for an evening I was sure to be unforgettable.

Timothy switched off his headlights as our tires softly rumbled over the thick steel railroad tracks and through the quiet rail yard. The light from Timothy's cellphone illuminated his bifocals as he quietly guided the Jaguar to our destination point.

Several locomotive engines silently rested alongside of their huge siblings like massive serpents waiting for their next travel orders from some distant rail master.

"That must be them down there," Timothy said, as he squinted above his glasses to the far end of the tracks. We crossed over two more sets of railroad tracks and came within view of a long narrow warehouse that had dirty white lettering printed on the side wall: *Royal Packers — Made for England.*

A few workers appeared to be waiting for something to do on the dark loading dock. A bright round light of a lone locomotive shined patiently about a half of a meter down range, provided the only sign of life to the dark lonely evening.

The buzzing sound of an electrical charge could be heard activating the signal lights on three adjacent train tracks. They changed colors from red and orange, as the engineer of the halted train waited for a green signal.

"We are going to have to hoof it from here," Timothy said, as he maneuvered the car into a dark parking lot and doused the engine. Timothy muted his cell phone and switched it to camera mode while winking at me to do the same. The morning mist bathed my face as I stepped out of the car and calculated our distance from where we stood to the warehouse.

Since Timothy and I both had been field reporters for a number of years, we moved well together as we jogged down the tracks towards the activity on the long loading dock. A single strand of boxcars stood dormant, directly adjacent to the loading dock. Timothy and I ran beneath the shadows of the buildings until we were safely hidden behind the stranded boxcars.

The mumbling locomotive that was fixating on the signal lights posted in front of the loading dock committed a short but startlingly loud air horn blast, which echoed throughout the rail yard with a vengeance. The huge diesel engines accelerate to life as the heavy chassis strained for momentum to drag its long line of cars forward. The groan of the engines relaxed just as the train gathered up enough speed to snuggle up between the loading platforms and the stranded rail cars.

The diesel locomotive looked different from most of the other locomotives I had seen over the years, even though I must admit I've rarely taken the time to notice any of them. It was massive, standing at least eight meters tall, from the rails to the top of the dual windshields. The exterior was richly painted light blue with a white center stripe detailing the face and sides of the engine. The name *EriTrain* was stylishly printed on the side of the locomotive. A round red and white logo proudly displayed in the center of the nose of the engine the letters *ET.*

Even though we were so close to the activity on the loading dock, we had a terrible view as we searched for a better vantage point. We soon heard the apparent footsteps of what sounded like hundreds of people being ordered off the train and onto the loading platform. A police whistle pierced the morning air as the passengers were directed along their way.

I scrambled along the side of the freight cars, lost my footing and fell on railroad gravel. My exposed knuckles dug into the rough stones on the ground numbing my fingers.

Timothy grabbed my arm and helped me back to my feet and up onto an awkward connection point coupling two freight cars. I grabbed a greasy hydraulic hose which was covered in black grime and leaned out as far as I could to catch a glimpse of the activity on the loading dock. It was buzzing with activity as workers unloaded luggage and large pallets of provisions which include wine, liquor, produce and meat. A huge crowd of women and children inadequately dressed for the season, flowed off the train in clusters as officers waved their flashlights in the direction of parked Mercedes-Benz busses in the distance.

We jumped from the train onto the loading dock and ran hand-in-hand to an entrance on the far end of the building. The door was unlocked so we disappeared into a dimly lit hallway and closed the door behind us.

Suddenly we found ourselves engulfed in a putrid cloud of human sewage. The horrible vapors assaulted our eyes and nostrils with a burning cloud of ammonia.

I covered my mouth and nose with my hands and attempted to block the chocking presence of methane emanating from a cesspool of urine and feces. The palms of my hands and knuckles were still bleeding from the cuts and scrapes I had received from my fall outside on the tracks. Timothy covered my face with a silk handkerchief that he pulled from his lapel pocket. He then removed his own tie and wrapped it around his face like a bandit.

We stood staring at each other trying to comprehend the source of the stench and the layout of the long narrow building. The building appeared to be made up of a series of narrow rooms with a central hallway running through the entire length of it, with each segment separated by doors. The walls were cinderblock and painted with thick green paint.

The floors, comprised of brown washroom tiles, were filthy and with mostly clogged drains positioned about every ten feet. Each door had multiple coats of brown paint with wire reinforced glass viewing windows.

The long hallway ran for hundreds of meters with compartmentalized storage rooms on both sides. Observation windows lined the hallway, reminding me of a tour I had once taken through a livestock processing plant.

The ambient sound of the building was indistinguishable at first but soon took on the horrible tune of a moaning choir.

What was it about this horrible odor that seemed so oddly different from what one would consider as normal sewage? I had never experienced such an awful smell in my life. The stench had increased two fold as the molecules of the air burned my nostrils and caused me to buckle over and vomit on the floor. There was something more here than sewage and that I knew full well. Death was in our midst, rotting atrocious death was surrounding us.

Timothy and I stared at each other's blood shot eyes above our makeshift gas masks. The expression in Timothy's face had changed drastically from that of a seasoned investigative reporter to a dumbfounded human. We each realized that we had stumbled into a tomb of the dead and dying.

Timothy took the lead, directing me further down the hallway and opening the first door to the next storage segment. Each room on either side of us had an observation window running the entire length of the hallway. The weathered tile flooring of each room resembled a public shower with mucky drains dotting the floor. The room next to me was empty and appeared to have been recently hosed out by a loosely coiled length of fire hose on the floor. But the room on the other side of the hallway was stuffed to the ceiling with what appeared to be blue laundry bags.

Timothy tugged me along to the end of the hallway segment and opened the door to the next set of rooms. Each room on either side of the hallway was stuffed to the ceiling with the same mysterious bags. At about midway through the fourth hallway section the choir of human voices became almost deafening and distinguishable as I could now identify groans of human suffering and nonverbal cries for help.

For as long as I can remember, even as child, whenever I entered a large room, movie theatre or public auditorium, I always make a metal note of the exits. It was my survival rule and one that I finally broke. I was now in a situation of zero exit points and I began to panic.

"We need turn back, Timothy; we're in way too far!"

"Just a little further Goli, I have to see what in the hell is going on here."

Timothy opened the door to the last storage segment, where the rooms on other either side of us were illuminated. The humidity levels were uncomfortably high and the temperature was sweltering.

I knew what was in those rooms from the moment we entered the building but my mind would not allow me to go there. Slowly we advanced down the hallway in the direction of the suffering. It suddenly became frightfully obvious to me that that each room was completely saturated with the heavy presence of suffering human spirits.

Low wattage yellow light bulbs hung from the ceiling of each room painting them with a sickening mustard tinge. The stark realization of what I was now observing caused me to suddenly question my definition of reality, as Timothy frantically began snapping photos with his cell phone.

The rooms were filled with women of all ages ranging from toddlers and adolescent teenagers to what appeared to be completely expensed women. Most were sitting on the floor in their own waste, while others leaned up against the wall with their knees crouched up against their filthy faces. Many of the children lay lifeless in the laps of the older ones. Their groans of despair were beyond heart wrenching, as they huddled together resembling one huge dying human heart.

These people were not simple casualties of some mistaken civilian bombing raid. They were drained human beings expensed like humanoid carnival rides that had been run down to a salvage value of zero.

Many of the women still had signs that scarcely translated their onetime beauty. However, every bit of their god given loveliness had been chewed and sucked off of them like the chrome from a rusty trailer hitch.

One woman who had lost most of her hair was having a pitiful conversation with herself. "Why," she moaned again and again. The single tooth on her lower jaw stood out as testament of her complete loss. Her vocal articulations were so pitiful that I felt so dreadfully sad for her.

Oh my god, I thought as I studied the poor woman struggling to understand her own position under some vacant god. I was so completely affected by the appearance of that destroyed women that I buried my face against

Timothy's chest and wept. I moaned so desperately into what seemed like a tragic human abyss.

A door opened and shut at the far end of the hallway as two workers in blue jumpsuits appeared and walked with their heads down in our direction. We were just meters away from them as Timothy pulled me back to life and rushed me away.

We ran, holding each other's hand, back down the hall from where we had come. Suddenly another light switched on in the first hallway segment as a worker wrapped in loops of fire hose slowly labored in our direction with his eyes also cast to the floor.

We quickly knelt down and I grabbed the first door handle within our reach and opened it. We moved into a room as if backing into a tiny closet. The strange shaped laundry bags were directly next to us and piled to the ceiling. Each bag had a long single zipper which ran along the entire edge.

Footsteps of the approaching worker became louder and closer to where Timothy and I were hiding. My hand brushed against the side of bag and I felt what I thought was a melon or some sort of produce but to my terror I suddenly identified the unmistakable form of a human nose.

The worker carrying the length of fire hose passed by our doorway and entered the next hallway segment towards the suffering humans. The sound of his footsteps coupled with the metallic sound of the hose nozzle which trailed along floor by his side, reminded me of the Grim Reaper.

"Timothy, my god---what's in this bag! Help me unzip this thing," I whispered. I knew what was in that bag but I was unable to summon up the courage to even look at it. I spun around and again, like a baby, and buried my face in Timothy's chest.

Timothy boldly reached over and grasped the end of the longer plastic zipper and opened half of the top of the bag revealing the hideous contents. Lying in the bag, like a dried flower was the smashed flat face of what was once a vibrant young woman.

I didn't have the tears to cry as I attempted to wrap my mind around this crumpled human figure. It wasn't the smashed facial structure of the poor child that unhinged me the most. It was her delicate hands that were still pressed against her destroyed face as if she was shielding herself from someone. Her carefully manicured fingernails were painted with pink nail polish will remain in my memory for the rest of my days on earth.

"The coast is clear, Goli," Timothy said, as he snapped off another dozen shots of the body bags. We staggered out of the room and down the hall running backwards as Timothy held my wrist with one hand and fired off rapid camera shots with the other.

"We have to go now!" Timothy ordered.

We left the rooms of death with a feeling as if we had both been pummeled with blunt force mental trauma.

As we ran I noticed the man with the fire hose opening the door to the room of dying prisoners and positioning himself in a fireman's stance with his right hand gripping the water valve.

A long fire hose trailed along the floor and through the entire length of the hallway like a rigid snake pleading for relief. The sound of water bursting through the cold metal nozzle whistled and screamed like sick monster breathing fire on the helpless human captors within the room.

The sound of high-pressure water blasting against the human masses echoed through the building with visual character. Choruses of screams and moans increased exponentially as the water blasted against their filthy bodies with a relentless force.

I couldn't take it any longer as I broke away from Timothy's hold and ran as fast as I could in the direction of the horrible hose-man. I wanted to kill him with my bare hands as I struggled with the doorknob to the next chamber. How could this traitor of mankind dare treat those people with such disrespect, I asked myself as I stammered helplessly towards the heart of the abuse.

Timothy tackled me from behind me and forced me to the floor. I helplessly strangled the fire hose beneath my body with my hands, in a futile attempt to stop the flow of water.

"Stop it, Goli, stop it! We have to get out of here---now! We can't save them," Timothy yelled, as he lay on top of me as the murderous force of the water traveled through the hose beneath me and against the doomed souls in the room of death.

"Oh my god, I have to help those people," I cried as Timothy dragged me away from the songs of human madness.

We reached the end of the hallway and stumbled into the black morning air expelling the fumes of the dead and desperately retrieving fresh moist air into our starving lungs.

Chapter 33

GOLAREH: A MIND ALTERING EXPERIENCE WITH SIDE EFFECTS

The train stood motionless alongside the busy loading dock as workers performed their tasks of moving pallets of body bags as if they were nothing more than loads of horse feed.

"This way, Goli, follow me," Timothy said, as he held my hand and led me along the darkened edge of the building. We skipped beneath the shadows of the building and alongside the motionless train. The low groan of the locomotive engine reminded me of a snoring giant resting before his next travel order. We ducked into a tiny dark alleyway within perfect view of the loading process.

Between ten and sixteen Mexican workers performed separate tasks requiring no supervision. Two men were constructing large cardboard boxes used for packing what the box indicated was swordfish. Each box had a stamped logo on each side, depicting the picture of a swordfish in the center of a large blue circle. *Epic Seafood Industries - Mexico City* was printed below the logo with a slogan saying *Enjoy the taste of the ocean!*

Another two men shoveled ice from a large container on a mobile platform into the boxes below. Each container was then positioned in single file along a processing line.

Body bags on pallets were staged into position in front of each box, as two men at the head and feet of each bag, lifted and tossed the bags over the top of each box as if it were nothing more than a simple game.

Timothy desperately captured every movement of the process on his cell phone, which was recording in video mode. Once each box was stuffed with four body bags, the ice crew arrived and topped each box off to its capacity while building a large cone of ice above each box. The boxes were then tethered together with metal fasteners, and tagged with bills of lading. In total we counted forty-five ice packed cargo boxes loaded by a large expansion arm into the base of six grain cars.

Just when I thought that my mind had absorbed as much as it possibly could, Timothy directed my attention to a long line of soaking wet refugees. Slowly they advanced from the building towards a group of empty box cars. Three dock workers angrily directed the pitiful humans through the doors of each train car as if they were nothing more than a herd of unhealthy goats.

"Ándale! Ándale! Arriba! Arriba!" They ordered as they pushed the exhausted humans through the doors of each car. There appeared to be no food or water available for them in the boxcars and the floors were covered in hay. I lacked the ability to count the number of departing souls, but before it was all over, four box cars were filled to capacity as the doors were slammed shut and secured with double crossbar security locks.

In the shadows we sat watching and recording this hideous show of organized human disposal. Timothy gently wrapped his arms around my back and held me close, as my mind tripped along the peaks and valleys of my turbulent emotions. I quivered and rocked in pain as my horrible thoughts began to position themselves throughout my mind like venomous bats clawing at my mental architecture.

As horrible as it was for us to witness, the seemingly oblivious dock workers seemed nonchalant with the stench, dead and sinful jobs they were performing.

Little did they appear to notice the gravity of their own actions, as they completed every one of their tasks flawlessly. Some chewed tobacco, sang songs and smoked cigarettes as they worked through the night.

I realized that day, why those workers were so hardened to their actions. It was because they were also human slaves of Henri's empire, who had lost their will to care a long time ago.

I trembled and shivered with my face pressed against Timothy's body, whimpering like a child, unable to observe any more horror. Soon the loading dock was empty of all cargo and personnel as the engine of the locomotive awoke from its restful slumber.

The huge locomotive carcass, with its multiple diesel cylinders, slowly moved into ignition mode with all systems building to positioning strength. The metal couplers slammed together in sequential order from the front car down to the very last one, as the long train organized itself into a sleepy crawl in reverse.

An overhead grain shoot positioned itself over the top-center of each of the grain cars and deposited a complete load of pungent cedar shavings into each rail car up to its capacity. Loads of chips climbed a narrow conveyor belt and dropped through a funnel opening into each car to one by one.

After the last of the six grain cars were loaded to capacity the fifteen-hundred horsepower diesel engine accelerated up to station-departure speed and moved away from the loading dock. The mighty engine pushed the long line of rail cars into the classification yard with ease.

The strong locomotive pressed the long line of train cars onto an intricate layout of disposition tracks. Car after car of empty freight units were dispersed in directions from right and left as other cars were spawned off and attached to other trains.

In the end, twenty completely loaded general shipment cars were now attached to the newly configured AriTrain before sounding its air horns and disappearing into the darkness of London's mass transit rail channel.

Timothy and I were now completely exhausted, slumped in our narrow alleyway on the wet concrete with our backs against the brick wall. I rested my head against Timothy's comforting body, which had become both welcoming and most importantly, alive.

My mind was racing in so many directions, trying to organize what we had just seen and also desperately trying to forget as much as was humanly possible. I felt as if I had become 20-years older in the space of only 20-minutes.

We sat in our hidden crevice completely out of view of the vacant loading dock, cloaked in the darkness as we slipped off into a dream-like stupor. What else was there to see as my newly rearranged mind unraveled dreams of mutilated carcasses and dying people? My stomach churned with nausea as my mouth baked with the remnant taste of human sewage and rotting flesh.

I couldn't recall whether I was sleeping or experiencing a nightmare when I was suddenly jolted awake by the sound of two people arguing within meters from where we were hiding. A man and a woman spoke in a mixture of broken Spanish and French.

"...Welcome it? Well I guess I do sort of welcome it----a little bit I expect," the elderly man, standing just out of view, said. "And yes I do think these stupid reporters are imbeciles and have nothing better to live for."

"He just thinks you're getting sloppy, Henri," the female voice responded in a stern tone.

Timothy and I listened intently to the couple, who were standing so close to us we could smell the woman's perfume. Might this be Henri and Ari? I wondered. The weight of my cramped body pressing against Timothy made it too difficult for us to reposition ourselves to view the conversation without producing a sound.

"He's just not happy with you, Henri," the woman scolded, as she flipped open her metal lighter, lit a cigarette, and then snapped it shut, producing the classic metallic snap. "Santo just needs some assurance that you have things under control." The distinct smell of her menthol cigarette entered our dark hiding place.

"That I have things under control," Henri scoffed. "Ari darling, never ever question my devotion to my brother Santo again. He should know by now that he can trust me with his fucking life. Besides---I have made him wealthier than he would have ever dreamed. But now---he must also trust me! Frankly my dear, I'm insulted that he would send you to pass along his concerns to me. How dare him---that coward!"

"Henri, darling, my cousin Santo trusts no one and you should know that by now. You---my friend, even you, must understand the importance of being loyal to my cousin. He trusts no one. He also doesn't understand this organization you are trying to establish with the UN. Why Henri? Why, he asks me. Why---must you be trying to create an army against us?"

"Because, I as I've told you Ari, I run my side of the business---my damn way. Tell him it's for our own security, it's an insurance policy! I now control the press, I now control the borders and *now*---control the law," Henri yelled.

"This organization within the UN, presents no threat to us, but will damage the hell out of our competition. The whole thing is designed to keep us all safe. Tell him that Ari! Tell him! Loyalty, fuck him! Santo should understand my motivation----goddamn him!"

"Well he's just having trouble understanding your logic and thinks you are being foolish and sloppy," interjected Ari. "Even here tonight, Henri, the spoilage factor with these objects has simply become unacceptable! Our last shipment of these objects could barely be used for fertilizer. The place reeks to high heaven, Henri; I hate to even come down to this god forsaken place anymore, it even makes my clothes smell. Henri, listen to me! I collect these objects, so the least you could do is ship them out of here before they begin to rot!" She paused. "Henri for your own good, tighten up on your end of the operation. You know how much I love you---but you can't keep missing calls and scheduled meetings with my cousin! Santo said that you are fucking up way too often and that you are showing a lack respect for him, Henri--- and he will not tolerate that!"

"Oh my god---Ari, I never thought I would here these words coming from you," Henri yelled. "Santo needs to show me some goddamn loyalty too. I will not tolerate such treatment any longer!" Henri stomped his feet like a child. "Please Ari, I'm tired and I want to go home and go to bed. Please let's go home now, I am tired of this ridiculous line of scolding by of all people---you," he pleaded, as they kissed each other quietly.

"Come let's go home, Henri, I'm going to fuck you until you are unconscious," Ari promised, as the sounds of their footstep faded away.

Timothy and I remained in the alleyway for several minutes, allowing them to leave the property. It was 4:30 in the morning when we made our way back to the car. Timothy was grinning as he opened my car door and helped me in. "I recorded that entire conversation on tape, Goli, but damn, I still never saw what she looked like."

I was completely lethargic when I collapsed against the comfortable leather seats during the drive back to Timothy's apartment. All I needed was a safe place to sleep, a shower and time to get my thoughts in order. I had so many unanswered questions about this ever-expanding industry which Henri had developed, but it would have to wait until after I slept when Timothy and I could begin reconstructing all of what we had witnessed at this death terminal. Now I must sleep, I thought, please God---let me sleep.

"Wake up sunshine," a distant voice whispered in my ear. "Rise and shine, sleepyhead, its way past noon," the voice said louder. My eyelids slowly began to open to a completely foreign environment. All aspects of the room were unrecognizable to me including the mirror on the ceiling above me and the oversized, round bed.

"Girl, you were out like a light, I must say," Timothy said, as he handed me a cup of coffee.

Oh my God, I thought, what in the hell am I doing in Timothy's bed?

"No worries---love, you are quite safe and together, I might add," Timothy cheerfully said.

What did he mean by the phrase: *quite together?* I quickly performed a quick inventory under the blanket and realized I that my clothes were still on.

"Darling, I'll have you know that I was a very good boy and only removed your shoes. You were out like a light."

I laid there in disbelief trying to gather the reality of both where we were the night before and how I got into Timothy's bed. The events of last night were so cluttered in my mind that I was clueless as to what was happening.

"Goli, darling, please drink your coffee and give yourself time to wake up. We have much to unravel here. We saw so much last night that we need to process this together."

Timothy poured more black coffee from a pot into my cup, took in a deep breath, stood up from the edge of the bed and began walking across the room.

"Oh by the way, can I can tell you something, Goli?" I nodded from above my coffee cup.

"You are the most beautiful woman I have ever had in that bed, without being in there with you! And let me tell you something else--- girly-girl, I have had some damn good looking women in that bed!" Timothy rolled his eyes and left the room.

I glanced up at my hideous reflection in the mirror above and let out a huge sigh of relief, realizing full well that Timothy really had a good heart somewhere in his nutty soul. His male urges, however, were just way out of control for his own good and his impulsive lifestyle worried me.

I knew he was becoming frustrated about not being able to put his name on a big story and his anxiety was only going to get worse. That was why I couldn't give him too much information at any one time, because he would run off halfcocked. But, last night he treated with me with the utmost respect and care so I really couldn't ask for more.

As the caffeine began to wake my extremities and clear my mind, details from the night before started to come alive. How was I going to stay in that apartment of mine with all of those cameras recording my every move, and why did Henri choose this moment to increase his surveillance on me. Might he think I was behind some of the many press gaffs? Quite possibly, I thought, but perhaps there was more. Maybe he was sensing Homayra's subconscious awareness of me and wanted to keep a closer eye on me. I'm sure she was dreaming visions of me as well and Henri was most likely beginning to notice it.

While those dreams and memories were frightening, they paled in comparison to what we witnessed last night at the rail yard. I also thought of how fortuitous it had been to be sitting so close to Henri and Ari as they argued over their concerns about Santo Gordo. Perhaps these fateful opportunities were a sign of the gods lining up the stars for us. Perhaps NOT, I concluded. God had rarely lined up any damn thing for me for my entire life. My fate was always oriented in one direction and that was downward towards hell.

I rested against my pillows and quietly sipped my coffee. Danielle and Frédéric popped into my mind along with my dear sister Homayra. There was now so much to give Frédéric for Interpol to process and so much that Danielle and Homi needed to protect themselves against. But I had to wake up first and compare notes with Timothy. Everything needed to be done properly, with the utmost precision; otherwise we could all be destroyed and too many lives would continue to fall victim to Henri's human disposal.

"Goli," Timothy called from outside the door. "You might find this odd but I've laid out some clean clothes in the bathroom for you to wear. Don't worry love, they're all perfectly clean. They're just leftovers from some of my more successful evenings at home. Please feel free to take a long shower; it will do you a world of good."

You must be completely mad, I thought. Take a shower in Timothy's bathroom and put on the clothing of the women he's had his way with? The thought seemed simply ridiculous if also a bit humorous. But, I could smell the remnants of death and rotting bodies from the night before in my hair and soon realized that a long shower was not a bad suggestion.

I undressed and took one of the longest showers I had taken in many days. I washed my hair twice and cleansed my entire body with soap, scrubbing away the horrible remains of the night before. Timothy tapped on the door outside and said, "Goli, you should find everything you need in there so please help yourself."

To my surprise, Timothy's bathroom was appointed like a five star hotel. The many women Timothy had invited to his condo over the past several months were at least pampered, even though he would probably never see them again.

I squeezed the water out of my hair and fashioned it in a single braid which hung down the center of my back. A clean pair of Calvin Klein jeans fit like a glove and I actually liked the black tank top. Timothy even provided me with a brand new bra and a package of panties.

When I entered the kitchen Timothy was busy cooking breakfast and pouring juice into a glass. The breakfast bar was set with fine breakfast china and the kitchen had a pleasant aroma of flowers and vegetable omelets.

Timothy stood frozen when he saw me walk in.

"What are you looking at?" I asked, as I walked into the kitchen in my bare feet.

"God almighty, Goli, you look so amazingly beautiful. Danni is one lucky girl, I must say."

"My lady, let's have coffee outside on the patio shall we?" Timothy asked, as we stepped out with our cups.

Thick billowy clouds slowly moved against the dark blue sky above us as Timothy lit two cigarettes in his standard fashion and handed one my way. I sat my coffee cup down on the stone wall and took a long drag off my first cigarette of the day. What was it about smoking that I found so refreshing? I knew full well that it was bad for me, but it seemed to both calm my nerves and wake up my thought processes at the times I needed it the most.

I stood there looking into Timothy's eyes with feelings of both gratitude and humility. We stared at each other with a renewed appreciation for each another, almost as if we were sole survivors of a terrible airplane crash. We had created an odd blend of familial love and kindred respect for each other in just the last 24-hours. I reached up and kissed Timothy on the cheek.

"Thank you, Timothy. Thank you very much for everything you have done."

We looked into each other's eyes as if we were two children trying desperately to comprehend the meaning of life. I reached for Timothy again and hugged him, knowing full well that he was suffering for answers just as much as I was. For the first time since I met Timothy we were now working together on a common goal.

We slowly released each other and studied each other's eyes in bewilderment.

"Timothy, what in God's name did we witness last night?"

Timothy took a long drag off his cigarette and stared towards the sky as he slowly released a steady stream of smoke into the morning air. I did the same as we both studied the peaceful activity of the people on the streets below.

I wondered how different we had just become from the world around us. How completely altered the structures of our brains were that morning as opposed to how they were just the day before?

"*Bête sauvage*," I said aloud, as I sipped the last taste of my coffee. "*Savage beasts* they all are."

A BRIEF INTERMISSION OF SORTS

HOMAYRA:

Present day, 9:50 p.m. - The Palais Garnier Opera House - Paris, France – UNESCO Foundation Dinner

Frédéric's blurry human figure came into focus as he slowly entered through the brightly lit entrance in the back of the opera house. The door behind him closed and he stood motionless, resembling a sentry at a guard post.

Just moments earlier, six of Henri's security officers were approached from behind and simultaneously disarmed by a strikingly attractive team of female officers from Interpol. Some of Henri's men, dressed in their custom made black suits, white shirts and dark ties, were still wearing their sunglasses.

Radio communication among the armed guards was suddenly jammed, as a combined team of officers from both NYC and Paris retrieved each man's Ruger P89 Semi-Automatic pistol without incident. The completely oblivious audience continued to stare intently at my sister and me as we traded off our heartfelt stories from each side of the stage.

Zooli confidently stood up and left her post on the side of the massive marble stage and followed the center walkway to the far end of the opera house to meet Frédéric. The dignitaries who had been sitting next to Henri had been quietly escorted from the table shortly after the program began, without Henri even being aware of it. Henri was engrossed in listening to the unexpected life stories unfolding from the identical twins on stage.

As the lights from one of the two major lighting groups swept across the lower seating level, Henri took notice of the two newcomers sitting on each side of him. His initial reaction to the two beautiful women was one of excitement; however his expectations soon wilted as he realized who they were.

Henri recognized the women's classic style because he had actually retained their professional services in the past. The two blondes were known as RF Units who performed services alright, but not the type of services Henri was accustomed to providing. They were each highly trained members of an elite all-female, Interpol retrieval unit known as The Royal Flush. Henri's face also flushed to a pale shade of red, especially when he noticed Zooli and Frédéric casually pass by his table on their way to the front of the room.

I'm sure that the emotion Henri was feeling at this particular moment was one that was almost completely foreign to him, one of embarrassment. I would also suggest that at this point in the evening, Henri still possessed a high degree of confidence in his ability to evade any level of downstream fallout; simply because of the sheer number of people he had under his thumb and the complete lack of any substantive proof of his involvement.

The one concern, however, that I'm sure Henri simply could not shake was his rapidly decomposing relationship with his dear friend and business partner, Santo Gordo. Gordo's zero-tolerance court-of-law placed him at the top of Henri's hierarchy of problems, with Gordo playing the judge, jury and executioner. Gordo's court followed his own due process, which was instantaneous and void of representation, delays, or appeals.

Henri knew that he was extremely vulnerable against these malicious reporters, but still confident that he would fix the matter. But time was not on Henri's side when it came to Santo Gordo. Henri knew that the moment Gordo detected any crack in his own shield, his death countdown would begin, and even Henri's own mother wouldn't receive his ashes. His body would become part of the gold alloy in Gordo's 22 kt crown-gold toilet bowl.

It was now 10:30 in the evening, and my sister and I had been speaking for exactly 94-minutes, according to amber colored numbers on the digital stopwatch attached to our podium. I considered providing an intermission to the stunned guests; but with the immeasurable amount of interest of the entire audience, I decided against it.

Henri gazed down at the table with a look of embarrassment, as he fumbled with the now obsolete, gold lettered program under his fingertips. He was now beginning to realize that his own personal program was becoming obsolete as well.

-We continued our story

Chapter 34

HOMAYRA: THE SUFFERING NON-OFFENDER

Colombier-Saugnieu, France

The mere thought of heading back home to Paris and spending a second in the same room with Henri caused chills to climb up my back. However, the consequences of not following a precise plan of action would have been absolutely devastating. Not only did my entire family's welfare and safety depend upon our success but so did the lives of the many people who were in the clutches of Henri's machine. I had to maintain my usual schedule and outward behavior with Henri as if I knew nothing at all.

Not only was it vitally important for me to keep my major discovery of my long lost sister a secret but also the fact about Frédéric's formal involvement with the international police. It felt incredibly empowered to know that the authorities were actively working behind the scenes as my sister and Timothy provided information. It was no longer *we victims* struggling under the weight of this horrible monster. The forces were now mobilizing around Henri Lepan.

The very next day I was scheduled to speak in front of another group of governmental slobs who clearly could care less about my mission. What is it about fighting evil that is so unfashionable and distasteful to the masses? Henri now personified the picture of evil dressed in a costume of good. I had to prepare for my opening statement at Ministry of Finance.

The new organization clearly must be endorsed and financed, especially in light of everything I had just learned about human trade. While Henri's desire for the creation of the commission was motivated by his own dark forces, removing him from the equation was completely necessary, but at just the right time.

Frédéric, Danielle and I spent a peaceful morning relaxing from our exhausting epiphanies the night before. As Frédéric and I walked through the horse pastures, we talked about the many wonderful horses we once had at the castle. We also reminisced about the wonderful Zooli, who had tried her best to save us from falling victim to the trade as well. Frédéric told me that Interpol had assigned a special investigation group to develop a history profile on Zooli and any possible living family members she might still have.

Who was Zooli really and where did she come from? Was she even still alive? Was Zooli still in harm's way, and if so, what sort of chain did Henri have on her to keep her in check for so many years? Frédéric was already working on the answers to those questions and expected a preliminary report within the next few days. It was somehow becoming apparent that Zooli might be called upon to play a role in the mechanics of the big lock we all were determined to crack.

Since Frédéric's country house was almost three hours south of Paris, I realized that I had a real problem with meeting my scheduled appointment in Amiens, which was 120 km north of Paris. I simply had to find a way to appear at my meeting the next day looking both fresh and on point. It was time for me to call upon the only resource available to me, my traveling office which Henri was always pushing for me to use, the Gulf Stream G650 Jet now stationed somewhere in France.

The closest airstrip to me that was capable of allowing a Learjet of that size to land was in Lyon at the Saint Exupéry Aéroport. I searched through my hand bag for my special instructions card with the disgusting picture of me embossed in the center of it. A call was placed and answered on the second ring and with no questions asked I was told I could expect the jet to be available at 2:00 p.m. in Lyon.

Danielle and Frédéric dropped me off at the airport like any other traveler in a hot-pink taxi cab. I cried when I kissed them both and said farewell for the time being. We agreed to use our cell phones for communication but only for short, non-descriptive conversations. It was heartbreaking to leave them behind but we had no choice. We each had to go on with our plan regardless of how sketchy it was.

The huge tail section of the Gulfstream G650 stood prominently off to the side on a dedicated runway. I flashed my special instructions card to the airport security guard and was granted immediate access to the tarmac leading to the open door of the jet. No one inquired about my lack of luggage or why I was in Lyon in the first place. Just a pleasant handshake from a handsome and extremely welcoming pilot and we were on our way.

My voicemail had a message from Henri who told me that he missed me terribly and hoped that I had a nice time on my shopping spree. He also said that he had heard of the nasty comment by the minister of Finance who insulted me the day before, about how sexy I looked when I showed passion about rape, human slavery and child sexual abuse. He said that he completely understood my anger and vowed swift revenge.

Henri said that he had been called away on business and hoped to see me in Amiens. If he failed to make it back in time, then he wished me the very best of luck with my speech.

"Good luck my darling, I can't wait to see your beautiful face again. I love you so very much," he said, as I held down my intestinal bile. Henri's face which had gradually become tender to me during the months past, suddenly changed, within a space of 24-hours, into the face of Satan.

As I entered the spacious quarters of the Gulfstream jet I was amazed by sheer luxury. The cabin was 16 meters long with an interior that was all state-of-the-art. The jet was paneled in mahogany with more than 14 extra-large windows. The attractive captain chuckled as he told me that the jet even provided me with 100-percent fresh oxygen, guaranteed to cure even the worst of hangovers. I'm sure he'd seen his share of hedonistic spoiled brats spending precious tax money while acting like drunken kings.

The rear of the jet was comprised of a bedroom, dressing room and a spacious bathroom with a shower. I also found a complete supply of clothing meticulously arranged for any business setting. How was all of this suddenly available to me? Who was paying for this insane luxury well before our organization was even approved?

I went in the dressing room and changed into a comfortable pair of jeans and a nice cotton top as the pilot sat in the cockpit entering his flight plans into the bright colored array of touch screen navigation monitors. I went back to my seat and buckled my seatbelt as the captain fired up both jet engines and proudly maneuvered the beautiful plane onto our approved runway.

The twin Rolls-Royce BR700 turbofan engines increased in velocity with the rich sound of both power and technology. We moved down the runway in a quick burst and catapulted into the dark blue sky like a bird into the heavens.

We arched around the airport as if we were on a roller coaster. I gazed through the window at the French countryside and could actually see Danielle's bright pink taxi cab slowly making its way along a major highway far below. That tiny pink dot so far beneath me contained my saviors, I thought, as it seemed to move so slowly back home to my dear sister and our brand new lives ahead. I was feeling stronger every moment as my entire purpose in life began to reenter my previously vacant soul. I was finally going to get my life together and I would hold my dear sister Goli in my arms one day very soon.

After the jet leveled off at 7,200 meters I sat down at my desk and logged on to the internet to check my messages. I located a copy of my prepared speech for the next morning and printed it out on a laser printer which was ergonomically designed into the wall panel of the cabin. I made a few edits and then dropped down to the news highlights of the day. My attention was immediately drawn to yet another news article about Henri. This time, however, the news was not about some tasteless remark he made about homosexuals or a joke about race, color or religion. This news item seemed to have teeth:

UK Deputy Prime Minister questions French Trade Minster Lepan about unclassified train

3:29 p.m. BST — In a surprise strike from left field, Louise Hebberling, the Deputy Prime Minister of the United Kingdom, charged France's Trade Minister, Dr. Henri Lepan, of flagrant misuse of AriTrain, a state-owned transportation utility. Hebberling accused Lepan with privately separating train operations from the railway infrastructure and providing transportation privileges to unknown corporations including a trading partner in Mexico identified as Santo Gordo. The bold claim surfaced just two weeks after the French Trade Minister leveled a shocking remark about Hebberling's sexual orientation to which Lepan immediately responded with what many in the gay and lesbian community described as a comedic apology.

Hebberling referred to Lepan as a rail privateer who extends favors to others while paying himself £ 2m last year alone from unaudited rail revenues. The statement touched off a firestorm of formal inquiry with the French Minister of Public Works and the Ministry of Transport.

EriTrain is classified as a French owned freight railway service connecting London with Paris and Brussels; however, with a fleet size of only one, coupled with the fact that EriTrain operates free of any home station, Hebberling's remarks caused many people to demand answers.

An unknown reporter contacted the deputy prime minster early this morning with the news after a source spotted the train taking on freight cars at the Hither Green Rail Yard in the south of London. The French Office of Trade has not yet commented on the inquiry and Dr. Henri Lepan has not released a statement to the press.

This latest press flap is one in as many as a dozen shocking reports that are causing many party members to question Lepan's mental stability. When questioned about extravagant trips and dinner parties, Lepan simply laughed off the questions as being politically motivated. However sources close to the office of trade report that Lepan is beginning to show frustration and even anger over the many news gaffs in the press world on an almost daily basis.

The flight from Lyon to Amiens was rather short but very comfortable. Flying around in this sort of luxury liner at the complete expense of the taxpayers was something I could never do on a regular basis. I packed a few of the things that I needed from the plane into a travel bag and approached the bulkhead to disembark.

"Well, did you enjoy your maiden flight, Miss Parastou?" asked the pilot in a noticeably polite American accent.

I lowered my sunglasses and said, "Oh, absolutely, it was a wonderful trip. I simply cannot believe this plane, it is so magnificent!"

"Well it is certainly my pleasure to fly such a wonderful woman around this country and I look so forward to your next call," he replied.

"Do you plan to stay long in Amiens?"

"Oh not long, I plan to return to Paris tomorrow evening."

"Will Dr. Lepan be joining you this evening or are you on your own, Ms. Parastou?"

"Well I'm not sure, I was expecting Henri but he was apparently called away on some emergency business affair, so at present I'm not sure exactly what my schedule is going to be."

"Ms. Parastou, I saw you on television the other night during an interview and I just wanted to tell you and Dr. Lepan just how much I appreciate what you are doing."

I took his warm hand in response. "Why thank you so very much for caring, sir." His words had taken me off guard and hit me with tenderness as I immediately felt his emotion beginning to build.

"Ms. Parastou, ten years ago my sister's daughter, Kelly, went missing. I loved her so much but she was so very hard for us to handle. My sister Lisa could not control her anymore so Kelly came to live with us. Her depression and drug use was much more than my ex-wife and I ever expected. We tried so hard to snap her out of her downfall but she became too hard to reach.

She was such a beautiful child, Ms. Parastou, with so much potential. But she would also strike out in anger at my ex and me for no reason. It soon became apparent to us that we simply could not be of help to her anymore. We were working on sending her to a support home in Asheville, North Carolina, for troubled women when she met a flashy man in a bar, who said that he was from California. My ex-wife called him a gigolo. You know, a ladies' man, with a fancy car and lots of money.

Before we knew it, she had vanished, completely disappeared without a trace. About a month later we began receiving letters from Kelly saying that she was doing well. She said that she was working for some art dealer in Los Angeles, but never gave us her address."

He took a deep breath and looked off at the terminal in the distance through the open door. "On Christmas day two days later my sister called me and said that the police had located her body in a wooded area near a popular beach in San Diego. She had been brutally beaten to death.

My sister lived in Charlotte, North Carolina and I lived in Beaufort, South Carolina and we were both pinching pennies at the time. We drove across country in my Ford pickup truck and arrived three days later. Her body had been placed in a refrigerated morgue for us to identify her. Identifying her body was the hardest and most horrible thing I ever had to do in my life," he said, as I pressed the knuckles on his hand. Tears came to his eyes and his voice crumbled as he continued.

"Her face still contained aspects of that beautiful fresh look that we all loved so much. She was a natural blonde with the cutest smile that re-minded me of a day at the beach. She was a day-at-the beach! God---I loved her sweet look," he said staring at the sky. "It was the condition of her body that shocked us both. It was as if she had been completely over-drawn by something very powerful.

She never had a desire for a tattoo, like the rest of her friends, and that was always a good sign, telling us that perhaps she respected her body. However, in her mouth, under her bottom lip there was a rather crude Spanish symbol along with a number. The homicide investigator said that it had something to do with a brand. You know the sort of brand animals like cattle or sheep would have to identify them.

Apparently, Ms. Parastou, she had been under the complete influence and control of a Mexican prostitution ring."

My body shuddered as I reflected back on the conversation I just had the night before with Danielle and Frédéric. Might it be the same organization that was responsible?

"Who killed her and why she died was never determined, but it appeared that her death was not due to a crime of passion. She looked as if she was simply extinguished because she had nothing more to give," the pilot said.

"We later learned that she had been held captive in some sort of organized sex trafficking gang. The girls were severely mistreated, beaten one minute and then raped the next. Why were they beaten so much? I asked the investigator and we were told that it was their way of keeping the girls in line. They wanted to break them down. Many of the girls were actually locked in cages and water boarded. Ms. Parastou, can you even imagine this sort of brutality," he said, as he gathered my hands in his.

"When we returned home from California, my sister Lisa was never the same. She acted like she was doing better, but it was all an act. She even wrote a book about Kelly, about how she was free again, like a humming bird. The theme of the book was about how humming birds are very beautiful but can never be caught. She also wrote about how she actually forgave the murderer.

Last year, Ms. Parastou, Lisa visited a sexual trauma center and gave a speech to a group known as *non-offenders,* family members of victims of rape and murder. People were very touched and also confused by her ability to forgive the perpetrators and put aside her anger so well. How could she be so forgiving they wondered as they watched my sister's expression suddenly turn blank. She quietly stood up and walked out the front door. The entire the group watched in horror as my sister purposely stepped into the busy rush hour traffic directly in front of truck and was killed.

Non-offenders are what the support groups call us. My dead sister Lisa and I are among this sad population of non-offenders! There are millions of us suffering non-offenders out there today praying for your success, Ms. Parastou. We desperately want you to succeed," he said, as lowered his head and broke down.

"I hate being a goddamn non-offender, Miss Parastou! I hate it with all of my soul. I am not like my sister; I will never forgive those monsters for what they did to my dear Kelly. Never in a million years!" he said as he turned his head away from me and wept.

"Oh my god," I said, as I drew this poor man into my space. My arms went around his shoulders and I pressed my hands deep into his upper back and felt his pulse and elevated heartbeat. "I'm so very sorry to hear of this, my dear man. I am so dreadfully sorry for your pain and loss."

As we hugged each other I felt an immense desire to never let him go. I wanted to talk to him much more. It felt so wonderful to finally have a man ask me about my life; to have a man be human again and show his heart. The fact that he cared enough to recognize who I was and what I was devoting my life to was overwhelming to me. He had seen me on television and wanted to know more about me.

"So when I saw you on the news the other night, I thought that if I ever saw you again, I wanted to learn more about you. I don't know what your motivations are and why you feel that you must take on such a difficult task, but I'm sure there must be a major reason. If you ever feel like sharing your story with someone, consider me as someone who would listen and understand."

"I plan to station here overnight and certainly could be available to fly you back to Paris tomorrow afternoon if needed. So please understand that I can be available at your request. Ms. Parastou, what happened to my niece haunts me every single day. I have never really been able to talk to anyone about it, even to my ex-wife." He paused. "I witnessed something else when I was in San Diego identifying my murdered niece. Would you like to know what I saw, Miss Parastou?"

I suddenly found that I could not speak as I looked into the soulful eyes of the pilot and nodded my head.

"I saw a homicide detective and a small police force completely under equipped to battle the powerful forces that destroy so many lives. I witnessed these lovely men and women in law enforcement simply catching the burned bodies as they fell from the sky.   So many burning souls falling from the sky at once. Someone must go after these organizations which are killing these pitiful victims and stop them at their root. I pray for you, Miss Parastou. I pray for your success."

We held each other in our arms in silence for what seemed entirely not long enough.

"Oh, Miss Parastou, I know that we briefly met once before but I was rude not to introduce myself formally. My name is Richard, Richard Edward."

"Well, it is certainly a pleasure to meet you, too, my dear Richard. I'm not sure if I do have your direct number on my special instruction card here but--," I said fumbling through my purse.

"Well please take my personal card, it has my email address and direct number on it and know that I am entirely at your service," Richard said, as he pressed the card into the palm of my hand.

I didn't even want to get off the plane. There was something just so wonderfully attractive about this man and the mysterious chemistry we both suddenly had for each other. His thoughtful honesty and kind way was something I suddenly so desperately wanted at that point of my life. I found myself gazing into his eyes thinking about myself sitting in the park with him and just holding his hands.

It was now definitely time for me to get off the plane. I was feeling parts of my soul opening up faster than what I thought was considered appropriate. I felt like a frozen flower covered in the snow for a wintery lifetime, finally coming to life.

Perhaps the release from the night before with my darling Danielle and my wonderful cousin Frédéric had loosened a major clog in my soul. I felt myself waking up for the first time in years. In the midst of everything that was happening in my life, with everything that I've learned with regard to Henri and my poor sister, I still had the capacity to, just maybe, love again.

I left the airport and checked in to the hotel that was attached to the airport. I entered my room and arranged the few things that I had for my next day's meetings. I turned the light on in the bathroom, which was average but comfortably appointed as a spacious studio atmosphere. I glanced in the mirror and could hardly recognize myself, I was actually smiling. I appeared happy and refreshed. Something new was happening to me, something healthy and unexpected.

My cell phone, muffled by the deep confines of my handbag, began to ring. I rushed into the other room searching in vain for it. Just before it went to voicemail I found it and answered.

"Hello, this is Homayra," I answered politely.

"Hi Homi, this is Danni, any problems with your flight? Did you get there okay?"

"Oh most definitely Danni, all is well. In fact---very well. Oh Danni, I'm feeling so absolutely different today! I feel almost as if I can breathe again," I said, with a giggle. I thought about telling Danielle about my remarkable encounter with Richard but decided to keep it to myself for now. I wanted to savor it in the privacy of my own mind.

"No really I feel so different. I just saw myself smiling just now in the mirror and feeling better than I have in years. Oh Danni, what is happening to me? I feel as if I'm waking up from the dead," I said, laughing and looking out the window at the airport in the distance. I could picture it off to the side of the airport, the Gulfstream G650; I wondered if he was still on the plane and when I might see him again.

"Well, Homi, it's time for you to live again. You have been through so much in your life and it's time for you to feel love again." She paused. "Homi, there's another reason why I called. Frédéric and I talked to Goli just after you left this morning, and they had an unbelievable experience last night, to say the least. Whatever they saw was too hot for conversations over cell phones so we plan to meet with them tomorrow in Oxford for dinner. Did you happen to see the news about Henri on the wire today?"

"I read something about some train? Yes, what was that all about?"

"Well apparently this is just the tip of the iceberg. There's going to be a lot of questions about that train over the next few days, so I want you to be extra careful. We will call you with more news as we get it. This is going to be a very big deal, Homi," Danielle said. "This train thing is being used for some pretty hideous stuff according to Goli and Timothy. So trust me baby, guard yourself and be very careful around Henri. There are things I haven't even told you yet about Henri but soon will.

———

The next day, my meeting with the members of the Ministry of Finance was rescheduled three times. First from 8:30 a.m. to 10:45 a.m., then moved to 2:10 p.m. and finally to 3:40 p.m. Clearly since Henri was not expected to appear with me I was being pushed aside like a stray dog with a pretty smile.

Promptly at 3:30 p.m. I entered the room and found my spot in the center of an awkward seating arraignment. Each table had its own microphone and a bottle of drinking water. Seven men and two women sat at their assigned seats which were scattered around the mostly empty room. Three camera men with bored expressions on their faces were stationed around the room with their video cameras poised on various areas.

Jules Perrault, the Minister of Finance, who chaired the meeting, was the very same man who announced to the entire room in a meeting just few days earlier that I looked so sexy when I was passionate. Mr. Perrault sat to my right almost out of appropriate range, while the others were positioned in equally uninviting locations around the room. The meeting was called to order as Jules Perrault formally read a statement referencing the state's current understanding of the purpose of the meeting.

I fully expected this level of almost designed ignorance. Why was there no pathway of information to and from the almost dozen other departmental meetings in which I had poured my heart out to over the last few months?

Every single meeting I attended always seemed to have the same start and finish: Who are you? Why should we care? Who is the organization in which you represent? What are your credentials? Why do you believe the problem you see is relevant the French government? What is the purpose of your organization? Can you better define the problem as you see it? What do you believe the solutions are and how will you be able to validate your success? Can you justify to the panel members, without any shadow of a doubt, why the French government should appropriate even a single Euro to your cause?

How long do you expect the funding to be allocated to you....you pretty-little-girl with your long sexy hair, nice breasts and cute ass? *She does looks so sexy when she's passionate, doesn't' she,* the chairperson seemed to convey with his eyes, from his seat on the other side of the room.

I wish she would stand up so I could get a better view at that nice ass of hers, Perrault said with his wandering eyes.

Henri could not be sent to jail yet, I thought. I needed him desperately to bring what influence he still had left into these chambers and kick this commission into gear. Nothing I could ever say would have any effect on this haughty group of fat government bureaucrats. Only a person of Henri's stature could move the gears of government forward and influence the wheels of change for the millions of abused victims throughout the world.

Talk is cheap to these gate keepers. Influence and power is what matters in these chambers. My god, why was Henri not here today, I wondered, as I sat in my seat fuming. Henri's power was ironically exactly what I needed in this sterile meeting, but he was gone, his influence lost!

Little did I know that day, how exactly correct I was about Henri's enormous power and influence. Further, little could I have imagined what would transpire over the next 24 hours, as our meeting concluded without a hint of success.

Fuck them all, I thought as I sat and stared at the blasé expressions on the faces of these overweight bastards. *Fuck them all,* I said to myself, as I looked back at the pompous asshole, Jules Perrault, scanning my body with his wandering eyes, the very same man who has his hands on the financial controls of the entire French government.

Fuck them all, was the very first phrase that I had heard from fourteen-year-old Danielle's frightened mouth, after she had returned to our room at the castle night after night in tears. *Fuck them all,* she would say as she dove on to her mattress and screamed into the pillow. *Fuck them all*, she cried as she began to fall asleep after a night of being manhandled by the highest bidder.

And most of all: *fuck you* Henri Lepan! When this is all over with, for raping my dear sister Goli and destroying my entire life, I hope you rot in hell!

Chapter 35

GOLAREH: THE SACRIFICE

7:30 p.m. - Brixton, South London

Frédéric arrived with two individuals. Rahda Shabur, a female law en-forcement officer with Interpol and Heath Wilson an American officer from the U.S. Department of Justice, Office of International Affairs. The two walked into Danielle's tiny apartment as if they were heading into a war zone. Rahda, a stout black woman in her mid-thirties, was wearing police issued field pants with side cargo pockets and retention snaps, steel toed boots, and a black tee-shirt under a blue wind breaker.

Heath, a towering and extremely handsome young man, was dressed in the same outfit but sported shoulder length blond hair tied back in a pony-tail. He looked as if he could have doubled for a lead singer of a rock band. The officers donned visible brass police shields, identification cards and high caliber pistols with custom grips, neatly tucked into holsters strapped around their legs just above the knee.

"Hi guys," Frédéric said, as the three entered our tiny kitchen. "Homi and Danni, I would like to introduce you to Rahda and Heath; they have been assigned to me under the coordination of Interpol.

"Wow," I said, as I shook their hands. "You two look like you have come prepared." I was struck by Heath's impressive build and Rahda's police-like demeanor.

"Please come in," Danielle said, as she stepped aside and directed them around the tiny kitchen. While leaning over the fire escape railing, Danielle gestured to Magda in the dispatch yard below, "Yes Magda, I'll ask them if it's alright.

Magda really wants to come up and meet you guys. She's the owner of the taxi service and I really can't keep anything from her. Would you mind if she just came up and said hello? Magda is the eyes and ears of Brixton and we trust her with our lives."

"Sure thing," Heath said, as he looked for agreement from Rahda.

Magda soon appeared, along with six other women climbing the fire escape behind her. "Cool it, girls! This is none of your concern! Now go back to work---this instant!" she demanded, as the girls reluctantly trailed off to their duties.

"You can't hide a thing from those girls of mine," she said, as she walked in and kissed both Danielle and me on the lips.

"Magda, this is my dear cousin Frédéric, he's an attorney with the Ministry of Trade in France and these are two of his associates working for Interpol."

"Well, it's a pleasure to meet both of you," Magda said politely. "I am so glad that you all are involved in with all of this mess with Goli's dear sister Homi. Don't worry about those girls out there; they're mostly interested in this handsome man." Magda shot a flirtatious wink at Heath.

"The pleasure's all mine, ma'am," Heath said, smiling and shaking her hand.

"Magda, Goli and Timothy saw some bad things the other night and they need to talk with these fine officers. Goli, where is Timothy, he should be here by now?" asked Danielle.

"Oh, you never know with Timothy. I tell you guys---he drives me up the wall!" I said, as I nervously glanced at my watch.

"Well, I can tell an Austrian when I meet one, am I correct?" Magda asked, as she sized up Heath.

"Wow, Frédéric, I guess we had better include Magda in these discussions, she's probably a better investigator then we all are. Yes ma'am, you are correct, I am Austrian. I was born in Malchin but moved to Vienna when I was very young and then to Richmond, Virginia. I guess I still have that look, yes?"

The five of us moved into the living room and sat around the coffee table.

"Well, you kids must be hungry," Magda said, as she turned and patted Rahda on her back. "Let me run down and bring up a nice pot of Austrian stew. And when I do come back I'd love to know more about you, dear, but if you are with an Austrian, you must be fine." Magda walked through the kitchen and out the door to the fire escape.

"She's really something, isn't she? But I have to ask you, why are all of the cabs bright pink," Rahda asked.

"Because she is our lifesaver, Rahda; she took in every single one of us from the streets. We were all on death-row, so to speak. We all, with the exception of Yolanda and of course Goli, were dug deep into the fashion circuit.

"Fashion circuit?" Heath asked.

"Yep, runway models, the lot of us," Danielle said. "Four of us were lingerie models, five girls were strictly runway models. Ginger and Brooke made it to top of *Playboy, Penthouse,* and *Lui.* Yolanda was the only one of us who didn't model. She was a professional boxer used in the gambling circuit. Yolanda works as our dispatcher and is also our *point* driver when times are tough."

"What do you mean by point driver," Rahda asked.

"She sets our plays when we are running our routines on the streets of London. She keeps an eye on the girls and the property here too," Danielle said with a smile. "She is also as tough as any man in these parts and can take an intruder apart in seconds. She can float like a goddamn butterfly and sting like a fucking bee," Danielle said, already reverting back into her linguistic comfort zone.

"Danni," I said, as I sat down next down on the couch next to her. "Girl---you really need to give these nice officers some time to get to know you---baby."

God, how I missed Danielle, she'd been away too long. I couldn't help myself, as I put my arm around her and held her hands tightly.

"Yolanda goes out with us when we have problems with the enemy. She was a super middleweight amateur boxer headed to the Olympics until that one hit to her left eye damaged her optic nerve. But she's much better now," I told the newcomers.

Danielle stood up and walked over to the kitchen to make sure that Magda was out of range before she spoke. "Magda is a breast cancer survivor, and after her husband died of a stroke a few years back, she almost died herself. She would have lost everything had it not been for Yolanda and the girls. Yolanda nursed Magda back to life and ran the taxi service as the other girls put in everything they had to save the company. The competition was fierce as our competitors did everything they could to destroy our business. They would come in at night and smash the windows and spray paint our cars. When they started terrorizing the girls---that's when they met their match. I wasn't on board at the time but I heard that Yolanda came into this very apartment and saved two girls that were being raped. She burst in here like a bull and beat the ever-living shit out of those bastards.

She took her time with them too. Each one was thrown out of that fucking window right over there. Then over the fire escape they went too! The first guy came out holding his jaw together in shock. After another minute passed the next dude was pushed out! Both of those mother-fuckers went over the edge and landed on their own fucking cab, completely smashing their windshields and flattening their damn roofs." Danielle was laughing at the top of her lungs as she recalled the story.

We could hear the sound of Magda's feet as she climbed the iron fire escape outside. Danielle jumped up and opened the door for her.

"An unbelievable woman---Magda is," I said.

"I even brought you kids some fresh baked corn bread," Magda said, with a welcoming voice as she carried in a large pot of stew.

While Danielle and Magda were preparing for dinner I stepped out on the fire escape and called Timothy. He was late and I was really concerned.

The first ring went to voice-mail, but rather than leave a message, I decided to quickly call back again, and after the fourth ring he answered.

"Hey Goli, Timothy answered, sounding clearly drunk. "I'll be there in just a few--- baby, I just needed to stop off and calm my damn nerves," he said, with the sound of a dance band in the background.

"Damn it, Timothy, you were supposed to be here an hour ago and now you sound shit-faced. Timothy! How could you do this to me? Frédéric is here with some police officers and they need to talk to both of us! I need you to be here Timothy, where in the hell are you? Are you still in Oxford---at Zelz?"

Danielle stepped out on the porch to check on me. "Are you okay---baby? Who are you talking to, sweetie?"

"It's Timothy, he stopped off at Zelz, Danni, and now he sounds like he's drunk as shit!"

"Give me that goddamn phone, baby," she said, as she snatched it from my hand. "Timothy, this is Danni! Now you listen to me you shit head! Where in the fuck are you?"

"Well I just stopped off at Zelz---Danni; I really needed a quick one to relax."

"Damn it---Timothy you are needed here! Now stay, the fuck, where you are! I'm sending someone over to pick your drunken ass up!"

"Danni, don't worry, baby, I'll be there in a little bit. I'm okay, Danni, just tell Goli to start without me.

"You keep your ass there, Timothy; I have a car on the way right now!"

"Danni, it's too late, he's at least an hour and a half away," I said, feeling deflated.

"Baby, go down there and tell Brooke to call Zelz and hold on to him! I'll try to keep his ass on the phone." Danielle said.

"Danni, Danni, don't worry baby! I'm fine, you're too far away. Just go on without me," Timothy pleaded, as the phone was suddenly snatched away from Timothy's hands.

"Wait Timothy---don't hang up on me! You need to at least talk to the officers!"

"Hey, who the hell are you talking to, Timmy baby, come back over to our table and order us another bottle of chard. Hey, who's on this damn phone anyway? Is this your so-called wife again, Timmy? Let me talk to that bitch!" The drunken woman blasted. "Hey listen to me you bitch, this is Sheila and I just want to tell you that your husband is currently un-disposed! Or is it in-disposed, awe fuck-it, he can't talk right now! You got that? He is with us---bitch! So fuck off! Besides, he said he's divorcing your flat-ass!" The phone went dead.

I ran down to the office and told Yolanda to call Zelz to try to get him on the phone again. When I returned, Danielle and I walked back into the living room and reluctantly sat down on the couch next to Frédéric and investigators. I was so pissed off at Timothy that I couldn't even see straight. The nerve of him for treating this whole thing so lightly!

"Stopping off at Zelz to calm his damn nerves, I'd like to calm his fucking nerves with my fist." I mumbled.

The thought of Timothy, sitting in a bar shit-faced, at a time like this, is he kidding me? I bet he's staring down the blouse of some drunken bimbo.

"Calm down baby," Danielle whispered, as she rested her hand over my clenched fist.

"Relax, cousin, to tell you the truth, I didn't expect him to show up here anyway," Frédéric said, as he placed his hand on my shoulder.

"Either did I, Goli," said Heath, from the other side of the dining room table. "Reporters like your friend Timothy hate to divulge their information to the authorities until they have squeezed the material for all of its worth to the media. Did you say that he also had taken pictures and videos of what the two of you saw at the train yard?" Heath asked.

"Yes, and that's why I wanted him here. He has the damn photos on his phone! I wanted you to see them so you could identify the damn train! Those people on that train need to be saved!"

"Ma'am, I hate to tell you this, but we've already found the train, well at least the locomotive," Rahda said.

"You did, well did you find the people on board?"

"No ma'am, we didn't and to be honest, we didn't expect to find them either. The people that run these transportation operations reclassify those trains at least three times before they move out of London proper," said Rahda.

"What do you mean reclassify," I asked.

"Well, Ma'am, there are about three or four hump-yards within close proximity of each other. Each time the train enters one of those yards the cars are shuffled off to other trains in order to confuse our immigration officers. Think of a train as like huge deck of cards which are reshuffled every time they enter one of those yards. There are so many trains delivering freight throughout Europe a single car can be spawned off to many other trains before it reaches its final destination," Rahda said, as she sampled another taste of potato.

"Guys," Heath said, putting his empty bowl down on the table and taking out his note pad. "Let's talk about what you actually saw out there that night and at least get that part into the system, okay. We will get those pictures from Timothy soon."

Thankfully Heath brought some semblance of order to my chaotic mind. "Okay, but damn-it, I wish that Timothy was here to help, because much of what we witnessed I couldn't even look at. I swear, I wouldn't have made it out of there alive had it not for Timothy dragging me out by my hair."

I told the investigators every single thing I could remember from the night before, including the dark monster bugging my apartment. I told them about finding the warehouse in the rainy and foggy freight yard and all of the horror inside.

I described the huddled weak women and children sitting against the wall in that filthy holding tank as a dock worker blasted them down with a fire hose. Danielle wept as I described this poor woman moaning for her life as she tried to comprehend what was happening to her.

My body shuddered as I described how they were loaded on to the boxcars and driven away. I gave them my best replay of Henri's and Ari's conversation that had taken place only meters away from us. I also told them how frustrated we were at not being able to shoot a picture of them together.

"Why were you not able to see them, Goli", Rahda asked, as she wrote on her note pad.

"Because Timothy and I were hiding in this extremely cramped alley. When we heard the voices of Henri and Ari we couldn't move because we were tangled together," I said.

Magda knocked at the kitchen door and emerged into the living room. "Goli, Brooke called Zelz in Oxford and found out that Timothy has left the premises. Some of the customers tried to stop him because he looked like he was very drunk.

"Yeah right," I said, as I retrieved my cigarettes and lighter from the table and stepped out on the fire escape. "Drunks, helping drunks ---He probably already has one of those bimbos on his way to his fucking bed---right now as we speak!" I began to cry, again, as I lit up a cigarette and placed a call to Timothy. His phone rang five times and then went to his voicemail.

"*If this is a salesman, hang up now and save yourself the effort. Otherwise, leave a message,*" said Timothy's stupid recorded announcement, followed by a beep.

"Hello Timothy—please, please---please call me back! I need you to call me back. We need you to talk to the officers. Please Timothy; please don't strand me here with all of this shit!"

I lit up another cigarette way before the other was half gone. Then my phone rang.

"Hello Timothy, Timothy, talk to me baby! Are you there?" I asked to a horribly long pause.

"Yeah Goli, I'm here. I'm sorry baby; I just couldn't wait to have a drink."

"Wait? How much have you had to drink? Hey, pull off the road and turn your car off, right now! I'll come and get you, baby," I pleaded, trying desperately to keep him on the phone.

"It's all right Goli. Wrecking this goddamn car is the least of my problems. I'm afraid the cat's already out of the bag, Goli."

"What did you do? What do you mean? Oh my god Timothy, please don't tell me that you put your name on a story? You are too drunk to make any sense right now. Just stay there and I'll come and get you. You can stay in Brixton with us," I pleaded.

"Goli girl, I already wrote the story and it's probably already hitting the wires."

I felt my legs become weak as my body flushed with sweat.

"Listen Goli, someone has to stop that mother-fucker and it might as well be me."

"Timothy, please pull off the damn road before you kill someone."

"It's alright, baby, I'm not driving anymore."

"Timothy I need you to come here and give your photos and videos to the police. These guys are specialized in this sort of stuff. They are with Interpol and ICE! They are much better equipped than we are---baby. Don't you understand the position you just put us in? Damn it, Timothy, how could you do this to me. Now hang on and let me put you on the phone with the officers!"

"Fuck the officers, Interpol, Europol, ICE or whoever the fuck else is over there. We can't wait for them to do shit! We have to act now Goli, through the court of public opinion. Henri evades every goddamn due-process of law that exists! If we wait on those assholes to do their damn jobs then how many more people will die?" Timothy asked, as his speech became very clear.

"Goli, Henri is already on to you. You know that! He's bugging your fucking apartment. How long until he takes you out, or your sister Homayra. How long until Danielle is picked off by a sniper? Baby, we don't have time for the fucking police to act. We have to act on our own!" Timothy firmly ordered. "I took the plunge tonight Goli, I did it to put more heat into Henri's fucking world. He needs to feel some real heat to come down on his ass. Not some namby-pamby questioning by some stupid officers!"

"But Timothy, we at least have to let the authorities go through their process of investigation. We can't do this all by ourselves!" I said, wondering about whatever that process was.

"Fuck their process Goli! I told you, Henri is bullet-proof to almost everything. Baby, I saw him on the news today, laughing uncontrollably about his so called private train-of-death. Hell, even the reporters were laughing their asses off.

"Hey, listen to this---Goli, Henri even took another shot at the deputy prime minister today! He said that she has a nice ass and thought they would make a great couple in bed regardless of whether she's a lesbian or not! Don't you see it, Goli? Someone has to make a sacrifice, and go after that prick! And that someone is going to be me!"

"No," I pleaded.

"Goli, as I've told you in the past. It's time for me to make a difference in this stupid world I'm living in. I've made a living out of destroying other people's reputations. I'm a goddamn mess, Goli! You know it and I know it. You see how I get all of my super news. I cheat! I don't investigate these people I break into their own privacy and take it! I'm living on borrowed time, Goli. I'm not even a barely functional drunk. I'm a full-fledged alcoholic with a dangerous addiction to sex. I don't know what it is about women; I just have this overwhelming urge to fuck them all! I can't help myself, baby. I just want to have sex---and a lot of it! I'm also a cheating bastard of a husband, who up until I looked into those beautiful eyes of yours, I couldn't tell the difference between right and wrong. My god, baby, I have to tell you something, Goli. I love you more than I have ever loved any other woman in my fucking life," Timothy said, as his voice began to struggle. "But I love you in the most pure way, baby. I love you like you are my own sister. I want the best for you baby, and that goes for Danni too. But I've have these demon around me that constantly push me towards women and booze."

There was a long pause after his admission as I felt my heart wrench for Timothy. For the first time in my life, I witnessed a total and complete transformation of a human being. This poor man, who I once considered to be the enemy, began to reveal a core of a tortured angel.

"Oh thanks a lot Timothy! Now I'm a total mental wreck." I blurted, to add some levity.

"Listen Goli, the sooner we can get the facts about Henri out into the media the safer all of us are going to be. Public opinion will protect us! Goli baby, we need to work on the next step," Timothy said, now sounding completely sober.

"Well, what's next then, Timothy --- if you are dead? How am I supposed to do this alone?" I screamed into the phone.

"Goli, listen to me baby, I'm not dead yet and I don't plan to be! You guys need to come up with a plan to get in that goddamn castle and find Henri's satellite phone. That phone is our *skeleton key* into Henri's world. That phone is the only link Henri has to Santo Gordo, and we need to record those bastards doing business together. We have absolutely nothing on Henri without a recording of a deal being made between Henri and his Mexican brother!"

"Girl--- listen to me, you guys need to find a way to get into that castle as soon as possible and locate Henri's satellite phone."

"But I'm worried about you Timothy; you need to be with us. We need to stick close together!"

"No we don't, Goli, we need to stay away from each other, we need to be spread out," Timothy demanded. "You need to stay close to me in London and send Homayra and Danni to the castle and try to get in there and find Henri's fucking phone. Maybe they can link up with that horse trainer woman, you know, that Zooli character you guys are always talking about. Hell, your sister may even still know her way around that place. I don't know! Just figure it out and call me back when you have a plan! But you have to get there---ASAP! I think Henri is heading there in the next two days. Don't you remember what Ari told Henri about some meeting that is scheduled the next day or two? Call me, baby. Just come up with a plan and call me," Timothy said, as his phone went dead.

I stood there in silence staring down at the empty parking lot below. I had a lit cigarette in both hands, so I threw one of them to a rain puddle below. My hands were shaking as I sucked the last bit of smoke out of the remaining one.

Danielle stepped out on the porch with glass of red wine. "Here, baby, sip this, and let it calm your nerves. Tell me baby, what's going on?"

"Oh Danni," I said, as I dropped the other cigarette into an ashtray. "We have some work to do now."

Danielle looked at me as if she knew exactly what we were supposed to do next. "Oh my god, baby, there you go again with those eyes again. You know exactly how to turn my keys, don't you, baby?

Chapter 36

HOMAYRA: SPONTANEOUS COMBUSTION

Amiens-Glisy Airport - Amiens, France — 8:50 a.m.

Scotland Yard stakes out Hither Green Rail Hub for body bag shipment
Timothy Edwards - ENTERPRISE NEWS SERVICE

*L*ONDON, South Eastern Main Line —— Three people have been apprehended and a fourth person remains at large following an early morning stakeout of a warehouse at Hither Green marshalling yard in South East London. Scotland Yard deployed a squad of officers to the Royal Packers Stock House after an anonymous tip claimed that dockworkers were loading what were described as body bags onto train cars.

The three suspects, who were arrested, spoke in a rare Spanish dialect, making it difficult for investigators to question them for details. The fourth suspect crawled through a window in the back of the warehouse and ran 300-meters down the track. He then climbed down into a drainage pipe and was last seen running under a high-way overpass.

The witness identified the train as being AriTrain, a Class-56 diesel locomotive freight system owned and operated by French Government. AriTrain has also been the center of controversy for the embattled French Trade Minister, Dr. Henri Lepan, who *has been fighting accusations of wrong doing in the court of public opinion for weeks. The unknown source also claimed that they observed a large number of female passengers being offloaded to awaiting busses.*

Dr. Lepan is scheduled to deliver a major closing speech to the United Nations on Monday, and it is expected that he will vigorously defend all charges and attempt to exculpate himself from any futures charges of wrong doing.

A death train just entered my world. The monster has been buying and selling human beings as if they were livestock and then destroying them when they were fully depreciated.

Henri is a madman capable of incomprehensible evil. How sick was he, I wondered. Although he clearly shows indications of genuine mental distress, the more I considered what I learned about his childhood, the more I understood why he possesses no conscious awareness of his sickness. Henri truly blames others, including his father, teachers, and coaches for his own failings.

Henri frequently told me that he had only two things in his life that provided him with a semblance of good. One was his mother, who he deeply treasured, and the other was me. He often described me as being his last bastion of pure good in his life.

All of the daily papers ran the same dreadful article which included horrible pictures of human tragedy. I bought three of France's largest papers, the *Le Monde, Le Figaro*, and the *Libération* and tucked them under my left arm. I flashed my travel card to an officer at the central security checkpoint and passed through an exit and into the back seat of a midsize Toyota Limousine.

It had been raining heavily since before I woke up and a storm cell was reported to be stationary over a large portion of northern France. Our limo approached the jet and came to a stop and then waited for the rain to slow down to a downpour. My phone beeped once in my handbag, indicating an incoming text message. The message was from Danielle: "CALL ME ASAP!--DANNI"

A bolt of lightning flashed in the sky directly above the limo followed by a deafening crack of thunder. I flinched and replied to Danielle's text: "ABOUT TO BOARD A FLIGHT BACK TO PARIS. DREADFUL WEATHER. WILL CALL YOU ASAP." The rain was intensifying and it was obvious that I was going to be stranded in the limousine for quite some time.

A human figure in a blue coat approached the door of the limo and tapped on the window. I squinted through the downpour and recognized Capt. Richard Edward. He was standing under a large umbrella with a welcoming smile. My body tingled with excitement as I gathered up my belongings and dove into the storm.

The tarmac was flooded and the rain blasted against my face from the side. Every one of my newspapers flew out of my arms and scampered down the tarmac like a flock of wet geese. Richard put his arms around me and held the stressed umbrella between us and the storm, like a gladiator with a rickety shield. The force of the storm soon overwhelmed the umbrella, collapsing it into a helpless wet flag, instantly drenching us.

We ran, hand in hand, towards the steps of the jet and held on to the railings as the weather dared us to continue. We were being pelted with hail and to our anguish we found the door half locked. Richard slid his hand through the small opening between the hatch and the fuselage and pulled a lever releasing the door.

We dropped into the bulkhead of the jet like wet rats as Richard pulled the door closed behind us and sealed it for departure. I stood starring at Richard's soaked face through the strands of my matted, wet hair, while realizing that every stitch of clothing I had on was drenched. Richard turned and faced me with the cutest expression, saying, "Well now---that went well--- didn't it?" We stood still reviewing each other's soaked bodies and suddenly burst out laughing.

For the first time in many years I actually heard myself laughing as if I hadn't a care in the world. My once pristine sleeveless white silk top now clung to my body like a layer of wet rice paper, rendering a detailed view of my entire upper torso. My nipples added to my embarrassment by becoming hard and visibly protruding through my invisible bra. All details of my ribcage were now on display for our private world with a population of two.

Richard stood studying my clinging, soaked jeans and exposed midriff. I'm sure that I appeared totally vulnerable as I studied Richard with a surprised but serious expression. Richard slowly approached and gently ran his fingers through my wet scalp like a human comb, sweeping my wet hair to the side of my head and down my back.

"Your mascara is running," Richard said, as he offered me a soaked cotton handkerchief from his saturated coat pocket.

"Yeah---like that's really going to help me now," I joked, as I suddenly burst into an even more elevated belly laugh. For at least an entire minute, Richard and I laughed uncontrollably, as we instinctually moved closer to one another.

I found myself wanting to skip all semblance of formality and touch Richard as I looked into his beautiful eyes.

My imagination began generating entire love scenes of Richard removing my wet clothing and caressing my breasts with the tips of his fingers and the palms of his beautiful hands. My thoughts turned erotic as I welcomed images of Richard's mouth and tongue against my wet breasts and nipples.

How were these emotions possible? I had firmly considered those types of desires gone from my soul, never to return.

I suddenly had enough with my code of behavior and lunged at Richard clutching his body in my arms. I pulled Richard in, as if I were a drowning child grasping for a life ring. Richard responded in matched movements as his hands explored my electrified body. The hail storm blasted against the outside of the aircraft, while inside, we explored each other's bodies in search of something magnificent.

My fingers dug into Richard's back as if I were trying to collect every remnant of human energy coming from his body. I wanted him so badly that I could feel my mouth water with pleasure.

Richard's hands flattened against my rain soaked back as he drew me closer into the warmth of his heaving chest. We held each other as the cadence of our heartbeats transitioned into groans of need.

Richard led me along the mahogany walls of the jet until we entered the sleeping quarters. I lifted my soaked silk shirt over my head and helped Richard roll my wet bra over my shoulders and head. He moved his hands up each side of my torso claiming each of my breasts in his palms, compressing my nipples into erotic points. I was alive with desire, wanting to laugh and cry at the very same time, as he gently sucked the tips of my nipples and clutched me with excitement.

I felt the texture of his tongue scrub the base of my nipples as I strained with desire and moistened with anticipation. I sat down and laid back on the white coverings of the divan bed, unbuttoning my jeans and desperately pushing them off. I wanted Richard inside of me so badly that I brazenly reached for his testicles and gently massaged his engorged penis on the outside of his pants.

Richard stood above me, kicking off his shoes, removing his pants and dropping down to his knees. I was now lying on my back looking up at his handsome face as I watched him remove my soaked panties and pitch them across the cabin.

Suddenly, the unexpected happened, like a flashing dream come true. Richard's mouth landed in the center of my vagina, pressing against my moist opening as if it were a perfumed pillow. I was instantly overwhelmed with desire.

My body trembled with want as his tongue gently gratified my clitoris. Never before had I experience such pleasure as he gently caressed the inner recesses of my vagina. I widened my legs with acceptance and pushed my vagina against his face, welcoming a flood of moisture while I pushed for more.

Richard moved his hands from the small of my back to both sides of my rear end as his tongue tormented my pleasure limits, extending me dangerously close to completion. But I didn't want it to end, I wanted more. So much more, as he gripped both sides of my butt with both hands and gently massaged them.

"Oh---enough---stop it!" I teased, desperately fighting back a major eruption. I was now experiencing a string of mini-orgasms, as I moved dangerously close to the vicinity of the *big-one*. I could no longer stand it any longer, for I was about to explode. I wanted him inside me now, deep inside me.

I directed his face towards mine and desperately kissed his mouth while tasting my own bodily fluids on his lips. My insides broke loose and exploded into a full blown orgasm.

"Make love to me Richard—oh my god---I want you. I need you inside of me now," I insisted.

My insides pulsed and contracted as if enough-was-enough. I directed and welcomed the head of his penis against the entrance of my vagina. "Now Richard, make love to me---now!"

I felt the tip of his hard penis gently penetrate my throbbing vagina as he entered. I could both feel and hear him moving slightly within and then completely out of me in a wonderful rhythm.

I was soaked with desire as I moaned and squirmed with excitement. I wanted him so much more as I reached around his legs and lightly stroked his testicles. I welcomed him entirely into my deep recesses while at the same time considering more activities on top of him. I needed to actively consume him with everything I had and pleasure him with all of my being, but our joint excitement exceeded our capabilities as I felt him explode within me and flood me with his warmth.

The sound of hail against the rain drenched plane tapered off as our beautiful love making came to a wonderful conclusion. He leaned against my body and rested his head against my heaving chest. I was beside myself in disbelief as I buried my fingers in his scalp. Never before had I experienced such a highly charged, spontaneous, truly beautiful and loving event.

I stared at the ceiling of the cabin as our bodies relaxed and blended together for a restful aftermath. I thought about my life up until this point as I considered the beauty of this precious encounter with this wonderfully caring man. In the midst of everything that had transpired over most of adult life, I was still able to have the capacity to open my soul and body to another human being with such freedom, excitement and intensity.

I held Richard in my arms and felt years of pain transferring from our connected souls as we gently tugged the torture and sadness away from each other. I was feeling beautiful again under the eyes of God and most especially Richard, as we held each other within the private confines of our private jet.

The sun broke through the top of the dark curtain of clouds which were now marching off to the east.

It was the beginning of a new day, as the warmth of the sun illuminated our wet runway of the Amiens airport.

Chapter 37

GOLAREH: THE ROGUE REPORTER

Oxford, England – 4:20 a.m.

Overnight almost all of the momentum regarding the possible connection between Henri and his questionable activities had shifted in the public's eye to none other than Timothy Edwards.

Agence France-Presse, Associated Press and Reuters, each had reporters posted at the *Enterprise* office in London, waiting for a chance to talk with the famous reporter. Who was Timothy's source of information for the infamous *train-of-death* and how was he or she connected to Timothy? That seemed to be the most important question of the day.

I had been working as a columnist for the *Enterprise* for twenty-three years and had never once met Rémi Masson, the company's global news director. But there he was, along with Walter Petit, the paper's chief counsel, on late night television, debating international laws surrounding press confidentiality. The 150-year old news organization appeared to be fighting for its life over ethics in journalism, while some angry judge on behalf of the Henri Lepan was threatening to order a disclosure of the sources ruling on the *Enterprise*. Both Masson and Petit were vehemently standing by Timothy Edwards, while threatening to invoke the protection of sources rule under a reporter's privilege law.

I now had enough of the news and left the flat with my cell phone in hand and began walking down the dark streets of Oxford desperately looking for the ever elusive Timothy Edwards.

Three large canisters of French roasted coffee were being filled as I entered *The Attendee* at 5:50 a.m. Freddie was just opening up, but looked as if he had been up all night long grinding coffee. "Hey Freddie….*tchetori*," — "*good morning*," I said, in our native tongue.

"Hi Goli." Freddie mechanically placed a cup in front of me and began filling it with fresh brewed coffee. "What brings you in here so early? Oh, let me guess, Timothy right?"

"So you must have seen him on the news as well---huh?"

"Saw him, hell; Timothy was here all night long, along with an entire television news crew. I never closed down. I almost ran completely out of coffee," Freddie said, as he poured a huge bag of coffee beans into a grinder.

"Well where he is now?   I really need to talk to him?"

"He's living the life, Goli, living his perfect high-life. Timothy is riding this whole death train thing like it's the story of a lifetime. He's swears he's got the goods on this Henri Lepan character. Hey, do you know that guy, Goli? Isn't he some big shot with the Ministry of Trade in France?

I felt flushed hearing Henri's horrible name coming from my dear friend's mouth. Up until that point Henri's name had been restricted to another country and within the confines of my own mind.

"Goli, if you think Timothy had an attitude before---well you should see him now."

"Tell me more Freddie---no better yet, save it.   I can't take it any longer; I need to smoke a damn cigarette."

I stepped outside on to the dark sidewalk and was desperately searched my purse for my allusive lighter, when suddenly someone approached me from behind and slipped a lit cigarette between my lips.

"Timothy---Jesus Christ!   You scared the ever-living shit out me! Where in the hell have you been and why have you not called me back. I must have called you a goddamn---million times!

"Calm down Goli, it's all good, everything's cool."

Timothy waved to Freddie through the window, letting him know that I was safe, and then placed his arms over my shoulders.

"It's all good? Timothy! Jesus Christ---everyone in the London is trying to find you. Some judge is trying to force the *Enterprise* to make you give up your sources! It's far from fucking all-good ---Timothy!"

"Shhhh!---Walk with me baby."

We headed down High Street into the theatre section of town. Early morning art dealers were turning on their lights and placing their street signage on the sidewalks in front of their shops. We skipped over puddles from the rain the night before, as we moved deeper into what is known as the curtain district. Timothy looked pretty energized, despite the fact that he had been awake for nearly 72 hours.

"Give up my sources!" Timothy laughed as he lit up two more cigarettes and directed one my way.

Around the corner we went, towards the bright marquee of the Oxford Flick Theatre off in the distance.

"My sources are the goddamn criminals, Goli, that's who my fucking sources are---you asshole judge!" cursed Timothy.

The *Flick*, as the theatre was named, was known as a *grindhouse*, a 24-hour continuous running movie house known for grinding out mostly gay and lesbian cult films and long forgotten musical classics. In the morning it served as one of the best coffee houses in Oxford, but in the evening it transformed itself into one of the swankiest pizza, movie and beer joints in all of London.

Big Ben Arnold, a huge man with a thick beard and curly gray hair, was a gay, ex-rugby player and owner of the movie house, who could always be found leaning up against the wall outside of his family owned building in a rickety, ladder-back chair. At 6' 6" and 395 lbs. he had a commanding presence, still maintaining the look of a halfback. Most passers-by avoided eye contact with Big Ben because he looked so massive and threatening. But in reality, he was no threat unless provoked. He was a huge and very sweet man with an ultra-feminine voice who loved me and absolutely adored Danielle.

"Hello, Goli-girl, and where may I ask is that super-hot sweetie of yours?" Ben asked, with the uncanny sound of a female cabaret singer. "I didn't know that you were friends with our local hero---Timothy."

Big Ben extended his hand to Timothy to kiss, and on instinct Timothy dropped down on one knee and kissed Big Ben on his championship ring finger.

"Oh my god Timothy, do you know Big Ben?" I asked.

I would have thought of Timothy as one of the biggest homophobes in the world, as I hugged Big Ben's huge body. I was perplexed as I stood between the two vastly different individuals while trying to comprehend the strange connection.

"Goli, sweetie, had it not been for Timothy, I might have lost my entire business almost two years ago," Big Ben said, as he awkwardly got off his chair, stood up and towered over the both of us like a huge grizzly bear. Ben draped his massive arms over Timothy's back and kissed him on his forehead.

"Years back the mayor of Oxford threatened to tear down this old theatre to make room for a sidewalk. A fucking sidewalk, mind you! The mayor along with this asshole developer had some big plan to turn this whole area into a park. They were going to build this ugly ass suspension bridge across that polluted river over there and make it look like some goddamn place in Italy. The city leaders said that my building here, which has been in my family forever, didn't fit the new plan and so they wanted to demolish it. I called Timothy at his office up north and asked him for help. This developer guy was buying up everything around here like a damn vacuum cleaner. He was a real hood, Goli, you know, a real mobster type? Well....just twenty-four hours after I contacted Timothy, we came to find out that this asshole developer was connected to some huge Italian crime family in London with other connections in both New York City and Venice!"

"Oh god, yes, I think I do remember something about that. Didn't they just want the water rights of the river running through here so they could hold on to a rug manufacturing plant downstream?"

"You got it, girl, and overnight the entire plan came tumbling down like a huge house of cards. The developer tried to fight the charges in a war of words but was later caught working a deal with the mayor himself. Somehow Timothy got the whole conversation on tape, with pictures to boot! Would you believe it, Goli---he was even able to videotape the filthy bastards!"

"I'm curious, Big Ben, what made you think that Timothy could help you?"

Big Ben suddenly got serious and glanced over to Timothy for approval to continue his story. Timothy nodded slightly as he looked down at the pavement.

"Well, Goli, I read somewhere that one of Timothy's twin sons was bullied for being gay. The nice young man was being brutalized by classmates on a daily basis. Well, one thing lead to another until Timothy found his poor little boy in his bedroom hanging from an extension cord."

I stood shocked, frozen, feeling a powerful force of tears as I looked at Timothy in disbelief. Why had he never told me this before? I stared at the both of them in disbelief.

"Listen, baby, there's still a lot you don't know about me, but in this case I never had the strength to tell you. I thought with all of your problems, you didn't need to hear anything about that."

I lacked the power to move. I felt like such a selfish bitch for treating Timothy with such disrespect and coming so dangerously close to calling him a homophobe. I turned on my heels and leaned against the window of the theatre and hid my eyes. Timothy and Big Ben walked up behind me and placed their hands on my back and comforted me as I wrenched with a large combination of sorrow, embarrassment and guilt.

"Goli—girl, it's okay. You should have known there must have been a reason I'm so fucked up."

The three of us stood instinctively pausing as if we were offering a moment of silence to Timothy's son.

"Guess what girl, Big-Ben, here is my new landlord and body guard too!" said Timothy, patting Big Ben on his back appreciatively.

"There was just no way I could stay at my place until this all blows over. What better place to hide out---than here?"

"Oh Timothy, I'm so very sorry about your son, I wish you would have told me."

"Okay sweeties---you both look like you could use a little breakfast. Come on in the house, everything is on me." Big Ben covered both of our bodies with his huge arms and walked us into the brightly lit theatre.

It was old-home week as we entered, recognizing many of my friends from work and several others from the theatre district.

Smithy Greene sauntered up and gave me a big hug. "Hey, baby, where's your sweetie, Danni-girl this morning--- huh?"

Smithy Greene was one of London's most promising actresses and also the most gorgeous. Timothy was beside himself with awe, as he performed a visual inspection of her body.

Smithy, a *trans-person*, was not only the biggest flirt in all of Oxford but also the most beautiful flirt as well. Four years prior she had been also one of the most strikingly attractive men in the London theatre scene. She was a master Shakespearean actor by trade who could play dual roles of either Olivia or Hamlet flawlessly. Tortured by her assignment to her male gender, she had spent years conditioning her body to become a woman.

She suffered through some of the most painful transitions that doctors in the UK had ever seen, with odd reactions to drug therapies and post-surgical complications that almost killed her. But Smithy's consistent, persistent and insistence for change payoff in spades.

Those days were all behind her and all she does now is just continue to become even more beautiful than ever. It seems that her true beauty blossomed exponentially once her soul was plugged into its proper housing. I always loved Smithy, but damn if she wasn't as much of a flirt as Timothy was.

"Hi Smithy," I said as I kissed her on the cheek. "Danni had to go out of town on a family matter and I had to spend at least one night at my boring flat."

"Goli, you should have called me, darling, I would have come over and we could have had a pajama party. Who's this handsome hunk-a-man?"

"Oh, I'm sorry, girl; Smithy this is Timothy, one of my co-workers at the *Enterprise*."

"Oh my heavens, aren't you the dude whose been reporting all of those wild stories about that French dude with the death-train?" Every bit of Smithy's charm was now engaged as she seductively bit the tips of her meticulously manicured fingernails and gazed into Timothy's eyes. "Ouuu, darling, you are one picture-perfect hunk of a man."

"Why thank you---you pretty little thing, the pleasure is all mine. May I call you Smithy as well... that is such an interesting name for a woman? But I wouldn't care if your name was Bruce. You are one fine looking dame." Timothy purposely circulated his eyes around Smithy's teardrop shaped breasts and appeared to actually be drooling.

"Honey-baby, you can call me any damn think you want to---any time you want---and anywhere you wish."

"Guys, please, excuse me, but isn't it just a bit too early for this? Its only 6:15 in the morning and I really could use some breakfast!" I maneuvered Timothy's body away into another room while his brains stayed behind.

"I'm starved too, Goli, so when you're done with Timothy, send him back to me. I want to buy my new heartthrob a beer."

"Oh my god, I've died and gone to heaven." Timothy walked backwards, totally plugged into Smithy's eyes while sending sexual sign-language for as long as he could keep her in view.

"I'm not sure she's exactly your type Timothy, but you never know, I could be way wrong. Anyway, we have other things to talk about right now."

We sat down at a breakfast bar, picked up a menu and ordered some much needed coffee.

"Timothy, listen to me! You have got to slow down with the stories. The whole thing is turning into a story about *you*. The *Enterprise* is under so much pressure to reel you in and yank your sources."

I caught the eye of the waitress behind the bar and pointed to a picture of an order of two eggs over-easy, a side of grilled potatoes and some rye toast.

"Yeah right, Goli, you think so--do you?"

"Damn right---I think so!   Reporters are staked out all over London, just waiting to corner your ass. You Timothy!   Not Henri! You!   What's up with that?"

"Goli, it's all a game with the management.   Don't you see that by now? When are you going to understand that all they are interested in is selling fucking papers?   They couldn't give two-shits about my sources, they love this attention---and so do the advertisers.   They haven't had a story like this in years. They're just playing poker with the French government. They don't want me to stop; they want me boldly come up with more. Which is exactly what I'm going to do," Timothy said as he pounded his fist down on the bar.   "It's all a game of brinksmanship at my expense!   Who will crack first, me or the French Government---and surely not our stupid publisher!   I've seen all of this before! What the fuck do they have to lose, Goli? Nothing! "

Timothy pointed to his coffee cup for a refill.

"Timothy, you need to eat something too.   You look like shit!   You can't live on coffee in the morning and booze in the evening!" I signaled the waitress for a double order of eggs for Timothy.

"Oh my god---Goli, who would have ever thought that you would be caring for me as if you were my own wife? Just my damn luck that the one woman I would give my left nut to have---is gay." He reached across the table and took my hand.   "Okay, girl, let talk, do you have a plan worked out with Danni, like I asked you for?   Who is going to the castle and when? ---Oh and by the way, someone had better be on their way by tomorrow!"

"Well, thank you for finally paying some attention to what we are doing.   Okay, Frédéric had dinner with us last night and he's on his way back to Paris as we speak.   He's now working with two officers from Interpol and ICE and has put together a research team in a classroom in Amsterdam dedicated to following up on every scrap of data we come up with," I said, as our eggs arrived. "They have already dug up a whole lot of horrid shit on Henri thus far, including testimony from his child psychologists—who was murdered, mind you!   But they still have absolutely nothing that can tie him to any crimes with."

"Okay so who's going to the castle and it had better not be you--- Goli? I need you close by to transfer information to---and to do whatever footwork we need," Timothy said, like a quarterback in a huddle.

"Well, it's so nice to see you taking charge again, Timothy." I kissed him on his shoulder.

"Oh baby, don't get me started," Timothy laughed, as he jokingly squirted some ketchup on his potatoes.

"Danni is at Heathrow—right now, waiting for Homi to fly in and pick her up and take them to Dijon."

"Wait a minute, what do you mean, fly in?"

"Oh, I forgot to tell you that my sister has her own jet airplane."

"Well, okay then," Timothy said, as he munched on his toast.

"From there they will drive to a town called Montbéliard, which is at the base of the castle. We think there still is this lovable guy that we all knew as kids who still works at the castle. His father was the long time hunt master for the fox hunts they organize for the guests at the castle. His name is Becker and his father died years ago.   We believe that he is now the new hunt master on the castle grounds. We also think that he might be able to get Danni and Homi onto the castle grounds. We also believe that Zooli is still on the grounds as well. Hopefully she will be able to help the girls get into the castle itself.   That reminds me, what does a satellite phone look like anyway, Timothy?"

"Well, I would expect that Henri would keep his phone in his office where he does his business, mostly likely plugged into rather sizeable charger. Knowing Henri, I would expect that it's a government issued model. They should be on the lookout for a phone that resembles a cross between an older model cell phone and a walkie-talkie. Satellite phones usually have a rather sizable looking thick antenna on them too."

"So again--- what are they supposed to do when they find this damn thing?" This was the part that was really making me crazy. I had no idea what a SIM card was and why we needed to remove it from Henri's satellite phone.

"Like I've told you, I need for them to remove the SIM card from Henri's phone and install it into either one of their phones. Just long enough for me to *express* in their phone and transfer his registration data onto my phone. Am I making myself clear, Goli?"

"Like mud? Okay, so you're asking my sister and Danni to find Henri's mysterious satellite phone, wherever in the hell that may be hiding. Then you want them to take some damn *thing* out of Henri's phone and install the same damn *thing* into one of their phones? Right? Are you fucking kidding me?"

The entire plan sounded completely ridiculous and entirely impossible. "How are they going to know how to do all of this and what in the hell is a goddamn SIM card?"

"Don't worry about it Goli, it's simple and I'll walk you through it. All they need to do is find the damn phone and have a paperclip handy."

"Okay so tell me more about this SIM card, Timothy and why you need to do this transfer again? I mean I have no fucking idea what in the hell you are talking about?"

"Goli, most satellite phones use the same SIM cards as all of the other cell phones on the market do. Don't you remember when I told you that all phones run almost the exact same software? Well, satellite phones use more of the features on a SIM card than standard phones do. The SIM card is what my son calls a *Subscriber Identity Module*; it's like this tiny-ass computer that sits in the body of a cellular phone and fucking does everything. It's this tiny little square flat electronic chip. It's easily ejected and installed by using the end of a paperclip.

Now this is a wonderful example of just how secure our entire fucked up communication industry is these days. These tiny SIM cards contain all of owner's user identity, including account information, stored phone numbers, passwords and IP addresses. They are registered specifically for that user and provide their own data encryption capability to the outside world.

One would expect that the SIM card itself is secure---right? Wrong! Guess what? Not!

Henri's SIM card is our ticket, Goli; it's our skeleton key into Henri's slimy world, Santo Gordo and the rest of his shitheads. Once Homi or Danni installs Henri's SIM card into one of their phones, I will *express* into their phone and make an exact image of his registration data on to my phone. When I'm done with my transfer, all the girls will have to do is install it back into Henri's satellite phone and get the hell out of there. When I have his SIM card registration I will easily be able to express in to his phone and pull every goddamn trick in the fucking book on Henri. Cool right?" Timothy asked, as stared at me. "Now, here's the real kicker, since we are dealing with a satellite phone, I can only express in to Henri's phone when he's actually talking to Santo Gordo. It's a session dependent operation----he must be using the damn phone at the time."

We sat chewing in silence considering the plan in front of us. Me--- scared to death and Timothy confident as hell.

"So," Timothy said, breaking the silence. "You say that your twin sister has her own jet airplane, does she? Am I hearing this correctly?" Timothy asked, as he cleaned his plate with his last piece of rye toast.

"Yes she does," I answered, knowing full well where he was going with this.

"Well my, my, my---she must be pretty well off---I would guess," Timothy said with a look of male curiosity. "And did you say that she is your exact twin, and looks just like you?"

After a long pause Timothy looked at the wall in front of him and thought for another lingering pause. "Maybe after our little adventure is all over with, I might get a chance to actually meet your sister? I mean she's not gay too, is she?"

"Forget about her, Timothy, you asshole! Homi is hands-off to you — you pig! I swear Timothy; Danni and I will hunt you down and put you out of commission if you ever lay a hand on my sweet sister!"

"Don't worry, girly-girl, it's all good. I'm just yanking your chain," Timothy said, as he stood up and stretched his back and arms, while glancing down the hallway for Smithy. "I have a little someone I need to get to know in the other room." His classic player-grin was returning with vigor.

I stood up to face Timothy and pulled his big body over to me. "Now listen to me you big dolt. Please be careful and watch your ass. Henri has a horribly dangerous reach and has many people working for him. I'm not kidding you, Timothy, watch your ass!"

I began to reflect back on the day I first met Timothy. I also thought about the other night, what a transition there had been, from one opinion of him to quite another. I thought of Timothy leading me through that horrid warehouse snapping pictures of the dead and dying. I thought of Timothy handing me coffee the next morning as I lay there half asleep in his bed. Then I started imagining his poor son who I just learned had ended his own life, by hanging himself from an extension cord in his bedroom.

I didn't want to ever lose this strange dichotomy of a man who was one-part genius, two-parts loving parent, three-parts skirt-chasing pig, and four-parts a brother to me. I was now more afraid for his life than I was for all of our lives combined.

Timothy had extended himself way too far out into Henri's world. He had identified himself as the press-thorn in Henri's side. He was now a marked man. I was seeing visions that this might be the last time I would see Timothy again. I felt myself starting to panic but tried to shake it off as distracting thoughts.

"Call me the moment Danni flies out of London and take care of yourself baby," Timothy said, as he gave me a light kiss on the tip of my nose.

"We will get through this, Goli-girl. You just watch and see. We are going to get this guy, Henri, once and for all."

As he looked deeply into my eyes, I saw the sweet and very protective side of Timothy that was invisible to the rest of the world. I also knew that he could finally see the real me, for who I was, once and for all.

Timothy quickly regained his composure and headed down the hall in search of Smithy. It suddenly occurred to me, that it was now my turn to yell out a cat-call at Timothy. He was in my domain anyway.

"Hey Timothy, you know that you are just about the hottest dude in this establishment, don't you know?"

Timothy looked from side to side realizing that he was also the only straight person in the entire establishment.

"Oh---and there is one more thing you should know, you good looking---hunk of man! Be gentle with my friend Smithy, she's been going through so many changes these days, if you know what I mean?"

I'm not sure Timothy understood my last remark as I passed by them both, and to be honest, I didn't care. Timothy was a big boy and he could take care of himself a far as that was concerned. I was smiling as I passed by Big Ben and slapped him on his massive butt as I pushed the glass door open and left the theatre.

The early morning sun was waking up the town of Oxford as I hailed a cab and told the driver to take me directly to the London office of the *Enterprise*. I needed to put myself directly into the epicenter of international news where all of the stories about Henri were germinated and disseminated. My office was going to serve as my own little control center. It was going to be a very busy day for us all.

As I sat in the back of the cab and I thought about Homayra and how much I wanted to call her. I desperately needed to hear her voice and combine myself with her in conversation, but I also knew that now was not the time.

Chapter 38

HOMAYRA: DISENGAGEMENT

"Gentle in what you do, firm in how you do it"

— *Buck Brannaman*

During my short flight from Amiens to Paris, I had a brief and much needed conversation with Danielle on the phone. We talked about the continuous headlines that were striking Henri like a barrage of machine gun fire. It was also quite evident that everyone had been working over-time, planning the next steps of our mission.

I was instructed to fly to London's Heathrow Airport and retrieve Danielle early the next morning. From London we were to fly to Dijon where we would rent a car and drive directly to Montbéliard. Danielle said that she would fill me in on the rest of our plans once she was on board at Heathrow.

I took my time getting off the jet but decided to exit well before Richard did, in an effort to minimize suspicion. It was difficult to part with Richard but time was of the essence. I wanted to tell him everything about my situation but simply could not. We would talk at a more appropriate time. For now I needed to love him for who he was, but work appropriately with him as my pilot on a very important assignment.

I thought it would be better to request my trip to London through the standard flight services rather than through Richard directly. Why I had to go to Dijon might raise some suspicion with anyone who might be monitoring me, so I decided to talk to Richard about the next flight to Dijon, once we had Danielle safely on board in London.

Richard seemed embarrassed as we said goodbye to each other. "Homayra, I do hope you understand that my feelings for you are in total control with the rest of my emotions. Oh hell, Homayra, who am I kidding, I can't wait to hold you again in my arms. My god today was just so incredibly wonderful."

As I walked through the bustling activity of the Charles De Gaulle Aéroport, I scheduled my early morning flight to London-Heathrow and told the scheduler to hold the jet until I arrived, just in case I had a conflict with Henri. I had no idea how I was going to break away from him in the morning and was feeling sick to my stomach about seeing him. I was heading into Henri's world once again and the thought of actually hearing his voice haunted me so much that I actually began hearing his voice as I walked through the busy terminal. My eyes wandered to the many televisions screens that were flashing breaking news in the airport bars and restaurants on the main concourse. News stories about Henri were playing out on all stations in every bar. Travelers stood engrossed as they watched live images of Henri battling it out with the hungry media.

I stepped into the closest pub and stood by bar while staring at Henri's face on the television screen. A buxom bartender in a ridiculously short skirt, retro-fishnet stockings and an over-the-top cleavage mechanically greeted me. "What can I get you honey?"

My mind was tracking so intently on the news that I barely heard her speaking to me.

"Excuse me love, I said, what can I get you to drink?"

"Oh, I'm sorry. Would you please bring me a white wine of some sort, I really don't care what?"

I couldn't remove my eyes from the screen. I simply could not believe what I was hearing. There was Henri, in all of his glory, standing on the steps of UNESCO-France, extoling the successful approval of our brand new organization.

"What the fuck?" I said aloud, as the bartender sat a glass of wine on a napkin in front of me.

The bartender swiveled around on her heels and studied the television screen.

"Oh, I just love that man----don't you, my dear?" She adjusted her bra as if she were fixing herself exclusively for Henri. "And what that man is doing for those poor prostitutes is just wonderful, don't you think? I mean someone needs to take a stand for those filthy whores out there on the street; selling their bodies for sex. I mean, oh my lord! I would never stoop that low for money. I work hard for my money and I take care of my body."

Did I miss something, I wondered, as I watched Henri thanking me publically for my support of *his* mission. How could it be possible that the funding was approved so soon, when I had just met with the finance panel the day before and was convinced that we were on a path to nowhere?

"I bet the son-of-a-bitch threatened the finance minister if he didn't sign the order," I mumbled under my breath.

"What's that you say--- love?"

"Nothing ma'am, I was just talking to myself, sorry."

"I am so mad at those damn reporters having the nerve to question that wonderful man about that stupid train of death thing. I mean just because some stupid wino said that he saw a train full of body bags---why would anyone think that Dr. Lepan is involved? I ask you, sweetie, just look at that beautiful man putting this stupid reporter back in his place. Go Henri---baby! Go! You hot thing!"

The bartender was yelling at the television as if she were watching a soccer game.

"My god, to have a piece of that man for just one evening----ummmm. I would tear him apart. Oh---and have you ever seen his so-called girl-friend? What a wet-fish she is! Some stuck-up, reclusive fashion bitch who's afraid to leave her house. She always seems to be so bored with that man. She must be crazy. I would be all over that man if he were mine, and I would never let him go."

Directly in back of me, another television showed Timothy Edwards being questioned by a television crew at a coffee house in Oxford. It was the first time I had ever seen the man and he appeared excited but extremely exhausted. The volume on the television was muted but the bi-line read: Veteran ENS reporter, Timothy Edward, maintains his position and refuses to give up his sources, regarding the Train of Death.

I glanced at my watch and saw that it was 8:30 p.m. I was now dreadfully late for Henri and I needed to be on my way. I dropped a handful of cash on the bar and walked out.

"Goodnight honey! Hey, that woman looks familiar? Hey wait a minute---wasn't that Dr. Lepan's girlfriend?"

I left the bar and joined the human race moving though the busy concourse. I exited the airport and caught a cab to Henri's residence.

As we approached the gated community my heart was pounding so hard that I could hear my blood surging through my eardrums. I practiced the same breathing exercises that Zooli had taught me when I was a teenager, whenever I was about to work with an aggressive horse.

"Now take a deep breath Homi, and then let it out very slowly," Zooli would instruct me. "Okay, now take your second breath and hold it in much longer. Good girl, now let it out very slowly." The exercise failed now, just as it did then. I was more scared than ever with an added dose of nausea.

Zooli had also taught me to set my boundaries with the horse, while allowing the beast the room to move away from me. "If he advances on you, bump him sharply on his nose until he backs away. You *must* establish leadership at all times Homi, and be assertive! He *must* respect you Homi. If he does not respect you, then he will run you down!"

I opened the front door of what I considered to be Henri's corral and was surprised to find the lights off throughout the entire main floor. I walked quietly through the large foyer and into the stateroom where I saw Henri sitting alone at the dining room table with his back to me. The room was dimly lit, illuminated only by an overabundance of spent candles which were bleeding wax at their base. A table was set with two large vases of drooping roses and trays of uneaten appetizers. An empty champagne glass was sitting at my place setting along with sealed envelope. Two magnum size bottles of champagne were stuffed upside down in an ice bucket, resembling dead soldiers, while the third bottle was within reach of Henri's left hand. Henri slowly turned his head towards me as I stepped into the room.

"Well, well, well, my little queen has finally arrived home to her castle."

I stood in the doorway watching the flickering candles reflecting off his reading glasses.

"Tell me my love, don't you find it just a little humorous that it takes almost eight hours to fly only 250 kilometers." Henri's elbow slipped on the table, causing him to miss the side of his glass as he tried to fill it.

"Well the weather was very intense, Henri, and there was a delay."

I approached the table acting like there was nothing to be afraid of.

"Delay, I'm sure."

Henri turned in his chair and faced me. His face looked large, red and saturated with alcohol.

"I hire one of the best goddamn Gulfstream pilots all of the way from Daytona, Florida, where ever in the hell that is, and he can't fly my goddamn jet through a French rain storm. This guy was supposed to be one of those top-gun fighter pilots. And he can't bring my beautiful queenie home to me through a little weather cloud?"

"Henri, he was only doing his job and being safe."

I walked over and placed my hand on his shoulder to calm him. The touch of his body was revolting to me and caused a stinging sensation.

"Well you're home safe and sound, that's what matters---darling." Henri attempted to stand up, but lifted the leaf of the table with the side of his hip. The silverware rattled and the bottle of champagne fell over on its side, leaking the contents onto the table and over the edge.

Henri stood up and moved into my personal space as I moved away from him in alarm. Wrong response I thought, as my vision of Zooli reappeared into my conscience. I regained some of my composure and took his hand and guided him back over to his chair.

"Everything looks so beautiful Henri, what a wonderful thing you have done here. I am so dreadfully sorry that I was late coming home."

Henri was clearly drunk and appeared to have been sitting in the candle lit room for quite some time. He inspected me with a level of frustration and began appraising my clothing with a syndical expression on his face. "Why on earth are you wearing those tight blue jeans and that skimpy little shirt? You look as if you had just come from a rock-and-roll concert."

"Oh this," I said, as I looked down at my cotton tank and visible bra straps.

"Well Henri, we were---I mean---I was caught in a downpour at the airport this afternoon, and my clothes were soaked. This was all I could find on the plane to wear."

"And so you were dressed like this on the plane; all alone in that tiny cabin with Captain Top Gun? I'm surprised he was able to keep his hands off those sexy jeans of yours. No wonder you were so late getting home. Exactly how long was your *layover* anyway? It all sounds a bit too cozy for me."

"Oh stop it Henri! Capt. Edward was the most appropriate pilot and you should be happy that we are both safe. The weather was terrible."

Henri's eyes wandered to my place setting where the envelope with gold lettering was sitting unopened. "Oh, my god, I almost forgot what this whole celebration was all about. I wanted to surprise you with the wonderful news, but some loud mouth reporter let the proverbial cat out of the goddamn bag."

Henri picked up the envelope and handed it to me. "May I purpose a toast to the most beautiful woman in the world, and the next presidente of Mission of Mercy?

> *UNESCO - Paris announces the founding of Mission of Mercy*
> *You are cordially invited to attend an evening of celebration*
> *to formally announce the successful creation of Mission*
> *of Mercy. This new organization will provide the much*
> *needed support for the helpless victims of rape and torture*
> *due to the growing industry of human trafficking.*

Ms. Homayra Parastou, the newly installed Presidente,
will be the host of this fine event which will include an
introduction of purpose, entertainment, and dinner.
All of the proceeds from this event will be donated to:
Paris Children's Hospital Foundation
Saturday, 9th at six-thirty in the evening
The Palais Garnier Opera House - Paris, France
Formal attire

I read the invitation with a look of shock, which was both contrived and genuine. I simply could not understand how the approval for funding was possible. Not even 24-hours had passed since that unproductive meeting had ended resulting in absolutely nothing and suddenly everything has been stamped and approved?

Even the gold scripted invitations to the event had been prepared well in advance. How could this be, I wondered; finally understanding the true power of Henri. Henri is good, I thought. Henri is really good.

"Darling, you mustn't forget to finish our toast." Henri tapped his glass against mine.

I took a sip of the champagne just to appease him.

"How could this have happened in such short order, Henri? Yesterday the Minister of Finance gave no indication of approval, as a matter of fact; I thought that we were getting nowhere."

"My dear, you should know by now, that I have zero tolerance for those who challenge me."

Henri refilled both of our glasses and looked me dead in the eye. "If I ever set my eyes upon that Jules Perrault prick again, they will have to send an ambulance to take his pitiful body away."

Henri maneuvered his hand around my waist and moved me against his body. "The nerve of that man saying such sexist remarks to my precious jewel." He lightly kissed me on the back of my neck. The touch of his face against my neck repulsed me as I gracefully turned around and faced him.

Henri stood looking at me as if he was planning to seduce me. I moved forward, directly into his space and backed him up a few steps. Zooli referred to that move as "disengaging a horse's hind quarters."

Henri clearly had the expression on his face that he anticipated the plans for the evening to execute flawlessly:

He envisioned Homayra walking through the door smiling with delight to see him. They would watch the sun set over western skies and hold each other as she begged him for his fantastic news. Henri would hold the envelope behind his back and tease her as *she* giggled and reached for the proof of his success. Henri would take his time opening an expensive bottle of Goût de Diamants.

She would finally be released from those horrible demons that haunted her dreams every single night. Those suspicious messages which were coming from that selfish sister of hers. That insolent and distrustful carbon copy of the beautiful Homayra; the one that needed to silenced and relocated long ago.

It was finally going to happen, after 32 years of first living like father and daughter, to celibate roommates. Tonight was going to be the night to remember between Henri and *her*. Everything would unfold perfectly, as if by design, it would all come together as *she* savored the good news.

She would drop the card on the floor and slowly pull for Henri's touch. All of the reasons that froze her emotions for Henri in the past would dissolve away in an instant as *she* surrendered her body to Henri.

She would be the one to advance on Henri this time, not like all of the times before, where she had always mechanically just performed her duty. *She* would be the one opening up her body and soul while desperately reaching for true love from Henri. *She* would be the one who would aggressively make love to Henri in a lustful and marginally violent way.

They would make love all night long, all throughout the house, spontaneously starting on the cool tile floor of the kitchen. Then, they would have intercourse on the stairway, which would finally culminate in their bed. Not Henri's bed but their bed!

She would be the one lusting for Henri, with a look of erotic nastiness. *She* would be the one struggling to hold back that grand orgasm which *she* never, ever, made available to Henri. *She* would be the one to see visible signs of anger in Henri's eyes for starving him from her sacred orgasms. *She* was the one who kept Henri away from this mystical never-to-happen explosion like some blessed covenant. But that was then and this is now.

She would be the one to beg Henri to exact some level of punishment on her for starving him for what seemed like a lifetime of sexual torture. Finally it would happen. *She* would growl like a wild animal as the two of them battled it out in bed, exercising the selfish spirit of her selfish sister out of her soul and away from their peaceful home.

She would convulse and squeal with an uncontrollable appetite for any movement that Henri would be willing to extend to her. Henri would hold her at bay for once in her goddamn life, as she begged for Henri to give it all to her. Henri would finally be in total and complete control of the one woman in the world he could never own. The one honest and most pure woman that he placed on a pedestal, directly at the heels of his own mother would be finally his.

Henri would then release himself strategically after *she* exploded with the one and only climax *she* ever had ever experienced from the right man in her entire life. Now it would be Henri's turn to make her beg for his long awaited grand finale.

That scenario was not to be and Henri knew it, as he sat across the table and leered at me through his drunken eyes.

"My dear Henri, I just love these stuffed grape leaves, and this beautiful tray of Iranian thin breads. The feta cheese and herbs look just marvelous."

Henri was now drinking vodka on the rocks and stirring the cubes with his fingers as he watched me scarcely nibble on the appetizers, now realizing that l was never going to nibble on him.

"So---you are very proud of me for giving you this little news?" Henri asked, as he cocked his head to one side, in an effort to block a nervous facial tick.

"Henri, where on earth did you find Nargesi Esfanaaj? The fried spinach with eggs and onions remind me of home," I said, further infuriating Henry, as he sat across the table weighed down by the alcohol.

Henri sat tapping the base of his martini glass on the table cloth. "I am just so happy that you are pleased with my unimportant news about the organization." He looked up at the slow moving ceiling fan. "It seems as if everyone in France is so fucking pleased for my news as well." He was now banging the base of his glass firmly on the table top.

"Oh stop it Henri, you've had too much to drink. Of course I'm excited about your news."

"I'm sure you've heard all about my stupid train of death."

"Yes, what in heaven's name is that all about---Henri?"

"They want to open a formal investigation on me! Fuck those stupid bastards---they don't have a clue where to look. They are so damn far away from anything." Henri was now talking as if he were alone in a room. An evil laugh began emanating from the depths of his chest and out of his nostrils. "This fucking little prick---newspaper boy in London, seems to think he has some goddamn thing on me? All of those little bastards in the press are fucking clueless! They have been screwing with me for weeks now, trying to make me look like a goddamn fool! They will never beat me! I will beat them!" Henri slammed the base of his glass down on the table, ejecting all of the ice cubes onto the table and floor.

"Henri, please, give me your glass, you've had entirely too much to drink---darling!"

"And like you really care----darling!" Henri stood up and stepped away from the table, carefully avoiding the wooden leaf.

"You are always trying to watch out for me, aren't you my little Iranian nurse maid? I'll give you my glass when there's something in it to give you! Now, I'm on a mission for another bottle of Russian vodka," Henri said, as he wavered out of the room and into the kitchen. "Oh---and by the way, my dear, I meant to ask you, did you ever find those wonderful boots you went shopping for the other day? I was so looking forward to a little fashion show from you tonight."

Henri was slamming cupboard doors and sifting through liquor bottles in the kitchen. I froze in my seat wondering how I was going to respond to his inquiry. "Oh Henri, I really couldn't find what I liked; besides I really just needed to get away."

"Damn it! Well it certainly appears that I have run out of all of my favorite Russian vodka. Well okay then! I guess I will just have to switch to another one of my favorite countries! "

Henri staggered back into the room holding slices of lemons, a stack of shot glasses and a bottle of Patrón Tequila. He fell back down in his chair and pushed a lemon and shot glass in front of me. "My dear, I've had such a dreadful day, would you please honor me in a drink to the wonderful country of Mexico."

Henri reached over and filled my glass to the very top. "Come now darling, I insist that you at least provide me with some level of gratitude for what I have done for you."

Lifting my glass with extreme displeasure, I placed my glass against his.

"To Mexico--- and all of those filthy little horny bitches! Oh---and to my dear friend and trusting brother! Salud! " Henri tossed his head back and poured the entire shot down his throat as if it were nothing more than water. After repositioning his wobbling head to center he checked to see if I had performed my side of the agreement.

"Henri, you know that I can't drink alcohol like this, what with all of the champagne, I'm getting dizzy.

"Please, you beautiful thing, I demand that you share a drink with me for my brother in Mexico." Henri refilled his glass and challenged at me to follow suit. "My compadre, my fucking brother! Another loved one who now questions me about my loyalty! Just like the rest of the people in this god forsaken country."

I had no choice this time but to comply. I hesitantly held my glass to the side of his and waited for more rambling dialogue.

"To my beautiful Homayra, the one who keeps her distance from me, as she successfully evades my officers assigned to protect her. Just because she just had to get out of town! Tell me Homayra, why you were running away from Paris in that stupid little pink taxicab the other day?"

I sat at the table feeling fury building in my chest. The monster was now waking up and turning on me.

"I want to know, my darling! Why were you in such a hurry to leave Paris the other day?"

I was done with his drunken rants and rallied my first shot over Henri's thick wall of alcohol. "I thought that was you who was following me you---bastard!"

I stood up from the table and leaned over him. "How dare you, Henri, I never dreamed that you would be spying on me! How dare you for invading my privacy!"

I turned around and walked towards the door.

"Princess, I'm just trying to keep you safe!"

"Safe from what, Henri, your own private army?"

I climbed the stairs and rushed towards my bedroom. This was my time to exit Henri's domain. He was drunk, dangerous, and completely unaware of his actions. I ran down the hallway and entered my bedroom, throwing some of my most precious belongings into my travel bag. Off the wall I snatched my precious riding crop which Miss Cathy had given to me when I was just a child. I draped my travel bag and handbag over my left shoulder and gripped the riding crop in my right hand.

Henri was now yelling from the dining room below as he was struggling to stand up. "How many times in one blessed day will the people around me treat me with such disrespect? First it's the press and now it's Homayra's turn! Our Lady of Goodness!"

Henri was struggling to break free from the confines of drunkenness and the crowded table above him. A huge crash resounded with the sound of broken dishes, empty champagne bottles and crystal goblets smashing on to the marble floor. The entire table sounded as if it had been violently overturned.

"I was only trying to protect you---Homayra! Why won't you ever let me protect you?"

Henri was now walking through the downstairs hallways yelling at the top of his lungs. "Now that you have become so public, everybody wants a piece of you. Including that stupid Timothy Edwards reporter in London wants to catch a story of you. I almost expected that little pussy to walk in here with you tonight! Now you are turning into that selfish sister of yours! Homayra, darling, please come down stairs and share a glass of sherry with me!"

I left my room and ran down the hall way in the opposite direction from where I had come. Henri's voice was following me from the floor below as if he knew exactly where I was in relation to him.

"Homayra, please come and sit with me. I need you to be with me tonight. Please give me one night of your company. I must leave tomorrow again for another trip to that god forsaken castle. I hate that horrid place and all of those selfish pigs. Please Homayra let me spend a wonderful night with you in my arms."

I reached the stairway on the other side of the house only to find Henri standing at the foot of the stairs refilling his glass with the last remnants of tequila. He leaned against the wall and snarled at me.

"Hello there you sexy little thing; you look so hot in those tight fitting jeans! My dear Homayra, I had such expectations for us tonight. Why my darling, will you never give yourself to me? After all I have done for you!"

His confidence vanished when he noticed my travel bag hanging over my shoulder. "Well now, where in the hell do you think you are going---you little bitch?

Out of everything I have given you for your entire life and you think that you have the right to just walk in and out of my home at will? You owe me some of your precious time for all of the years you have pretended to tolerate me!"

Suddenly my familiar vision of Zooli appeared in the doorway just to the left of Henri, acting as my guardian angel.

"If you take one step past me, it will be the last step you ever take. I wanted you tonight Homayra. I wanted you more than I ever care to admit, and now you have the nerve to walk out on me, at a time like this?" Henri was beating the base of his bottle against the wall violently as he challenged me to advance.

I held the riding crop close to my leg and gathered up all of my emotions. There he was in all of his glory, Henri, the massive stallion, waiting for me to enter his stall. I could see it in his eyes, he was going to toy with me and gently lure me into striking range for the kill.

The instructions from Zooli became audible as I took a deep breath and drew my thoughts together. "Define your objective in your mind Homi," Zooli said. "You must own the moment. You must make the horse know that you are in control him, that you are the leader of the heard. Start your mission when you are ready and then complete it. You are now bigger than the horse. Define your objective and do not look into the eyes of the stallion," said Zooli.

"Own your position over the horse and gauge his breathing," said Zooli as I took my first steps forward.

Henri roared at me at the top of his lungs with his eyes raging. "Come to me you selfish little cunt and let me take you apart!"

I ignored his perverted neighing, but gauged his behavior and position within the confines of his imaginary stall. The beast's face cringed with anger as his entire countenance crumpled up like that of a huge paper doll. His upper body snapped forward as he hurled his glass directly at my head. I watched the glass move through the air and confidently ducked to the side as it flew past my temple and smashed against the large painting in back of me.

Shards of glass and liquor shattered against the wall and mixed with the air around me. Down I stepped as I kept my eyes on the doorway and away from the frightening eyes of the beast. When I reached the last step the stallion threw himself in front of me blocking my path to safety. I continue on with my progression as the beast launched his body towards mine.

With complete control I maintained the same pace directly into the face of the horse. "Move through him girl," Zooli said, as I approached the beast's huge and drunken head. Forward I went as if I owned the crowded stall which housed the crazy stallion.

"Move it---Henri," I demanded, as I approached him face to face. "I need you to move over *there!*"

I locked my eyes on the very spot that I needed him to move to. The beast now stood with a rigid hesitation as an explosion was about to ensue. I was now completely prepared to meet his violence and render him harmless.

"I told you---that I need you---to move over *there!*"

I moved my riding crop into motion. The flat leather tip of the crop sung through the air and slapped the beast on the right side of his face instantly producing a raised welt, well before my arm fully extended.

The beast fell back, meeting my intended goal, but advanced on me once again. The full force of my recoiling riding crop slammed against the opposite side of the beast's face piercing the skin this time, as my arm returned back to neutral. The impact of the crop ejected Henri's glasses off the bridge of his nose and dug into his face making bloody contact. Henri was totally overcome with shock, disbelief and pain. He fell passively against the wall and sunk to the floor like a loser in a boxing match.

"Now you stay there! You sick bastard!" I stood above him almost taunting him to move. "Henri, you have changed me into a stronger person and you have no idea how much I appreciate that!"

The imaginary vision of both Zooli and Goli appeared in the doorway seemingly urging for me to join them.

"I'm leaving you now. But! I will see you at the opening event!"

I pinned my eyes on the beast's drunken pupils which were now becoming weaker by the second. Exhaustion, humility, embarrassment and a large volume of alcohol had reduced this once powerful control figure into a wilting parade float.

My mind was clear and concise as I left the apartment and walked down the street towards town as I reached for my cell phone and the card of Captain Richard Edward. I smiled as I turned the corner, feeling as if I were completely armed with guns and ammunition.

I had neither, nor did I need them. I was now armed with strength and confidence to carry on.

Chapter 39

HOMAYRA: DANNI UNLOAD

London-Heathrow Airport - 7:48 a.m.

Danielle was not as impressed with the Gulfstream as much I was, as she walked quickly across the tarmac towards the resting jet and climbed the steps into the cabin. She began reminiscing about her days on the wings of luxury the moment her eyes adjusted to the interior lighting. She said that she had way too many horrible experiences flying from country to country in similar airplanes with the high rollers in and around the modeling industry.

She said that the beds in the sleeping quarters were designed for everything else but sleeping. Admittedly, I was a bit embarrassed over that comment.

It was now Danielle's turn to let out some of her most painful memories that were provoked by the environment of the luxurious airplane. She vividly described times of snorting extra-long lines of cocaine and drinking ultra-expensive bottles of champagne as men and women studied her body through their own cocaine bleached minds. She recalled needing a heroin fix so badly one time, that she agreed to have sex with two bookers and another model as they flew from Russia to Switzerland and then on to Eastern France.

As much as my sister had poured out her painful memories of the past to the welcoming ears of Danielle, few stories, if any, of Danielle's tragic past had ever been discussed with Goli. She said that she had never wanted to burden Golareh with her own past. Her comment sort of shocked me as I watched Danielle stowing her luggage away and taking a seat next to me. I have learned that some of the best listeners of stories of abuse keep their own pasts extremely close to their own vests.

I asked Danielle if she had ever been physically injured during the many rapes she had endured in modeling industry. "Oh, I simply can't tell about you any of that, it's just too horrible," Danielle said, as tears welled up.

I held her hands and looked into her eyes as the sound of the jet engines increased in velocity and our jet taxied into the departure pattern. Richard opened the door and glanced back at us with a caring look. "Are you ladies comfortable?"

Danielle looked at him and then followed his line of sight directly across the cabin to my eyes. "Oh, why yes captain, something tells me that at least one of us is more than just comfortable."

"Well, we are going to be on the ground here for a short while, so feel free to take care of whatever you need, and I'll check back with you in just a bit. Welcome to Heathrow, ladies, the largest airport in the U.K. and the third slowest in the entire world. But once we get airborne the flight will take us only about an hour."

Richard closed the door and Danielle smiled and looked directly into my eyes. "You need to clue me in on what's going on between the two of you. I can see it all over your face---girl?"

All I could do was smile as I wondered how amazingly attracted I had become to the man in the cockpit, all in the space of what seemed like a few hours. "Danni, that story is meant for a more appropriate time. But let me just say that I am feeling so much more human now."

As the jet slowly edged behind a long line of different size airplanes, Danielle continued to unload her stories of abuse at the castle. It was apparently time for her to empty the rotten garbage in her memories.

She described being burned with a cigarette on her back as the animals that controlled her destiny treated her as if she was nothing more a rented appliance. Brief descriptions of nightmarish acts of oral sex with fat rich men in expensive suits made us both want to vomit. She even talked about losing her virginity with a patron at the castle on of all days, her thirteenth birthday.

"I had a void in my soul and Henri knew exactly how to fill it. I was confused, scared, and willing to do anything for my father and then ultimately my new parent which was heroin."

My body shivered as she talked about the day she met Henri and how magnanimous he was. She described her first impression of him on a busy street in London's lower market district, presenting himself as some lifesaving messiah. I could so relate, having similar experiences with Henri at the age not much older than Danielle was at the time.

"Although I appeared much older than my actual age, I was only 12-years-old when I noticed Henri watching me from a distance on the far end of the market with my father just out of reach. I was a master of the streets, even then, and always on guard. But for some damn reason, on that particular day, I left myself wide open as Henri approached me from behind. He spared no time with introductions and immediately set the hook by telling me that he thought that I was the most beautiful woman he had ever seen. He read me like a book as he reached for my hand and studied my fingernails. 'My dear, you look as if you haven't had a bath in days. My heart aches for you my poor dear lady. Please take me to your mother and father; I would so very much like to see how I can help you.'

On the rare occasions my father was sober we would both be out desperately seeking employment with anyone who would hire either one of us. I was too young to be considered for employment and my father was always passed off as a drunk. My father and I were walking separately through the market that day taking handouts of fruits and vegetable from the local vendors who we had known for years. We never stole from the vendors because my father had once owned a stand in the very same market.

Everyone was aware of the fact that my mother died of ovarian cancer when I was only seven-years-old and how my father had lost his entire meat business trying to pay for her medical bills. We were pretty well off prior to my mother's illness. We lived in a big house and even employed gardeners and maids. We owned and operated two meat stands at two of the largest markets in London. But after my mother died, none of his friends were there to help him out, so he began to disappear into his own pity. Bar owners, who knew him well in the good old days, did what they could to help but one by one dropped off the radar. My father was just too far gone.

A bartender called me in the middle of the night, telling me to come down and fetch my drunken father. It was an evening that I will never forget. When we returned home my father passed out on the living room floor and I went to bed. In the middle of the night, I heard my father rummaging through his dresser drawer searching for something. I knew the sound of that drawer well, because that's where he kept his gun.

I got out of bed and stepped into his room. My father's sorrowful eyes met with mine with a look of embarrassment as he slowly put the gun back in the drawer and closed it. I slept in the same bed that night with my father, starring up at the ceiling for the remainder of the night until the sun came up the next morning. I made sure that he would not wake up later on and go for that gun again. I loved my father dearly.

Henri introduced himself to my father and told him how he would like to send me off to school and later the university. My father had stars in his eyes for what Henri was offering his only child. I remember thinking years later; that if my mother had been alive at the time, Henri wouldn't have been able to buy a side of beef from us, much less her own flesh and blood. So off I went with this king of kings, out of the squalor and into a fantasy land of royalty.

When I first arrived at the castle I thought that I had been reborn. Henri gave me expensive clothing and treated me like princess. He referred to me as his amber princess, for I was the only black girl at the castle at the time. I also think that I was Henri's first and only attempt to appreciate a female of color.

Henri began flirting with me and spying on me while I was dressing. Later, during social occasions he would find hidden ways to fondle me behind chairs and beneath table tops. It made me uncomfortable at first, but he was so wonderfully kind to me that I got over it. I hate to admit it,

Homi, but there was something about Henri's touch that felt good to me. Homi, Henri was successful at grooming me."

I fought back tears as I remembered my own experiences with Henri when I was just seventeen.

"Why Henri hid his groping hands confused me because fondling was the normal protocol for all of the guests at the castle no matter how old they were. The castle itself was one huge sex-party where everyone could engage freely in sexual activity. It was an orgy atmosphere and a sick one at that.

Henri's behavior suddenly changed for reasons I could not understand. He walked in on me while I was getting dressed one quiet afternoon. I was bent over naked, pulling up my panties from my ankles. I froze when I saw Henri standing there gazing at me. In a low voice he told me to drop my panties to my feet and stand up straight. He closed the door behind him and entered my room and began slowly walking around me surveying every inch of my body.

I'll never forget what he said to me that afternoon, because it hurt me so terribly.

'Oh my, young lady, you are one shining example of the mysteries your kind. If I was not of sound mind, I would savor every single inch of your beautiful black body. I have always wondered what it would be like to screw a negro. It would be ever so simulating to press our starkly different colored bodies together.'

Henri placed the palm of his left hand on the lower part of my stomach. He moved his body closer to me and lightly touched my bare rear-end with his fingertips.

'I'm embarrassed to admit this, even to myself, but I have always found you people very erotic in a strange sort way. Those rich lips you people have. And those overdeveloped gluteus-maximus muscles. Your perky little nipples are also so tempting.'

Henri paused as he stood directly in back of me. He slowly moved his hand from the tips of my shoulders down my sides and around each of my hips, flattening his right hand just above my pubic bone.

'But would I ever pleasure myself with your kind? No! I will never stoop so low as to pick the common fruit of a nigger.'

Homi, his remarks were so startling to me. He always seemed that he cared so much about me, but suddenly his entire opinion of me shifted from a person with so much potential to a worthless black tramp. I believe that he lowered my own opinion of myself on that very day.

'Too bad my little Amber Princess,' Henri said to me. 'I know what you have been hoping for but that will never happen. For you---my dear---you are meant to be sold to those who have a taste for your breed.'

He turned and left my room and never looked back.

I'll tell you Homi, Henri is one sick man with combustible personality and a brain that follows no rule of common sense.

Soon other staff members were in control of my destiny at the castle. I was never sent off to school as he had promised my poor father, and no way in hell was he going to place me at a university. Instead he dressed me up like a fucking stripper and sent me out to fuck his guests.

They periodically took me to the infirmary to be tested for sexually transmitted diseases. Can you believe that, Homi, a 14-year-old child being tested for venereal disease---which I would have only caught from one of them? They also--- always seemed to pay so much attention to our teeth. They wanted to make sure that we all appeared outwardly healthy, well dressed and somewhat refined.

Everything had to do with our market value. How we looked, how we smelled, and how much we could fetch. Our handlers taught us how we needed to present ourselves to the customers.

'You must appear as if you are not interested in them whatsoever,' they would instruct me. 'Provide them even with a hint of disinterest. That's what these people were really attracted to.'

At the time these instruction made no sense to me but later I realized that they wanted us to appear challenging to the customers by presenting them with an expression of unavailable nastiness. Apparently, they wanted the customer to experience the thrill of the hunt.

The entire activity between the girls on the floor and the clients were completely contrived. It was a stupid show designed to provide the customer with a sense of conquest. Forget the fact that we were already bought and paid for, we had to make the customers believe that they had won our attention because of their own wonderful looks and qualities. Far from it! Fuck them all, I always screamed. I thought all of the men were rich gluttons for sex, and I hated them all from the depths of my heart.

They were getting me stoned on pot when I first met the two of you, but had not yet pushed me into full time guest services. It wasn't until Henri decided that the two of you would be much more appropriate for the fox hunters, rather than some little black tramp spoiling the view of the landscape. That's when they began ordering me to the floor every single night and switching my drug regimen from pot to cocaine. The drug that really put me on the direct path to heroin was the amphetamines. They fed *speed* to all the women of the castle! Every single damn day we were always expected to be happy, horny and ready to fuck!

Henri had me sold off to clients in other countries many times but Miss Cathy wouldn't hear of it. My dear Miss Cathy was and probably still is Henri's Achilles heel; he would never say no to her---ever. I had lost the ability to fight and was simply doing whatever they told me to do, up until the night Goli came looking for me in that room. The room they called the Grand Circus.

The activities in that room were indescribable. It was the primary launching pad for all of the new arrivals. It was in that horrible room that women were paraded around in a large circle and sold to the highest bidder. Many of the women were plucked from the ring and used for the entire week by the guests. Those poor girls had no idea what was in store for them. Many of them believed that they were being initiated into some sort of life of luxury.

Most of the guests were government officials from all over the world, brought in by the French government to fatten them up. Others were CEO's of some of the largest corporations in the world who wanted screw an underage girl to death during the week, then take her home to use as eye candy for their conventions and business parties.

Goli was on a mission that night to find me and get me the hell out of there. I yelled at her to leave but she wouldn't take *no* for an answer. It was entirely too dangerous for her to be in that goddamn room. She begged me to leave with her and desperately tried to drag me out of there, but at that point, I was in way too far over my head.

I also knew that both Henri and Ari had spotted her as she ran from the room crying. That was the night we were separated and moved away from that god forsaken castle.

I was moved to London and sold to a French magazine publisher and never knew what happened to Goli. I found myself in the same room with well-known designers like Versace, Giorgio Armani, Calvin Klein, Valentino and Yves Saint Laurent. At first I hated to be photographed but knew that I had to look good in order to stay alive, so I forced myself to be better than the best in front of the camera.

I was nothing more than a Barbie doll with all of the working anatomical parts. It wasn't until I was rescued by a woman named Magda Hulls that my life changed for the better. I later learned how Henri and Ari had buried your existence from Goli and it broke my heart. Your sister saved my sanity, Homi, and I will never ever stop thanking her."

Danielle and I held our hands tightly together as Richard received the final orders from the control tower to take off. As the jet screamed down the runway and launched into the sky, I sank into my seat and melted. Danielle leaned over and wrapped her arms around me as if she was trying to protect me from the storms in my mind.

There was just simply too much news for me to comprehend, all of the many horrible things that Henri had done to so many people. I leaned into her body and ached over our intersecting sorrowful lives.

"It will be okay, Homi. We're gonna get that bastard and I'm gonna enjoy every goddamn minute of it."

We leveled out at 7300 Meters and Richard began speaking over the intercom, waking both of us from our joint dream.

"Ladies, the lonely pilot up here in the flight deck graciously requests the pleasure of your company in the front seat. Please join me in the cockpit with a cup of fresh brewed coffee."

For the rest of the flight the three of us huddled in the cockpit while Danielle informed us all of what was next for us once we landed in Dijon.

I brought Richard up to date with an abbreviated explanation of my family tragedy, and I also told him about Henri's drunken tirade the night before.

"Goli told me that it would take a lot to break Henri down and that's exactly what was happening. Every day Timothy was publishing some new story in the headlines about Henri's secret life. He was delaying and deleting Henri's important emails, text messages and even rearranging his appointment calendar. Timothy was making Henri look like fool to everyone associated with him."

Danielle unzipped her pocket book and pulled out a note pad with an action list.

"Okay, so here's what's next. We have got to find a way to get on the other side of the castle walls and find Zooli. She should be able to get us into the castle itself and help us find Henri's satellite phone. There's a rental car waiting for us when we land, complements of Frédéric. He has also made us a reservation at a hotel in the heart Montbéliard. Homi- -- I want you to think back to when we were kids. Do you remember Stash, the old black Hunt Master? Please tell me that you remember that old wonderful man who raised the foxhounds and ran all of the fox hunts? Stash was the only person outside of Miss Cathy that Zooli ever trusted with her horses.

Stash had this adorable son, Goli! You have got to remember Becker? The one you had a crush on?"

Suddenly the face of Becker came into view as if I was watching a Polaroid picture developing in mind. "Oh my god---Becker! Yes I do remember him, and you are right, I did have a crush on that boy. My god---he was so cute."

I remembered watching him working alongside of his father; he was in charge of the foxhounds.

One day in particular, I remember experiencing abnormally painful menstrual cramps and felt terrible. All I could do that day was lie on a cot in the isle of the stables. I loved being around the horses so much that I didn't want to leave. I remember Becker being so kind to me that day. He asked me in a sweet tone if I would mind if he just sat with me for a while.

All day long I rested on the cot, slipping in and out of dreams, listening to the stable sounds all around me. Becker sat peacefully with me the entire day telling me lovely stories about his family and lightly touching me on my hand.

"You will feel better soon, Miss Homi, you wait and see," he told me. I will never forget that innocent young black boy being so kind to me.

"Stash died several years ago and now Becker is the Hunt Master."

"What about Zooli, what do we know about her", I asked.

Danielle pulled up an email from Frédéric on her smart phone and began reading it intently. "Frédéric ran some background reports on Zooli, and it's beginning to flow in as we speak. Okay---according to Frédéric's research group: Zooli was legitimately recruited by Henri in 1974 to provide equestrian training for the National Gendarmerie. She graduated three classes of officers on horseback in the areas of crowd control."

Danielle continued reading. "Zooli Trahm was born in Cairo/Egypt on August 25, 1950. Her father was a well-known French-Hungarian trainer who conditioned horses for many of the countries upper-class. Zooli's mother was from Iran."

"That explains her ability to speak French and Farsi, so well," I mentioned under my breath.

"Zooli attended the Egyptian Academy of Equestrian Arts and graduated with a degree in Equestrian Defensive Phycology. She developed a patented training technique that perfected the cooperative communication between the horse and human. Zooli soon became well known in the larger equestrian circles for what she called protective dynamics, where the horse develops an enhanced level of protective instinct over the rider.

"Zooli moved to Tehran after graduating from the academy and married Dr. Raman Trahm, a physician assigned to Zendān Evin, which is a prison located in northwestern Tehran. They had a son named Alexander. Shortly after his birth, Zooli was heavily recruited by Henri Lepan with the expectation that her family would soon follow. After Zooli moved to Paris, Dr. Trahm was accused of providing drugs to inmates. He vehemently fought the charges against him but was found guilty of selling drugs and sentenced to life in prison.

In the fall of 1978, Dr. Trahm was found dead of an unknown cause. There were conflicting reports as to the exact cause of his death, whether a heart attack or suicide."

Danielle looked up at me in shock and continued to read from her tiny screen. "Listen to this shit, Homi! There's not been a single request from Zooli to the Iranian government to have her son Alexander moved to France, and the report also indicates no public request from Zooli to return back to Iran either. Homi, I'm sure you know why Zooli never made a damn request for her son to come to France or for her to return home?"

"Because Henri told her not to---and she did what she was told! Just like we all did!"

"You are goddamn right, Homi, that bastard has held that poor women in chains for her entire god forsaken life. Hell, girl, Henri probably had her husband framed and murdered!"

"Danni, please reply back to Frédéric and ask him to find out as much as they can about Zooli's son! I want to see if we can locate him and get him out of there."

How bad can Henri possibly be I wondered as Richard sent a landing request to Dijon.

Danielle and I left the cockpit and settled into the seats in the cabin.

"Why was Zooli held at that damn castle for so many damn years---Homi?"

"Henri's probably holds the life and well-being of Zooli's son over that poor woman's head till today! Why Danni---why would he do that?"

"I'll tell you why he keeps Zooli there, Homi! It's because she is Miss Cathy's personal baby-sitter! That's why!"

What a control artist Henri truly is, I thought as I visualized Zooli's poor son who now must be in his mid-thirties. I wondered where he is now and whether Zooli has any contact with him. All of these questions would soon be answered once we get behind the walls of that dreadful castle. Everything was now moving extremely fast as we began our final approach into the air space around the Dijon Bourgogne Airport.

Chapter 40

GOLAREH: BIG BEN'S CODE OF CONDUCT

Big Ben knew that the family theatre which he had worked in for his entire life was his to lose after both of his parents had passed away, so he invested smartly in the business for the long haul. He replaced the old pair of Brenkert-Enarc carbon arc 35 mm movie projectors with a state of the art digital cinema projector which was subscription-based and remotely controlled by a film distributer in London. The projection room, where Timothy slept, was now only used as an observation post to make sure that the customers acted appropriately while on the premises.

The Flick was considered to be one of the most well-known gay and lesbian movie houses in the region and Big Ben strived to retain the theatrical ambiance of the setting, offering quality film art, specialty coffees, craft beer and delicious food. He would not tolerate belligerent drunks or over the top displays of sexual misconduct. He wanted to cater to everyone who appreciated film while pushing out all the riff-raff.

The regulars were well aware of Big Ben's rules of conduct and abided by them fully. Occasionally, however, Big Ben's rules were challenged, usually by some ignorant fool who was misled by Big Ben's feminine speech patterns. Perhaps the fact that he sounded exactly like a woman was a sign of weakness and that maybe Big Ben could easily be taken advantage of. The few who tested that theory, soon found out that they were terribly wrong.

On one particular occasion a group of drunken hoodlums on motorcycles came roaring through the curtain district of Oxford and paid a rambunctious visit to the Flick Theatre, thinking that it was some sort of racy strip club that showed X-rated smut.

After coming to the conclusion that most of the people in the establishment were transgender, the trio exploded in anger and decided to remodel Big Ben's business. One of the bikers, after realizing that the person in his arms wasn't at all Marilyn Monroe but a kissing cousin, lost his cool completely. He furiously pitched her aside as if he had just been infected with the plague.

His fellow biker friends began flipping tables upside down and throwing plates of food against the screen and walls. Glass shattered everywhere as they paraded the Marilyn Monroe look-alike around the room as if she was a witch about to be burned at the stake. One of the bikers began breaking the legs off the chairs for kindling wood and was in the process of building a bonfire in the center of the theatre.

Enter Big Ben, via stage-left, like a mother grizzly, sparing no time at all in gathering up two of the three troublemakers by the scruffs of their neck. The two were suddenly held captive in Big Ben's trademark vice grips. Miss Monroe was suddenly released as Big Ben towed the two compressed human heads in the direction of the third biker who was on the verge of lighting a bonfire.

"Are these two brats friends of yours---sweetie?"

The confused pyromaniac gazed up at Big Ben who was now towering over him as some sort of feminine giant. The blood ripened faces of his leather clad travel companions turned a darker shade of purple as their legs flailed wildly.

"Look at these little boys---would you?" Big Ben gazed down at the two purple faces almost appreciatively.

"Sweetie, these are what I would call my little *brothers- in-arms*. And would you know that this sort of reminds me of the new recipe I have been preparing for my Sunday marinara sauce. I have always prepared my sauce with canned tomatoes, but now with everything going organic, I feel the need to make my pasta sauce with only fresh tomatoes."

Big Ben sounded remarkably like Julia Childs as the two men screamed under the pressure of his massive arms.

The lone biker backed away and studied Big Ben as if the image he was witnessing simply did not add up. How could the voice of woman be coming from the body of a hulk? He kicked the pile of wood in front of him, scattering pieces of splintered furniture across the floor.

"So the recipe goes as follows. Are you listening to me, sweetie? I usually start with two large tomatoes. Not those huge hybrid one. I try to find those small, vine ripened tomatoes. You know the really juicy ones, sort of like these two veggies right here."

Big Ben showed off his blood bursting captors as the lone biker reached behind his back for his switch blade knife. Miss Monroe was terrified and began screaming.

"He's got a knife---Big Ben!"

The bold biker circled Big Ben in show of new-found confidence.

Big Ben looked over at the knife wielding intruder, threw his head back and laughed like woman standing in the center of an opera stage. "Sweetie, do you really think that it's necessary for you interrupt me, just when I'm about to reveal to everyone in this fine room the secret to my Sunday sauce? Now, as I was saying, some like to cook the tomatoes whole, while others like to dice them into tiny pieces. But me---well, I prefer mine---crushed. Sort of like this!"

Big Ben intensified his hold on the two men's necks as their feet kicked wildly. The lone biker decided to make his one and only assault just as Big Ben gave each man under his arms a final compression crush, rendering them both unconscious. They dropped to the floor like lifeless marionettes.

The biker thrust his knife directly at Big Ben once and only once. Out flew Big Ben's foot as if he was kicking a football, knocking the knife out the confused man's grip.

Big Ben advanced on the surprised intruder, grabbing him by the throat and holding his swinging body high above the floor as his massive fingers dug deeply into the fleshy part of the screaming man's neck.

On rare occasions when he had trouble makers, Big Ben refused to simply kick them to the curb and set them free. "Why in the world, would I let these blokes go free?" He always declared. "They'll just go next door or down the street and cause more trouble. Nope, I want these sweeties to spend a comphy night in jail and then report back to me in the morning to repair their damage."

At this point he asked, "Who says we can't rehabilitate my three-little-pigs here? Now I want you to apologize to Miss Monroe here for your rude behavior!"

Big Ben was holding the full grown man high above the floor with his single and fully extended hairy arm. The cheap leather skull cap on the biker's head had slipped over one of his eyes as he dangled above the floor, realizing full well that the balance of his life now hung by the single grip of Big Ben.

"I thought I told you to apologize to Miss Marilyn!"

The totally deflated hell-raiser squeezed out his remaining words to the applause of the people in the room and the arriving police officers: "I am sorry, Miss Monroe!"

The local police force didn't see if often, but they had witnessed it long enough to know, full well, that Big Ben was a force to be reckoned with. They also knew that Big Ben would never hurt anyone unless they deserve it. He was massive, well balanced, and unbelievably strong. The Flick Theatre was Big Ben's way of life, his home and no one was going to control his domain, injure his clientele or insult his staff.

Big Ben considered Timothy a welcomed member of his own family as he rolled over on his side in his bed. He was worried sick over Timothy's whereabouts that night along with everyone else. Slowly his concerns were placed on-hold, as sleep finally swept Big Ben's troubled mind away.

Chapter 41

CHANGES

Changes are taking; the pace I'm going through

— DAVID BOWIE

Timothy hadn't planned to sleep after being awake for nearly four days straight, but it just happened. At 3:30 in the morning Smithy Greene tapped lightly on Big Ben's bedroom door and whispered into the darkness. "Big Ben? I'm so sorry to bother you---but I need your help with getting Timothy up to his bed."

"Did that poor boy finally get home?" Big Ben dropped both of his large feet on the floor and stood up in the darkness. All that Smithy could see from her vantage point was the shadow of a naked man the size of a mountain walking through the darkness. Big Ben's longtime partner, René Ghislain, lay fast asleep under his covers, never stirring as Big Ben kissed him on his cheek and replaced the covers on his side of the bed.

"Hand me my robe baby girl, it's hanging on the back of door. Oh my lord, what time is it, Smithy?"

"It's way after three. I'm so sorry for waking you Big Ben, but there's no way I could get him up the stairs by myself. The poor man is exhausted. I'm just really worried about him."

Smithy handed Big Ben his baby blue robe which sported a large embroidered pink flower on the lapel. Big Ben stepped into to his fuzzy pink slippers and slowly moseyed down the dimly lit hallway towards the main foyer of the theatre.

A French version of *Annie Hall* with English subtitles was showing to a sparse audience as Timothy sat slumped over in the back row of the dark theatre. His head was perched downward and he was completely asleep. His fingers still gripped the pen in mid-sentence on his notebook. An ear pod was plugged into his right ear as the other one dangled from his other ear.

"He's been transcribing interview notes all night long, Big Ben. The poor man has been killing himself for days over this Lepan fiasco. He also needs to eat something soon before he dies of starvation."

Smithy leaned over the sleeping man. "Timothy darling, Big Ben's gonna take you up to your bed, okay baby?"

Timothy's ears registered little of her voice as Big Ben bent down and scooped Timothy out of his seat as if he was a mere child. "Make sure that we get all of his belongings sweetie and follow me up stairs. This poor boy is spent---Smithy."

Big Ben effortlessly carried Timothy's lifeless, 230 pound body up the narrow staircase to the projection room on the second floor.

Smithy followed, still talking. "He arrived just after midnight and immediately went to work writing down everything he had recorded during the day. I'll tell you Big Ben, I'm worried about this man. Reporters are looking for him all over London, just hoping to get an exclusive on him. Poor Timothy has been moving from place to place, evading most reporters while meeting with others. He's also been pumping out stories about this Henri Lepan--sleaze bag--like there's no tomorrow."

"Well darling, it looks like *tomorrow* has finally caught up with this poor boy---he's done. Do me a favor Smithy and go down to my room and fetch me my cell phone. It's charging on my end table next to my bed. I've got to call Goli and let her know that Timothy is safe and sound. That poor child's been worried sick about him."

Big Ben cradled Timothy's large body in one arm as he turned the knob on the door of the projection room with his other hand. He walked into an

extra-large closet which once served as the sleeping quarters for the projection-
ists and placed Timothy on the bed and then covered him with a comforter.
He gently lifted his head and slid a pillow with a silk covering beneath it. Big
Ben then kissed Timothy on his forehead and slowly ambled out of the room.

Smithy was rushing back up the stairs just as Big Ben was coming down.
She realized that there was no possible way that she could pass by his massive body in the stairwell so she retreated back down the steps to the main
floor and handed Big Ben his cell phone.

Big Ben bent down and kissed Smithy on her cheek. "Thank you for
taking care of Timothy; I was worried about him too."

He squinted at the illuminated keypad on his cell phone for Golareh's
phone number and pressed the *send* button. "I'm going back to bed after I
talk to Goli, thanks, Smithy. You're a sweetheart"

Big Ben walked slowly down the hallway towards his room, sliding the
soles of his fluffy pink slippers on the cold linoleum floor as he chatted
softly to Golareh.

Smithy glanced up the dark stairwell at the doorway of the projection
room and immediately started to scurry up the steps; but suddenly paused
as she reconsidered her actions. Abandoning her concerns, she continued
up the steps and slowly opened the room to the projection room.

Timothy's eyes opened slightly as Smithy opened the door of the room
where he was resting. The light and sound of cooling fans of the projector
briefly filled the room as she closed the door behind her and began to slowly
remove her sweater.

Through the vail of darkness, Timothy eyeballed Smithy removing her
silk top, revealing her firm breasts within her lacey white bra. She draped
her shirt over the foot of the bed board and then dropped her black skirt to
the floor, leaving nothing on but a thin pair of black panties.

Smithy stood in the partial darkness, illuminated only by a line of
light emanating from the base of the door and considered her next move.
"Timothy, would you mind if I stayed here with you tonight? It's too late for
me to walk home and I just want to lie next to you?"

Timothy looked up at Smithy trying to capture the image that contained the carefree spirit of a tiny winged fairy.

Although Smithy had much to do with the modifications of her new body, her natural growth took over and created the most beautiful metamorphosis her surgeons had ever seen. Being born a male was a design flaw of the gods that even her doctors agreed upon. Although her previous physique as a man was equally beautiful, the lines of her true architecture had always been that of a female. Her surgeons offered the option of larger breasts but Smithy declined, saying that she needed a body that was more suited for theatrical performance. The result was a well-proportioned physique which projected tantalizingly star like qualities.

Even though Smithy came off as a flirt, it was mostly a show. She never wanted to present herself as a woman for good-times but sometimes she just couldn't resist. It was the actress in her.

"Come here baby and lay next to me."

Timothy lifted the blanket revealing his far from toned belly. Smithy stood there with a look of humility on her face. She bowed her head to the floor and held her breath with awkwardness.

"Smithy, please come over here and lay down with me, I can't hold this blanket up forever."

Smithy slowly moved to the side of the bed and sat down with her back to Timothy. She searched the darkness for some distant spiritual help. Slowly she leaned back on the pillow and lifted her legs and feet from the floor and placed them under the warmth of the blanket.

The room was dark and quiet as she lay on her side motionless, staring at the light at the base of the door.

"Timothy, I need to tell you something, baby, and I'm not sure if you will ever understand."

A few seconds passed before she continued. "I don't know how you are going to take this and if you want me to leave, I will certainly understand."

Smithy gently pulled Timothy's arm over the top of her body. "Baby, I have gone through some major changes in my life. Not just mental changes but physical ones as well."

As Smithy spoke she looked off into the darkness as tears filled her eyes.

Timothy took a deep breath as if it were his last second awake for the day. He gently pulled her in closer to him, warming her now shivering body. "Smithy, I want you to know something and I ask you to take this to heart—okay?"

Smithy nodded her head in quick agreement as she fought off the desire to cry.

"I want you to put all of those concerns about the changes that you speak of completely out of your head from now until eternity. You are a wonderful woman encased in a body that came from heaven---if there is such a damn place. Smithy, you might not be aware of this but I'm considered be one of the best investigative reporters on this side of the Atlantic Ocean."

Timothy chuckled quietly as he continued to fight to stay awake. "But guess what? Most people here firmly believe that I am also one of the biggest assholes on both side of the Atlantic. Even Goli thinks that---most of the time. What I'm trying to say--- Smithy, is just as you desperately needed to change your body into what you believed it always should have been, I need to change the person within my soul into what I apparently was never meant to be. I was designed by some cockeyed god to be a drunk, selfish pig and a womanizing fool. And this---he, she or it, did a goddamn good job at it, don't you think? Now go to sleep you beautiful thing and realize that you and I both need to find that joy in our lives that we lost a long time ago."

Timothy's voice began fading off as he was captured by sleep.

Smithy moved back against Timothy's body and formed the remnant of a once-in-a lifetime smile, as her body finally relaxed. The last thing she could remember before slipping off to sleep was Timothy whispering in her ear.

Through the darkness she listened to Timothy weakly whisper:

"Just for the record, Smithy: you were lucky to have had the help of some damn good surgeons. I, on the other hand, have been trying to change who I am---on my own. Maybe you can stand in as my own personal surgeon, whatcha think?"

Smithy pulled Timothy's hand against her tearful eyes and smiled.

Chapter 42

GOLAREH: MISTAKEN IDENTITY

Enterprise News Service Headquarters, Thomas More Square, London

Unsubstantiated reports suggested that the Prime Minister of France was about to launch a financial audit into the castle but was evaluating the relevance and validity of the accusations. Many in the press corps doubted that the Prime Minister would carry on with any investigations; for fear that what might be uncovered could implicate him. Protesters were hitting the streets in force, staging peaceful sit-ins in front of government buildings, holding signs that read, *Lepan is a sexist pig! Dump the hypocrites, and Charge the castle!*

Rather than spending my evenings at my flat in Oxford, being spied upon by electronic surveillance, I chose to embed myself within the confines of my tiny cubical at the *Enterprise* Headquarters in London. Timothy was right on the money when he said that the editors and publisher could care less about some loudmouth French judge demanding the identity of anonymous sources. Advertising sales were booming, the killing floor was bustling with activity and that was all that mattered to the staff and management of the *Enterprise*.

Timothy was executing the role of a one-man news room, churning out story after story about Henri's secret life and anyone tied to him by name was already lawyering-up and going silent. Unfortunately, nothing brought under the light of day was yielding anything that Interpol could move on.

What was Henri's connection with Santo Gordo, who was identified by Interpol as a well-known Mexican kingpin? How long has Henri been involved with the Castle and how much control does he have over it? Why did some high ranking officials within the Prime Minister's inner circle know so much about the castle while the public was oblivious to its existence? Exactly how wealthy was Henri Lepan and why were his tax records impossible to obtain and seemingly immune from the freedom of information law? These were the questions that were actually slowing down the transaction speed of the internet, because of the more than 197 million visitors to the ENS social media site alone.

The reporters on the killing floor were following up on every single story that Timothy was pushing their way. I was keeping an extremely low profile, monitoring the senior level management activity at the headquarters while trying to keep Timothy up to date with everything.

My job was also to keep Timothy's stories alive in the media by re-directing all of them to news aggregators worldwide. The plan was working very well, especially when gossip magazines and late night talk shows began publishing comical skits of Henri and his government cohorts quaffing expensive bottles of wine while twirling strippers around extravagant dance floors.

I was certainly relieved to hear, from Big Ben, that Timothy was safe and getting some much needed rest, but how long could he hide from Henri's henchmen who might also include the deceivingly dangerous Ari?

The mechanics of our carelessly constructed plan seemed so completely farfetched to me. All we had to do was secretly record Henri conducting crucial business dealings with Santo Gordo over the only form of communication the two ever used. We were also unaware of the level of sophistication the two men maintained in order to be completely invisible. The tax payers of France were unknowingly funding a scarcely detectible, highly encrypted, ultrathin frequency band, which stretched like a shoe-string from Santo Gordo's private residence in Mexico to Henri's castle-office deep in the mountains of southern France. Henri Lepan had single handedly constructed an unregistered, highly controlled, international communications portal, utilized exclusively by the top order of human brokers.

Thousands of people were trafficked to all segments of the human exchange industry. Sadly, as huge as Lepan and Gordo were, they were just average size brokers in a world of trade commerce which was comparable to a monetary currency with its own distinguishable exchange rate.

I had little faith in our chance of success while Timothy always seemed to be so damned optimistic. He was always so incredibly positive about a successful outcome and it drove me nuts.

"I think our chances for success are actually quite good! Don't worry so much, girly-girl!" he always told me, which pissed me off to the nth-degree.

How our plan would come together seem so farfetched. Homi and Danni would somehow find their way into this highly secured fortress in the mountains of France and find Zooli, a woman whom none of us had seen for more than 32 years. The three of them would sneak into the castle, find Henri's mysterious cell phone and pull the guts out of it so it could be remotely examined by Timothy? Really?

A large portion of our success rested on the shoulders of Timothy. If he were removed from the equation, ended up dead, or both, our demise would soon follow. Timothy was the only one who knew how to hack into Henri's phone. The rest of us were just clueless runners operating on a wing and a prayer.

When my cell phone rang, my heart lifted as I saw that it was Timothy calling in.

"Hello beautiful how's the weather in your parts?" He sounded upbeat and remarkably rejuvenated.

"Oh my god, we have thick fog, rain and zero fucking visibility."

I needed a smoke badly, so I reached for my handbag and headed for the elevator. "Hang on! I'm about to take an elevator ride down to the smoking area, so if I lose you, call me back---alright?"

Luckily my signal didn't drop as the doors to the elevator opened and I walked briskly out in the open courtyard. I lit up a cigarette and searched for a private place to smoke and talk. The entire area was alive with activity. Reporters from all over the UK and France were poised everywhere hoping to snatch an interview with Timothy, his anonymous source or Henri himself.

Television crews from CNN-France, BBC-TV and CBC were all set up for remote broadcast, hoping to talk with the famous reporter who was single handedly bringing down one of the most powerful government officials in Western Europe.

"Holy Shit—Timothy! You can't imagine the amount of media out here looking for you. If they had a clue that I was on the phone with you, they would chase me down like a rat." I finished one of my cigarettes and quickly fired up another one.

"I know Goli, they're all over Oxford too, but I will only talk to those ass-holes on my terms, not theirs."

"Alright talk to me Timothy---what, in the fuck, are we supposed to do next?"

"Okay Goli--- first, you have to relax and take a deep breath. For your information I'm tracking Henri via GPS---as we speak, mind you! And he has just arrived at the castle and was instructed by Ari to place a satellite call to Santo tonight."

"Fuck! Tonight? Timothy! The girls aren't even there yet!"

"I know that Goli---that's alright, baby! I've got their sweet asses covered. That's why I took the liberty of delaying Ari's messages to Henri. He'll never receive the damn message, which will really piss off Santo Gordo." Timothy chuckled with a dastardly laugh.

"Well at least that's some good news. I'm going crazy with this whole damn thing, Timothy. I'm sitting on pins-and-needles waiting on a call from Danni. Look, Timothy, can you hold off their conference call until, at least, tomorrow evening? Danni and Homi still have to get behind the walls of the castle and find Zooli who they haven't seen in more than 30 fucking years! Oh my god, Timothy, we don't have a chance in hell of pulling this stupid plan off." I heard myself growling through my teeth while I desperately sucked on the filter of my cigarette as if it were my only lifeline to sanity.

"Goli, would you please get a hold of yourself and relax! I told you--- time is on our side!

There he goes again with that ultra-positive attitude. I wanted to reach through the phone and strangle him. "What in the hell do you mean---we have time on our fucking side---Timothy? Are you fucking crazy?"

"Goli, don't you see by now that I'm in charge of Henri's clock? I've just given him a new task, something more important than kissing the ass of Santo Gordo. Oh and when Santo finds out that Henri blew him off again, he's really going to blow his fucking stack! Goli, as we speak, Henri's limo is searching for a parking spot on *Rue du Docteur Flamand Street.* Once they park I will actually be able to track Henri on foot as he passes through the hospital entrance to check on his dear, dear mother."

"My god, Miss Cathy, what happened to her, is she alright?"

"Well---that's what Henri wants to find out. His mother was removed from the castle about two hours before he arrived! She was *reportedly* having a massive heart attack and on the verge of death. I'm sure, by now, she is completely hooked up to all of those tiny wires and blinking monitors. Isn't this just perfect, Goli? I took the liberty of placing a call, which originated from Henri's own cell phone. The call went to a hospital-emergency number, requesting an ambulance to come to the castle where an old woman appeared to be dying. I played the part of Henri perfectly, who was completely out of my mind with concern for his dear, dear mother. 'My mother---oh!! She is having a heart attack, send someone here at once,' I ordered, in my best Henri-voice. The last I heard, the ambulance had arrived at the castle and carted the old woman off to the hospital for a complete examination, CBC, chest panel, the whole works! Don't' you just love modern communication technology, Goli?"

"You are really something else, Timothy! Listen, I need to come back to town and meet with you somewhere, we have got to come up with some contingency plans."

"Contingency plans---for what Goli? Everything is running great."

"But what if something happens to you, baby?" I actually caught myself calling Timothy--- *baby.* What was up with that?

"Relax Goli; nothing is going to happen to me. Just sit tight and stay where you are; it's much safer for you to be my eyes and ears at the

Enterprise. Plus, like I told you before, baby, we can't be seen together. Listen girl, you know where I am and believe me no person in his right mind wants to tangle with Big Ben. Plus last night was the first time in a long time I had a truly relaxing evening."

"Okay, Timothy, I guess you are right, but please be careful and answer my calls from now on! I worry so much when you don't answer!"

"Okay, sweetie, take care and I'll call you as soon I hear from Danni and Homi. Hey listen---there's just one more thing I must tell you?"

"Yes, what's that?"

"Watch that hot ass of yours, everybody else is! Ha Ha!"

"Oh my god, Timothy, you are such a damn pig!"

I smoked my cigarette down to a remnant, stuffed the butt into a receptacle and started walking towards the back entrance of the building when I noticed a young female reporter and her fat cameraman staring at me from the upper deck. The bleach blonde reporter was yelling something at me as she stumbled down the steps and ran across the mezzanine in my direction. "Hey, that's her! Miss! May I have a word with you?"

Other reporters glanced at her, then me, and that's when pandemonium set in.

Several other reporters seemed convinced that I was my famous sister. "Miss, may I have a word with you? Aren't you Henri Lepan's girlfriend? What's her damn last name?"

"Homayra," yelled her disheveled camera man.

"That's it! You're Homayra Parastou, Dr. Lepan's girlfriend? What brings you here to London? What do you have to say about Dr. Lepan? Is he a murderer?"

"Hey!---That's Pocha over there!" Other reporters yelled, as they flowed towards the steps of the upper deck.

"Why are you here? Is Lepan a cold-blooded murderer?"

I had suddenly become extremely popular as a wave of reporters rushed towards me like a small army. I spun around and ran in the opposite direction towards a metal framed door. The door was locked and only to be opened by the flash of my electronic access key. Luckily the sensor beeped and allowed me in. I dove into the building and pushed the door closed behind me feeling the electronic locks engage. The blonde reporter with her perfect camera-face reached the door first and pounded on the window desperately trying to enter the building as the rest of the mob reached the door and peered through the glass at me like a pack of monsters.

I rushed towards another set of doors and ran as fast as I could down the narrow hallway towards the front of the building. The sound of my boots echoed through the empty hallway as I struggled towards an exit sign in the distance. I burst through the doors of the main entrance as if I were a woman on fire and flagged town the first taxi cab I could make eye contact with.

A surprised cabbie noticed me as I ran towards him through the oncoming traffic. A panel truck slammed on its breaks, sounded its horn and screeched to a frightful stop just missing me. I flung the door open and threw myself into the back seat as the driver stared at me in disbelief.

"Go! Go! Go!---Take me to Oxford, please sir—go!"

The driver sat there staring at me with a stupid expression on his face.

"Please sir! I said take me to Oxford---at once! Go! You fool! Go!"

My body collapsed in exhaustion as I fell against the back of the filthy seat and redialed Timothy's number.

"Hi Goli, what's up?"

"What's up? I'm on my way back to Oxford to hide out with you! That's what's up?"

"Oh come on, Goli. Will you please try to relax and tell me what's going on?"

"The reporters saw me right after I hung up the phone with you and they were convinced that I was Homi! Timothy, I'm coming to the Flick to hide out with you! What in the hell are we going to do now? Shit, they probably think that she is being interviewed by someone at the *Enterprise*."

"Wow, I never thought about that happening---and who would ever imagine that Homayra has an identical twin sister working for the *Enterprise?*"

"What if Henri sees me on the fucking evening news tonight? He'll think that Homi is off ratting on him to the London press! What then, Timothy---tell me---what the hell then?"

"Relax, Goli, will you please slow down. The chances of that happening are nil. But listen girl, we must take this whole thing one step at a time."

"Oh come on, Timothy! Who are you kidding? We have no damn--next steps!"

"Goli! You need to stay at Danni's apartment tonight, not with me. Tell Magda and those hot little taxi-chicks over there to watch over you. Even if you did make the evening news, the chances of Henri seeing it are very slight. It's not like the guy is sitting around watching television all night long! Listen, did they take your picture?"

"I'm not sure! Who knows? As soon as I saw them all rushing at me I ran for my dear life."

"Well then don't worry about it so much---girl."

I noticed the driver spying at me through his rearview mirror. I suddenly had enough of everyone invading my privacy. I launched my body forward and placed my mouth directly against to his right ear. "Listen to me, asshole; can you do me a fucking favor and keep your god-damn-eyes on the fucking road in front of you---and not me? Can you do that for me---asshole? Thank you!"

The driver meekly diverted his eyes back to the traffic and shrunk down in his seat.

"Oh---damn it, Timothy, I'm getting so tired of everyone in this fucking world watching me."

"Will you calm down this instant, Goli, and be nice to that driver. Give him a tip and wink at him and you'll be just fine. Also, girl, watch your language, you are sounding more and more like Danni every single day! Listen, maybe what just happened will work to our advantage! Henri might think that Homi actually is in London, rather than at the castle about to spy on him! Don't you see it baby, it's like I told you before: The more we throw on Henri's plate, the more he's going to itch. The more he itches the more he fucks things up. The more he fucks things up, the more upset Santo Gordo becomes with him. His whole life will soon turn into a vicious tornado with Henri in the center of it all. We are creating a perfect storm for both of those bastards!"

"But Timothy, he's going to know it was me! Don't you see that?"

"Well maybe he will, but so what if he does? He's the only person who knows that Homayra has a twin sister! Even the editors of the *Enterprise* don't realize the connection---yet. Don't worry about it. Trust me girl."

When I finally began to see Timothy's point, my breathing returned to normal. I also knew that Timothy really didn't realize exactly how much I resembled my sister. I didn't just resemble Homayra; we were mirror images of each other.

Feeling that I had better do some damage control with the driver, I moved up behind him and gently patted him on his shivering shoulder.

"Hey listen, buddy; I'm sorry for my mood. It's my boyfriend, Timothy; he's driving me completely mad. I'm dreadfully sorry for snapping at you. It's just that relationships can sometimes bring out the worst in me. I'm sure that you can relate to what I'm saying? You've been there right?"

The driver's face slowly began to change from a sour frown to a slight smile.

"Sir, would you mind if I made just one last request?"

"Why sure, how can I help you?"

"Please change my destination from Oxford to the Angell Town community in Brixton."

The driver's eyes suddenly widened with surprise, as if he had just been asked to drive to me the gates of hell.

Chapter 43

HOMAYRA: THE LIBERATION WAR DANCE

10:15 p.m. Montbéliard, Fr. - Fox and the Hound Pub and Grill

Danielle grabbed my hand and pointed above the bar at a large flat screen television monitor. To my amazement I recognized what appeared to be a close-up, mirror image, of myself. The spirit that inhabited the shocking image disposed of her cigarette and walked towards the cameras. Appearing startled, she quickly turned around and ran across a courtyard and disappeared through a doorway.

"Oh my god that was Goli! That is your fucking sister---Homi!"

Danielle gripped both of my hands as we both stared at the television. I was dumbfounded as I as soaked in the images of my sweet Golareh, whom I hadn't seen in nearly 33 years.

Everything about her looked exactly like me. She was the same size, same weight and wore the same color make-up. Everything from the length of her hair to the cut of her jeans was my exact image. She was wearing a black tee shirt under a brown leather jacket, exactly like the one I had draped over the back of my bar stool.

She also wore a pair of black boots, which were the exact same ones I had been searching for all over. The only thing that set us apart from each other was the fact that she was smoking a cigarette. That was a habit I never picked up, mine was sleeping pills.

I thought it so amazing that although I had not seen my sister in nearly a lifetime, I still had the presence of mind to notice her shoes, clothing, makeup and jewelry. What was it about shoes that always seemed to claim at least some major segment of my consciousness?

The volume on the television had been muted but the scrolling text on the bottom of the screen read: - - - *members of the media who were seeking an interview with ENS reporter-Timothy Edward spotted Homayra Parastou. The reclusive fashion icon can be seen running from reporters and entering ENS headquarters in London. France's embattled foreign trade minister, Dr. Henri Lepan, just yesterday announced that Miss Parastou will be named the president of a UN sanctioned human rights organization whose mission is chartered to crack down on human slavery.*

The video switched over to a split-screen display showing the two of us side by side. One image was a recent photo of me exiting an airplane in Paris, while the other was a grainy telephoto shot of Golareh walking towards the reporters. There was no mention of Golareh's name identifying her as the image on the right side of the screen, just my name as being the same person in both shots.

Questions surrounding the reason Homayra Parastou was visiting the news organization has not been verified, but many members in the media expect that she has been sent by Dr. Lepan on a damage control mission. -----MORE BREAKING NEWS: Henri Lepan has just been accused of railroading the French Finance Minister Jules Perrault out of office in an effort remove him as a barrier for Lepan's human rights commission...

Seeing my sister for the first time dumped an unexpected amount of anxiety on me as I watched the video of the both of us staged next to one another as if we were a single person. Apparently the press had not yet picked up of the fact that I had an identical-twin sister living and working as a reporter for the same news organization in London.

Golareh must have lived an even more private existence than I did, perhaps under a different last name. Possibly she was programmed by Henri to never even consider her true identity, because of threats over her parents and the lie about my death.

Chances are the people she worked for at the *Enterprise* never knew that she had a famous twin, until now. Suddenly both of us were making the headlines in two separate countries under a single name. Soon, if not already, both identities will be made public and the chase will begin.

Danielle and I had landed in Dijon at around 9:30 a.m. and told Richard to remain at his location until further notice. In the event that questions arose over his nearby location of the Gulfstream, Richard was confident that he could justify everything by scheduling a routine maintenance procedure which included test flights in and around our airspace.

We sped away from the Dijon Bourgogne Airport in a VW Polo. The other rental car choices available were a Ford Focus and a Citroen C1, but Danielle only wanted the VW because of the power and the manual transmission. "You'll never see my ass in a car with an automatic transmission," she said, as we motored down the A36 highway for our 166 km drive to Montbéliard.

The town had changed significantly from the time Golareh and I first passed through as timid teenagers. It was much smaller then, and the entrance to the castle required a short drive through the country. Now, with the town's proximity so close to the border of Switzerland, Montbéliard's population had swollen. The construction of a nearby Peugeot automobile plant also accounted for the changes in the major highways systems.

The sprawl of the town, which dated back to the 11th century and the days of the Holy Roman Empire, had crept to the base of the massive castle. The Castle, as it was even referred to by the town's people, was once the home of the Duke of Württemberg and had fallen into extreme level disrepair. Henri discovered the decaying treasure and brought it back to life in the form of a government owned entertainment facility that was never mentioned to the public at large.

Danielle and I stood together on the side of the road holding hands and staring in awe at the magnificent but powerfully disturbing fortress in the distance. Danielle was reading an email that she had just received from Frédéric, as I surveyed the roads and access points around the castle:

The castle is closely monitored with an advanced security system and the fortress employs a private contract police-force from the United States. There is only one entrance to the grounds of the castle and every car is searched upon entry, no exceptions. All invited guest are told never to leave the castle grounds and explore the surrounding town for safety reasons.

"Can you believe this shit, Homi? All of those rich pricks up there, fucking up so many people's lives at the expense of the French government are worried about the honest, hardworking people down here being a threat? Give me a fucking break!"

We dropped our luggage off at the hotel and immediately went on an information-gathering trip to try to locate this young black boy that we had known more than three decades prior. Good luck, I thought.

To our surprise almost everyone we asked, whether it was at a local tack shop, trailer service garage, or feed store seemed to know Becker well. We were given a surprise education of his entire family history. Becker's father, Stash, had been the hunt master for more than 45 years at the castle. Becker served as what was known as a *whip*. He managed all aspects of the hounds, before, during and after a hunt. They both knew the land like the back of their hands and the footing of the entire terrain.

The hounds were akin a vintage wine to the sport of fox hunting and every one of the hounds was owned, bred and treasured by Becker and his father for generations. Up until the day he died, Stash was highly respected as a humble man with a quiet disposition and huge heart.

During the fox hunting season Becker was rarely seen in town. However in the off-season, Becker was supremely popular and the most in-demand private bartender in town. Every event demanded the presence of Becker behind the bar. He was known for his wonderful Bloody Marys.

Danielle knew both Stash and Becker better than my sister and I did, especially since she was the only black girl at the castle at the time. She said that outside of Zooli and Miss Cathy, Becker and Stash were the only other people at the castle who treated her with any dignity and respect.

Danielle began to further explain buried facts about Becker and Stash which were returning to her as we learned more from the town residence.

"Homi, since Stash was the completely irreplaceable hunt master, he had Henri by his miserable balls. No one could tell Stash or Becker what to do or how to act. Stash never said shit about Henri or any of those asshole-guests. He just raised the hounds, helped Zooli with the horses and ran the hunts. Zooli told me that once Henri tried to pay Stash off, by offering him lots of money to come mix with the guests, but Stash wouldn't hear of that and was highly offended.

Zooli said that Stash told Henri to never, ever, try to buy him, as if he were Henri's personal slave. He got right in Henri's face and told him that he was not there for Henri, the castle, or his rich white guests. He was there for horses, fox hounds and foxes, nothing more and nothing less."

As Danielle was explaining all this to me, I noticed a line of ogling men sipping their drinks and eyeing us from the far end of the bar.

"Stash and Becker were the only employees of the castle who lived outside of the castle grounds off in the country miles from town. Further, both father and son were allowed to venture into town for whatever reason. Stash was an exceptionally private person with no desire to socialize outside of his responsibilities as the hunt master, so Henri was never concerned.

Becker, on the other hand, was the complete opposite of his father, with a huge appetite for friends and conversation. The town's people were so impressed with Becker for being so well read. He was never formally educated or sat in a classroom a day in his entire life. Becker was home-schooled by his mother up until the day she died of massive stroke. He was 11-years-old at the time of her death and armed with a strong educational foundation. It was up to Stash to instill the wisdom of hard work and a cautious eye into those around him at the castle.

All of the town's people spoke highly of Becker, claiming that if he ever wanted to run for town mayor he would win by a landslide."

A cute brunette girl from behind the counter of a tack shop told us that we would recognize Becker when we saw him, "because he is *appallingly handsome.*"

"Appalling handsome, what do you mean by that?" I asked.

The female shop owner stared off in the distance as if she were in a dreamlike trance. "Oh, I'm sorry; perhaps I shouldn't have said that? I really should have said that Becker is *appallingly beautiful*, does that better describe him to you, ladies?"

We each smiled at each other and giggled like school girls.

"He usually shows up at The Fox and the Hound after he's done bartending. Look for him just after 11 p.m., that's when I usually search for him." The tack-shop girl gave us a wink and said, "I'll see you ladies tonight!"

So here we sat relaxing at bar named the *Fox and the Hound*, drinking virgin strawberry daiquiris, watching my sister and me on the news and waiting for the *appallingly-beautiful* Becker to grace the entrance of the establishment.

The crowd was getting thick and the atmosphere was slowly building to a party momentum as the men at the other end of the bar rearranged themselves around us.

A tall man with wavy brown hair and a kind face leaned over and asked if I was planning to dance later on. His buddy next to him started laughing loudly and mocked him for his comment. "Hey Billy, stop being forward with these pretty ladies! I'm afraid that you'll scare them off!"

"Hush you mouth, Jackie! I was just wondering if these fine ladies are planning to dance on the bar later tonight."

"Danni, what in God's name are they talking about? Dancing on the top of the bar? Who does he think we are?"

A woman with a large glass of white wine in her hand and pleasant smile weaved her way through the crowd and came to our sides as if she wanted to let us in on their little secret.

"Hello, ladies, don't mind these boys, they're harmless. They do this to all of the new ladies in the bar. Please allow me to introduce myself. My name is Bee Judges and I own this fine establishment."

She graciously extended her hand to Danielle and me and we shook it firmly.

"Hi Bee, my name is Danni and this is my soul sister, Homi. Excuse me, but can I ask you why this gentleman asked us if we were planning to dance on the bar-top this evening?"

Suddenly the attention of every person in the bar reoriented their line of vision to the front door as a large and very attractive black man walked in.

"Attention! Becker vient d'arriver!" - *"Becker's in the house!"* The crowd chanted.

Becker was dressed in black tuxedo with no tie. The top two buttons of his shirt were undone partially revealing his handsome build. The volume on the juke box seemed to increase as Becker made his rounds. He moved through the bar as if he owned the place, shaking hands with everyone. Women and men circulated in his direction to greet him with handshakes, hugs and kisses. Every woman he came in contact with was met with a personalized greeting, which included a long embrace, some quiet dialogue and a kiss on the cheek.

Bee tapped Danielle on her shoulder with a curious grin on her face. "Please tell me what brings you pretty ladies to our fine establishment this evening?"

"Oh, we're just visiting," Danielle said, as she stared at Becker in disbelief. "Oh my god, Homi, the girl at the tack shop was right! Becker is *appallingly handsome*."

All I could do is gaze at Becker. "No Danni, that man is *appallingly beautiful*."

"Oh my god, are you ladies talking about Becker? Here, let me call him over here and introduce him to you."

"No, no, no please, Bee, don't say a word. Let's just see if he remembers us."

Danielle sank down in her seat as if she were a shy teenager.

"Do you two ladies know Becker?"

"Yes, but from a long, long time ago."

I watched Becker circumnavigate the entire room.

"A damn long time ago—Bee," I said.

Danielle was beside herself as she blindly reached for her daiquiri and tracked Becker as he moved around the room.

Becker was more than beautiful; he had grown up to be a very distinguished black gentleman with a proud face and a wise expression. As he moved closer to the bar, he scanned the room as if he were doing a complete inventory of everyone in the bar, while waving at those he missed.

He instantly got the attention of the well-endowed bartender and made a broad motion with his arm. *"Faites une tournée de service à mon compte et pour moi ce sera une Guinness"* - *"I've got this round bartender and make mine a Guinness!"*

Every person at the bar clapped their hands and rose their glasses high in the air for a toast. "To Becker! To Becker!"

He was stationed on the opposite side of the bar, appearing to look over our heads at the people coming through the front door. Two male customers smiled at him and proudly tapped their pint-glass against his as the trio sipped their stouts. Becker again refocused his eyes on the front of the room and then lowered his line of sight towards the two of us.

When his eyes landed first on Danielle and then me, he looked as if he had seen a ghost. He stared in confused wonderment, as he stumbled towards us. He now stood next to us staring at the two of us as if we were strange creatures in fish bowl.

For a few seconds he appeared to be fading into the privacy of his own world, trying to validate everything he seemed to know about his own history. "Oh my Lord in heaven."

He carefully set his pint glass down on the bar next to him and placed his large hands against both sides of his face. "Are my eyes deceiving me or have I just seen two ghosts? Oh my god it simply can't be Homi and Danni?"

Danielle and I jumped off our bar stools and drove our bodies into Becker's welcoming arms as passionate tears of our past burst forward with a vengeance. He folded himself around us as if we were on fire and he was attempting save us from our own flames.

All eyes were on us and most especially those of Bee Judges who was witnessing the king of the room, suddenly looking as if he was going to break down and cry.

"For the love of Christ!" Becker gazed at us through his flooded eyes. "Homi and Danni, I don't know what to say? I thought---I mean---I was told that---the three of you were dead! Henri told me that all three of you had been murdered!"

Becker was swelling with delight as he pulled our faces against his *appalling beautiful* face. "I didn't know what to think after I heard the news. I was just a dumb kid and my father warned me to mind my own business. Is it really you, Homi and Danni? Oh my god, please tell me that your beautiful sister Goli is still alive as well?"

Danielle kissed me on my cheek as we both moved deeper into Becker's embrace. "Goli is fine. She is healthy and just as beautiful as Homi is."

From across the bar, the two men who asked us earlier if we were going to dance on the bar were clearly tuned into our conversation. "Oh hell, imagine that---she has a damn sister! Hey bring your sister down here baby, I want to buy her a drink too!"

"She's taken!" Danni winked at the men and then grinned at the both of us as if she was harboring her own exciting secret.

Becker stared at Danielle and pondered her comment. "Is that right---Danni? I always thought there might be something going on between the two of you. It was the way you smiled at each other."

Becker continued to embrace the two of us, as if he had just reclaimed a missing portion of his own heart. "If only my dad were here today to see you girls."

Becker hid his face from the crowd which had suddenly become an audience. "When Henri told us about you girls, I thought my father was going to take matters into his own hands and murder Henri."

The tone and volume of the entire bar had dropped to only the sound of the jukebox, as everyone watched the three of us move through what looked like a painful but pleasurable reunion. Becker realized that he was portraying his most personal and vulnerable side, as he slowly took in a deep breath. He positioned himself between us and addressed the entire crowd. Clearing his throat and regaining a minimum level of composure he proudly began to speak. "My friends---let me introduce to you my wonderful sisters, Homi and Danni! Who are so very much alive, would you not agree?"

The room exploded in applause as everyone raised their glasses to the three of us. "To Becker and his living sisters! Welcome to the Fox and the Hound!"

The volume of the jukebox increased as the room pounded to the sound of a pop song of which everyone seemed to know the melody to, but few knew the English lyrics. The room exploded into dance. I looked over at Danielle as she began to laugh uncontrollably as we both moved to the rhythm of the music.

As the music intensified I noticed the audience shifting their focal point to top of the bar as three women stepped off a bar stool and on to the thick wooden surface. Bee Judges stood squarely in the center of the two provocatively sexy bartenders, who had shed their aprons and started to dance. The trio laughed and strutted up and down the bar to the sound of the tempting music.

Bee Judges taunted the both of us from the stage to join them. I reluctantly avoided eye contact with her until I saw Danielle being lifted to the bar top by Becker. There she stood in all of her glory, as if she were a magnificent model on fashion runway. The room roared with excitement as Danielle's gorgeous body mimicked the movements of the others.

The crowd whistled and went wild with delight as she blended in with cadence of the female posse. I could not believe what I was watching as I felt the sound of the music saturate my newly discovered soul. I thought of Richard and how I wished that he were right there with me, with his arm around me, holding me tight. I became charged with an overwhelming load of sensual excitement. I wanted to join in and broadcast my feminine existence on the bar top with the rest of my new found sisters. I could not help but move closer to the bar hoping for the boost from Becker to the top of the bar, which came in an instant.

I was finally liberated and standing right next to my sweet sister Danielle along with the rest of the wild lovely ladies. The entire room of wonderful revelers jammed to the backbeat of the music.

No worries existed during that magnificent moment in time, on the eve of one of the most dangerous days of my existence. I laughed out loud and yelled over at Danni who was moving her body like a fanatic.

"Free at last Danni, we are finally going to be free at last! Free at last!" I yelled to Danielle as I reached for her hand and poised it high above us, up towards the ceiling in a sign of powerful defiance. Never in my life had I felt so happy, so powerful and so ready to reclaim what was truly ours.

"I'm coming for you, Goli! God almighty, I am coming for you!"

Chapter 44

GOLAREH: OFF THE GRID
TO ANGELL TOWN

" **B** rixton, why must you go there? No one goes to Angell Town, especially a woman!" The cab driver was visibly concerned as he changed course to one of the most dreaded communities in Lower London.

"I'll be fine; I have friends and family there. Just drop me off at a place called the Hoot & Nanny. It's near the corner of Acre Lane and Brixton Hill."

Brixton provided me with a feeling of home, almost as if I had lived there during another lifetime. I respected the culture of Brixton, where nearly one quarter of the population was of African-Caribbean descent. The people are deeply devoted to their music and art, even though many live below the poverty level. However, Brixton also had a dark side. Two-thirds of an estimated 250 gangs in London proper are based in Angell Town.

Danielle inherited her bluish-green eyes and striking beauty from both her mother, who was an African-Caribbean from Jamaica, and her father who was a handsome man deemed by the census bureau as a *Black-Brit*. Her mother also provided Danielle with the gift of independence and confidence. "Never let anyone control your life," was the lesson her mother constantly impressed upon her.

Danielle's father, on the other hand, taught her to take care of herself on the streets of London. He also impressed upon her the colorful use of profanity. The words somehow stuck with Danielle and provided her with a sense of verbal empowerment. Each of Danielle's choice curse-words served as tools for her emotional release and remnants of loving memories of when her father had been healthy and strong. Danielle once explained to me why she cursed so often: "When my father was strong and confident he would often curse, but when he became sick, he said nothing at all. After my mother had passed and my father was on the decline, I prayed often to God for just one more curse word to come from my father's mouth."

Danielle was watched over by her first cousin Swoop Bennett, one of Brixton's most revered gang leaders. As children, Swoop and Danielle shared a playpen together, which was set up in the back of her parents' meat stand at Brixton's central market. Danielle's mother and aunt watched over their beloved children as they both worked behind the counter.

Swoop claims that rap music is his passion these days, rather than being at the helm of one of the largest gangs in London; however, his song lyrics suggested otherwise. Whenever Swoop was interviewed by reporters in the entertainment industry he would claim in his thick Jamaican accent that he was there for the children of Angell Town. "Everybody calls themselves the boss now-a-days, that's just what they do. I am no longer the boss. I work for the little people of my hood."

It is a well-known fact, especially within the local police department, that Swoop Bennett keeps order among three of the largest rival gangs in Angell Town. The most notorious was his own gang, GAS, which stands for *Grip-And-Shoot*, *OC*, *Organized-Crime* was the second largest, followed up by *ABM*, which was an acronym for *All-Bad-Money*. All three gangs had become way too violent and it was becoming all too clear, to everyone involved, that there were no gang winners, just losers, in the form of dead teenagers.

Through his own recording label, Swoop became an icon of hope after he was arrested and almost went to prison for a crime committed by a rival gang member. During an interview with the BBC on the steps of the courthouse, Swoop made a pledge to the community to do something that even the police force couldn't do: gain control of the overwhelming gang violence and stop the deaths of innocent children. "I just suddenly realized how easy it would be for me to lose my freedom, so I became the voice of reason to the collective gang members. Hey, we are all in *dis* together and I don't want to see any more children die."

Squirt Terhune was another important caretaker in Danielle's life. Squirt, the longtime proprietor of the Hoot & Nanny, loved Danielle and was proud of her for turning her life around. Squirt was the one who had called Magda to come pick her up on that fateful day Danielle came dangerously close to overdosing on heroin. Squirt and Swoop, while vastly different, were best of friends and both had attended Danielle's graduation ceremony on the day she was promoted to the position of full-time driver.

While most of the bars in Angell Town were open to the public, few doors were left unlocked. In order to enter an establishment, one had to issue a secret knock on the door and be recognized. The Hoot & Nanny was no different from any of the other establishments, requiring its own authentic, quick, audible tap directly beneath the sliding metal observation slot.

I paid the taxi driver and sent him along his way with a generous tip along with another quick apology for my verbal lashing earlier. He quickly rolled up his window and left the neighborhood as fast as he possibly could. Two teenage girls wearing high-top tennis shoes dribbled a basketball around me as I walked down the sidewalk and climbed the stoop to the door of the bar.

From inside the bar I heard an angry voice of an irritated man as he stomped his heavy feet across the wooden floors towards the front door. "Fucking-A! Who in the hell is it this time?" The spring loaded metal observation cover dropped down as a pair of unfriendly eyes belonging to Terrance, the busboy glared at me from the other side of the door.

Terrance seemed a bit more agitated than usual. But his eyes softened as he recognized me and released the metal plate, snapping it tightly shut. "Oh it's you, Goli, I am sorry, the man in the back is driving me freaking out of my mind!"

"It's Goli, Squirt!" Terrance yelled, to the back room while rolling his eyes in exasperation.

"Well don't just leave that poor child standing out there in the cold, you dumbass! Let her in!" Squirt was in his usual crotchety mood as the door rattled shut and the deadbolt snapped shut.

"Oh my God---Goli, I'm sorry about that! There's just no pleasing that old prick. He's always telling me to check on every single person that knocks on that blasted door, but when it's one of his friends, he kicks my ass for doing so. I tell you, Goli, there's no *win for losing* with that old son-of-a-bitch."

"Oh don't give it a second thought, Terrance; you know he loves you like a son." I kissed him on his cheek and headed for the other room.

"Hey dumbass, bring the kid over here to me! What in the hell is taking you so goddamn long?"

"Oh---come on Squirt, when are you going to ease up on Terrance, he's the closest thing you have to a son." I ran into Squirt's open arms at the end of the bar and gave him a huge hug.

"There's no changing a rock, honey. That kid just aint right!"

Squirt snapped Terrance on the ass with his bar towel as he passed by us on his way to the kitchen. "You just can't get decent help anymore, Goli; you know, like the way we used to? Oh---I should have never hired the damn kid in the first place, he's a train wreck. Sometimes I think he tries to piss me off on purpose---and the curse words the kid uses on me!" He shouted toward the kitchen, "Hey Terrance, heat up some of that wonderful stew you made last night. Could you at least do that for me? Hey in there---I'm asking you a goddamn question? Did you hear me?"

Swoop Bennett, who was sitting at the bar drinking a cup of tea, jumped down off his bar stool and gave me a hug. Swoop was a handsome man, with an extremely dark complexion and pearl-white teeth, unlike Danielle, who had a lighter skin tone. Swoop spoke with a heavy Jamaican accent, which he purposely maintained. Danielle, on the other hand, had been forced by her many handlers to lose her accent.

"Damn, girl, you are all over the television news these days. I didn't even know that you had a sister until Magda called me this afternoon."

Squirt watched me anxiously searching through my handbag for my cigarettes. "Shit, I'm out again!"

Squirt lifted a half of a pack of Benson & Hedges Blue from his shirt pocket and slid them across the bar next to my clenched fists. "Here take the rest of mine; I have plenty more back where those came from."

My hands were shaking as I lit my cigarette.

"Damn Goli, you're shivering. Have you had anything to eat, sweetie? Hey Terrance, where is that bowl of stew I asked for an hour ago? Oh and also bring out a bowl for Swoop and me. Can you at least do that, you lazy-ass Italian wop? At least the kid can make some damn good soup! "

"So Magda saw me on the news, did she? Damn it, Squirt, I can't believe this is happening to me."

"Oh yeah, everyone thinks that this Lepan guy from France sent his girlfriend over to London to smooth things out with the press. The dude has apparently done some pretty warped shit!"

"Oh my god, Squirt, things are just moving so fast for me right now. My head is spinning." I took three quick drags off my cigarette and finally got rid of my shakes.

"Goli, relax, I just texted Magda and she's sending Brooke over here to pick you up and take you back to the depot. Just relax and eat some stew. Then you can go home and get some rest."

"Is your sister some sort of fashion mogul or something? I've never heard of her before. What's her name?" Swoop asked, with a look of confusion.

"Well it's really too much for me to go into right now, but a long time ago I was led to believe that my twin sister was dead. Or at least that's what I was told--- by Henri Lepan."

Terrance brought out three large bowls of deliciously looking stew and went back into the kitchen to fetch some Italian bread.

"Do you actually know the French Minster of Trade?" Squirt asked.

"Well, it's a long story, Squirt, and a little too painful for me to talk about right now. But let's just say that you will soon meet my sister, Homayra, if things go the way we plan."

"Well you just tell me whenever you are good and ready sweetie," Squirt said, as he kissed me on my cheek and yelled off in the distance. "Hey dickhead, get your ass out here and kiss Goli goodbye before she leaves, can you do that, you lazy-ass bum? He knows I love him. But sometimes the kid just needs a swift kick in the pants."

Terrance came around the corner smiling and from behind Squirt's back shot him a *bird*.

Swoop motioned me over for a hug and a semi-private conversation. "Listen to me---my *lil sista*. If you *ever* need help from me in Angell Town, you make sure *dat* you call *me*. Anytime of day, I don't care what for! You call either me or you call Squirt. Okay? Because you are part of our family now and we love you. I will take care of any problems *dat* you find yourself having in my town. You understand *dat?*"

As soon as I my head hit the pillow I was out. Danielle's fragrance was still evident on her welcoming comforter as I drifted off to sleep. I felt safe and settled into my surroundings with Magda and many of the other girls sleeping in their apartments below.

Just after 3 a.m. the land-line started to ring, launching me into an upright position and back into a world of concern. Who could be calling so late? Danielle would be calling me on my cell phone.

"Hello? This is Golareh."

"Hi Goli this is Big Ben, I'm sorry to call you so late, baby doll, but we may have a bit of a problem over here. It seems that Timothy has gone missing again. Could he be over there with you? We haven't seen him all day?"

Big Ben sounded as if he were standing outside on the street in front of the theatre.

"No, Big Ben---why, what do you mean? I thought he was with you guys."

My mind was still struggling to wake up.

"He's been gone since early this morning. ---Hold on Goli, Smithy is standing next to me and she really wants to talk with you."

Why would Smithy Greene want to talk to me? I wondered, as Big Ben passed her the phone.

"Hi Goli, Smithy here, I'm so very sorry to wake you---darling, but I'm worried sick about Timothy. He called me around dinnertime and said that he was on his way back here, but he never showed up. He was calling from some bar and said that he needed to stop off for a Bloody Mary and watch the news."

Smithy sounded a bit shy about sharing her concern with me over Timothy's wellbeing.

I started picturing Timothy at Zelz, sitting at a table, drinking wine and drooling over the boobs of one of those blonde bimbos. Perhaps he had gone home with one of them. Could he be capable of doing such a thing at a time like this? With everything that was going on? Absolutely!

"I've been calling him all night long and he won't pick up. Oh Goli, I know this might be hard for you to believe, but Timothy and I have been sharing some wonderful time together and we just--. I don't know what to say---Goli, I just really care for him, and I believe he feels the same way about me. Smithy's voice was trembling and it was clear that she was being quite sincere.

"Wow Smithy, I didn't realize that you two had become serious. Have you told him that you are--? I mean does he know about your transition?"

I felt stupid asking her that question and thought about retracting my entire line of query. "Listen girl, I'm sorry, forget I even asked; that's entirely none of my business. Smithy, please try not to worry too much about him at this point."

I had known Timothy for a while now and knew that he had a problem with alcohol, especially when he mixed it with women. Surprisingly though, I never saw him smashed out of his mind. He always had the ability to take himself right to the edge of disaster and get home safely.

"Smithy, please try to get some sleep. It's very late and I'm an hour and a half away from you. There's nothing either of us can do right now, anyway. I'm sure he will show up sooner or later."

I placed the phone back in the charger, laid my head back down on my pillow and felt myself quickly dozing off. With the many challenges facing me, I noticed an interesting phenomenon surfacing in my behavior: I was beginning to take things in stride and not wilt under the pressure. In the past I would have been standing on the fire escape freaking out and chain smoking myself to death. Now, I seemed to be using more of my own common sense. I also remembered a lesson my father once told me: "Goli, when things get really bad, remember---you always have time to think."

At 6:20 a.m. my cell phone started ringing. It was Danielle.

"Talk to me Danni? What's happening?"

"Well you sound relaxed and in control---baby. How is the love of my life doing this fine morning?"

"Missing you badly, Danni---- my god, do I wish you were in bed next to me---baby!"

I rested on my head on the pillow with my eyes closed and savored the sound of her voice.

"Well Homi just went downstairs to the bakery to get us some coffee and breakfast and I'm about to jump in the shower. Oh, my god, Goli, you would not have believed last night---girl! We found Becker! ---and Goli, he is so beautiful! Homi and I were up until two-in-the-morning dancing on a bar top like wild girls."

"You were what?" My eyes sprang open and I lifted myself upright in bed.

"I know, right? It just happened, we found Becker and you would not believe that boy today. He is so fucking gorgeous! Let me tell you, he almost fainted when he saw Homi and me sitting at the bar---checking him out."

He asked about you---baby and he's so on-board with our plan. Oh-- and guess what, baby?"

I got out of bed and walked naked across the loft into the kitchen and turned on the coffee maker.

"Becker told us that Henri had convinced his father that the three of us were all dead! Can you believe that, girl? Becker thought that all three of us had been murdered! God damn, what a son-of-a-bitch Henri is!"

I was cursing under my breath, as I walked around the loft searching for my cigarettes in my always-illusive handbag.

"Anyway, baby, Becker says that he thinks he can get us behind the walls and on to the hunt-grounds in just a few hours from now!"

"Thank God, how does he plan to do that?" I finally located my handbag on the other side of the room and grabbed for my cigarettes and lighter.

·"Goli---Becker is the hunt master for all of the fox hunts; and guess what, baby, they're hunting later this morning. Becker's gonna pick us up in about an hour and smuggle us onto the castle grounds. He also says that he will put us directly in the hands of Zooli!"

"Goli, you are all over the news; did you know that?"

"I know it! That's why I'm here at your place, Danni. There was no way I could stay in Oxford. Even my editor is wondering who the hell I really am. No one had a clue that either one of us had a sister."

I noticed a shadow of someone moving around on the fire escape just outside of the kitchen window. "Oh my God---baby, its Magda and all of the girls! And--here I am again standing in the kitchen butt-naked. Listen Danni; call me back as soon as you can. I miss you, baby, and I love you so much! I have got to run and put some clothes before Magda and the crazy girls storm the place."

I skipped out of the kitchen, grabbed Danielle's night shirt and slipped it over my head, just as Magda started tapping on the glass.

"Goli, darling, are you in here?"

I unlocked the bolt lock on the door as Magda and a sea of crazy girls flowed into the tiny kitchen.

"Oh my sweet darling-girl---are you quite alright? We have been worried sick about you, my child. Have you heard anything from Danni yet, is she alright?"

Magda and the crowd filed into the tiny kitchen and blocked my way to the fire-escape for a much needed morning cigarette. They were carrying a box of scones and a pot of coffee and Brooke was jumping up and down, waving the daily paper over Magda's head. "Goli, have you seen the headlines? You should see the morning's stories that Timothy just published, you won't believe this!"

"Please lower your voice girls and give Goli some time to wake up!" Magda set the box of pastries on the table and began searching the cabinets for some coffee cups.

"Danni's fine, Magda, I just got off the phone with her. She and my sister were dancing on the top of a bar last night. She sounds great! Let's just step out on the porch and get some air, I really need a smoke badly!"

I lit up my cigarette and took my first drag of nicotine for the day as Brooke excitedly unfolded the newspaper and pointed to the major headlines. To my shock and surprise I saw four large, high-definition color photos of a large pile of human corpses blatantly displayed on the front page. Another large photo of that poor child with the freshly painted fingernails caused my knees to buckle. Magda ran forward and wrapped her large arms around my waist to catch my lifeless body.

Chapter 45

HOMAYRA: THE MEET'

Montbéliard, Fr. 9:00 am, 12-miles (20 km) north of the Castle

It was pitch black as the pack approached us from the distance. We knew they were coming and that they would soon be upon us. Ravaging our vulnerable bodies and exploring us with their anxious, hungry mouths. We hunkered down beneath a filthy waterproof tarp and prayed that it might serve as a protective barrier between us and them. Danielle and I huddled together with our hands gripped together as the excited voices drew closer and more deafening. We were told to expect fifty of them. Not 49 or 51, but 50.

The voices were becoming louder and completely primed for the hunt. Becker referred to their relentless baying as *mouthing*, but Danielle and I considered it alarming. They had bell-like voices which covered the spectrum of vocal range: alto, baritone, soprano, tenor and bass. They knew that we were in here and that we would soon be under their complete control. It will just be a matter of seconds until they invade our tiny, private space and ravage our bodies.

"Just relax!" Becker instructed. "Let them examine you and do not push them away. They will respect you as long as you respect them."

The cage was only the size of a midsize automobile and was about to be completely filled with a pack of overly excited foxhounds. All sides of the compartment were constructed of plywood as we pressed our backs against the wall of the fortified foxhound truck and braced ourselves for impact.

"Take a deep breath ladies and just play dead, because---Here they come!"

The latch rattled and the base of the cage door rolled upward on its metal tracks, allowing the bright morning sun to fill the vacant interior of the foxhound truck.

The first one to first make his acquaintance was *Smokey*, who served as the primary scout. Smokey was the alpha-hound and spared no time aggressively poking and sniffing every centimeter of our bodies.

"Just relax girls and let him explore you." Becker's instruction contained a hint of humor, which provided me with at least a minimum amount of comfort. "Smokey's job is to determine whether the two of you are a threat to the rest of *his* pack."

Smokey's sharp, nudging, nose soon became noticeably playful and even ticklish, as he heaved his entire body on top of the both of us and began to roll and scrub up our combined scent. The tarp became worthless as the two of us lay completely exposed to the oncoming pack.

The second in command was a large male named *Taskmaster*, whose job it is to be the primary communicator to the rest of the pack; but only when Smokey gives Taskmaster the all-clear signal. Through the ticklish-turmoil, I notice the active communication between the two animals as they took turns having their way with the two of us.

As if on cue Taskmaster sent off an invisible signal and suddenly the entire compartment was filled to capacity with the teaming madness of the frolicking foxhounds. Danielle and I were screaming with a blend of terrified-laughter as our daunting canine experience became comical.

We lost hold of each other's hands as we were pushed around the floor of the truck as if we were play toys. Wet snouts, flopping tongues and friendly eyes sniveled, blew out, and licked every centimeter of our bodies. The only thing that Danielle and I could do was try to cover our faces, laugh our asses off, and enjoy the ride.

"I didn't hear you ladies say *Uncle?*" Becker was clearing enjoying himself, as he closed the lower grading of the door and locked it into position. Neither Danielle nor I could render a response as we completely gave in to the insanity of playful hounds.

Finally Becker switched off the madness of the entire pack by letting out a loud "whoop." In an instant the hounds halted their crazy probing and stood completely silent, waiting for Becker's next command.

"Wow, Danielle said, as we lay on the floor of the truck bed panting. But we were the only creatures breathing heavily as the entire pack stood frozen in the moment, holding their combined breaths. Danielle and I had suddenly become secondary to Becker, an afterthought with no interest in us.

"Well aren't they just like all of the rest of them?" Danielle sarcastically gasped, as she stared at the top of the cage. "They ravage you one minute- -and leave you the next! *Wham bam thank you ma'am!*"

Becker slapped the side of the truck with the palm of his hand and walked to the front of the truck. "Congratulations ladies, you have just been accepted into the royal pack and we are on our way to the gathering."

The gathering was another term Becker used to describe the first phase of the fox hunt. This was where the hounds, hunt master, whipper-in, and the field of hunters meet to establish the ground rules of the fox hunt. This was also to be our connecting point for Zooli.

Since Becker grew up being a *whipper-in* for his father, he had gained the ability to be in complete control of his hounds at all times. While most hunt master's required the assistance of a *whip* and perhaps a *huntsman*, Becker rarely required either one. He was a one-man show working only with Zooli, who oversaw her side of the hunt by delivering all of the horses to the fussy hunters.

I can still recall those torturous days, working late into the evening, preparing the horses for the hunt the next morning. Each horse was bathed, brushed and clipped only for the selfish demands of fox hunters. I also can remember Henri telling Zooli, "I want those horses looking good, feeling good and smelling good!" We dressed their hooves, pulled and braided their manes and did everything we could to please the snooty hunters. It was an arduous task that took a daily toll on us girls, Zooli, Miss Cathy, but most especially those poor dedicated horses.

"Move to the back of the truck and put your backs against the wall," Becker said, as we motored away from Becker's country home. "Now, when we get to the castle entrance we will hit a security check point so expect a little excitement."

"Do you think they will see us back here, Becker?"

Becker began laughing out loud as if my concerns were ridiculous. "Oh no, Smokey will make sure of that. You will see."

During our drive to the castle, Becker told us about the history of his beloved foxhounds. They were a breed of French foxhound known as Grand Bleu de Gascogne. To the onlooker they appeared completely out of control; however, Becker told us that they were probably the smartest living creatures at the castle.

I hated to think that Becker would allow these creatures to destroy the poor defenseless fox, but Becker assured us that they would only kill if he issued that specific command. "These are tracking hounds used purely for the game of tracking foxes not killing them. But I can tell them to track down and kill almost anything. I've even used Smokey and Taskmaster as a pursuit team for the local police department. Last year a man broke into a home and kidnapped a young girl as she was asleep in bed. It was a horrible scene as the man left the home on foot with the child in tow. The chief of police called me out and asked me to track them down. I gave Smokey and Taskmaster the command to *seek and retrieve* and the two exploded off on their own mission of glory. In just twelve minutes my guys had the man trapped and locked under-jaw. I came so close to issuing the kill-order on that guy, but officers talked me out of it."

We traveled down the main highway towards the primary entrance of the castle. It had been thirty-three years since I'd last seen the main gates and even then I remember seeing them only once. When my sister and I ventured through them we didn't leave the confines of the castle grounds for almost a year. I still have no recollection of actually leaving the castle; I was too engulfed in so much mental trauma and anguish.

From our vantage point, we could see little of the castle through a small porthole in the back of the cab. Becker slid open the window as the sound of the engine slowed down.

"Well what do have we here?" Becker asked as he squinted off in the distance.

We slowed down to a crawl behind a long line of supply trucks in front of us.

"There appears to be an ambulance leaving the permanent residence parking garage. I wonder if Miss Cathy's okay."

The hounds were completely quiet as they lay in piles resting peacefully. The only hound that appeared alert was Smokey, who sat with his head erect and sniffing the air for his next order from Becker. Danielle and I peered through the opening just behind Becker's right shoulder and watched the activity in the distance.

"Holy shit, Homi, that must be the ambulance that brought Miss Cathy back from the hospital," Danielle said.

"What happened to Miss Cathy?"

"Oh sorry, Homi, I forgot to tell you guys. Timothy called in a fake emergency call that originated from Henri's cell phone. Timothy pretended that he was Henri requesting an ambulance for his mother!"

"Are you kidding me?"

"Yep, it's all part of our stall effort to keep Henri busy until we can get in there."

"Unbelievable! I would guess that Miss Cathy is at least 90-years-old by now?"

"Ninety-four and a half, to be exact," said Becker. "And she still rides horses every single day, rain or shine."

We slowly moved within range of the infamous drawbridge.

"Are you kidding me, that woman still rides? Does she still have that strange memory problem?" I asked.

"Well she may not be able to tell you what she had for lunch but can tell you everything she has done for her horses during the day. The medical world says that she has Alzheimer's but I think it's all due to her injury long ago and simple old age."

"Any chance she will remember us?"

Becker smiled and stared at us through his rearview mirror. "Oh yes, Danni, who could ever forget the three of you? She still asks about you almost as if you guys never left. Yep, Miss Cathy has an odd brain. She is completely self-sufficient with her horses, not forgetting a damn thing. But outside of her houses, she has a window of recall that spans just fifteen-minutes. Zooli will tell her to do something and she will complete the task flawlessly but beyond that tiny window of clarity, she forgets everything. It's like everything is washed clean from her mind."

"Do you talk much with Zooli?" I asked.

"No need to, I wouldn't understand a damn word she says. She speaks only in Farsi these days. Ever since the three of you left, she has sunk into her own world and refuses to communicate with anyone except Miss Cathy. Hell, I bet Miss Cathy speaks Farsi now too."

"I bet she's depressed, just like the rest of us have been."

"Zooli, depressed? Hardly, Goli, I'd say she's broken and *done* with the human race. Well, look at it this way, guys, that poor woman has lost every-thing that she ever cared about, all at the hand of Henri Lepan---that fucking bastard. You three were suddenly gone, and then of course her husband. God only knows what happened to him. Committed suicide? Yeah right! She has a son, did you know that? Well she hasn't seen him in forever. Apparently he's kept away from her, back in Iran. I mean just how much can that poor woman take?"

Becker slowed down for the checkpoint. "Okay girls, get back to your posts, put your fingers in your ears and brace yourselves. I can't stand this new security guard they just brought on board. He thinks he's some kind of hot shot, super-cop. I'm really going to let him have it this time, just for you girls, and also because I can."

As Danielle and I sat back down, we noticed Smokey and Taskmaster standing at attention on all fours on opposite sides of the truck. The rest of the brood had changed their configuration but were still zoned-out as the truck advanced to the check point.

We listened as the truck came to a squeaky stop. Becker whispered under his breath, just before he rolled down his window: "You guys are really going to love this."

Bonjour Monsieur; vous devez être Becker, le fameux maître de la chasse?

Hello sir, you must be Becker the famous hunt master?

Oui, bien sur que je le suis, j'ai été dans ce château juste toute ma vie!

Well of course I am! I have only been here at the castle for my entire life!

Ne jouez pas au malin, montez moi votre pièce d'identité!

Don't be a smart ass! Show me your identification!

Je dois aussi fouiller le camion!

I also must search your truck!

The security guard stepped away from the window and walked towards the rear of the truck, tapping the sides with his wooden nightstick along the way.

"Well you asked for it you little asshole." Becker softly mumbled.

The officer purposely took his time as he slowly meandered around the rear of the truck.

"This guy's really trying to piss everybody off."

Slowly the guard arrived at the back of the truck as if he was sending out a message to the rest vehicles in line, that they too should expect a similar amount scrutiny.

"This prick really thinks he's the king-of-the-fucking-hill."

Carefully, the guard moved the sliding latch on the iron safety grid. From the cab I heard Becker speak directly to Smokey in a sharp but quiet tone: "Up!"

The hounds immediately advanced themselves to a standing position and attentively watched the silhouette of the human figure as if they were watching their prey coming within striking range.

Each hound eagerly awaited Becker's next command, as the pompous security guard positioned his head through the dark opening.

"Yoo-hoo! Is there anybody in there?" The guard sounded as if he just found something that would earn him a gold star from his commanding officers.

It was now Becker's turn as he quietly issued a single command while Danielle and I girded ourselves for an explosion: "Cast!"

In a fraction of a second the entire pack charged iron grate, biting and growling at the metal grid which served as the surprised human's only barrier of protection. Their combined breath and saliva sprayed out of the back of the truck and onto the face of the baffled guard as if he had been hit with a cloud of terror.

The hound's yelping became deafening as they burst against the back of the cage displacing the weight of the back truck and dropping it downward. The guard fell upon the hood of car directly behind us, as if he had been shot in the chest by a high caliber bullet.

The surprised drivers down the line blasted their horns in applause. They jeered the officer from their car windows as if they were watching a scene from the Keystone Cops. The hounds did not back down, but only increased their pressure on the terrified officer with even a more ferocious fervor.

The befuddled officer desperately attempted to stand up but was restrained by his leather holster which held his pepper-spray. In the melee the officer's thick utility belt had become wedged within the grill of the automobile patiently waiting behind us. Then the worst happened, as the canister began expelling a thick cloud of biting gas. The line of on-lookers was exploding with laughter as the humiliated officer fell to the ground and choked for assistance.

A senior-ranking officer stormed from the guard house and angrily waved our truck forward, as Becker slowly accelerated through the main gate and towards our next destination.

Danielle made our first successful milestone known to Golareh in the form of a text message: *we are now on the castle grounds.*

From the cab Becker issued his termination command to the chaotic pack: "Whoop!" The hounds halted their voices as if it were all part of a movement in a musical score.

We were astonished by how different everything now looked. The landscaping in the front of the castle was immaculately groomed and much larger than I remembered. The woods which had once embraced the front of the castle had been drastically cut back to make way to an over produced, plastic-town complete with coffee shops, café's, and pubs.

"What in the hell have they done to this fucking place, it looks as if they're trying to create a gaudy version of the town outside." Danielle said, as we squinted at the sights through the small opening of the cab.

"Welcome to Henri's personal utopia! Since the visitors are told never to venture out to Montbéliard, Henri decided to bring the town inside."

"This looks like some sort of weak imitation!" I said.

"It's a fucking fantasy land." exclaimed Danielle.

We passed through the bogus town, spying on the super-rich as they strolled about with their noses held high.

When my sister and I had first arrived at the castle it seemed that the equestrian grounds were rather close to the castle entrance, perhaps within walking distance. However, the layout seemed to have been completely re-architected. There was much more activity on the outside of the castle with guests strolling on foot, motor scooters and even golf carts. Supply trucks moved freely through the castle grounds providing a stark contrast to what I once remembered.

As we approached an intersection I saw a sign that read *aerodrome*. "Do they have their own airport here?"

"They added that about ten years ago, about the same time they expanded the other airport in town to accommodate the Peugeot plant. And---oh my lord let me tell you about that stupid automobile plant! What a farce that has been. It was supposed to bring so many jobs to the people of Montbéliard but that never happened. I heard that the deal to build that plant was done on a cocktail napkin in some strip bar inside the castle.

So much money poured into the construction of that plant and even more money went into the castle. The town's people didn't get shit, except a property tax increase. Listen to this, girls! No jobs were given to any of the people of the town, none whatsoever! All of the workers came here from someplace else, 25,000 of them and all from Mexico. It's all cheap labor! They don't even live near town to shop and buy food.

They all live off in some cheap tenement up in the mountains. It's a fucking joke! Sorry for my language girls, but it just pisses me off to no end. Henri had government money flowing out of his ears, so he built his own private airport. Landings are supposed follow a strange flight pattern, but I have seen them land huge cargo planes there too. I can't even imagine what they need that much cargo for. None of the guests arrive at the castle by limo anymore; they're all flown in by helicopter, airplane or jet. It's a fucking joke! The people in town can't understand why in the world there are two airports, so damn close to each other. What a waste of the taxpayer's money, they all complain. And yes, the taxpayers of Montbéliard are paying for that as well!"

"Where is the control tower?" I asked, surveying the terrain.

"They don't have one; it's what's known as a non-towered airport. It's apparently up to the pilots to communicate with one another as they come and go."

As I listened to Becker give us a full rundown, I sent off a text message to Richard, letting him know about the airstrip and the lack of a tower.

"Becker, are you allowed in the castle anymore?" Danielle asked.

"Are you kidding me, not only am I not allowed in there, but neither is Zooli and Miss Cathy, and we all could care less. I have no interest in seeing what goes on in that horrible place. Those people in there are dirty, rich slobs, with no morals! And prejudice! Girls you won't believe how prejudiced they all are. My real name isn't Becker, its *nigger*. Even the women call me that as if it's my birth name: 'Could you ask that nigger over there to adjust my saddle?' and 'Hey, nigger, can you clear away this sick manure! When is the nigger going to give us a chance to kill the bloody fox?'

"Well why, on earth, do you stay here, Becker?"

"Because I love the town's people and I promised my father I would stay here for the foxhounds, Zooli and Miss Cathy. I love those dear women, even though neither of them talk to me anymore. I know it's not me, guys, it's just that Zooli has just given up with the human race."

I thought it to be so ironic that Becker would feel such a devout obligation to watch over Henri's mother. What a wonderful women she must be and how completely broken Zooli must have become. I also couldn't imagine why in the world Miss Cathy, Henri's own mother, was not even allowed to set foot in the castle anymore.

"Okay, ladies, you better get back to your posts, we are about to enter the *meet*."

Danielle and I slowly slid down the back wall of the truck and sat silently watching the resting pack of foxhounds. We were numb with disbelief over what we had just seen and heard.

How powerful and controlling Henri is. How can one person take advantage of so many? What a completely selfish man Henri Lepan had not only become, but had been for his entire adult life.

ENS NEWS WIRE

Dear Golareh:

Below you'll find a collection of the most popular topics trending on the Web today. ENS Online-Edition: From Entertainment to Sports, if people are chatting about it, we are reporting on it:

News Tidbits-

(Tags: Henri Lepan, Sex, Politics, Nude)

London, United Kingdom- "Although the gruesome pictures of nude prostitutes are quite disturbing, Enterprise New Service (ENS) has made the decision to release more explicit material to the public. More images are expected to develop over the next 24-hours, according to our anonymous news source. The staff and management of ENS believe that we have the responsibility to report what has been described by Scotland Yard as the dumping of human victims caught up in the snare of sex trafficking." - Rémi Masson, e-Magazine Section Editor - ENS.

. . .

(Tags: Henri Lepan-Quotes, Sex, Nude)

"It's during times like this that I am sickened by the media for publishing nude images of carnage. We as children of God must come together as an army of good, rather than a cowardly assembly of pigs! We must flush out these vermin from wherever they may be hiding. I am also calling on the press to stop condemning the people who are desperately trying to curtail the horrible activities of human sex trafficking." - Dr. H. Lepan.

. . .

(Tags: Jules Perrault, Henri Lepan, Sex)

Amiens —Partial loss of body parts: The apparent cause of death for French Finance Minister - French Minister Jules Perrault's dead body was found naked and gruesomely disfigured in a posh hotel. Police from both Amiens and Paris opened a joint investigation into what some are calling a mutilation death following a bizarre sexual encounter.

Chapter 46

. . .

GOLAREH FERTILE FINDINGS

Brixton, South London - 8:22 a.m.

A white Volvo V60 Sports Wagon moved slowly into the dispatch-yard below and came to a stop as Magda and I sipped coffee and hardly nibbled on our pastries. I had already smoked a half of a pack of cigarettes and was lighting up another one when I noticed Frédéric and the two officers step out of their car.

They had somber expressions on their faces as they walked towards the steps of the fire escape. "Hi Goli, could you spare a cup of coffee for your old cousin and his straggling officers?"

"Absolutely guys, come on up."

As Frédéric climbed the steps a cold chill flushed across my body. I could tell that he was about to inform me of something horrible, as my mind flashed through the inventory of faces belonging to everyone dear to me. What terrible news was he about to share?

"Hi Ladies, I'm sure that you remember officers Rahda Shabur and Heath Wilson?"

"Why sure Frédéric, how could I forget? Please, we have plenty of coffee and pastries in the kitchen, help yourselves."

Frédéric took a deep breath and glanced up at the sky. "I'm afraid we have some unfortunate news to share with you this morning, Goli. I'm sorry to tell you this but we've found the bodies of the people that you and Timothy saw at the rail yard the other night."

Suddenly the newspaper in my lap felt as if it were about to burst into flames. "What do you mean---Frédéric? Did you find the train?" I held up the paper and pointed at the graphically disturbing pictures of the huddled and dying people in the storage room at Hither Green.

Heath walked over with a folded report containing a NYPD stamp posted on the front cover. "Not the train, Ma'am, but the bodies---all one-hundred and ninety-one of them."

The numbers didn't add up. I suddenly felt the hair stand up on the back of my neck. "I don't remember seeing that many body bags."

"No ma'am, we're not talking only about the ones in the body bags, we've found all of the people that you saw at the rail yard that night," said Rahda.

"What do you mean by---all of the people? Are you referring to the ones that were still alive?" I gripped the rolled up newspaper in my hand and waited for the dreaded answer.

"I'm afraid so," said Rahda.

"But the people I saw were not dead! What happened to them, how did they die?"

"Well it appears that they had all been shot in the head execution style."

"Oh my god, Rahda, this is horrible!" I jumped out of my chair and ran over and gripped the railing of the fire escape. "Who could have done such a terrible thing to those poor, innocent people? I could have saved those people! Oh my god, I could have saved their lives!"

I stared in disbelief at the faces of the pitiful women and children in the article.

"Their bodies were found in a grain container on board a cargo vessel in international waters. They were all, apparently, buried in wood shavings," said Heath.

I stood on the deck, staring off into the trees as Magda sat motionless with a blank expression on her face. I had nothing more to say, as the newspaper fell from my fingers to a puddle of dirty water below.

"Goli, we now have reason to believe that the bodies were destined for a rendering-fertilizer plant in Mexico City."

"Oh my Lord, how awful," said Magda, spilling her coffee on her robe.

Suddenly I remembered Ari discussing with Henri, something about fertilizer quality, the night on the dock. *"Our last shipment of these people could barely be used for fertilizer!"*

"That's what *she* said..." I mumbled under my breath.

"That's what who said, Goli?" Frédéric asked.

"Ari said something about the spoilage factor and how much she hated to come to the train yard because it always made her clothes smell gross! She was complaining to Henri, that the last shipment couldn't even be used for fertilizer! I thought that she was kidding! I didn't think she was seriously talking about turning people into fucking fertilizer! My god these people are all crazy! This is too fucking unbelievable!"

I reached for my hand bag and searched for more cigarettes. "Well, do we know who owns the rendering plant or this fertilizer factory you are talking about?"

"Yes ma'am, we think that we do. We believe that the company is owned by Santo Gordo," said Officer Wilson.

"Well then why don't you just arrest him? Surely you can get him for that---for God's sake? What else do you fucking need?" My hands were now shaking terribly as I tried to light another cigarette.

Magda stood up and put her arms around me. "Please don't smoke so much my dear child, you are going to make yourself sick."

"Oh Magda, what in the hell does it matter anyway? My mind can't take any more of this horrible news!"

I felt another weeping spell approaching and I was becoming sick of them. "Oh---God damn it, here I go---again!"

"Now stop using the Lord's name in vain, Goli!" Magda scolded, as she held my face against her robe.

"Oh---why not Magda? ---There is no lord anyway! What sort of lord allows such--such, shit to happen? I thought the bastard up there was sup-posed to protect us down here, in this horrible place---rather than, fucking, destroying us!" I was losing my voice with anger.

"It's called biofuel, ma'am" said Officer Wilson.

"What?" I realized that I might be offending everyone within range, but I just didn't care anymore.   I was so pissed off at this loving lord that I was trained to trust so much. "What do you mean Heath? What the hell is biofuel?"

"Well believe or not, it's legal to convert human remains in Mexico into not only fertilizer but cosmetics and fuel too. It's becoming common practice."

"What in the hell are you talking about, Heath? Does this world actually think that it's acceptable to use human beings as fertilizer for their goddamn tomato plants?" I was now seething with anger, as I heard my voice echoing off the building next to us.

"Goli, please---please try and calm down. We don't agree with this practice either. But in Mexico the economy is so distressed that the citizens are actually redeeming their own corpses to offset future costs of burial. This is why it's important for us to catch Santo Gordo and Henri Lepan arranging a business deal together. Even if it were illegal, getting the Mexican government to cooperate with our investigation would be next to impossible. We have now learned that Santo Gordo is almost as powerful in Mexico as Henri Lepan is here in Europe, if not more. Gordo has his fingers in so many levels of the Mexican government it's ridiculous. That's why what the four of you have been able to accomplish is so remarkable. These men have spotless records and leave no trace of their activities anywhere. They never send emails or text messages. They never even delegate orders to anyone in writing. The only time they communicate with one another is either in person or over that dedicated satellite link," said Frédéric.

I realized it was way past time to contact Timothy, but my call was immediately sent to his voicemail: *"If this is a salesman, hang up now and save yourself the effort, otherwise leave a message."*

Timothy's recorded announcement was now making me sick and completely frustrated.

"Timothy, why don't you answer your damn phone?" I was now yelling into my phone and losing all control. "You were supposed to let me know when the next meeting is set for Henri and Santo. Call me as soon as you hear this message! Danni and Homi are now on the castle grounds! Call me back when you get this! Please Timothy---Please!"

I was so upset that I felt like heaving my cell phone directly against the metal dumpster on the far side of the taxi yard.

"Where is Timothy now?" Frédéric asked, as he tried to calm me down.

"Oh--- who in the hell knows? He's been gone since yesterday morning. He's been hiding out at a theatre a friend of ours owns in Oxford, but even they don't know where he is now! He may be dead for all we know!"

"Well let's go to Oxford right now and find him." Heath said.

Chapter 47

HOMAYRA: DELIVER US FROM EVIL

Montbéliard, France — Castle grounds — 10:10 a.m.

I felt the terrain change as the truck exited the paved road and labor up a grassy knoll towards a crowd of riders on horseback. The hounds knew exactly where they were in relation to the hunters, while as if on cue, they burst into full voice. It was apparently all a show for the enjoyment of the foxhunters. Danielle and I huddled beneath our brown tarp, watching the butts of the entire pack as they faced the back of the truck, readying themselves for an explosive exit.

Becker found a level point to unload and came to a stop. The engagement of the emergency brake and the dousing of the engine finalized the first step of our mission. I listened to Becker's boots move across the grass towards the back of the truck as the hounds watched every movement of the cage door with their eyes wide open and their tails held high.

Becker flipped the latch downward and slid it to the side and then slowly lowered the door to the ground to serve as a ramp. The entire pack of hounds flowed out of the back of the truck like a black and tan blanket and immediately searched for places to stretch, scratch and relieve themselves.

Becker appeared as a silhouette against the bright sunny morning. He was wearing a black hunting cap, scarlet red coat, canary vest with brass buttons, tan pants, and handsome boots.

"Stay hidden and wait. The next person you will see will be Zooli. Do not exit the truck for anyone but Zooli and that includes me."

Becky moved his stag antler dog whistle close to his lips and walked away as the hounds obediently followed.

Danielle and I were clocked in darkness in the back of the truck, peeking through the tiny holes of the tarp at the activity just a few meters away from where we sat. Men and women in perfectly pressed clothing pretended to primp, brush and polish their immaculately groomed horses as if they had stayed up all night long doing so. Others were on horseback, soothing their hangovers with cognac, reading their text messages, and trying their best to look the part of a true foxhunter.

Only about nine meters away from us stood a wooden table that served as a makeshift bar. Several people were hovering around it, sipping cognac and laughing. With his back to us and almost within reach was Henri. He was in full uniform, chuckling graciously as if he hadn't a care in the whole wide world. His clothing was impeccable, as if every item he wore were brand new.

"Lepan, you old coot, you have really outdone yourself here, this place is nothing short of incredible," said a man with a familiar face.

"Flattery will get you everywhere my old fellow," bellowed Henri, as he approached the gentleman who looked completely out of his comfort zone, wearing an unflattering foxhunter's costume. "Well, I'm glad that you could finally make it out here with us, my boy."

Henri positioned the man for introduction in front of the others at the table. "Ladies and gentleman, I'd like to introduce to you my dear friend Richard Alain. I'm also proud to announce that Richard is now France's newly installed Minister of Finance!"

The other raised their tin cups in a toast, "Here, here!"

"Oh please Henri; I'm only the interim Minister of Finance for now---but whenever Henri summons me for service, I rush to his beckon call." Alain bowed to his majesty as if he were a cheap Shakespearian actor on stage.

"My son, consider the job yours! The interim title is merely a formality for the public. You must know by now that our constituents always demand change, but few want it too quickly. We must ease you into the position slowly."

A tall and highly aristocratic looking man with silver hair patted Alain on his back and furrowed his brow with a look of contrived concern. "What an odd tragedy it was for your predecessor. What was the chap's name again---Jules something?"

"His name *was* Perrault---Jules Perrault," Henri answered coldly, as if he hardly knew the man.

"They're saying that the poor man was involved in some rather disturbing sexual activities. Dear me, what a peculiar thing to happen to the chap! What on earth was that man involving himself in?" asked a woman with a face that appeared as if it had been under the care of an overly aggressive cosmetic surgeon.

"The police found the poor chap's body in a hotel room bloody and naked. Did my ears deceive me but wasn't his penis missing? Hadn't it been bitten entirely off by someone?" The silver-haired aristocrat appeared to be pondering his own question, as if he wondered whether any part of the man's demise was pleasurable.

Henri seemed to have little interest in the shocking details of Mr. Perrault's demise, as he studied the label on the cognac bottle. "Well, you simply don't know what goes on within the minds of the younger generation. Apparently the man liked to overindulge a bit with the bazaar. It's a shame really. I actually found the man to be quite handsome, especially when he spoke so passionately from his heart," said Henri with a mocking tone.

I felt my chest tighten as I remembered Henri's drunken threat a few nights prior. "*My dear, you should know by now, that I have zero tolerance for those who cross me. If I ever set my eyes upon this Jules Perrault prick, they will have to send an ambulance to take his pitiful body away.*"

I gripped Danielle's hand and whispered, "My god---that man died at the order of Henri. I'm quite sure of it."

The pack had moved off to the staging area and was about to enter the field as Becker pulled the hunt together for the blessing of the hounds.

"Bow your head, one and all:

Bless, O Lord, rider and horse, and hounds that run, in their run-
ning, and shield them from danger to life and limb.
May Thy children who ride, and Thy creatures who carry, come to the
close of the day unhurt and give thanks to Thee with grateful hearts.
Bless those over whose lands we hunt, and grant that no deed
or omission of ours may cause them hurt or trouble.
Bless the foxes who partake in the chase, that they may run
straight and true and may find their destiny in Thee."

The hunt was now under way with Becker in command as all of the riders broke off into two separate groups. The groups were known as flights and only the most experienced hunters were allowed to be a part of the First-Flight. The Second-Flight was left for the novices riders who followed safely behind.

The flights were noticeably imbalanced with, of course, Henri and a select few riding along side of the hunt master. The balance of the riders, of at least 20, made up the second flight. They were instructed to follow along quietly, so as to not distract the hounds. Most of hunters looked like tourists, clueless, half inebriated and praying they wouldn't fall off their horses.

Danielle and I were now left hiding in silence in a landscape littered with empty cups, garbage, hound feces, horse manure, and empty bottles of liquor. The scene was both peaceful and disturbing, reminding me again of the spoiled side of humanity.

Several minutes had passed as we continued to hear the distant sound of Becker's whistle and brass horn while holding hands and waiting for our long lost instructor to arrive.

The name Zooli was short for Zoleikha and it originated from a legendary feminine figure. A Persian Juliette, absent of a Romeo, is how literature described her. Zooli's watchful eyes had become more important to me in recent days. Up until my broken past began rearing its ugly head, I had rarely thought of this wonderfully charismatic woman with the odd name. But it was her instructive voice that returned to me with frequency, always instilling the confidence I desperately needed to be able to stand up to the dreadful force of Henri.

I was shivering with anticipation as the sound of footsteps approached the dark opening of the truck. The female figure was standing just outside of the truck gazing in at us as if she, herself, were a mesmerized wild animal. It was Zooli, whose physical stature appeared larger than life, but whose spirit looked guarded and unavailable to humans.

Zooli stood in silence, gazing upon us with her dusty ball cap and dark sunglasses. Danielle took it upon herself to move the tarp and expose our concealed bodies. On impulse Danielle slowly rose to her feet and faced Zooli directly. We were now in a world of our own as Danielle humbled herself in the presence of Zooli. She stood entranced by her image which was silently studying the two of us from the opening of the truck. Danielle respectfully extended her hand to the woman who had tried so desperately to protect us all.

"Oh my god---Zooli, what in god's name has happened to you?" Danielle asked, as she stood in the darkness studying our once protective mentor.

I rose from the floor and stood next to Danielle as if we were two children who had just been delivered from evil back to our loving arms of our guardian angel. "Zooli, please say something? We have come to see you again," I whispered, afraid that I might actually frighten her away like a spooked horse.

Zooli looked more beautiful than I had remembered her. Her face beamed with beauty, her long brown hair flowed down her back, reminding me of a Native American Indian. Still no sound, as Zooli removed her sunglasses and studied us with her dark brown eyes. Her eyes will suspend themselves in my memory for the rest of my life, the eyes of a person who had turned away from people. Zooli had an aura about her, much like that of an unbroken Mustang, highly intelligent but deeply distrusting. She appeared far from tame as her lips remained closed.

"Zooli, do you know who we are?" Danielle asked, as she moved closer to the guarded image. "Oh please Zooli; please tell me that you remember us?"

Finally, Zooli's lips began to mouth the words: "Danni." Slowly her voice became audible in her native tongue of Farsi: "Vay Khodaye Bozorgh - *Oh my god!*"

Zooli slowly climbed up onto the bed of the truck and stood directly in front of us. "Biyain nazdik bezarin baghaletoon konam. *Come let me hold you!* Bachaham barghashtan.

My dear children have returned. Shoma ra bekhodah, baghine Golareh ham khoube?

Please tell me that my dear Golareh is okay? Pass Khoda vojood dare? - *Might there be a god after all?*"

It had been nearly 33 years since I had spoken full sentences in my native language of Farsi. Using the language was unbearably painful. But as she spoke the words were received so naturally. The two of us carefully put our arms around our wonderful Zooli.

Knowing that the first words coming from Zooli were unintelligible to Danielle, I realized that she was at a disadvantage. I put my arms around Danielle and held her close as I humbly made a request of Zooli.

"*Zooli aziz, midounam delet por haste, vali ma be komake to ehtiaj darim. Khahesh mikonam, ghaboul mikoni ba ma inglisi ya farancavi chohbat koni? Hade aghal baraye Danni?* - *My dear Zooli, I know that you are hurting. We are here in need of your help. Please would you consider speaking to us in either French or English? Please Zooli, for the sake of Danni?*"

Zooli stood before us completely humbled as the dim light of her distant soul began to intensify as if it were receiving energy from us. Her response was unsettling as our suspicions were confirmed. Her voice broke as tears filled her eyes:

"*Homayra joon, midouni k shoharamo as dast dadam dar daste adamhaye Henri. Pecareh golamo nadidame as vaghti Bache bood. Har cetaye shomara az daste dadam. Tasmime ghereftam maghzamo az daste nadam. Cedamo az daste dade boodam. Vali alan k tora ba cheshamam mibinam - dobare harf kham Zad. - My dear Homayra, I have lost my husband by the hands of Henri's people. I have not seen my precious son since he was just a baby. I lost the three of you. So I would not lose my mind, I chose to lose my voice. But, now that I see you with my own eyes, I will open my mouth and speak again.*"

Chapter 48

GOLAREH: A KILLER QUEEN

The armies of those I love engirth me, and I engirth them

- NIETZSCHE

Oxford, England 11:18 a.m.

"It's called a jammer. It's a frequency scrambler ma'am." Officer Heath Wilson said, as he slowly opened the door to my flat.

"Heath, will you guys please do me a favor and call me Goli from now on? I have an aversion to being called ma'am."

Rahda, Frédéric and I followed behind Heath into my heavily bugged apartment.

"It scrambles the video signals of most of the latest video surveillance systems. I'm not saying all systems, but most. We will know in just a second how effective this jammer is with these things."

Heath held the small hand-held unit in front of him as if it were a gun, as the three of us tiptoed into the living room behind him. Heath turned his face towards us with his extended index finger over his lips and motioned to us to not make any sound. The tiny indicator light at the base of one of the fake smoke detectors changed from being constant to blinking.

"Cool, cool, cool, cool," Heath said, as he slowly walked around the entire apartment disabling each bug. I stepped outside and started to gather up my uncollected junk mail piled by the door.

"Goli, I think you'd better leave that mail where it is for now, we need to keep the outside appearance just as it was." said Rahda.

Heath walked back in the room with a smile and a sense of relief on his face. "I love technology don't you? This jammer was apparently invented by a high school kid in Miami, Florida, and now he's a millionaire."

I was growing weary of calling Timothy and never receiving a call back. I figured that his phone was either powered off or muted during interviews. But still, a simple text message back to me, saying that he was at least alive would be wonderful.

Coffee was brewing in the kitchen and the four of us were sitting on the couch talking about the places where Timothy might be hiding out when the doorbell rang. Rahda shot off the sofa and stood with her back to the wall next to the door. She had both of her arms raised and her pistol pointed towards the ceiling. She moved towards the side of the door and took a quick look through the peep hole.

Heath had positioned himself directly in front of Frédéric and me with his eyes fixed forward and his revolver also pointing directly at the ceiling.

"It's some girl," Rahda whispered, as she motioned me over to the door.

Heath reached for my hand and led me over to the side of the door with his arm around me and his gun aimed toward the top of the door.

It was Smithy Greene and she was standing on the other side of the door, kicking the mail around with her toes. She appeared anxious and concerned as she glanced from side to side and pressed the doorbell again.

"I know her, she's okay. She's a friend of mine."

Heath and Rahda were taking no chances as they remained on guard. They briskly opened the doors to the suddenly terrified Smithy Greene.

"Oh shit!" Smithy screamed, as Rahda approached her and pulled her into the room. "Oh my god, Goli, you scared the living shit out of me!" She stared at the four of us surrounding her with concerned faces, guns and badges.

"Smithy, what are you doing here?"

"I just thought I'd check to see if you were here and if you were okay. Timothy still hasn't returned home and Big Ben and I are scared to death for him. What's with all of the guns, have you found him?"

I approached Smithy and comforted her. "No we haven't, but we are on a mission to find him."

Smithy studied the four of us with a confused expression.

"Smithy, this is my cousin Frédéric from Paris and these two guys are police officers of sorts. Guys, it's okay, this is Smithy Greene. She's has been staying with Timothy over at that theater I told you about earlier.

"He never came home last night. I tried to go back to sleep, like you told me to, but he never came home." Smithy was now weeping with concern.

"Calm down, Smithy, we are going to fan out and try to find him. Has he called or texted you?"

"Only once when he was at that bar and that was it. I've been calling his apartment all day and leaving messages, but I've heard nothing back from him, I'm scared something bad might have happened to him."

"Well listen, Smithy; we think that he's okay, at least for now, because his stories are coming out on an hourly basis. We think that he's moving from place to place publishing articles, giving interviews and hiding from view. Do me a favor, Smithy, just go back to the theater and tell Big Ben that we're in town and we're all looking for Timothy. Tell him that we will stop by the theater later on this evening after we've searched the city. Also tell him to call me if he hears anything. Okay baby? Smithy, you have really seemed to have fallen for Timothy. I'm curious and forgive me for asking, but how did this happen so quickly?"

"We have only known each for a few days but we seem to have a powerful connection. He knows all about me but sees the true me. The other night we fell asleep in each other's arms. I never have felt a touch like that before in my life. The last thing he told me when he left yesterday morning was that he must be the *sacrifice*. What did he mean by that, Goli?"

—◦◦◦—

It was decided that Frédéric and I would search the local community on foot while Rahda and Heath checked out Timothy's apartment, which was about 20 minutes west in the Greenedge section off Vernon Avenue. Timothy could be anywhere, but perhaps he made a stop back at his apartment to retrieve some of his belongings.

When Timothy was not drinking or chasing after some woman's skirt, he was very proficient at his job and even kept an eye over his shoulder. But the moment alcohol touched his lips he resembled a plane trying to fly with one wing.

At 1:30 p.m., Frédéric and I sat down at the counter of the *Attendee* coffee house, where Freddie was cleaning up after a busy lunch rush. I leaned over and whispered into Frédéric's ear, "You are really going to like this guy. I promise you."

Out from the kitchen emerged Freddie with a welcoming smile on his face. "Hello Goli, my sister! Are you here for a little late lunch?"

Freddie leaned over and placed two glasses of ice water in front of us and glanced over at Frédéric.

"Maybe so," I said.

I eyed Freddie's famous Oxford sausage special. I hadn't eaten anything, except a bite of a scone and my blood sugar was beginning to drop. "Freddie, this is my cousin Frédéric and I think the two of you have a few things in common other than your name."

"Well, it's nice to meet another member of the *Fred* club, my friend! Tell me, my brother, where are you from?"

Freddy shook my cousin's hands with both of his.

"Actually, Freddie, my cousin's real name is Jalal, Jalal Abbasi."

Frédéric looked as if he were searching for words and appeared to be asking for help speaking English. I hadn't realized it before, but Frédéric really struggled with languages. He understood English, but having extended conversations was challenging for him.

"Frédéric, it took you forever to learn to speak French when you moved from Iran and now you can barely speak English, what gives? Have languages always been so difficult for you to learn?"

Frédéric looked at Freddie and me and for the first time in a long time my shy cousin began to laugh out loud. He abandoned English for French and attempted to explain his linguistic predicament:

"Lorsque je suis venue m'installer en France et ai quitte l'Iran - j'ai appris la langue francaise avec tant de difficulte. Maintenant que je parle francaise - j'ai du mal de parler farsi - et la - vous me demander de parler anglais? C'est une plaisanterie? "

"When I moved from Iran to France, I had hardest time learning French. Now that I speak French I have trouble speaking Farsi. Now you ask me to speak English? Are you kidding me?"

Freddie and I both laughed as Freddie spoke directly to my cousin in fluent Farsi.

Hich masali niste baradar Man Farsi, Inglisi va Farancavi harf mizanam. Rahat bachid. - "That's alright my brother. I speak Farsi, English and French! Please relax and eat!"

Freddie's lunch special was two sausages with a substantial dollop of well-worked, creamy mashed potatoes, gravy and a heaping serving of fried onions, and it was exactly what my starved body needed, but Freddie surprised us when he returned from the kitchen with a large colorful bowl.

"This is from my bride to you and Jalal and it's on the house!" Freddie said, as he presented a plate of Kashke Bademjoun, an eggplant, onion and walnut dip with wonderful feta cheese. For desert I must treat you with Bastani Chirazi, which is her homemade ice cream with saffron, it's to live for!"

Freddie smiled, as he grabbed two menus and escorted two new guests to their table.

"Your friend is a wonderful gentleman," Frédéric said, as he dug into the spicy dip.

"Few people know of his nationality; he is actually from Beirut and his wife is from Iran. Some patrons have been harsh about his wife's nationality and it makes him feel bad. So he keeps much to himself. I just love him."

My phone started to vibrate as soon as I took my first bite of eggplant.

"Hi Rahda, talk to me," I answered, with a full mouth.

"Hi Goli, we just arrived at Timothy's apartment and found it totally ransacked."

"Really---How badly?"

"Big time! The place has been completely turned upside down. The place is trashed beyond belief. Whoever is after Timothy obviously doesn't care who knows it. We're going to look around and ask some questions. Oh, and by the way, Heath found something interesting outside on the terrace, two spent menthol cigarettes butts. Would you happen to know of anyone who smokes a brand called Royale Menthol 100 Extra Longues?"

Something about the smell of menthol cigarettes had always disagreed with me. I hated the fact that I smoked as much as I did, but I truly detested the scent of menthol cigarettes. Someone recently had been smoking those nasty things very close to me, but I couldn't remember who and where it was.

"Let me think about that one Rahda and call me when you get back to town."

"What's up," Frédéric asked as he dug into the tasty dish.

"Someone broke into Timothy's place and tore it apart searching for something."

"Timothy has his computer with him---right?" Frédéric asked.

"Oh yes, I'm sure he does. He does all of his work on his laptop and smartphone. I don't know if he has a desk top computer at his apartment or not. If he does, the only thing they will probably find on that would be smut. Rahda did say that they found a couple of menthol cigarette butts out on Timothy's terrace."

Freddie was passing by us and seemed to key in on my statement about the menthol cigarette butts. "Goli, have you seen Timothy lately?"

"No---that's why we're here. We're searching everywhere for him. Have you seen him?"

"Well, I haven't seen him since the two of you were here the other morning, but there was this super-hot broad here earlier this morning asking about him?"

"Really? What did she look like?"

"Man, she was one hell of a *looker,* I'll tell you. She was dressed to the max and had a body to die for. She had shoulder-length platinum-blonde hair. She told me that she was some kind of a news reporter trying to track Timothy down for an interview. I thought the girl was really something until I saw her standing outside of my shop smoking those smelly menthol cigarettes and tossing them on the sidewalk with no regard to my store. She could have at least had the decency to throw them in the ashtray instead of leaving them for me to sweep up!"

Finally it hit me as I jumped out of my seat. "Freddie, I have to look through your trash for those cigarette butts! I now remember smelling those disgusting things and it was just the other night at the rail yard! Ari was smoking those damn things!"

A poisonous thought suddenly came to mind. Might it be possible that Ari had been sent on a mission by either Henri or Santo Gordo to silence Timothy and perhaps maybe even me? The job of clean up was what Ari did best, but, I never considered that she would be sent on a mission to eliminate Timothy.

Certainly Henri has the motivation to silence Timothy---but to have him killed? Henri would be considered the prime suspect. All questions aside, Timothy was now in danger and we had more reason to find him.

Next to the dumpster in back of the coffee house, Freddy emptied the garbage bag that contained the sweepings from the sidewalk, and *lo and behold, there* on the ground were three half smoked Royale Menthol 100 Extra Longues.

Frédéric was searching for something on his smart phone and walked up to Freddie and showed him a photo. "Any chance this was the person asking about Timothy?"

Freddie stood up and brushed off his apron while squinting at the small picture on Frédéric's phone. "That's her, but her hair is much longer now and she looks even better in person!"

As the three of us stood next to the large green trash dumpster gazing at the picture of this incredibly attractive woman, I found myself in wonderment. How could such a person of such outward beauty be such a cold blooded murderer?

Frédéric broke the silence by speaking to us both in Farsi: *"Vali Khodaye bozorgur - Goli, in zan kheili khatarnake - adam bokoshe haste!"* - *"My god, Goli, this woman is supremely dangerous. She is a killer queen!"*

I put my arms around the shoulders of both my cousin and Freddie and prayed silently to myself, that Timothy would never find himself in the clutches of this brutally evil woman named---Ari.

Chapter 49

HOMAYRA: PATHWAYS

Montbéliard, France – Castle hunting grounds – 1:15 p.m.

I was riding a wonderfully forgiving blanket-Appaloosa gelding as I followed behind Danielle and Zooli who were riding matching bay Warmblood mares. The trees and wilderness canopy that surrounded us provided a protective vale from anyone who might be watching from the castle grounds below. Each horse knew instinctively where we were going as we followed the grass path gradually up the slope of the mountain.

The feel of the horses brought back fond memories of those not so peaceful days at the castle prior to us being torn apart from each other. Everything about the moment was rich in movement and texture as I leaned forward and hugged the large neck of my horse. I breathed in the wonderful scent of his large body which carried me deeper into the wilderness.

I eased up alongside Zooli and Danielle as the horses settled into a matched cadence for a comfortable climb. "Zooli, I was just thinking back on that old black thoroughbred gelding that Henri once owned. Atticus, wasn't that his name?"

My question seemed to jolt Zooli, as she removed her sunglasses to catch a sudden tear. "Yes, poor Atticus---oh what a beautiful horse he was. He was so forgiving and such a wonderful guy. Well I'm sorry to tell you this, Homi, but that poor horse met a tragic demise shortly after the three of you left."

"Oh my, Zooli, what happened to him, was he hurt?"

"Well brace yourselves girls. Atticus came up lame one day and Henri ate him." Zooli abruptly returned her sunglasses over her eyes and let her statement simmer in our minds.

"Holy shit, what do you mean, he ate him! Who ate who? What are you talking about, Zooli?" Danielle barked.

"Girls, it pains me to tell you this, but, Henri sent poor Atticus to slaughter for one of his damn Pony Club dinners---and I believe that he did it from spite."

"Oh my god! ---Zooli! Are you kidding me? Do you mean that Henri actually ate Atticus-- like—like for dinner?"

"Henri is a member of the infamous Pony Club in Paris," Zooli said, as she maneuvered her mare around a washed out section of the path. Apparently, Henri owns a restaurant in the 12th arrondissement of Paris, where his shameful pony club meets once a month for their sinful dinner. About thirty perfectly dressed men and women sit around an oval dining table and eat the horses they once rode."

I felt so sick for poor Atticus, who was the very first horse I ever rode. Such a smart and playful horse he was with his huge black face and sensitive eyes.

"Why would they do such a thing?" Danielle asked.

"Well girls all I can tell you is---that these reprobates say that *they* taste good. Horse meat is a delicacy in Eastern Europe and most especially in France. Last year alone more than 5,000 horses were slaughtered and consumed by the likes of pony clubs of which Henri belongs."

As we followed Zooli's lead horse I heard Zooli quietly speaking to herself in Farsi: "*Be jaii recidam k az encaniat gozachtam.- I have come to despise Homo sapiens.*"

I allowed my horse to drop back behind the others as we continued up the narrow trail with the snowcapped western Alps above us. My body suddenly felt limp with sorrow as I bounced in my saddle and stared sadly ahead at Zooli and Danielle. I was thinking about what Zooli had just said under her breath: "*I have come to despise Homo sapiens.*"

Homo sapiens, what a pompous Latin term it is: *knowing man, wise man, thinking man*. Far from that we are, I thought, as I pictured poor Atticus' face. Far from it!

We rode in silence for the next several minutes listening only to the sound of the horses' hooves and the breeze blowing through the pine trees above. We emerged from the forest onto a grassy plateau which overlooked the majestic castle below. It was time for us to tell Zooli why we were there and what we needed from her to accomplish our seemingly impossible mission.

We dismounted and allowed the horses to graze freely as the three of us sat on a large boulder and looked down at the castle. Off to the east I noticed a faint vapor trail from a small jet forming on the horizon. The plane clearly appeared to be rapidly approaching the castle.

"Homi, look, that looks like Richard," said Danielle.

The sound of the engines increased as the jet moved into range and began descending to about 3,000 meters. As if Richard knew exactly where we were sitting, the jet advanced upon us dropping even closer to the surface of the earth. My heart pounded as I recognized the configuration of the aircraft. As if he were flirting with me, Richard veered the jet to the south, climbed into the heavens and then accelerated out of sight.

The oldest section of the castle below matched the image that had been branded into my long-term memory, with its massive towers, stain glass windows, and rich detailing. However, it was the additions that shocked me. Two new wards had been added to the main castle, each maintaining the original medieval design. Enormous towers with linking stone walkways connected each ward as if it were a sequestered community. Although the lower, middle and upper wards of the castle were a vision of magnificence, the fortified structure as a whole seemed to contain an evil mystique. Almost is if the inhabitants within the stone walls were at war with world around them.

What a massive cost it must have been to renovate and expand such an ostentatious monument of sin. Tax dollars alone couldn't have possibly funded such a grandiose expansion. Might it be possible that Henri Lepan's and Santo Gordo's small share of an economic system under which people are treated as property was capable of generating such immense revenue? Apparently so, especially with the help of French tax money and a direct pipeline to the government coffers.

"I thought of killing him after the three of you were taken away from here. And I would have killed him, had it not been for Miss Cathy. I had lost my battle with him. 'You win--- Henri,' I once told him. All I ask of him now is to be left alone with the horses and Miss Cathy." Zooli said, as she gazed at the castle below.

"That was the day Henri called me to his office to watch something on his television." Zooli carefully removed her riding helmet and fluffed out her long brown hair in the wind.

"Yes Zooli, will you please tell us more?" I asked, as Danielle and I settled in around her.

"Henri told me that he had a dilemma. He said that I had spoiled his relationship with his own mother and that I was aware of way too many of the activities of the castle. He actually admitted to me that he was jealous of me. 'You would never have anything to do with me, Zooli! When I first saw you, I thought the world of you, Zooli. You were so beautiful and so remarkable with those horses, but it was the way that you have always looked down on me. Almost as if I was an idiot. I bet you even believe that you're a better horseman then I am, don't you Zooli? You think that I'm too rough with them, that I don't care about their wellbeing, and that I'm abusive to them. Zooli---you also think that I'm a bad rider. I see you watching me, judging me all the time, like I'm some sort of beginner. You are always correcting me about something that I should or should not be doing with those stupid horses. You have even trained my mother to think that I'm a clown on horseback. At first I thought it was cute, the way you both use to scold me. But over the years I have become sick of it, with your pompous, know-it-all, attitudes. Well let me tell you something, Zooli, you are no longer attractive to me, and you are *not* a better horseman than me! Not by a long shot! If only my mother didn't need you as much as she does; you would have been gone a long ago. Oh, and by the way, Zooli. Atticus was delicious.'"

We shook our heads in disbelief as Zooli continued, "Henri walked across the room and turned on the television. 'I want you to watch something, Zooli, and I want you to realize who you are dealing with here. If you must remain here, Zooli, then you had better understand the rules of *my* castle. I want you to see what you have forced me to do. All you ever had to do was treat me with some level of respect. But instead you have made even my own mother believe that I'm a selfish fool! So for that, Zooli, damn you!' The television was tuned to the Islamic Republic of Iran Broadcasting System, as a group of soldiers stood with their pistols pointed at heads of five men kneeling on the ground at their feet. A soldier was reciting a prayer as the camera panned over the group of half-naked captives, one of whom was my husband. The prayer ended and the weapons discharged, dropping four of the men to the ground. My husband was the only man spared. Two soldiers grabbed him by his emaciated body and stood him upright, flaunting his pitiful face in front of the camera. 'I decided to spare your worthless husband, Zooli. The good doctor will live his days in prison where he belongs, all for your selfish crimes against me. And---as for your son? Well, your son will be there to join him if you ever cross me again. If you so much as utter a word to anyone about what you have witnessed here at the castle, I swear to you, Zooli, I will kill your son and send his teeth to you!' Henri said that my son's life was now mine to lose. I must stay here and care for his mother, whom he has even grown weary of, or watch my son murdered like the others. Four weeks after Henri's vicious threat, my husband was found dead in his prison cell. He had apparently hung himself."

Danielle and I held Zooli in our arms and could not repress our tears. No words were available to me as I searched the sky for the guilty god that had completely abandoned Zooli.

"Zooli, may I please ask you a question?" Danielle quietly asked, as she rested her head against Zooli's shoulder.

"Yes, my child."

"How do you do it?"

"How do I do what, Danni?"

"How can you take care of Miss Cathy the way you do? How can you help the mother of someone who has been so terrible to you?"

"Because I love her, Danni--- I love her. She is an angel who just happened to have birthed a demon. Her mind is not like yours or mine, Danni."

"Does she love Henri?" I asked.

"She knows that Henri is her son, but nothing much more. She views Henri as if he's a spoiled adolescent. The older she gets, the younger he appears to her. She still is the only person in the entire world who can scold him. Her mind is quite odd, how it performs so properly with her horses, but so partially with the outside world. She has been like a mother to me, just as I have become a mother to her. I will take care of her until the day she or I die."

The three of us sat on the stone ledge overlooking the castle discussing our connected history and our joint mission ahead. Zooli's spirit brightened with excitement when she learned that Frédéric was quietly working with the Swiss Embassy to secure a possible release of her son.

Zooli was suddenly an entirely different person than she was just a few hours prior. She was now in control of her own destiny and our pathway into the castle. She was working on a plan of entry as we mounted our horses and traveled on to her home.

Chapter 50

HOMAYRA: ENTREVUE

Montbéliard, FR – Castle Ground - 2:58 p.m.

S hocked, was the opinion that I had when I saw the home which Ms. Cathy and Zooli shared. I had expected to see a sprawling chalet built off in the forest, away from the castle in honor the mother of a billionaire. However what we found was a cramped two-bedroom, one-bath, log cabin within spitting distance of the main stables.

"Is this where the both of you live?" I asked.

"Of course, what more do we need?" Zooli seemed oblivious to my question, as if nothing more were required. In the kitchen sat a wood burning stove, a table and just two ladder-back chairs sitting across from one another. A worn leather sofa with a matching overstuffed chair and ottoman were arranged in a cozy group in the living room. Each of two small bedrooms on either side of the cabin contained a bed, a tack trunk and a small closet for minimal belongings.

There was no telephone, television or radio connecting the women to the outside world, only a huge collection of equestrian magazines, books and periodicals covering every aspect of the care and wellbeing of the horse. A vast array of literature on equine massage therapy, saddle design, hoof care, dental and anatomy filled the shelves and end tables of the home.

The walls were covered in drawing, posters and detailed charts of equine foot anatomy, equine confirmation and the digestive system of the horse. I'm sure Henri required that Zooli and his mother kept their equine knowledge up to date for the benefit of his assets, and the two reclusive women must have been happily studying for the last thirty-plus years straight.

"Zooli, forgive me for saying this, but I was expecting the two of you to be living in a much larger home. I mean, my god, my apartment is larger than this and Goli and I barely have enough room for our clothing. Do the two of you have enough room to live in here with all of this reading material?" Danielle asked.

"I must agree with Danni, Zooli; I mean why Henri would put his own mother in such cramped living quarters is beyond me. You hardly have any room to move with all of these books. Why would Henri treat the two of you like this? "

"It's because I embarrass him," came an old woman's voice from behind us. Miss Cathy was standing in the doorway dressed in dusty blue jeans, red leather chaps, a red and black plaid shirt, and suede boots. She still had that regal quality about her that could easily win a best-dressed contest for the over-ninety's cowgirl.

Danielle and I turned and starred at Miss Cathy in amazement, as she impatiently inspected us with her ice blue eyes. She showed the strong hands of a worker as she entered the room with her thumbs hooked through the belt loops of her jeans. She extended her strong hands towards us as Danielle and I slowly moved forward into her welcoming arms.

"Oh my god in heaven, where on earth have the two of you been? I have been waiting for you all morning. I was starting to get worried about you girls. I'm so behind schedule and I have so many chores to do today!" Miss Cathy exclaimed as she studied our faces with her piercing eyes. "Homi, where is Goli? Did that sister of yours sneak off to that blasted castle again? Danni, would you please try to keep Goli away from those awful people in that horrid place. I don't trust those men in there with their roaming eyes and hands. I don't at all like the company my son keeps. ---And the women he invites, trollops they all must be---ladies for good-times! My friends, if any of them were still alive today, would never dress as those heathens do--- and not in a million years would they ever insult my wonderful horses the way those people do!"

Zooli closed the front door and walked to Miss Cathy's side. "Calm yourself, Miss Cathy, and please don't worry about our dear Goli, she'll be along very soon I'm sure," Zooli said, as she straightened Miss Cathy's vest.

"My dear, would you please try and stand up straighter. Have you been doing those core exercises I taught you? You simply must keep up with them if you want to continue to ride. We cannot afford another fall if you don't exercise, Miss Cathy".

"Oh, Zooli, I guess I'm alright; it's just that foolish son of mine called the doctors on me this morning! They came out here in an ambulance and kidnapped me! They took me away from my horses, against my will, mind you! Never should I be pulled away from my poor horses! The fools said that my son thought I was having a heart attack. Can you believe that, me having a heart attack? I was so worried about my poor horses while I was stuck in that stupid infirmary! I had to get back and feed them their grain rations and pick out their stalls. I had so much work to do today. I think that boy just wants me dead and gone. He told me that he's embarrassed by me and that his guests are complaining about my clothing!"

"Oh he's not embarrassed by you Miss Cathy, please put that man out of your mind, Miss Cathy," Zooli said, as she straightened her shirt.

"I'm not allowed in the castle dressed like this! No---no! He tells me to wear those ridiculous things hanging over there on the wall, whenever I visit him." Miss Cathy was pointing at pair of kitchen uniforms hanging on a hook next to the door.

"Why would he do such a thing?" I gasped, imagining this poor, kind woman skulking through the services hallways of the castle, dressed like a dishwasher.

"I think my little boy is just waiting for me to die so he doesn't have to put up with me anymore! But I'm just too stubborn die. No way! Not yet!

As long as I have my horses to ride and Zooli at my side, it will be a cold day in hell before I ever leave!"

"But I thought he loved you, Miss Cathy. I always believed that you were the only person in his life that he cared about." I said.

"Homi, that boy is my son, but something about him reminds me, more and more, of his father. My late husband was a loving man to me, but--- oh, he had such a temper with Henri. Anyway, I really don't care what he thinks about me! I can still turn him over my knee and spank his bottom!"

"But why do the two of you take so much abuse from Henri, I mean, why don't you just leave this damn place? Zooli, do you guys even have enough food eat around here? You can't eat these damn books!" Danielle was beginning to lose her ability to curtail her cursing.

"Oh Danni, calm down, we do pretty good for ourselves, don't we old girl. We have great soil and golden manure! Everything we eat, we grow right out there on the other side of the barn. We don't need his help any-way," Zooli proudly said.

Miss Cathy was standing by the window glaring at the majestic castle in the distance.

"Well if he so embarrassed by you, Miss Cathy, why do you even go see the selfish bastard. For that matter why in the hell don't you both just leave this fucking place?" Danielle's vocabulary was now in full flower.

"Because of the horses!" the two blurted out in unison. "We stay here only for our wonderful animals and we will never, ever abandon them! These horses are under our care and I will never allow any of them to founder or colic on my watch! We are blessed to be with them each day. This home serves only as a shelter from the weather and a place for us to study, wash and rest. Our home is outside of that door---with them!" Zooli announced.

<hr />

Danielle and I desperately needed to wash up after spending the morning with a pack of drooling foxhounds. We bathed and put on extra clothing belonging to both Zooli and Miss Cathy and sat around the table dining on tasty salads and delicious breads, as Zooli executed our initial plan of entry.

"Miss Cathy, I just had a wonderful idea for the girls tonight! Wouldn't it be fun to have a costume party and dress up like those rich women in the castle? We could drive right up to the main entrance of the castle in a horse drawn carriage and walk straight through the front door. Then we could teach that son of yours a lesson, by making off with some of his delicious pies and cookies? We could dress you up like the Queen of England, and the girls would be your maids of honour. No one would ever be the wiser."

Miss Cathy's face began to change as if she was imagining herself as an elegant queen. "Well my son would never allow it, but I will let you girls in on a little secret. I still make my way in that cold tomb from time to time to stock up on a few things we need. Just look at this beautiful salad bowl we are using just now, I nabbed it last week. Oh, and I declare, Zooli, I believe we have run out of fine chocolates."

Miss Cathy was clearly gloating as she slowly rotated the porcelain and gold salad bowl in the center of the table.

Danielle picked up on Zooli's strategy and joined in. "Oh my god, Miss Cathy, we would have so much fun! Maybe we could even snatch some of Henri's cheese cake from his private stock. Homi, don't you just love those wonderful cheese cakes Henri always keeps on hand in his pantry?" Danielle was cueing me to join in as the three of us adlibbed a plan for the benefit of Miss Cathy.

"And then we could bring it all back here to snack on before we go to bed tonight. Oh Miss Cathy, might it be alright if we could stay here to-night with you?" I asked with stars in my eyes.

Danielle began acting out the part of an invited guest one second, then a naughty child the next, hiding behind the living room furniture with a sneaky smile.

"Oh that would be fun and simply marvelous! Yes! Yes! Let's do this--- shall we?" Miss Cathy happily announced.

Zooli had remarkably completed our initial plan of entry with Miss Cathy playing the lead role, and was now on to the transportation and logistics phase of our mission. "Homi, please get Becker on that telephone of yours. We must arrange for a horse and carriage!"

I found Becker's number and placed the call. The phone rang three times and Becker's voice answered. "Is that you Homi? Talk to me girl, are you guys okay"

Without saying a word I held the cell phone to Zooli's ear and prayed that Zooli would speak to Becker in French.

Salut Becker, c'est Zooli, je me demandais si ce soir vous aurez de l'équitation ou balades en calèches au centre?" - Hello Becker, this is Zooli. I was wondering if you were providing horse and carriage rides to the castle this evening?

There was an extended pause as Becker determined who he was talking to. "Why yes ma'am---Zooli, is this really you? You sound so different! I haven't heard you speak French in many years. I guess those girls must have made you smile once again?"

I could picture Becker's broad smile on the other end of the line.

"My dear Becker, don't you remember when you were a young boy, I told you, time and time again, to never call me *ma'am?*

Becker paused a few seconds and then followed up with a hearty laugh.

"Oh Zooli, you really must be back in the saddle again. Now what sort of mischief are you ladies planning for this evening?"

As we continued to plan out our entry mission, Miss Cathy's mind continued to amaze me as after each ten-minute interval she would forget all parts of our conversation. Zooli told us that Miss Cathy never seemed frustrated with her condition and could be easily put back on task by simply replaying the conversation exactly how it was related to her in the first place. "You must repeat everything to Miss Cathy, word for word, much like the lines from a play? Do you understand girls? Now go write out your script and be prepared to act it out to Miss Cathy whenever required."

"My lord---girls, I'm 94-years-old! If I forget things from time to time----than so be it!" Parts of Miss Cathy's strange mind were childlike as she planned out our evening's adventure, while other parts were stern and sharp as she excused herself to tend to her horses.

Chapter 51

GOLAREH: THE SUITS AND THE BLONDE

St Clément's St, Oxford, United Kingdom - 3:34 p.m.

*P*ARIS *(ENS) — (Timothy Edwards): Republished: Associated Press Acapulco, 12.47 EDT*

Santo Gordo, Mexican Slave-Lord, questioned about connection to French Trade Minister- Dr. Henri Lepan. Gordo is also being sought by U.S. authorities for the kidnappings and deaths of hundreds of American slave victims. Notorious Mexican sex-trade lord Santo Gordo was released from jail after spending only 28-minutes behind bars, according to sources in an early morning interview with ENS-London's Timothy Edwards.

I must be the sacrifice, were the last words any of us had heard from Timothy in more than 48 hours and I feared the worst. I lit a cigarette as I stood on the sidewalk peering through the windows of Zelz's, not at all expecting to see him. The popular night spot was closed and not scheduled to open until 5 p.m. The likelihood of Timothy showing his face at Zelz seemed absurd to me, as Frédéric and I slowly walked down St Clément's Street towards the curtain district.

Frédéric was finishing a phone call with a research team in Paris who he had tasked with locating Zooli's son, Alexander.

"Wow! Well it looks like our man Timothy really came through for us this time! Big time!" Frédéric ended his conversation, switched off his phone and placed it back in its holster.

"Has your research group been in contact with Timothy?"

"Yes, but they lost contact with him two days ago. Listen to this, Goli! Before the Shah left Iran, every country had an embassy there, but one by one, they all disappeared. Only the Swiss Embassy exists in Iran today and you had better have some real clout to have a contact there.

So that's when I decided to cheat and put Timothy in touch with our research group. He *expressed* into Henri's cell phone and somehow found a personal contact at the Swiss Embassy in Iran! So he calls this woman from Henri's own cell phone, mind you! Can you believe this guy? Timothy has gotten pretty good at sounding exactly like Henri. So the woman's name is Monique Nassell, and oh my lord, is she ever fond of Henri, almost as if she's a current lover of his or something!"

We turned left onto High Street, with Flick Theatre down range about two kilometers, and crossed the street to the other corner.

"Do you think she can find Alexander?"

"She told Timothy, or should I say Henri, that she would be most happy help Henri, or should I say Timothy! Goli, are you following all of this? I must say, this guy is really good! Oh, and guess what else she told Timothy?"

"What?"

"She said that when they find Alexander she will fast-track his travel visa and drop the processing fee."

"Wow, did Timothy do all of that? Holy shit! Talk about the power of technology! How much would the processing fee have been?"

"A fortune, Goli! Somewhere between 4 to 5 million rial! I have to tell you that things in Iran have really gotten out of hand. The rial has been devaluated more than 4000 times since the revolution. Can you even imagine such a thing? The rial is no longer an exchanged currency! They don't even have a normal postal service in Iran anymore. I've even tried to send my mother pain medication but when the packages arrive, they are broken into and the contents are stolen by the mail workers. My heart bleeds when I think of our family there."

About seven people were sitting at the far end of the bar sipping pints of dark beer as they studied the two of us while we walked in and took a seat. Just as my eyes were adjusting to room my cell phone began to ring. Up the steps I went and back out on to the street, leaving poor Frédéric behind to fend for himself.

"Hi Goli this is Heath, we've just got back into town and we're looking for you guys."

"We're at a place called Gully's Pub & Tavern. It's near the corner of St Clément's and High Street. Come join us, we'll be at the bar waiting for you."

"Guinness, my lady?" the bartender asked, as I reentered the pub and sat down on stool next to Timothy.

"Oh no, I simply couldn't drink alcohol at this time of day, might I just have a cup of green tea?"

I noticed the men at the far end of the bar staring at their pints and quietly chuckling to themselves.

"A cup of green what?" The sarcastic bartender asked, scratching his head and laughing out loud. "My lady, this is bar, not a health spa! Guinness is much better for you than a green whatever!"

As if I had no choice, Gully-the-bartender sat two pint glasses of stout down in front of Frédéric's and my nose. Frédéric had a slight grin on his face and appeared as if he was hoping that Gully wouldn't hear him quietly mumbling to me in French.

"Mais Goli, tu te moques de moi ? Tu me laisses seul ici avec Gully et tu t'attends à moi voir boire du thé vert?" - "Are you kidding me Goli? You leave me in here all alone with Gully and you expect me to order you a cup of organic green tea?"

"Okay, I give up---why not? Hey, let me ask you something Gully; is it alright if I light up in here?"

"Young lady, this is a bar not a hospital room, we smoke, we drink, we sing and we cuss, but we never---ever---drink green tea."

The rest of the patrons at the bar lifted their glasses in a toast of acceptance.

"To green tea!" the patrons chanted, just as Heath and Rahda entered the bar and stared at us in disbelief.

"Don't ask guys, just sit down and have a stout with us. Hey Gully, would you set these two up with Guinness as well? I said.

Heath and Rahda awkwardly took a seat on the stools next to us and looked completely out of place.

"Are you sure I couldn't talk your fiends into a cup of green tea?" Gully sarcastically asked, while everyone in the bar applauded.

"Okay, guys, I'm afraid our man Timothy is a bit more in demand than we thought," Heath said, as he took a small taste of his beer. "Wow, this beer is really good!"

"Yeah, why do say that?" I whispered to Heath, as I lit up a cigarette.

"Well according to the neighbors, yesterday morning, some blonde bombshell was seen smoking on the back terrace of Timothy's apartment. They had no idea who she was but figured that she was just another one of Timothy's many girlfriends. She spent about a half an hour inside the house and then drove away in an expensive white Mercedes-Benz sedan."

"And that would be---Ari," I said, as I took a long, nervous drag.

"It appears so, but then later in the day, the neighbors said they saw two black government vehicles with French license plates arrive at the apartment with two men in each car. The neighbors said they saw the men kick down Timothy's front door as if they had every right to do so. The men then proceeded to tear the place completely apart. The neighbors did nothing because they figured they were part of some government secret service detail. These guys were all dressed in dark suits, sunglasses and earphones."

"And, of course, these guys must be from Henri's own police force---I would expect."

It was way past time to warn Timothy so I placed another call to his cell. But this time the recorded message was different: *We are sorry but the party you are trying to reach is not accepting messages from callers at this time because the party's mail box is full.*

"Damn it! His voicemail box is full! Where in the hell can Timothy be?"

"Oh Goli, that reminds me---regarding Timothy's voicemail," Rahda said, staring at my cell phone. "We found Timothy's answering machine smashed to pieces on the floor of his kitchen. The tape had been removed. Now, I have to ask you, Goli, have you ever called and left a message on Timothy's home answering machine?"

I had to think back on the many phone conversations I'd had with Timothy and never remembered calling his land line once. "No-luckily I don't believe I ever have, thank God."

While lighting up my third cigarette, I considered her question. A vision of Smithy Greene popped into my mind: *I've been calling his apartment all day and leaving messages for him to call me back, but I've heard nothing back from him, I'm scared something might have happened to him!*

"But Smithy has!"

"Oh my god, you are right! Let's get out of here!" Heath said, finishing his Guinness in a final gulp.

Chapter 52

HOMAYRA: THE QUEEN AND HER NEGRO

05:21 p.m. – Montbéliard, FR – Mezzanine level - Castle

At 64-years of age and 118 pounds, every muscle in Zooli's body was toned to perfection. She said that her physical condition was by design. "I'm a tool, more or less, and only for the good of my horses. What good would I be for them if I were broken?"

We could dress Zooli up in anything in their closets and she would look stunning. We did find it a shame, however, to make her look like a high-climbing aristocrat, because it was not at all like the Zooli we loved and respected. Every dress we put on her fit perfectly and when it was all over we all looked as if we had just arrived from Buckingham Palace, with Miss Cathy playing the part of the Queen.

Five years ago when Zooli and Miss Cathy were effectively banned from the palace, Zooli had thrown nothing out, only because she was too busy to do so. Ms. Cathy, on the other hand, said that she would never part with her massive inventory of clothing and jewelry.

Henri pleaded in vain for his mother to relinquish her vast fortune of jewelry to his safe keeping, but she vehemently refused. Zooli spoke of a time when Henri had threatened Miss Cathy, causing her to slap her son across the face in the presence of Zooli. Henri had become humiliated, lost his temper and pushed Miss Cathy off her feet and onto the floor. Zooli rushed in to protect her and threatened to shoot Henri with Miss Cathy's shot gun if he didn't leave the premises at once. That was the straw that finally broke the camel's back and sent the two ladies packing.

"Girls, never think that I would be stupid enough to part with my jewelry. To me they are much more than diamonds, pearls and gold, they are my memories."

We followed Miss Cathy into her tiny bedroom and with the end of a wire coat hanger she removed a floor board in the center of the bedroom uncovering her bounty. Tucked within the subfloor was a privately stashed, elaborately arranged, treasure chest filled to capacity with priceless diamonds, gold, pearls and platinum jewelry.

"We horse-girls must always have a saving account," Miss Cathy said, with a wink.

From the moment I had received my first of too-many presents from Henri; I vowed that if I ever had the opportunity to see Miss Cathy again, I would return that wonderful diamond necklace Henri had seduced me with when I was just a teenager. The precious necklace along with my coveted riding crop were the only valuables I had snatched from my bedroom the night I left Henri during his drunken tirade.

"Miss Cathy, I have something of yours that I have wanted to return to you for many, many years." I searched through my large hand bag and retrieved the purple felt pouch.

"What do you mean my darling Homi, what on earth are you talking about?" Miss Cathy was peering at me with a quizzical expression.

Miss Cathy's knowledge of Henri's and my relationship was not only hidden from the entire world but from her as well. In her mind it seemed that I had only been gone from the castle for only a few hours.

I, on the other hand, had pushed Miss Cathy from my memory completely, just as I had done with the dreadful castle and my entire family. It was only the mere mention of returning back to the castle that reactivated my memories of Miss Cathy.

"Oh Miss Cathy, Henri gave this necklace to me as a gift a long time ago. He said that it was yours and that you probably had forgotten that you even owned it."

I emptied the contents of felt pouch in the center of Miss Cathy's wrinkled hand as she gazed at it in wonder.

"Oh, my heavens, this was my grandmother's necklace. It's called the *Emperies* and my mother gave it to me on my sweet-sixteenth birthday."

It appeared as if the crystal clear memories of Miss Cathy's childhood were bursting forward and connecting to the painful ones that had long since been deleted.

Miss Cathy turned and gazed out window at the horses grazing in the distance. "I always thought that my son had taken this from my jewelry box."

"Oh, Miss Cathy, I didn't mean to upset you. I'm so sorry. I just never thought that he had the right to give it to me."

"Homi, it's quite alright, please forget about it. Besides, I want you to have the Emperies. My mother would have wanted an angel like you to have it. Please keep it with you, my darling child, and think of my precious mother whenever you wear it."

"Miss Cathy, I'm sure your mother must have been such a simply marvelous woman."

As I gazed into Miss Cathy's sparkling blue eyes, it occurred to me that her long term memories were remarkably intact. Perhaps the reason she is so capable of taking care of her horses on a daily basis was due to the fact that those same responsibilities are directly connected to her equestrian memories of long ago.

Even though Zooli despised horse drawn carriages, she devised a plan which employed them. "I have always hated the way people torture those poor horses as they hook their tired bodies up to those dreadful carriages. And those manure bags they strap under their tails are completely inhumane."

Ms. Cathy was singing and dancing around the cabin as we readied ourselves for our grand performance. We witnessed her mind, like clockwork, go completely blank.

"Girls, did you write down your script as I instructed? Well it's time for you to put it to good use," said Zooli.

Danielle ran to the kitchen table and snatched up the script as she and I reenacted our plans for the evening for the benefit of Miss Cathy:

Homi: "Miss Cathy, I just had a wonderful idea! Wouldn't it be fun to dress up like those rich women in the castle and spy on Henri! We could dress you up like the Queen of England and no one would notice us!"

Danni: "Oh my god, Miss Cathy, we would have so much fun! Maybe we could even snatch some of Henri's cheese cake from his penthouse. Homi, I'm sure you remember those wonderful cheese cakes Henri always kept on hand in his kitchen?"

Homi: "Oh my heavens yes, Henri just loves to have the cheesecake and chocolate!"

Danni: "And then we could bring it back to the cabin to snack on before we go to sleep tonight! Wouldn't that be so much fun Miss Cathy, wouldn't it?"

It had been a long time since Henri had seen Zooli on the inside of the castle walls, and decades since he'd witnessed her dressed to the hilt in formal attire. Tonight would be the night that we hoped Henri would not recognize Zooli, even if she might be standing right next to him. We styled her hair in a way that she had never worn it before and covered her in pearls and gold. She wore a full-length, dove grey silk chiffon evening gown which featured a pleated fitted bodice and a wide pleated strap. Two props were also employed which would finish off Zooli's new look: satin evening gloves and a golden 35 cm, theatre-length, cigarette holder which held an expensive slim cigar.

Danielle and I disguised ourselves in equally garish costumes and dressed Miss Cathy up to look like epitome of a royal Queen Bitch.

Becker arrived at the log cabin just before 6 p.m. driving an elegant horse drawn carriage. He was to play the part of our *negro* chauffeur, wearing a rich black suit, starched white shirt, bow-tie, white gloves and black derby hat.

Just as the sun was dropping behind the mountain tops, we left the safety of the log cabin in our elaborately decorated horse drawn carriage and slowly descended to the majestic castle below. Four of the haughtiest and most decadent bitches one could ever imagine, each smoking female cigars and casting ridged orders at our black carriage driver.

Miss Cathy was playing her role flawlessly, causing Becker to hold his glove over his mouth to suppress his laughter. "Boy---would you please improve the diet on these filthy beasts. Their wind is completely intolerable!"

"Oh, yes Mum! Whatever you say, Mum," Becker responded, while holding back his tears.

"You needn't address me at all--driver! That will be all from you---*boy!*" Ms. Cathy snapped, as she held her golden opera glasses to her face by the delicate ruby tipped handle.

When we arrived at the grand entrance of the castle, we sat patiently awaiting our *Negro* to help us down from our lofty perch. Miss Cathy held her royal nose high as the three of us assisted her highness from the carriage to the red carpet below. The four of us traipsed through the main entrance of the castle and on to the mezzanine area leaving our Becker to tend to our horses.

As the four of us joined the crowded forum a young man in a dark suit approached us and rudely asked Miss Cathy for her identification.

"*Madame Veuillez m'excuser, puis je voir votre invitation? - Excuse me madam but may I please see your invitation?*"

"Who in God's name do you think you are talking to, you fool? Stay away from her Excellency--you idiot! No one is ever permitted to address our lady head-on. Now back off you vagrant and never--- ever refer to her Majesty as Madame!" Zooli viciously demanded.

The young security guard backed away with his eyes flinching with embarrassment.

"My dear man, please go out and instruct my nigger to hold our carriage at bay. I simply don't know how long I wil be able to stand being in this cold and dank mausoleum," Miss Cathy said, as she covered her nose with her silk handkerchief.

Chapter 53

HOMAYRA: A WELCOMED MEMORY LAPSE

Zooli split off on a mission of her own to try and locate Henri and let us know of his location at all times, as the three of us moved along with the natural flow of the crowd towards grand ballroom. Earlier in the day we had given Zooli a crash course in how to operate a cell phone and also set her up a speed-calling code for easy contact to Danielle.

The crowd was bustling with activity with people from all over the world speaking in different languages. Two Asian women were walking along side of us carrying on an animated conversation. They looked as if they might have been sisters, with one having short cropped hair and the other with long straight hair down to her waist. They appeared amazed with everything that was going on around them as they moved along with us wearing shockingly revealing clothing, leaving little to the imagination.

The one with the short black hair glanced over her shoulder at the other and handed her a cigarette. They quickly lit their cigarettes and began to rush in front of us, anxiously searching for a private place to smoke and talk. The apologetic one was paying more attention to her cigarette than to where she was walking and ran directly into me.

"Oh—so sorry. I—so sorry! Please forgive I—so very sorry," said the one with the short hair.

She looked as if she had been staged to look much older than her actual age, but as I studied her childlike features I could tell she must have been no older than sixteen.

She desperately searched for her partner who had witnessed the mishap and ran off. "I so sorry, please don't tell on me!"

I tried to steady her shivering shoulders and help her relax but to no avail.

"Shhhh---My dear! It's quite alright. There's no need to worry, you have done nothing wrong."

Around her neck, I noticed a strange round electronic device hanging from a lanyard. The object had a small LCD screen in the center of it, displaying a seven digit number. A tiny red light was blinking on and off every few seconds. I assumed the device was used both as a form of identification and also a means of communication, instructing her where she was expected to be at all times.

"Please relax my dear child!" I continued to try to help her calm, but she panicked, broke away from me and ran off in the direction of her missing friend. Her level of terror unsettled me and reminded me of a terrified horse, eyes wide open, ears pricked forward and tail flagged straight up in the air. The poor child was a portrait of *fight-or-flight*.

Miss Cathy was beginning to fade with confusion so Danielle and I took her aside and quickly read to her the lines from our script. As promised by Zooli, she snapped back to life as we continued along.

The behavior of the crowd around us was beginning to resemble a market place atmosphere as we entered the huge ballroom. Tables and small platforms were assembled throughout, with naked teenage boys and girls standing upright on each pedestal. My mind stumbled with disbelief as I tried to grasp what seemed entirely fictional.

The children appeared statuesque as they slowly moved their young bodies for the pleasure of the onlookers. Each child wore the same electronic lanyard that the oriental girls wore, with his or her own flashing red lights. Some lanyards were actively flashing bright green lights, prompting those individuals to leave their posts immediately and report to some higher authority.

"This is a goddamn travesty, these people are selling these poor children for sex," Danielle whispered in my ear; as she directly Miss Cathy and I along.

We moved through the crowded room, watching platform after platform of naked young girls and boys presenting their prepubescent private parts to the shameful men and women surrounding them.

Miss Cathy looked stunned and confused as she studied the naked children poised right next to her.

"Are you alright Miss Cathy," I asked.

"What's going on here, Homi, where did all of these children come from? Someone needs to cover these poor things with blankets. Where are their parents?" Miss Cathy quietly muttered.

"We need to get her out of here now," Danielle warned, as we both began to escort the suddenly angry and highly confused Miss Cathy to the nearest exit.

"Excuse me sir, would you please find some blankets and cover those poor children in that room at once!" Miss Cathy ordered, as the people surrounding us became confused by her reaction.

With Danielle holding one side of Miss Cathy and me the other, we swept the horrified woman through the packed forum as she exploded into an uncontrollable rant. Faster and faster we moved Miss Cathy along, praying that we wouldn't be stopped by security. Danielle grabbed the first door knob we could find and the three of us dropped out of public view into a service hallway.

Miss Cathy's breathing was elevated and her eyes were wide open with concern.

"Relax, Miss Cathy, it's all right. Please Miss Cathy, please, take a breath and relax," I said, as we searched for a quiet place to rest. Danielle stood by the corner and kept watch, while chatting on the phone with Zooli who had yet to locate Henri.

"Hey Homi, I just received a text from Timothy: *From T. Edwards To: Golareh, Danielle, Homayra-06:03 P.M. - Hi pretty girls...I just expressed into*

Henri's domain and hijacked a message from Ari. The meeting between Henri and Santo is set for 02:00 a.m. your time! Good luck!"

"How in God's name are we going keep Miss Cathy going for that long? That's almost six hours from now!" I said, as I looked at my watch in horror.

I was sitting on a folding chair next to Miss Cathy, tightly holding her hand as her mind softened to a blank expression. Miss Cathy's color was returning, but, as expected, her memory was not, as she gazed at us with a confused look. "Girls, I need to do a night check on my dear horses," she said, with concern.

"Miss Cathy, they are fine. Danni and I have already picked out their stalls and filled their water. They each got a thick flake of hay and a nice juicy apple."

We allowed time for Miss Cathy to completely relax in her own private fog. Then Danielle and I acted out our third theatrical performance of the evening to Miss Cathy, and like magic she again returned to our world:

Homi: "Miss Cathy, I just had a wonderful idea! Wouldn't it be fun to dress up like those rich women in the castle and spy on Henri! We could dress you up like the queen of England and no one would notice us!"

Danni: "Oh my god, Miss Cathy, we would have so much fun! Maybe we could even snatch some of Henri's cheese cake from his penthouse. Homi, I'm sure you remember those wonderful cheese cakes Henri always kept on hand in his kitchen?..."

She was up in an instant while returning to full royalty as she led the three of us to the destination of Henri's ground floor office. The rapidly moving service personnel scurried past us as if the three of us didn't exist as we reached the service entrance of Henri's office.

The heavy metal door had no identifiable markings indicating what the room was used for. Danielle and I searched the door and found no indication of a lock or key access.

"Miss Cathy, have you any idea how we can open this door?" I asked.

Miss Cathy confidently placed her hand against an odd blue scanner causing the tiny lights to change from red to green.

"Girls, all it takes is my magic touch," Miss Cathy said, as the lock released and the door popped open.

A motion sensor in the dark room detected our movement causing the energy efficient lighting system to illuminate above us. The ground floor office was the very same room that my sister and I first met Henri in more than thirty years ago. The room was plush and luxurious as always but appeared as if it hadn't been used for quite some time.

"Miss Cathy, are you sure this is Henri's office?" I asked.

Miss Cathy also seemed confused as the three of us wandered through the offices activating the lights above us.

"I'm not sure anymore, girls, it's been a while since I've been here," Miss Cathy said.

"Well, we are certainly not going to find any cheesecake here," Danielle said, as she continued to search the room.

"And no decadent chocolates either," I added, with a pitiful look of sadness on my face.

"Now don't you girls worry about a thing, I know where we will certainly find some. Follow me to my son's penthouse where I'm sure we will find the motherload!"

Just before we left the suite I gently moved Miss Cathy aside and checked to see if she might be still concerned about the welfare of those poor naked children.

"Miss Cathy, I was wondering if I could ask you a question that has been bothering me?"

"Of course my dear child, you should know that you can ask me anything."

She was studying me with her bright blue eyes with her mind as sharp as ever.

"Well Miss Cathy, I just wanted to ask you what you thought of that big room that we were in just a few moments ago. Do you remember seeing anything upsetting in the ballroom just now?"

"Homi, my dear, what on earth are you concerned about? I told your sister and Danni just the other day that if you ever want to visit the castle, just ask me, and I'll give you a tour. Now come along, girls, we need to push on and steal our tasty treasures."

Chapter 54

AND LEAD ME INTO TEMPTATION

Zelebritiez Tapas Restaurant, Clement's St, Oxford, United Kingdom - 6:45 p.m.

Michelle and Hans had already danced with her twice and were chomping at the bit for their next opportunity. Timothy was completely hidden from view in the far back corner of the dining room portion of Zelz. He had just published his last story of the day, clocked in the darkness of his booth, with his back facing the public. Only the glare of his computer screen reflecting off his reading glasses made him scarcely noticeable to even his waitress, who had been serving him coffee since she let him in the door before they even opened.

He didn't even turn his head as she strutted through the front door and raised the ambient temperature of the room. Timothy was busy hacking into Henri's email domain controller and was completely oblivious to the excitement of the bar.

The vital conference call between Henri Lepan and Santo Gordo was now scheduled for 2:00 a.m. CET, mainly to accommodate a highly exasperated Santo Gordo, who claimed a time-zone advantage of seven over Henri. He most likely demanded that the meeting be set that late to purposely piss off Henri.

Timothy pressed the send button and fired off a message to the girls and was finally done for the day.

With the new meeting time finally established and all of the news he could possibly push out to the media, it was time for Timothy to shut his brain down, relax and go home and rest for the big night ahead. He closed his laptop, unplugged his mouse and power cord and stuffed everything into his leather backpack. He removed his reading glasses, rubbed his eyes and leaned against the back of his booth and chilled.

It must have been a full moon because Zelz was already jammed with people at the beginning of happy-hour. Most of the band hadn't arrived except for Tim, the drummer, who was busy setting the stage for the night. To the gawkers fixated on the blonde, it didn't matter what was playing on the jukebox, just as long as it had lyrics that rhymed and a rhythm to dance to.

A drunk man with a fat belly and blunt-style hair bangs stood directly in front of the other spectators with his eyes glued to the rear-end of the blonde on the dancefloor. "Goddamn! Who in the hell is she? Would you just get a load of that ass!" he yelled.

Would you just get a load of that ass? ---was the phrase that woke Timothy from his momentary catnap. He twisted his sore neck around to the front of the bar and caught his first glimpse of the spectacle on the dance floor.

She was a sexy silver-silhouette with an incredible body that demanded further inspection. Three men were prancing around the dancefloor as if they were dogs chasing a bitch in heat.

At first glance Timothy couldn't believe his eyes. Never before had he seen this extremely attractive woman in Oxford. She had long platinum-blonde hair that flowed over her shoulders and rested upon her explosive breasts and cut biceps. She was wrapped in a frighteningly short, black and silver metallic dress with vertical stripes that could have been painted on her body.

Long silver strips of leather originating from her high heel sandals twisted and crawled their way up her legs as if they were hungry vines claiming ownership of her toned calves. Her porcelain skin blended perfectly with the silver-metallic dress as her inviting breasts arrogantly emerged from top of a shallow silver bra.

Her face projected a disturbingly blank expression that suggested an obvious level of disinterest in the salivating men around her. She danced with a dead stare and a far-off expression on her face, which solicited a feeling of frustration amongst the entire male audience who were praying for any slice of her attention.

The table of the bimbos across the room from Timothy seemed put-out by the silver-comet on the dancefloor. She had successfully lured every single one of their dedicated fans away from them and on to her, and because of that she was now considered the enemy. They nursed their Proseccos, pursed their lips and glared at the backs of the men who had abandoned them for the evening.

"I've had it girls, and I believe it's about time for me to call it a night," Sheila whispered, as she caught her first glimpse of Timothy sitting by himself in the darkness.

Michelle, the Frenchman, shot an angry look at Timothy from across the room as if he were holding up a neon sign that said: *stay away from this one, you pig, she's mine!* Michelle was just one in a long line of competitors who had made it their primary mission for the evening to become the lucky winner of this super-hot sex-bomb on two legs.

For the first time Timothy could remember, mixing in with the others was exactly what he did not want to do. Timothy was expended, exhausted and totally spent. In the last 48-hours, he had given 14 interviews in six different locations with media groups from at least three different nations, including a news group that flew in to meet with Timothy from Mexico City. During the same period of time, he had self-published twenty-four new-blasts to three of the largest news aggregators in the world. All were picked up like birdseed by the likes of the BBC, Fox News-France and La Jornada, the largest media group in South America. Timothy was now done for the day having effectively advanced Henri Lepan and perhaps even Santo Gordo into the number one trending political topic in the world.

All Timothy had to do now was patiently wait for a call from Homayra or Danielle telling him that they had found Henri's satellite phone and installed his SIM card into one of their cell phones.

Timothy was about to leave Zelz and head back to the Flick Theatre for a quiet evening with Smithy, when his waitress placed his favorite cocktail on a napkin directly under his nose.

Timothy surveyed the bar for a familiar face and then glanced over at Sheila and the table of blonde bimbos. He raised his glass with a look of questionable appreciation and considered whether one of them might have bought him the drink. That would have required a bar tab, and in all of the years the bimbos had been coming to Zelz, rarely had they spent so much as an English Pound on their own drinks.

The drink was known as a Rum-Runner and was prepared exactly the way Timothy had designed it. Timothy's patented cocktail was much different than the usual recipe by the same name, made up of rum, blackberry liqueur, crème de banana liqueur. His had a powerful reputation, which he taught to only a select few of the bartenders at Zelz how to prepare. It was concocted with every clear, 100-proof, liquor on the top shelf, and would cause a woman to sing after just a few sips. Timothy called the drink his *love-potion* and the cocktail was highly successful in maneuvering lovely ladies from their dizzy barstools to Timothy's big round bed at home.

Sheila beamed a smile back at Timothy along with a flirtatious wink and casually excused herself from her table. She was mindful of her flawless competition on the dance floor as she sucked in her midriff bulge as best she could and sauntered up to Timothy's booth.

"Hey---honey doll! What's a sexy guy like you doing sitting over here all by his lonesome? I think you could use a little company?"

Sheila leaned over and kissed Timothy passionately on lips, introducing a noticeable amount of tongue action. Her commanding perfume and large breasts covered Timothy's face as his nose poked through the center of her cleavage.

Perhaps forty-eight hours earlier Timothy would have reveled in such an environment but tonight was different, he needed to leave and get back to Smithy so he politely tried to disengage himself from her overly perfumed bosom. Timothy had promised himself that he would stay sober and avoid women at all costs. He was now being tested and had a strong suspicion that he was going to fail miserably.

"Thank you so much for the drink, Sheila."

"What drink?" Sheila asked, as she signaled the rest of her brood over to Timothy's booth.

"Hey girls, it's Timothy! Come on over here and join us, the party's just getting started!"

The rest of women adjusted their hair and sequin dresses and marched over to their new found bar tab.

Sheila slowly maneuvered her hand up Timothy's inseam and rested her fingers on his crotch, taking full liberties with his testicles.

"Hey, slow it down baby-girl, the night's still young." Timothy cursed himself for absorbing the contents of his glass as if it were his normal, automatic, reflex. "Damn it! I just can't to this tonight. Okay, ladies, I really can't stay with you all tonight. I have a lot of work to do."

Sheila's friend, Julia, skidded in on the other side of Timothy and slid her hands up his other inseam as the two ladies began teaming up on his manhood.

"Did you see that showboat on the dance floor---girl?" Julia said to Sheila. "She looks like a bitch to me, and probably anorexic one at that."

"Yeah, those boys over there had better be careful with that one, I tell you---she looks pretty dangerous to me," Sheila replied.

Timothy's cocktail waitress arrived at the table with a large tray of Goldschläger cinnamon schnapps.

"Doubles shot for everyone from a fan of Timothy's."

The waitress stooped over and whispered into Timothy's ear.

"Well it seems that you have a secret admirer in the bar somewhere. She or he wanted you to have this special Jägerbomb. Whoever she or he is has been slipping me notes for the last hour or so."

The waitress dropped a shot glass of Jägermeister into the center of another glass of something even more dangerous.

Without even considering the consequences, Timothy said, "Well then! Thank you to my sexy admirer whoever she or he might be!"

He threw his head back and tossed down the contents of the glass and instantly felt the jolt of something very potent. Timothy ignored the powerful effects of the drink and hammered it up even more. He stood up and allowed the smaller glass of German liqueur to drop and remain in his mouth as a sign of total abandon.

"Hey girls, guess what?" Timothy yelled, as he popped the small glass out of his mouth and into his hand. "I think my favorite drink is beginning to work on my ass this time! Now don't you lovely ladies start thinking that you can advantage of me now that I'm getting a bit shit-faced!"

The table of women applauded Timothy for his playful antics as the waitress returned with another tray of drinks. "Oh, and by the way, your secret admirer wants me to give you one of these for the road."

Timothy thought that his waitress must have received a very huge tip in advance when she gave him an over-the-top French-kiss and seductively poured the next shot of unknown liquor down his welcoming throat.

Chapter 55

HOMAYRA: CONFIDENT CONTROL

Montbéliard, FR — Castle interior - 8:41 p.m.

Traveling upward--to where we prayed we would locate Henri's satellite phone proved to be an arduous task as Miss Cathy, ever so slowly, guided Danielle and me through the meandering service hallways of the castle. The service elevator that was dedicated only to Henri's master penthouse utilized the same bio-scanner that was found next to the door of his old ground floor office.

Miss Cathy pressed her 94-year-old hand against the scanner and we were automatically granted access. As the cramped elevator labored its way to the top floor, I found myself studying the back of Miss Cathy's head. How strange it was, I thought, that everything around us had been brought to life by this old woman's son. The fact that this kind human being, who once changed Henri's diapers, wasn't even allowed to show her face to Henri's own guests seemed utterly shameless.

Further, how was it even possible that I could have spent so many years as Henri's play toy and know so little about his life's involvement in such a terrible industry? The mind works in mysterious ways for those who are abused; it opens only slightly for those of us who are under the thumb of someone evil.

The doors to the service elevator finally opened and we found ourselves in the back of a large industrial kitchen. As the doors of the elevator closed behind us, so did the mind of Miss Cathy, who had suddenly become totally unware of her surroundings.

"Where are we, girls?" she mumbled.

Danielle and I quickly replayed our one-act-play and as expected, Miss Cathy returned back to consciousness, but this time, at only at about half-strength. Miss Cathy's previous royal form was quickly wilting like a stale bouquet of flowers. Although she was aware of where we were and what we were doing, her physical strength was giving out and she was quickly powering down for the day.

"Alrighty now, let me just see where my son stores his stash of cheese cakes, shall I? I do hope that he has something fresh and truly decadent for us to munch on tonight, don't you, girls?"

As Miss Cathy went to work in the kitchen, Danielle and I pushed our way through the double wooden doors and into the dimly lit forum. The room that I had once spent time in when I was a teenager had been completely transformed into a massive dining room for entertaining very special guests. There were more than a dozen tables arranged around the room, all surrounding a large golden gazebo in the center.

Each table had a dozen chairs set around it and was immaculately set for a lavish multicourse dinner. The settings were comprised of golden flatware, sparkling crystal goblets and fine china with a red velvet booklet neatly placed upon each plate. Every table featured a huge vase of red roses, with the entire setting being dimly illuminated by a massive crystal chandelier above.

An elaborate lighting system painted the ceiling and walls with a prism of red, blue, indigo and violet lights. All of them were tuned to perfection from a primary control center in the back of the room.

Marble, sandstone, limestone and granite statues depicting men and women copulating with children and animals were staged throughout the large room. Each figure portrayed a dark theme of a forcefully, selfish orgy. Many of the statues looked to be original pieces from ancient times.

One intricately carved half-horse and human figure was so perverted and lifelike, I had to turn my head away in disgust. Disturbing portrayals of horned demons, performing cunnilingus on young girls, goats and lambs, to brutal monsters having intercourse with unwilling children, populated the large forum, with each sinful character frozen in time.

"This is really some sick shit," Danielle exclaimed, with a horrified expression.

We paused next to one statue that depicted two adult males holding down a struggling child at the feet of a naked and obese paganistic creature that wore a crown of thorns.

"What in God's name goes on in this room Danni?"

We weaved through a configuration of tables towards a large doorway on the far end of the room, praying that we wouldn't be seized by any evil spirits that might be watching us.

"There aint no god in this room, girl." Danielle whispered, as she clung to my arm.

I suddenly felt nauseous and was about to faint, just as our sightseeing tour through the perverted forest had come to an end. We had finally come upon Henri's private office.

"Get a hold of yourself Homi, and do not pass out on me! I will not be left alone in here! Do you hear me Homi?"

Danielle grabbed my cheeks tightly with her fingers and cranked down on both sides of my face, desperately trying to keep me from drifting away.

Henri's office was as fanatically organized, as were the other offices he maintained throughout France. He was known to be a devout enemy of computers, never possessing a single desktop computer, laptop or CPU of any sort. Henri insisted that computers were an inherent evil and that if he was ever forced to use one it would be to his ruination. Henri refused to touch a computer or even be in the same room with one. He considered them a violation of his personal privacy which served an example of a perfect paradox.

The mere fact that Henri carried a smart phone was a miracle in itself and a direct violation to his strict code of conduct. But since every single person in his line of command used no other form of communication, he was forced to comply. The days of doing business face to face was now a thing of the past and completely out of Henri's control.

Henri despised his cell phone so much that he vociferously refused to be taught even the basics of the security features of his smartphone even though he was ordered to do so, time and time again.

"I don't need to know how to use all of these stupid bells and whistles. Just show me how to read a text and make a goddamn phone call." I remember Henri always saying. Little did Henri realize that through his own stubborn defiance he had slowly become a perfect hacking target for someone of the likes of Timothy. Henri was the classic example of dumb-user of a very powerful communication device.

Danielle and I scanned the room for anything closely resembling a handheld transceiver or satellite phone and could find nothing. Although it was painful, I tried to put myself inside the mind of Henri as I carefully searched his neatly arraigned office. If I were Henri, where might I keep such a device which I loathed?

Henri always had an appreciation for fine wood and his office clearly portrayed that theme. He adored meticulously polished Honduras mahogany, Bolivian Rosewood and rich black walnut and his office featured all three. But sitting on the floor directly next to his desk sat a very old and noticeably distressed dogwood box with a tarnished brass latch.

I could recall seeing that same box before in his old office many years ago. It was during the time when Henri smoked and used it as a humidor. He told me that he had made the box when he was only 12-years old during woodworking class at school. The box still displayed the faint name of Lepan that had been burned into each side.

The entire box appeared to have been fastened to the floor by shiny brass fasteners. A power cord ran from a hole in the base of the box to an electrical outlet on the wall. I moved the latch and lifted the lid and sitting within my own grasp, was Henri's all-powerful satellite phone.

"I found it, Danni---Look!" I whispered, as I lifted the transceiver from its charger and showed it to Danielle. We both stood with our backs to the door examining the infamous device.

"That's it? That's Henri's fucking satellite phone," Danni exclaimed, as I searched my purse for the paperclip which I was instructed to use to remove the mysterious SIM card.

I was expecting a device that was capable of connecting with dedicated geostationary satellites under harsh conditions to look a bit more significant than what I was holding in my hand. The unit was of the brand, *Inmarsat IsatPhone Pro*, and it looked more like any other smartphone one might find at a department store.

"But where is the SIM card slot supposed to be? Timothy told us to look for a tiny hole through which we are to insert a paperclip," Danielle said, as we both squinted and inspected all sides of the device.

"I don't see any goddamn hole---Homi!"

"Shit, this phone is probably something different than what Timothy thought Henri might be using," I said.

I glanced back in the wooden box for further inspection and found a small booklet.

"Look Danni, this must be the operating instructions," I said, as I searched the index, looking for anything having to do with a SIM card.

"I found it Danni! Listen to this! It's here in the trouble shooting section. Okay Danni, listen," I announced, as I began reading from the booklet.

"I found it as well---girls," came a loud voice shouting from the doorway. Danielle and I sprung around and faced the darkened figure in terror. It was Miss Cathy sporting a huge grin and standing in the doorway holding a round cheesecake pan.

"Holy shit! Miss Cathy--- you just scared the crap out of us," Danielle said, as she held Henri's satellite phone behind her back.

"Would you girls like lemon raspberry cream, chocolate tuxedo cream, key lime, or a tiramisu cheesecake? ---I just love taking orders!"

"Oh, why don't you just surprise us, Miss Cathy? I'm sure they will all be scrumptious. Won't they, Homi?"

Danielle was prompted me for my next line.

"Oh---absolutely Miss Cathy, why not go back to the kitchen and put each slice in a nice cake dish or box and cover it very tightly with cellophane?"

"Fun, fun, fun, this is just so much fun, girls," Miss Cathy said, as she scampered off to the kitchen singing a familiar French war tune out loud.

"Does that woman ever stop singing?" I asked, as I listened to her trail away in song.

"It's okay with me if the woman sings; it's when she stops singing--- that's when I worry," said Danielle.

"Okay where were we, Danni," I said as I continued my dictation from the booklet:

Make sure your phone is fully charged and turned off.
Next:

1. *Remove the battery cover using a coin or screwdriver to loosen the screw on the back of the phone. Gently lift and slide the cover off. Remove the battery.*
2. *Remove the SIM card from the tray with the notch up and the gold plate facing out.*
3. *Push down the SIM tray and slide the tray back to lock it in place.*
4. *Replace the battery and the battery cover, and screw it into place.*

"Homi, I don't have a coin or a screwdriver! Quick, take a look in Henri desk drawer and see what you can find."

I ran to the back of Henri's desk and opened the top drawer and snatched a few stray coins from his tray. Just as I was placing a coin in Danielle's hand, a door opened in the forum just outside of the office and a person entered.

"Who in god's name is that in my kitchen," a baritone voice boomed from the forum.

Danielle and I realized immediately that it was Henri as we ducked behind the desk.

"What in the hell," Henri yelled, as he pushed opened the doors to kitchen. "Mother--- what in the world are you doing in here?"

Danielle's hands were shaking as she fidgeted with the coin, desperately trying to remove the battery cover.

"Mother what in the hell are you doing here at this time of night?"

"What? My god son----you scared me to death!"

"Mother, why on earth are you dressed in such a strange costume and what are you doing in here all by yourself? One of my security guards told me that they thought they had seen you on the main floor with some other women. I thought ---that can't be possible! Why are you here, mother, and who were those other woman you were with?"

Henri's voice was booming and filling the kitchen with terror. I was quite sure he was freighting Miss Cathy to death.

"What son--- why are you asking me all of these ridiculous questions?"

"Mother! I demand an answer this minute! Who were you with on the mezzanine earlier---and what in the hell are you doing up here in my damn kitchen at this time of night?"

Henri was losing his patients as the sound of a dish crashed to the floor.

Danielle had the just removed the battery cover and was extracting the SIM card as I was about to run into the kitchen and defend Miss Cathy.

"Mother I asked you a goddamn question and I demand an answer!"

Henri was yelling at the top of his lungs and when he slammed his fist down on the steel counter, that's when I'd had enough.

"That's it Danni---I'm going in!"

"Wait Homi; don't go in there just yet! ---Wait and let's see how Miss Cathy handles her son."

Danielle replaced the cover on the back of the phone and placed the satellite phone back to the base of the wooden box. She then carefully placed the tiny SIM card in her bra.

A large crash emanated from the kitchen as Danni and I ran towards the kitchen in pursuit. We were about to push through the kitchen doors and jump on Henri's back when Miss Cathy suddenly became the *alpha mare* and made herself known.

"Back off Henri, you just back off at once! Do you understand me? You will never raise your voice to me in that sort of tone again! You remind me of your father! Back up Henri and never charge me again."

Her voice was so striking and assertive that it brought back vivid memories of Zooli instructing us all how to control a frantic horse on the attack:

Step into his space and move him off you! Watch that temper girl.

Be confident and skillful, Miss Cathy and give him space to move away. Control all four feet with your body language and move Henri's head with just a slight bit of pressure.

"But mother, I was just asking you a simple question. Why are you up here this evening? And who were the other women you were with downstairs?"

Zooli's instruction continued:

Disengage that forehand, Miss Cathy and move Henri's hindquarters. — Zooli's image continued to instruct.

"Now move out of my way you snarky thing," Miss Cathy ordered, as Henri backed up and skulked out of the kitchen like a broken horse.

Danielle and I were hiding in the darkness as Henri walked right past us disgusted with the entire situation. He knew it was useless getting answers from his forgetful mother, because there were none to be found.

The three of us were now on our way down to the ground floor service tunnel with the SIM card neatly stashed in Danielle's bra, a large tray of mixed cheesecakes, a completely confused Miss Cathy and a huge sense of relief.

Chapter 56

CLEAR SHOTS

Zelebritiez Tapas Restaurant, Clement's St, Oxford, United Kingdom - 8:45 p.m.

B ody shots were well underway as Timothy licked a generous portion of salt from the top of Julia's breasts and began sipping from a shot glass of tequila that was wedged within the confines of her cleavage. When he came up for air, Timothy leaned over and snatched a small slice of lime from Julia's mouth with his teeth. "Have I just died and gone to heaven?" He asked, as he appraised the women on all four sides.

Timothy was back in full form, lit up like a sparkler, and enjoying every second of it. The women surrounding him were becoming more desirable with every shot, which were arriving at the table on silver platters. The bimbos edged their large assets closer to Timothy's wandering hands as they cranked up the heat and asked for more.

Bottles of expensive wine were raining down upon the table, one after another, as the hour hand on Timothy's watch magically skipped from 7 p.m. to eleven. It was quickly becoming Timothy's night, whether he wanted it or not, as his hands and fingers were traveling up the legs of every inebriated woman at the table.

Timothy always knew that he was a bad dancer and tonight wasn't any different as he stumbled around the dance floor to a cheap rendition of *Brick*

House. He had all but forgotten about the mystery women who had caused such a ruckus during happy-hour until he found her in his arms. She had been dancing with a field of men, who were moving their bodies to beat of the music and sending off their own special mating calls. The dance floor was saturated with people, all blending together in a feeding frenzy as every male on the floor was being drawn towards *her*.

The edge of the dance floor was lined with drunks; three deep, holding their drinks and sizzling with interest in the mystery woman who was maliciously teasing each one of them with her seductive derriere. Out of the corner of his eye, Timothy took note of two men dressed in dark suits with sunglasses who appeared to be observing him rather than the temptress on the dance floor.

The suits didn't fit the standard profile of the population of drunks in the bar as they slowly moved around the circumference of the crowd working their way towards him. But Timothy's concern in the strange men disappeared just as soon as the mystery woman's luscious lips lightly brushed up against the side of his face.

Her body felt fabulous as it molded against Timothy's chest perfectly, causing his penis to become partially erect. Her breasts felt firm and natural as he stared down at them neatly tucked within her silver bra as he considered his next move. Just when Timothy was about to formally introduce himself, a frustrated bald man took matters into his own hands and shoved Timothy to the side lines.

Michelle became the first casualty of the evening as Timothy collided with him and knocked him off his feet. Michelle fell to the floor as if he were on ice skates, bringing down Sheila's drunken friend Julia with him.

Michelle was desperately attempting to reorient his dignity by clinging to Julia's clothing when the worst happened. Julia's entire dress, along with her 38DD bra were suddenly relocated to her waistline as her queen-sized, pasty white breasts went on full display to the thrill of the crowd.

The impatient bald maniac who had just set Julia's nightmare in motion took full advantage of the melee to place his large hands around the front of the mystery women and directly upon her chest. The surrounding competition watched in astonishment as he fervently massaged each of her breasts to the rhythm of the song. Surprisingly, the mystery woman showed no interest in the placement of the man's hands and even less to the owner of the hands. The bald man, surprised by her lack of protest, decided to up his ante and go for more. He began kissing the mystery woman on shoulders, neck and face as his hands explored her every detail of her buttocks.

The bald man's successful acquisition fueled the frustration of the wide-eyed man with the bangs who had been drooling over the mystery woman ever since she walked through the front door. Certainly she must feel violated by the hoodlum's show of force. Someone must jump in there and save that poor woman's life, and that someone was going to be him.

When the lucky competitor cupped the mystery woman's buttocks in the palms of his hands the man in bangs turned into the *man of steel*. Just when he was about to leap forward and save the day, a pushy man in a black suit with sunglasses forced his way in front of him blocking the hero's access to the mystery woman.

The fuse had been lit and an explosion was forthcoming as the two sexually frustrated drunks, came together with the suits and sunglasses in a collision of pushing and shoving, flailing fists, flying glasses, broken beer bottles and boots.

The entire dance floor exploded into violence as drunken men attacked whoever was within striking distance. The mystery woman was pushed to the side and thrown to the floor as the onlookers moved in for a closer look. Her skirt had been moved above her waist line revealing her entire silver thong which glistened under the brightly colored lights of the dance floor.

The dynamics of the crowd had suddenly changed as half of the drunken men were running to the aid of the damsel-in-distress while the other half was rushing in for a quick feel. The room burst into frenzy, as bar stools took to the air, tables were overturned and the worst was yet to come. The two men who put the rumble in motion were now locked together in a strangle hold as they charged the stage to the horror of the musicians.

Tim, the drummer, was the first to go through large picture window onto the sidewalk. His snare drum and cowbell skipped across the sidewalk and rolled into the path of an oncoming car. Smokers, who had been standing on the sidewalk chatting, scattered like frightened sheep as shards of broken glass, broken musical equipment and bodies exploded through the window.

Next to be ejected through the opening was the cute blonde vocalist, still gripping her microphone. The piano player, bassist, lead guitarist along with a man in a dark suit and broken sunglasses were ejected from the window like cattle in a hurricane.

Timothy missed being thrown through the window by tripping over Michelle's bloody face and hiding under a table. He was now feeling the full effects of his mystery drinks and wondered if he was even capable of standing up. He crawled on his hands and knees towards the back door hoping to retrieve his laptop computer.

There was no shortage of people tripping over Timothy as they rushed to the aid of the half-naked mystery women. The police would soon be arriving along with their proverbial patty wagons. Anyone remaining at the scene of the crime would surely be arrested and taken off to the trunk tank.

It was now close to midnight, and Zelz, along with Timothy's brain, were completely demolished. Timothy grabbed his backpack and staggered out of the back door onto a second story wooden porch. No matter how inebriated Timothy had ever been, he was always conscious of his bill and never left a restaurant with an open bar tab. Little did it matter since the cash register had been unplugged and relocated from the checkout stand to a sink full of blue rinse water.

Timothy was surprised by how drunk he had become in such a short period of time. Who had paid for all of those bottles of wine and what were in those powerful drinks that seemed to set his brain on fire? The bimbos certainly couldn't have afforded to pay for all of those top-shelf brands. The only thing they ever put money into was the tampon dispenser in the ladies room.

As Timothy felt his way to the back door he was reminded of something his waitress had said to him earlier: *Oh—and by the way, she also wants me to give you one of these, as well.* Whatever *one-of-these* were might have been the cause of his total inebriation.

The wooden porch that was attached to the back wall of restaurant overlooked a narrow dark alleyway. The small wooden structure was crowded with the injured and stressed under the weight of the bar room casualties. Men and women triaged the wounded as others smoked their cigarettes and theorized as to who was the main culprit of such a barroom disaster. Others stepped around the carnage and down the wooden steps to their awaiting automobiles.

Sheila had her arms around Julia and was trying to comfort her best friend who was wailing in an overly dramatic call for help. "I have never been so demeaned in my entire life!" Julia bellowed, as she kept one eye open for that special man in shining armor.

Michelle and Hans were standing off to the side smoking their cigarettes and quietly ranting. They had bloodied-up, angry faces and glared at Timothy as he emerged from the scene of the crime. .

"It was him! Timothy is the cause of this---this---disaster!" Michelle pretended to lunge at Timothy like an angry French animal as Hans easily held Michelle at bay. "You are the cause of all this---you---you--- you--- filthy pig!"

The sound of fire engines and police sirens filled the cool night air and provided a sobering wake-up call to anyone still on the premises to pack it up and leave immediately. Guilty or innocent, drunk or sober, anybody remaining would soon be placed in plastic handcuffs and taken off to jail.

Timothy knew that he was within staggering distance of his temporary hideout, but even walking there was becoming a concern. He also realized that as every second that clicked by, his level of drunkenness seemed to be intensifying and his sight was diminishing to tunnel-vision.

A police cruiser slowly entered the far end of the one-way alley and was advancing on the remaining drunks on the porch as Timothy knocked over a garbage can and stumbled out of sight.

Chapter 57

HOMAYRA: THE COVERED DISH

Montbéliard, FR — Castle interior - Pantry

At 9:05 p.m. Miss Cathy reminded us that she was nine and a half decades old, when her body completely gave out. Although Miss Cathy's drive and physical endurance was incredible during the daytime hours, she had a strict bed time and that time came the moment the elevator doors opened on the ground floor of the castle.

Danielle saw her collapsing first and caught her wilting body just before she went down. I jumped in and saved the box of cheesecakes which was tumbling from her arms. Expecting Miss Cathy to be able to keep up with us for the long haul was a mistake on our part. Zooli had warned us that her bed time came fast and furiously and---my god was she ever right!

Danielle held Miss Cathy's drooping body in her arms. "Wow---this poor woman's lights are totally out! Homi--- quick! Grab that table over there and pull it over here---fast!"

I swiftly retrieved the large portable banquet table along with a huge stack of tablecloths and rolled it over to Miss Cathy. I raised her feet while Danielle held onto her torso and we hoisted our sleeping queen onto the top of our makeshift gurney.

We covered Miss Cathy's slumbering body neatly under several table linens and rolled her down the hallway towards the mezzanine entrance.

"Homi hold up! We can't leave here without her cheese cakes!"

"Good thought, Danni, it just wouldn't be right for us to drop our end of the bargain with Miss Cathy."

A peak under the table cloth assured us that Miss Cathy was sleeping soundly and then we were off. We had one actively working cell phone between the two of us while Henri's all important SIM card was safely tucked within Danielle's bra as the three of us approached the entrance to the mezzanine.

"Where in the fuck is Zooli?" Danielle whispered, from the side of her mouth.

"I don't know, but I've got a sinking feeling that the cell phone I gave her---is dead."

We emerged from the service hallway into the middle of a party that was going all out. Guests were wearing 18th-century French costumes and celebrating to the sounds of rap music blasting from the speakers mounted on the mezzanine walls. People were mingling, dancing, drinking, smoking and blatantly snorting lines of cocaine served on large silver platters.

To the onlookers we must have looked as if we were nothing more than two extravagantly dressed hostesses pushing along a covered table full of appetizers. Several hungry people noticed us moving through the throngs of people and moved in for a closer look.

A distinguished looking gentleman, who was escorting an overly made-up femme fatale, boldly took it upon himself to grab one end of the table cloth and begin removing it.

"Well what might you have under here, you gorgeous ladies, perhaps a lobe of Henri's infamous Duck Foie Gras? He's been bragging about that ever since he arrived here this morning? I just love that old sport, he throws the best parties, doesn't he darling? Of course you know that I am one of Henri's closest friends and advisors?" The gentleman announced this loudly for the sake of everyone standing nearby.

Danielle quickly stepped between the man and the table and glanced at me for any defensive maneuver I might be able to conger up.

"Well I don't believe we are serving that, sir, but I do think that you and your beautiful lady friend will just love our delicious Atlantic raw seafood medley." I said.

I gently patted the table cloth which was covering Miss Cathy and prayed that she would not suddenly wake up and rise from the dead. "We are serving salmon tartar bites gratis, served on a layer of sardines. Oh and I bet the rest of you lovely people might like to sample some our raw seafood, it's to die for. Tell me miss, don't you just adore raw octopus? Especially when they're still wiggling and squirming, aren't they absolutely scrumptious? But I must warn you, my dear; this little fellow is a little tricky to get in your mouth. Here, reach over and touch the slimy beast, I do believe the poor creature is still breathing! Does anyone know if an octopus breathes air? I swear this one does!"

"Oh my lord----Robert, that sounds disgusting--- and simply horrible! Please get this mess away from me this instant! Who in their right mind would ever eat such a gross beast and a living one that breaths air?" the angry woman snarled.

"Oh you are so right, my lady, and to think that they actually eat these creatures when they are still alive! I myself would rather eat one of those lovely horses outside!" I said, venting a bit of anger from earlier in the day.

I taunted the crowd with the table covers in the hopes of actually scaring the crowd away. My maneuver seemed to be working perfectly as the couple edged away from the table in disgust.

"Perhaps her highness would rather have the fish and chips or maybe some bologna, cold cuts from our deli tray. All of our wonderful processed food is being served over on the far side of the mezzanine." The haughty guests took my cue and gazed off in the distance for more palatable alternatives as they all moved quickly away.

We continued our trek towards the court yard entrance where we hoped Becker was still stationed, when I saw Zooli rushing through the crowd towards us with a look of both concern and relief.

"Oh, thank god, I found the two of you! I was worried sick! Where is Miss Cathy? I have been trying to call you all night long, but your phone doesn't seem to be working properly." Zooli said, as she privately pressed the cell phone into the palm of my hand.

"Oh my god, I was right! The phone's dead alright, Danni. I'm so sorry, Zooli!" I searched through handbag praying that I hadn't forgotten my charging cable as the three of us rushed for an exit to the service hallway, pushing along our table of appetizers.

"Girls, please, where did you put Miss Cathy?" Zooli asked, as the three of us navigated the table through the busy service hallways. "She must be dreadfully exhausted by now. I'm going out of my mind with concern for her!"

"She's right here Zooli. You're pushing her!" I gently lifted the edge of the table cloth just enough for Zooli to see Miss Cathy sleeping comfortably beneath the coverings.

"What!" Zooli said, as she let out a loud and boisterous belly laugh, which was highly contagious to the rest of us, excluding Miss Cathy, of course. "Oh my god, you girls are just---way too much. I simply can't believe this! Oh my sweet, daring Miss Cathy----she most certainly is down for the count!"

<hr />

Danielle found a vacant room that was apparently dedicated for feeding the staff member's scraps of garbage during their long work days. Zooli told us that the lower level servants at the castle were fed barely enough rations to stay alive. She spoke of a time she came upon some servants hiding in the forest roasting a cat and eating leaves.

We locked the door behind us and pulled down the shades. Miss Cathy was sleeping soundly and, according to Zooli, would not make a move until 5:00 a.m. At that time her biological alarm clock would go off with vigor and send the old woman off to tend to her horses. This was the routine Miss Cathy had followed every day for last 40 years, rain or shine and sickness or health.

"Zooli, I'm so sorry for not charging my phone before I gave it to you. You must think of me as an idiot," I said, as I plugged my phone to an electrical outlet.

"What do you mean Homi? What is a charge?"

Danielle and I glanced at each other and smiled. We knew that Zooli was behind the technological curve, but we never imagined her to be that far behind.

"Forget it, Zooli, it's too hard to explain," I said, as I kissed her on her cheek.

As the four of us hunkered down in our temporary sanctuary waiting for the time to pass, it occurred to me that although we all were fighting for our lives and deep within the walls of fire, our human spirit soared. We laughed, smiled and joked with one other as we worked our way through some of the most complex aspects of our plan which were all being constructed on the fly. For it was our camaraderie, dedication and love for one another that fueled our optimism and protected our sanity.

"Homi, I do believe I found that tiny hole on my cell phone that Timothy was referring to. Please tell me that you still have the paperclip?"

Danielle carefully inserted one end of the paperclip into the center of the tiny hole of her cell phone and applied a slight bit of pressure as her tiny SIM card slowly ejected from the body of the phone, just as Timothy said it would. "Alright, Homi, let's just hope that Henri's SIM card fits my phone."

To our delight and with the help of all of all of the gods watching, Danielle successfully installed Henri's satellite SIM card into the body of her cell phone as we all let out a collective sigh of relief.

At 9:21 p.m. my cell phone had just enough power to allow me to send off a text message to Timothy and Golareh, wherever in the world they might be to receive it:

TO: Golareh, Timothy-9:21 p.m. - Success! We have successfully installed Henri's SIM card into Danni's phone!!! Do your thing!!!

Chapter 58

TEMPTING FATE

What a day it had been and what an evening it was becoming, Timothy thought, as his feet stabbed the asphalt of the dark alleyways and side streets that separated Zelz from his temporary hideout at the Flick Theatre. As he staggered down the center of the winding street, the diminishing cognitive portion of Timothy's brain was examining his drunken side in his classic clinical fashion. Timothy was always good at assessing his miserable condition and often examined himself as if he were his own personal therapist.

Timothy had a long standing theory that he had tempted fate far too many times, and as a result, he was being paid back in spades. He had somehow personally offended a particular spirit he was beginning to know very well. Something he had said or done to he, she or it, was now taking full revenge on his soul. But this time the revenge would affect the welfare of other innocent people, and that didn't sit very well with Timothy.

Even though his career in media was soaring, everything else in his life had slowly fallen apart ever since the loss of his son. His marriage, which he never dreamed would ever end, came apart at the seams; his few friends in the world rarely called him anymore; he considered himself an alcoholic and had recently come to the conclusion that he was a sex addict, which in the past made little sense to him.

"Okay goddamn it! I'm sorry for whatever I did to piss you off---you bastard! But why, in the fuck, did you have to pick tonight--- of all nights, to get me drunk as shit?" Timothy was yelling at the spirits above and below, his voice breaking the silence of the sleeping neighborhood around him.

The malicious spirit, who most likely was in cahoots with Satan, was well aware of the fact that Timothy had been trying his best to remain sober and stay as far away as possible from the temptations of the flesh. But the high octane cocktails and tempting female body parts came raining down upon Timothy's weak condition, relentlessly, one after the other, for the sole purpose of rending him stupid and worthless.

Why had he not received any phone calls from the girls, Timothy suddenly wondered, as he reached for his cell phone in his pants pocket and activated the screen. To his horror the amber screen displayed a warning message:

WARNING YOUR TEXT MAILBOX IS 100% FULL. PLEASE CLEAR YOU'RE OLD MESSAGES; YOUR MAXIMUM LIMIT HAS BEEN REACHED!

Timothy was shaking as he scanned a very long list of unread text messages. His son Joseph had been trying to reach him because Timothy had requested a special app that he needed to replicate the data from Henri's SIM card to his own cell phone. Unread messages from Homayra, Danielle, Frédéric and more than a dozen from Goli had silently stacked up in his inbox.

"Fuck, I can't believe I didn't hear these bastards come in! Why wasn't I notified? Oh my god---the fucking ringer's muted! Why the hell did I switch my phone to the fucking silent mode?" Timothy was cursing loudly in the center of a dark neighborhood caring little about who he might be disturbing. He angrily stomped his feet on the ground and swore into the black heavens, as he struggled to focus his bloodshot eyeballs on his phone's main menu.

He fumbled with his phone and squinted through the lenses of his severely smudged and bent bifocals as he read the most recent of a long list of critical text messages:

From: Golareh-9:23 p.m.- Timothy!! Danni and Homi have installed Henri's SIM card and they are waiting for you to copy the SIM card!!... Please don't forget that Henri's conference call is at 2:00 a.m.... where in the fuck are you?

From: Danielle-9:21 p.m. - Success! We have successfully installed Henri's SIM card into Danni's phone!!! Do your thing!!!

From: Joseph-7:23 p.m. - Hi dad attached you will find the latest version of the mobile SIM card replicator that you asked for. Click on the link and it should automatically install. Let me know if you have a problem>>>>><u>SIM Rescue Restore 3.0.1.5 (latest version)</u>

Timothy felt his entire body heating up with embarrassment as he deleted several messages, located Golareh's phone number and pressed *send*. The line was busy.

"Fuck, fuck, fuck!" Timothy was now growling aloud as tried to reach Danielle. Her phone, for some reason, went straight to voicemail. Back over to texting, Timothy decided, as he verbally dictated a drunken text message to all concerned:

To: Golareh, Danielle, Frédéric, Homayra -12:07a.m. .- Hi guys sorry I'm late. I am—I was tied up with parties- I mean reporters all day. I also had to download some software from my son in order for me to replicate the SIM card data. I'm good to go.

Timothy made one final attempt to call Golareh and Danielle but to no avail. Perhaps it was for the best, for if they had picked up, they would know immediately that he was entirely smashed out of his mind. The only thing for Timothy to do now was safely make it back to the Flick Theatre and desperately try to sober up.

The SIM card data transfer app downloaded quickly and installed without a problem as Timothy dropped his cell phone back in his pocket and veered around the corner of High Street and Oriel Street in full view of the theatre marque in the distance. Down range, he could see Big Ben leaning back against the wall in his uncomfortable wooden chair, surveying the people as they walked past his establishment.

A taxi cab slowly passed by Timothy and pulled into the VIP parking lot of the exclusive Oxford Tablemate Inn, which was cattycorner to the theatre. A tall and extremely attractive blonde woman slowly stepped out of the taxi and walked towards the entrance of the inn. The yellow light from the flame of her lighter illuminated her face as she stood in the shadows, lit a cigarette and paused for a moment to smoke.

As Timothy got closer, he recognized the woman as being the very same mystery woman who was the source of all of the excitement at Zelz. She appeared to be completely intact, showing no signs of trauma from the barroom explosion earlier. She slowly puffed on her cigarette and looked up at the evening sky as delicate whiffs of smoke slowly drifted from her tempting plump lips to the dark sky above.

From the second Timothy watched the mystery women get out of the taxi cab, he had already answered the critical question that was about to be asked of him by that offensive spirit that was hounding him. Should he ignore the temptress and return to the safety of the theatre or should he deviate, just a slight bit, and check on the safety of this poor, battered woman from the bar?

"Fuck it! I won't spend too much time with her," Timothy justified to the spirit, who was pursuing him with a vengeance. "Just let me stop long enough to make her acquaintance. Okay? Is that too much to ask of you? Perhaps we can meet up later on for a drink and celebrate my successful recording of Henri and Santo Gordo doing their big-time deals. Hey, you only live once," Timothy jokingly mocked his stalking spirit.

Timothy stood wavering by the side of the busy street as he anxiously waited for a group of cars to pass by him before he piloted himself across the street. When he reached the other side of the street he squinted over towards the theatre, noticing Big Ben standing up under the lights of the marquee glaring at him. Surely he can't recognize me from this distance, Timothy thought, as he approached the mystery woman who was looking sexier by the step.

"Hello there," Timothy said, as he sucked in his stomach and desperately tried to form his words properly.

The mystery woman totally ignored Timothy as she took another seductive pull from her thin menthol cigarette. There was something oddly familiar about that menthol scent, Timothy thought for a fraction of a second.

"Excuse me Miss, I'm sorry to bother you, but wasn't I dancing with you earlier this evening at Zelz? There was a terrible brawl there and I just wanted to see if--- I mean ask, if you were alright?"

The mystery woman totally ignored his entire question and said nothing.

"I'm sorry Miss; I was only concerned for your safety, is all--- I'm so sorry to bother you, Miss."

Timothy's drunken apology was rudely ignored and returned undelivered, as the mystery woman looked away and refused to make even the least bit of eye contact with Timothy.

Perhaps she couldn't even speak English, Timothy thought. Maybe she was from Russia, Bulgaria or someplace like that. Timothy reluctantly passed by her unnoticed. There was no greeting, no acknowledgement and no hint of a possible date set for his celebration party.

Big Ben had left his post temporarily as Timothy walked away from the mystery woman a bit dejected but also sadly relieved. He was on his way back out of the theatre when Big Ben noticed Timothy staggering in.

"Oh my god, Timothy, I thought that might be you crossing the street down there. What were you doing at the Tablemate? Where have you been, sweetie? Goli has been worried sick about you."

Big Ben rushed over and caught Timothy just as he tripped on the curb and fell forward. "Darling, you are really drunk!"

"I'm okay, Big Ben, I just was being my normal fucked-up self again tonight. I'm drunk as shit, so---the fuck---what! What else is new? Hey, do me a favor, Big Ben and please don't tell Smithy, she's the only person who hasn't given up on me.

"Have you checked your phone Timothy? She was here earlier today looking for you. She's been calling you constantly."

"What do you mean she's been here looking for me? She who---Smithy?"

"No Goli---Timothy! Goli and her cousin Frédéric have been looking for you for the last two goddamn days!"

Timothy quickly retrieved his cell phone from his pants pocket and noticed a completely new list of text messages that had just come in.

"Son of a bitch, I did it again! I forgot to turn my goddamn ringer back on! Again!---Oh my god, Big Ben, I'm such a fucking idiot," Timothy said, as he squinted at the latest line of text message from all concerned.

"Oh my god, Big Ben, I'm so fucked up and I can't even see straight. I can hardly read the numbers on my damn phone. Please tell me what the messages say. Please, Big Ben; help me get my messages across to those poor girls. Oh my god, what have I done?"

Big Ben moved Timothy's drunken body over to the wooden chair in front of the theater and began reading the text messages aloud for the benefit of Timothy:

> *From: Homayra- 12:20 a.m. - Timothy this is Danni...I'm texting from Homi's phone... where the fuck are you; I have installed Henri's SIM in my cell phone. Don't know what to do next? Help!!!!! Hurry!!! We don't have much time!!*

Timothy quickly sent off a reply message through the help of Big Ben's sober fingers:

> *To: Homayra, Golareh- 12:42 a.m. - Sorry for delay guys!! I'm replicating Henri's SIM card right now!!! Danni...leave your cell phone alone and let it finish! Do not turn off your phone for any reason!! Sit tight! ...T*

"Thanks Big Ben---now hand me the phone—I have to do this part myself."

Timothy located the icon for his newly installed SIM Rescue Transfer app and activated the program. Immediately he was presented with a menu screen which prompted him for a target cell phone number. Timothy invoked his contact list and selected Danielle's phone number. Once the connection was established a main transfer menu was presented:

You can now transfer your saved data to this device
Tap on the choices below to select or deselect content:
Contacts   Text Messages   User IdentificationPhotos   Videos
-Start Transfer-

Timothy's index finger was shaking as he nervously checked each box and pressed the Start-Transfer button. To Timothy's horror, a transfer status was displayed with an estimated transfer time much longer than he had ever expected:

Transfer in Progress
Approximately 59-minutes remaining

Chapter 59

GOLAREH: SEARCH TEAMS

12:45 AM – Blueboar Street, Oxford, United Kingdom

It was the way that he looked at me that got my attention. The man in the car had a surprised look on his face, as if he'd just seen a ghost. Frédéric noticed him as well and recognized the kid immediately. Actually he was no kid at all, but a hired gun from Henri's private police force and the youngest one to be added.

Earlier in the evening we agreed that Heath and Rahda would search the north-end of Oxford while Frédéric and I covered the areas of the city that I knew best. The plan was to keep in contact via cell phone and reconvene at the Flick Theatre no later than 1:00 a.m. If neither of us had found Timothy by then, we would cancel the mission for the time being and tell the girls to leave the castle for safer grounds.

The bald hired gun spotted Frédéric first and then his eyes drilled a hole in my forehead as he accelerated into a side street and screeched his tires, reorienting his black Ford Town Car in our direction. Frédéric grabbed my arm and pulled me in to a crowded, smoky pub. He navigated me through the bar and out the back door into a dirty alley way.

"Those guys mean business and they just put you and me together," Frédéric said, as he spun me around and escorted me through the back door of a yarn shop.

"Hello ladies," Frédéric said, as we rushed past five elderly women sitting in comfortable chairs, drinking tea and knitting.

The ladies were concentrating so hard on their knitting that they scarcely noticed us standing in the room next to them. We stood to the side of a large window overlooking the street as two men in dark suits and sunglasses ran past.

Frédéric told me that after looking into Henri's private security force he was shocked at what he found. Every one of the tightly groomed, stiff-dressed men in black suits and shades had either worked for a mafia-based crime family or some corrupt politician at one time or another. Each had the eyes of a shark, experience with a kill and an anxious desire to take someone out.

"That's Stephan Yoden, he just turned 23-years-old and really wants to make a name for himself with his peers," said Frédéric, as he watched the two men trail across the street in the direction of a false lead.

"Why do these guys always wear the same get-up? I mean, what's with the dark suits and sunglasses? Don't they realize that everyone can tell exactly what the hell they do for a living?"

"They want people to know what they do for a living, Goli. I don't think they'd even do it if they couldn't dress the part. Dressing up like someone on the Prime Minister's security detail makes these guys think they're doing something righteous."

Frédéric and I carefully stepped back out on the street and walked quickly in the direction of Zelz's.

We had almost covered a full circle, searching every single bar, restaurant, and coffee house for the illusive Timothy. Almost every other place we stopped had some person who remembered seeing Timothy somewhere in town during the last 48-hours. Somehow I felt that we were getting closer to Timothy, because his tracks seemed to be getting hotter by the step.

Even though I had just received a text messages from Timothy, I still had no clue as to his whereabouts and not getting him to pick up his phone was really pissing me off. His voicemail box was at capacity as my calls and text messages continued to bounce back to me as being undelivered. I was now completely frustrated with Timothy as the evening was getting dangerously close to the scheduled time Henri Lepan and Santo Gordo were to have their long delayed conference call.

I made one final attempt to call Timothy and like before it went straight to his saturated voicemail. As I was angrily stuffing my phone back into my handbag, I noticed a throng of police cars and fire engines, lighting up the evening skies in front of Zelz's. My heart sank as I pictured Timothy dead from a gunshot wound.

At least three large rectangular police vehicles, which Frédéric identified as modern day paddy wagons, were staged in front of a scene of broken glass, smashed windows and injured patrons. Everyone who wasn't in uniform was bloody, inebriated and under arrest. Wrap-up appeared to be in the final stages as the last few people were being led towards the opening of the mobile jail. Two men were crying like babies as they were being cuffed with plastic zip-ties and led to holding tanks.

"Ask her," one yelled in his recognizable French accent. It was Michelle along with Hans, each showing battle scars from a turbulent evening.

"Goli---please!" Michelle yelled, as he directed the attention of a female police officer to Frédéric and me. "Goli, please tell this kind and very pretty officer that it was not me who did anything wrong. I did nothing wrong! It was *her friend*, officer, it was Timothy! It was the pig! He started the whole thing over that girl," Michelle said, as if he were spitting flames.

The female officer loosened her hold on her prisoner, allowing Michelle to relax and speak freely in hopes that the cause of the brawl might be further explained.

"What the hell happened here tonight, Michelle?" I asked, as we approached.

Frédéric politely flashed his identification to the female officer as Michelle, who was clearly drunk, tried to represent himself. "It was Timothy, that—that pig. He was so drunk, Goli, my god! He was tripping all over the dance floor, lusting over that—that---that woman!"

Michelle was doing a poor job at pretending to be sober, hoping that some new information from me might provide some fair trade for an immediate release. He would be wrong.

"Timothy was trying to have his way with every woman in there. Oh my god, this man never stops with his forceful ways with the women!"

"Who was the woman---Michelle?" I asked, hoping and praying it wasn't Ari.

"Oh my god, she---she was so beautiful and everyone around her wanted to dance with her, but Timothy would not allow it! But not me, Goli, I was a gentleman; I was just standing by the door minding my own business. Tell this pretty officer of my gentle ways! Please---Goli---tell this beautiful officer that I am not a troublemaker!"

"Michelle! Would you please shut up and tell me---who the woman was that you saw with Timothy?"

"I'm not sure, Goli, I have never seen her before---but she was so beautiful. She told me that her name was Reneta and that she was from Russia. Oh my lord, she was so sweet and very shy. A treasure with platinum blonde hair all dressed in silver!"

"So were you also dancing with this woman you're describing---sir?" the officer asked.

No no no no noI I am a gentleman! I did nothing! It was Goli's friend--Timothy, who is to blame! He could not wait to put his hands all over that poor woman's body and that's when the fights broke out. Now I must go to jail---for what he did? Why, tell me, and for what?"

"Michelle, Michelle! Where is Timothy now? Has he been arrested?"

"No-no-no---- he ran from the police like a cowardly drunk! He was drunk, oh my god, Goli, he was so drunk. I've never seen this man so drunk before, officer! He must be arrested for this---not me!"

Michelle's pleading was becoming pitiful as he realized that his time as being his personal attorney had just ended.

"Okay sir, we're all done here. It's time to load up----little man," the female officer said, as she moved Michelle and Hans through the door of paddy wagon #4.

"But why---what are you charging me with?"

"Public drunkenness, sir, you have had way too much to drink, and plus, you're lying through your teeth," the officer said, as she shook her head and carefully lowered the top of Michelle's head through the door of the mobile jail.

Through the corner of my eye, I noticed two thugs dressed in dark suits and sunglasses, I hadn't seen before. They were arguing with a police officer as if they were trying to find out who had been arrested. One had a bloody nose while the other was shaking shards of glass out of his hair. Suddenly they spotted Timothy and me and quickly made hand gestures to a black Ford Town Car which was parked behind us, on the other side of a police barrier.

"Let's get out of here, Goli! We've got to go---now!"

Frédéric and I ran across the street and into a dark neighborhood. The Ford Town Car instantly squealed its tires in reverse and charged after us into the sleeping neighborhood about three streets down from us. The two thugs, who had been arguing with the officers, left the scene of the crime on foot and were chasing us at full sprint.

The screech of the tires on the Town Car echoed through the neighbor as their headlights flickered and flashed between the long line of homes, as it raced to our location. We left the street and ran across a dew covered lawn and around the back of a large Gothic style home with large dark square windows and a gabled roof. The Town Car slowed to a crawl in front of the home and activated a search light which lit up shrubbery next to us and the front of the homes down the line.

On the far side of the home we found shelter within a broad leafed, giant rhubarb plant. The two men on foot had caught up with the Town Car, showing no signs of exhaustion, and still wearing their sunglasses. They conversed with the very same young driver who had spotted us earlier downtown and then slowly continued on opposite sides of the dark street.

When the back side of the Flick Theatre came within view, Frédéric and I made a break for it. Luckily the door was unlocked and we found our-selves in the back of a messy storage room where Big Ben stored his retired Simplex XL film projector. Empty film reels cluttered the dusty shelves along with old movie posters from every film Big Ben had ever shown.

Pieces of discarded celluloid, from burned film clips, littered the floor as an old film re-winder sat dusty and unplugged next to the exit.

A dark hallway led us to the door of the kitchen where René Ghislain, Big Ben's partner of 28-years, was chopping a large pile of red onions. The gas from the onions burned my eyes and caused me to cough. René turned around in terror and shrieked while accidently dropping onions and his chef knife onto the floor.

"Holy shit, is that you, Goli? You just caused scared the pee out of me!"

"Oh, I'm sorry we frightened you, René; we just came in through the back door. Are you aware that it's unlocked?"

"Oh, I keep telling Benny to make sure that damn door is kept locked but that man has A.D.D. or something. Why were you coming through the back door anyway? Are you okay and who's this handsome young man with you?"

"I'm sorry René; this is my cousin Frédéric from Paris."

The three of us got down on all fours and began picking up the pieces of onion which had fallen on the floor.

René was a rugged, handsome looking man, with a long thin face and wavy brown hair. He was a director during the day and a chef at the theatre on his off nights. Most of the regulars were aware of the fact that René and Big Ben were legally married but to the average person on the street, they would never guess that the two were a couple, mainly because of their sheer size difference.

Suddenly Big Ben opened the door to the kitchen and screamed at the top of his lungs as he stared at Frédéric standing over René holding the large chef knife. "Who are you---and what have you done to my René?"

Big Ben grabbed an oversized iron skillet from a pan rack and began to make his way towards the terrified Frédéric.

René and I quickly jumped to our feet and ran to the aid of my petrified cousin.

"It's okay Big Ben, this is my cousin Frédéric! Everything's fine! There's nothing to worry about!"

Big Ben's expression slowly switched from murder-mode back to gentle giant.

Frédéric gently placed the chef knife on the cutting board and let out a noticeable gasp while quietly speaking to me in French, *"Ah mon Dieu, Goli, je pense que moi aussi je me suis pissee dessous! - Oh my god Goli, I think I just peed my pants as well!"*

"Oh, I'm sorry Frédéric," Big Ben said, as he approached my cousin and gave him a playful hug. "What are you guys doing back here? Timothy's out in the front lobby---but I have to warn you, Goli, he's really drunk!"

As we approached the lobby, Rahda and Heath were entering through the front door.

"Did you guys see Timothy out there," I asked, as I stepped outside on to the sidewalk and squinted into the dark night.

"No? Why--was he here?" Heath asked, as Big Ben stood there with a look of disbelief on his face.

"Look, Goli, there's Timothy's backpack on the chair over there; he can't be far. Listen Goli, I've got to go over to Smithy's house and check on her. I've got a really bad feeling that something is terribly wrong!" Big Ben said, as he ambled back into the kitchen to tell René of his plans.

"Timothy is fucking missing---again!" I yelled, cursing out loud, as I lit up a much needed cigarette. I continued to yell in vain to distant street lamps and parked cars along the vacant street. "Timothy! Where are you---goddamn it?"

Big Ben returned to the front of the theatre with René cursing at him. "Benny, don't go! Please stay here---please---it's just too dangerous."

"I've got to go, just stay here and keep an eye out for Timothy and Smithy!"

"Benny---please stay here!"

"Just go back inside René! Please René! Just---do as I say!"

Rahda instructed Frédéric to stay behind with her as Heath, Big Ben and I left on foot.

As we were walking away, Big Ben yelled over to Rahda and Frédéric, "Hey guys, keep your eyes on the Tablemate Inn, across the street! Timothy was over there chatting with someone in front of the place earlier."

Chapter 60

HOMAYRA: THE MASTER KEY

Castle - Central ward service corridor - 12:45 a.m.

"Well I'll be damned! It looks like the bastard's alive after all!" Danielle's sudden announcement rescued me from a horrible nightmare that I was having about Miss Cathy. I had lost control of Miss Cathy's roll-away bed and was helplessly watching her frail body tumble down a large staircase to her death.

I had dozed off while waiting for some indication that Timothy was going to remotely replicate the data from Henri's SIM card, which was staged within Danielle's cell phone.

Danielle never closed her eyes, but stood watch over us, much like a guardian horse remains awake while rest the of the herd rests. I wished that I had never fallen asleep, as I jumped to my feet and ran to the side of Miss Cathy.

Danielle's cell phone had just become active, as if it were being controlled by a ghost in the same room with us. We were crammed into a tiny space which Zooli called a larder where centuries ago had served as a large walk-in refrigerator to store cheese, dried meats, fruit and grain.

Thankfully, Miss Cathy was safe and sleeping sounding, with her face peeking through a hole in the covers and her head turned to the wall. Zooli and I crouched around Danielle's cell phone and squinted into the tiny screen, as lines of cryptic nonsense scrolled across the screen:

SIM Rescue Restore 3.0.1.5 (latest version)
Start.....
SIM Card ATR: 30 20 95 00 0F FF 06 A3 83 II
Read/writer operation in progress...
Please, do not turn your phone off during this period!
It may cause the SIM card to be unusable or damaged!
Status: Read Record DF_TELECOM (7F20), please wait...

Our hideout was situated on the ground floor in the northeastern side of the central ward. The entire section the ward was cold and eerie and hardly welcoming to even the spirits who were unfortunate enough to be dispatched to our haunt. Unglazed, permanent openings along the walls were covered with weather stained mesh as it vented in century old moldy air. Across the hall from us, was an even more unwelcoming room, which was known as an undercroft, with vaulted ceilings, brick walls and a cold stone floor. Zooli told us to be thankful that we were not in there because that room was once used as a morgue.

"Okay girls, we have got to get Miss Cathy back to Becker and home to her bed. I just had a most dreadful dream about Miss Cathy! We can't just keep rolling this poor woman around the castle like she's nothing more than a main course on a dinner table! My god, the woman's 94 years old! What if something happens to her? I would never be able to live with myself!" I found myself vigorously protesting as my nightmare still lingered within the darkness of the dreadful room.

"Well then---I'll take Miss Cathy out of this goddamn hell hole! I'll walk down the center of that fucking room and straight out the front of the goddamn door! If any of those mother fuckers ---mess with me---I'll knock their fucking lights out! I've had it with all of these perverted assholes!" The pressure of our constant uncertainty, coupled with the haunting effects of the malicious spirits, was making all of us crazy as Danielle's voice trembled and her eyes filled with tears.

"Oh my god, Danni--- please baby---it's going to be alright! We're going to get through this. We'll all take Miss Cathy out to Becker. There's more power in numbers---you know? Then the three of us will go back up to Henri's penthouse and----"

"Whoa, girls!" Zooli interjected, as if she were schooling us on horseback. "Look at me? Look at me, girls! None of us are taking Miss Cathy out to Becker! We're all going up to the penthouse together, like one big happy family -----and we're taking Miss Cathy along for the ride!"

"Why?" Danielle and I responded in unison.

"Because, we need her---hand!" Zooli firmly announced, as she gently lifted Miss Cathy's limp appendage from beneath the covers. "This old treasure, girls, is the only key we have to Henri's penthouse! Have the two of you forgotten about her magical touch?"

Danielle and I stood stunned as we starred at Miss Cathy's wrinkled hand in disbelief. Henri's penthouse entrance, along with all elevators, every single restricted passage way throughout the entire castle, was off limits to almost everyone, except for Henri Lepan and his old, forgotten, and absent-minded, 94-year-old mother. Only the size of her tiny fingers, the lengths of her life lines, and her average body temperature, would unlock the doors of the castle.

<hr />

It was amazing to me just how soundly Miss Cathy was sleeping as the four of us left our temporary safety zone and made our way back to Henri's service elevator. Luckily for us, the unusual blend of a brain injury and advancing Alzheimer's, cause this precious woman to plunge deeply into an almost comatose slumber.

We had just about reached Henri's service elevator, when three security officers, including the officer who had asked us for our invitation when we first arrived, came rushing around the corner and spotted us immediately.

"That's them---over there! Those are the ladies   ! I saw them earlier with Dr. Lepan's mother," the panicked officer announced.

We quickly changed course and rolled Miss Cathy's covered body through a doorway and onto the rich marble floors of the upper-great hall. The room was so enormous that it stopped me in my own tracks, spellbound.

The upper-great hall, as Zooli called it, was a rectangular architectural masterpiece with massive stained glass windows which traveled the length of the wall up to a meticulously decorated ceiling. The room resembled a huge cathedral with renderings of God and Adam along with a multitude of angles both clothed and nude, seemingly peering down upon us with an expression of pity.

The size of the crowd had expanded exponentially, along with the smell of human energy, which reeked with the effects of sex, alcohol, drugs and abuse. Clothing seemed optional as the rich and decadent laughed, talked, grunted and moaned.

The room stunk of cigarettes, marijuana and intimate body odor as many were deeply immersed in group intercourse. When we made it about midway through the orgy, I glanced back and spotted the three officers fanning out on both sides of the room and pointing at us with excitement.

Zooli became the pilot of Miss Cathy's table while I guarded her feet and Danielle protected her head. People were dancing, sitting, standing and copulating on the floor around us as we slowly maneuvered Miss Cathy through the swampy quagmire of immorality.

Still there were those who stepped around the madness with indolent and fussy expressions on their faces, as if it would be impossible for any person in room to meet their lofty requirements. Others seemed eager to feast on anyone they could get their filthy claws on, as they plunged themselves into sexual activities with partners half their ages.

In the midst of the fleshly free-for-all, I suddenly observed an elderly man who was deeply engaged in the masturbation of young girl who had not yet reached puberty. The sight was so vulgar and disturbing to me that I felt my reality shutting down. The deeper we moved into the crowd, the more I felt as if we were on a pathway towards pandemonium.

A man, who was lying flat on his back on the floor, reached for my legs and slid underneath my dress. His hands traveled up my inner thighs and grabbed my crotch and rear end. My protective instincts immediately kicked in and ejected me from the floor, as if I just realized that I had been standing upon a serpent. My calf muscles burned in pain from the over exertion as I landed a few meters away. I felt as if I had been suddenly thrust into the center of a perverted hell on the edge of sexual chaos. I gasped for breath and choked on my own bile as it started to make its way out of my core.

Somehow through my private terror I felt the lifesaving touch of Zooli's hand as she confidently gripped my wrist and directed me onward. "Homi, wake up! ---and get a hold of yourself! And you too---Danni! Keep your eyes on the far exit and walk with me, girls! ---Walk with me!"

Amazingly Zooli was able to transfer both my and Danielle's shattered minds into an imaginary safe-zone where we might be qualified to comprehend our situation. We had been transferred into the bodies of panicking mares, recognizing only the presence of Zooli, our alpha-owner as our guide. In the midst of the turmoil, I no longer saw the people around me as aberrant humans, but only frantic horses as we ambled our way down a dangerous trail.

"This is the tricky part of the trail, girls---so stay alert. Just keep calm and follow my lead, ladies. Do not look into the eyes of the enemy---girls! Are you listening to me? Move with me!" Zooli instructed, as we moved through the turmoil and finally came within range of the penthouse elevator.

The glass elevator was absent an operator, leaving the bio-scanner close by and available to us. We aligned Miss Cathy's makeshift gurney alongside of the bio-scanner as Danielle lifted Miss Cathy's limp arm out from underneath the tablecloths and placed her wrinkled palm against the panel of the bio-scanner.

The four of us quickly entered the elevator and allowed the heavy doors to close behind us. I didn't realize it until the elevator had built up to speed and was climbing the wall that I had been crying out loud.

The melee below reminded me of a lake of sin, as the glass elevator moved up to the top floor. From our perch I spotted the three confused security guards below who appeared to be admonishing the young officer for being careless and the cause of the security breach.

When we reached the top floor we carefully rolled Miss Cathy's table onto the smooth marble hallway and began pushing it towards the entrance of Henri's penthouse entrance where yet another bio-scanner was waiting. The wheels of Miss Cathy's banquet table were beginning to squeak making it difficult for us to remain unnoticed.

When we were just outside of Henri's main entrance, Danielle handed me her cell phone.

"Here Homi, take this phone in there with you and give me yours. As soon as the two of you get inside, I'll take Miss Cathy back downstairs and out of this god forsaken place."

"Are you sure, Danni? Do you think you can make it out safely?"

"Oh---you're goddamn right, Homi; I'm going to get her out of this shit hole---even if I have to kill someone to do it!"

We switched phones, leaving Danielle with the only phone that could make outgoing calls. Danielle said that when she returned, she would tap three times on the front door with a coin.

It had been three hours since we had last seen Henri in his penthouse and we were praying he was away at some party. Our hopes were suddenly dashed when we heard the sound of his footsteps approaching the other side of the door.

The locks started to move and the huge mahogany door began to open. Danielle dashed down the hallway and hid behind a large potted plant, while I dropped to the floor, lifted the linens and crawled beneath the table. The door widened and there stood Henri, shocked and staring at Zooli, who appeared to be standing all alone in front of a covered dinner table.

Henri stood speechless as he starred at Zooli in disbelief.

"Zooli, is that you? What on earth are you doing here?"

Henri stepped into the hall and glanced in both directions to see if Zooli were alone. Hearing Henri's voice so close by caused my body to shutter.

Chapter 61

LOST IN FLIGHT

Watch and pray so that you will not fall into temptation.
The spirit is willing, but the body is weak.

- MATTHEW 26:41

The High - Queen's Lane, Oxford, United Kingdom - 1:05 a.m.

"Danni--- it's me--- I'm sorry I'm getting back with you so late."
"Timothy! Where in the fuck have you been?" Danielle's voice was hardly a whisper, but was shrouded in heavy breathing as if she was about to hyperventilate.

"Danni, I've just started the transfer---but it's going to take a bit longer than I expected--maybe twenty-minutes or so."

"What? Are you fucking kidding me?"

"Danni, I somehow got all messed up today ---I'm not even sure how it happened. I'm sorry----Danni. I didn't mean to get so fucked up --."

"What? What do you mean by--- fucked up?"

"Danni---Danni---Danni, I know! I don't know what happened to me---I tried so damn hard to be good---but things just got out of hand."

"Oh my god, you're drunk, aren't you?"

"Listen to me --- Danni, don't worry. I'm gonna be okay; just give me a little time to get my shit together."

"Timothy, for Christ's sake! You---- need time to get *YOUR* fucking shit together? Are you fucking kidding me? We may all be dead in twenty-fucking-minutes! And you need some time to get *YOUR* shit together?"

"I didn't think the transfer process was going to take this long, Danni----I'm sorry."

"Well listen to me---you fuck-head; everyone's ass is on the fucking line here. All because of something you didn't fucking *think* was going to happen! Now, I'm separated from the girls and talking to a drunken fool on the phone."

"Well---where are the girls?"

"They just went into Henri's penthouse! With Henri! And they rolled Miss Cathy in there with them too! And now you show up---drunk? Tell me this, Timothy, how are they going know when you are done with your transfer--shit, you drunken fuck?"

"Danni, Danni, listen to me, the transfer is working fine, *so far*, and the phone *should* power off when the transfer is finished," Timothy slurred.

"Oh--it's working fine---SO FAR! And---it SHOULD power off! I swear Timothy; I don't think you know what the fuck you're doing! I swear Timothy, if anything happens to those girls, and I'm still alive, I gonna hunt you down and beat the living shit out of you! Why, in the hell, did you pick today, of all days, to get yourself shitfaced? Tell me Timothy---- you a fucking idiot? Where in the fuck have you been all night? Oh----never mind Timothy—it doesn't even matter anymore. You son of a bitch! Listen to me---you asshole. You had better be sober up enough to record the conference call at 2 a.m. I mean it Timothy! You had better get your shit together. Goddamn you---Timothy! ---Shit! I have to hang up right now and try to stay alive."

Timothy needed a smoke and he needed one now. He had successfully pissed off every human spirit in his life, including his own. Even the mystery woman across the street thought he was a drunken fool and for good reason, because he was one. But something very strange was happening to Timothy's mind, his mental condition was moving from a state of confusion to even more of a drunken stupor.

His sense of confidence had plunged to a new depth, of a hopeless failure. Luckily his cell phone was working properly and the battery was charged. Timothy always made it a point to work near a power outlet. Timothy thought it ironic that he took better care of his cell phone and laptop computer then he did his own physical wellbeing.

The most important thing at this very moment was to complete the replication process. Everything relied on this process completing successfully. For if it failed, there would be no way to way to express into Henri's satellite phone, no ability to connect to his vital contacts, no messages to retrieve and no incriminating evidence to be gathered.

Timothy's hands were shaking as he desperately lit a cigarette and walked further away from the Flick Theatre. He had to find a quiet place where he could sit down and try to sober up. He was drunk and completely disgusted with himself. The last thing he wanted to do was show his demolished condition to the likes of Smithy and most especially Golareh. Smithy was the only person left in the world whose shit-list didn't contain Timothy's name.

In a dark alley directly across from the Tablemate Inn, Timothy found a city park bench where he flopped his drunken body down upon and collapsed. The theatre was clearly the best place for Timothy to be, but even there he might find more women and a constantly flowing supply of beer. Timothy couldn't even imagine drinking another drop of anything, but then he also couldn't imagine how he had gotten so completely wasted.

Alcohol had always been a friendly demon to Timothy, for as long as he could remember. It helped him during social settings, freed him from his normally shy disposition and always made him the life of the party. It never really caused him much of a problem until now, as once again he was revisited by the voice of that pretty waitress at Zelz who said "Oh, by the way, she also wants me to give you one of these drinks."

Nineteen minutes remained in the transfer process, reminding Timothy of how download time estimates were always worthless. Minutes and seconds never corresponded with the actual clock time. All transfer times fell under the mercy of the internet's ebbs and flows. Timothy was at the mercy of the gods of cyberspace and all he could do was wait.

Visions of the girls began playing with Timothy's drowsy mind as he imagined Danielle running through the dark hallways of a mid-evil castle. Other images of the girls ducking behind dark corners and running for their lives as some evil Sheriff of Nottingham character chased after them with a bloody ax. So many people's lives were in play and everything was dependent upon Timothy, as his worries chased him off to sleep.

He had slipped into another dimension and was dreaming of a successful outcome. Golareh, Danielle and Homayra were congratulating him in a victorious group hug. But just when the girls tried to kiss him on his cheek he would wake up to an even more intoxicated reality, with a slew of unfinished business in front of him.

Time remaining on the transfer: 10-minutes.

"Thank god," Timothy mumbled, as he gave cyber gods above a thumbs-up.

Back to the castle his stoned mind traveled as he dreamed that he was listening to a real-time conversation between Henri Lepan and Santo Gordo. The entire conversation was lively and full of incriminating evidence about their entire dynasties, past, present and future. Every syllable of the juicy conversation was being recorded onto electronic media in the form of a valuable digital present, which Timothy would proudly gift wrap and hand over to Frédéric and the authorities.

"We've done it, Goli; we have captured Henri's flag!" Timothy mumbled in his sleep, as he squeezed the Golareh's dream like hand.

Her hand felt warm to the touch as he brought it closer to his face and kissed her silver fingernails. Another hand gently touched the side of Timothy's face as the scent of her perfume transported him into yet another dream zone.

It must be Golareh, forgiving him for all of his drunken missteps of the past. She was stroking his hair and nibbling on his ear. Or maybe it was

Danielle joining in as well; as she kissed his neck and gently massaged his back.

"Oh my god, girls, we have finally done it. I love the two of you so much!"

Timothy was moaning loudly in his sleep, as he took in the wonderful fragrance of the mystery woman, who was kneeling over him in the form of a blurry mass. Her hands smelled like a bouquet of flowers as she gently massaged his neck, back and shoulders sending him off into another cock-eyed reality.

The mystery woman looked beautiful as he studied the outline of her long toned legs, flat stomach and wonderfully shaped breasts through the slits of his swollen eyes. Her silver lips were only centimeters from his mouth as the lights from a passing car provided more detail to the woman's face. "Who is this person?" Timothy wondered, as his eyes scanned the outline of her fine-looking face.

Whoever the person is, she's definitely not one of the girls, but some mirage of an erotic angel sent down from heaven, to comfort him in his terrible time of need. Timothy knew full well that he resembled a drunken bum, slouched over on a park bench as he lifted his head and tried to identify the beautiful image closing in on him.

"Excuse me sir, but are you in need of some help?" The mystery woman asked with a thick Russian accent. "I am so very sorry for not speaking to you earlier, when you asked about my wellbeing. I was afraid of you and thought you were one of those horrible men from that bar. Stupid pigs they all were to me."

Although she said she was there to help, the mystery woman appeared frightened for her life and on the lookout for some mugger. "They wouldn't stop touching me!" She cried, as she covered her breast with her hands. "They were grabbing me everywhere and touching my body with their hands and fingers. I told them to stop but they ignored me."

"Oh my god, I must have passed out," Timothy moaned, as he raised his head and glanced at his phone: *Nine-minutes remaining — Please wait.*

Timothy was now seeing double as he covered one of his eyes with his fist and stared at the blurry image through his other.

"You were moaning in pain. I heard you from across the street. I thought that you might have been beaten up by that huge man in front of the movie theatre."

"I've been beaten up, pretty lady, but not by Big Ben. I think I tried to drink myself to death tonight. I'm sorry, but did I ever get your name?"

Everything about her perfumed body was towing him into her sexual harbor as she moved in even closer. Timothy's erotic spell was suddenly broken by the sound of his cell phone striking the concrete sidewalk below.

"Oh fuck, Timothy yelled, imagining his valuable device in shattered pieces.

The mystery woman watched as Timothy dropped his wobbly head to the side and surveyed the darkness beneath the park bench.

"Please sir, allow me to help you with that," the mystery woman said, as she knelt down on the ground in front of him and extended body in the direction of his phone. The further she stretched for the cell phone the higher her short skirt crept up her hips. Her shiny metallic thong was on full display and sending Timothy mind off in his most obvious direction.

"My god, you are one gorgeous woman."

Timothy was again, lost in flight, as his bloodshot eyes studied the outline of her toned hips and tempting rear-end. He surveyed the thin wisp of stitched silver material which was comfortably parked between the cheeks of her buttocks and disappeared into the tempting recesses of her crotch.

"It seems to be working fine sir," said mystery woman, as she slowly repositioned herself even closer to Timothy's drunken body.

Timothy no longer cared who the erotic temptress was in the magical lingerie. His mind was already serving up erotic sex-scenes of the two of them engaged in aggressive sexual intercourse right there on the private park bench.

"My name is Reneta Yorgonoda and yours is?" Reneta asked, as she shivered and glanced over her shoulder as if she was expecting some impending danger.

"Reneta, now that's one beautiful name, but you could have had man's name for all I care, because you are one damn good looking woman. I'm Timothy," he said, considering whether he should provide his real name or not. "You know, Timothy Edwards, the world famous investigative reporter!" Timothy's bad-side bragged, as if his identity meant nothing.

The stupid remark about him not caring whether she had a man's name, bounced back at Timothy's conscience with a vengeance, in the form of Smithy's sweet face. For the first time in his life, he began experiencing the rare and unmistakable feeling of guilt.

"Damn it! Stop it," Timothy cursed under his breath. "I just can't do this shit anymore," Timothy protested to his bad-side as he struggled to pull his spinning mind to his feet.

"Where are you going, wait please don't leave me here all alone. I am so scared!" the mystery woman begged as she moved her body even closer to Timothy, stabilizing his balance.

"Listen, Renova, I mean Reneta. As much as I'd love to stay here with you---I simply can't. I've got to go home; I've got way too many important things that I must do tonight. I'm sorry but I really must go home---now."

"Oh please, I am so freighted of those perverts at the bar and that huge monster in front of the movie theatre. Please don't leave me here all alone---I need you. Come; please help me back to my room, there we can rest and be safe."

Timothy feared he might crush the platinum beauty under the weight of his severely out of shape body, but, to his surprise, the mystery woman had an amazing amount of strength and was able to almost effortlessly set him back down on the park bench.

"Please help me back to my room, mister reporter, I am so frightened," Reneta pleaded, as she pressed her firm breasts against Timothy's face.

"What are you so afraid of, Reneta?" Timothy asked, as he glanced over at the theatre in the distance.

"There was a huge man staring at me just a while ago. He looked like a monster from a horror movie. Please help me back to my room before he comes here and murders the two of us."

Reneta was begging Timothy for help, as she guided his hand over her breast as if to shield it from danger. She kept her hand on to top of Timothy's and began massaging her breast in small circles.

As Timothy was allowed free access to her breast, his crossed-eyes zeroed in on a narrow strip of material that served as a metallic bra. The soft material covered only the center of her perfectly proportioned breasts, taunting Timothy's imagination with her visual treats.

All concerns associated with Timothy's good-side were now under the complete conservatorship of his bad-side, as he moved his face closer to her plump and shimmering lips. Her lips were covered in a silvery, sticky gloss, which containing hints of golden glitter and magical taste. Her breath was warm and moist and gave off a fragrance of hunger.

Timothy was weak with desire and at the complete mercy of the mystery woman as his lips brushed the side of her sticky lips. Her tongue slowly emerged from her mouth like a snake and licked Timothy's lips as if he were a melting block of chocolate.

"Please come to my room, mister reporter, there we can both rest and be safe. You need to be off the street before you fall asleep," she begged, as her hand travelled south and slowly unzipped his pants.

Her fingers entered the opening of his boxer shorts and eagerly traced the outline of his firm penis as Timothy turned his head towards her and pressed her richly painted lips against the side of his face. She seductively opened her mouth and let out a moan, while displaying her perfectly straight teeth. Her fingers firmly clasped his manhood with her long silver fingernails.

Timothy gazed through the shadows of his dark hiding place to the lights of the marquee in the distance. Most likely, Big Ben, the so called monster, had retired for the evening and Smithy and Goli probably had given up their search for his drunken ass.

Timothy knew full well that he was breaking the last cardinal rule which he had left in his soul as he wondered why in god's name was he was actually hiding from the only people in the world who truly cared about him? It didn't matter anymore, for all sense of reasoning were now under the control of the erotic fingers tips which firmly held his rock hard penis.

Reneta's touch soon advanced into a wild grip, squeezing Timothy fully engorged penis as if it were a throttle on a motorcycle. Her strong fist bent his fully stimulated organ backwards and forward and in and out of the opening of his pants.

Timothy studied the mystery woman's aggressive behavior with curiosity as she savored his saluting actor making its debut on stage. Her attitude was so very different from that mystery woman on the dance floor at Zelz, who paid no attention, whatsoever, to anyone. But here on the park bench, her actions were drastically different as she gazed down upon his penis and testicles as if she was about to eat them for dinner.

The mystery woman's sharp fingers nails scratched Timothy's chest as her head slowly descended to the level of his overly bloated penis. She worked his genitals as if she owned them, kneading them like bread dough while stimulating every nerve ending his reproductive organs had to offer.

Timothy grabbed the back of her head with both hands and moved her face against his manhood, praying that she would take him in to her silky warm Russian mouth.

The warmth of her breath moistened the head of his penis as she placed both of her hands around his throbbing testicles and teased him intensely with a preview of what was yet to come. Timothy was now on autopilot while she boldly plunged her mouth up and down and carelessly clamped down on his engorged shaft while compressing her teeth into his vulnerable foreskin.

Timothy's formation increased to an even higher level of excitement while sending him dangerously close to completion as he listened to her muffled groans and slurping.

By some strange miracle brought on by some tiny remnant of Timothy's good-side, coupled with the deadening effects of alcohol, Timothy suddenly found himself leveling off to a sexual plateau. He now had the ability to examine the reason why he was in the dark ally in the first place.

Tonight was different, Timothy thought. It was as if the alcohol was actually working in favor of his mission, increasing his level of stamina and allowing him to place the erotic activity below his beltline on hold. His proud penis, which was fully employed in the mouth of the mystery woman, had become noticeably separate from Timothy's mental being.

Suddenly the word *transfer* snapped him back to some semblance of reality and reminded him of the tasks at hand. My god, Timothy thought, had the SIM replicator process completed? He steadied his drunken body against the mystery woman's head and reached over and retrieved his cell phone from the park bench.

To his delight the transfer process had *finished* successfully.

"Yes!" Timothy loudly groaned, causing the mystery woman to suck even harder on his overly activated penis. She had almost completely engulfed his entire being within the confines her mouth and throat.

"Talk about multi-tasking," Timothy mumbled aloud.

Timothy was gloating with pride, as he felt the beginning stages of an orgasm notifying him that his night may soon be coming to a premature end. With both hands he gently pushed the mystery woman's mouth away from his saliva soaked appendage and began willing away an upcoming explosion. Timothy then performed what he considered to be the impossible. While desperately fighting off a major ejaculation he accurately composed a text message to Homayra and Golareh.

At 1:21 a.m. Timothy's final text message was sent: *transfer complete!* This part of his job was done while another job was scheduled to-be-continued in a bed across the street.

Timothy dropped his phone back into his pocket and pulled the mystery woman's face directly in front of his. She appeared frustrated with desire as she licked her lips and moaned for more.

"Baby, might it be time for me to assist you back to your room and away from all of these dangerous muggers?"

Timothy was proud of his sexual dominance over the mystery woman and was beginning to tease her with a full serving of his classic machismo. The mystery woman helped Timothy to his feet and gently tucked his penis back in to its cage for future use.

Timothy suddenly felt his distorted mind shift to the vantage point of a mere spectator. He watched his hands independently lift the curtain of mystery woman's shiny metallic bra. Her large round breasts burst into view and electrified Timothy's desire for more as he watched them drop without restrictions into a tranquil position. Timothy studied her tantalizing and amazingly tiny nipples as both of her breasts seemed to move independently to the rhythm of his pounding desire.

"Oh yes, please take me to my room, Mr. Reporter. *I want to fuck you until you are unconscious.*"

That same phrase seemed oddly familiar to Timothy, as if he had heard that voice saying the very same thing to someone else entirely. The dream girl confidently gripped Timothy's belt buckle and began towing him across the street. Timothy was seeing double again as he starred at the outrageously inviting blonde temptress with a strange feeling of doom.

Who was this sexually charged vixen who was aggressively leading him across the street by the front of the pants for a sexually charged evening he would be willing to die for? Everything about what was transpiring seemed wrong, with red flags flying everywhere. But Timothy could care less.

"Could this be really happening? Can it really be this easy? Timothy wondered as the mystery woman escorted him across the street in the direction of the Tablemate Inn. Nothing this fantastic is ever this easy. Everything must come with a price, Timothy thought, as they walked off towards his destiny.

Chapter 62

HOMAYRA: PEACE TREATY

Castle – Penthouse suite - 1:15 a.m.

"Dinner --- you must be joking---at this time of night?" Henri said, as I watched his feet suddenly move out of the way of the table.

Zooli didn't miss a beat as she boldly pushed the table past Henri and directly down the hallway towards his kitchen. I crawled along underneath the table on my hands and knees desperately trying not to fall, or, hit my head on the bottom of the table. Finally Zooli came to a stop as Henri followed along in amazement. Little did Henri realize that lying on the table, beneath three starched white linen table cloths, was his own mother.

"Oh please Henri, dear, you mustn't ruin our surprise, it would be so upsetting to your dear mother. We've put together something very special for you, an arrangement of fruit, a fine selection of cheeses and some of the juiciest cuts of aged meat you've ever tasted. Please Henri --- oh please---give me the honor of preparing you a most wonderful late night snack? Don't you think that an apology is completely overdue---from me?"

Henri stood in the foyer shocked and speechless by Zooli's sudden invasion into his private domain. After 30-years of privately fantasizing about Zooli, never once had she returned even a hint of interest towards him. Finally, Zooli was giving in to Henri's magnificent charm and awesome power. Zooli was no different from all of the rest of the stubborn women

Henri had acquired, used up, and then disposed of over the years. Everyone has her price and breaking point.

"Henri, I was just thinking about how long I've known you and how selfish I've been. How frustrated you must be with me and how horrible my behavior has been for all of these years. I've been so disloyal and quite ungrateful for everything you have done for me. Henri, what can I ever do to win back your friendship and trust?"

Henri studied Zooli with a hint of mockery, as if finally she were coming to her senses. But even now, Henri could not ignore her gorgeous figure, picture-perfect posture and magnificent way she filled out one of his mother's finest evening gowns. Rarely had Henri seen Zooli looking more superb than she looked at this very moment, and never had she paid him the least bit of interest.

From the first day Henri saw Zooli, during a recruiting trip to Iran back in 1969, he had wanted her for his own, but that had never happened. Everything about Zooli was about those damn horses, and he had finally realized after many years, that she was much better on horseback than he would ever be. He once thought she would be impressed by his equestrian skills, handsome control and striking masculinity, but Zooli was blind to it all. She hated the way he treated the horses, thought he was a terrible rider, and never could accept the way he rode too far forward in the saddle.

Zooli had a long list of personal rules and convictions which she would never deviate from. She rarely drank alcohol, never smoked cigarettes or flirted with anyone of the opposite sex. She was strict vegetarian, always stayed in superb shape, and was always in bed by 10 p.m. She had a body that most men would kill for to possess, but she never made it available to anyone. She was off limits all because of what Henri considered as those stupid marriage vows, which she mistakenly took with her skinny little husband back when she was a senseless child.

The good doctor was to be Zooli's only soulmate for a lifetime and no man would ever take his place. Henri briefly met the little man and instantly considered him to be a roadblock to Zooli. What she saw in her husband was a total mystery to Henri. He was nothing more than an emaciated little know-it-all, who just happened to have the most beautiful woman in the world at his side.

After years of frustration Henri finally had enough and applied way too much pressure on Zooli when he admitted to her that he was the person responsible for her husband's incarceration which ultimately led to his death.

Henri's concentration was broken as Zooli light heartedly offered:

"Your mother thought that perhaps it might be the right time for you and me to put our petty little differences aside and become, shall we say, friends."

I noticed her heels lift off the ground as she stood on her tip toes and gave Henri a seductive peck on his cheek.

"Um--- Zooli, I don't know what to say, other than I appreciate your sudden change of heart. Did you say that mother instigated this? Well she must know what's good for you after all."

"Oh---no no no no! I agree with Miss Cathy, Henri. I've been thinking about this for quite some time, and I'm sure that its way past time that we became, you know, reacquainted."

"Was that you--- with my mother on the mezzanine earlier this evening? I found her in my kitchen rummaging around. I had no idea what she was doing and was sure that she had completely lost her mind."

"Well, if you must know, yes---yes it was your mother and me. I think that Miss Cathy is finally beginning to realize that she doesn't have that many years left and she just wants to make sure that I still have a place to live after she passes on."

I parted a small opening in the table clothes and peeked up at Zooli as she confidently composed one of the biggest lies I've ever witnessed. I was amazed as I listened to Zooli adlibbing the performance of her lifetime and how Henri was chomping down on it like he deserved every bit of it.

"Well Zooli, I have to admit that a small part of me was expecting this from you sooner than later, but I never dreamed it would be tonight. My mother, it seems, still has some common sense left in that batty brain of hers after all. But, make no mistake, Zooli, I welcome it; and I must say that you look remarkably beautiful this evening in that dress. Yes, Zooli, yes, I would enjoy your company this evening. But unfortunately, I have this damn business call I'm forced to take in a short while, but I promise to cut it short---trust me. Please, Zooli; please let me help you with that table." Henri said, as his feet suddenly moved towards the table.

"No, no---Henri, please, you dear thing. You must allow me to be in charge, I would love the opportunity to pamper you tonight. Why don't we have a little drink and perhaps you can give me little tour of your beautiful penthouse, it's been so long since I've been here?"

"But Zooli, I've never seen you drink alcohol before?"

"Oh Henri, I rarely do, but tonight seems rather special and we should celebrate our peace treaty. Now you must promise me that you won't take advantage of me if I get a little tipsy. I've been known to get a little naughty at times."

"Oh, ho ho ho---- you can trust me, darling. Tell me, Zooli, what have you stored down in this little box, my dear," Henri asked, as he leaned down and opened the stainless steel desert bin.

"Cheesecakes! ---Oh my lord! So that's what my mother was doing up here in my kitchen. I must tell you my dear, that woman is getting nuttier by the day. I simply can't imagine where she might pop up next? I actually feel a bit guilty for the way I treated her earlier this evening. She still has some spunk though. I thought she was going to come after me with an iron skillet."

I wished she would have beaned that son-of-a-bitch with that skillet; it would have saved us all of this trouble, I thought, as I watched Zooli trying to move Henri out of the room.

Please, Henri, show me around your wonderful penthouse. I simply can't wait to see all of the improvements you've made over the years. You know, I don't believe that I've ever seen where you sleep. I bet your bedroom is quite comfy."

"Well Zooli, I would love to take you on a tour, but not until you allow me the pleasure of holding you in my arms. A peace offering would mean nothing without a hug from you. Besides, I must see for myself that you are in fact real."

Cautiously, Henri put his arms around Zooli and gently moved her against his chest. "My god, Zooli, I can't tell you how many days I've dreamed of holding you in my arms. You simply cannot imagine."

⁂

My neck and back ached because of my awkward position. Their voices were far enough away for me to determine that it was safe to move out from underneath the table. I took a short peek under the white linens at Miss Cathy, whose mouth was slightly moving to the rhythm of her snoring, which was quickly intensifying.

I ran down the hallway to the main entrance, hoping that Danielle was still standing nearby. Carefully I turned the bolt lock on the door and lowered the latch. Down at the far end of the hallway I spotted Danielle angrily stomping her feet towards me. Her eyes were cast to the floor and she appeared to be seething with anger.

"Fucking---stupid, drunken prick---mother fucker! Stupid son-of-bitch! Why did we ever trust that bastard?"

"Hey---Danni!" I whispered, waking her from her muffled temper tantrum. Her eyes finally lifted from the floor and connected with mine. "Oh my god, Homi! Are you okay?"

"I'm okay, but now it's Zooli I'm worried about, she's in there with Henri. She's trying to buy me some time so I get in to Henri's office. Danni, you could not imagine how she's leading Henri on! She's doing everything she can possibly do to keep Henri on the far end of the penthouse and away from his office. Zooli is one hell of an actress, I'll tell you. Danni; we have got to get Miss Cathy out of here---now! She's already starting to snore. Have you heard anything from Timothy?"

"Oh, I just got off the phone with that bastard and guess what? He's smashed out of fucking mind--- drunk!"

"Drunk? What! How can that be? Are you kidding me?"

"He's promised me that he'll be okay. He said that he's transferring the data as we speak, but it might take twenty minutes to finish."

"Twenty minutes! My god! We're running out of time, Danni! I don't know how Zooli will be able to keep Henri occupied for that long without actually taking him to bed."

"Homi, listen to me, one way or another Henri will be on that call with Santo and that SIM card had better be back in his phone!"

"How will I know when Timothy is done doing whatever he's doing?"

"He told me that the phone should power off automatically once his replication is complete. Do you still remember how to swap out the SIM cards?"

"Yeah, I think so. Don't worry, Danni, I can do it."

The two of us slipped back into the penthouse to Miss Cathy's side. She was still sleeping sounding but her snoring had become noticeably louder. We rolled Miss Cathy down the hallway and out of the penthouse as the wheels of the table vibrated and squeaked.

"Danni, when you get her out to Becker, call Richard on my phone and tell him to pick us up at that private airstrip we spotted when we first arrived. I'm sure he's already spotted it from the air. Tell him we will be there at 5:30 a.m. His number is stored in my phone as *Captain Richard!* Also tell Becker that if Zooli and I aren't out of this dreadful place by 4:00 a.m. to send in the hounds!"

"What do you mean, send in the hounds?"

"Just tell him Danni, he'll know what you mean. Now go baby, go!"

I kissed Danielle on her cheek and rushed back into the penthouse.

I could still hear the squeaky wheels of Miss Cathy's traveling bed rolling down the hallway as I closed the door and made a mad dash for Henri's office.

Chapter 63

ONCE BITTEN, TWICE SHY

Abduction; a carrying off
Oxford, England — 1:34 a.m.

The Oxford Tablemate Inn is one of the top five most luxurious hotels in London with an average price tag of £2,126 per night. The five-story, 16-room inn boasts of having one of the finest French restaurants in the UK. Every suite is different than every other, each designed by the renowned Kelly Faustus, one of London's top interior designers. Each bedroom features custom oak flooring, Robert Langford's handmade beds and award-winning furniture by Channels. A full bar awaits guests, which Timothy was determined to stay away from.

Reneta was staying in the penthouse which accommodated the entire top floor of the magnificent inn. The restaurant had closed at its normal time of 11 p.m. and the building was silent with most of the guests retired for the evening.

With the swipe of an electronic security fob, Timothy was granted access to both the top floor and the intricately carved wooden door of the penthouse. From the doorway, he took in the view of the magnificent interior of the luxurious penthouse. "Wow, Reneta, this is one hell of a nice place."

Timothy steadied himself along the back of a long black leather couch as he guided himself to the far side of the room, while Reneta excused herself and stepped into the powder room to freshen up.

The impressive four-bedroom suite was rich to the point of being garish. Timothy opened the French door and gazed out on to a large stone terrace which featured a spectacular view of the town of Oxford in the distance. Blue lights from a large infinity pool illuminated the entire surface of the water as it disappeared off the edge of the top floor. A continuous gas burning fire pit gently lit up the area around yet another fully stocked bar on the terrace.

The living room featured some of most costly paintings Timothy had ever seen in a private residence. The entire suite was kept fastidiously neat and tidy, appearing as if Reneta had just arrived and never unpacked. A closet door in the master bedroom was slightly opened, revealing a wide selection of expensive clothing which clearly could only be worn by Reneta.

Next to the front door, hidden almost out of sight, Timothy happened to notice two pieces of luggage. One appeared to be an expensive black leather backpack which appeared to be packed. The other piece of luggage could only be described as a heavy duty stainless steel gun case which had two security latches and a custom gripped handle.

Timothy briefly thought about the gun case along with the strange placement of both pieces of luggage and wondered if Reneta had just arrived or was about to leave. Both questions vanished from Timothy's drunken mind as soon as he saw Reneta emerging from the powder room. She appeared even fresher and more provocative then she did before she went in.

"How long have you been staying here, Reneta?" Timothy asked, as he held on to the latch of the French door and studied what appeared to be an original Rose Period, Picasso hanging on the wall adjacent to him. The owner must certainly be extremely wealthy, Timothy thought, as he identified a huge Claude Monet painting hanging above the bed in the master bedroom.

"I've only just arrived; this is one of my sponsor's many condos." Reneta began acting the part of a spoiled daughter as she spun around the room in front of him like a ballerina. "He owns this entire inn."

"Well you don't say, Reneta; well he must be one hell of a sponsor. What exactly does this big sponsor of yours do?"

"My sponsor is an extremely wealthy collector of, shall I say, perishable *objects* and he sends me on trips to tie up some of his loose ends."

Yes---I bet he does like to send you around the world to tie up loose ends. I wish you would tie up some of my loose ends ---tonight, you sexy little bitch, Timothy thought, as he cocked his head to the side and watched Reneta struggle to unhook the long silver leather straps which wrapped around her gorgeous legs and attached to her gladiator sandals.

"Speaking of loose ends, I was hoping that you might leave those sandals on."

Timothy could barely contain himself as leaned against the wall and watched Reneta remove both of her sandals and toss them onto the floor of the powder room.

"This dress is becoming way too restrictive for what I have planned for you; I just can't wait to get out of it. Would you do me a favor, Mr. Newspaperman, and unhook me from behind?"

Timothy used the back of his head to push his drunken body away from the wall as he weaved his way across the room to the back of Reneta.

"It doesn't matter how fucked up I may be, baby, this is the one job I'm always a professional at." Timothy suddenly took note of the fact that while he was well aware of what he was trying to say, what he heard coming from his mouth was nothing more than a bunch of garbled nonsense. Why was he still continuing to become more and more disoriented as the minutes ticked by?

In an instant her tight dress was unzipped and lying on the floor at her feet, leaving Reneta standing in the center of the room wearing nothing but that tiny silver thong and a swath of silk which barely covering her large breasts. Reneta's body was the most incredible thing Timothy had ever had the pleasure of being alone with. Never before had he been able to score such a hot bombshell for an evening of steamy, raw sex. If he could only stay conscious long enough to enjoy it, Timothy thought, as he watched the room around him begin to spin.

She had a picture perfect rear end which complemented her chiseled mid-section and muscular back. Under her silky vail were those perky breasts, which were perfectly shaped and had enchantingly tiny nipples, which he couldn't wait to devour.

She removed a clip from her long blonde hair and fluffed it out, letting it fall down over her cut shoulders and her smooth back.

Timothy was nothing more than astonished as he studied her spectacular physique and erotic qualities. Other than her breasts, every muscle in her body was toned to flawless perfection. Even the gluts in her hind end appeared to be conditioned for either ballet or battle.

"Wow, Reneta, you are in damn good shape."

Her toned abs, forearms, biceps, middle back, and shoulders reminded Timothy of one of those erotic super-heroes he used to drool over in comic books. "Why do you keep yourself in such great shape? Are you one of those body builder chicks or something?"

Timothy couldn't help but move in closer to examine the rippled geography of her back with the tips of his fingers. Time came to a halt as Timothy invited Reneta closer in towards his chest. She moved into Timothy's arms as if she had been trained in the art of seduction. Timothy placed his hand over the top of her right breast as Reneta let out a sensual moan.

"Well, let me just say that my work requires for me to be able to move a lot of *dead* weight, so I must keep myself fit."

Reneta reached up and unexpectedly grabbed both sides of Timothy's face with her thumb and forefingers. Timothy's lips pooched out through her fingers as she gathered them up and squeezed his face hard. Timothy eyes sprung open with surprise as she tightened down on both sides of his jaw and forcefully moved him forward and bit down on his lower lip, causing him to recoil in pain.

"Ouch, baby, be gentle!" Timothy snapped, as he tasted blood oozing from a cut on his bottom lip. "Hey---what the fuck, are you some kind of wild animal or something? Take it easy, girly girl, and don't damage the merchandise!" Timothy scolded, as he pulled out a handkerchief and pressed it against his bleeding lip.

Reneta appeared to be studying Timothy as if he were suddenly some sort of enemy. Her face contained an unmistakable expression of disgust as she looked down at his fat belly.

"What's wrong, girly girl, I exercise every day too----can't you see?" Timothy said, as he jokingly slapped his gut with his hands and shook it from side to side.

Reneta didn't buy into his feeble attempt at humor, but turned her head in disgust. "Yes, right, I'm sure you do. My god, how I sometimes hate my job." Reneta whispered under her breath.

"So tell me, girly-girl, what exactly does this sponsor of yours collects anyway, art, classic cars, what?"

Reneta ignored his question and continue to hold an expression of disgust.

Timothy thought he might be safer if he placed himself in a higher position of control as he placed his hands over both cheeks of her rear-end. He slowly began spreading them far apart from one another as if she was some sort of fleshy accordion. He lightly touched her anus with his index finger, causing Reneta to angrily snap backwards.

"So how do you like that---bitch? Did that get your attention?" Timothy growled, feeling for the moment that she had met her match.

"Hmmm, Mister Reporter, so---I guess you want to get a little rough with me---I like that." Reneta said, as she snatched Timothy's hand away from her back side and placed it to the base of her crotch. Aggressively she positioned his index finger underneath the material of her thong and then through the wet lips of her vagina.

"I have no problem with that order, Mister Reporter, no problem with that order whatsoever. But beware, Mr. Edwards, once you start something with me, you had better damn well finish it---because I don't like quitters."

Timothy noticed that even though the foreplay was exciting, Reneta appeared agitated to the point of anger as she aggressively inserted Timothy's middle finger into her vagina and began stabbing them both fiercely up inside of her.

Suddenly, Timothy felt faint as if the blood in his head had fallen to his feet. Perhaps it was shock from Reneta's overly aggressive sexual behavior or maybe it was because he had reached a new level of intoxication. For whatever reason, Timothy lost track of reality and passed out.

When Timothy came to, he was lying on the bed in the master bedroom with his nose tightly pressed against the interior regions of Reneta's vagina. She was moaning with excitement from above and painfully grinding her pelvis against Timothy's face with increasing intensity.

"Oh you've got it baby! You know how I like it!" Reneta growled, as she gripped handfuls of Timothy's hair in her fists and shook his head from side to side. Violently, she grinded the base of her pelvic bone against Timothy's nose as her fingernails dug deeply into the skin of Timothy's scalp.

Timothy turned his head to the side and gasped for air as he watched her large breasts dancing above him in her sweat soaked covering.

"Come on baby, slow down and tell me more about this sponsor of yours," Timothy asked, in a weak attempt to buy some time to catch his breath and free his scalp from her painful grip.

"Well let's just say that my sponsor collects something a bit more in demand than art."

Reneta smiled and arched her body back, as if she were purposely allowing Timothy time to live.

"Well what's more valuable than art?" Timothy slurred, as he again felt faint and a bit nauseous.

"Oh come on, Mister Reporter, you tell me, you nosy little fuck! I think you know a lot more about my sponsor than you are willing to admit!" Reneta was now clearly angry and freakishly in command, as she unfastened the tiny clasp on her covering and slowly began aggressively massaging her breasts with both hands. "I think that you know what's more valuable than art, you dumb fuck!"

Timothy had no idea who this frighteningly powerful Russian nymphomaniac was referring to, as the room around him spun by as if they were both in the center of a carrousel.

"Oh come on Timothy Edwards, don't pass out on me now. I have big plans for you tonight," she wined. I know how much you want this, baby, and I know that you like it rough! So come on baby, stop punishing me any longer. Lick me baby, conquer this pussy you idiot. Do it you stupid fuck! Do it---now---you fucking fat bastard."

Reneta was loudly shrieking at Timothy as she violently slapped Timothy across the side of his face, letting her fingernails snag long rows of his flesh.

Timothy's drunken mind was muddled by her wicked assertiveness, but he continued to dismiss her as a danger, thinking this was all part of some sort of kinky, dominatrix game which would come to a happy ending. Besides, she's just some sort of crazy bitch, how bad can it get?

Even though his mind was out of order, his body seemed to be playing the part extremely well, remaining staunchly erect while demanding more. Reneta let out an erotic squeal which reminded Timothy of a voice he had heard on a recording sometime and somewhere in the not too distant past.

"Oh you are good, Mister Reporter, you are really good, you crazy little man---you! Come on big shot; let me show you what that nose of yours is really meant for---you nosy little prick." Reneta charged, as she gripped Timothy scalp in her tight fists and forced Timothy's sore nose into the interior of her wet vagina again.

"Here we go Mister Reporter; you had better enjoy this, because after tonight you won't have a cock to fuck with anymore! Do you understand me you stupid mother-fucker! I mean you will be fucking done, you fat piece of shit! Because you have been fucking with the wrong man---Mr. Timothy-Fucking-Edwards! And I have been sent here to take you out of this fucking world."

"What? Timothy yelled in a weak attempt to understand what or who she was referring to. Over the years Timothy had made so many enemies who were spending many years in prison thinking of all sorts of creative ways to snuff him out. But none of those crooked politicians were Russian?

Timothy was fighting for his life as he helplessly watched the erotic monster mount his miserably sore shaft and pump away with an angry intensity. Blood was flowing out of his nose and lips while his insubordinate penis remained bravely erect and blindly charged him deeper into battle.

"Come on Mister Reporter. Let's give all of your fans something newsworthy to read about in one of your fucking newspapers tomorrow morning!" she said, as she raised her arms and slammed her hard knuckles against the sides of Timothy's drunken head. Down came her head, landing on his chest, as she gnawed and ripped into his bloody nipples with her sharp teeth.

Out of control cries of some past resentment burst out of Reneta's mouth as her entire body perspired profusely. She quickly withdrew from Timothy and then dove down and on his engorged scrotum baring her teeth, violently biting into his testicles as she moaned, laughed and cried.

Her anger intensified the more she clamped down on his scrotum with the full force of her jaws. She then moved to his torn shaft as if it were nothing more than a frozen hunk of bloody meat. Off she sprung again as she violently grabbed his bloody remains in her fist and stuffed it violently back into her selfish vagina.

"Stop it you crazy bitch, you're killing me!" Timothy begged, while clearly hearing himself pleading for his life.

"Stop it," Timothy begged as he felt the bloody abstract of an unwanted orgasm approaching. "Oh, my God! No! Please no! Stop!" Timothy begged, as tears flowed from his eyes and he finally gave in to the sexual predator's demands from above.

"Come on you fucker! You're not done until I say you are done. You are my personal slave tonight! I own you now---you fat bastard! Give me what you've got---Mr. Reporter! Fuck me---you worthless prick. Fuck me---you fat piece of shit," she yelled as she finally became independent of Timothy and drove away from the bloody crime scene for her own selfish climax.

Timothy fully realized that he had suddenly become a victim of rape as he let go of most freighting death ride he had ever signed up for. Although he was terrified, freighted for his life and completely violated, his drunken mind still could not stop the most unwanted and disgusting orgasm which painfully exploded in a bloody fury, causing Timothy's world around him to go black.

Chapter 64

HOMAYRA: THE SWAP

Castle Penthouse - 1:53 a.m.

The multitasking ability of the human brain never ceases to amaze me. In the midst of high anxiety and apparent danger I'm frequently able to remove myself, and for just a fraction of a second, consider things completely unrelated to the matters at hand.

It was during a physiology class which I had taken during my freshman year at Oxford. We studied the remarkable durability of the human heart muscle. Among the many other seemingly irrelevant facts I had filed away in my brain, one came to mind:

During an average lifetime, the human heart will beat more than 2.5 billion times.

With that number lodged in my mind, I caught myself listening to my own blood surging through the four chambers of my heart as if it were desperately trying to warn me that I was rapidly closing in on my final number.

The penthouse was quiet, except for the distant voices of Zooli and Henri having a conversation at the far end of the residence. I was sitting on the floor and leaning against the back of Henri's desk, rereading the user's manual for removing the *ISATPHONE SIM card*. Danielle's phone had already powered off, just as Timothy said it would, once his remote replication process had finished.

I had left Henri's desk lamp on and the center drawer open, as I removed the back cover plate of the satellite phone and positioned the pivoting bracket upward. Very carefully I slid the tiny SIM card back into the delicate bracket and pressed it back down into place, making sure that the gold contacts were facing downward. I replaced the cover plate and then returned the phone back to its charging base at the bottom of the wooden box.

With the SIM card slot on Danielle's phone now vacant, I quickly realized that for at least for the time being, her phone was useless. During the heat of the excitement of swapping out Henri's SIM card earlier, I had allowed Danielle to carelessly toss her tiny microchip into the bowels of my cluttered pocket book. Finding it now would require yet another act of god, and since my luck with him these days was at an all-time low, I didn't even attempt to search for it.

As I was rushed towards the door, I suddenly realized that I had accidently left Henri's desk drawer open and lamp still on. I hurried to the back side of his desk and while closing the drawer I noticed a stylishly bound booklet tucked against the right side of the drawer. It appeared to be of the same style as the other booklets which I had seen neatly placed upon each place setting out in Henri's bizarre dining room.

I opened the booklet and moved it under the desk lamp. The pages appeared to be laid out much like a dinner menu, each with detailed pictures and inflated descriptions of the items being offered. But instead of pictures of delicious entrées or tempting desserts, the pages displayed disturbing photographs of young men and women posing in a variety of offensive positions.

At the bottom of each page I noticed standard pricing information, delivery and return instructions and an entire section on disposal policies. This horrible piece of evidence was coming with me, I thought, as I stuffed the booklet into my cluttered handbag, turned off the light and headed once again for the door.

I had barely touched the latch when the office door suddenly opened and Henri entered. He was so close to me that I could feel the heat from his body and smell his familiar cologne. As if on cue, Henri turned his head to face Zooli, who was driving Henri away from the office entrance.

"Really Henri, it's dreadfully late, let's please make it a rain check for another night? You mentioned that you have some sort of business call to attend to. I can bring dinner another time."

"Oh, nonsense, Zooli, I wouldn't hear of it. This is a very momentous occasion. Come---please sit with me, darling. We'll have a glass of cognac. It's really too late to eat."

Henri leaned forward and snatched Zooli's hand and directed her into the dark office. Seeing that I was in the room with them, Zooli switched over to trainer mode and broke free from Henri. Instantly Zooli disengaged Henri's hindquarters, turning his body and directing his eyes towards her.

With Henri's back to me, Zooli treated me as if I were a vulnerable mare and Henri an equine threat. Assertively, Zooli led Henri to the opposite side of the room as if he were a wild and unpredictable stallion on a lead rope.

I dropped to my knees behind the base of a large bronze statue. The headless cast metal fragment depicted a nude woman's busty torso, impaled upon an iron rod above a stone pedestal. Each of the arms had been broken from its torso, leaving the limbless figure defenseless to the world around it. The artwork fully defined Henri's deviated perception of a human being, as nothing more than a null and void object with neither a mouth to protest nor feet to escape.

Zooli was now in full command of Henri as she marched him around the room allowing him to vent off his anxiety.

"Zooli, would you please relax and let me hold you. I can't tell you of the many days I have dreamed of holding you in my arms."

Henri moved in on Zooli and lunged at her in an attempted to capture her. But Zooli was prepared for that response, as she confidently moved backwards keeping Henri at bay by the length of her imaginary lead rope. Suddenly the satellite phone started ringing from the base of the wooden box.

"Damn it, is it that time already? Please Zooli; don't move---please stay where you are. This will only take a second---I promise you."

Henri reluctantly left Zooli's side and walked over to the far side of his desk and angrily snapped opened the old wooden box. The lid flew backwards and slapped against itself, breaking free of its hinge.

"Hello—hello—this is Henri---Hello?" Henri answered, as he inspected his damaged wooden keepsake.

Henri was angry and distracted by the interruption as he fumbled with the buttons on the phone. A second ring rudely demanded Henri's full attention as he angrily stabbed the glowing keypad hoping for the proper response.

"Oh---damn this miserable phone! I hate these goddamn things!"

"Santo! Hello Santo! Are you there?" Henri's greeting sounded rude as he yelled into the phone and demanded a response from the caller on the other end.

"Yes, yes, I'm here, Santo. I'm sorry my friend, I ah, I just didn't realize it was that time yet. Forgive me, my friend. I was just in the middle of dinner. I mean---a meeting."

Henri's usual commanding character had oddly diminished, as if he were nothing more than a mere soldier reporting to his angry senior officer. "Why, yes of course---Santo my brother. Yes--I am certainly able to talk with you now. Please my brother calm down. ---No, no---I was only asking you to relax my brother----I meant no disrespect."

Henri glanced over at Zooli with a helpless expression. The call was clearly not going to be short, because of Henri's many cancellations. Henri could tell that Santo was angry and quickly becoming a mortal enemy. He flailed his arms and motioned for Zooli to stay and wait for him to conclude his call.

"No--no Santo, I have not heard from Ari, why do you ask? Yes, of course I was expecting your call. Please Santo, relax! I'm here now, so let's talk, shall we? No Santo! I told you! I have not been trying to avoid you!"

Zooli spared little time in moving towards the door as Henri helplessly watched.

"No, I'm not upset with you my brother. Please tell me---Santo, how is your wonderful family these days."

I was sure that Henri saw me as I followed Zooli through the doorway with my head facing the opposite direction.

Unexpectedly, Zooli turned on her heals and poked her head back into Henri's office. In a highly uncharacteristic fashion, Zooli appeared to be taunting Henri, by sending off a mocking wink. It was as if she was both bidding farewell to Henri and telling him to rot in hell for an eternity. Henri stood staring at Zooli in helpless disbelief.

"Zooli! Wait! Where are you going? Who is that person with you? Zooli, stop! Mother was that you? Come back, you two! Please come back! I demand it!"

We ran to the kitchen and pressed the button for the service elevator and painfully waited for the slow moving elevator to reach the top floor.

"Do you think he saw me, Zooli? Do you think he recognized me?"

"No! I don't think so! But honestly, Homi, do you really care if he did?"

On our way down to the ground floor we clung to each other, both shivering with excitement and fear.

"Zooli, how were you able to allow yourself to be touched by that man?"

Zooli looked at me with her beautiful dark brown eyes and whispered in Farsi: *Gahi adam majboureh, khodesho fada koneh baraye digaran.* - *Sometimes you must sacrifice yourself for the welfare of others.*

The further the elevator traveled from the top floor, the more I felt a false sense of security, as the elevator car finally reached the ground floor and settled into its connection points.

"What now?" Zooli asked, as the door of the elevator slowly opened.

"We've got to find Danni and get the hell out of here!"

With our next objective in mind we stepped off the elevator and found ourselves standing directly in front of a very angry security officer. The officer was the very same man who failed to detain us when we first arrived. This time the anxious officer was not going to take any chance in losing us for a third time. He fumbled with pistol and two-way radio and began spewing orders at us in poorly spoken French:

Et bien, qu'est ce que je vois ? Mesdames, vous m'avez presque fait perdre mon travail tout à l'heure, maintenant vous venez avec moi toutes les deux, vous êtes dans de sales draps, je vous le promets, suivez moi immédiatement! - "Well look who we have here? You two ladies almost cost me my job earlier this evening. You two ladies must come with me at once. You ladies are in big trouble. I promise you! Now come with me this instant!"

The American officer appeared visibly nervous and desperately unsure of himself as he trained his service revolver on our backs and directed us towards the entrance of the heavily populated upper-great hall.

Chapter 65

SELF-DIAGNOSIS

He woke up to darkness --- in a bed with his pants and underwear down around his ankles. The room was spinning as Timothy grabbed the side of the bed and squinted at the clock. The tears had finally stopped flowing from his eyes from the traumatic event earlier. As he glanced at the bright blue numbers on the digital clock by the side of the bed, his brief mental intermission provided him with an unusual amount of clarity, even though the room around him was still violently tumbling overhead.

The time was 2:18 a.m. and Timothy had missed his mark. The scheduled conference call between Henri and Santo Gordo had already started without him, while there Timothy was, half naked and violated from the waist down. The head of his penis was burning with pain as his fingers traced the deep lacerations all over his male organs. Then Timothy realized that he was lying in a pool of his own blood.

The door to the master bathroom was closed and he could hear the shower running. Timothy stuck to his mission and grabbed the outline of cell phone which was still lodged within the pocket of his pants which had been tangled in a mass around his ankles. There was no time to piece things together, Timothy's only concern was for the girls at the castle, as he struggled to free his feet from his tangled clothing.

The power on his phone was at about 43 percent as he activated the SIM Profile menu and pressed the user icon. A bright blue button with the symbol of a stethoscope appeared and Timothy pressed the button causing the auto-hack feature within the SIM card's firmware to connect with its duplicate brain on Henri's satellite phone and digitally monitor the transmission in progress.

"Thank god for these child hacks, they really do make things easy," Timothy mumbled, as he raised the phone to his ear.

Timothy clutched his bloody groin in pain as he rolled out of bed and landed on to the cold wooden floor. The international point-to-point satellite call was going through as a piercing carrier wave squealed into his ear. Another blinking amber icon appeared, prompting Timothy to join the dedicated session already in progress. The SIM Assistant's automatic phone hacking feature, which he had adopted from his son, was working perfectly as he began listening to a live conversation taking place as if he were sitting in the same room with them.

The sounds of the two men's voices were clearly audible as they concluded their stilted greetings and moved on to the more important matters of the day. Timothy pressed the record icon and proceeded to drag his bloody body across the slippery wooden floor into the living room.

The sound of the shower in the master bathroom continued to run as Timothy unsuccessfully attempted to stand up. Who was this crazy woman who referred to herself as Reneta, and why did her moans seem so oddly familiar? Timothy was now sure that he had heard that phrase before: *I want to fuck you until you are unconscious!* Everything about the Russian seemed oddly familiar but still she remained a mystery.

Timothy's mind was turning summersaults as the entire room rotated end-over-end, while he crawled on his hands and knees like an injured animal towards the powder room near the main entrance. His knees slipped on his own blood as he grimaced in pain from the waist down. The bloody injury of what he expected to see caused him to become nauseous. He threw up the contents of stomach onto his hands and floor beneath him.

Losing his balance, Timothy fell on his side, splashing in a pool of his own vomit and blood. While tightly gripping his cell phone in his right hand, Timothy continued crawling his way towards the safety of the power room. The lights of the city lit up the living room as he came within reach of his hiding place. Grabbing the edge of the door frame Timothy heaved his injured body on to the cold marble floor and closed the door behind him with his bloody feet.

Fearful of what he was about to see, Timothy reached up the side of the wall with his bloody fingers and switched on the overhead light. His eyes flickered to the intensity of the light as he adjusted his focus on his mutilated private parts. The sight caused him to convulse in horror. His entire penis had deep lacerations all over it causing his entire organ to appear completely un-functional.

How he was able to reach an orgasm after receiving such a traumatic injury to both his penis and scrotum was a complete mystery to him. Perhaps he took it as some sort of idiotic challenge when he heard the erotic monster tell him, that after she was through with him, he would no longer have a *cock to fuck with.*

Although his anatomical body parts were still intact, a massive amount of blood was flowing freely through a gaping hole on one side of his scrotum. Having once been a medic in the military, Timothy had seen bloody injuries before. Although he was shocked by the sight of his injuries, he quickly switched over to medic mode and began triage. It was easy to for him to establish, from his third party vantage point, that this patient was in the most need of critical care, because the man was, most definitely, bleeding to death.

Timothy fell back against the wall and took a deep breath, trying desperately to clear his vision and mind. Surprisingly, Timothy realized that he was actually sitting upon one of Reneta's silver leather sandals, which she had discarded earlier in the evening. Timothy no longer admired the sandals as much he did when she was strutting around the dance floor at Zelz, but now considered them only to be material for emergency first aid.

Timothy grabbed one sandal and wrapped the long length of a leather strip around his wrist and tore it away from the sandal. The thin leather strap seemed long enough and would certainly serve as an emergency tourniquet, as he tied the two ends of the straps together into a square knot. One more item was needed for his rudimentary tourniquet. With all of his strength Timothy broke off the six-inch heel from the base of the sandal and positioned it on the far end of the loop and began rotating the heel. As if the heel were a handle, twisting the straps together, the mechanics appeared to make sense.

Fighting back searing pain, Timothy looped the other end of the strap above the flowing bloody gash, to the base of his scrotum and up against his groin as far up as he possibly could. Holding the heel of the sandal in his right hand, he rapidly turned the makeshift handle clock-wise as the loop tightened like a noose around the base of his scrotum. A sick old rhyme began haunting Timothy as he tightened his own noose: *Righty Tighty, Lefty Loosey.*

The remaining blood squirted out of the numerous lacerations on his perforated penis as he tightened his rudimentary tourniquet until he could no longer physically stand it. Shocking jolts of pain shot through his lower extremities as dead portions of his drunken brain began to wake up. He quietly cried out as he pulled both of his knees against his chest and suffered through excruciating pain while bathing in a warm pool of blood. The pressure tourniquet appeared to be working as the rapid stream of life-blood which was flowing out of his many lacerations began to shut off like a valve on a gruesome garden hose.

Timothy wrapped the tightly twisted cord around the base of bloody scrotum and stowed it secure. Falling backwards against the wall of the small powder room, Timothy began feeling the effects of his brain rapidly losing its grip on life.

"No way, you fat bastard," Timothy growled, scolding himself for the horrible predicament he had placed himself in. "You deserved everything you got tonight *Mister Reporter!* But I'm sorry you sick Russian bitch, or whoever the fuck you are? I'm not willing to leave this earth yet," Timothy grumbled as he pulled his weak body to a standing position.

Turning both faucets on, Timothy filled the sink and shoveled waves of water over the edge of the counter onto his bloody genitals. The first few waves washed most of the bloody mess away from his injuries allowing him to validate the success of his life saving tourniquet.

The following splashes of water went directly against Timothy bloody face, beaten head and carved up chest.

"God damn, what did you do to me---you monstrous bitch?" Timothy wondered as he stared at his pitiful expression in the mirror.

Ironically, Timothy began to derive some sort of sick humor from his critically injured condition. Perhaps comedic relief was Timothy's strange way of saving his own sanity, as he spotted Reneta's makeup bag hanging by its strap on the door knob.

Perhaps there was something in her little bag that might be of some help for my situation, he thought. When he overturned the bag on the counter and began studying the contents, a prescription bottle rolled off the edge of the counter and dropped into the toilet bowl. He bent down and retrieved the small brown bottle and read the ingredients from a torn and faded prescription label: *Vicodin, acetaminophen, hydrocodone*. Of course the patient's name was missing, having been scratched away.

"Just what the doctor ordered," Timothy said, as he opened the bottle and tossed three large tablets down his throat.

"I need this way more than you do---bitch! What else do you have in your little pursy--poo?" Timothy said, as he verbally identified each item on the counter in front of him.

"Let's see---what do we have here? Oh, you have some sexy silver lipstick, two joints, a business card from that skinny little French prick at Zelz, a small plastic container of what looks like cocaine, some rolling papers, another medicine bottle and a small pink aerosol can of pepper spray. You certainly do come prepared, don't you?" Timothy mocked, as he held the other bottle under the light.

Flunitrazepam, Rohypnol, what the hell is this shit? Tim asked himself, as he watched the bloody water flowing down the drain.

Finally it hit him when he vaguely started remembering a story he had once written about a class of drugs used for date rapes on college campuses. *Narcozep, Rohypnol, Rohipnol* and *Roipnol* were the names that came to mind.

What were those drugs which each rhymed with the street name *Ruuff--Rufinol. Roofies?*

"That's it," Timothy said out loud, as he stared at his dilated pupils in the mirror.

"You slipped me a fucking Roofie--- you evil bitch!"

Suddenly the events of the entire evening began to make more sense. But who exactly is that monster taking a shower in the next room, and why was she trying to kill me?

Chapter 66

FACE-OFF

Oxford, UK – Tablemate Inn

Timothy never fashioned himself to be a collector. Stamps, coins or jewelry never really appealed to him. But during his high school years he was introduced to the Zippo lighter, which from that day forward, changed everything in his life.

The wonderful look and design of the smooth metal lighter appealed to Timothy from the first instant he held one in his hand. He liked everything about it, from the way the flint igniter wheel felt spinning beneath his thumb, to the precision sound of the metal lid when it flipped open and snapped shut. Timothy even adored the fragrance of the burning lighter fluid and the full yellow flame which warmed both his hands and soul during those cold winter days as an awkward teen.

The Zippo was responsible for Timothy acquiring friends, impressing girls and introducing Timothy to smoking, a habit which he had both loved and hated for more than 40 years. At 57, Timothy could still make out the remnants of that faded rectangular scar on the right side of his neck, put there by a showoff bully during a gym class in high school. The malicious little tyrant thought it would be funny to heat up the cover of his Zippo lighter to the point it was red hot and place it against the side of Timothy's neck, branding him for life.

Because of those experiences, both good and bad, Timothy became a lifelong collector of Zippos dating back to the vintage models which were made during the mid-thirties. It was also because of those imbedded memories that Timothy was able to distinctly identify the sounds that each classic Zippo lighter made when opened, closed and ignited. The very same sound that Timothy clearly remembered from when Ari lit her cigarette only ten meters away from where Timothy and Golareh lay hiding, in the alley at the Hither Green Rail Yard.

Even though Timothy desperately wanted to catch a glimpse of that super-charged erotic hottie, whom Golareh had warned him to avoid, he was unable to, for fear of being discovered. But the sounds Ari made while having wild sex with Henri remained with Timothy as he recorded every grunt, moan and groan coming from that sexy little vixen's mouth. How dangerous could she really be, he wondered, as he recalled Ari promising Henri that she was going to *fuck him until he was unconscious?*

Timothy finally got his wish the moment he lowered the latch of the powder room door and quietly stepped into the dark living room. The city lights dimly illuminated the living room floor and reflected off his blood, sweat and vomit which trailed across the floor from the bedroom.

Then came the sound of that classic Zippo lighter. The broad yellow flame illuminated the face of a woman sitting on a ladder-back wood chair on the other side of the room. The light showed only the lower portion of her face as she lit her long menthol cigarette and snapped the metal lighter shut. In a flash Timothy identified the female monster which had previously gone by the name Reneta, as being the one and only Ari.

"Well it appears I'm finally getting my wish," Timothy quietly mumbled, as he leaned against the wall, wrapped only in bloody towel. He was gripping his blood crusted cell phone in his left hand and another object in his right. The dark figure remained silent, appearing only as a shapely silhouette as she sat with one leg casually folded over the other. The two observed one another as Ari gently pulled another slow drag from her cigarette which slightly lit up her eyes.

"The blond maiden," Timothy quietly announced, as he studied the evil shadow silently observing him through the darkness.

The effects of the 30-milligrams of hydrocodone along with three healthy snorts of Ari's cocaine was finally bringing much needed relief to Timothy's horribly mangled sex organs. The disabling effects of the Rohipnol, date-rape drug, was finally wearing off and providing Timothy with the clarity he most desperately needed.

"Consuelo Ari Balencia, I should have known it was you." He spoke in a medically-relaxed manner which ironically matched the tone and cadence of the monster on the other side of the room.

"Oh, you are the perceptive one, aren't you mister paperboy?" Ari casually took another slow drag from her cigarette and quietly studied him. "Tell me mister paperboy, how did you know it was me?"

"Well before I answer, I'm wondering something. Might I ask you of a favor?" Timothy asked.

Timothy suddenly felt a deep jolt of pain breaking through his Lortab barrier, subtly reminding him of his critical condition, as he patiently waited for her response.

"Most certainly, Mister Paperboy, anything I can do to make your remaining time on earth more comfortable."

"I'll make a promise to you that I won't refer to you as the blonde-maiden, if you could refrain from calling me *Mister Paperboy*. I actually was a paperboy when I was a kid and I hated the job with a passion. I also expect that you would like to be called anything but a maiden?"

"My, aren't you the perceptive one? Okay, my love---deal."

Another minute passed as Timothy curiously studied Air's ironically beautiful profile on the opposite side of the room. How something so well designed by God could be so cold and brutal, was a mystery to Timothy.

She was dressed in a sleeveless, black turtleneck sweater with tight leather pants and rugged leather motorcycle boots. Long gentle strands of hair stylishly framed her flawless face as a single loose braid adorned her right shoulder. Her lips contained a fresh coat of that once delicious lipstick, which shimmered from the light of the city. But despite her beauty

Ari was no blonde maiden at all, but a black widow and a perfect killing machine.

"Well if you must know, I hate the brand of cigarette you smoke. Royale Menthol 100's, I can't stand those nasty smelling things. But it was your lighter that really gave you away."

"Oh, really, is that so?"

Another minute passed as the two studied each other from opposite sides of the dark room.

"Yep---I can still recall the sound of your brass lighter the night you were drilling your so-called sponsor a new asshole on the loading dock at Hither Green. By the way, how is Henri these days, I've been reading so much about him in the news lately."

Ari felt the sting of that remark and became a bit agitated as she shifted her position on the chair. She struck her lighter and held the flame closer to her face, examining the bottom and sides. "Why yes, I guess it is brass, how about that. You really have a mind for details, don't you, Timothy?"

"I believe that would be the 1938 brass military-issue model. They sold a slew of those during the Second World War." Timothy said, as he felt his body shiver and sweat at the same time.

"And you must be the mysterious, unknown source, who demands not to be identified for fear of some sort of retaliation? You really have become quite a pain in ass to my sponsor, but more than that, you have crossed the line of no-return with my cousin."

Ari puffed lightly on her cigarette and then suddenly glanced at a fingernail on her right hand.

"Oh damn, it looks like I broke a nail. I guess you got me a little too excited this evening--- Timothy."

"Oh well--- I'm sure I could find the fragment still implanted somewhere underneath my flesh. Somehow I expect that Henri doesn't get you as excited as much as I do, otherwise he would be dead. Lucky me! Tell me Ari, what was it about me that causes you want to devour me so?"

Timothy couldn't help but chuckle at his own humor, causing another sudden jolt of pain to electrify his mid-section.

"Oh you really are the funny man; I'm impressed by your stupid optimism. Tell me Timothy, before I break your jaw, what makes you so confident with yourself?"

Ari's speech pattern was gradually shifting from Russian to her native language of Spanish.

"Well, it sort of goes this way---Ari. You see for years, I worried about losing everything I ever had. And now that I have nothing more to lose, I guess I'm sort of at peace with myself. My only regret about meeting you is that I wish I didn't excite you so much in bed! Tell me Ari, was it good for you?"

"Shut you filthy mouth---you smart ass bastard! You are a funny man aren't you? Well I don't like funny men! Were you aware of that, Timothy?"

Ari stood up and slowly walked across the room. "And what I especially don't like are nosy, funnymen---Timothy. Do you understand what I fucking mean by---nosy men? Timothy?"

Ari gracefully switched her stance into a position that resembled a ballerina about to perform a pirouette.

In what seemed like a graceful dance of athleticism, Ari launched her left leg into a powerful backwards rotation as her body spun, landing the heel of her boot against the side of Timothy's jaw. The force of the impact dropped Timothy's weak body to the floor as if he was nothing more than a bloody side of beef.

Ironically, although Timothy's front teeth were missing, he felt no pain, but felt a renewed sense of clarity arriving to his previously cloudy mind.

"Oh I'm dreadfully sorry Ari, but perhaps you are mistaking me for someone who has something to live for?" Timothy moved his contorted face and purposely spit his two front teeth out between Ari's legs and across the floor.

"Mister Paperboy, I'm curious about something?" Ari said, as she stood above Timothy's broken body in yet another offensive stance.

"Why yes---my dear *blonde-maiden*. I'm all yours?"

Timothy's light hearted joking was beginning to surprise even himself, as he realized that she had, in fact, severely broken his jaw.

"I'm just dying to know how you have been able to gather so much information on not only my sponsor but my cousin as well."

"Well I'm dying to tell you too, Ari---and no pun intended, of course. But Henri, your sponsor---you know, the guy you constantly threaten to *fuck unconscious*, has become a fountain of information on your kissing-cousin. Tell me Ari, did Santo teach you to fuck people to death like that?"

Timothy had just gone over the edge, as his humor was turning into resentment. All he was focusing on now was the pearl handled pistol Ari had tucked in a leather holster under her left arm.

"Stop it--- with your jokes and questions you stupid man, because I'm tired of your silly tone!"

Ari pressed the heel of her boot against the bath towel covering Timothy's mutilated genitals. Timothy groaned in pain and crouched into a fetal position as he desperately tried to protect his emergency tourniquet.

"Oh, would you look at that, Mister Paperboy; it appears that my little reporter does have something to live for---after all? Don't you, you worthless piece of shit! Now I want you to tell me how you have been obtaining so much information on my cousin! And I want you to tell me---now!"

Ari was done playing with Timothy as she collected her knee upward and kicked Timothy directly in his injured groin. Timothy felt the room fade as all of his strength dissipated from his body and a willingness to die surfaced.

"Well, what do we have here?" Ari asked, as she noticed Timothy's cell phone dropping from his bloody hand. A status message was flashing a notification to Timothy, as Ari stooped down and studied the bloody phone from above.

"Well Timothy---you do like to be called Timothy? Tell me, what have you been doing with your little cell phone here all evening?"

Ari moved her head closer and examined the cryptic status message flashing on Timothy phone. "It appears that whatever you have been recording here tonight has ended successfully? Successfully, hmmm, is that a good thing, Timothy---yes?"

Ari casually walked across the room and slid the ladder-back chair back to the side of Timothy's fading body. Timothy watched in horror as Ari removed her high caliber pistol from her shoulder holster and pressed it against his temple.

"Perhaps it would be nice for you to play back whatever it was you were recording here this evening, Timothy? Oh, I bet I know what you were recording, you naughty little boy---you. You were recording our magical lovemaking session. Is that it ---Timothy? Oh I just love to hear to myself begging for an orgasm! Tell me Timothy did you cum during your news-worthy performance with me this evening, I really can't recall? Was it good for you? Let's listen together shall we? Perhaps the sound of us fucking might get us both a little horny again---yes?"

Ari was playfully mocking Timothy as she pressed the end of the gun barrel painfully against Timothy's temple.

"Make no mistake Timothy; you are going to die very soon, so you might as well just relax and enjoy the show. Would you like your last ciga-rette, Timothy? Oh, that's right, you detest my brand, I almost forgot. Oh well, that's just too bad for you, my fat little friend. Let's listen to this together shall we?"

Ari pulled back the hammer on her pearl handled magnum and pressed the end of the barrel even deeper against Timothy's skull. "Play the god-damn recording you dumb fuck, before I blow your fucking brains out!"

Timothy managed to press the play button while Ari sat back in her chair and lit another cigarette with her now infamous Zippo lighter.

The recording began with excellent clarity as two unidentified men bantered back and forth. A confused expression suddenly developed on Ari's face as she appeared baffled and surprised while she flicked her burn-ing ashes on Timothy half-naked body. For the next nine-minutes and 26-seconds, Ari and Timothy listened intently to a very private and remark-ably revealing conversation between Henri Lepan and Santo Gordo.

How such a recording was captured was a disturbing mystery to Ari, but the highly incriminating evidence stored locally on Timothy's cell phone had the potential of bringing down the entire industry which Henri Lepan and Santo Gordo had carefully built for the last 35 years.

Chapter 67

GOLAREH: FULL CRY

Central North Oxford - 2:40 a.m.

By any stretch of the imagination Smithy Greene was not struggling to make ends meet. Her father, Paul Greene, died on Smithy's 50th birthday and left her with a sprawling home within walking distance of the city centre, along with a hefty portfolio of investments. Paul was a famous producer-director who had made seven major motion pictures and six stage productions all commissioned for the Royal National Theatre.

Although Smithy had a bold and extremely flirtatious personality, she was actually quite reserved and somewhat conservative. She lived quietly in a beautiful three-story, six bedroom estate in Walton Manor, just six blocks north of the Flick Theatre. Her home retained the charm of her beloved father, reflecting his artistry and classic style while featuring large rooms, rich furniture and traditional design.

As we approached her home, I knew immediately that something was terribly wrong. Every light in the house was on and two black Ford Town Cars sat in the driveway. Each was empty causing Heath to make the assumption that all of the men were inside the home. He instructed us to stay safely behind, as he drew his gun and ran ahead of us. Big Ben and I cut across a yard two houses down and worked our way through the woods until we were directly behind Smithy's large home. We saw Heath run to the back of the house and begin looking through the windows on the ground floor. While Big Ben and I could see most of the activity occurring on all three floors of the house, Heath could see only into the living room.

On the third floor, two men in suits appeared to be moving from room to room, systematically searching for Timothy and most likely me as well. The same bald man, we identified earlier named Stephan Yoden, was holding Smithy by the scruff of her neck and shoving her through each room, demanding answers. Heath saw none of this as he ran to the corner of the house and disappeared around to the front.

Smithy looked absolutely terrified as her captor threw her up against the wall and harshly interrogated her while soaking in her body at the same time. We stood helpless in the woods watching the drama unfold as two other men searched the first two floors.

Suddenly, the sound of a gunshot, coming from the front of the home, cut through the early morning darkness like the crack of a whip, terrifying both of us. Immediate I was convinced that Heath had been shot. The men inside of the house flinched and temporarily froze, giving Smithy the opportunity to break free and run for her life. All of the men in the home leaped into action, desperately trying to retrieve Smithy.

"That's it! I'm going in!" Big Ben said, as he grabbed my hand and dragged me across the lawn towards the patio. When we arrived, Smithy was passing through the living room screaming at the top of her lungs. Big Ben tried to open the sliding glass door but found it locked. He knocked on the glass with his fist, almost breaking it, as Smithy turned and stared at us in disbelief. Frantically, she unlocked the door and was about halfway through the narrow opening when her bald assailant snatched her from behind by the hair.

Big Ben lunged at the intruder, grabbing him by his face and yanking both of them through the narrow opening to the patio. Both glass doors became dislodged and smashed onto the patio's brick floor, shattering glass everywhere. Immediately, Big Ben passed Smithy's tiny body from one hand to the other and repositioned his grip around young Mr. Yoden's neck.

The bald henchman, still gripping his gun, suddenly found himself helpless, as he twitched and screamed under the pressure of Big Ben's powerful grip.

"What do you plan on doing now, little fella--- shooting me with your little pop-gun? Guess what?---Not!"

The gun was no pop-gun at all but a 9mm, semi-automatic pistol. Big Ben gracefully moved the three of us over to the side of a round stone table.

"He looks so cute with his sexy little sunglasses, doesn't he, girls?" Big Ben's ultra-feminine speech patterns clashed so oddly with the brute strength of his frame.

"Well I'm sorry to say this to you, honey, but you won't be cute for long!" Big Ben announced, as he swept the man-in-black off his feet and slammed his face down on the surface of the stone tabletop. The sight was gruesome, and the sound was even worse, reminding me of a grapefruit hitting a concrete surface.

"How do we look now, sweetie?" Big Ben asked, as he held the dangling man by his neck and inspected his broken face.

The helpless man's pistol fell to the ground along with two of his teeth. His broken glasses were smashed against his flatten face as he stared at us in disbelief.

"Goli, honey, do me a favor and grab this little man's gun. I don't believe he's a responsible gun owner. Oh, I just love these little bald bad-boys, don't you, girls? They look so macho---especially when they fly away like bald eagles!" With that, Big Ben tossed the man into the air like a rag doll and kicked him across the lawn into the flowerbed.

Heath suddenly appeared from the corner of the house. "Get down on the ground---now!" He yelled, as he ran toward us. Three other thugs followed behind him in pursuit with their guns drawn.

"Heath—look out! --- In back of you! He's got a gun! Get down!" I yelled, as the action down-shifted to slow motion.

One of the thugs squeezed off a round from his powerful hand gun and struck Heath in his back, just below his right shoulder. Heath was thrown forward by the force of the blast and tumbled helplessly to the surface of the patio.

"No!" I screamed, as I stared at Heath lying motionless on the ground.

Realizing that I was holding a completely foreign pistol in my right hand, I gathered my thoughts and considered my next move. Everything that I had ever learned about guns had come from movie theaters, and never in my life, had I held a firearm in my hand. As the three men charged us, all of the action seemed to be moving from frame to frame, as if I were watching a slideshow.

Smithy's eyeballs appeared to be popping out of her head as Big Ben shielded her from danger. Big Ben's eyes, were trying to lock in on mine with an expression of dread. The world became silent as I waited for the next blast from the enemy, which would have blown at least one of us away. For a full second, I was convinced that I was going to die.

Suddenly, the voice of my guardian angel filled the caverns of my terrified mind and seized my full attention. It was the voice of Zooli, as I imagined her sitting on a horse bareback, critiquing my every move through her dark aviator sunglasses while tightly gripping her riding crop. "Center yourself Goli. Stand firm and think about your objective at hand. Take it piece by piece. Do you hear me girl? Remember what I've taught you, Goli. You always have time to think! Now stand square, girl. Extend your arms, take a deep breath and take command of your situation."

Every single element of my private world was staging up for my next move as I watched the charging killers close in on my loved ones. I curled my index finger around the smooth trigger and held the molded grip into my palm. I took a deep breath, fully extended my arms, and pulled the trigger. As my life flashed across my eyes, I suddenly realized that I had left out the most crucial step---which was to take aim.

The gun went off in a blinding blast. The burst of the gunshot shook me to my core. When the smoke finally cleared, I saw the three assailants running from the scene, as a thick terracotta rain gutter which had been molded to the corner of Smithy's house, exploded into pieces.

The young bald man lay moaning and recovering in the flower garden while Heath's motionless body lay, lifeless, on the cold bricks.

While not even thinking, I stuffed the warm pistol into my handbag and raced to Heath's side.

"Heath!—Heath!" I cried, burying my face in his windbreaker. I was so sure that he was dead that I was afraid to even look at him.

Suddenly, the unimaginable happened. Beneath me, I felt Heath's lungs expanding with air, followed by a distant groan.

"Heath, Heath, please don't die on me! Please, lord! Oh my god, Heath---please don't go!"

Big Ben arrived at his side and gently turned Heath over on his back while elevating his head. Heath's eyes were flickering as he started to cough and come to. Big Ben gently lowered his body to the ground, took his pulse and put his ear to his chest. Heath took an even deeper breath and then slowly opened his eyes.

"Holy shit, don't tell me I'm still here? Did I actually make it?" Heath stared off into the distance and slowly began to grin.

"Heath, honey, you've been shot. Do you know if the bullet penetrated your back?" Big Ben asked, as he inspected a hole in the back of his wind breaker.

"Well I'm hit alright, but I think my armor took the bullet. Help me out of the damn vest."

The three of us gently brought Heath to his feet and led him over to the stone seat next to the table. We unzipped and removed his windbreaker, revealing his bullet-proof vest. Heath was now sitting up as his long blond hair fell over the back of his shoulders.

"This, my friends, is the latest in bulletproof technology. It's a stab proof, bullet proof, Kevlar vest, and this will be the second time one of these babies has saved my damn life. Am I lucky or what?"

The amazing white nylon vest was made up of two ballistic panels, one in front and one in back. Three Velcro straps held the vest firmly against Heath's body as we carefully unfastened them and removed the body armor.

"My god, sweetie, you took one serious hit," Big Ben said, as he examined a growing bruise on Heath's back. "Let me check you out, honey." He carefully flexed Heath's right shoulder inward and outward.

"Wow, Big Ben, I didn't know that you knew so much about this sort of stuff!" I watched in amazement as Big Ben checked the various muscle groups of Heath's shoulders and upper back.

"Well, baby girl, don't forget that I was the biggest and meanest, gay football player in all of the United Kingdom. They didn't call me the *fear-less-fairy* for nothing! You're going to be sore, Heath, honey, but you will live to see another day." Big Ben carefully helped Heath's sore body to a standing position.

"Thanks guys, but we'd better get back to the theatre; I've been thinking about that hotel that you saw Timothy at earlier in the evening."

As we slowly trekked back to the Flick, Smithy started crying.

"They were coming after you too, Goli, and also some woman named Ari. I heard one of them talking on his radio to Henri Lepan! Henri was telling them to take out someone called Ari at all costs! Oh my god---we have got to find Timothy! All of these fucking people are trying to kill him!"

The notion about Henri ordering his men to take out Ari confused me entirely. Why he would order the death of a woman who had been fiercely loyal to him for what seemed like my entire lifetime seemed implausible. There was way too much for me to understand and finding Timothy was now paramount as our disheveled search party slowly moved in the direction of the theatre.

When we came within view of the Flick Theatre a crowd of people, many in drag, saw us emerging from the darkness. Rene spotted Big Ben bracing one side of Heath's body and ran towards us in horror.

"Oh my god Benny, are you okay? I told you not to go over there! But you wouldn't listen to me---would you---you big dumb fool?"

The entire procession of theater district patrons surrounded us under the bright marquee lights. Rahda and Frédéric were standing away from the crowd in the middle of the street trying to calm the manager of the Tablemate Inn. The poor man was dressed in a blue night robe with matching slippers and anxiously pointing at the top floor of the Tablemate Inn in amazement.

"What are those guys doing over there?" Heath asked, as Smithy and I walked towards them.

"People, you all need to go inside---now!" Big Ben yelled. "It's not safe to be out here--- people! Move it! Please go back in the theater!"

Suddenly a powerful gunshot blew out a large glass window on the top floor of the Tablemate Inn. A reflective mass of shattered glass fell from the top floor to the sidewalk in front of the main entrance of the inn.

"What the fuck?" Big Ben yelled.

"Get down, people!" Heath yelled, as he sprang into action and ran towards entrance of the inn with his pistol drawn, followed by Rahda. Frédéric tried to hold back the frantic manager but he broke away and ran through main entrance of the hotel, just as three more powerful gun shots exploded from the top floor.

The fire alarms came on, returning the elevator cars to the ground floor and unlocking all emergency exits. Lights in the darkened rooms came on as the out-of-control manager chased after Heath and Rahda.

Several police sirens screamed in the distance as Smithy and I broke away from the crowd and ran towards the entrance of the Inn. Frédéric caught up with us and tried to hold me back. "Stay back Goli, don't go up there! It's way too dangerous!"

I ignored Frédéric's order and ran over the broken glass and through the hotel entrance. Smithy and I were going up to that room even if it meant being shot ourselves. We were convinced that Timothy was up there clinging to dear life and we needed to be up there with him.

Smithy and I opened the door to the emergency stairway and climbed up several flights of stairs as terrified hotel guests flooded past us attempting to get out. Some were dressed in nightgowns while others were wearing nothing but their underwear.

Several more shots were fired from the top floor hallway as Smithy and I arrived at the far end of the scene. We watched in horror as Heath and Rahda traded off rounds with an angry blonde woman dressed in a sleeveless, black turtleneck sweater, black pants, and boots. She appeared to be holding a wet wash cloth against her eyes as she blindly fired off rounds in every direction and then disappeared back inside to reload. Heath and Rahda barricaded themselves within an alcove and waited for the right time to gain their next position.

Forward the officers advanced, posting themselves on opposite sides of the penthouse door with their guns drawn and ready. As the smoke cleared in the hallway the elevator door just across from the entrance of the penthouse opened as the irate hotel manager stepped out and walked right up and knocked on the door of the penthouse.

"I am the manager of this hotel and I demand that all of you leave my property at once!"

"No! Get back---sir!" Health yelled, as the angry manager ignored his commands.

"Get down on the ground, sir---this second! Do as I say!" Heath yelled, as the door of the penthouse opened and Ari stepped into the hallway still holding the wet cloth against her face.

As if she was struggling to focus, Ari raised her 44-magnum-revolver and began firing randomly from side to side. Heath and Rahda dropped to their knees, out of her direct line of fire. Distracted by the hysterical hotel manager standing directly in front of her swearing, Ari pointed the end of her long barrel at the manger's head and fired pointblank. In an instant the powerful blast blew his head completely apart, as a cloud of blue and gray brain matter covered the splintered wooden doors of the elevator. Ari retreated, slamming the door behind her as Heath and Rahda fiercely maintained their position.

The demolished body of the hotel manager lay wilted and leaking on the floor in front of the elevator, as an eerie silence filled the hallway. Heath glared over at Smithy and me and issued a stern order to drop to the floor and stay there. From inside the room we heard Ari screaming, as if she were in pain.

Another shot was fired from inside the room as Ari's screams suddenly intensified and then faded off in the distance. Heath and Rahda took that as a cue and each kicked one side of the penthouse door in. The door flew open as the officers entered the suite with guns blasting and reports flashing. In seconds everything ended in a dreadful silence.

Smithy and I were lying on the floor with our faces pressed against the smelly hallway carpet for what seemed like an eternity. Smithy was weeping uncontrollably as Rahda emerged from the suite with a somber face and dark expression.

"Goli, I think you two girls had better get in here---but I want to warn you, what you are about to see is bad. Hurry girls," Rahda ordered as Smithy and I sprang to our feet and rushed down the hallway towards the crime scene.

I felt both frightened and nauseous as I entered the dark penthouse, dreading what I was about to find. The room was filled with the smell of blood and spent gunpowder which burned my nostrils. Heath reentered the penthouse through an open set of French doors which apparently led to a stone terrace. He looked both exhausted and frustrated.

"She got away---Rahda. I'm going down stairs to get some help. Talk to him, Goli. See what you can find out, because he doesn't have much time---at all!"

Heath took me in his arms and hugged me and then left the penthouse. I rushed over towards a mangled bloody mass leaning against the door of a small bathroom. The mass looked nothing like a human body until I got a closer look.

It was Timothy, sitting on the floor in a pool of blood. He was half naked and wrapped in a bloody towel. His breathing was labored as his right eye tracked me kneeling down to study him. He had been shot at least four times in the abdomen with puncture wounds slowly spewing blood down his body and on to the floor. His head was resting against the corner of the wall with his jaw clearly knocked out of alignment with the rest of his skull. At least two of his teeth were missing and his left eye was swollen completely shut.

"Timothy, my god, what did she do to you?"

I slowly extended my hands to the side of Timothy bloody face and was almost afraid to even touch his mutilated body. Timothy was murmuring something under his breath that was unintelligible.

"What baby?" I moved in closer and held my ear closer to his bloody mouth. "Tell me--- baby, tell me honey. Tell me what you're trying to say!"

I could see that his face had been badly beaten and his body was riddled with bullet holes, but why he was naked and wrapped in a bloody towel was a mystery to me. His neck and torso were covered in strange lacerations, resembling bite marks from a wild animal.

"Timothy, my god, what happened here tonight?"

I felt myself becoming sick and was about to throw-up until I cursed myself for being such a damn coward. I was such a pitiful fool for getting Timothy involved in my ridiculous life in the first place. And now I don't even have the strength to look at the man dying on the floor next to me. "Damn you Goli---just goddamn you!" I softly cursed.

"We have it, Goli." Timothy gurgled, as he somehow managed to move his mouth to a strange smile. "I got the bitch with this---." He lowered his only working eye to his bloody hand and allowed it to open as a small pink aerosol canister of pepper-spray fell out of his hand and rolled across the floor.

"Hold on baby---help is coming!"

I dropped down to the side of his injured body and desperately attempted to hold his bloody head upright in an effort to prevent him from aspirating in his own blood.

"Hang in there my dear sweet love. My god, baby, I'm so sorry I got you into this whole mess! I love you so much!"

Not once did I consider what I was telling this person who I once believed to be the scum of the earth; for I now loved this person with my entire being as if he were my own brother.

"Goli, we've got Henri," Timothy said, as his voice began to fade.

"What do you mean, Timothy? What do you mean, baby---tell me what you fucking mean!" I was now yelling at poor Timothy out of love and frustration, thinking that he was entirely delusional. Even in the process of dying, Timothy still maintained his ridiculous trait of optimism.

"She tried to take it from me but I wouldn't let her! It's all been recorded right here on my phone. The recording is stored locally and nowhere else. Do you understand me? This phone has to make it to Frédéric---and no one else! I don't trust---no goddamn police department either! Take it now and run with it. Take it to Frédéric and nail Henri's fucking ass to the goddamn wall---Goli."

Smithy dropped to the other side of Timothy and stared at him in disbelief.

"Oh Smithy, I'm so sorry, baby, I love you so much. I was trying to be true to you. I swear to hell I was. You are too damn good of a person for me. I was---tempted and I couldn't be true to you!

Timothy pleaded with his last breath until his eye lowered and closed.

Timothy's left hand fell open just as the paramedics arrived at his side. His bloody cell phone slipped from his sticky hands and dropped into my lap. I looked down at it in disbelief and grasped it with all of my being. It had just become the skeleton key to Henri Lepan's entire empire and suddenly the most valuable thing in my world.

Smithy lost it and started bawling. She threw herself over Timothy's unconscious body until the paramedics pulled her away.

"It's okay, my love, stay with us, darling. Don't leave me, Timothy. Please baby, don't die! I need you! " Smithy was wailing and almost out of her mind, as the paramedics loaded Timothy's bullet ridden body onto a gurney and rolled him out of the room onto the elevator.

As the blood stained doors of the elevator closed I noticed Frédéric glancing at me from inside with a surprised look. I was suddenly alone in the hallway holding Timothy's cell phone tightly in my hand as I ran for the emergency exit and headed down the dirty stairway.

My mind was whirling with images of everything that had happened to us over the last 48-hours, as I raced down the steps to the exit. So much had to be done as I thought of my sweet Danni and my dear sister at the castle, probably wondering what in the hell was happening.

As I left the ground floor emergency exit of the Tablemate Inn, I was shocked to find a huge crowd shuffling around the sidewalks and streets. Police cars, emergency vehicles and fire engines cluttered the streets all the way from the inn to the theatre and beyond. I saw Big Ben in the distance trying to keep his anxious patrons at bay.

The police had set up extra lights to illuminate the entire area while officers cordoned off the front of the inn with crime scene tape.

I looked around for Frédéric but he was nowhere to be found. I wasn't even sure that he had even made it out of the building as I blindly moved through the crowd searching for a place to hide. As I was making my way through the throngs of onlookers my eyes ironically landed on Ari. She was standing alongside the crowd of onlookers, on the other side of the street, calmly smoking a cigarette.

When Ari's eyes locked in on mine, she casually dropped her cigarette on the ground and then slowly started walking towards me. I turned in the opposite direction and started to run.

Just as I was about to cross a major intersection a black Ford Town Car containing the four thugs we had tangled with earlier, passed right by me. The bald man, now with extensive facial injuries, saw me as he was resting his head against the window. I made a beeline to the other side of the street, just as the car slammed on its brakes and began spinning its tires in reverse.

I was now on the run, and being chased by both Ari and Henri's thugs as I stuffed Timothy's blood stained cell phone into my hand bag and ran for my life.

Chapter 68

GOLAREH: THE BUMP, LIFT AND SLIP

3:05 a.m. – Oxford Station, United Kingdom

I was fueled by the force of terror as I ran through the dark, early morning streets of Oxford. I crossed Frideswide Square, adjacent to the Saïd Business School on Oxford University's western campus, and continued north. The "square", as it's called, is actually triangular and once served as my old smoking hangout back when I was a student in my early twenties. Even though I was familiar with the area, I felt no element of safety.

My boots pounded the concrete as I ran as fast as I could to escape the killers behind me. Killers they most certainly were, as I had witnessed two of them in action. I found myself crying out loud while I ran through the darkness. I was so very sure that I was going to be shot, just as the confused hotel manager and Timothy had been.

The Town Cars that I had seen earlier, along with Ari, were somewhere close behind, but I refused to look back as I ran down the adjacent streets towards the Oxford Railway Station. The bloody images of the evening blended in my mind as I played back the unnerving sounds of those horrible gun shots. I had been so dazed after Heath took a blast to his back that I completely forgot that I had stuffed the Glock 17- 9mm pistol into my handbag until I felt it slamming against my hip as I jumped the curb and sprinted down Cornmarket Street.

I'm sure that the young bald thug with the smashed face and broken teeth hadn't forgotten about his ill-placed firearm, after his partners had pulled him from Smithy's flowerbed. It wasn't until I reached the entrance of Oxford Station that I felt safe enough to stop and catch my breath. My mouth was dry and my throat and lungs were burning in pain from my long distance run.

The building was mostly empty as I entered the quiet Oxford station and headed for the woman's restroom. It was 3:20 a.m. when I opened the door of the stall, closed the filthy lid of the toilet and locked the door. The possibility of being relaxed enough to even pee was out of the question, as I lifted my feet to the top of the seat, pulled my knees against my chest and began to cry. Every horrifying image in my mind had to be tended to before I could go any further.

The door to the restroom opened and the sound of a woman's heels entered the lone restroom and opened the stall door next to mine. Whoever the woman was, she was wearing dress heels, not boots, so I ruled out Ari as the woman next to me.

Once she locked her door, I took it as my cue to leave mine, so I dropped down off the seat, flushed the toilet, and left the stall. I walked over to the sink and looked at my face in the mirror. I looked dreadful; my hair was a complete mess and my face still had blotches of Timothy's dried blood all over it. There was not much I could do to make myself look even halfway presentable, so I just rinsed my face off with some cold water and hoped for the best.

The toilet flushed in the stall and the door opened as I was drying my face with a paper towel. She was a pretty woman and most likely an undergraduate-coed from the university. I was too exhausted to even consider why such a pretty girl was alone at the train station so early in the morning. Perhaps she was there to pick up someone from an arriving train. She approached the sink next to mine and noticed that I was a wreck.

"Are you quite alright, my dear," she asked, as she glanced at me with her pretty face and caring eyes.

"Oh, yes, thank you."

"I do hope so, it's dreadfully late and you appear to be, shall I say, a bit frazzled."

"I'm fine--- it's just been a very long day."

"Well---do be careful, miss, this is not the safest place to be at this time of the morning."

"Yes, indeed. Yes---and thank you."

I quickly gathered up my belongings and headed for the door. "But---thank you, so much for caring, dear."

I left the restroom and ordered a cup of black coffee and a bran muffin. I found a quiet booth where I could sit and collect myself. I grabbed my phone from my pocketbook and sent a single text message to all parties concerned, telling them where I was and that I was safe for the moment.

A train arrived and suddenly the station was alive with activity, as people lined up at the counters and ordered coffee and pastries.

"Holy shit! What a fucking horrible day it's been." I whispered under my breath, as I retrieved Timothy's bloodstained cell phone from my pocketbook. I placed it on the table in front of me and just stared at it.

"Oh god---why did I ever ask you to get involved with me? My poor, poor Timothy," I softly said. Tears came to my eyes and I was about to cry until I stopped myself for fear of being noticed.

This was not the time or place to mourn, I thought, as I carefully pressed the power button on Timothy's cell phone and was relieved to find that is was still working, even though the battery-power was quite low. I turned the phone back off to conserve power and then haphazardly stuffed Timothy's phone, rather than mine, into the back pocket of my jeans.

I took an extra-large gulp of coffee and accidently inhaled some of it into my lungs. Although I was coughing uncontrollably, the people around me couldn't have cared less. They were all plugged into their own private worlds of laptops, cell phones and digital devices. A murder could have occurred, right then and there, in the center of that very room and there would have been not a single witness.

I surveyed the crowd around me for any sign of Ari or Henri's men and saw neither. It was then I noticed the pretty coed from the ladies' room. She seemed to be studying me intently as if I were in some sort of danger. Perhaps she saw something I didn't see, as she gestured to someone on the other side of the room.

"Goli," came a voice, from the other side of the room near the entrance. "Goli--- over here!" The voice called again, as I spotted Brooke, one of Magda's taxi drivers. For the first time all day I felt a sense of relief.

I was excited to see Brooke as I weaved my way through the crowded terminal towards her. My mind shifted back to Danielle and I imagined the drama playing out at the castle. I thought of my sister, Henri and everything else that had to come together before we could all be together again.

Suddenly, I was pushed by someone on my right. I lost my balance and fell against a person to my left. The person I fell against, ironically, turned out to be the pretty coed.

"Whoopsy daisy---easy there sweetie," she said, as she caught me in her arms and prevented me from falling.

"Oh my, I'm so dreadfully sorry."

I regained my balance and brushed myself off, making sure that I still had my handbag in my possession.

"Excuse me ma'am, but you look so familiar to me. I swear I know you from somewhere, may I ask your name?"

"It's Golareh, but my friends know me as Goli. But, I'm afraid we've never met. Now I really must be going. I'm so sorry for bumping into you just now. Oh, and thank you so much for your concern earlier."

The parking lot, which was empty when I arrived, was full of taxis and busses all creeping towards the loading areas. Brooke's tiny pink cab was parked alone in a taxi-zone with its emergency blinker's flashing. I walked briskly up to the cab and waited for Brooke to unlock the passenger door of the trademark pink Mini-Cooper Clubman.

I dropped into the passenger seat and locked the door immediately. Brooke ran around to her side and jumped into driver's seat and we were off.

"Brooke! I am ever glad to see you!"

I leaned over and kissed her on her cheek. Brooke was another one of the gorgeous survivors on Magda team of hotshot drivers. She sported large golden hoop earrings beneath her ball cap. She had on a pair of tight fitting black jeans and a black tee-shirt with leather driving gloves. She was chewing gum and gripping the steering wheel in the exact same manner as the rest of the drivers on Magda's team.

"Magda sent me--- and guess what? We have seven girls here in Oxford all searching for you guys! Magda just picked up Frédéric and that gorgeous blond officer---Heath! Oh my god, is he ever cute? We're all meeting at the *Attendee* coffee house in 20-minutes."

"That's great, Brooke, but I'm being followed by some really--really bad people, so please be watchful!"

"I've got your back---girl! But guess what? We've already tagged them! "We've got a total of three Ford Town Cars and a white Mercedes all on the field and Magda's running our plays.

"Three Town Cars---you say---and a Mercedes? Goddamn it! Ari must be in her car now!"

I turned and studied the traffic on all four sides.

"Look at me Goli---do I look scared? I can drive the shit out of this car, and I know I can beat their asses on the stretches! So just sit back, relax and enjoy the game!"

The game, I thought, what game?

Brooke reached over and picked up the microphone tethered to her radio and began to speak.

"Brooke to Mobile-Mag?"

"Mobile-Mag here, Brooke, did you pick up the stranded package?" Magda's voice returned, in a relaxed and controlled tone.

"10-4, Mobile-Mag, the package is onboard and we're inbound."

"Roger that."

Suddenly, I heard my phone ringing from within my handbag.

"Now---who in the hell can this this be?"

I opened my handbag and carefully maneuvered my hand around the large pistol until I located my cell phone. I pulled it out and glanced at the name of the incoming caller. It was *Timothy*, and he was somehow calling me from his phone. But that would be impossible because Timothy's phone was in my back pocket.

"Hello," I answered, in a state of confusion. There was a long pause and then the sound of a woman's voice:

"I thought this number might be yours. Is this Goli?"

"Yes, hello, yes this is Goli, who is this?"

"What kind of a stupid name is Goli, anyway?"

"Hello? Who is this?"

"Shut up---you stupid, rich bitch! I'm the person who was so concerned about your welfare at the train station."

Although I recognized the voice her angry tone confused me entirely.

"Oh yes, I remember you, yes—but why are you calling me and how did you get my phone number?"

"Well it turns out I have your fucking, nasty ass phone—you stupid bitch! It's the one all covered in dried blood, or some kind of shit?"

I quickly felt my pants pocket for Timothy's phone and was shocked to find it missing. "Do you have my cellphone miss? Did I somehow lose it?"

"I sure do have your phone, and yes---you did somehow lose it! Goli, Goli, Goli! That sure is one fucking, weird-ass name! Goli!"

"Well, can I come back to the train station and get it from you?"

"You sure can Goli, Goli Goli! Meet me at Frideswide Square at 4:00 a.m. on the fucking dot, Goli! I'll be waiting there for you in that glass shelter in the center of the square. Do you understand me, Goli?"

"Why---yes of course, certainly, I will be there shortly and thank you so much for calling me."

"Oh---and there's more thing, Goli! Bring along £2000.00 cash! Do you understand me---bitch? I'll give back you back your bloody-ass phone when you hand over £2000.00 British fucking Pounds. Cash only, bitch! You bring me the cash, and I give you this nasty ass phone back to you."

Chapter 69

HOMAYRA: POWER CORRUPTS

3:24 a.m. Central Ward - Upper Great Hall

The party atmosphere was in full throttle as the rookie officer pushed us along though the drunken crowd in the great hall, with his eyes nervously darting from side to side and his pistol visible to everyone.

"Hey girls—what did you get busted for —being too dang sexy?" asked a drunk wearing an overstuffed pinstripe suit. He rose to his feet and approached the anxious guard. "Hey junior---what's with the gun? Listen here---whatever---in the hell, these sexy ladies are under arrest for, I will gladly pay their bail!"

"Please sir, this is of none of your concern. These ladies are under house arrest, please sir, step aside!"

"Sonny, who in the hell do you think you're talking to here? I'm telling you--- I want to pay their bail."

Two additional officers arrived at the scene, along with their highly irritated commanding officer: *J'esperes que tu n'osera plus brandir ton arme devant nos invités, espèce de fou. Remets ton pistolet dans sa poche immédiatement. C'est moi qui prends les choses en main dés cet instant, tu es idiot! — Don't you ever brandish your firearm in front of our guests you stupid fool! Put your gun in your holster this instant. I will take it from here, you idiot!*

"Now move along ladies, just do as I say," the tall ranking officer ordered, as he shoved Zooli and me towards the exit.

In the middle of the room I saw another officer struggling with an angry woman in the middle of a crowd of hungry onlookers. It was Danielle and she was far from cooperating.

"Get---your goddamn hands off me--- you fat fuck! Hey, everyone, this officer's manhandling me!"

"Sir, I was just trying to retrieve the lady's cell phone, but she started to act all out of friggen control. She's one of ours, sir---and she just bit me on my damn arm!"

"Miss, cell phones are prohibited on the castle grounds; you should know that by now! Now do as my officer ordered and hand over that phone!"

"Yeah---that's right; give me your damn phone---bitch!"

The pinstripe drunk, who was watching the action unfold, jumped to the center of the conflict. "Hey! --- Just what in the hell is this idiot trying to do with this fine lady here? Calling her all of these horrible names? I want to know what the hell is going on here. I happen to know the Minister of Trade personally, and I'm sure he would be surprised to see this young lady being treated in such a manner."

"Please sir, I told you---this is NONE of YOUR concern. These ladies are ours! Now back off!"

"What did you just say to me, you little shitwad? And what do you mean by--- she's one of yours? Do you actually think you own these ladies?"

"Get back---all of you! You, sir---are interfering with police business!" bellowed the senior officer.

"Police business---are you kidding me? Do you fashion yourself as some sort of real cop? Don't make me laugh, you fool, or I might wet my pants. You're nothing but a goddamn night watchman who's about to lose his job! Do you see that elegant charmer standing over there by the bar? Well that's Director-General Claude Valles, are you even aware of who in the hell he is---you little prick? That man, my little deputy friend, is the highest ranking police officer on the National Gendarmerie. He has more than 95,000 men reporting to him! I think it's high time that you and he get acquainted---don't you? Hey Claude! ----Claude, come over here for a second, this little nimrod says that he works for you!"

The ranking officer quickly turned, corralled his men, and began barking orders: "Come along men; let's get these ladies out of here---Now! Move it!—Move it!"

The incensed, pinstriped man could no longer hold back his rage. He snatched a cocktail tray full of drinks from a nearby waitress and smashed it over the top of the senior officer's head, dropping him to his knees.

Pandemonium ensued as fists, feet, knees, chairs and tables overwhelmed the officers, forcing them to the floor where they were punched, beaten, kicked and bitten. The three of us saw our opportunity to flee and we took it.

The youngest officer ran past us with a nasty bloody nose and look of dread. He pulled a fire alarm and a chorus of sirens and red lights charged the castle environment to emergency status.

The three of us ran for temporary refuge in the service hallways on the eastern side of the castle where Danielle said that she remembered being before.

"That's it! That's same room that Goli and I hid in, back in the day. Follow me!" Danielle led us to what looked like an observation room with a one-way glass window. "Holy shit, this is it! I can't believe it! Goli and I once hid in here when we were kids!"

The room was filled with boxes of cleaning supplies, paper towels and miscellaneous plumbing parts. Danielle locked the door behind us and we all settled down in front of the one-way glass and watched people scurrying about in the alley outside.

"That was the old parking garage across the alley there," said Danielle, as she moved her face closer to the one-way glass.

"There was a restroom just up that ramp on the left where we would hide out and change clothes. We were just kids back then, what did we know, but some of the shit that we saw in this alley---oh my god."

"Danni, is Miss Cathy safe?" Zooli asked.

"She woke up and demanded to be taken to the horses. Becker took her straight to the stables. Listen to this, Zooli; she had no idea where she was and why she was wearing a dress! I felt so bad for her."

"Oh god, Danni, I was going out of my mind with worry! But as long as she's with the horses, I'm sure she'll be okay. She won't remember any of tonight, trust me," Zooli said.

"Oh, and get this, that guard that caught me, stole her goddamn cheese cakes---the bastard!"

"Danni---Danni, were you able to reach Richard?" I asked.

"Yep--- he said he will be at the airstrip at 5:00 a.m. Oh, and I did tell Becker what you said about the hounds."

The fire alarm stopped as the three of us remained in the office and waited for things to settle down. Ten minutes passed before we were on our way to our next hiding spot in the restroom in the old parking garage. Piece by piece, we planned to slowly extricate ourselves from the castle.

What was once the main parking garage is now used as a maintenance garage for all of the landscaping equipment. We hurried up the concrete ramp only to find the restroom locked. When suddenly:

"Put your hands up ladies! Over your head and turn around slowly," an anxious voice blasted from behind. "I'm warning you, I will shoot you if you make one false move!" It was the young officer and he looked as if he'd been through the night of his life. "I mean it ladies---I will pull this trigger!"

The officer looked terrible: dried blood was caked on his shirt, he was sporting a black eye and he was suffering from a severely bloody nose. He called his commanding officer on his lapel microphone. "Officer Wilson here---sir, I'm reporting from the first floor of the maintenance shed. I've apprehended the escapees and need an immediate assist." His attention reverted back to us. "You ladies are in a lot of trouble, I'll tell you that. This night has just been unbelievable!"

After his call Officer Wilson looked relieved but blood was freely flowing from his nostrils onto his coat, shirt and tie.

"My dear officer, your poor nose is bleeding. Here, please let me help----," I said, as I lowered my hands and began to open my hand bag for a handkerchief.

"Keep your damn hands up, lady, and don't try anything or I swear I'll----,"

"Sir, she's only trying to help you. There's no call for you to be so angry with her," Danielle said.

"Oh---no need to be angry? I may lose my damn job after tonight, and I've only been on duty for a week! All because of the three of you! Stealing food and trying to escape! Now shut up and keep your damn hands above your head!"

Two police golf carts rolled around the far corner of the castle and approached us.

"Over here sir," Officer Wilson yelled, while waving them in. "I just caught them, sir, they were trying to hide in the maintenance shop. Be careful, sir, one of them just tried to reach in her purse for something."

"Jesus Christ---Wilson, don't tell me these ladies beat you up? I'll tell you, Wilson, you beat it all! Do you know that? Getting beat up by a damn woman? Now get the hell out of my sight, you little pussy. I swear, Wilson; you Americans are a weak bunch. Officer Smith, get this asshole to the infirmary before he bleeds out in front of us all, can you do that for me---Smith?"

Smith and Wilson peeled away from the scene and left the three of us with the three of them. The officers appeared strangely off-purpose, as they scanned our bodies with their lurking eyes.

"You ladies are the property of the castle and are never allowed to leave the grounds for any reason," the senior officer said, as he approached the three of us and moved around to the rear of Danielle. "And capturing you is exactly what makes my job interesting."

Mesdames, je voudrais voir vos jolis sexy bras bien en haut sur la tête! - *Keep those sexy arms up high over your heads, ladies!* Another officer surveyed Zooli's body with the beam of his flashlight and a dirty smile.

"Apparently you ladies are nothing but petty thieves," the senior officer said, while leaning over and appraising Danielle's rear end. "Damn, I don't know where the man upstairs finds you bitches, but he must have the corner on the market. *Objects* are what the man upstairs calls these beautiful ladies. Do you know that, Murphy, fucking objects? Well I like those objects right there----a whole lot," the senior officer said, as he studied Danielle's breasts.

"You touch me and I'll kick the ever living shit out of you," Danielle, said as I shot her a signal to settle down.

"Oh, aren't you the feisty one here," the senior officer said, as he spun her around to face her. "A sexy little nigger with an attitude, I like that! We don't get many nigger bitches around here, so tonight must be my lucky night."

"Officer Murphy, don't you think some interrogation is in order?"

"Oh---yes sir, very much in order!"

"So this is what it's all about? You assholes actually think that we are property of this damn castle, oh—my—god, this is fucking unbelievable! Well we are not property!" Danielle charged, as she shoved the senior ranking officer against the wall. The third officer charged forward and grabbed me by the arm.

"Will you all calm down? You will have plenty of time to prove to us who you really are---and what your strong points are. Now you listen to me you little bitch! Do you know what this is?" the officer asked, as he pulled his pistol from his holster and held it in front of my face.

Danielle glanced at me and officer with a look of helplessness. "Please sir! I meant no harm."

"Now you ladies, along with this hot black number, are going to do exactly what we tell you to do--- or I'm going to put a bullet in the brain of this sexy little piece of ass, right here," said the large officer pointing the barrel of his gun directly at the center of my eyes.

"Now come with us ladies, we're about to put you all back on the clock!"

"My god, talk about fine fringe benefits," said the senior officer, as the three officers marched us up the ramp into the maintenance area.

Each officer quickly claimed his prisoner, with the senior officer selecting Danielle, Officer Murphy snatching up Zooli and the third and largest officer training the barrel of his revolver to the base of my neck.

"Now you ladies can make this difficult, in which case Officer Wesson over there, will blow a tiny hole into the side of that Egyptian bitch's head; or you can all relax and enjoy what we have planned for you," said the commanding officer.

"Officer Wesson, why don't you start by asking your prisoner exactly where in Egypt she was purchased from? You know I have a nose for accents," said the lead officer, as he kissed Danielle on her neck. Come to think of it, I've had at least nine--- no make that ten, Egyptian bitches during my tenure here at the castle and I must say that they were all pretty amazing against the ropes."

"Uh---listen bitch, I think you had better tell my commander where you're from. And may I add that you have the most amazing lips I have ever seen. I can't wait for you to wrap those lips of yours around my cock. Now, tell the superior officer where you are from!"

"Iran," I quietly answered.

"What's that you said, Miss Egypt? Speak up, I didn't quite get that?"

"I said, I am from Iran."

"Well, holy hell, did you say that you are a goddamn Iranian? Well I'll be god damned! You will be a first for me. I don't think they've ever had any Iranian bitches here, but I might be wrong. Hey, Murphy, have you ever fucked an Iranian before?"

"Nope, can't say that I ever have."

Officer Murphy was grinning from ear to ear as we rounded the corner and entered the second level and proceeded up the stairs to the third and final level.

"Well tonight's our lucky night, gentleman. Because, tonight is Persian night and we've got us a little black pepper too!"

Chapter 70

GOLAREH: MIND SHATTERING

Oxford, U.K. - 3:30 a.m.

The one night to be robbed by a common pickpocket had to fall on this very night. I was being followed by at least six of Henri's henchmen and Ari, a woman who had probably lost track of the number of people she had killed.

At first, I couldn't even believe it actually happened until Brooke informed me that I was almost asking for it. "But why---why would she take my cell phone and not my handbag? I mean, just how valuable can a cell phone be to anybody?"

"Well, that all depends on how valuable that cell phone is to you? And I hate to be critical, Goli, but why did you put Timothy's cell phone in the back pocket of your jeans? You should never have anything of value in your back pocket---especially at a train station in the middle of the night!"

"I wasn't thinking straight, Brooke--- I know! I meant to put my phone in my back pocket and Timothy's into my purse! Damn it!"

"Well ----now that woman is holding Timothy's cell phone prisoner and demanding a ransom from you. I hate to say this, baby doll, but you asked for it." Brooke said, as she changed course to Frideswide Square and radioed Magda: "Brooke to Mobile-Mag."

"Go ahead Brooke," Magda responded.

"Change advisory. Occupant clipped. We're outbound to Frideswide Square to meet up with an Artful Dodger at 400 hour."

"10-4. Ginger, Yolanda, Samantha, Pink, and Misty provide a false-nine at Frideswide Square for Brooke who is meeting up with Artful Dodger at 400 hour. Magda out!"

"Who is this Artful Dodger character you're referring to and what's a false-nine."

"Haven't you read Oliver Twist? Well, we call your slick pickpocket an Artful Dodger and the false-nine is the play strategy we use for dealing with this sort scenario. This happens to our clients all of the time. You see, Goli, we talk in code, because we never know who might be monitoring this frequency."

"Don't beat yourself up, Goli, that woman at the station does this sort of thing all of the time. She works with others and they have their scam down to a science. They probably saw you looking all nervous and scared. You were probably clutching Timothy's cell phone as if it were the most important thing to you in the world. Am I right?" Brooke asked, as we quickly buzzed through the dark side streets of West Oxford.

"Okay Goli, we have a situation here and this the way it's going to play out. Think of Timothy's cell phone as the soccer ball, which Artful Dodger possesses. We have other opponents on the field but we can't get a reading on them just yet. By those other players, I'm referring to Henri's men and the bitch in the white Mercedes. We are simply two teams on a huge soccer field." Brooke checked her rearview mirror for anything out of the ordinary.

"But, Brooke, this isn't a soccer game and those people are cold blooded murderers!" I was now becoming sick with fear.

"Oh but Goli, that's where you are way wrong. Right now, you and I are playing as centre-forwards to Magda, while Pink and Samantha are inverted wingers, Ginger and Yolanda are supporting-strikers, and Misty is our set-back striker."

Brooke was actually smiling with excitement; but everything she was telling me was going through one ear and coming right out the other.

"Look Goli, I know none of this makes much sense to you right now, but we must have a play strategy because our opponents sure as hell do. How do you think we've been able to stay in business all of these years. We play these games every single day on the streets of London. It's our livelihood. If it's not the thieves and thugs after us, then it's the competition that will stop at nothing to take advantage of us and run us out of business. Girl, we play to win! Now just sit back and relax and tell me where to stop to get some cash for Artful Dodger."

I had a total of £46 in my change purse, while Miss Artful Dodger was demanding £2,000 in the space of twenty minutes? There was no way I was going to be able to withdraw that much money in a single transaction, much less multiple ones from different machines. I figured that I could withdraw some money from National Westminster Bank and perhaps the same amount from HSBC, which were both on the way, but certainly not £2,000. Any cash in hand would just have to suffice as the minutes flew by.

Brooke dropped me off at the south end of Frideswide Square and quickly drove off. The square was nothing more than a glorified bus stop with several small trees growing through small cutouts in the concrete. It was dark and quiet, with no one around, as I walked towards the glass shelter near the center of the square.

It was now 4:12 a.m. and I feared that my tardiness might have ruined the deal. I stood under the shelter and lit up a much needed cigarette while I waited for my malicious scam artist to arrive. My hands were shaking as I took long drags from my cigarette and desperately tried to calm my nerves. I felt exhausted from the long day and fatigue was quickly setting in.

At 4:20 a.m., I heard someone whistle from the corner of the large tan building across the street on the far end of the square. I flipped my cigarette into an ashtray and proceeded in that direction.

The streets were dark as I walked beneath the tall light posts and across a five lane thoroughfare towards a lone female figure standing under a street lamp. The closer I got to the person the more I became confused by the entire situation.

She looked as if she was no more than 21-years-old with beautiful shoulder length blonde hair. She was wearing a conservative red dress with practical black shoes. Her face projected an innocence that set me back. She resembled a sorority sister with bright friendly eyes, straight white teeth and an almost childlike expression.

She was smiling at me as I approached and that confused me even further. I was beginning to wonder if she was the wrong person entirely.

"Do you have my phone?" I politely asked, as I stepped up to her.

Her pleasant smile continued to puzzle me as she appeared to welcome me in. Perhaps I misunderstood this young woman's intent and the whole thing was nothing but a bad joke.

"Did you bring the money?" she politely asked.

"I did---I did, but I'm afraid that I was unable to get the full amount that you requested, I do hope that is alright? The ATM has limits you know? I could only withdraw half of what you asked for."

As I was pulling the bills from my wallet, I noticed the woman staring at me with a look of sadness and for a second I felt sorry for her. "My dear, why are you doing this, are you in some sort of trouble? If something's wrong then perhaps I can help you another way? You shouldn't have to resort to this sort of thing?"

"Wrong! And shut your fucking mouth, bitch! I told you £2K and I meant £2 fucking K! So I'm calling the deal off---right now---bitch!"

Her tone was so harsh and her actions so counter to appearance that it shook me. She quickly turned on her heals and began walking away.

"Wait! Please! Come back! I'm sorry! I can get more money when the banks open in just a few hours! Please, I need my phone back!"

"The deal is off, bitch! I told you, Goli! I wanted £2K in cash and nothing less---you rich bitch! Now---you owe me £3K! Do you understand me, bitch, the price has just gone up to £3K"

She was now running away from me and I began to chase after her. "Wait, wait---please don't leave! What's wrong with you? I'll get you the money when the banks open!"

As I was running I noticed a white Mercedes-Benz parked on the other side of the street. The vehicle was empty and appeared to be misaligned with the side of the curb with the driver's side door slightly ajar. At that moment I saw the platinum-blonde killer standing on my side of the street about 9 meters down range from the unknowing Artful Dodger. It was Ari and although one of her arms was behind her back, I was convinced that she was fully armed and extremely dangerous.

On impulse I turned and ran in the opposite direction, causing the pickpocket to turn back and watch me in amazement. Both women were now chasing after me with the confused pickpocket being the only one unaware of the third party.

"Hey! Goli---stop running! Where are you going? I was just kidding! Don't you want your phone back? Stop Goli! Come back!"

I picked up speed and turned the corner, gaining distance between the two of them.

"Hey Goli, it's okay, I'll take whatever you have. Stop! Stop Goli, I just really need some cash badly, I'm sorry!"

I turned and watched her turn the corner and run toward me with a look of desperation. Her right arm was extended in front of her and she was waving Timothy's cell phone from side to side. Ari had not yet arrived at the scene as I boldly advanced on the hysterical pickpocket.

"Stop this---young lady! We are both being followed! You don't have any idea what's going on here---do you? You need to get out of here this second---before you get yourself killed!"

Ari rounded the corner and was casually walking in our direction as the pickpocket starred at me in a state of confusion. She was completely unaware that Ari was even behind her preparing for her next move.

"Get down on the ground! Get down---you fool! Please---do I say! Now! There's someone after us both!"

"Goli---I'm not going to hurt you! Just give me whatever money you have and this whole thing will be over."

Ari was now standing about eight meters behind the pickpocket with her legs straight and her feet a shoulder-width apart. Her body weight was distributed evenly with her back bent slightly backwards. Her head was erect and her arms were fully extended with both hands wrapped around the grip of her large caliber, single-action revolver.

"Get down!" I screamed, as I ran toward the clueless female and dropped to the ground.

"Please---do as I say! Hit the ground!" I ordered as I crawled on my knees towards the front of her pretty red dress.

A deplorable explosion filled the dark square with impressive decibels as the flash from Ari's large caliber gun caused the surprised pickpocket's eyes to widen just before a single 124 Gr/9mm bullet penetrated the back of her skull. In what seemed like a stretched-out second, I watched as the once a beautiful woman's face changed into a bloody tunnel, and a bullet ripped through her skull and exploded through the front of her face, covering me in her blood, brains and bone fragments.

The force of the impact heaved her lifeless body towards me as if she had been struck an automobile. Her distorted and incomplete body collided with mine as we both hit the pavement. I struggled to breathe and my ears were ringing as the smoke cleared. I could see Ari slowly walking towards our horrid death scene while pulling back the trigger on the revolver. She appeared completely relaxed and was wearing a winner's smile.

I have no idea why my thoughts went this direction, but as she pointed the long barrel of her gun at my head, I couldn't help but admire the smooth quality and mechanical workmanship of her firearm. For some very strange reason my brain refused to let me panic as I laid there under the bloody corps of that pitiful young woman and held my breath for my execution.

Ari squeezed off a final round which resulted in only the sound of a single snap of the trigger, striking the center of a spent percussion cap. The dead girl's hand was ironically still clutching Timothy's cell phone as I snatched it from her disgusting fingers and scuttled out from underneath her. I struggled to my feet and ran off.

I knew full well that Ari was a highly trained marksman who rarely miscalculated the number of live rounds in her pistol. But the blunder of running out of bullets was enough to humiliate even the most highly trained assassin. I could hear her cursing out loud as she ejected her spent rounds on to the concrete and reloaded.

"Okay Goli, run along, you spoiled little Iranian bitch! Because I'm coming for you, my little superstar! You have something that I want and I will get it! Run along for now, you hot little bitch!"

I ran like a mad-woman down the street, taking every opportunity to confuse the efficient predator behind. I weaved around corner after corner of dark buildings until I found myself standing directly in front of a pink taxi cab which had come to a screeching halt.

My heart went through my throat as I turned and saw yet another one of Magda's taxi cabs. This time it was Ginger who was at the wheel of her cab signaling for me to get in. I threw myself into the cab as she starred at the tiny pieces of bone fragments covering my hair, face and blood stained clothing.

"Are you okay, Goli, were you hit?" Ginger jammed down on the gas and blasted us forward.

"I think I'm okay, Ginger, but I don't know--- Ari just killed that poor girl back there! She was just a kid and had no clue what she was doing. Ari's a fucking monster, I'll tell you; it was so horrible! That poor kid had no idea what she was in the middle of."

I was yelling and gripping Timothy's cell phone with all of my strength as I felt the walls of my mind closing in on me.

"Goli, lean over and put you head between your knees before you faint." Ginger moved my pocket book from my lap and placed her hand on the back of my neck, moving my head forward and over.

"Give me the phone and I'll put it in your handbag," she ordered, as I handed her Timothy's blood stained phone and fought to keep myself from passing out.

"Oh my god this is horrible, I can't take any more of this, Ginger."

I could actually taste what must have been human brains on my lips, as I inhaled the terrible scent of the bloody bone fragments still clinging to my face and clothing.

"Take some long deep breaths, girl! It's going to be okay. We're still in the game. Breathe in deep, girl," Ginger said, as she accelerated down the dark road with the engine roaring next my head.

Oh---there's that damn game reference again! This is no goddamn game! I thought, as Ari's demonic voice repeated her warning to me over and over: *I'm coming for you my little superstar! Run along, you little hot bitch!*

"Deep breaths Goli, relax, girl. Take deep breaths."

I took one final deep breath and came dangerously close to vomiting as I slowly gained enough confidence to raise my head and glance out of the windshield and spot two sets approaching headlights.

"Oh my god, those are Henri's men, watch out Ginger!"

Ginger showed little concern as she down shifted into a high performance gear. "Well how do you like that? It appears Henri's boys are heading for the wrong side of the playing field!"

Ginger had an even larger smile as we shot past both automobiles at a speed of 153 kph.

Now in full control, Ginger grabbed her microphone and reported our status: "Ginger to Mobile-Mag."

"Mobile-Mag here, talk to me."

"I'm cutting infield to space-left and maintaining our false-nine. Artful Dodger was removed from the field-of-play and we are now in possession of the ball—over."

"10-4 Ginger. Team members: reset your formation to conventional set-up and proceed to home-field. Good job, girls, and prepare for advancing opponents."

I rolled down the window and leaned my face into the cool morning wind to dry my tears.

"Oh my God, Ginger, you guys are something else. What's the play now?" I asked, as I took a deep breath and slowly closed the window.

"Magda wants a home-field advantage and is directing us back to Brixton. She expects a fight and would rather do it on our own turf than here. You okay, Goli? Why don't you close your eyes and try to relax?" Ginger said, as she winked at me and patted me on my knee.

I leaned my head back and took a look at Ginger as my heartrate began to normalize. She was a beautiful young woman with flowing long brown hair and the face of a fashion model. She had once made the cover of the

Sports Illustrated Swimsuit issue and was the last girl to be saved by Magda before Danielle came along.

She noticed me studying her and glanced over at me as a swath of her beautiful hair fell over her right eye. "What, Goli, what are you looking at?" she asked, as she gripped the steering wheel and aggressively chewed her gum.

She had on a gray tank top which exposed her muscular arms which would have made any man envious. "What wrong girl, why are you looking at me like that?"

"Guess what Ginger, I'm all out of tears and done with crying like a damn baby. But---you girls are the best to me, do you know that? I love you all so much."

And sure enough, I began to cry.

"I thought you said that you were done crying?"

"I know---right? But at least now I'm crying with a sense of relief."

I let it go, as if I were the biggest cry-baby in all of the United Kingdom.

With all seven pink taxis moving in an orderly formation, we rapidly traveled back to the home field of Brixton with our dangerous opponents not far behind.

Chapter 71

HOMAYRA: THE HOG'S BREATH

*The world, that understandable and
lawful world, was slipping away.*

— WILLIAM GOLDING, *LORD OF THE FLIES*

I was quite sure that Zooli had a higher level of receptive consciousness than most humans do. She was able to witness consciousness within the minds of the creatures that she interacted with on a daily basis. From horses to dogs, cats, foxes, coyotes and snakes, Zooli appeared to have a kinship with them all. But when it came to the lower orders of nature, Zooli seemingly fell short, as Officer Murphy pulled her dress down to her ankles and threw her against the ropes of the makeshift fighting arena.

"Oh! Ho-ho-ho! Now that---was a good move, Officer Murphy! Did I not teach you that one?" The commander cheered as Zooli's feet became tangled in her clothing and she tumbled to the mat.

It pained me to witness this strong, beautiful person with such powerful qualities being overcome by such a dreadful force. I was never worried about Zooli's welfare when she was in the midst of chaotic animals both large and small. But Officer Murphy was not just some large animal; he was a loathsome freak of nature.

"Well thank you sir! You know, I think you might have taught me that move!" Murphy sneered.

I struggled to break myself free and rush to side of Zooli, but froze when I felt the cold barrel of a gun enter the center of my ear canal and press against my skull.

"Now don't you even fucking think about fighting me--- you little cunt, or I will be forced to lose my evening's fun with you and blow your god-damn brains out," said Officer Wesson, as he dug the barrel deeper into the base of my ear canal.

The top floor of the maintenance garage had been cordoned off to allow only foot traffic and was known by only a select few of the highest levels of the security staff. Large pallets of grass seed and bulky bags of fertilizer formed a private secondary enclosure which surrounded some sort of deviant playground.

The officer's chortling began to resemble the sound of grunting hogs as they nudged Zooli and me towards an elevated boxing ring. The fighting ring was covered with filthy mats which reminded me of a blood-spattered butcher block. Thick ropes, which were meant for both barriers and torture, were attached to posts on each corner of the ring.

Hanging above us were articles of discarded clothing. Stretched stockings, torn bras and soiled panties, filled the ceiling with symbols of past conquests. The room reeked of urine, beer, body fluids and tobacco.

The concrete floor, which surrounded the boxing arena, was littered with bloody gauze, human teeth, beer cans and cigarette butts. Judging by the number of looming spirits in the room, I had the distinct impression that many of our predecessors had never made it out of the room alive.

It was now our turn to be stripped of our clothing and thrown to the center of the melee as Officer Murphy and the commander unfastened their belts and removed their pants and underwear.

"It's time for the fun to begin---ladies," the commander yelled, as he knelt down, dropped his shorts and grabbed Danielle violently by her hair.

Out of a protective response, Danielle lashed out at the commander with the only weapon she had.

"Ouch! ---Did you just bite me you filthy little slut?"

The commander shoved Danielle away and examined the side of his arm, revealing a bright red ring of teeth marks.

"Goddamn it---what is with you people? Do all you niggers bite---you nasty bitch? You are nothing more than a wild animal that needs to be fucking tamed," the commander said he kicked Danielle in the side of her small and feminine ribcage.

"Stop kicking her! Please, stop!" I screamed as I watched my dear, sweet Danni being brutalized.

"Never mind about that nasty bitch, ladies, it's time for us to get down to some serious business!" Announced the commander, as he left Danielle writhing in pain and rushed over to the side lines. He grabbed a metal hammer which was attached to a cord and held it to the side of a large brass bell.

The three of us stared in horror at the commander as he stood on the sidelines gripping his erect penis in one hand and the hammer in the other. As if pretending to be an announcer of a nationally televised boxing match, the commander yelled for the games to begin:

Mesdames et Messieurs! Bon et maintenant, préparez vous, que la lutte commence! —*Ladies and gentleman---Let's get ready to rumble!*

The commander struck the bell with face of the hammer and dove into the center of the ring. Instantly the mayhem began as the three officers pounced on their prey and began wolfing at our souls. The remaining clothing around Zooli's ankles were torn off and discarded over the edge of the ring.

Officer Wesson struck me on the side of my head with the butt of his gun and rendered me temporarily bewildered. His large meaty hands ripped my dress open and down to my waist as his repulsive face leaped to the center of my chest. He groaned with exhilaration as he bit the center of my bra and began chewing on it. His head lashed from side to side, tearing my bra from my body and exposing my vulnerable breasts.

"Oh yeah baby----you're going to get it---because you are one hot little bitch!"

For the first time in my adult life my guardian angel, in Zooli, was missing in action as the revolting body on top of me transitioned into a wild boar. I was being mauled and aggressively pounced upon by a dreadful hog with its enormous snout, huge tusks and disgusting tongue. I lost sight of Danielle and Zooli as the wild boar flipped me over on my stomach and yanked me backwards against his furry hind legs and bot belly.

I pushed myself up on my elbows and glared back at the wild animal, as he slapped my bare rear end and growled at his male counterparts to stay away from his feast. His claws trekked down my bare back and yanked my panties to my knees. Tears were flowing from my eyes as the hog violently spanked the cheeks of my buttocks with the base of its paw as if he were punishing me for blocking him from a much deserved meal.

The center of the ring turned into a power play of perverted brawling as the officers fought to maneuver each one of us into a position of forced copulation. I could hear myself screaming for my life in direct unison with my loved ones, as we struggled to stay alive.

Instead of shouting for help from a godless universe, I pleaded in my native tongue for my parents to come save me: *Madaram – pedaram! Tamana mikone - be dadam berecin! Mano az daste in div nejat bedin! - Mother, father-- please help me! Save me from this beast!*

The voices of our collective screams filled the room with a chorus of horror as each officer struggled to gain control over his captive. Suddenly, however, it seemed that the number of voices in the room outnumbered the collection of humans, causing my captor to sit up on his haunches and take note. "What in the fuck is that?"

The two other hogs stopped what they were doing and squinted over their snouts across the room at two four-legged creatures standing at attention in the entrance way.

Smokey, the lead alpha hound, and Taskmaster, his long-time companion, had entered the room and appeared to be planning out an attack strategy on the three wild hogs. The two large hounds spared little time advancing across the room as the surprised hogs considered their situation.

"Those are goddamn dogs, Murphy! Shoot those fucking things," yelled the commander, as he rolled over on to his side and searched for his holstered firearm. It was now Taskmaster's job to signal the rest of the pack, notifying them that the two leaders had found the mark.

Taskmaster began to yelp and bray madly as he went for the throat of officer Murphy. Smokey went airborne and landed on commander's head driving his powerful jaws around the screaming man's throat. The communication link between the lead hounds was successful as a sea of aggressive hounds filled the room and went to work on the three officers while amazingly singling the three of us out, as being off limits.

Becker's entire pack of 50 hounds were now in full control of the attack domain as the flaying bodies of the three half-naked officers were dragged from the mats and onto the concrete floor.

The face of the commander swept past me with a look of terror as he desperately tried to keep the strong jaws of Taskmaster from piercing his neck. He fell to the floor as the three other officers were consumed in a sea of attacking hounds. Each hound not only gripped and shook the necks of their victims, but growled and fiercely bit all exposed body parts as blood began to paint the color of the battle.

Zooli, Danielle and I rolled around naked on the bloody blue mats watching the feeding frenzy in both shock and awe as the pack of destructive hounds went to work on their prey.

Suddenly, a huge crash on the opposing side of the fertilizer wall caused the make-shift house of torture to collapse and barely miss me, as I rolled out of the way and onto the floor.

A second crash toppled the rest of the wall as the headlights of Becker's foxhound truck advanced on us and came to an abrupt stop. Becker jumped out of the cab and ran to our aid. Several hounds were already surrounding me as if they were trying to warm my naked, bloody body.

"Get in the back of the truck girls---now!" Becker yelled, as he removed his coat and covered Zooli.

Once we were safely on the truck, Becker jumped up onto the fighting ring and looked down on the melee, as the hounds continued to demolish their prey. Becker slowly raised his stag antler hound whistle to his mouth and reluctantly placed it between his teeth. Appearing as if he was struggling to follow the moral rules of right and wrong, Becker removed the whistle from his mouth and openly scowled at the suffering officers on the floor.

"Call them off, Becker! That's enough," I yelled, believing that Becker was going to let the pack of angry hounds complete their kill. "Becker! Stop them! That's enough! Please call them off!"

Finally Becker came to his senses and placed the end of the whistle back in his mouth and sounded off two short tones.

The entire pack immediately disengaged with their targets and stood at attention, smelling the air and listening for their next command. "Up!" Becker ordered, in a clipped, staccato voice. Realizing that we had to make way for the hounds, Danielle, Zooli and I scooted our way to the back of truck bed.

Simultaneously, the entire pack of hounds filled the compartment of the truck and settled themselves around our bodies as if to protect us from another threat. Becker closed the back of the truck and *tended* to the injured officers. After a few minutes and many curse words, Becker returned to the driver's seat, started the engine and slowly backed up and twisted around the obstructions and down the parking levels until we were safely out of the maintenance garage.

Chapter 72

GOLAREH: IMPECCABLE TRANSIT

M40 Highway inbound to Brixton

Possession is paramount when a team wants to score points during competition. The longer either side has possession of the ball, the better their chances are in winning the game. Magda constantly drove that principle into the minds of her girls every single day they took to the streets of London.

Magda likened the game of soccer to the way her drivers should deliver their passengers to their intended destinations and the strategy they employ in order stay alive.

The competition was brutal and filled with angry and often unlawful competitors whose main mission was to eliminate *impeccable transit*. The existence of a fleet of a dozen hot-pink taxi cabs, driven by highly skilled and extremely attractive female drivers, put the fear of God in the competition, whose objective was to maximize their own billable hours. The fact that the drivers were beautiful meant nothing to the angry competition that would stop at nothing to slow them down.

"Cabbies can be a ruthless and sick bunch!" Magda would often say.

In the beginning, customers were captivated by the idea of being picked up by a hot pink taxi cab driven by a gorgeous ex-model. But the excitement soon faded after a few disastrous mishaps made the news all over the

London, describing smashed vehicles, angry competitors, vicious assaults and high-speed chases.

Early on, the all-female taxi service became more of a joke in England's capital city than a legitimate business. False stories of the girls providing more than transportation became rampant. Rumors of sexual benefits, mobile prostitution and everything else went viral in the media, way before the internet was even born.

Several times a week Magda would angrily hang up the phone on adult magazine publishers or creepy movie producers asking for her girls to pose nude in X-rated photo-spreads or be filmed acting out naughty taxicab fantasies.

Local pimps, rich patrons and wealthy business execs tried to cash in on the popularity of this so-called mini-bordello on wheels. It wasn't until Magda went underground into Angell Town's organized crime circuit and called for a meeting with the family heads, that things were finally brought to order. Her dear friends Squirt Terhune, owner of the Hoot & Nanny and Swoop Bennett, a reformed gang leader, arranged for the meeting.

Squirt wasn't actually in the mafia but could have been anytime he wanted to. The crime family considered Squirt a *good-fella* who always paid his bills on time. Swoop, on the other hand, was never formally invited into the family, mainly because he was an Afro-Jamaican, but since he had such a firm grip on the street gangs in Angell Town he was voted in as an honorary member.

The only thing that Magda asked for was to be left alone by the many underling, wannabe pimps, drug dealers and mob startups. She said that she could handle her competition though legitimate means but needed their help in exterminating the local vermin exploiting her girls.

The family respected what Magda had done for so many kids struggling with alcohol and drug addiction and felt it their *moral* obligation to support her. Further Magda knew everything about what was going on in Angell Town and information was considered golden to the mechanics of organized crime. From that meeting forward Magda's pest problem was neutralized.

Magda ordered each girl to adopt her own play strategy when handling her customers in play. She said that the game of soccer dictated that individual skill is vital to winning because of the rapidly changing dynamics of the game. Anything could happen when a player is driving the ball down field; so it is the responsibility of each team member to defend, block, receive and confuse the opposition as best as humanly possible.

The strategy proved to be invaluable as the injuries and near fatal mishaps began to subside. The highly skilled and passionately devoted fleet members also proved to me more professional, efficient, and safer to be with, than their rude and often foul-smelling counterparts.

The clientele of *impeccable transit* matured to only regular customers, mainly consisting of middle-class female professionals. The services of *Impeccable Transit* became in such demand that there was an application process and two-year waiting list to become a valued customer. Although Magda was both loved and hated by some city officials, the majority of the business community considered her to be an incredible businesswoman with a slick service offering.

<hr />

As our six cabs silently traveled from Oxford to Brixton, Magda put the cabs into an inverted W-formation with Magda accommodating one of the two taxis one Kilometer in front of us. Two other cabs cruised slightly behind us, covering our flank, as a lone cab a half-kilometer behind watched our backs. Magda was in the sixth car and was considered the captain and fullback when ever missions were considered treacherous and called for her mobile coaching.

Frédéric had safely reconnected with Heath and Rahda several miles ahead of us. We planned to connect somewhere in the vicinity of Windrush Square near the center of Brixton. The newly renovated square is just beyond Brixton's underground station and sits between Central and Southwest London.

The location is densely populated and tricky to maneuver within. Magda felt especially familiar with the traffic patterns and considered it a perfect place to rendezvous. Most importantly, the square was only 18 kilometers from London's Heathrow Airport where Frédéric and the two officers could catch a flight back to Paris headquarters.

After we had traveled an hour at legal speeds, Yolanda's voice broke radio-silence and woke me from a restful sleep. Yolanda had the position as our sweeper-lookout in the lone car in back of us. It was her job to keep an eye out for approaching invaders.

"Ah---Yolanda to Mobile-Mag--over"

"Go Yoli--over," responded Magda.

"I've got two ---a---make that three inbound black Fords, two-kilometers down range, tailing us on a rapid approach---over."

"Roger that, Yoli. Leftwing, Rightwing, drop back to cover our Sweep-lookout and triangulate---over."

Like fighter pilots, Samantha and Ginger, who were flanking our sides, rapidly dropped back and formed an inverted triangle directly in front of Yolanda.

"Okay, ladies, the ball is now in play. Remember, girls, keep that triangle tight," ordered Magda.

Magda quickly changed her position of being one of the two fullbacks and gradually dropped back in front of the V-formation to gain a better view of the play action.

"Fullback, give me your status," Magda called, as she glanced over at us and pointed at Ginger from her car as she rapidly dropped past us.

"Fullback now in control of ball and waiting on orders, Mobile-Mag--over," Ginger answered, accepting her newly assigned position. She sat up at the wheel and stuffed a fresh stick of gum in her mouth.

"Fullbacks--- increase speed to Brixton borders, prepare for mid-attack---over."

"Roger that, Mobile-Mag," Ginger replied, as she placed the microphone back in its cradle and accelerated ahead of the secondary fullback. "Well, Goli, my dear, let the games begin! You may now have a chance to watch us in action."

"Ginger, exactly what did Magda mean by a mid-attack?"

I unbuckled my seat belt and twisted around to watch the cars in back of us.

"Goli! Secure yourself this instant! And never do that again, do you hear me?"

Ginger's stern order gripped my attention and somewhat embarrassed me.

"I'm sorry, Ginger; I guess I sort of lost my head there for a second!"

"Oh---You'll lose your head alright--- if you're not buckled in and we fail during our attack. Now turn around and keep your eyes on the road in front of us! We don't care where we've been; we only care about where we are going!"

Good life lesson, I thought, as I tightened my seatbelt and took a deep breath.

"Remember Goli, Timothy's cell phone is our proverbial soccer ball and it's my job to drive it and you---down field. When we come within striking distance of Windrush Square, I'm going to attempt to score a goal. When we have all of the drivers in place and the ball is being driven in, we say that we are driving at full-strength. Right now we are at mid-attack, just picking up speed to gain our home field advantage.

Magda will also be covering us on GPS and determining our exact pathway to the destination. She is also the most likely player I will pass the ball to if I fail to hit the target," Ginger said, as she picked up the pace to 128 kph.

"Ginger! What do you mean by *pass the ball*, how do you pass the ball? You don't mean me--- do you?"

"You got it, baby. You are now the ball-in-play, girl, so be prepared to be kicked to Magda! Hang on to your belongings, darling, stay alert, and get ready for some play action.

Chapter 73

GOLAREH: SLIPSTREAMING

"Hands-free girls---and go to seven," Magda ordered.
Ginger opened the glove box and took out two sets of white ear-pods, handing one pair to me. She then plugged both male jacks into her Delcom car-to-car taxi radio and dialed in channel seven, a dedicated frequency originating from the Brixton dispatch office. The play action continued:

"Come on girls, move it! Tighten up that triangle and lock in on your partners--- and ladies, please don't forget to use your obstacles. If you see them--- use them!"

Obstacles to Magda were pieces of trash, tire fragments, loose gravel and water puddles. Anything along the highway that could be could be lifted off the surface of the highway and deposited on the hoods and windshields of the vehicles in back of them.

"Yoli---- give me your status?"

"I've got three, black Ford Town Cars advancing on my ass – hot! Where are my wingers? I need you guys---now!"

Yolanda's shouting unnerved me bit, especially when I heard what sounded like bullets piercing through the glass of her rear window.

"Shit guys! I'm taking on fire back here -- window distorted with a two bullet holes!"

"Climb out of it, Yoli!" Brooke yelled, from her position in front of Yolanda.

"Pull me out of this shit, Magda, goddamn it---they're firing on me---big time!"

"Wingers, I want you to drop back and hug Yolanda's nose! Come on now, girls---get with it!" coached Magda.

Like partnering racers on a high performance track, the two side-wings dropped back to the front of Yolanda's front bumper and formed a tight aerodynamic package.

"Yoo-hoo girls, I'm – ah-- waiting on your collective asses here!" Yolanda yelled.

"What the hell are they doing back there?" I asked, as I watched the action from our vantage point unfold.

"Magda's attempting to set up a slipstream in front of them. She wants to reduce their drag and pull them out of there fast. She gonna boost them out with a drafting column."

"Pull up, Yoli, and tighten that damn triangle—girls! Please, please clean up your driving girls! Hesitation will kill you!" Magda sternly scolded.

Yolanda advanced forward as the two other speeding cars quickly aligned themselves in back of her.

"Okay---I need everyone to push up to 1-4-5! I'm going to draft these girls out of this mess in about 10 seconds."

Magda raised her sunroof upward, creating a slightly larger wind column directly in front of the three vehicles.

All seven taxis were now moving at 145 kmh.

"Okay, Yoli, pull up to lead position--- just a slight bit more. I want to see those big blue eyes of yours! I'm talking to you, Yoli dear; I need you to concentrate."

Suddenly Magda spotted a puddle in the center of the highway and aimed for it. "Hold on, girls, I want to wash those cars in back of us. Here comes a water feature in--- three-two-one---now!"

The tight arrow configuration suddenly grabbed the water source from the highway and pulled it off the road surface and into the air, covering the Fords in a dirty cloud.

"Thank you, girls, every little bit counts!"

The lighting configuration on each Mini-Cooper made it easy to distinguish between the girls and the Fords on their tails. Two main headlights on each side of the grill, followed by two touring lamps slightly lower down and dual amber fog-lights all blazed a pathway in front of them.

"Come on girls---On my count---three-two-one--- Draft! Go—go—go—go—go!"

Like a slingshot the four taxis, with Magda in the lead position, blasted forward and past our car at an incredible rate of speed.

"Good job---girls," Magda said, as the four cars settled in around us. How much did we gain that one, Ginger?" Magda asked.

"I'm thinking about a half-kilometer, Magda."

Magda's slipstreaming stunt on the A40 Westway, bought us just enough distance from Henri's men, to provide Magda with the confidence to order Ginger and me off at the first Brixton exit.

Through the sunroof, I noticed the welcoming evidence of dawn, providing my dark world with hope. I was thankful to see a new day emerging, but I felt weighted down with sorrow over Timothy. Perhaps when the sun comes up, my world would look a little brighter.

It felt like days since I had gotten a good night's sleep and I was covered in dried blood from three human casualties. But I felt exhilarated by witnessing the performance of these highly trained women. Never before had I seen such a well-choreographed team of drivers executing their moves with such precision. My heart glowed with pride for these fine women who were risking their lives for the benefit of my family.

I was confident that Timothy had successfully recorded a vital conversation between and Henri and Santo; I could imagine the excitement in his eyes. The mere fact that the recording had been done at all meant that Homayra, Zooli and Danielle must have done their jobs as well; but were they safe and out of harm's way? I hadn't a clue.

Ginger and I separated from the rest of the team at the Westway highway and hugged the inside corner of the turnabout on to the Earl's Court Road exchange. As we entered West Brixton a large flock of pigeons burst into the early morning sky as if they were fleeing from the mouth of a pink monster.

With only 11 kilometers to go before Windrush Square, Ginger eased the car down to legal speed, as I removed an ear pod and placed a call to Frédéric.

Frédéric picked up on the second ring, under a weak frequency.

"Frédéric can you hear me?"

"Goli, we—at-----rush square, where are..."

"We've got a bad connection, Frédéric! We're about eleven kilometers out, coming in from the west. Where exactly are you?"

"We are in front of the Electric on Town Hall----"

Frédéric' voice was broken, cracked and sputtering.

"Say again --- I can't understand you. You're where? You're breaking up badly!"

"I said -we---are at—Electric Brixton on Town ---Parade! We will meet you--- in---of ---marquee---"

The call dropped.

"Where are they?" Ginger asked, as she spit her gum over the top of her window and stuffed a fresh stick in her mouth.

"I couldn't make it out. He said something about an electric parade?"

"Okay--- I've got it. ---Ginger to Mobile-Mag, our rendezvous point has just been updated to the Fridge over on Town Hall Parade Street."

The Fridge, as the locals continue to refer to it, is the newly renovated Electric-Brixton Music Hall. The venue is now a prime music venue after a £1,000,000 facelift. It's also one of the latest, state-of-the-art, music venues in London. While the inside is magical with the latest in lighting and sound technology, the outside still retains its original blank exterior, resembling a large refrigerator.

A mild sense of motion sickness invaded my mind as I successfully sent off a text message to Frédéric confirming our rendezvous point. The cool misty-morning air blew against my eyelids as I rolled down the window and pressed my face into wind.

"So where is Magda now, Ginger, did she follow us in?"

"Nope, she always works the alternate routes."

No sooner had I moved my head back into the car than a white sedan emerged from a side street on our left and shot directly in front of us, blocking our entire field of vision. The long vehicle slipped across the road, missing our front bumper by dumb luck.

"Holy shit! What the fuck was that?" I screamed.

The event happened so quickly that it took me a second to grasp what had just occurred. The white Mercedes, obviously driven by Ari, entered a side street on our right-rear and dropped out of sight.

"Ginger to Mobile-Mag, we've just been marked by Ari, and I'm requesting guidance," Ginger said, as she switched on her in-dash GPS navigation system.

"Roger that, what's your twenty, Ginger?" Magda calmly replied.

My mind quickly flashed back to the bloody images of Timothy, the hotel manager and that clueless pickpocket at the train station who had each been executed by Ari.

"Okay, we're heading southeast on Edith Grove about to cross Kings Road—over."

Ginger sat further up in her seat and glanced over at the buildings on the neighboring road running parallel with us on the next street over.

"Okay Magda, she's ghosting us now, one block over on Fernshaw Road."

Ginger concentrated on her driving as I watched Ari's white Mercedes, to the right of us, picking up speed and flash between the open spaces of each building.

"Ginger, I need you to take a left on King and proceed to the Battersea Bridge---I'll intercept you there."

Magda remained surprisingly cool and collected, as Ginger cut a vicious left, producing an alarming squeal on the pavement under our tires.

"Damn it! I hate when I lose grip like that! Think---Ginger ---think!" Ginger was cursing at herself for the least bit of driving error, as the powerful Mini Clubman, with its heavily modified engine, charged down the quiet road past dozens of sleeping apartment houses.

"What's wrong, Ginger?"

"I keep making stupid mistakes and Magda knows it! I just lost maximum tread coverage on that turn---and she's gaining on me now! I should have known better!"

Through the rearview mirror we spotted the headlights from Ari's vehicle making the same turn on to King Street and narrowing the gap between us.

"We didn't lose her, Magda---she took the same goddamn turn on King and she's advancing on me fast."

"Ginger I want you to pass me the ball when you get to the other side of the bridge at Albion Riverside, do you copy?"

"But Magda, I know I can get her in closer!" Ginger pleaded, as she turned and cut me a look of frustration.

"Ginger, sweetie, you did a real good job, and I'm proud of you, but I need to take Goli in from here. Brooke, Yolanda and Heather, I need you girls to form a *wall* on Battersea Bridge northbound--- please confirm!"

All three drivers immediately responded as if they had been listening intently to every word.

"How did they all get there before us?" I asked.

"Goli--- if you want to win, you've got to know the territory! Okay, Goli, in about three minutes we'll be crossing over the Thames. Just on the other side of the bridge, we're going to pull off and I'm going to kick you to Magda. So gather up your stuff and be ready to go! Do you understand me?"

My heart sunk, as I nodded my head in approval. I opened my hand bag and verified that everything was in place.

"Ginger, what's a wall?"

"No time to explain, but let's just say, you're about to find out!"

"Ginger, I want you to know that I think you did an incredible job back there---and I love you so much!"

Ginger scrunched her eyes together, pushing back tears, as she gripped her steering wheel and prepared herself for action. I could tell that she felt horrible for not shaking off Ari, but there was nothing more I could say.

I vaguely remembered having dinner with Danielle, one evening, at a place called the Albion Riverside Restaurant. It was in a weird, high-end, mixed-use complex, on the south bank of the Thames adjacent to the Battersea Bridge. From the north side of the river, the Albion Riverside looked like an ugly piece of modern art. The completely vacant real-estate flop resembled a cross section of an ugly steel shell and a true architectural nightmare. This was to be my apparent transfer point and where I was either going to be killed or successfully passed to Magda.

Ari had gained on us and was only about one block behind us as our tires screamed around the corner of King Street on to Beaufort Street. The foot of the Battersea Bridge was now well in view and about one kilometer down range. The high-end performance of the engine on the tiny Mini-Cooper roared like a lion, causing me to wonder just how fast these tiny taxis could actually go.

Ari's Mercedes also turned the corner, but extra wide, in an effort to avoid a man on bicycle walking his dog on a leash.

"She's gaining on us, Ginger," I yelled, as I stared through my rearview mirror and clutched my handbag.

"Goddamn it, that bitch is good! I've had it with her ass----hold on, Goli!"

Ginger kicked down on the clutch as if she was stamping out a fire, while down-shifting into a lower gear. I felt the momentum of the small automobile push me back into the folds of the black leather seats. We entered the Battersea Bridge at maximum speed, as the sound of the road under our tires switched from pavement to the rapid rhythm of corrugated steel bridge plates.

At the midpoint on the 220-meter bridge we were passed by Brooke, Yolanda and Heather, each traveling north bound in the direction of Ari who had just crossed the foot of the bridge. The only cars on the bridge were Ari's Mercedes, traveling southbound, and the three northbound taxis, which suddenly fanned out across both lanes of the narrow bridge.

The headlights from Ari's Mercedes were blocked from view as the three taxis advanced on Ari like a solid wall. As the wall approached the

Mercedes, Ari flinched and brushed against the side of the protective metal barrier. Sparks flew as Ari slowed to a stop to avoid loss of control. The three cars quickly transitioned into an arrow formation and shot past Ari's left side.

"Ha Ha!—we got the bitch! We're coming back via Albert Bridge and rejoining you guys!" yelled Yolanda, as the rest of the girls cheered.

I watched as the three taxis left the bridge and traveled along the north bank of the Thames to the sister bridge up stream. The Albert Bridge was the next bridge over and within short order; the girls could be seen advancing across that bridge to our side of the riverbank.

As we left the bridge, Ginger caught a visual of Magda rapidly flashing her headlights from the center of an empty parking lot in the back of the Albion Riverside Resort Towers.

"Fuck, something's wrong! I think we have company!" Ginger cursed.

"Wagon-wheel, Ginger! Wagon-wheel!" ordered Magda.

We crossed the highway onto a service road and advanced into the parking lot at full speed.

To my shock and dismay, as we entered the parking lot, two Ford Town Cars were already there waiting on us. The black vehicles entered the center of parking lot as if they were pit-bull dogs in pursuit of Magda.

"Those bastards must have hacked our frequency!" Ginger cursed, a she picked up speed on one side of the vacant parking lot with Magda directly across from us. With Ginger and I on one side of an imaginary wagon-wheel and Magda on the other side, we began rotating around the two Fords.

The drivers sat in the center of our circle, apparently trying to decide which one of us to go after.

"On three, circle out--Ginger," Magda ordered, as our speed increased the g-forces within the interior of our speeding cab.

"Okay, one---two---three!"

We broke off into two separate circles and followed a new arc around in separate directions. A wide figure-eight pattern was forming as we were about to meet each other at the point where we had just had split off from.

"Get ready, Goli, when we come together, I'm going to slide in damn hard! And I want to you get out and drop into Magda's car fast! She'll be ready for you, I promise."

I watched Ginger purposely switch off her anti-lock braking system and dynamic traction control, as I grabbed the door latch and watched Magda close the gap in front of us.

"Here you go Magda, the ball yours in three: one---two---three!"

Ginger pressed down twice on the brake pedal and then pulled her emergency break up, sliding us to controlled stop just to the side of Magda. I pulled the lever on the door, jumped out and ran in the direction of Magda's open passenger side door.

"Hold on tight Goli," Magda yelled, in her strong Austrian accent, as both cars launched themselves around their imaginary circles and out of the main exit.

I had successfully been kicked to Magda's car and we were on our way to Windrush Square. We had gained some distance, and dropped from their line of sight, giving us a small space to breathe, but, Ari and the two Ford Town cars were still in hot pursuit and not too far behind. I knew that at least one more of Henri's cars was out there somewhere, perhaps even at Windrush Square, but I refused to even worry about it.

For the time being I needed to fill my lungs with some much needed oxygen and try to gain my bearings, while the posse behind us had at least one kilometer to reclaim.

Chapter 74

GOLAREH: REST STOP

"God ---I'm so sorry Magda."

"What are you sorry for, my dear?"

Magda checked her rearview mirror and studied the large-screen GPS monitor mounted within her dashboard.

"I'm sorry that my problems have become yours! I never thought it would come to this."

"Goli, I want to tell you one thing, and I want you to calm down and listen to me!"

Magda quickly veered off to the left and drove to the back of a church parking lot. She doused her lights and crept behind a group of trees and some thick bushes. The amber lights of the taxi-radio reflected off her glasses as she calmly issued an instruction to the rest of the girls: "Magda to crew, continue in formation to the goal, spread out and orbit two blocks out until further notice."

She lowered the brightness on the GPS monitor and turned to face me.

"Now you listen to me, young lady, and you listen good! I am going to tell you something and I want you to take this to heart. We're engaged in a fight right now whether you like it or not. And it's important that you give it everything you've got. Now, we can't be boohooing at our challenges. We have to work through what life throws at us!

Now Goli, I don't follow that old adage that everything happens for some sort of cosmic reason. Sometimes bad things happen to people for no reason at all. We get sick, people die and we lose everything ---that's what we call life! I also don't follow the belief that everything gets better with time. Guess what, Goli, sometimes we suffer for the rest of our lives over the loss of someone. This is why we must protect those we love and fight for what's right."

I closed my eyes and listened to her much needed words.

"I had to fight for my freedom when I was a child too, did you know that? My parents sent us away when I was just a small child. We had to leave Vienna for England because the Nazis annexed Austria in the late 1930's.

My father lost everything in the worldwide depression all because of that horrid regime. My parents were convinced that the Nazis were brain-washing children against their own parents, so they tried to send us both away."

"What do you mean by---both, did you have other brothers and sisters?"

"I lost my parents and the one person in my life who meant everything to me."

"Oh---I'm so sorry, Magda?"

I lost my dear sweet brother, Johannes."

Magda pointed to a small black and white photograph dangling from a chain below her rearview mirror.

"Is that your brother, Magda?" I asked, as I sat up and studied the face of the young man in the tiny photo. The picture was very old and embossed onto a faded travel visa. Below his photograph were his descriptions:

Occupation: Student
Place of Birth: Vienna
Date of Birth: May 20, 1929
Place of living: Vienna
Size or Body form: Normal
Face: Oval

Eyes: Blue
Hair: Blond
Special Marks: None

"He was the eldest of my siblings and was detained as we boarded the train for Switzerland. He pushed me onto the train and told me to leave him behind, just as he was taken away. He sacrificed his life for mine. Perhaps in the same way Timothy might have done for you."

"I never knew this, Magda, I'm so sorry? But, I didn't want Timothy to die for my problems. Don't you see? I brought him into this whole mess never dreaming what we would find! If it wasn't for me, he'd be alive today! Magda, I'm the person responsible for putting all of you in so much danger---and for what? Just because two Iranian refugees washed up somewhere on the shores of France, other people have to die?"

"Young lady, one of these days, I'll tell you my full story---when the time is right. Look at me, Goli. Look at me---my dear."

I gazed into Magda's caring eyes which were lit by the early morning light.

"I believe that you are worth fighting for, just like Danni and every one of my girls. I would die for every single one of you. Do you know that, kiddo?"

I felt a mixture of embarrassment and humility building up in my chest as if an explosion were forthcoming.

"My dear, when I look into those magnificent eyes of yours do you know what I see?"

Magda was looking into my eyes like few ever do; as if she were looking directly into my soul.

"What? I whispered.

"I see your wonderful soul, my dear child. Listen to me, Goli. You are a loving and caring soul." she said, as her pupils drove through my eyes and into my heart. "Can I tell you what else I see when I look into those beautiful brown eyes of yours?"

"What?" I said as I, of course, began to cry.

"I see myself." she said, as she leaned over and kissed my tears.

Again, I was reminded of what my sister had said, when we were just kids, about these mysterious eyes of mine. She had said: "when people look into your eyes they often see themselves." I never could understand what she meant by that, but as I began putting the pieces of my life back together again; it was beginning to make sense.

"Now you listen to me, young lady, it's time to get tough and get going. It's time to make things right and bring our girls home. Okay, Goli?"

"Okay, Magda."

"Okay then, now blow your nose and let's get back to work," Magda ordered, as she reached in the back seat and retrieved a box of tissues and threw it into my lap.

Chapter 75

HOMAYRA: FARE THEE WELL

She sat with her legs tucked up close to her chest and a look of terror on her face. Zooli could tell immediately that Danielle was not coping well with what had just happened.

The three of us were sitting on the floor of the truck, half-naked and bleeding from small wounds, fingernail scratches and teeth marks. Zooli removed the coat which Becker had covered her in immediately following his rescue and wrapped it around Danielle in an attempt to calm her down. Not only did Danielle have a nasty bruise on her side but Zooli did as well.

Danielle was rocking back and forth, shivering as Zooli and I held her in our arms and cuddled in close to her. There were no words to comfort Danielle as I looked into the troubled eyes of Zooli as she held Danielle's cringing face against her bare breasts.

As for myself, the assault had not yet sunk in, and thankfully the attack was abbreviated by the arrival of Becker and his well-trained hounds. But for Danielle, the attack kicked off some very real nightmares which were bitter, acidic and violently sharp.

When I first met Danielle, she was she was a cocky and extremely boisterous little 14-year-old, bursting with youthful fire and enthusiasm. She had already been assaulted several times by the time we met, but masked her pain very well under a blanket of profanity. Her spirit and mannerisms appeared to be about the same the day we reunited in Paris, even though what she had witnessed as a girl was just the start of Danielle's lifetime of abuse.

However, now poor Danielle looked pitiful. Perhaps she believed that she had successfully evaded the demons from her past by simply out lasting them and cursing them away. But witnessing Zooli and me also being attacked right next to her might have been the final nail in her emotional coffin.

"Let it out--- my sweet Danni-girl," Zooli whispered as she brushed Danielle's long beautiful black hair away from her tear soaked face. My heart sank as Danielle's emotional cork slowly slipped out. A long and overdue release of repressed pain and suffering burst to the surface and evacuated her soul. Her cries of despair were painful to hear, but entirely necessary as a transformative healing process began unfolding before our very eyes.

From the cab, Becker tapped on the window and slid it open. "Homi, is that Danni I hear crying back there ---is she going to be okay?"

The truck bumped through a washed out trench in the dirt road and bounced over some exposed tree roots. The entire hound-pile absorbed the movement and slid from side to side as if they were one large resting body.

I rose up to the window and peeked through at Becker. It was dawn and the deep blue sky was just beginning to illuminate the forest around us.

"Oh my god, Homi, did that officer do that to you? You are going to have one hell of a bruise on that face of yours!"

I had so many aches and pains I had forgotten that I'd been pistol whipped in the side of the head by that nasty guard. "Oh, I'm alright, I think I'll live."

"Well I can tell you that the bastard that did that to you feels a whole lot worse this morning than you---by a factor of ten. So tell me about Danni?"

"I think Danni's finally connecting the dots on what could have happened---to what actually did happen to her so many times during her life. She's finally letting it all out and it's probably about time," I explained, as the lights from the horse stables came within view.

Becker told me that the clothing that we had arrived in was still in the back of the truck in a canvas bag and we would be arriving at the stables in just a few minutes. Danielle's weeping began to slowly subside as we came to a stop by the doors of the main barn.

Inside I could see Miss Cathy walking into the feed room. A long line of horses poked their heads out of their stalls, patiently watching her every move. Zooli gently helped Danielle get dressed as I slipped back into my jeans and tee-shirt.

It was great that Becker had the presence of mind to keep all of our clothing together. I located my cell phone and thought of calling Richard but saw that the battery was dead. Thankfully, Danielle had made contact with Richard earlier so he would be set to meet us at the airstrip. I closed my eyes and prayed that he would be able to land such a large jet on what was considered a tricky approach.

Zooli covered herself in Becker's coat as the three of us carefully stepped around the pile of resting hounds to the back of the dark truck where Smokey and Taskmaster sat on their haunches watching us. The touch of the two hound's warm tongues appeared to wake up something in Danielle as she dropped down on her knees and held both animals in her arms. They eagerly licked her face and nuzzled up against her body as if they knew she had been suffering terribly.

Zooli and I knelt down and hugged the wonderful hounds, as well, and thanked them for saving our lives. The large pile of canines recognized that the ranking hounds were at ease so they quickly approached. Soon we were covered in 50 sets of playful eyes and lapping tongues, all bidding us farewell.

The three of us scooted off the edge of the truck and dropped into Becker's welcoming arms.

"You girls really had me worried there for a while."

Becker gently drew Danielle onto his chest and hugged her extra fervently. She buried her face into Becker's chest and released her last tears as she slowly lifted her head and opened her beautiful green eyes to Becker.

In the same way Zooli had given up speaking to anyone, Danielle had given up speaking French, largely because hearing it reminded her of Henri, but like Zooli, she felt it was time to get past it: "*Becker - vous est un vrai seigneur - un vrai dans le monde entire. - Becker, you sir, are the most wonderful man in the whole wide world.*"

Becker escorted Zooli to the tack room where she could find some fresh clothing while Danielle and I stepped through the narrow opening of the double doors and stood in the aisle watching Miss Cathy work. Four horses were saddled up on crossties in the center of the aisle and she was moving through her morning rituals as if nothing had ever even happened the night before. She was holding a large coffee can of grain in one hand and a hoof pick in the other when she caught us staring at her.

"Well, don't just stand there gawking at me girls, get to work! ---Danni, please go check the runny nose on that mare down on the far end. Tell me if she has any more snot dripping from her nose. I have to make sure she's over her sinus infection before l release her to the trails. Also pull the thermometer from her butt and give me her temperature."

Danielle stood in the aisle dumbfounded as she stared at Miss Cathy in amazement.

"Danni-girl, I'm talking to you! I'm not going to allow the four of you to go out on a trail ride, this early in the morning, unless I know that the mare is sound. Now chop---chop!"

Danielle snapped back into gear and moved along the line of sleepy horses to the last resting mare. She grabbed a cloth from the top of a tack trunk and gently located the end of a long blue cord which was tied around the mare's tail, with the other end attached to a rectal thermometer.

As if she had done many times before, Danielle held the cord securely and carefully removed the thermometer from the mare's rectum. She wiped off the thermometer and announced her reading. "She's just under a hundred, Miss Cathy, and there's still is a little snot coming out of her nose but at least it's not green."

"Alright then, Danni, I'd say she's probably okay to ride. Besides, the early morning exercise will probably do her some good. But listen to me, girls, she's on her last day of meds so if she starts breathing heavy or appears fatigued, I want you to get off her and let her graze. Do you understand me, ladies?" Miss Cathy asked, as she stepped out of the stall and tossed a rake of manure into a muck bucket.

"Who's going on a trail ride?" I asked, as Miss Cathy barked more commands at Danielle. "You are! At least that's what Becker tells me."

"What? Did you say---we're going on a trail ride?" Danielle asked.

Danielle showed expressions of both excitement and hesitation as she gently began massaging the mare from her withers to the front of her hips. "Miss Cathy, she's feeling a bit tight on her top-line; so I'm going to see if I can work some of this tension out."

Watching Danielle instinctively massage the mare made me believe that my friend was finally on the road to recovery.

"Good girl, Danni, you haven't lost your touch. She's starting to chew and soften a little. Finish up on that side and then move to the other," instructed Miss Cathy as she smiled.

"Homi, grab that rake over there on the wall and get to work! Well---don't just stand there staring at me, Homi! Take the rake and help me pick out some of these stalls before Zooli and Becker get back. Don't be like your sister, Goli; she's always trying to sneak away from her work! When you are done with that--- fill the water bucket in that last stall and sweep off the aisle." Miss Cathy instructed.

Zooli soon arrived with Becker, holding three riding helmets under her arms. "Girls, do you remember these?"

"Oh my god, those were our old riding helmets! I can still make out our names on the back! I can't believe it!" I said.

"I never had the heart to throw them out. This one's Goli's and I can't wait to give it to her!"

The sun was just about to peek out from above the snowcapped mountain tops as the four of us came to a stop along the ridge of the plateau overlooking the sleeping castle. It seemed as if nothing had ever happened as the four of us sat in our saddles and studied the resting giant below.

Becker told us that the three officers had not been entirely destroyed by the hounds but were left with wounds they would wear for life. He said that he had tied each officer's hands behind his back with bailing twine and warned the senior officer that if anyone came after us, he would be back to end their lives. He also told them that their hobby of raping the captive girls was soon to become public knowledge. The senior officer signaled that he completely understood Becker's warning, just before Becker beat him to a bloody pulp.

The 525 meter airstrip had an 18% gradient and was surrounded by tall mountains. There was no control tower, but only radio controlled runway lights which were automatically activated at the request of the jet's onboard navigation system before we even saw the Gulfstream G-650 drop nose first from the stratosphere on approach to the earth below. The acoustics of the French Alps along with a significant headwind silenced the majestic bird as it lined itself up with the runway and implemented final approach. As the beautiful jet came in closer, I felt my body shudder with excitement for Richard. I couldn't wait to hold him in my arms again.

The four of us sat on our horses at the base of the tree line and watched as the jet lowered its landing gear, approached the airstrip, and came in for a perfect landing. The plane utilized every bit of runway space while its twin-sister flaps gathered up as much breaking wind as possible to come to a stop.

The four of us eased our horses out from the cover of the forest and moved up to a full gallop across the open ground toward the awaiting jet. The powerful body of the strong mare beneath me lifted my spirits as I glanced over at Danielle, who was yelling at the top of her lungs, "Let's go home, Homi!"

Zooli glanced back at us, as the four of us lined up in single file and galloped along a long wooden, two-slat, fence line.

"Let's jump it, guys," Zooli yelled, as she dictated commands from her lead horse. With Zooli in the front and Becker in the last position, we curved off to the right into a large arch. We each claimed our target along the four-foot fence line. The powerful necks and bodies rhythmically moved back and forth and picked up speed as we approached our take-off points.

It had been years since I'd been in a saddle but it felt as if I'd never left it. My exhilaration soared as my mind became completely clear with control as the fence line drew closer.

Just as it always happened during the many challenging times of my life, the voice of Zooli reentered my mind and provided me with instruction. "Find your rhythm, Homi. Keep that chin up and keep your eyes on your target. Chin up, girl, and don't lose your focus! Watch that hind-end, Homi! Good girl---now jump!"

My beautiful mare found her correct rhythm as her hooves hit the ground for her last four-legged revolution just before takeoff. Up we traveled, clearing the fence line with ease as I settled in for the flight.

The front hooves of each rider's horse met the turf and landed successfully as I, once again, heard the voice of Danielle, screaming for joy. "Whooohooo! ---we did it!--," she yelled with delight, as all four of us gathered up speed and raced towards the jet at the far end of the runway. Captain Richard Edward appeared in the doorway in his dark blue suit and tie, beaming with amazement as the four of us galloped towards the jet like a posse on a mission of good.

We slowed our horses to a stop and dismounted as the three of us women took off our helmets and ran to Becker.

"Take good care of Miss Cathy, my love--- and we will soon meet again," I said, as I kissed this wonderful man on his warms lips.

"I will Homi, now you make sure that you tell my Goli that I will be seeing her real soon," he said, as he gave me a tearful departing hug.

I was the first one up the steps of the jet as I threw myself into Richard's awaiting arms. "Oh my dear--- lovely Richard! Guess what? We did it--- Richard! We did it!" I was yelling with delight, as I hugged and kissed my new new-found lover.

From the ground I heard Danielle slapping and rattling the hand rail with her riding crop. "Hey---you two! Break it up and let us on the plane!"

The last thing that Becker had said to me played over and over in my mind as the jet moved down the runway with the push of a strong tail wind. We burst into the early morning sky and into a steep climb up and to the left. The wings of the jet were nearly vertical as the landing gear retracted and the powerful jet curved up and over the runway.

"Now you make sure that you tell my Goli that I will be seeing her real soon," replayed the voice of Becker, as I gazed down at the far end of the runway. There was Becker far below, sitting on his horse waving up at us as the three other horses peacefully grazed.

"You will see my sister again soon, my good friend, very soon." I whispered against the window as I watched him vanish from sight.

Off to the west, sat the mysterious castle which was just now coming to life in the early morning sun as the three of us stared through the same window at the ground below. Richard deliberately altered his course to provide us with the opportunity to bid farewell to that stone chamber of evil.

Somewhere within those walls was Henri, waking up to a new day, wondering about my whereabouts. He most likely was also trying to validate the unbelievable encounter he had with Zooli just hours before. Also, perhaps, in his selfish mind he was assessing the condition of his decaying relationship with his long time business partner, Santo Gordo.

As we felt our way through the mysterious maze of the days and weeks leading up to this point, we thought that we had done our job well. Hopefully Timothy had been successful in recording the conversation between Henri and Santo Gordo and maybe---just maybe, he had captured something incriminating.

I had no idea what was going on in London with my sister, Frédéric and Timothy, the man who had made much of this possible. But at least, we were safe and on our way to London to find them.

We were able to rescue our longtime friend and mentor, Zooli, from the terrible grip of Henri. I couldn't wait to hold my loving sister in my arms again after 32 very long and extremely painful years. We had come and gone without Henri even knowing it. Miss Cathy was safe and back to work with her horses with no memory of the night before.

Finally my exhausted body gave out and I drifted off to sleep. I slumbered between my two lovely soulmates holding their hands.

While I slept, our jet reached 15,500 meters above eastern France and continued through the heavens on an emergency mission to London's Heathrow airport at nearly the speed of sound.

Chapter 76

GOLAREH: HIDDEN RIVER

St. Matthews Peace Gardens - Brixton, London

Windrush Square was coming to life with early morning motor and pedestrian traffic as we came within range of the Fridge, just before 7 a.m. The six other taxis were patrolling the square in four separate locations in an effort to provide cover for Frédéric, Heath and Rahda.

Ginger was on Saltoun Road to the south, while Brooke was to the north on Coldharbour Lane. Two others were stationed around St. Matthews Peace Gardens, a triangular park, just southwest of the Windrush Square. The rest of the girls were directed back to home base for further instructions.

The plan was that wherever Frédéric and I would finally meet, we would be within a quarter kilometer of an available cab with a direct shot to London Heathrow.

The three Fords and Ari's Mercedes were nowhere to be found and that concerned Magda very much. She always said that during the game it was vital to always know your opponents' whereabouts.

We had just entered the square from the North within range of the Fridge, when Magda suddenly veered to the south, to the eastern side of St. Matthews Gardens, and came to a stop in one of the very few available parking spots.

I hadn't eaten a thing since the day before and I was suffering with the hollow feeling of low blood sugar. Magda always made it a point to carry a thermos full of coffee, a pack of rice crackers and a jar of peanut butter, specifically for those occasions when a customer needed a quick sugar fix, so I helped myself.

The Electric "Fridge" Brixton was located on the opposite side of the park and was completely blocked from our view by the St. Matthews Church. I knew that Magda was uneasy about not knowing the location of all of the players on her mental playing field, so I made a suggestion. "Magda---just let me run over there and peek around the side of the church to see what I can see?"

"Alright---go ahead, but just get right back here fast! I have no idea where our opponents are."

I grabbed my handbag, opened the car door and ran through the entrance of the gardens to the back side of the church. I moved along the shadows and caught a decent view of the Fridge, but I was still too far out of range.

Traffic was moving along briskly, as people on foot, bicycles and scooters were rushing to their destinations. Everyone was so plugged into their social media gadgets that reality was secondary and irrelevant to them. I scanned the sidewalk along the front of the Fridge and saw no sign of Frédéric.

I decided to venture a bit further and seek an even better view from beneath a group of dwarf maples, directly across from the music hall. Magda was now out of view and, I'm sure, upset by my absence.

Suddenly, my phone rang within the depths of my handbag as I struggled to fetch it. "Hello---Frédéric, where are you? I'm in front of the Fridge waiting for you."

"Goli, get out of there fast! It's not safe!"

"What?"

"---They've got the whole area staked out! Leave! Get out of there---now!"

No sooner had I taken my eyes off my phone than I saw a man in a suit, running across the street in my direction. He was angrily stabbing the air in front of him while directing another man to where I was standing.

I flung my handbag over my neck and ran for the exit. At the base of a ravine I saw a sign that read, *Brixton Water Lane – Storm Access*, so I ran for it.

My knees gave way and I lost my footing, as I slipped and tumbled down the steep embankment made of sharp quarry stones. My hands and knees were scraped and bleeding as I revolved to my feet and limped towards the entrance of the Effra storm sewer.

Although the interior of what was known as *the hidden river* was dark and frightening, I had just enough light to find my way to the other side, just as I heard the sound of my assailant's feet entering the pipe behind me.

Puddles of putrid water splashed against the black slime smeared along the belly of the grey concrete conduit as I made my way through the tunnel. Judging from the orientation of the pipe, I presumed that I was set to pass directly underneath the foundation of the St Matthew's Church and exit out the other side of Coldharbour Lane.

My feet slipped on the goo as I thankfully slid to a stop just before the lip of the pipe. I watched as the smelly water flowed past me, over the edge of the pipe and down to the Effra River below. To my left, I spotted some narrow stone steps covered in vegetation leading up to the main road.

As I climbed the steps, the first of the three men chasing me misjudged the sudden drop off and slipped over the edge. He passed over the lip of the pipe like a helpless animal and streaked down the side of the slick concrete wall into the black waters below. His partners appeared to care nothing about his fate as they glanced up at me escaping to the road above.

Back on the street, it became clear to me that I had emerged on the southern side of the gardens and out of range from Magda. I was at the 1900 block of Brixton Hill Road, just four city blocks from Angell Town, the single most crime infested area in all of the United Kingdom.

Few people ever ventured into Angell Town, most especially a terrified Iranian woman running for her life. Not even the police would patrol the area on a regular basis because of the sheer number of gangs which outnumbered the law. I, thankfully, knew the area pretty well, even though I still had to remain diligent of the winos, pimps and early morning prostitutes all around me.

If I could just remain relatively unnoticed for the next nine blocks, I just might be able to seek refuge at the Hoot & Nanny.

My cell phone rang and I quickly answered it.

"Hello---Magda? Is that you? Where are you?"

"Well hello there, my little superstar. I just wanted to tell you that I'm really enjoying our little adventure ride through this shitty little town of yours. God, do I hate this filthy place," Ari snidely remarked.

"How did you get my number?"

"Well let's just say that I helped myself to your little headless pickpocket friend's purse. It seems that she saved you as one of her favorite contacts on her phone. I'm so looking forward to seeing you again you hot little Iranian slut. And make no mistake, Goli, dear, I will find you. And when I do, I plan to have my way with you---for all of the trouble you and your stupid reporter-friend have caused me. So keep your eyes peeled for me, will you? Oh and guess what, Goli----darling? I'm actually getting moist thinking about you." The phone went dead.

My face flushed with that remark as I gripped my phone and called Magda. She answered on the first ring.

"Where are you, Goli?"

"I'm on Brixton Hill heading south about to enter Angell Town, I'm going to try to make to Squirt's as long as I can stay alive----oh shit," I cursed, as I noticed another one of Henri's black Ford Town Cars passing by me on the opposite side of the street. "I have two men on foot, about three blocks behind me, another one of Henri's cars just passed by me heading north on Brixton Hill and I just received a sickening call from Ari, promising that she was going to have her way with me very soon! Magda, I'm not sure I'm going to be able to make it," I whispered, as I ran across the intersection towards a news stand on the corner.

"Just keep moving south and keep you head down, I'm calling Swoop, right now, for some backup. I'm also sending Brooke and Ginger your way, so keep an eye out for them."

Chapter 77

GOLAREH: AN EYE FOR AN EYE

Angell Town, Lambeth, London — 7:28 a.m.

"Hey sweet pants, it looks like you need some directions? How about taking a detour into my pants," yelled an anemic looking, bald, twenty-something, in a tight fitting black tee-shirt and filthy blue jeans. "Hey girl, I'm talking to you! You know---those hot boobs of yours look pretty heavy, why don't you let me hold them for you?"

The punk was skipping backward on the sidewalk in front of me, with both hands over his crotch. Without acknowledging his presence I raised my arms above my head and moved through him as if he were a snarky colt showing off his dominance to the rest of his herd.

"Hey baby, do you like your meat glazed or cream filled," the nasty hood persisted.

"Back up!" I ordered, as if I was disengaging the hindquarters of an imaginary horse. He yielded to my command and fell back on his tailbone in the center of the intersection.

In the equine world, one should never lose ones temper with the horse, be direct, have patience and be persistent. But in the human world, I had finally had enough. Something snapped within me at the thought of this stupid kid thinking that had every right to treat me with such total disrespect. I stood above him seething in anger as he sat on the pavement staring up at me in shock. It wasn't just him that caused me to snap; it was everyone who was taking advantage of me.

I asked myself: "Am I naïve, brave or stupid? Which is it going to be today----Goli?"

"Go ahead, you little bastard, keep on talking! Because, I'm---DONE--- TAKING---ALL of your--- SHIT! I yelled, kicking the snotty brat in the side of his head with every word.

Brooke's taxi pulled up alongside of me, but I couldn't care less as I continued to vent my anger. "Get in the car, Goli," Brooke yelled, as Frédéric jumped out and pulled me away from the shocked kid.

"Oh my god, Frédéric, am I ever glad to see you? I think you just saved me from killing that little bastard!"

The tiny cab picked up speed and continued down Brixton Hill Street.

"I'm taking you guys to Squirt's; Magda thinks that you will be safe there," Brooke said, as Frédéric and I glanced back at the kid in the intersection.

"Heath and Rahda are going to meet us there too, and then we're off to the airport," Frédéric said, as he turned to me and smiled.

"Frédéric will you turn around and fasten your damn seat belt! You too, Goli, things are far from over here," Brooke ordered, as we approached a red light of another busy intersection.

"Brooke to Mobile-Mag, I have two players in hand and we are sitting next to the Corpus Christi Catholic Church about to cross Brixton Water Lane. We're inbound to Squirt's place---over."

"Rodger that, Brooke," answered Magda.

Diagonally across the intersection, on the left, was a multilevel parking garage with a garbage truck blocking the road about 15 meters further down. The light turned green and Brooke stomped on the accelerator, advancing us into the intersection in hopes that we could squeeze past the garbage truck in the distance.

I had just secured my seatbelt when I felt the impact. It was forceful, loud, and overwhelming, as the front of what appeared to be a white Mercedes-Benz hit us broadside on our left. The force of the impact sent our car flipping through the air and landing us back on our wheels, as the shatterproof windshield flew through the interior of the Mini Cooper like a sheet of diamonds.

My body molded against the smashed left side, as the grill of the Mercedes continued to shove our destroyed vehicle into the path of an oncoming delivery truck. As if I were observing the entire action on a movie screen, I braced myself for impact as horns blared and the tires of the truck came to a screeching to a halt.

When the explosive nightmare ended the left-side of our car was resting on the hood of the white sedan. A man poked his head through the opening of our sunroof and checked for survivors.

"Hey in there, are you all okay?" the driver yelled, as he removed shards of glass from the window frame.

"We're okay---I think?" Brooke moaned, as she glanced back at Frédéric and me. "You guys---get the hell out of here now! Don't' worry about me, just get out of here!" she ordered, as blood from a laceration on her forehead dripped down the side of her face.

"No Brooke! I won't leave you here! You're bleeding!"

"Goli, I'm going to be okay. Now---you and Frédéric need to get the hell out of here---now!"

Two men on the roof of the car already had their hands on Frédéric's coat and were hoisting him through the narrow opening of the sunroof. Once his legs disappeared through the opening I glanced back over at Brooke for one last look.

"Are you sure that you're going to be okay?"

"I'm okay, Goli, trust me. I'll meet you at Squirt's---now go!"

Another set of hands reached under my arms and lifted me out of the top of the wreckage.

Traffic was at a standstill as the men from the garbage truck down the street were helping a platinum-blonde driver out of the smashed Mercedes and to her feet. Our eyes met as she shook off the effects of the crash and smiled at me. It was Ari, fully composed and primed for the kill.

Frédéric grabbed my hand and we both took off running. Police sirens from various parts of city were tangling with one another as Frédéric and I raced towards the dark opening of the parking garage.

My legs ached with pain, as I glanced back and saw Ari casually walking in our direction with her hand reaching for the revolver parked in her holster. Everything about her appeared relaxed as she pursued us with a chilling calm.

A line of slow moving automobiles were creeping up the concrete ramp of the main level of the parking garage, their brake lights and turn signals treating one another with mutual respect. Frédéric and I ran past the oblivious drivers, not a single one of them realizing that a female assassin was hunting us down for the kill.

Exhaust from the garage, mixed with the cool morning air, stung my nostrils as my heels slipped on the oil-stained floor. Frédéric's fingernails were digging into my palm as the floor leveled out and we ran past a never ending line of automobiles.

At the far end of the parking garage a man was standing next to an elevator reading a newspaper and sipping from a cup of coffee. The light above the elevator turned green and the door began to open.

"Sir," Frédéric yelled, as we reached the midpoint of the parking level. "Sir, please hold the door for us!"

"I'm terribly sorry but this elevator is heading up, guys," the man said, as he studied the shards of glass in my hair.

"That's fine sir, whatever," I said, as I bent over in exhaustion and grabbed my knees to catch my breath.

"You two seem to be in a bit of rush this morning," the man said, as he casually sipped his coffee through a tiny hole in the lid of his cup.

"Yeah I know, right?" I answered, as I shook more glass from my hair onto the elevator floor. The elevator came to a stop at the 5th floor and the door slowly opened.

"Good luck you guys, I hope you don't miss your appointment," the man said, as he rolled his eyes and left the elevator.

Just before Frédéric was able to press the button for the main floor, the 8th floor button lit up and we were summoned to the very top.

"Oh----damn it, someone up there beat me to the punch," Frédéric cursed, as we watched the floor numbers tick from the 5th floor to the 8th.

Finally the elevator came to a stop and the doors slowly opened to no one standing nearby. Somewhere out in the dark parking level we heard a coin hitting the concrete floor. Frédéric slightly stepped out of the elevator while I held my thumb on button keeping the door open.

As if Frédéric's head had been hit by a flying object, his body was violently sent to the concrete floor, landing face first. Instinctually I moved out of the elevator to help him.

"Frédéric," I yelled, as I rolled him over on to his back, just as the thick leather heel of a woman's boot smashed into the base of my stomach. The powerful impact disbursed what felt like every bit of oxygen from my lungs. I was left completely unable to breathe, as the insides of my lungs felt as if they had been fused together.

The full weight of my body landed on top of Frédéric as Ari stood over us casually lighting a cigarette. Still, I continued to struggle for air but my collapsed lungs stubbornly ignored my demands.

"You two amuse me," Ari said, as she snapped the lid of her lighter shut and casually took a drag from her long skinny cigarette.

I stared up at Ari through my gaping eyes as if I were attempted to breathe through them. Then it came, the smell of her menthol cigarette, which served as an ironic catalyst to opening my oxygen starved lungs.

She grabbed Frédéric by his curly hair and hauled him up to his feet with surprising ease.

"Get up, bitch, we're going for a little walk!"

I was spellbound by Ari's strength as she kicked me to my poor cousin's side.

"Aren't you going to ask me why you amuse me so, my dear Frédéric?" Ari asked, as she led the two of us towards the center of the parking level. Frédéric said nothing as we walked side by side into the darkness.

"Well, I always seem to find disloyalty oddly humorous," Ari said, as she casually checked the number of bullets in the chamber of her gun. Perhaps she remembered her miscount from the night before when her gun failed to comply with her order to execute me on the campus of Oxford.

"The way I understand it, Henri saved you from that cesspool country of Iran. Didn't he treat as if you were his own son---Frédéric?"

Ari's voice was intensifying with anger. "Didn't he put you through law school and give you a job of a lifetime, you ungrateful piece of shit. I'm asking you a question, Frédéric, and I believe that I deserve an answer?"

Ari shoved him forward into striking range as I helplessly watched. As if she were highly trained in martial arts, she spun her body into a complete rotation and connected the back of her boot against the front of Frédéric's already bloody face.

Frédéric's limp body fell sideways as his forehead again struck the concrete floor.

"Are you aware of the fact that the man who considers you his own son, to this day, has no idea that you and your filthy cousin here, have set out to destroy him? This is what I find so humorous about the two of you. You both have a total disregard for those who have tried to provide you with a better life!" Ari scolded, as she brutally kicked Frédéric again in his head.

"Stop it! Please---stop kicking him! You're going to kill him!---Stop it!" I screamed as I threw myself on top of Frédéric to absorb her next strike.

"Get up---you filthy little bitch," she yelled, as she grabbed me by my pony tail and hoisted me to my feet.

"You must remember how this feels---don't you---you little cunt? Do you remember how it felt that night I caught you trying to save your little nigger girlfriend? I should have killed you back then, but oh no----Henri wouldn't think of it. He thought that you and your spoiled sister were something special! I never could understand what Henri saw in the two of you? But I know what I saw--- two worthless Iranian con-artists using their cute little bodies to get whatever they wanted! " Ari yelled, as her powerful arms violently shook my scalp. "You ungrateful little bitch, you have no idea how much trouble you have cause so many people, do you?"

Ari let go of my hair and violently slapped me across the side of my face. I lost my balance and began to plummet to the floor when she caught my ponytail in her fist and yanked me back to a standing position.

"Now you listen to me you filthy little Iranian---dyke. You have something that I want---and you know what it is! So hand it over. I stared at Ari and studied the truly organic evil present within the dark recesses of her angry eyes. The longer I inspected her eyes, the more I seemed to gain an odd level of control over her.

"Oh, I remember those eyes of yours, Goli. I remember them having such an effect on Henri. So you want to try them out on me--- do you? Go ahead, Goli, tell me what you see in my eyes!" Ari said, as she jerked my face directly in front of hers. Her fingers curled around my hair and dug into my scalp.

"Tell me---you selfish little bitch! Tell me what you see in my eyes!"

Ari pressed her nose against mine and allowed her pupils to connect with mine. Her breathing intensified as her face cringed and her eyes locked in on mine.

"Do you think you have me figured out? Do you think you know what I'm made of? Tell me then, you all-knowing little bitch! Tell me something that even I might not know about myself?"

I drilled into her mind through her eyes until she couldn't stand it any longer and looked away.

"Well, then, if you're too stubborn to tell me what you see in me, how about I show you what I see in you?"

Ari's behavior was suddenly transitioning from anger to an odd level of humility. We were now locked in with each other as our opposite emotions collided in joint communication.

Suddenly with an explosion of involuntary passion, Ari advanced on me and pressed her lips against mine. Her mouth molded with mine, as she forced her tongue into my mouth. Her kiss was fueled with passion but tempered with anger, frustration and a noticeable amount of pain. She fiercely sucked air through her nostrils, as she desperately probed my mouth with her tongue for answers.

Her tears began flowing as if she were beginning to recognizing the root cause of her own evil. At the height of her kiss she opened her eyes and stared at me as if begging me for help. Ari was inadvertently dumping her soul to me, while at the same time receiving nothing in return.

Realizing that I had most likely seen too much of her, Ari appeared deflated, mentally violated and perhaps even used.

Her protective response finally returned to the vacuum of her mind which resulted in uncontrollable anger. Breaking her tormented kiss, she exploded into rage, pushed me backwards and snarled at me. Growling like an angry beast, she struck the side of my face with her pistol.

My vision flashed as the impact of the heavy gun spun me around and dropped me to the floor on to my stomach. I fell on my handbag and I struggled to keep from passing out. Both Frédéric and I were lying side by side on our stomachs with our faces pressed against the oily floor while Ari stood above us fully redeemed with evil.

The entire area around us was completely dark as Ari pulled back the trigger on her revolver and directed the end of the long barrel at our heads.

"Ahhh! I hate you, Goli! I hate you so much it hurts!" Ari screamed, continuing to call me by my nickname. "You sicken me, Goli! You always have---and you always will!"

"I've had it with the two of you," she yelled, as she stepped directly over the top of us with both legs spread. "Now give me what I came for, Goli! Give me the cell phone belonging to that nosy reporter friend of yours!"

I could hear Frédéric struggling to breathe through the blood leaking from his nose. The surface of the handbag beneath my chest felt hard and uncomfortable as I suddenly remembered the Glock, police issue, service revolver which I had mistakenly stowed.

The soreness from Ari's blow to my face caused me to let out an involuntary moan. As I fought to stay conscious, I slowly maneuvered my right hand through the opening of my handbag to the hidden gun.

"I'm waiting on you Goli! If you want to see tomorrow, I suggest that you give me the reporter's cell phone today!" ordered Ari, expecting that I was searching the contents of my handbag to fulfil her demand.

My fingers followed the custom handle of the revolver as my index finger curled around the polished metal trigger. I was now in complete control of the firearm as I lay motionless on the floor, carefully orienting myself with the firing mechanism.

The silence of the top floor of the parking garage was suddenly broken by the sound of an approaching automobile emerging from the floor below.

The headlights broke the darkness and shifted the shadows on the walls around us.

Ari glanced over at the headlights of the car as it entered the far side of the parking deck and approached the corner. Her momentary interest elsewhere caused her to break her concentration with the two captives lying on the cold concrete floor beneath her.

As she followed the movement of the car, I followed the movement of her head as I removed the gun from my hand bag and aimed it awkwardly as far in back of me as I possibly could. My shoulder strained and I felt my right eye swelling as I locked in on Ari's dark figure.

Realizing that she had broken a cardinal rule of taking her eyes off her prisoners, she quickly snapped her head back to me as I pointed the powerful gun in the direction of her torso. In the darkness of the room we connected once again, as the whites of her eyes widened like the aperture of a camera lens.

With all the strength I could gather up, I squeezed the trigger on the gun as visions of my life flashed before my very eyes: My sister and my lost parents sped through my mind like ghosts in a fast moving slide show. I saw a replay of Ari holding that heavy baton on the back of the bus as she bludgeoned the life out of that poor defenseless woman at the castle so many years ago.

Images of Ari and Henri raping me so many years ago filled the walls of my mind as I studied the evil in Ari's surprised eyes. I thought of the gunshot wounds and the strangely mutilated body of my dear Timothy, as I pulled the trigger with the full strength of my index finger.

"This is for all of the human beings you have destroyed---Ari! Go back to the hell from where you were conceived!" I charged at the top of my lungs. "And let not a piece of your evil soul to be saved by the lord above!"

The huge explosion of the high caliber cartridge in the chamber of my gun did not distract my aim as I directed the bullet directly into the center of Ari's chest.

Off, went the exploding 9MM bullet from my powerful equalizer.

"Off---I send you," I screamed, at the completely stunned Ari in a language that she could fully understand. Out followed my next demand in my mother tongue which only Frédéric and I could understand: *"Miravi beh jahanam, az hamanjaiyeh ke azash miyaie!* " - *"To the gallows I send your filthy soul!"*

Chapter 78

GOLAREH: THE WRONG HOOD

The warm pistol dropped from my hand and clattered to the cement floor. My heart was pounding as I closed my eyes and refused to even look at what was left of Ari.

What fueled her madness, I wondered, and was she somehow reaching out to me for answers? The kiss seemed almost involuntary on her part, but it was her tears that really took me back. Perhaps her kiss was a planned prelude to my death or possibly it was a strange cry for help. I will never know.

The headlights of the automobile drew closer and lit up the area around us; while simultaneously the elevator doors opened and four men emerged with their pistols drawn.

The black Ford Town car came to a stop, just centimeters from Ari's body and within seconds Frédéric and I were surrounded by six of Henri's men.

The youngest of them men rushed over and kicked what had been his firearm out from beneath my hand. He anxiously recovered it and stood next to the rest of his team members aiming his gun directly at my head. He was frowning and spitting fire as if losing his gun to me was the worst thing that could have ever happened to him.

"Well--- it appears that your lost gun was finally put to some good use, Officer Yoden," the squad leader joked. The humiliated officer glared at me even more, as if he'd been the brunt of jokes for hours.

"This should teach you what can happen when you lose your gun to a woman! Just look at what happened to this poor---poor thing. This bitch was next on our list to take out, but thanks to you, young lady, our job is pretty much done. I'm not sure what she wanted from the two of you, but whatever it was, must have been pretty damn important."

The squad leader knelt down to Ari's side and carefully removed the pearl handled revolver from her hand using his gold plated Cross Pen.

"Damn, I've always wanted one of these pearl handled babies and now it appears that I've finally gotten my wish. This bitch was supposedly Dr. Lepan's maid---that's what they called her---you know? That's right--- she was the one who tidied up after Dr. Lepan. She was apparently very good at it too, and by the looks of that nice ass, I can see why. Damn, such a waste of a fine looking woman," the lead officer said, as he picked up her purse and handed it to another officer."

"Sir, for the record, I just wanted to say--- that this woman didn't take my gun from me! It was this huge, monster of a guy, twice my size," exclaimed Williams.

"Yeah right, Yoden, that's not what we heard," barked another officer in a damp suit. "The way I heard it, you dropped your gun after some faggot slapped you across the face!"

"Shut the hell up, Warren! You're one to talk! We wasted a half a damn hour dragging your smelly ass out of that river. So how about the two of you just grow up and get Hansel and Gretel on their damn feet and into the car?"

Officers Yoden and Warren advanced on us and brought us to our feet as the ranking officer studied Frédéric's face. "Wait just a damn minute; I've seen this asshole before. Get him over here in front of the light so I can take a look at him."

Frédéric was just coming out of his fog after falling on his face twice and being kicked several times by Ari.

"I've seen you before at a few of Dr. Lepan's functions? What's your name, asshole?"

The lead officer shined his flashlight in Frédéric's bloodshot eyes as my poor cousin said nothing.

"I asked you a question, fuck face, and I expect an answer. Now who the fuck are you and where are you really from?"

"My name is Frédéric and I am from France."

"Yeah right, and my father's the fucking Pope. You don't look like any Frenchman I've ever seen before. How 'bout you tell me what your real name is? Yoden, grab that bitch's handbag and bring it over to me. I want to know what was so god-awful important that Blondie here got herself killed over"

Frédéric stiffened up to defend me as officer Yoden reached for my handbag.

"*Bon, d'accord, je te dirais ! My vrai nom n'est pas Frédéric, mais Jalaj, en fait Jalal Abbasi, je suis de Téhéran, Iran!*" - "Okay! Okay I will tell you! My birth name is not Frédéric, but Jalal. My name is Jalal Abbasi and I am from Tehran, Iran," Frédéric blurted out.

"Well---you don't say? It looks like we've got ourselves a bunch of fucking French-Iranians. I didn't think they allowed you people out of that fucked up country of yours. So what was it that the blonde bitch wanted from you that caused you to shoot her down in cold blood?" the senior officer asked as I held my handbag closer to my chest.

"William's---don't just sit there staring at me--- bring me her goddamn purse!"

Officer Yoden now meant business as he went for my handbag, but there was no way in hell, that I was going to lose it to Henri's officers even though they appeared to have no idea what they were looking for. I wrapped my arms around my handbag and dove to the floor.

Frédéric's protective side kicked in when he saw the two officers manhandling me. Officer Yoden jumped on my back while the other officer grabbed me by my hair and pushed my face against the cement. In a rage, Frédéric broke free from another officer and managed to kick officer Yoden directly in the center of his already broken face.

Yoden flipped over on his back as his gun, once again, fell from his hands. The pistol spun on its side within in range of my right foot, so I kicked it across the smooth concrete floor into the darkness.

"Oh! Ho! Ho! Ho! If this isn't the most ridiculous thing I've ever seen! Twice in one fucking night, an officer under my command loses his gun to a goddamn woman! Not once, mind you---but twice!"

Officer Yoden was overcome with pain as he held his broken face together in his bloody hands.

"This is fucking ridiculous!" yelled the squad leader as he suddenly noticed a man standing in the darkness. Turning his head, he saw a bald, black man squatting down to pick up Officer Yoden's pistol.

"Hey you---over there, leave that alone! ---Put that down!" The squad leader yelled, as he stared at the man in the darkness.

"Hey, boy, I'm talking to you!"

All of the action came to a halt as the squad leader shined his flashlight in the face of the black man in the distance.

"Hey Bumpy, turn the house lights on!" ordered the black man in the distance.

On the far end of the parking area a switch was thrown and the room suddenly came to life.

"Brother, my name aint *boy*. Do you understand me---white boy? The name is Swoop---Swoop Bennett ---to be specific. And you white boys are in the wrong hood. Do you know *dat?*"

Swoop was all about confidence as he casually stood alone in the center of the room casually examining the high caliber pistol in his hand.

"I don't give a shit what your name is, nigger, or whose hood you think we're in. Now just put the gun on the floor and leave!"

"Oh, are you referring to the murder weapon here, belonging to the dude with no teeth?" Swoop chuckled, as he removed the Glock's 9MM magazine from the base of the gun and stuffed it in his back pocket. "Nope---*dis* piece stays *wit* me, for safe keeping."

"Hey---who the fuck do you think you're talking to you little street punk? Do you think you own this neighborhood or something?"

The squad leader approached Swoop and grabbed him by his over-stuffed down-filled jacket in a futile effort to show Swoop who the boss was.

"You better cool it down white boy, because my boys *be* willing to teach you a lesson for messing with my sister. We've got some black tempers rising here and my boys are fixing to get violent with you. I've got a hundred rounds with 20 niggas that will turn up the sirens on your asses," Swoops said, as he placed his nose into the face of the ranking officer.

"Well, all I see right now is just one Jamaican—ass, mixed-breed, standing here all by his lonesome."

The squad members who were struggling to hold Frédéric and me down, suddenly paused as they noticed at least twenty other gang members, heavily armed coming into view on all sides.

They wore hats of all types ranging from oversized ball caps and stocking caps to stylish fishing hats. Some of the young men wore sunglasses but all carried an expression of power and confidence. This was clearly no ordinary street gang, but a well-organized militia apparently working on the side of good. They were employed by a single leader, and that person was Swoop Bennett.

Each gang member, with the exception of Swoop, was armed with not one, but several weapons, each much more powerful than the munitions in the hands of Henri's security detail. From my days as a reporter I recognized an Agram 2000 9mm sub-machine gun and a Walther P99 German revolver in the hands of at least two gang members.

The youngest of the gang members, whom Swoop considered too young to carry guns, were armed with chains, pipes and pepper spray.

"Now you listen to me---boss-man. I don't appreciate the prejudicial comments you're handing down to my sister over there on the floor. I happen to have a soft spot in my heart for the country of Iran. But, even more, I don't like the way your playmates have my family pinned down on the floor like *dat*. It's now time for all of you suits to make a contribution to our church, so tell your sisters to slide their pieces my way."

"Oh---and like that'll happen--- nigger," said the squad leader as he glared into Swoop's eyes.

"Well then, it looks like I have no choice but to charge your white ass for the crimes you have committed within my jurisdiction."

As if Swoop were performing a slight-of-hand magic trick, a rectangular shaped police TASER materialized from his sleeve, immediately firing two electroshock wire probes into the center of the squad leader's chest.

The tiny copper barbs dug in like fishhooks in two separate locations and delivered a debilitating electronic pulse which traveled from one probe to the other. The squad leader dropped to his knees and then on to his side, screaming in terror as his muscles contracted to the buzzing and zapping sounds of 5,000,000 volts.

"Oh and guess what---white boy? I've always dreamed of having one of these pearl handled Magnums---too," said Swoop, as he kicked the pistol out of the officer's hand. "Let's get the hell out of here, Goli. I'm going to leave it to my crew to clean up *dis* shit."

Swoop stepped over and reached for my hand while Bumpy helped Frédéric to his feet.

"Hey Bumpy, I almost forgot, I like *dat* white boy's sun-shades, they're pretty cool. Snatch them off his ugly face and give them to me, I think he's done cooking now."

"Oh and Bumpy---one more thing. I need you to call the chief superintendent down at the station house. Tell him that Swoop needs him to come down here and clean up *dis* shit. And make damn sure to tell him *dat da* white boy with no teeth is the rightful owner of the gun that took that lady down. I always try to do my civic duty around my home town. Someone's got to keep *dis* place safe for my children. You know what I'm saying?"

Swoop, Frédéric and I were soon heading down to the ground floor of the parking garage with Swoop holding me in his arms. "It's okay baby girl. It's all over now. Don't you worry about a thing---Swoop's got your back."

It was business as usual at street level, as the traffic moved normally. People walked past us on the street, again, paying more attention to their latest gadgets than to the world around them.

The intersection where Brooke's tiny pink taxi had met its demise was clear with no sign of a past collision. Two high pitched car horns sounded off just to the left of us as three pink taxis sat patiently awaiting our arrival.

Magda was in the lead as she moved forward and rolled down her passenger side window. "Come along you three, we have some visitors meeting us at Heathrow," Magda instructed, as Frédéric and I slid into the back seat.

"You too Swoop, get in and keep me company. I need someone's hand to hold." Magda patted the passenger seat as Swoop surveyed the streets around him.

"Swoop, will you please stop standing there with the door open and get in the damn car! Danni is asking to see you!" ordered Magda.

My heart burst into my throat as Magda applied pressure to the gas pedal and led the other two pink taxi cabs through our beautifully-filthy Brixton streets, towards the busy M4 expressway, just 19 kilometers from Greater London.

As we reached cruising speed and joined the rest of the traffic, Magda's eyes met mine in her rearview mirror. "Swoop, give this box of tissues over to *misty-eyes* back there. I swear that girl cries more than anybody I've ever seen in my entire life! And blow your nose, Goli, you look terrible! We have about 20 minutes---and I'm sure that you don't want your sister to see you looking like that?"

I rested my exhausted head on Frédéric's shoulder and held his hand tightly. We drove in silence as I tried to formulate an image of my sister's face in my mind, but for the first time in my entire life I couldn't. I felt as if I was on a fantasy ride for a rendezvous with a ghost.

I peered out at the highway in front of us and caught yet another glance of Magda's wonderful eyes peering at me through the rearview mirror.

"Some things are truly worth fighting for my child, don't you ever forget that." Magda smiled and slowly raised Swoop's large hand to her lips and kissed it.

I was speechless for the entire trip to Terminal 1 of the Heathrow Airport.

Chapter 79

HOMAYRA: FINAL APPROACH

I had entered the cockpit earlier and buckled myself into the co-pilot's seat shortly after Danielle and Zooli had fallen asleep. I was too exhausted to even speak as I sat quietly next to Richard with my eyes closed, listening to him communicate with a female flight controller.

We dropped down below the cloud canopy from the southeast and came in for a smooth landing along the North Runway. We touched down and sped past a long line of large planes all reminding me of a family of peaceful sleeping giants. I reached over and kissed Richard on his wrist and asked if I could unbuckle and go back to the cabin area.

"Sure, Homayra, but be careful and fasten up when you get back there."

Richard was smiling and studying me with an expression of wonderment. He was looking at me--- and not at my dirty, bruised and cut up face.

"Richard---you said something to me recently that touched my heart. You told me that you were *taken* with me, and I made note of that statement."

Richard's eyes lit up with interest.

"I'll have you know, that I've never felt the least bit beautiful to anyone until I met you. I now understand what you meant by being *taken*. I am also, as you say, *taken* with you."

Danielle was yawning, and excitedly scratching Zooli's back when I rejoined them in the cabin. They were gazing out of the oversized windows like kids in a candy store.

"Homi, look baby, we're finally home! Oh and Homi, listen! I just called Magda and she told me that everyone is waiting for us in the terminal. Everyone baby----everyone!"

Our jet maneuvered through the complex taxi lanes and came upon Terminal 2, which was named the *Queen's Terminal*. We turned left and traveled past five A320 Airbuses and around to the other side, where three other planes sat attached to their assigned gates like baby birds, snuggling up to their mother.

The three of us rushed for the bathroom and stood before the mirror in a state of alarm. We appeared as if we'd been through the battle of our lives. My hair was filthy with remnants of sweat, dried blood and grime. All we could do was wash up and cover our heads with ball caps.

After a cursory inventory of our cuts, scrapes, bruises and dried, dirty tears, we reached the conclusion that there was not much more we could do. Zooli lifted her shirt and showed off her bruised ribs, which resembled the shape of a man's boot. "Well I'm no stranger to bruises but this one's going to keep me from jumping any fences for a while."

"Girls, let's face it, we look terrible!" Danielle calmly admitted, as we posed together for a group selfie in front of the mirror. "Well I, for one, don't care what we look like! We're alive and we have each other---and that's all that matters to me--- so the heck with them all!" said Danielle.

It suddenly occurred to me, that ever since the three of us left the foxhound truck, I hadn't heard Danielle utter a single curse word. I said nothing, but only smiled and kissed Danielle lightly on her cheek.

Richard had already opened the bulkhead door and was lowering the exit stairs to the tarmac, as the cabin filled with the familiar thick London air. Zooli was second in line before Danielle and was cautiously studying the bustling activity outside of the aircraft. I wasn't exactly sure how she would react with such a starkly different environment after spending a lifetime on the castle grounds.

"Come in with me, Richard, I want you to meet my sister. Plus---I need you in there with me." As we walked towards the terminal I thought about the many times I'd been to London, never knowing that my own sister was actually living in the same city.

I glanced up and saw a crowd of people waving down at us from the windows above. We moved along the side of the building and I wondered what it will be like for me to finally see Golareh again? What will be the first words from of my mouth? "Hi Goli, how are you? Nice weather we're having—right?"

The entrance of the building was teaming with activity with officers from Scotland Yard, airport security, Interpol, and Europol. All were smiling and casually talking to one another as we made our way into the crowded room.

The room became electrified as I came to a stop, saturated in a sea of faces, hands and lips. Danielle's suddenly emerged through the crowd leading someone by her hand. Her smile was golden and beaming with joy, as she maneuvered a beautiful woman with long brown hair, fashioned in a ponytail through of all things, the back of a ball cap.

When Danielle moved the woman's bruised and injured face directly in front of mine, I saw that her skin tone had my exact signature color. A sudden jolt of adrenalin rushed through my body and caused my vision to blur. I felt as if I was having trouble comprehending who this identical image was, standing right in front of me. I whispered my sister's name as the woman stared back at me in bewilderment. My legs buckled and I dropped to the floor as my mirror-image caught me in her arms and followed me down to our knees.

I fell against my sister as if I were falling off the edge of a skyscraper, clinging to her body for my dear life. I was suddenly petrified to open my eyes for fear that she wasn't at all real. I felt the warmth of her face as I gripped her coat with my fists and pulled her head directly to the side of mine. I could smell her wonderful breath and feel our unmistakable genetic energy mixing together into a single spirit.

My eyes were clasped shut as I moaned and rocked my dear sister in my arms. I was becoming even more terrified to open my eye, fearing that everything was just a dream. What if it were just another one of those terrible nightmares, which I had experienced thousands of time before; when I would open my eyes to the darkness only to find her gone.

"Enough!" I thought, as I opened my eyes to the floor, fearing even to make eye contact with my sister. Our hands finally met as our fingers intertwined and only then did I realize that I was holding my sister.

Nothing else in the world existed when I finally looked into my sister's beautiful brown eyes as she graciously welcomed me back into her soul. We knelt together on the floor in the center of everyone, holding hands and staring into each other's eyes.

Finally I spoke to her in our mother tongue: *"Goli in toii? Tamana mikonam javab bedeh. Yani mishe ke khodet bashi va na rouhet, va na khilatam? - Is it really you, Goli? Please tell me that you are no longer a ghost to me?"*

The room was quiet with only the sound of sniffling and weeping spectators as everyone witnessed our long and overdue reunion. My line of vision finally let go of the center of her pupils and brought in the rest of her terribly bruised face. Just as we did when we were children, we carefully traced each other's injuries with our finger tips, desperately trying to heal our joint injuries.

The unmistakable sound of a champagne cork popped and broke our intimate reunion. We slowly rose to our feet and took in the smiles and applause of everyone around us. Within short order, we held our glasses high as Golareh wanted to announce something that was quite shocking to both Danielle and me.

"I just wanted to say—that. It takes an army to destroy evil. You all are my own private army. I sincerely hope that we have what we need to separate Dr. Henri Lepan from the rest of society. I just hope that we were able to obtain what we desperately need to serve as evidence against this vicious monster.

But I also must tell you that none of this would have ever been possible if it were not for my dear Timothy----who..." gasped Golareh. "If---he hadn't sacrificed----his own...life for me. What Timothy----did for all of us---I can't begin to even say----." My sister was heartbroken and could no longer speak, as I tightened my grip on her hand.

A trip to Paris was just minutes away as our departure party slowly proceed towards the doors of the gate. The resting Gulfstream G650 sat waiting for our return. It would fly our exhausted bodies and renewed spirits back to Paris, and then on to Frédéric's country home for a much needed rest.

I hoped and prayed that somewhere within the memory chips of Timothy's cell phone was an audible recording of Henri Lepan and the powerful Santo Gordo locked in a detailed conversation about their horrid industry. Two very powerful kingpins, responsible for the death and destruction of so many innocent people must be brought to justice. This is what we hoped. This is what we prayed for.

Chapter 80

GOLAREH: A VIEW FROM ABOVE

London Heathrow - West London

It had been a lifetime since I had been on board an airplane. The last time was when my sister and I flew from Tehran to Paris in 1979.

It occurred to me, as I was climbing the steps to the cabin entrance that I hadn't even been out of Great Britain since I arrived as a broken teenager. I never even considered going anywhere else and suddenly I knew why: It was because Henri had told me not to.

Never should I leave the borders of the U.K. for any reason. Never should I ask why, and never should I question Henri's authority.

Even as a reporter, the furthest I ventured from Oxford was to Northern Ireland, Scotland and Wales, and even then it was only for a night. The only time I felt the most worldly was the day I took a two-hour ferry ride from Troon to Larne.

This sudden and most elementary epiphany was further evidence to me, that the three of us had been almost entirely brainwashed by Dr. Henri Lepan and his dreadful companion, Ari.

"This is really unbelievable!" Richard studied Homayra and me as we stood side by side in the bulkhead. "The two of you are truly identical twins! And

I must say, the most beautiful women I've ever seen in my entire life," he exclaimed, as if he were star struck.

Homayra and I turned to each other and laughed. "Oh yes, my dear Richard, we are just the perfect spectacles of flawless beauty---now aren't we?" Homayra joked, as we brought our face together for an impromptu pose.

"Well aren't you two the lucky ones! Got that---got that---and got that!" Richard snapped off a few pictures of us with his cell phone.

"Oh---no you don't--- Richard! Give me that cell phone this instant!" Homayra said, as she charged Richard and wrestled with him against the cabin wall. I jumped in for Richard's defense and began pulling Homayra off him, as the three of us burst into laughter. The scene took me back to when we were kids, when I pulled my sister from the little boy who refused to be friends with her any longer simply because she had breasts.

The jet had a total of one hour's worth of hot water on board and the four of us took full advantage of every drop, washing days of trench warfare from our bodies. There was enough clothing on the plane to dress us all, before we settled into our seats for the short flight to Paris.

Pizza was delivered to us, jet-side, compliments of Magda, including a gluten-free option for Heath. We all thought it a bit humorous that such a gorgeous hunk of man was sensitive to wheat. It only reinforced the fact that we were not superheroes, just mere mortals trying to do what was right.

At 3:00 p.m. we blasted down the runway and ventured up to initial cruise altitude. The passenger manifest included Officers' Heath and Rahda, Frédéric, Zooli, Danielle, Homayra and myself. Any concerns I had about flying vanished the second I sat back in the rich leather seats and held hands with both Danielle and my sister.

Frédéric and Heath had been given the full responsibility of Timothy's, most valuable, cell phone. They found a way to easily attach the device to the Gulfstream's LCD entertainment system for an inflight review. We snacked on pizza and sipped champagne as Frédéric located the nine-minute and twenty-six-second audio file which contained the conversation between the two kingpins.

The earth below looked even more beautiful than I had ever imagined it would, as I soaked in the love of my family around me. But my heart ached for Timothy terribly and wished that he could have been there with us. The flight to Paris was to be only 50 minutes in duration but I didn't care if took 50 hours, as the audio recording cued up and was about to start.

To think, just seven hours earlier, every one of us on board had been struggling to stay alive in two separate countries while Henri had not a clue that we had pierced his private veil.

I thought of my parents and considered the possibility that perhaps, maybe, Homayra and I might see them once again.

The sound of a person coughing on the recording broke my dreamlike trance as I tuned in to the recording. I closed my eyes and saw Timothy's face smiling at me with a look of pride. I almost felt that I could reach out and touch his face as he excitedly exclaimed, "We did it girly-girl! We fucking did it!"

[Coughing]
GORDO: Okay, okay. Henri---it is not necessary for us to talk any longer about our families, we have problems to discuss.

LEPAN: How do you mean, my friend? Tell me about these problems we have.

GORDO: Henry, my friend, let me say to you---that I am concerned about your mental state.   Your logic appears skewed and peculiar.

LEPAN: Oh..hmmmm---and how do you mean, my brother?
GORDO: Well to start off with, what in the hell is this United Nations' watch-dog group you are setting up with that Iranian bitch---what's her name Homma—Hemma?   Who in the hell is this woman that you have been apparently living with all of these years? Who is she and what does

she know? Is she your wife, girlfriend, personal fuck-piece--- what? Tell me!

LEPAN: Santo, please do not refer to Homayra with such a nasty tone.

GORDO: Well then----who is she? *[Coughing; movement of furniture]*

LEPAN: She is a colleague of mine---and none of your concern.

GORDO: Mm-hmm. Well then, Henri, why has she been talking to the London press?

LEPAN: What do you mean?

GORDO: Well---I saw this same woman on television causing quite a stir at a news bureau in London? Do you even know that, Henri? Do you even know where this woman is at this very moment? *[Laughing]*

LEPAN: Well not at this very moment---no---but. I have been traveling---but I assure you she is not talking to the press about us! She knows nothing anyway, I assure you. Perhaps you saw her twin sister who stays in London and works as a reporter? She must be who you are referring to?

GORDO: Reporter! Are you kidding me, Henri? *[Coughing; movement of furniture]* Do you expect me to sit still while you set up an arm of the United Nations to go after me! This---this organization which your Iranian girl-friend is expected to be the president of?   You tell me that you don't even know where she is, and that she has a twin sister who is a reporter working at the very same newspaper that publishes all of your foolish bullshit? A twin sister---Henri---please. Come on! Do you expect me to believe this?

[Extended pause]

LEPAN: Santo, Santo! Relax! As I told Ari, this U.N. group is our insur-ance policy. It's our way to crack down on our competing cartels in Italy, Germany, Russia and the U.S. We now have the wheels of the law on our side, so we can crush these bastards while we remain safe and even more profitable. Again, Santo, this is all part of an insurance policy, which you have never had to concern yourself with.

GORDO: Well this is where we differ in our thinking--- Henry. I believe that what you are doing is entirely too risky. You have made yourself chair-man of this goddamn organization!

[Pause]
For weeks now, I have been reading so many, how can I say, stupid and embarrassing stories about you in the—the---the world news. I must tell you Henri....you really concern me.

LEPAN: Santo, my dear brother, you must understand that this is nothing for you to be troubled about, my friend. *[Laughing]*

GORDO: Well you may think this is funny, Henry, and up until just this morning I might have been laughing with you. For I have considered these stories to be your problem and not mine. But! My friend, I read in the *La Jornada*, one of my countries' largest newspapers, my name in the very same paragraph as yours. In my own country Henri! You are linking me to those sloppy shipments of rotting bodies on board my shipping vessel.

LEPAN: Sloppy shipments, what do you mean by this, are you kidding me? These shipments are a result of your rotten exports! Must I remind you that for as long as we have been doing business together, all costs, logistics and security have been left entirely to me? And all that has been expected of you is to supply me with quality objects, which, I might add, have turned to shit!

GORDO: No, no, no, no, no, no, no, no, no-- Shit, how do you mean? *[Sound of a fist hitting the furniture]*

LEPAN: You have been sending me sub-par humans, Santo! Shit! Sick women, whose minds are soaked with drugs and bodies infected with bugs and disease. They reek of cocaine, heroin, methamphetamines, venereal disease, and even AIDS! You have been sending me garbage, Santo. You send me men and boys who are pickled in alcohol and mentally retarded. How can I use these useless pieces of human shit----tell me how? We had a deal Santo, we had a deal!

GORDO: Mm-hmm. Okay, now you listen to me, Henry I don't like your tone of voice with me. If you think that that you can--- *[interruption; coughing; static]*

GORDO: *[Interruption; coughing; static]* Tell me Henri, why are you making such a mockery of yourself to the world press? Why must you draw attention to your expensive lifestyle? You are making yourself out to be a monkey of a man?

LEPAN: Goddamn it Santo, how dare you call me a monkey! I've just been being attacked by this little *newspaper boy* in London----and I'm putting a stop to it. Santo---this little reporter is nothing more than a nudge, an itch and I will take care of it.

GORDO: Henry--- think of our trade partners in Russia, America, Taiwan and the rest of the world---what must they think about you----and me, for that matter? I never will find myself in a vulnerable position by this little nuisance in London. This little news boy is much more than a mere nudge; he has successfully plastered your stupid face and my respected name all over the international news media!

LEPAN: I will take care of this!

GORDO: My brother, you need to know something about me. Okay? Okay, I don't wait for others to do a job for me, okay---okay? I don't ask others to fix my problems, okay? I get things done my way! Now your problems have become mine, and I'm going to fix them---now!

LEPAN: What do mean Gordo, what are you telling me here?

GORDO: Okay, okay, I have already dispatched for the elimination of your little nudge, as you call it. He will be dead and disposed of before the sun comes up on your side of the world, and I will no longer have to scratch your fucking little itch---okay--okay?

LEPAN: What? Who have you send to do this? Santo---I already have my men on this.

GORDO: I have sent Ari in to dispose of this Mr. Edwards, shit. He will be disposed of within the hour---okay?

LEPAN: Santo, listen to me---please! If he ends up dead---I will become the prime suspect! Call Ari off---this instant! Because if I go down----then we both go down!
[Pause]

LEPAN: Listen to me, Gordo, when I met you decades ago you were nothing but a shy little pimp operating out of the hovel in the weeds of Mexico. You were a small, stay-in-the-back-room hood. Your idea of business was nothing more than pimping children to the local tourists. You were hiding under rocks and behind trees from your own police department. Until you met me, you were nothing but a street vendor selling child porn to your local priests. I have changed your entire world, Santo Gordo. You owe me! Just look at yourself today. You are a billionaire and you tell me that I have lost it? How dare you, you---you---you Mexican fuck!

GORDO: Mm-hmm. Okay, now stop it Henry! Stop it this moment!
[Static; coughing]

LEPAN: No, you stop it---you little Mexican puke. What you and I have done together exceeds the imagination of what you and I ever dreamed of doing together. We have revolutionized the definition of immigration; we have populated entire vacation spots and resort communities with our own people. We have staffed automobile plants, aircraft facilities, casinos, resort developments and manned them with all of our own people. We don't have to rely upon your stupid little whores, earning money by sucking some dirty old-man's cock. We are selling flesh by the megaton and you have never had to worry about a goddamn thing. We've enjoyed a 1500 percent sales margin on a reoccurring revenue model, over the long-term, with every bit of the expenses paid for by my country of France! You need to just go to hell...Santo....go to fucking hell!

GORDO: *[coughing]* Mm-hmm. Okay, okay, my dear Henry--you bearded French fuck. I have had the power to dispose of you for many years now, but I've not done so because you were my brother and we had a kinship. Even my dearest cousin Ari, whom I installed there, to keep an eye on you, has begged me to allow her to put your fucking lights out! But! I have stopped her, mind you. She has wanted to kill you so many times that you cannot even to begin to imagine, Henri.
[Pause]
This is done---Henri. We are done! You are finished! You will be in jail or dead within the next week unless you fix things to my design. I'm giving you a chance to get out of this with your life--- you little French prick. I'm also giving you a chance to redeem yourself to me before I send Ari in to remove you from the face of my earth.

LEPAN: Gordo, please my brother! Please listen to us---we are acting like children. We are better than this!
GORDO: Henri, Timothy Edwards' destiny is already done. If I were you, I would ask your security team to step in and solve the problem before my cousin does. I will give you until noon tomorrow to make sure that your problems are no longer mine.
[Pause]
Now---*[Static]* All right? You get a hold of your men and tell them that I want this goddamn reporter silenced, and I want them to do it now! *[Static]* Get it done! *[Static]* Fix it---Henri---or you are a dead man. *[Coughing; Static]*
[Pause]
GORDO: Listen Henri, I have always loved you as if you were my own brother. I know that there are things about you that are, shall I say, peculiar. Like the way you hide behind that grey beard of yours, your shyness

and insecurities, that's all fine with me. Okay? Okay? But there has always been a trait about you which I have never been able to ignore.

[Extended pause]

LEPAN: Yes, go on, what is that, Santo?

[Pause]

GORDO: You---Henri, are a liar.

[Pause]

GORDO: You are a goddamn liar, Henri. You lie to people in order to gain an unfair advantage over them! Always---you do this! I've caught you in so many lies many times in the past. And you are probably lying to me now---about this---this—this twin sister garbage!

[Extended pause]

GORDO: Okay, Henri, you have until noon tomorrow---you lying cocksucker! Do you understand me, you son of a bitch?

[Pause]

Everyone that you hold dear to your fake and lying heart will be dead, Henri! And this includes everyone from your little Iranian play-toy to your old, forgetful mother! Fix it, Henri, goddamn it, or you will soon be in the hands of Ari.

[Pause]

---And I swear to you---Henri---she will not fail me.

[Extended coughing; call ends]

Chapter 81

HOMAYRA: TO FULL CIRCLE

The Palais Garnier Opera House - Paris, France — UNESCO Foundation dinner - 10:50 p.m. present day.

And then there was silence, an eerie hush. According to the amber clock timer on my podium, my sister and I had been speaking for a total of 161 minutes. For more than two hours and a half we captured the attention of an audience that had started with 1,979 semi-interested social-ites and had swelled to more than 2800 stunned souls.

Several press organization arrived hours before the program started and quietly positioned themselves at various points throughout the famous opera house, recording every word. TF1, the largest and most viewed television news station in Europe was among the first to arrive early this morning. Their broadcast engineers channeled into the Palais Garnier's sound system and positioned several of their television cameras throughout the opera house.

Two large format high-definition video monitors came to life above us, providing the audience with the ability to view the many photos, videos and sound bites which had been retrieved from Timothy's all-important cell phone. Page after page of images taken from Henri's pay-to-order sex menu, which I had taken from Henri's desk drawer, were intermit-tently displayed on the screens as well. The grand finale, of course, was the secretly recorded argument between Henri Lepan and Santo Gordo, and most likely the last conversation the two would ever have.

Every bit of digital details that we could find, portraying Henri's terrible empire, was edited, formatted and brought to life on the monitors above. In the space of two and a half hours, the once high and mighty Dr. Henri Lepan had been reduced to nothing more than a naked man, sprawled out on a large examination table with nothing left to hide except his disgusting family jewels.

But even now, after everything we had presented for the audience to see, Henri appeared utterly relaxed and surprisingly nonchalant. He looked as if the whole thing were nothing more than a prime time celebrity roast for which he was the guest of honor. He leaned over and casually poured what was left of his bottle of wine into his glass and then politely offered the last few drops to the two female officers sitting on each side of him, to which they declined.

The audience, however, was not amused or entertained by this evenings program; they appeared shocked and deeply disturbed by what they had just learned. Many sitting nearby Henri did their best to distance themselves from him, as if he were a savage beast strangling an infant child to death right then and there. A bright spotlight from above shone down and tightened in on Henri as he sat at what his event planner had promised to be the table of honor and the best seat in the house.

It was supposed to have been Henri's night to provide him the much needed boost back to the top, after months of being unfairly harassed by the nasty media. It was apparent that he thought the boost might still be possible, as long as he had the chance to take the stage.

The master of debate and the spoken word was now on a mission to recapture the trust and confidence from those who had all but written him off as being just another one of those corrupt, high ranking, government officials.

However, I could still see that familiar twinkle in his eyes which always exudes confidence and bold superiority. As far as Henri was concerned he was, is and forever shall be, larger than life and utterly stain resistant. Henri always considers himself as being at the forefront of the world's thought-leaders, especially in the areas of trade and governmental affairs and a fall from grace would be completely impossible.

As far as I was concerned, Henri never gave his victims time to defend themselves, so why should we? His time will come in the form of hundreds of pre-trial motions, delays, preliminary hearings and well-orchestrated public interviews. Hell, before this is all over and done with, Henri might even publish a bestselling book. No, no, not tonight, I thought, belonged to my sister and me, and I didn't want to hear a single word from his filthy mouth.

But to my surprise, Golareh had a different opinion. She wanted to give Henri a chance to say his piece. Turning to me she said, "Homi, this man raped me and turned our lives upside down. I want to face Henri, head on, and see what he has to say for himself. I need this moment so I can survive and hopefully heal."

Henri started his act by slowly clapping his hands as his lonely applause echoed through the vast dark arena.

"Very nice work Homayra, I commend you for your strength, dedication and attention to detail. I never thought you had it in you to do such a thing like this to me. You and your sister have certainly done some fine research on me, now haven't you? I must say that I truly underestimated you. I would have expected this from your sister, but never from you, Homayra."

Henri's voice was clear and powerful, especially since Golareh had asked to have a directional microphone trained on his mouth.

"I am so impressed with these two beautiful women, aren't you, ladies and gentlemen?" Henri asked, as he gazed off into the darkness around him. "They really have done some fine sleuthing; perhaps our own French National Police Force might want to hire these two ladies to look into their own internal affairs!"

No one seemed amused by that remark, especially the current Minister of the Interior who was sitting at the next table over, sinking in his seat and staring at his hands.

"And hello to you, my precious Golareh. Don't you do look ravishing this evening? How long has it been since we've last seen each other in the *flesh*, my little *superstar?*"

For as long as I've known Henri, he always kept a full supply of verbal darts, which he would viciously throw at his advisories whenever he deemed it necessary. There were many more to come, I was sure of it. The first dart hit the Minister of Interior and clearly stung him, but the dart meant for my sister missed her for the first time in her life, as she reached over for my hand and held it tight.

The two spot lights which had been beaming down on my sister and me all night, slowly narrowed in on us as we stood together at center stage holding hands.

"Oh, now this is a nice touch of ambiance---isn't it, ladies and gentlemen? Rather a cozy feeling here, wouldn't you say? Just the three of us back together again, just like it used to be. It makes me feel all warm inside," Henri taunted, as he squinted through the single beam of light capturing just the upper part of his body.

The entire room was dark except for Henri sitting at his table and Golareh and me standing on stage directly in front of him. It was the epitome of a well-orchestrated operatic face-off.

"It's your sister's fault, Homayra! She has always hated me! Even as a child, she never trusted me."

The room was silent as the audience held its breath and examined the three of us as if we were all under a microscope.

"Isn't that right, Goli? You detested me even when you were a child. Let me ask you something ladies---shall I? Do you even remember the day we first met?"

Golareh and I said nothing but continued to stare at Henri.

"No----not the day when you arrived at the castle, I mean the time way before that? Back when you were just children."

Where was Henri going with this line of inquiry, I wondered, as I studied his ugly face at the table below.

"I know that you won't remember, Homayra, because you are too stupid to look back that far into history and connect all of the dots."

And there was his next dart.

"Oh---you were barely conscious that day anyway and pretty banged up by those jagged rocks, just off shore. Oh the two of you looked so pitiful that day on the beach. You especially, Homayra, the way you clung to your sister's fingers as if you were nothing more than a frightened feral cat being pulled from the ice cold water. But you, my dear Goli---you stared at me as if I was some sort of monster! I will never forget those eyes of yours, even then, Goli. I still can't understand why you looked at me with such distrust, when all I was doing was saving your goddamn life! Did you actually think I was going to hurt you that day or help you? Why, why were you afraid of me on that day of all days? What was it about me---that you saw in my eyes?"

Suddenly an image surfaced of that day on the shore of the Caspian Sea, many, many years ago. It couldn't have been Henri who rescued my sister and me from the sea that day? Certainly not---not in Iran of all places! How could he have been there? Why would he have been there?

Finally it hit me why Henri might have been in Iran back then! He must have been there on a recruiting trip to take Zooli back to France with him. He was going to assign her to Cavalry of the French Republican Guard. That's it! The timing seems plausible.

"You really don't remember that day, do you, Homayra? Of course you don't; you were too naive and stupid!"

Next dart, but I felt no pain.

"But your sister remembers that day, don't you, Goli? You recognized me on the first day you arrived at the castle, whether you will admit it or not. I saw that you recognized me, Goli! I saw it in those all-knowing eyes of yours."

I felt Golareh's hand tighten around mine as if she were warning me of what was forthcoming.

"She knew me alright, she thought she had me all figured, but she never felt the need to tell you what she thought of me. Why was that, Goli? Why did you never tell your sister that you thought I was a monster? Were you jealous of your sister for finding me attractive? Perhaps you didn't want to break her heart! Oh poor, poor Homi! What would she do if she knew who I really was? Were you mad at me because your sister was falling in love with me---and you wanted to get the hell out of that god awful place! Why, Goli, why did you not tell your sister, then, why you hated me so?"

I was speechless, as the day he was describing came rushing back to me after traveling full circle around the universe. That was the day I have dreamt of constantly for my entire lifetime.

"It was I who saved you from the waters when you were just children! I was the one who rescued your drowning battered little bodies from those jagged rocks on the shores of the Caspian Sea, while your stupid parents lay sunning themselves on the beach! I was the one who hauled your little bodies out from those violent waters and took you back to the beach that day! I saved your lives and handed you back to your terrified parents --- and this is how you repay me? I saved your goddamn lives when the both of you were only nine-years-old and this is the thanks I get?" Henri bellowed.

Henri was receiving the rare burden of silence from an audience he didn't know anymore and something he had never experienced before. His breathing increased as he swallowed the last of his red wine.

As Henri spoke, several police officers moved in and positioned themselves just outside of his field of vision.

"Tell me ladies; why else would a powerful man in another country take such a passionate interest in the two of you? Who were you? Nothing---was who you were! What were you to me? Why would I open my home to two pitiful little girls from Iran and give you everything you ever wanted for the rest of your selfish little lives?"

A long awkward pause ensued as Henri milked it for everything it was worth.

"Would you like to know why? I'll tell you why? It was because I loved you! I loved the two of you more than anything on earth! You were the only things in my life that was decent, clean and honest. Everything else in my life was shit! I loved you both more than life itself."

Three policemen became visible as they came to the side of Henri and held both of his arms.

"Wait just a goddamn minute, what the hell's going on here? Am I being charged with some sort of crime here? Is that what this is all about? Do you people actually think that I'm going to go to jail for anything? Get your damn hands off me, you sons-of-bitches! I'm leaving here this moment and I'm going home! I swear to God, Homayra, you two owe me with your lives! You owe me with the very essence of your selfish souls." Henri voice suddenly began to crack! "Your parents owe me as well for saving your worthless little lives! Do you know that, Homi? Do you know that, Goli? Get your damn hands off me---you fools!"

The last remnant of spot light was cut just as Henri's microphone went dead. His voice resembled the cry of a spoiled child being dragged from a toy store. Out of the totally dark opera house Henri's struggling body was taken, as his heals kicked at the marble floor beneath him.

"Let me go you fool! Do you know who the hell I am? I'm Dr. Henri Lepan! You can't do this to me! I'm not the only one who should be arrested here tonight! There are many others in this very same goddamn room who will go to jail too! You just wait and see! If I go down, others will follow! Now, let me go! You're hurting me!"

His yelling suddenly became pathetic as if he were a whimpering child being punished by the spirit of his vengeful father who had just returned from the dead to render a long and much overdue punishment on his guilty soul. Henri screamed and cried as if something had finally snapped inside. He was going completely mad.

The main doors of the drafty opera house slowly closed as the sounds of the heavy locking mechanisms slapped back in place. The drama was over.

"The world is a dangerous place, not because of those who do evil, but because of those who look on and do nothing."

- ALBERT EINSTEIN

Chapter 82

GOLAREH: A NEW DAY

The Palais Garnier Opera House - Paris, France – present day

T he lights of the theatre slowly came upon us as if an electronic sun were on the rise. The audience was standing, sitting and staring at my sister and me as we stood on the stage before them. They seemed startled, disheveled and shocked.

Some had their palms resting on the tops of their heads as if they were desperately trying to hold on to their thoughts long enough to examine them again. Many had their eyes wide open and jaws dropped. Others looked confused as they gazed at one another in disbelief.

The scene took me back to a distant memory: seconds after a bomb had gone off, just meters from our home in Tehran. Our childhood friends lay scattered around our backyard, standing, kneeling and unconscious. Homayra was lying beneath me, semiconscious, as I desperately tried to drag her off to safety. But that was then and this was now.

Homayra and I looked towards the ceiling of the grand foyer and studied the beautiful angels painted more than a century and half ago by Charles Garnier's good friend, Paul-Jacques-Aimé Baudry. I imagined my mother up there alongside them, looking down upon the two of us smiling. My mother stood separate from the angels, wearing that familiar stained artist smock and gripping her paint brushes. She looked happy, joyous and most of all relieved. For the first time since my sister and I left Tehran, I imagined my mother finally at peace, knowing that her two girls were finally safe.

I, of course, was crying---and I know what you're thinking: I'm a big crybaby! And you would be correct! I cry, I laugh, feel joy, sorrow and pain. Most of all, I believe that I can love with much more of a capacity than ever before. Besides, I have much more to love these days, I thought, as I held my sister in my arms.

In the front row I noticed a man stepping forward and quietly applauding. One clap led to the other, until his lonely applause triggered a standing ovation.

At first, I was taken back by the applause, thinking that this was no opera, theatrical production or stunt; it was the end of a long line of tragedies caused by an evil man. But that's what we humans do, I thought, as I watched the entire crowd rise and cheer. Humans should applaud when good conquers evil. We should remember it and mark it down, because it's a rarity.

Danielle, Frédéric and Richard appeared at the side of the stage and began walking towards us, all holding hands and beaming with delight. They looked so beautiful and fresh, each wearing broad and genuine smiles. Zooli was next in line, but in the company of a handsome young man with a sweet smile and curly brown hair. As the group moved in closer, my sister and I rushed over to greet them.

"Homi, Goli---I would like to introduce you to my son Alexander," Zooli exclaimed, her voice shaking. Zooli instinctively tried to tame her emotions, just as she had always instructed us to do, but this time she fell short, tearing up, starting to cry. "This is my dear son, girls! This is Alexander! He is here with me now because of what all of you have done for me."

Frédéric moved forward and shook Alexander's hand and then gave Zooli an extra-long hug. Homayra glanced over at me with a *did-you-see-what-I-just-saw* expression on her face.

"Oh Frédéric, what can I ever do to repay you. You have saved my son's life and brought him home to me!"

"Zooli, there is nothing that you must ever do to repay me, for it was you who has saved my cousins' lives every single day. Bless you, Zooli, and thank you for being in our lives."

Frédéric had met Zooli only once before, when he had come to visit us at the castle; Zooli had been much younger then and we just kids. But this encounter seemed remarkably different as the two seemed magically caught off guard by one another. They stood staring into each other's eyes with a passion that seemed dreamlike and wonderful.

Before my very eyes, Frédéric began to glow with an interest for Zooli, while she seemed to be boiling over with curiosity for him. Could it be that Zooli had finally been released from the shackles of pain, sorrow and guilt for leaving her husband behind so many years ago? Whatever was happening between the two of them got Homayra's attention as she leaned over and whispered in my ear:

"Regardes Goli, est ce tu vois ce que je vois? Zoli a enleve la pancarte qui disait: complet. Esperons que c'est le signe d'une nouvelle romance!" - *"Look Goli, do you see what I see? Zooli has taken down her no-vacancy sign. Perhaps she may find romance again!"*

The microphone was noticeably vacant, seeming to urge both Homayra and me back for final remarks as our loved ones surrounded us by the podium.

"Ladies and gentlemen---" Homayra's voice was cracking as she paused for the next 30-seconds to allow the audience to settle. Richard appeared as if he wanted to step forward and assist her but held himself back. It was again Homayra's time.

She gently pulled her hair back over her shoulders, took a sip of water and composed herself.

"I didn't think that Henri deserved a chance to speak this evening, but my sister requested it."

Homayra gripped my hand and smiled at me.

"He will have plenty of time to defend himself in the days ahead. My sister and I have dumped out our souls to you on this very long evening; it was an opportunity for us to begin our healing process. We appreciate your sincere interest and we thank you for your patience and understanding."

The audience quieted down even more as they all took their seats.

"Now that I have my sister back in my life, perhaps the two of us will be able to assist in the prosecution of a man whose mission in life was to take advantage of the world around him. But unfortunately there is no punishment that can return the lives and hearts back to the many victims and families who have been destroyed by this horrible man.

Henri Lepan is a man who sees no difference between right and wrong. His mind doesn't work like yours and mine. Likewise, the crimes that he has committed far out strip the imagination of most everyone here tonight.

This lack of understanding of these sorts of crimes poses a challenge to our legal system, because for the most part, juries won't allow their minds to go there. Imagine what it must be like to witness a child being raped. Or try, if you can, to visualize an infant being molested by not one but many adults. Who on earth can allow themselves to see these sorts of activities? Certainly not you or me!

If you still have the stomach for it, then let's take a voyage a bit deeper into another level of hell, to an industry that purchases human beings for the sole purpose of beating, torturing, raping and even murdering people for money. A most unsettling thought, you must agree?

But for the good of all of those people we've displayed on the television screens here this evening, and for the many other victims around the world, we have an obligation to open our minds to all of these lurid activities and confront them head on. We must ventilate these putrid fumes from beneath their protective veils of which we as a society have inadvertently given them. We must have the stomach to study the forensics of human trade and most of all--- child sexual abuse. We can no longer turn our heads from it and pretend that it doesn't exist; we must deal with now---sooner rather than later.

Dr. Henri Lepan is not supernatural or an unstoppable demon. People like him don't have magical powers and fly around on broomsticks. They are real human beings who perform dreadful acts on others, knowing full well that society is much too afraid to even watch them.

Sadly, there are many other powerful people around the world today pushing this industry to its maximum. People like Santo Gordo, who runs his side of the organization from almost six-thousand miles away from here. Ladies and gentleman, might we be able to stop him? I certainly hope so, but I sincerely doubt it. Do I believe that the authorities in Mexico and around the world will join forces with us in bringing this criminal to justice? Realistically, no, I simply do not! But--- that shouldn't stop us from trying.

We must start by raising the awareness of the public that the industry of human trafficking is very much alive and flourishing. This was the primary reason we are gathered here tonight, ladies and gentleman.

Our mission is to help those fallen victims and families who have been crushed by this horrible industry. We also plan to hold our legal institutions accountable so that the people who commit these crimes against humanity are removed from society and punished accordingly.

Further we need to raise the awareness of people around the world so that we can no longer close our eyes to these crimes, but treat them like other crimes of passion.

Ladies and gentlemen, by some estimates there are close to a half-million slaves around the world today with at least 80 percent of them under age and being used for sex. Human trafficking ranks third, internationally, behind the illegal drug markets and the sale of firearms.

This industry is so large that it's become invisible to the human eye. By some estimates, global human trade generates close to $50 billion profit annually. I only hope that after this evening you will have gained a renewed appreciation for what this industry actually is. Now that Henri Lepan is no longer an evil force in this room, perhaps our new organization, which has been given the name, *Mission of Mercy*, will grow teeth and bite down on abuse and human trade within our reach. We may not be able to save all of the *starfish* that wash up upon our shores, but we can certainly save a few.

Henri Lepan will still be around to spit in our faces. Make no mistake of that! We can expect to hear much more from him before this is all over. He will be represented by some of the world's foremost legal minds. They will do everything in their power to release Henri Lepan back to the society from where he came. Wait for it, expect it, and make your voices heard when you see our legal institutions dragging their feet, shirking their responsibilities and failing to hold up their side of the deal!

Please, my dear friends, I ask you to stand up with Mission of Mercy and support us. We must put an end to human slavery if not around the world then at least here in France."

My sister then spoke in our mother tongue:

"*Mamnoune hastam az shome doustane aziz keh dastaneh mara bekhanide*" - *Thank you my dear friends for listening to our story. Ta bezoudi (till real soon)*"

Homayra dropped her eyes and humbly stepped away from the microphone. Our faces came together and we kissed each other's lips, cheeks and eyes.

"I love you so much, Homi. I am so very proud of the fact that I can call you my sister."

"Goli, you are and forever shall be a biggest part of my soul."

My sister and I held each other for the longest time in the center of the stage as the house lights came on.

Suddenly, there was a commotion and through the corner of my eye, I noticed Rahda Shabur rushing towards us with a shocked expression on her face. Next to her I saw Heath running by her side. They looked as if they had both just seen a ghost.

"Goli! Goli! Come quick! Oh my god! You won't believe who's in the back!" Rahda's rock hard spirit seemed visibly shaken, but crying with delight. She and Heath spun around and pointed towards the back stage area.

"Look, Goli! Oh my god in heaven! Look who is back there!"

In the darkness of the back stage area I saw what appeared to be a zippo lighter igniting a distant yellow flame. The warmth from that flame shot across the room and struck me in the center of my chest. The darkened figure with the lighter moved the flame closer to his face and appeared to be lighting not one, but two, cigarettes at once.

My heart ground with emotion as I studied the darkened figure in the distance, knowing full well that I was seeing a ghost. The dark figure appeared to be in a wheelchair and was being pushed towards the light by a beautiful woman.

My emotions heaved as I grabbed my sister's arm and pulled her towards the distant figure rolling towards us in a wheelchair.

He was dressed in a black tuxedo with a white shirt and bowtie. He was smoking two cigarettes at once and smiling at me broadly. One of those cigarettes was meant for me, because he was offering it to me!

"I know who that woman is back there!" I told Homayra. "I also know who that wonderful man is--- as well!"

I let go of my sister's hands and rushed towards the man in the wheelchair.

Smithy Greene greeted me with her magical smile and pointed down to her lover sitting in the wheelchair. I gazed upon my wonderful soul mate, brother and companion in amazement. Then I knelt down before him and held his face desperately in my hands, as if I never--ever wanted to let him go. It was Timothy Edwards and he was welcoming me into his open arms.

"This one's for you girly-girl---this one is just for you!"

If there had ever been a time in my life that called for a long and overdue smoke--- it was then.

EPILOGUE

I watch my sweet appy gelding from a distance as he notices everything around him from the moment his stall door opens and he's allowed to enjoy his time at liberty. Rarely has he experienced this level of freedom, but since the herd is stable and I am within range, I grant him this time to explore.

He has been dreaming all night long about the length and special taste of the grass on the far side of the pasture along the fence line. He knows exactly where it is because he saw the delicious patch of grass the day before. No decision making is required as his hoofs slowly step across the cool early morning mud past the main barn and towards his destination in the distance.

The wind kicks up and moves a limb on a tree at the edge of the forest causing him to stop in his tracks, look up and take note. What was that? He wonders, as he stares intently at the fluttering of a leaf on the tree. What is it about today that seems so vastly different from yesterday? What is causing that strange thing on that tree to move the way does? Is it safe for me to continue towards my destination or should I just call it a day, head back to my stall and rest? I can always go back there tomorrow but perhaps not! Perhaps tomorrow it will be too late; the grass may be eaten by one of my own. All of these questions go unanswered as he makes a clear decision to pursue his goal.

The winter grass is exactly how he thought it would be as he lowers his large head, sniffs the turf and grabs the tiny pieces with his lips and teeth, tearing them from their roots. The morning sun warms the portions of his back and hindquarters covered by his turnout blanket and it feels wonderful, warm and secure. The grass is plentiful here, on the far side of the farm, as he escapes from his fears and folds into the joy of the peaceful early morning earth.

He never loses sight of the barn and knows exactly where the rest of his herd are as he further relaxes and places his concerns on hold. Off in the distance, he knows that I am here observing him. He is well aware of the fact that I am watching him even though he makes no attempt to make eye contact with me.

The wind suddenly picks up again, causing that single dried leaf to break free from its branch and float through the sky in his direction. The large brown leaf drifts through the morning air and tumbles downward. Across the dormant field the leaf seems to take on a life of its own, appearing to have the gelding set in its own cross-hairs. Enough is enough, the gelding realizes as he raises his large head in alarm and studies the angry brown leaf advancing on him with seemingly malicious intent.

He is vulnerable and completely unable to protect himself. His herd is much too far away to protect him and I have become nothing more than a passive observer. He is now on his own, facing impending doom.

"I don't like it! I don't like it! I don't like it!" I believe he thinks.

The 24-year-old gelding concludes that the danger is much too forceful for him to contend with any longer. He explodes to his hind legs and finds his exit path and launches himself that direction.

Out, out, away and away the large, aging horse, with a touch of painful arthritis and occasional locking stifles, orders his large achy body to escape from probable death. Every aspect of his conscious is fleeing for his life, fully believing that the tiny leaf which is advancing on him has the full capability of killing him.

The gelding runs as fast as he can possibly push his body. He neighs, whinnies, kicks up dirt and calls for his herd for help. He gallops, bucks and discharges digestive gas with his eyes open in terror and nostrils flaring. He runs until he can see his herd again, his stall and me as well. And then--- and only then, does he come to a stop, feeling safe enough to drop his head for another snack. Only until he is convinced that he is far enough away from danger will he relax and live again.

I gaze down at that wonderful blanket appaloosa with pride and smile. His name is *Glowy*, which is short for *Glow in the dark*. Not only is Glowy, Zooli's favorite horse, but confidentially, mine as well. Zooli has had him since he was five-years-old and treasures his gentle way. He will be the school horse I will use with Laura, because he is wise, strong and caring. Glowy is the ambassador of peace and the one who provides balance to the many personalities within the herd.

More arrivals are due in around noon today, I consider, as I look off in the distance at the castle entrance. The guard gate has long since been removed along with the rest of the medieval accoutrements of battle which once guarded the castle entrance.

Along the secondary road leading to the castle I spot a long line of bicyclists carefully passing a mail truck, making their way up here to the castle where they may hike, picnic and enjoy this most beautiful day. The riders politely wave to the driver of the mail truck as they pedal further up the hill towards the main road to the castle. The castle is now open to the townspeople, visitors both near and far, and most especially to the many innocent victims of sexual abuse from around the globe.

The latter are in various stages of therapeutic development but they will all join in and work as hard as they can with our counselors. They will learn that this is not a vacation or a time to be pampered or even pitied. This is a time to address the demons that have haunted them since their assault and have driven many others to suicide.

Music, dance, yoga, painting and sculpture are just a few of the many activities that these innocent souls released from danger will spend their time doing. They will also hike the trails, work the earth with their hands and cook for one another. I hope that they will learn that there is still a world out there that welcomes them with respect, care and love.

Golareh appears at the far end of the pasture behind Laura, a partially disabled child from birth and a victim of life long abuse. She had a severe speech deficit and lacked the mobility and muscle control to fend off the man that took advantage of her for many years.

Laura, unknowingly, fit the perfect profile target for a predator on the borders of her own trusting family. She has witnessed the full spectrum of abuse which shattered the family unit which she always believed to be rock solid. She believed everything was her fault for only telling someone the truth about what happened to her, while other members of her own family refused to accept it.

Laura worked tirelessly with investigators, dumping her heart out to her therapists and testifying under oath, with the help of interpreters during her trial. She faced the man who had accosted her during testimony, but because she was a minor she was spared the sentencing phase, where the defendant was found guilty and taken away to prison, to the mixed opinions of her extended family.

Piece by piece she has been able to put much of what happened to her into perspective and slowly move through it. She is now in her mid-twenties and smiling from ear to ear as my sister pushes her wheel chair over the bumpy tufts of field grass towards me.

I've been told that she has been clinging to my sister, who I'm sure shared some of her own emotional secrets with her as well. Perhaps my sister told Laura things that she never told anyone else. I'm sure they cried together. Perhaps Laura was able to help my sister locate other neurons that have tightly gripped those memories of her painful past.

"Communication helps and talking about what happened---is what it's really all about," my sister always tells me, even though she has yet to share anything with me about that dreadful night that Henri raped her.

But---that's not my job this morning as Laura rolls up in her wheelchair and comes to a stop, smiling as if she is on vacation. My job is to teach this frail little person to be ready to work when she reports to me for her lessons. Riding helmets must be on and secured with not a hint of candy or gum in her mouth. We are here to work with creatures many times our size and gain the confidence we need to maneuverer them to where we want them go.

Most accidently, I catch myself instructing her with the rules of the farm: "Laura, never call me ma'am. I am Homi to you! Do you understand?"

For it is Laura's time to have her first of many lessons in art of passive persistence, confidence and control.

I can only hope and pray that my voice of instruction will remain with Laura for many years to come, just as Zooli's voice will remain with me for an eternity.

Illegitimate Advantage

ACKNOWLEDGEMENTS

I am deeply grateful to my friend Homayra Sellier from whom I gained so much inspiration to write this novel. She and her twin-sister, Golareh Ayazi Broujerd, who sadly passed away on October 13, 2006 at the age of 44 of brain cancer, personified the power of true love between expatriated sisters cast away from their homeland of Iran. The twins triggered a burst of vivid imaginings that made telling this story easier and completely fulfilling.

Special thanks to my story consultant, Bonnie Braendlin, who worked with me during my initial editing stages. Your proofing and validation gave me the confidence to move forward through the unknown.

To Lydia Juenger for helping me blend this story with a rich equestrian theme and to my other close friends who observed me during my concentrated creative process, I cannot thank you enough for your love and support.

Much thanks to Homayra Sellier for providing me with the many translations from English to both French and Farsi; along with additional insight into the Iranian culture. Also, thank you for contributing the Arabic illustration of the title.

To Pam Larson, who provided the artwork for the title page, you have a precious talent for capturing the souls of your subjects. I thank you from the bottom of my heart.

Thanks to Jonathon and Judy Funk for brainstorming with me during the very early stages of this novel. Also to my father for warning me to be realistic about my expectations and to remember that every author loves to read their own words.

Thank you, Harry Juenger, for your input on soccer strategies and how possession of the ball is paramount.

Much appreciation is extended to Sherry Eades and Ginny Haddis for being my first and second readers. Sharing the story that had been living exclusively in my mind for years with you was nothing short of amazing.

I would like to dedicate this novel to my daughter, Lauren, who bravely marches through the many challenges in her life. Certainly the old adage is true---that the truth shall set you free.

Lastly, I would like to thank the many coffee houses from Charleston, S.C. to Tryon, N.C. that welcomed me into their cozy settings to sip coffee and feel at home. The wonderful distractions within the walls of those lovely places only enhanced my creative process.

R. Kirk Gollwitzer

Kirk Gollwitzer is a freelance photojournalist and independent filmmaker. He lives and breathes on a horse farm in the foothills near Tryon, North Carolina.

29580811R00384

Printed in Great Britain
by Amazon